Evolutions Climb

BOOK II

Fear of Heights

By

L. Pelletier

Shirley
Thank you so much for opening up your barn to me to bring this story to life!

Little ol' Me Publications

ISBN-13:978-0-692-53908-8

DEDICATION

It's been a *long* and crazy ride from the whirlwind that was Book I, to the publishing of Book II! The fire burned just as brightly in me the entire time, but my hiatus from the real world had officially ended. The amount of time I was forced to spend putting it off while working another shift at my new job or filling out paperwork for school, both my children's and my own, was really hard for me but unavoidable. I wanted *nothing* more than to just sit and work exclusively on this book until I was finished I *promise* you! Unfortunately I simply didn't have that luxury this time around. Life is constantly changing and your only choice is to get flattened by it as it passes you by or to roll with it, wherever it takes you.

Well I'm happy to say that I'm still rolling along, but I would really like to thank every single loyal reader that waited *somewhat* patiently for Book II, while I learned to manage all the expanding areas of my life and my rediscovered love for writing all at once. It was a longer process than I had ever anticipated, but I absolutely refused to rush it or to cut corners in the story just to get there faster. In the end I know it was the right decision!

Of course I am already onto Book III as you are reading this, and hopefully as my life continues to adjust so will I, and I'll find ways to make the wait in between books much shorter for you next time around.

So until then, for your patience and your continually motivating enthusiasm for this book to come out, I humbly dedicate Book II to all my readers. This one's for you. Each and every one of you that have grown to love "Pinegrove" as much as I do.

Thank you for letting this story come to life in your own minds, as I let it out of mine.

ACKNOWLEDGMENTS

I would like to take this opportunity to clarify a little bit about what is "fact" and what is "fiction" in this series and how I chose to divide and depict them. It's a trickier subject in this case than you might think.

As most of you know from Book I, a lot of inspiration was taken from things around me in my own town, the *real life* version of "Pinegrove." There were references to many of the local places and people, including friends, family and well known town characters alike. I really enjoy being able to pick out things that I recognize from a book, so I knew immediately that I wanted to write my own story that way. I had a lot of fun with it too. Book II continues on in that trend and there are whole new areas of my beautiful, quiet town and references to many more colorful characters in here for you to explore and enjoy.

If along the way, you are lucky enough to be able to pick out for yourself a few of the local spots that are the backdrop for my story, or the real life inspiration for one or two of the lively characters that help me tell it, first of all good for you! Second, here is what you will find and why. As a basic rule of thumb *geographically*, things are represented true to life, and are identified accordingly. For instance in the story the Merrimack River is the Merrimack River and resides where you would expect to find it. Boxford is Boxford, and so on.

The town of "Pinegrove" is the only exception to that rule, since I would like to keep my towns' anonymity to some extent however miniscule, to preserve the peacefulness here that inspired this story in the first place. In the name of that goal, it crosses the boundaries from "geographical fact" to fall predominately into my other category, which covers *real people,* (current or historical) and *names of actual local businesses.* These types of names are "*eluded*" to or thinly veiled for those in the know, but all *real* names have been changed to *"protect the innocent"* so-to-speak.

So while you may very well recognize a familiar place or character, and think to yourself, "Oh I know who/where that is!" it will be because you are clever, not because they were listed under their real names. I really hope that you *will* figure a few of them out though, and that you will get to share in the little "winks" that have I put in here just for you. Just don't go giving them all away to everyone else. ;)

That covers people and places. As for the parts of this uncommon tale itself that are "fiction" verses what came from "real life experiences" personal or otherwise, well I'll just say this; I'll leave you all to guess at that stuff on your own, but when it comes to the most extraordinary parts, I can assure you that probably 90% of your guesses will be wrong. Why am I so sure? Because fact is truly *stranger* than fiction and at the end of the day, it was the small, extraordinary *facts* that made this *fictional* story so much fun for me to tell!

Last but certainly not least, once again I have a long list of musicians to thank for their inspiration in my life, and in my writing. I am eternally grateful to the many artists whose lyrics and melody continually help me to tell the musical side of the story, which is no small feat! Many thanks to *all* of them, including but not limited to; Lee Brice; Jim Croce; Eagles; Florida/Georgia Line; Dobey Gray; Imagine Dragons; Don McLean; Kansas; Lenny Kravitz; Lynard Skynard; Scorpions; and most especially for Book II, Maroon 5, who's song Daylight was a *perfect* fit this time around; as well as any and all of the previously mentioned artists whose songs recur from Book I.

REFERENCES

I would like to acknowledge my few resources including The New York Times article titled "Silos Loom as Death Traps on American Farms" by John M. Broder from 10/28/12, for its hard and cold truth about industrial accidents, found at; www.nytimes.com/2012/10/26/us/on-us-farms-deaths-in-silos-persist.html

Also the CDC's article on West Nile Virus and it's symptoms at www.cdc.gov/westmile/symptoms

Next I would like to *sort of* acknowledge a few other websites, without giving away any of my pseudonyms for any "real businesses" if I can. *(Not that one needs to be a genius to figure them out, but I have decided not to name names. So in the name of consistency, I won't name them.)*

I will just say thank you, to the *real-life* version of "Breezey Park" for the historical information available on their website which my fictional version follows quite closely, at least in that one aspect.
(You know who you are.)

I would also like to acknowledge the only other online resource for my little divergence into our local past, which was the *blogspot* of that families history, created by a direct descendant of our fair parks' namesake. *(Again, there was only one that I found so I'm sure it's obvious to that party, who I mean.)*

Between the two, I found all the historical and inspirational information that I needed and more!

Other than that vague connection to reality though, please note that the storyline in Book II surrounding the beautiful Breezey property is *entirely* fictionalized. The real-life version of "Breezey Park" is already a well-kept, historically fascinating, but widely functional and beautiful, multi-use public venue.
If you *do* ever figure out where it is, you should really check it out.

Lastly, I would also like to recognize Joe D'Amore for graciously opening his historically educational hikes to the public for those who were eager to explore the beautiful woods in our little town and all of their secret, forgotten places. I'm sure he will recognize a few of the areas and a few of the facts that he has shared along the way, specifically the reference to the *"Pinegrove' Gold."* I always knew a lot of that would end up in here somehow, so thanks again.

PROLOGUE

Evolution: The change in the inherited characteristics of biological populations over successive generations.

While we humans as a species are continually changing, along with every other living thing, the explanation for why we change does not.

So the story continues, as it always will. Sometimes the players change. Other times the original players simply change completely within themselves. Either way the struggle itself to grow and evolve never ceases, it merely changes locations and allies along the way.

Chapter 1

This is it, I'd thought nervously to myself, the big unveiling. It had been so long coming that it was hard to believe it was really happening. After all the time it had taken and all of our hard work, I still wasn't ready for it to end. A certain someone still wasn't there to share it with me yet. That certainly wasn't the only consideration or even the most important one, but I couldn't deny that it had a big effect on my overall enjoyment level.

It had been over a month since he'd left and the desire to see him again, to touch him, *hold* him was nearly all consuming by that point! I had never known anything like it before, and I wasn't sure anymore if it was a good thing or a bad thing, to know it then. It was astounding to me the amount of pleasure that I had derived from his physical presence, but just as impressive was the level of emptiness that his absence had created. It was absolutely *bewildering!* I had felt deep attraction to people before but never anything like what I felt in his presence! I had finally come to grips with the fact that it was definitely something *else*!

It was a truly extraordinary situation, any way you looked at it. But was it really *worth* it? I took a few deep cleansing breaths and looked up at myself in the *castle*-sized, gilded mirror that was leaning solidly against the wood paneled wall. I was still struggling with that one. It had gotten harder and harder to be sure, the longer he was away. Not because I was starting to forget about him. *Hmpf.*

There was not a single chance in hell of *that* happening. In fact the pain of missing him somehow actually managed to get stronger and stronger as time went by. No, it was because I was starting to seriously wonder if I was strong enough to maintain my sanity long term in a relationship with emotions so intense! I knew that I *wanted* to be, had recently decided to at least *try* to be. However there was no guarantee that my efforts wouldn't be in vain.

Could I really find a way to finally achieve some level of success in an intimate relationship? I felt pretty sure at that point that if any man on our crazy, crowded, wet and rocky planet really had a shot of being that man for me it was him, convenient or not. I was at least beyond trying to deny that fact. Standing there staring at my own reflection, I resigned myself anew. As long as I was physically capable, I *would* continue to hold on. Just the fact that success was even a possibility made it worth it to me.

I gazed back at the mirror. I knew that I at least looked the part. I appeared for all intents and purposes, to be someone who had their act fully together and was prepared to celebrate a very special occasion. My long, usually light brown hair that was most often found in a ponytail, had been professionally blown out and swept up into a dramatic twist, with random tendrils pinned perfectly in place. My normal summer highlights were even blonder than usual by then with all the time I'd spent working outside. The "windblown" up-do, combined with the bright golden strands made me look as if I had spent the day walking on the beach. It was designed to look like an accident, even though it had taken over an hour to accomplish such specific imperfection.

I wished then that that I could go to the beach for real instead of being where I was. I always felt more peaceful there with the hypnotic sound of the waves and the constantly moving air, especially... *wistful sigh...* if it was an *empty* beach! Oh well, it was a nice thought anyway.

I examined the makeup which I so seldom bothered with one more time. It was for a change, expertly applied. By hands much more skilled at the art than my own, of course. Viv had made sure of that. It was light and clean, in honor of the hot, mid-summer weather. No foundation, just a sparse dusting of a faintly glittery powder on my cheekbones and some shiny white eye shadow that looked surprisingly good with the tan that I was sporting, regardless of my compulsive use of sunscreen.

A little mascara and eyeliner were all that was needed to finish it off, except for a tiny swipe of lip gloss just for shine. I was never one to wear lipstick to begin with and I wasn't going to start then, no matter how many of Viv's lackey's ganged up on me. That I was sure of! The best part was that thanks to the sales lady who had originally and so thoughtfully pointed out all of the "*sweat-proof*" items to me, it was all actually holding up rather nicely in the heat.

I had chosen a dangerously thin, mid-thigh high, off white shift dress for the occasion. It had delicate spaghetti straps that were actually just thin strips of gold chain, connecting the gauzy fabric over my shoulders in the front and to a single point in the back. I picked it mainly because it was light as air and felt like more of a slip than real clothes. It was decidedly more revealing than I was usually comfortable with, but both Viv and the saleslady had worked hard to convince me that it was loose enough that I didn't look like the cheap streetwalker that I had pictured in my head.

"I mean streetwalker maybe, but definitely not *cheap!*" Vivianne had insisted. "Not in *that!*" She added getting a laugh out of the saleslady despite her desperate attempt to remain professional.

I had given in eventually when I grew tired of shopping for alternatives, but mostly just because it was also the coolest and most comfortable thing I had tried on. The extreme weather of late definitely helped make it less objectionable than I would normally find it. When they brought me what I now refer to as the "*miraculous*" strapless bra that somehow managed to keep things where they belonged without heavy rigging, I was out of arguments. Between the dress, the delicate gold hoop earrings my mother had lent me, and the designer high heeled, strappy sandals that I had splurged on at the last minute, I knew I presently looked more like a woman than I had in quite some time.

What the Hell I thought, at least approving of the overall effect. I spend an awful lot of time in work clothes and covered in dirt and I'm mostly good with that scenario. I'm actually quite comfortable with that, truth be told. But I am also the type of girl who truly enjoys *being a girl* on occasion, when I happened to be in the mood.

It was kind of a "*best of both worlds*" situation and it was actually a lot of fun for me to play dress up every once and a while! Even if the one person it made me long to twirl in front of, wasn't there to appreciate it. That was okay. I had taken a picture on my phone, to share with him at a later time. Not to torture him with in the meantime, but to *have* later so that he won't have completely missed it.

Sending it then wasn't really an option anyway. I wished for the millionth time that it was and that I could at least text him and tell him all about everything that he was missing. But the phone that I knew the number for was turned off and had been since the night that he left. I had tried it only once, from a payphone in the city, but I wasn't surprised when it went straight to a robotic voicemail. I knew that was intentional, if he kept it off of their radar, he wouldn't have to change it. I was actually glad for once that in typical Simone fashion, I had never gotten around to officially labeling "*unknown*" in my phone. After a while it was like a private joke in reference to my future with him so I had left it alone. At least it wouldn't be easy for someone to pick out. But he hadn't used it since then to call me and I knew he wouldn't until that whole mess was over.

He had called me exactly four times since that night and it had been from a different and new "*unknown*" number each time. I always knew for sure regardless, when it was him. Just from the ring, it was like somehow the electricity would come through with the connection. It was often like that for me with the people I was close to. If I knew the person calling well enough, I usually knew it was them before I looked. I also knew that as soon as we hung up, each new number would also be junk. I never wasted my time trying to call him back on any of them in desperation late at night. I dreamed about it, don't get me wrong, but I never gave in to the desire to complete the foolish action.

I had heard and seen on TV too often how easily they could

get my cell phone records and see the number of every call or text that came or went. They may not know which one was Ethan's, since I doubted that even at the source it was simply listed under his name, but they could work by process of deduction, by eliminating the numbers they *could* easily identify. Or they could simply wait for each one of them to ping again off of a tower somewhere and follow each and every trail until they tracked him down. Well, they could try anyway.

Ethan was too smart to make it that easy for them though and more than smart enough to make sure that I couldn't either, accidentally or otherwise. I knew it would be hard for them to get a location on him from me, if the same number never called me twice. Even if they traced where the last call came from, he wouldn't be anywhere near there when they arrived. He was like a ghost, barely even real. To Agent Anderson, to his own makeshift family, to his friends and coworkers, but most of all to *me*. He didn't really exist for anyone but Jeremy during that time. I knew he hadn't realized yet and probably wouldn't for some time, just how lucky a kid he really was.

So!... I couldn't send the picture to him right then, even if I wanted to, but I would make sure that it existed for when I could share it with him later. At least getting primped had given me something to do all afternoon to keep my mind occupied before the big night. Viv had come with all her well-meaning "*helpers*" and spent the entire day in my apartment with Liliana and myself. I had wanted Viv to come with me to the opening and she would have too, happily being both support and comedic distraction, but unfortunately she'd had an event of her own to attend the same evening. A family wedding that couldn't be missed. I understood but I can't say I didn't curse the bad timing, *vehemently*!

In the end we had decided to at least spend the day getting ready together, as *pre*-event moral support for us both. She'd had her newest employee with her too, who in spite of all her big talk, had turned out not to be a man after all.

On the contrary, Cindy was quite feminine and quite the opposite of the woman she was replacing. Where Andrea had been hard edged, and socially withdrawn, Cindy was soft, super friendly and equally as funny. She was as petite as Viv, with a short snow white blond lob, which I was told meant a "long bob," and a sort of plain but adorable face. What she lacked in exotic features, she made up for with creativity and perfectly applied make-up. Her edgy clothing had the same effect on her tiny, unimposing frame. She appeared bigger than she was, because you saw her uninhibited personality first and that came across as huge! She was also sharp-witted and had quickly become Viv's new side kick in her comedy show, her physical "*ba-dump-bump*" partner if you will.

They had met at the convention that Viv had attended in hopes of just such an occurrence. Of course she had been scoping out all of the male attendees, but by the end of the first day she had ended up at the hotel bar, despondently bemoaning her lackluster choices. As she sat sipping her scotch and scanning the passersby, the inhabitant of the next stool spoke up.

"They start to look a little better after the third one." Cindy had said as a conversation opener, holding her own shot glass up and clinking it with Viv's. Of course they'd hit it off right away.

I got the impression that the working atmosphere was much improved around the shop with her there. I was glad that my friend was getting her happy ending to at least one of her issues, even if mine continued to elude me at the moment.

All four of the other girls had come with her too and they all had fun treating Liliana and I to a day of beauty treatments. From nails to facials to makeup and hair, they had it all covered in their boxy metal cases. I laid out the three dresses that I had bought for her to pick from. She had been at camp when I had the chance to go, so I planned to just return whichever two she didn't wear.

Liliana had been a little bit upset at first that she couldn't change the color of her cast because she was sick of pink and didn't want a pink dress but she wanted it to match. In the end she settled on the pale yellow one since she said it complimented the pink cast without being the same color. I was just happy that my little fashionista was happy. In the end she had absolutely loved the whole experience which of course made me happy to endure it even with them all clamoring to claim their own piece of my make over. Most of them had seen me enough times in my muddy jeans and work boots with my go-to ponytail to be excited by the challenge. I understood that, but I was surprised to find that they were just as excited about getting Viv all dolled as they were me! Well in her case, it was more like "dolled *down.*"

The wedding was a collection of some of the most eligible men in the city and they were all hoping that she would find a new man there that would be willing and able to act as her new "*sometimes*-boyfriend." Their overwhelming eagerness to make that happen was like a fast moving positivity train. I couldn't stop it. I could only try to keep from being flattened by it.

Everyone who knew Vivianne knew that she was happier when she was not necessarily "*involved*," but at least being "*serviced*" on a semi-regular basis. She had always had a few, reliable back-ups that she could call on in an emergency, thank goodness! But she didn't like not having a regular thing. It made her antsy. It made sense that the people who had to work with her six days a week would want to avoid that scenario as much as possible. It made me smile to see her *not* in control for a change as they ganged up on her all at once and began to pull clothes on and off of her.

"You're not going to help me at all, are you?" She had asked dryly with one arm twisted halfway into what was most necessary for her transformation, a more modest, dare I say "*pretty*" dress. Viv didn't normally do "*pretty.*" I had to laugh, even though I was positive that her look would have caused a stranger to lose bladder control. Viv knew she didn't scare me.

"Are you kidding me? I can barely sit down in this thing without putting on a show, never mind wrestle four women at once! You'll get no help here." I joked. Liliana had just giggled by my side with her hands covering her mouth in an attempt to hold it in. She and Viv had always been close and she was fully aware of how unusual it was for her to sit still and let someone else take control. Viv on the other hand, was only mildly amused. But she gave up and allowed it to happen which made the excitable group positively squeal in delight! Liliana and I just covered our ears. I knew she only accepted it because she was also eager for a result that might last beyond sunrise. She wasn't against going to extreme measures to ensure regular future satisfaction.

There wasn't much hope of that in my immediate future though. After that night my calendar was wide open for the foreseeable future, I reminded myself as I stood staring into my own made up eyes. That was the scariest part for me. It was getting to the point where I really needed to stay busy or Ethan needed to come home, one or the other. It felt like there was very little *air* left in the in-between anymore and I was starting to miss the way it felt to truly *exhale.*

I did have to laugh at the fact that I had been so afraid to let myself get involved, or to really need someone again in the beginning because of course I was petrified of ending up in pain and alone again. Then there I was, living the repercussions of that very reality every day and yet I still couldn't bring myself to regret it, any of it. The fear at least, was completely gone.

I wasn't someone who was normally content with having their happiness so tied up in someone else's either, but it went beyond any of that for me by then. What I wanted, in theory or even just what looked good on paper was all completely irrelevant at that point. All of that was designed to help direct you to that perfect person who would make you happy, potentially for the rest of your life. I didn't need those preconceived notions to guide me anymore, because I knew without a doubt who that person was. I just didn't know how to get to a place where we could actually begin to be that for each other yet. It was beyond frustrating.

At that point, it would have been easier to get over a broken heart because although it's painful, you know it's done and that it wasn't meant to be and that there is still someone better for you out there somewhere. You also know that *eventually* it *is* going to heal. You suck it up and you move on.

My heart however, wasn't broken. On the contrary, it had found its' missing parts and was working more efficiently than it ever had before, until those parts suddenly went missing again. So surprisingly, I didn't spend my time cursing the fact that I had met him. But I did spend my time with bated breath, constantly waiting and longing for what I had miraculously found, to return. It was a lot harder than not knowing what you were looking for as it turns out.

I knew then what and who I wanted, and I wanted him so badly that I could taste, feel and even *smell* it! It was still extremely difficult even though it was completely different from what I had originally feared. That I realized, was mostly only because my imagination could never have conjured up such a situation like the one I was currently in!

It wasn't just some fantasy that I needed to accept wasn't going to happen though. He was real. *Amazingly* real! And thankfully he even felt the same way that I did about our incomparable connection. That was also real and it was incredible to me! He just wasn't occupying the same physical space that I was at the moment. That was the hardest part. I refused to feel weak or ashamed for wanting it or missing it though, even if the current situation did make me feel more helpless than I was comfortable with. Finding ways to hold on and hold myself together actually gave me something that I could work at, something that I could do. So that's what I did.

I knew as I made my way methodically through the mundane tasks of the day, weaving my way politely through the happy people that not everyone had to endure such difficulties. But I also knew that not everyone had a reason to that made every arduous trial seem miniscule in comparison! Just having him and his incredibly powerful feelings to hold on *for* had made me stronger than I ever would have been without them.

I stood, mesmerized by how deceiving looks could really be, even though I was more than familiar with that concept already. I had spent most of my life understanding only too well how often people felt one way, but projected something completely different out into the world. Being an empath made it obvious to me. Being a *heightened* empath made it absolutely unavoidable! I had become just as skilled at "*required improv*" as the best of them though, and the current situation was just another fantastic example of why I needed to be. *Here we go...*

I took a few more deep breaths and then pushed myself away from the counter. I *would* have to leave that palatial ladies room sometime, I knew. Whether I felt like it or not. It really was beautiful and all, incredibly well done. From the colorful, intricate oriental carpets under the plush velvet sofas, to the elaborate crystal chandeliers. All good reasons for why I had never wanted to go traipsing in there in my muddy boots during the actual *work* phase.

I gazed expressionlessly at my reflection, as it stood staring bravely back at me. At the moment, for better or for worse, I looked as if I truly belonged there. Only *I* knew that it didn't penetrate the surface. And, I reminded myself, I really couldn't stay in that sanctuary forever. Mr. Wu Xing would not hold off the opening ceremony indefinitely. Even if I hid in there all night, he would still have to cut the ribbon at some point, with or without me. The crowd was waiting.

Waiting. *Hmpf!* That was a word that I didn't care much for anymore. I had never been known for anything even remotely resembling patience, but I had still failed to realize before, what a truly torturous word "*waiting*" could really be! It was definitely only recently, that the mere mention of that word had begun to make me grind my back teeth into a fine powder. Surely I would regret that later in life!

I had noticed that unfortunate side effect the first time someone had asked me about Ethan. It had been an innocent enough question. A simple, "*How are things with you and Ethan?*" from Gabby in the market and I'd had to fight the urge to scream. Since no one around me had brought it up, I had avoided talking about it completely until then. The internal explosion at having to say "how it was" out loud had been almost instantaneous and completely unexpected. I had almost taken Gabby's head off and she would've had absolutely no idea why! That just would have made things worse. Especially since she was feeling bad enough since her own "boyfriend" had up and left town on her so unexpectedly.

Of course I wasn't surprised by that but I did feel bad for her. Personally though, I was extremely glad that he was gone. I wasn't stupid enough to think that he wouldn't keep tabs on me and any major movements that I made. That was why going and meeting with Ethan somewhere was also out of the question. That's what they wanted me to do, to lead them to him. We had agreed that we would *not* be weak and give them what they wanted. *Deep breaths...*

So I had ground my jaw shut tight instead of flipping out and I was relieved that I had managed to get it under control before she stopped talking long enough to pick up on it. But I had made sure to be more careful after that, much to the detriment of my molars, especially when I was picking up Liliana from Ben.

She had remained as cooperative as she had been in the beginning when it came to not asking about Ethan. But she *had* mentioned to Ben, however casually, a few of the exciting details from the last movie night. He brought it up only once, in passing. But since then I had noticed a slightly sharper look in his eye each time I came to get her, a slightly less trusting posture. There were a few more questions about what we were going to do or where we were planning to go. It was closer to that "monitoring" that I used to feel when we were still together and I hated it. It was that constant second-guessing in his attitude towards me that had done the most damage to *us* overall I'm pretty sure looking back.

I was right that we had taken a step backwards because of the latest mess, both between myself and Liliana, *and* myself and Ben. I cursed it, but only under my breath because that was all I could do. I knew that she would always come first with me, and I knew she was completely secure in that. Only I still had no idea how to convince Ben. He still didn't trust that I would always be able to separate myself from the storm of intruding exterior emotions and make good, responsible, conscious decisions where Liliana and her well-being were concerned. I had never been and would never be okay with his lack of faith in that, especially since in reality he had no grounds for that attitude what-so-ever!

In his view, he thought he was only voicing doubt because of the cursed things that were beyond my control, so I shouldn't take it personally. He thought he was helping me and being "on my side" when he blamed my abilities and not me directly. But that had always been the problem. He never understood that what he was really saying was that he had no faith in my strength to get past my circumstances and be a good person anyway That lack of faith would eat away at anybody after a while.

Not to mention that my skills are a *part* of me, not some foreign entity that you can demonize separately. But he never quite got that either. What I dealt with on a daily basis was hard, but I thought that I had learned to deal with it pretty admirably, and to have the one person closest to you continually not notice that effort was disappointing to say the least. It was just too defeating to have to face on a daily basis and it did a lot of damage to "us" over the years.

I knew that I was only human and as occasionally flawed as the next guy, but I had no doubts in myself that my fierce love and protectiveness for Liliana would always override everything else, even my *heightened* emotions. Nothing would ever change that in my mind, but only he could change whether he believed in that or not in his. Life could be a struggle sometimes sure, but I was not naïve enough to think that my struggles made me *different* anymore! We *all* had adversity in our lives. The only part we can be judged on in my view is how well we deal with life in spite of it and I had been working hard at that for a long time by then. Too long to quietly accept not getting credit for it anymore.

It was difficult, knowing I couldn't really defend the whole situation with Ethan more thoroughly. But I knew I still had never neglected to take care of Liliana or to put her first and I never would. I could say that honestly and I knew I would be able to until the day I died. But I *was* officially a part of Ethan's high-octane life at that point and that also meant that he was a part of mine, which by default made him a part of *hers.* I couldn't deny that alone upped the risk factor somewhat. But the truth was that he was likely to be a part of her life at some point in the future anyway, whether we were together or not, and there were no guarantees in life no matter what your circumstances were. I had to remind myself of that important aspect as well to keep Ben's doubt from poisoning my own confidence. I also knew that Ethan and his associates were much more likely to help her someday than to ever do her harm.

So somehow I had to find a way to make it all work and I knew I couldn't change who he was to do that, any more than I could change who I was or who Liliana would turn out to be. All I could do was absorb the hit and try to move forward from there. I *would* find a way to have a life with him, with her in it and still keep her safety a top priority! Somehow!

I was willing to try. It would be worth it, if it turned out to be even remotely possible. Although I had many moments of weakness, that was the only thing that I was still sure of.

Ben however, was going to need a little more convincing. There was still that ever-present warning in his eyes at first each time we pulled away from him on the curb. A "*don't make me decide what to do if you mess up*" kind of warning, that I couldn't mistake, even without being able to read him. We were working on getting past it though, tiny increments at a time, and I was confident that we would eventually succeed. We had to, because I still had to find a way to tell him about the *height* stuff at the very least!

We still had another big obstacle to tackle together at some point and he didn't even know about it yet. I was trying to figure out how in our precarious situation I could possibly tell him about it without driving him even further away! I had absolutely no idea how to do that yet though. So I was still biding my time there too.

I was growing tired of all the waiting in general. Waiting for that eventual talk with Ben, and the inevitable distancing that I was sure would follow. Waiting for Anderson to show up and finally decide to prosecute any or all of us. Waiting to hear from Ethan, until he thought it was safe. Sometimes it was long hours, sometimes it was endless days, sometimes *weeks! In... out...* Waiting to see him again, to hear his voice in person and not just over the phone. As grateful as I was for that each time I was blessed with the small but welcome treat, it wasn't nearly enough.

Of course life all around me went on as usual. My visits with Liliana did slowly begin to become more frequent again, as Ben's original wariness finally began to wane in the long, uneventful aftermath. Sometimes it simply required patience to make that progress, other times a tooth marked tongue at his accusing questions about "what I had planned for the evening" that I could not thoroughly refute, even with the current dullness of my days. But I would never jeopardize our mutual cooperation just to save face. It was far too important. So I let the little things go as much as I could. Let the looks of suspicion roll off me. Kept the peace and kept coming back the next time for the sake of our future as co-parents.

It helped the axis start to turn again and soon after that he started to need things to work between us as much as I did. His practice was getting even busier than usual with all of the good publicity he'd received over having saved Urgo, the city's heroic police dog. By then I was picking her up from school and hanging out with her until he got home, either at the farm or at her house at least two days a week to help him out more.

He was officially responsible for the city's K-9 Unit after that, on top of all the extra calls he was already getting just from having been featured on the news. It was a good thing though. I've said it before and I'll say it again, Ben is really good at what he does, and the world is in need of his services. I know I have my issues with him personally, but professionally I couldn't think of a single complaint. He's worked hard at building his practice to make it stable enough to at least sustain itself, so that he can stay in business and continue to *do* what he does so well.

I was happy to help make that possibility a little more probable, especially when it was just by spending more time with my sweet Liliana. That was the only thing I wanted in life more than I wanted Ethan anyway. That part was easy. The rest we would get to, I kept telling myself, eventually.

Then there had been the work at the gardens as well. Thank God for that! I dove into the work head first and with complete abandon until my hands were blistered, my shins cut and bruised. When that still wasn't enough to drown out the intensity, I pushed on further, single mindedly until my knees were stiff from the almost constant squatting. I pushed on when the dirt would no longer wash out from under my fingernails, even though I always wore gloves. I lived and breathed it completely and happily. Until one day last week, when I looked up to find to my complete surprise… that it was all done.

I was instantly a little lost then. Like gravity had suddenly just decided to let go of me like a small child's errant balloon, floating around without any anchor what-so-ever. I hadn't really stopped feeling that way since.

I worked hard daily at holding it together and not letting myself go all Mopey-Mary again. I knew it didn't do anyone any good, but I wasn't really sure what I was supposed to do with myself instead a lot of the time. Free time became my biggest enemy. Aside from my extra time with Liliana, there had only been the rare social obligation thrown in here or there. A night or two where there was a good band playing at The Tavern, or when Viv just plain forced me to leave my apartment. When your heart's just not in it though, it's just not worth the trouble. There was no satisfaction to be had in it. I was getting by just fine, but I *really* missed feeling "*satisfied!*"

At that admission, the memories of the last night that I had spent with Ethan immediately ran through my head for the thousandth time. It was all I had and I revisited them repeatedly, shamelessly. That last kiss on the little safe-house deck, that last time making love in his tiny, original bedroom at Kent's Farm. And the last time that his intense, electrifying, nerve singeing feelings had burned their way through me. From my head to my toes and all the way back out to my aching palms! The way his eyes would shine with his own satisfaction at the sight of it. I had held on tightly to all of it at the time, and I was glad for that then. It made it that much easier to recall.

I'd had too good of an idea what it had meant unfortunately, when we'd said goodbye that night. Still, I was not prepared for the extent to which I felt the lack of his presence. That overwhelming sense of "*something missing*" had been completely unexpected. I was simply not prepared for the *vast* negative space.

I'd had my share of break ups. I'd dealt before with being alone. None of that was new to me. I could suck it up with the best of them by that point. My separation from Ben and Liliana in the beginning had been like pulling myself apart straight down the center and permanently separating the pieces. I had never known a more painful sense of loss before that. It had taken me *months* to learn how to handle and overcome those devastating emotions. To get to a place where I could pull my shoulders back, open up my chest, lift my chin, and take a full deep breath into my lungs again. Just that ability is something that I could never take for granted after that.

But I had gotten there, eventually. We all had. And I had done a fair job of getting back to real life since then, once I let go of Mopey-Mary.

I'd managed to run her off again after Ethan left, but it wasn't easy. I hated being Mopey-Mary though so it was worth the extra effort to get rid of her. She was just too damn heavy to hold onto. It was too exhausting to keep her propped up and functioning. Eventually, I managed to drop her and I didn't look back. The first day that I felt the lightness of her absence, I picked myself up and quickly got back to the business of living before she could find me again. What was the alternative really, I'd asked myself?

So I had happily thrown myself back into my work, up until such time that it was suddenly not an option anymore. It had kept my days filled and my hands not just bruised, but busy. My mind however, refused to be so easily swayed. It held tight to the memories, to keep itself from reeling at the loss. As long as they existed inside my head, I could get by in the meantime.

There were days though, I thought as I finally walked out through the large, swinging stained glass door, that it was harder than seemed possible. Like when I had something really important happening and it may as well have been a trip to the market for all the enthusiasm that I felt.

Chapter 2

I was immediately surprised by the size of the crowd in the lobby when I came down the hall. The actual unveiling was by invitation only and it was still unbelievably full. That was about the only thing that could make the situation worse for me. *Ugggghhhh!* But I had known that would be the case. I had expected it. I could even see the TV cameras then, over by the grand entrance to the hotel where they planned to follow us out to capture the first images of the newest Wu Xing Garden. They were the main reason that Viv's posse had been necessary in the first place. *Deep breaths… whoa!*

There were *way* too many people there for *my* comfort level! I was already getting hit with so much excitement and anticipation that my heart was positively racing as I made my way over to my employer. I tried to focus on blocking some of it out the best I could. I began to sing one of Ethan's songs to myself, out loud but softly, while I continued to take slow deep breaths in through my nose. My heart settled down some then, but not a lot. Oh well, I thought to myself with all the courage that I could muster, *it is what it is. Just keep going.*

I walked up and shook hands with Mr. Wu Xing and we each gave a slight bow then stepped back.

"It seems our guests are very excited for the big reveal." He stated with a genuine smile at the interest the event had generated for his family's hotel. "I just hope the finished product turned out half as beautiful as you look this evening, Miss. Harrington. Quite the transformation." He added sincerely. I was praying silently that he would think so when he saw it, and that it would all turn out to be *good* publicity for them in the end.

"Thank you. I've done my absolute best to create a pleasant outcome I assure you, in both cases." I added with a sarcastic half smile. He offered his arm to me.

"Shall we go and see how it measures up then?" He asked simply. A couple more giant inhalations and I nodded.

"Let's do it."

As we walked past the front desk, the staff room beside it began to slowly empty out. The first to fall in behind us were an older couple that I had to assume from the pride they were currently beaming, were Wu Xing's parents. After that came his two younger brothers and then a woman I recognized immediately as his beautiful wife. We had only met once but she had been as kind as her husband always was. After that it was just a mass of children, cousins, aunts and uncles as the group continued to grow. One by one they walked out and filed behind us on our way over to the front door.

But we still had one more stop after the family joined us, at the V.I.P. section off to the side of the lobby where another fifty or so people were waiting to do the same. I knew the Mayor and his wife, who were both avid gardeners, were supposed to be there with their grandchildren, as well as a handful of other local politicians of varying importance. There was even a famous newswoman from one of the major stations in the city, who had apparently grown up nearby. She wasn't one of the one's working there that night though, she was there as a guest of the hotel. I had also heard, proving that not all my time in the ladies room had been wasted, that we had two New England Patriot's, and one Bruin's player in attendance, which was pretty impressive considering how far out of "town" we were up there. They had all come with their own wives and families as well.

There were patrolmen stationed all around the grounds as a precautionary measure. Mostly in response to the number of dignitaries present. The general public waiting outside wouldn't have access to the garden until after the official live presentation was over, and then only for a short introductory period, but they didn't seem to mind the inconvenience or the wait. They had come out in droves regardless. I had seen them already starting to line up earlier when I first arrived at the hotel. I had to shake my head at the patience of some people. There were some things that I would never personally understand even with my fairly impressive comprehension skills.

Inside, we had the local Chief of Police who was also off duty and there in the V.I.P. section strictly as a civilian. Most of the people I "*knew of*" but didn't necessarily recognize. It was even harder to recognize some of the faces that I had been seeing on a daily basis for the past two months, when I spotted them all spiffed up.

The whole crew was there of course and they were just as excited to celebrate the unveiling as the rest of the crowd. Like me, they just looked so different all cleaned up and dressed in their "Sunday best" that I had to look closely to positively identify each one. It helped that they were all standing together in a very handsome group by a giant potted palm tree right next to the doorway, as if they still didn't feel entirely comfortable *fully* entering the VIP section.

Doug, Mack and Tom were all in their dress khaki's and freshly pressed short sleeve shirts, hair all combed, gelled and haphazardly spiked. Sharon and Dale were standing next to the three stooges in matching light gray linen, Dale in slacks and Sharon in a short swingy skirt and silk top. And last but never least was Mickey. She stood on the other side of the stooges in a soft pink ruffled tank dress and heels. She looked like she was enjoying being a girl just as much as I was. I smiled at them and went over to hug each one hello. There were whistles and shocked looks at my appearance as well but I tried to ignore it as much as possible throughout the greetings.

Once we were done complimenting each other I made my way over to the next group of familiar faces. That one included my own personal miracle worker that I owed the much celebrated completion to, Gen. She was dressed as nice as the other guests in a light blue cotton dress, but it wasn't as shocking on her since it was more her normal attire. She stood talking with Jack and the rest of the workers that she had helped to connect me with when I needed more specialized help on the water harp. I hadn't spent too much time getting personal with them during my bid to drown myself in the work, but they had turned out to be a great group of guys in the end that got along with the others well and were very skilled at what they did. I went over to say hello and to thank each one of them again personally, grateful for the chance to make up for my earlier nonchalance a bit.

They were receptive to my apologies and I was relieved to have so many friendly faces there to support me through the circus act that was to follow. Jack was the last to come and hug me but he held on the tightest and the longest. It was a very fatherly type of pride that I felt from him as he smiled at me.

"Thank you for coming, and for all your help, heck for your offspring too!" I gushed while wrapping one arm around the shoulders of a blushing Gen. "Without whom this would not even be happening!" I finished honestly. She smiled in appreciation of my appreciation. Jack just grinned some more before he shrugged it off.

"Eh, I had some time to kill and I haven't worn this suit in a while. I was afraid the moths were getting more use out of it than I was!" He joked affectionately, trying not to take too much credit. I continued despite his attempt at modesty.

"Seriously, I know that words are cheap but I don't know where I'd be without either of you and that's the God's honest truth! So *thank you!*" I reiterated wholeheartedly.

"You'd be right here I'm sure, somehow!" Gen insisted teasingly. "You would have found a way to make this happen, with or without us, but I'm thrilled that I was in the right place at the right time to help you, and to get to know you along the way!" She added with an honest smile. "If you ever need my services again, you know where to find me." She insisted as she hugged me.

"You don't know how relieved I am to ear you say that, because I could really use a "friend/kick-ass lawyer" in my life!" I said as I laughed. I finally noticed then though, that one rather large crew member that I didn't recognize, was paying pretty close attention to our conversation and I started to get annoyed, thinking that he was being awfully nosy. Then I noticed that his attention was mostly on Gen and it was not *all* of a PG nature! That just pissed me off more! I knew Gen had a boyfriend and I was sure he wouldn't appreciate that!

I looked back at her with an eye roll and quietly suggested that we move to a different spot for a minute, so I could speak to her privately. I nodded towards the group of men standing behind us. There's something I should probably tell you before I get lost in the crowd." I whispered. I tried to pull her by her elbow but she didn't budge. I wrinkled my brow at her reluctance and she laughed.

"Simone, I'd like you to meet my fiancé' Travis." She reached back for his hand and he took it instantly, coming forward on cue. It was the overly affectionate man and his ridiculous grin made perfect sense then.

He was closer to Ethan's height than the others at what I guessed to be around 6'3" or 6'4". We shook hands and said hello officially as the pieces all started to fall into place. I took the time to notice then, his all-American football player looks, with his short, straight reddish brown hair and kind green eyes. It was clear that someday he and Gen would make beautiful babies together. I gave a secret smile for Jack and Shirley at that thought but didn't dwell there. The present situation demanded my full attention.

Travis was formidable in stature, being just slightly beyond what you would call "*slim*" but still not quite substantial enough to be considered "*hefty.*" He was *sturdy*, like he was wearing football pads, even though he wasn't. Contradictorily enough, he was also the quietest and definitely the most subtle of the group. While they all joked and jostled one another behind him, his demeanor was calm and pleasant, quietly amused. The strongest thing coming off of him was his desire for Gen.

"It's very nice to finally meet you." He said as he stood beside her, with his hand placed gently on the small of her back, making his affection for her apparent to everyone then and not just me. "This is quite a turnout. I've heard so much about this project lately." He joked looking down at Gen playfully. She just grinned sarcastically back up at him. "I'm very excited to finally see it for myself!" He added genuinely.

"Well I hope it lives up to the hype at this point. Either way, I'm done." I joked back, with my hands in the air. "I just have to get through tonight." I said with a deep breath. They all felt my anxiety to some degree I could tell, but Jack was the first one to try and talk me down.

"You'll be just fine." He cooed confidently. "That place is amazing! You've got nothing to worry about!" He finished with a chuckle and wink. I hugged him one more time and hoped desperately that he was right! I tried to calm my breathing and relax a bit. I was still searching the room while we chatted.

There were a few more V.I.P.'s in particular that I needed to find. After another moment of scanning the crowd, I could finally see them heading over. I sighed in relief at the comfort that it gave me.

"*Mama!* What took you so long?" The most important "*P*" of them all asked as they approached. She let go of my father's hand and ran over to me. I lifted her up carefully, making sure that my dress stayed in place and as gracefully as possible, set her on my hip. I refused to add "*horrifying wardrobe malfunction*" to the list of things I had to deal with that evening.

"Sorry." I said in response. "I just needed a minute by myself first to get ready." I admitted with a deep sigh. I could feel her forgiveness as she gave me a big hug and a kiss and then I put her back down just as carefully.

"Are you ready?" I asked her. She nodded vigorously but her overwhelming joy was answer enough. My parents followed her at a much more adult pace and each came up to give me a hug and a kiss on the cheek.

"Congratulation's honey. You look beautiful." My father offered with a calm smile. I could feel the pride emanating out from him already and he hadn't even seen what I'd done yet. You just had to appreciate a parent's unconditional love.

"Thank you." My mother was right behind him with her own hug and kiss, and her own beaming pride, both looking as neat and as polished as ever. Events like this were cake for them. It was having it be because of *me* that was different! It was a nice change for them though and they were both really happy to be there simply as proud patents instead of solicitors for once.

"I'm so glad there will be pictures of this!" My mother joked happily to the crowd, referring to my attire. I immediately blushed in the way that only a parent can make you blush. It always made her ecstatic whenever I took the time to dress up. Truth be told, it was probably at least a small part of what made it so satisfying for me on occasion, knowing that she got such joy out of it.

"Mom, Dad, this is Jack, my landlord and savior." I said with a lopsided grin as I finally introduced them all. It was definitely a little weird having them all together in the same place for the first time. "And this is his daughter Genevieve, the miracle worker and her fiancé Travis. I've just met him myself though so I don't know what *his* special qualities are yet." I joked, breaking the tension a little. My parents went down the line shaking hands. I was worried they would feel awkward but they handled it with grace, as always.

"Seth Harrington." My dad said, referring to himself. "And this is my wife Evelyn but everyone calls her Evie. It's so nice to finally have a reason to get together! I've heard such good things about all of you!" He gushed while shaking their hands. "Of course we are extremely grateful for all of the support and kindness your family has shown our Simone. It's nice to know, when your children are away from home, that there is someone looking out for them like you would." He said simply but sincerely and everyone could feel the intensity behind his words as easily as I could for once.

The familial bond was welling in the immediate atmosphere and it grew as I felt it from each person there as it bounced back and forth. I bit my lip and tried not to let it overwhelm me. *In... out...*

"You don't have to thank us. We consider ourselves very lucky to have her 'round here! You all have done a great job with that one." Jack replied affectionately as he stepped back. Gen backed him up.

'Absolutely. What he said." She added, breaking the seriousness a little as she came forward and took her turn shaking hands.

"Ah Genevieve, so then you are Gen, the incredibly talented lawyer that almost rendered my small bit of assistance completely unnecessary." He said without really being annoyed as he shook her hand. "It seems a lot of the people I've been waiting to thank are right here in this room." He commented with a warm smile. "Simone really did land in a good spot, didn't she?" He decided out loud. Gen took the praise in stride and glossed right over it.

"She's been just as good for the people here as we have been for her, I promise you." She proclaimed diplomatically with a quick wink in my direction. I could feel her deep appreciation for what she knew Ethan and I felt for each other and I didn't take that lightly either.

"Well we certainly tried to raise her right, but you never know once you send them out into the world now do you?" My mother said sarcastically as she shook hands with, Jack, Gen and then Travis. "It certainly is refreshing to find so many kindred souls so far from home." She finished honestly with her trademark smile.

Both Jack and Gen just nodded understandingly while Travis smiled in agreement.

Liliana ran up then and jumped up to hug Jack, almost taking out a passerby with flying pink fiberglass arm. Jack swooped her up and out of the way just in time for them to duck and smile. I quickly mouthed an apology and they laughed it off and kept going. "Hi!" She shouted completely unaware. "How's Cookie?" She asked excitedly. Jack didn't bat an eye.

"She's getting fat waiting for you!" He replied playfully. "Won't ride with anybody else." He added with a straight face. It was a bit of a white lie of course but I knew he was working to maintain their connection so I didn't interfere or object. He winked at me in appreciation. "So I'll tell her maybe you'll see her in a couple weeks?" He asked and she literally beamed!

"Yes sir, doc says two more weeks and I'll be good to go!" She affirmed with a tiny smile that beamed like the moon! Finally free of her cast, she was just slowly getting back to her normal activities which made me very happy, but it reminded me of a situation that made me very *unhappy*, so I put it out of my mind temporarily. I had enough to deal with for the moment.

She hopped down and went back to skipping around the room after that and I watched her with a pride that had no equal in my life. My daughter was generally a source of pure joy for me and one that I treasured. It was an unfortunate situation that we found ourselves in currently though, that much was for sure. At that, I thought of my own mother and I took in her feelings too.

She was extremely proud of me for sure, but of course I could feel her worry for me as well. Those emotions were warring inside of her when she spoke up.

"You gonna be alright out there? That's an awfully big crowd." She asked gently, knowing better than anyone how hard things like that could be for me. But I had known what to expect, and I had tried to mentally prepare as much as possible. I was working hard at "*control mode*" and I knew that was as "*prepared*" as I was ever going to get.

"Yeah, sure. What's the big deal? It's just a couple hundred people watching and waiting to see if I succeed or fall flat on my face. No biggie, right?" I chuckled in the end but there was a lot more nerves than humor in it. My mom just hugged me tightly once again, trying to absorb a little of my anxiety through her skin. She was a mother after all. That instinct to protect was just as strong in her. It didn't really work that way unfortunately, but just her desire to help, helped. I was a big girl though and I knew I had to do it on my own. I had learned how to get through those types of things long ago, and I would do it again. They couldn't defeat me anymore.

In... Out...

I smiled back at my mother, truly grateful for her efforts. "I'll be fine. Really." I was reassuring them at that point so they knew me well enough to let it go. We all took a deep breath as Liliana skipped around us in circles in her little yellow cotton sundress and her new "super-cute" but smartly rubber-soled, sandals. Her hair was up in one high swingy ponytail, tied with a piece of bright yellow silk ribbon. It somehow looked old fashioned and yet adorably fresh and modern at the same time. Don't ask me how.

I knew that she'd had had just as much fun as I did getting

ready with Viv and her whole "team" earlier in the day, and she was having a great time there already. I was always glad anytime I was in any way responsible for that. The anticipation at her seeing the garden for the first time was as intense as my anticipation of Wu Xing seeing it. I didn't know which I was more worried about pleasing or which I was more excited about showing it to!

Excitement wasn't the *only* thing I was feeling, not by a long shot. I did try to just focus on that for a minute though, and on how lucky I was instead of how empty that one certain place in my life currently was.

Mr. Wu Xing had stopped briefly to greet the attending dignitaries while I had been talking to my coworkers and my family, but he was ready to proceed. His own children came forward then to walk with him. His youngest son Min, who was three, was holding his left hand and his only daughter Hua who was seven, held his right. His oldest son Shen, the "*next in line to the throne*" so-to-speak who I knew was eleven stood independently next to his little brother as they all came up beside me. Mr. Wu Xing took his place on my left side once again.

"Ready?" He asked simply but with great meaning. I felt the excitement of the crowd reach a crescendo and spill through me at his question. I held it all in and simply nodded. It was all I could do. I took Liliana's hand while my parents, the Kent's and the crew all fell back in with the rest of the group and we started moving again.

One by one, people emptied out of the beautiful room and all fell into step behind us as we made our way out past the ropes and through the oversized doors back into the lobby. We formed a spring-fashion parade of short skirts, sandals and sharp but lightweight summer suits, as we continued out through the main doors into the hot summer night. There were flashbulbs going off on all sides from the photographers that were hired not only by Mr. Wu Xing to document the occasion, but also by the local newspapers and magazines as well to cover the event.

Well respected magazines like Country Garden and even prestigious ones like *Garden Design* had reporters present I noticed as we passed! *Yikes!* No pressure there! I also noticed that the TV cameras made sure they got a shot of each important face as they passed. Then they turned to get a wide shot of line as it moved up the stone walkway that curved around the main building and up toward the gardens. From that vantage we could all see a wide red ribbon that waited patiently to be cut hanging across the newest path on the left.

The crowd was chatting excitedly and Liliana was skipping merrily at my side as we made our way over there. Thankfully we could not have asked for a better night weather-wise. It was still as dreadfully hot as it had been every other day lately, but with the dusk came a glorious breeze, even if it was a warm one. It was at least strong enough to keep the mosquitoes from having an easy time landing, so it had a doubly-good effect. It was nice to get the chance to smell like the Ralph Lauren "*Romance*" perfume that Viv had spritzed lightly over me, rather than like bug spray for a change. No matter how "fresh" each brand decried their scent to be, it *all* still smelled like bug spray, if it worked anyway.

We reached the entrance and I stood on one side of the giant velvet bow while Mr. Wu Xing went and stood on the other. The related children all stood around us and the rest lined up eagerly behind them at the head of the winding concrete trail. The adults separated into two lines on either side to make room for them. The children knew that they were in the driver's seat for a change. The parents were just lucky enough to be able to tag along. I could feel how much fun they were having, just with that one circumstance and I grinned along with them.

I looked back at Mr. Wu Xing as he picked up the ridiculously oversized gold scissors. He brought them up between us and I held the other handle. We worked them fairly easily, with my half coming up and his half going down. The ribbon fell and the crowd clapped as flashbulbs went off in another blinding round.

With one final nod from Mr. Wu Xing, the children all began to scream and cheer and run freely up the trail. I felt their joy in a giant rush through my body as they ran past. The adults got a chuckle out of their eagerness but were completely content to follow at a leisurely pace. I was still slightly apprehensive at what the reactions from the adults would be, a few important ones in particular. So I was quite willing to dawdle along with them, delaying the inevitable.

We started down the path that was walled off on both sides with tall, dark green shrubbery like you would find in an English labyrinth. I wanted to take away all sense of where you were temporarily, as you prepared to enter the main area further up the trail, so that people would be more open to the alternate reality that we had worked so hard to create on the other end. All we could see so far were walls of tiny leaves and the smooth, shoe-friendly walkway but we could hear the cries of delight quite clearly as the children ahead of us, began to spill out onto the main trail.

I felt their surprise first and then their pure unadulterated delight at what they had found and I smiled a satisfied smile to myself. Nothing could keep me from feeling *that!* As half detached as I was from the celebration for my own reasons, I could not go untouched by the infectious elation that the children spread. I was secretly glad for that. I would take that type of involuntary overload any day. Especially if some of that was Liliana's.

Just another moment later and I was sure that it was. I smiled even bigger at the realization of that particular goal. Mr. Wu Xing saw my expression and his anticipation grew along with his curiosity. He grinned back at me as we got closer but otherwise exhibited the same supreme patience as always.

A few steps later and we rounded the last bend in the 'hedge-trail' ourselves, where it opened up into the forest and the concrete walkway widened to almost road-size. It also transformed from the plain taupe colored concrete that it was on our end, to a much brighter, livelier path. We had planted hundreds of yards of flowers and seven different types of groundcover all along both sides of the main trail that made it all appear to blend right into the greenery.

Then we copied that same bright color palette into the stain that we used on the walkway from that point on. One spring color washed seamlessly into the next and made for a much more organic feel. Although a perfectly smooth concrete path was obviously not exactly "natural" to the area, but between the way that it curved lazily back and forth, the colorful stain, and the surrounding flora, it at least felt like it was.

As the adults began to look up and take in the Tree-fort Village for the first time, *ooh's* and *ahh's* started to erupt all around me, but I was still waiting anxiously for a response to waft out of the ever-stoic Mr. Wu Xing to my right.

I held my breath a little, knowing he would never be rude and I started to think that his slow response may be an attempt on his part to come up with something positive to say to cover his displeasure. I checked again, just to see. It wasn't helpful though because despite his calm outward demeanor, his emotions were all over the place and I still couldn't be sure what he thought about it. He was feeling too many things at once and I didn't understand them all. I started to sweat just a little despite my liberal use of a heavy duty "*summer-proof*" deodorant during our earlier *battle preparations.* I turned and gazed back out over the whole thing myself once more, to check for any obvious flaws. It immediately made me smile.

The garden was made up of one continuous trail down the center and one shorter one that intersected perpendicular to it. Together they made a large, wavy cross that pointed into the forest, with the well and our solution to that little revelation sitting directly in the center of the intersection. It was really what you would call a triple-cross though because it was made up of three distinct paths that extended in each of the four directions. There was the center path that we were currently walking on. This was for the *not-so-young-at-heart*, or those in high heels, you know anyone who required a flat surface for easy walking but still wanted to appreciate the view and the ambiance.

In addition to that, there were the two upper "tree-fort" paths that were made up of long, suspended walkways running along either side. They extended across the entire length of the main trail and connected way up high in each tree as they passed. They were low hanging and free-swinging in the space between, with knotted rope sides and railings, but there was a "*fort*" at each spot that the walkways connected to the tree. A solid place where the kids could stop, sit or look out a window and appreciate the view. It wasn't incredibly high, but it was more than high enough for people under five feet tall!

We had excavated very carefully, a wide area underneath each walkway between the trees, removing all the loose sticks and rocks. We made sure all the tree roots were safe and sufficiently covered with a rich soil and padding over that. Then we covered that with three feet of fall-safe fill. First a layer of sand, then a layer of small mold resistant foam blocks on top of that, more sand and then finally a layer of recycled rubber mulch to finish it off and make it look nice. It would not only serve as extra cushion if necessary for a soft landing, but also would not need to be removed or replaced every year. It had the added benefit of *looking* natural, even if it wasn't. They would only have to add to it periodically to maintain it, to replace whatever nature took away with the weather each year. It was the truest outdoor playground I could imagine.

I watched as the children and a few of the more adventurous adults began to run up and across the suspended walkways with great delight. I rejoiced at the little happy faces that quickly began to peek out of every window and peer over every ledge.

It was built sturdy enough to hold every adult there, and then some, but it was really *designed* for the children. Everything was made to their height and from their point of view, for their benefit. That didn't mean the adults weren't enjoying it just as much though. We *all* have a child inside of us somewhere after all, every single one of us. No one gets to eighty, without first being eight. You just can't do it.

You would think the fact that two thirds of the attraction was poised up in the air would be the most unusual thing about the garden, but it wasn't. The thing that really set it apart was the fact that the whole Tree-fort Village was aglow, lit with thousands of strings dotted with tiny neon blue LED lights! *This* was the main reason that the opening was being held at night and the overall effect was absolutely stunning, even to me!

The lights were strung from all of the surrounding trees where they wouldn't interfere with future growth and would blend in nicely with the foliage during the daytime. They draped down in a hanging pattern so that it appeared to be a secret forest of phosphorescent weeping willows, with a tiny suspended village tucked safely in its branches. Sharon and Dale had done their job well and the lights truly looked as if they had blossomed from the leaves themselves. With the low light of the crescent moon for a backdrop, the whole glowing Tree-fort Village looked straight out of a fairytale.

That had been exactly what I envisioned when I had started the project. It was a dream brought to life, literally. My design was based originally on a dream that Liliana had told me about once when she was four years old. She had described a place where everything was built to her size and everyone lived high up in the tree tops and where the leaves were a pretty glowing "*blue-moon*" color.

Ever since then, I had thought about how cool it would be to try and create such a place for her in real life, before she was too old to enjoy it. The Tree-fort Village garden was the direct result of that wish. I was quite happy with it myself I reconfirmed, and as I caught Liliana's eye from one of the tree-fort windows I knew for sure that she was just as thrilled.

That meant that I had really achieved that goal and *that* meant everything to me! It was more than enough to make it all worthwhile.

I had told her of my desire to recreate her dream place once and I knew that Wu Xing Gardens may be the only chance I would ever get to make that happen. I could feel the satisfaction that I had been waiting for as her overwhelming approval filled me. She knew that I could feel it too, even though she was pretty far away in the second tree-fort landing. I'd never had a problem picking up her feelings, and short distances hardly seemed to matter between us. As long as she was within sight I could generally get whatever she was feeling clearly. She was so elated then that it was actually *beyond* easy. She was not just satisfied, she was *overjoyed!*

At that honest but completely accidental assessment, I thought of the song with that same name and the time that Ethan had sung it to me. I had to work hard for a minute or two after that to keep the longing out of my current attempt at being upbeat. But

I had found a way to keep that particular memory a good one and that part actually made me smile in anticipation. I didn't want to ruin that. I had yet to reveal that still.

As I stood lost in my thoughts and everyone else's, I finally felt the first real emotion coming off of Wu Xing and it was *good! Phew!* There was surprise and there was wonder but there was also a real happiness and a sense of satisfaction at the fantasy quality of it all. The adult in him wanted to resist the playful nature of it, but it was irresistible. It was pure fun on a level that you couldn't debate. You just wanted to run, laughing, from one tree-fort to the next. I had noticed the effect it had on one grown up after another throughout the process. Every full-grown adult in attendance that had worked on it in any way had already done it themselves, most numerous times. None of us were exempt.

As adults, we try to act like the mature grown-up's we know we're supposed to be, and in that vein we had the more conservative option to walk along the perfectly even path of the concrete trail as it meandered its' way through the center of the trees. And it was very pleasant. But it was the suspended pathway that beckoned and even *begged* to be traveled! That's when I knew it was a success, when I could feel that, not just from the children but from him and the other adults as well.

"It's wonderful!" He complimented honestly. He looked up then to the nearest tree-fort landing on the right where his wife and two youngest children called and waved playfully from different windows. He waved back and I could feel his happiness at the outcome. Seeing his children laugh and play and be so carefree was the ultimate goal for him.

He had made that very clear from our first meeting that that was the direction he wanted to go in for his personal legacy. He didn't know exactly what he wanted, just that his own kids had convinced him that there should be at least one garden on the grounds that was strictly for kids. One where they could run and play and not get scolded for acting inappropriately and he had agreed. Having Liliana's dream in my head for a design already had made the decision an easy one for both of us when we met. He looked at me again and his smile was contagious.

"There's more." I added with a smile of my own at the thought of the surprise that still remained. "Come and see what we've done with the aquifer and the well." I coaxed. He grinned at the reminder but I knew he hadn't seen it or asked about it since we had inadvertently discovered it. He had left that little disaster to me to work through and had simply requested that I "Let him know what I decided to do."

In the end I had decided not to tell him though. I just let him know that we had worked it out and that I thought it would make a nice surprise for everyone, including him. I was genuinely excited about getting to finally show that to him. I didn't have to work as hard at keeping a smile for the next few minutes as we made our way up toward the pergola-like structure that we had built over and around the well.

The suspended walkways in the trees had a ramp that fed from the closest tree in each of the four center corners of the cross, to the balcony level that wrapped around the outer edge of the pergola's rooftop. From there, each corner held a spiral stairway that led down to the main level on the outside. As the crowd of adults and cameraman made their way up the stairs to enter the pergola, the children and adventurous adults started to follow those ramps and spiral down to meet us at the very heart of the garden. It was the only section that had not been a part of Liliana's dream. That particular gem was all Ethan and I, born completely out of unexpected circumstance.

I had envisioned something that I wasn't even sure existed or *could* exist, and he had proceeded to very skillfully pull a million different little pieces from a myriad of varying disciplines together and somehow bring that vision to life!

I had heard music in the water from the beginning and I had imagined, in the spirit of the "dreamlike" quality of the whole design, actually being able to *play* it!

Ethan not only knew how to read, write and play music, but he also understood the basic construction behind many of the different instruments that he had mastered over the years. He also found enough information from books about the aquifer and weather patterns to understand the flow rate and figure out how to account for its' fluctuations. This enabled him to engineer a pump and regulator that would keep it flowing at a steady and controllable rate. That was important he had explained, for the regulations, but also for what we wanted it to do. I really hated that he never got to see it from sketch to completion, since I knew in the end he had been just as excited about it as I was.

It had been especially tough when it came time for the actual assembly and he wasn't there. The men that I had working on that new part along with my original crew had all been totally fired up about it when they first saw the plans. They were excited to be a part of it and no one could wait for it to be done so we could try it out and see if it would really work! I understood their reactions completely but it made me sad that so many strangers got to experience the joy of actually creating it when Ethan didn't. Especially when he's the one who made it work in the first place. It just wasn't fair. But *eh*, we all know how that one goes, don't we?

The breeze was still blowing and the children were still straggling down so we took our time walking up to the pergola, but we did eventually make it there and I had to get back to trying to be happy again then. One big breath and I headed up the four steps to the top. We had removed the remaining boulders that were originally covering the "*brook*" as Mack had first referred to it, with no further exposure thank goodness! Then we built a square structure on top of the opening with its' four walls each resting on solid ground.

The interior of the pergola was built like a suspended bridge over the whole exposed area of the aquifer. It opened up to the outer paths with the same four steps in all four directions. It was only under the structure and therefore inside, that you could tell the opening was even there. It felt fitting for it to be a surprise to visitors, just as it had been to us.

As we filed inside, adults and children began to mix again and fill the wide walkway that extended around all four walls of the square building making all sorts of surprised sounds and faces. The floating floor inside looked much like the suspended walkways outside having been built using the same wide wooden planks. The difference was that in there it was all perfectly flat and permanently affixed. The center of the structure however, was left completely open where you could easily see the water passing by tranquilly beneath us. That center square wasn't completely empty though. Just above water level, its span was crossed time and again by evenly spaced, overlapping rows of shiny metal strings. They were too thin to obstruct the view in any way but they glinted occasionally off of the light like giant strands of tinsel.

From the metal railing that stood at rib level, down to the bottom edge of the walkway, there was a solid glass wall separating the people from the chasm in the middle which gave a wondrous view of it all. From that railing up to the ceiling on two sides, there was a virtual wall that spanned the distance, made up of thin vertical light beams. They were also evenly spaced and were glowing the same neon shade of blue as the trees outside.

People stood in awe of the unusual sight but didn't make any moves toward the railing at first. From the two open sides they peered down to the impressive view beneath us. They were curious, but still wary, some just of falling in I noticed, but I knew that fear was unfounded. We had taken every precaution, inside and out to ensure the safety of our visitors. The glass wall was much too high for anyone to "*fall*" *in*. They would have to be over seven feet tall or intentionally "*climb*" to get over it and even that would not be easy. Hopefully the plainly visible, twenty four hour security cameras aimed directly at the center would deter, or if necessary, put a stop to anyone stupid enough to try it. I grinned as I felt most of the people admiring the beauty and the artistry of it, thinking that's all there was. They didn't know yet that there was more.

Jack walked up behind me then and whispered encouragingly. "This is my favorite part." He grinned mightily then rejoined the crowd with Gen grinning knowingly at his side. My parents filed in with the same look of delighted confusion that everyone else had though and they watched but didn't approach it.

It was no surprise to me that it was the children who were

the first to finally come forward to test it, not yet having completely tamed their natural curiosity. They were inherently unable to resist the urge to stick their hand through the beams of light.

Mr. Wu Xing's oldest son Shen was one of the oldest kids there and the very first to step up and timidly test it out. As he reached out slowly, the whole crowd held their collective breath. When his hand broke the light beam, the water dripped out from above us and played the corresponding note on the strings beneath us, they all responded as one, gasping in surprise and delight! It swept through me and I felt like a little girl with a big plate of birthday cake for a few seconds. *Ahhhhh...*

He did it again and they all looked down and watched as the water dropped past the strings and rejoined the slivery current below, playing a perfect note on its' way by. There was a round of approval and a handful of "*that's-so-cool's*" in the crowd. Shen passed his hand through the next beam over and the next note in the musical scale played. He laughed out loud then and began to try more of them with both hands. It didn't take the rest of them very long to come forward and join in, all sticking their hands in and out and running up and down the length of the wall with their arm out like they were passing a picket fence and creating moving scales. The adults backed up some and let them have their fun. Before long, they ran over to try the strings on the opposite side of the square, much to everyone's renewed delight.

The beams on the side closest to us were designed to play individual notes, but the laser beams opposite had each been programmed to trigger a whole section of a song when broken. There was another soothing round of giddiness at that discovery as the first one played. The adults were having just as much fun as the kids again with the added element of standing silently and listening to the first few familiar sections. Then they competed to be the first to identify the song. It was a good feeling, that win-win thing again. I stepped back and happily made more room for the curious.

I looked over at my parents who weren't surprised to see me backing off. They grinned and tilted their heads in understanding, but then they both gave me the double thumbs up as they looked around in awe. That made me feel content enough to sigh another deep sigh and fall even further against the back wall.

I was afraid to trust it at first though, like maybe it was just an "*only a parent could love it*" kind of thing. My parents were pretty honest in general but you never know. I gave a quick sweep of the entire range of emotions flooding the room, instinctually looking for the most negative in the bunch to gauge my success or failure by. Sometimes even a roomful of positivity, was not enough to outweigh the heaviness of one souls' negativity, *if* they had a valid point. I didn't find any of that there though and that made the relief real. All I felt was genuine joy, amusement and a sense of surprise and fun. I finally felt like I could relax, just a little more. *In... out...*

I looked over and I saw Mr. Wu Xing and his wife holding hands and grinning at their children's enjoyment. They were giving off some of the best feelings in the room. I gave a small sigh in silent thanks and left everyone to their fun. The photographers had a field day shooting it all while the cameramen got everything on film.

I was glad but I was mentally done, exhausted. I backed all the way into the corner and just quietly observed. My parents were working the crowd as beautifully as ever and I wondered why I had inherited the *height* gene instead of that one, when it was obviously so prominent in both of them. I guessed maybe it skipped a generation. Anyway, I didn't need to constantly entertain them and Liliana was still playing with Wu Xing's children and having the time of her life.

The laser water harp had been just as much of a surprise to her as it was to the other children and I was just as happy as the Wu Xing's to simply sit back and enjoy that coming from her. Seeing her so happy and Mr. Wu Xing and his family also enjoying the success of the design was all I could ask for. Everything else was gravy. Quite frankly, I was ready to go at that point. I wondered how bad it would look if I skipped out on the whole dinner reception being held in my honor in the hotel after the opening?

Mr. Wu Xing came over to me a few minutes later, before I had a chance to think up a plausible excuse to bow out though. I knew right away, that I would have to abandon my escape plan. Oh well, we were almost there, I thought knowing that at least that was the final photo op of the evening. He stood to face me and I stood up straight again as the crowd fell silent.

He extended his hand to me and I shook it. "Thank you, Miss. Harrington, for a job *well* done!" He said in official acceptance. *Alrighty then! Thank goodness for small miracles, I thought with a great sense of relief.* He was back to his usual calm demeanor and gave another slight bow while the crowd clapped. The words were simple, but the true honesty and appreciation that I could feel behind them were overwhelming. The photographers got a few more shots of us shaking hands and then a few of the family all together in front of the harp. Slowly people began to break up and socialize more while each of the kids got a turn.

Thankfully, we had programmed the electronic brain that controlled the water flow over the strings to not play more than one song at a time. We had also set it up so that while the individual notes could be played together, they could not be played when a song section was playing. Otherwise we would be being bombarded with a symphony of musical madness.

That little feature had been a last minute suggestion of Ethan's as well and I couldn't agree with that foresight more after the fact. Not only did it force the children to exhibit just the slightest bit of patience, having to wait for one song to finish before they could play another, but it also saved the sanity of the accompanying adults as it kept the music pleasing instead of annoying.

I stood smiling to myself at that when the famous newswoman came over and introduced herself.

"Hi! I'm Marina. Marina Stavros." She said enthusiastically offering her hand. She was about my height but she was obviously a pro in heels as hers made her about two inches taller. She was much thinner too, even more so than she looked on TV. I guessed it was true what they say, about the camera adding ten pounds. I tried not to think about what I was going to look like in that dress at ten pounds heavier when it aired. *Uggghhck!* Oh well, lesson learned.

"Hi. Simone. It's nice to meet you and thank you so much for coming." I said politely as we shook hands. She was in a great mood and her energy was like a bright pink light bulb. It was nice enough to be around though. Certainly much better than some of the other available options I have encountered in my life.

"Oh you're welcome! I heard about it and I really wanted to be here so badly that I arranged to borrow my nieces for the night!" She confessed with a genuine smile. She was obviously pretty but didn't come off as presenting that to others first as her most important asset and I liked that. She was aware that she was attractive, don't get me wrong, but I could already tell that she was not dependent on it to get by.

She had dark, shiny hair that had clearly been professionally straightened, and then re-curled just on the ends. To go with it there were big brown eyes and skin that was a beautiful shade of light golden brown. It was hard to tell how much of that color was tan and how much was natural for her due to her ethnicity. She didn't try to hide her Greek features though or to homogenize herself like a lot of other TV personalities did. She was a smart woman who knew how to make her own natural beauty work in her favor.

Her originality and her exotic appearance got peoples' attention, but it was when she would proceed to give an insightful and intelligent interview, that she would really shine. I had always admired that about her in her work and it was refreshing to know that I felt the same way in her presence. She would be foolish in her line of work *not* to have used it to her advantage though and she definitely did not strike me as foolish.

Sorry, this is just what's it's like to be me. This is what's going on in my head in the first few seconds, every time I meet someone new. There is this whole in-depth inner conversation of incoming information and analysis going on, often before they've even said hello to me and they have no idea. It'd been really hard to get used to originally but I had become completely accustomed to it by then. It made me think of other new *heights* though who might face the same kinds of things and how long someone else might take to adjust. Then that made me think of Jeremy which of course, instantly made me think of Ethan. I sighed and switched my focus back to the conversation starting up outside my head instead before the longing could show on my face.

"I don't know if you know who I am or not but I wanted to tell you personally how much I just love what you've done here!" She gushed sincerely and I was instantly flattered since I knew exactly who she was, just like everybody else there!

"Of course I recognize you! I admit that I don't watch a lot of news in general, it's just too much for me most days." I added without explaining further. "But I've seen a handful of segments of yours over the years. You're very good at getting the facts but still being a lot of fun to watch, especially when you go after the bad businesses and stuff. You're like a graceful pit-bull! I love it!" I added in genuine appreciation of my own. "And thanks, I'm really glad you like it." I finished with a real smile.

"Well being in the line of work that I am, I can honestly proclaim that I'm not one of those types who'll say something unless I mean it." She insisted. I knew she was being completely honest already, but of course she didn't know that I knew that. I let her continue to convince me just a minute more before I changed the subject.

"So you grew up around here?" I asked, successfully switching the focus back to her again.

"Yup. Well part time anyway. The other half was spent down in Massachusetts, in a little town that most people haven't ever heard of. But we had a vacation home up here that was only about five miles from the hotel. It was perfect because when I say "vacation home" I really mean cabin with no electricity until I was five and no running water until I was nine! But we would still spend all of our weekends and summers there anyway and this place was a Godsend to us!" She beamed.

"It was smaller then, but whenever we needed a break from "*nature*" we could get a hot meal in the restaurant or for a real treat we would come stay the night. Then we could shower or if it was raining or something we could use the indoor pool where the parrots flew around free! It was so cool! Whatever the reason, it was always memorable whenever we got to come. I grew up loving it here and I still love to come back every once in a while when I'm in town. It's certainly only gotten better over the years." She said and I nodded.

"I believe it! Mr. Wu Xing has been a great man to work for. His other employees must feel the same way because it definitely shows in their level of dedication. I imagine that many of his family members have probably shared that personality trait throughout the generations, for the family business to have done so well for so long. They've done a great job of growing *and* maintaining it over the years." I said, wondering if I would ever have anything that vast or important to be proud of, or to pass on.

I wasn't sure where that thought came from and I tried to chalk it up to just the things that "*real adults*" probably think about, but I still got lost in my own head again after that and the conversation died. A moment later, Marina smiled awkwardly and excused herself.

A few more people came over to talk to me, Gen, Mack and a few dignitaries, but most of the conversations were similarly successful and just as short. One at a time the reporters each came over and asked a few questions about my inspiration and I briefly explained about Liliana's dream.

I really wanted to explain about my friend Ethan too, and to give credit where credit was due in the design of the completely digital laser water harp that everyone was so excited about, but I wasn't sure if that would help or hurt his situation so I kept silent, not willing to accidentally do more harm than good.

Eventually, once everyone had gotten a turn to play the room sized instrument, they were ready to move on. A few small groups at a time, they began to proceed back up the main trail and inside for the dinner portion of the festivities which was about to start. I tried to remember to smile somewhat convincingly at each one as they passed.

Chapter 3

Phew! I had done it. I had survived the unveiling without ever letting on that I wasn't *really* happy to be finished. Not one person was any wiser to that fact as they hugged and congratulated me over and over. Not even my parents suspected my true feelings. They knew me the best and of course were well aware that I didn't really want to be there, but I knew they conveniently chalked it up to the effects of the crowd. I was fine with that misconception though. I knew it was not the time to try and correct them. The Kent's had a better understanding of my current state of mind, but of course they would never mention it so my secret was safe with them.

One after the other, I had accepted the praise of the attendees as humbly as possible. I *had* worked really hard to earn it but it didn't seem to matter as much as I wanted it to at the moment. I had been extremely excited about what we had set out to accomplish there from the very beginning, and I was truly thrilled with the results. It was just the celebration of that accomplishment that I wasn't ready for. I couldn't deny that it felt somewhat hollow for me under the circumstances and I really wished that weren't the case.

I had always been excited to forge my own path in life and to embrace every new encounter along the way, despite the obstacles. Not just by celebrating life on certain occasions either, but by really *living* it to the absolute best of my ability every day! The only problem then was that the new path that I yearned to bravely travel was not a "*one-person*" trail anymore. Life no longer seemed entirely complete just being by myself. By that point I knew I wanted my family by my side, like my parents that I was so lucky to have, but not just them. I wanted more than that. I wanted to have a family of my *own* again. I wanted my daughter back in my life *completely* where she belonged, and I wanted Ethan there just as fully! On top of that I really hoped to always maintain a good relationship with Ben and his family for the sake of our extended family as a whole. It wasn't enough for me to try and get by on tiny separate bits of each of them anymore. I really wanted all the pieces to come together and make up one full life! I just had to figure out how to do that. *Hmpf.* Yeah, that was all.

I stood and swiped my own hand through the light stream and triggered the one that I knew played Matchbox Twenty's "*Overjoyed.*" I backed up and leaned against the edge of the opening and listened to the beautiful tinkling of the water over the strings. Once the crowd had thankfully moved on, I finally got to play one, my personal favorite.

I had shooed the last groups on ahead, begging a quiet moment alone at the well. All of them, including my family members, Harrington's and Kent's alike who were having a great time getting to know each other, smiled as they willingly complied. Most of them just assumed that I wanted to bask in my big moment for a bit before I moved on. Feeling that from so many of them had almost made me laugh out loud, but it got them moving away so I held it in and again, I left it uncorrected.

The excitement was officially over and it was time for everyone to go eat and drink. Their attention on me was already a thing of the past, for the most part. I sighed deeply and laid my head back wearily against the corner beam. I was finally alone again and it was absolutely blissful. I was so relieved to have a just few minutes where I didn't have to keep up the smile, a small break from acting like I was nothing but thrilled with the completion of such a humongous job.

All you could do when someone gushed over your work excitedly, was act gracious and try to *be* the kind of "*happy*" that they expected you to be. I thought that I had done a pretty good job of faking it so far too, but I was really ready for a break.

The design was officially a success. The Tree-fort Village was completed on time thanks to the help of *many, many people*, and had turned out even better than I had ever dreamed! Literally, since I personally had not had any premonitory dreams of the actual finished garden either before or throughout the process. That was another reason I tended not to rely on them, I could never control what I saw or when. It could be very frustrating when you not only wanted but needed to know how something would turn out. It was never that easy though. It had been the same in that case and I was just as surprised as everybody else by its true beauty in the end.

It was definitely a huge hit with visitors, young and old. That *was* extremely gratifying. I couldn't let that personal victory go by entirely without stopping to experience it. I knew moments like that in life were too few and too far between. I would not turn my back on the good graces of the universes' latest good mood, just because mine wasn't the best. Instead, in genuine appreciation I would at least acknowledge the successful outcome. Far be it for me to throw a pissy wrench into the giant turning wheel of life. Karma could be a real bitch and I did not need to get her attention and end up her latest example! In that spirit I had shown up, smiled, and accepted their accolades as graciously as possible. I knew it was the right thing to do.

Too bad it still wasn't enough to lift me out of my current state of "*No, no, everything's fine.*" That "grey place" where I had been existing stubbornly for the last month or so. I had been eating, breathing and living that project for the past *few* months and once it was finished, I was already worried about what I would do next. Instead of feeling joy and the usual sense of completion that's supposed to be there, all I was feeling was *worried!*

What on Earth was I going to do to keep from thinking about him then? I wondered for the millionth time.

I sighed and closed my eyes while I remembered our last time together again. Contrary to what one would expect, it actually helped me to calm down. I remembered one thing in particular just then, with my nerves as frazzled as they were, and it was the way he had drawn one finger down my cheek and across my chin to calm me down that night. It had been an extremely effective, non-verbal "*Shhhhh.*" I could almost feel his gentle touch slide across my skin as I relived it in my mind.

It was the small moments like that one that I found I missed the most. The way he could not only *figure* me out but also *bail* me out, instantly, with just the simplest of gestures. No one else had ever been able to do that the way he could, and no one else had done it successfully since. I wished it weren't the case so definitively, but nothing had ever been truer. I was still somewhat surprised by that, but I had finally come to terms with the fact that denying it was both childish and pointless.

I sighed again and was about to open my eyes and head down the trail to catch up with the crowd, when I felt a ripple of that remembered heat cascade lightly over me. I was a little surprised by the sensation. Even though it was faint, it had almost felt real for just a brief second! Damn! That was cool! The thought that maybe my mental replays were getting *that* good from the constant repetition, made me smile contentedly to myself.

I decided then to linger a moment longer with my private thoughts and I kept it up, reliving it all mentally, moving further back to when we had been together in the little twin size bed. I had felt ridiculous at the time for the lengths that we had gone to just to be together. *Hmpf.* I hated to even think of what I would do for that opportunity *lately!* The thought of seeing him for the first time in a *public place* had started to give me waking nightmares from worrying that I wouldn't be able to physically control myself! And that I wouldn't *care!* At that thought, another strong, almost real wave of desire washed over me again. *Whoa!!*

I was still blown away that even my own memory could come that close to those feelings that I had been missing so very much, but I was not complaining! If it was some new progression of my skills, being able to recreate and re-*experience* previous feelings so completely just from memory, then maybe I could hold on a little longer after all! If I could continue to conjure them up at will, I could almost pretend that he was really there.

Yeah sure, it was almost the same. *Hah*! It was a nice thought anyway, I accepted with a smile, but I knew that even if it was really possible, it wouldn't be enough to sustain me for very long.

Seeing his face for real would be like a dream come true by that point. *Literally*, for me! Since visions of him were what did fill my dreams almost every night! I had seen him so many times in my dreams lately that I had started to try and nap in the middle of the day just on the off chance that I might see him. I was even willing to risk the possible nightmares that sometimes replaced the good dreams half way through. But even the good dreams were always fuzzy, too unclear, which meant that they were still way too far away. The only thing I was sure of at that point was that I wouldn't see him *any*time soon.

I decided then in the familiar grip of frustration that I'd had enough "*alone time*" and I started to push away from my sturdy beam of solitude. Strangely though, as I did I felt that familiar wave a third time and I hadn't been imagining him just then so that really confused me. If it had been weaker, I may have assumed it was just the first waves fading away. But strangely it had been even stronger than before! I stood momentarily frozen and entirely perplexed while I contemplated it.

"*I thought you'd never lose the damn paparazzi!*" There was a *huge* wave just then! It hit me like a God damned fucking *tsunami!!* Took my breath away *completely*! My oxygen supply was expelled like it had been rocketed out of me! I held on to the frame with one hand and my eyes fell shut to protect themselves from the force.

Ethan!!! Huaauhhh!

He was there??!! But how…!! How was he there?!! I felt him walk up behind me and those feelings hit me fully, without restraint for the first time in over a month! It was like being hit with *defibrillator paddles! Holy freakin' shit!!* I grabbed the post tighter and my eyes flew open. I heard and *felt* him get even closer but I was incapable of reacting while in the midst of the powerful surge. I tried in vain for a second to catch my breath. I was still afraid to believe my own *average-at-best* ears and petrified that when I did manage to turn around, I would really be all alone with my obsessive fantasies, like usual! My heart held still for a half-beat at just the thought. It started up again with a heavy thump, but I was still frozen in fear and shock.

It wasn't just my ears that told me he was there though. The voltage that was pouring through me then could have come from no other source. Not even my own overactive imagination I realized, suddenly feeling very stupid. It was impossible. No one else had *ever* felt like that or made *me* feel like that! I did get my breathing back under control then. I pulled in a long slow chest-full of that energy and I held it there for just a beat before I let it out slowly.

I had finally regained my composure and started to turn around when I froze again in shock as I felt his fingers slide slowly down the side of my exposed neck, completely *real!* It was super light, but definitely *not* imaginary! Next I felt his lips follow suit and the second his hot breath hit my sensitive skin my knees buckled like toppled cards beneath me. The sensation caused a complete overload. I would have hit the floor for sure in a graceless, overexposed heap. But he really was there after all, *thankfully* and of course he didn't let that happen! In one fluid movement he reached one arm around my waist, stepped inside and slid us back into the farthest, darkest spot of the corner, behind the cameras view. He held me tightly against his body as he moved and I was beyond thankful as all of my own muscles promptly hit the picket line. *Stinking traitors!*

It wasn't their fault necessarily though. I had never been one of those weak, *faint-y* types of girls. Not, *ever!* Dammit! *Ever!* But the long pent-up feelings that were emanating off of him then, especially once he pulled me close against his body, combined with the relief that *I* felt, well they just weren't your average everyday feelings! I mean, I considered myself to be a pretty strong person, stronger than most if I was really being honest. At least in that one area, just from the amount of extra stuff that I'd always had to deal with. But those feelings were still *so* much stronger than anything I had ever known! I didn't even understand how we managed to physically make each other feel the way we did, but it was powerful to the point of absolute *ridiculousness!* So I forgave myself the weakness where I would normally have no mercy for someone acting like me.

I reached up behind my head and held around his neck as the air rushed right out of me again temporarily, along with my strength. One more kiss further down my neck though and one full deep inhale of his singular and amazing scent later and I had recovered enough strength to stand and turn around in his arms and look my greatest desire in the eye for the first time in over a month!

Those grey eyes were burning fierce and bright and they were as beautiful as I remembered them to be. The only thing they were missing was his usual calmness. He was struggling mightily to keep his own desire under control, and for once I wasn't sure that he was going to win that battle.

Whoa!! My insides started to dissolve into a puddle just from the look alone!

Hmpf! I had experienced the iron will of his control before. I've been shocked by it, counted on it thankfully, and even cursed it once or twice. But its ability to last right then was far shakier than I had ever known it. That was a definite first! When he spoke he let a great wave of it out with his simple words.

"Nice *dress!*" He complimented with an enormous amount of enthusiasm. He practically growled looking down at me while his true and deep appreciation washed straight through me. I could suddenly feel my lungs stretch against my ribs as they expanded to their full capacity trying to breathe it all in.

The sight of his face before me in the shadows was nearly overwhelming! I had been so sure that I wouldn't be seeing him for a long while. *So sure*, and yet there he was! In the flesh! I still couldn't quite comprehend it.

"You're here! You're really here!" I said restating the obvious repeatedly in disbelief. "*How? When? I… I don't…*" Every thought made me inhale deeper until I feared that I would hyperventilate, pass out and wake up alone. That thought was the scariest of them all.

"*Shhhhh.*" He said out loud, reminding me of my earlier memories again. I didn't need those just then though, because he was finally standing right in front of me! I reached up on my tip-toes and threw myself against his chest while I tightened my arms around his neck. I felt his appreciation grow and I felt just as happy to be that close to him again!

"I can't believe you're here!" I whispered vehemently into his neck. "Can you stay?" I pulled back and asked a second later.

"Not long." He answered sadly but honestly. He knew how I would feel about that answer and was quick to explain. "They're expecting me to show up for this Simone. They're waiting in a few strategic places right now as a matter-of-fact, eager to catch even a tiny glimpse of me. We don't want to make it *too* easy for them now do we?" He asked sarcastically with a weak but happy smile and for a second, I was crushed.

It felt so good to have him there though, *really there*, that it only lasted for a second. I refused to waste any more time than that being sad. I recovered quickly and went back to holding him as closely as I could again.

"I don't care. You're here now!" I said gratefully and I meant it.

"Believe me, it really goes against the grain for me to be so entirely, disgustingly *'predictable,'* but I just couldn't miss your big night." He explained softly. "It means too much to you. You should be happy tonight!" He pulled back that time and looked at me intently while his sincerity washed through me. "*You deserve to be.* You've earned it! This place turned out amazing!" He gushed and I positively beamed!

I'm sorry if your one of those people who wants to think that I need a man's approval to be happy and *blah, blah, blah.* Whatever. Truth is, you can read all kind of things into it if you want to, but when he said he liked it, I could finally feel the happiness and that sense of completion that had eluded me before, and it felt *goooood!*

"I wanted you to enjoy it and I was really afraid you wouldn't. That you would let the present situation stop you from fully celebrating your accomplishment. I'm taking a big risk by being here, but I'm already the reason that you're suffering on a daily basis.

I didn't want to be the reason that you missed out on this too. Not after working so hard to get here. Don't bother being hard on yourself about that either." He continued, trying to spare me any possible guilt. "Because I would feel the same way at this point and I *never* would have said that before I met you, so I know how crazy it feels." He confessed looking down and feeling terrible about the situation he had put me in.

I still hated that he always blamed himself first, then I hated that he was always so right about me, but I didn't bother to fight either circumstance anymore. I would take both of those character traits right along with all the rest at that point if I could get it. I wanted it *all!*

"Unfortunately though, I'm quite sure our friend Anderson is counting on all of this, so I won't actually *stay* here and ruin this night for you. *That* would not be very smart. And while I may occasionally allow myself to be predictable, it's only because I am always *smart* enough to pull it off!" He joked while backing me up another step to make sure we stayed out of the cameras range. He was feeling more generous then, and added to that.

"Truth is I wouldn't have lasted much longer anyway. Lately I've been searching for *any* excuse to come! *Hmpf. You don't know how many times I have gotten in my car in the middle of the night and made it halfway here!*" He confessed in a fervent whisper and I could feel how much he had wanted it just then. I thought of each and every fuzzy dream I'd had of him and realized that I probably did know *exactly* how many times. I couldn't help wishing silently, that just once he would have made it all the way there! But he had made it there for the opening after all and that meant everything to me at the moment!

"I always stopped myself before." He explained, logically of course. "I didn't want to endanger you any more than I already had and I'm still too afraid to leave Jeremy alone for too long. I never had a good enough reason before tonight to justify doing either one of those things. But I was pretty damn close to throwing caution to the wind and doing it anyway, good reason or not." He admitted with another low growl. "So this will do." He said happily in a deeply satisfied voice and smiled down at me.

"Nice job, Simone. *Really!*" He added looking out at the gently swaying, glowing gardens. "It looks incredible!" He offered happily. "*Especially* this!" He said in awe looking up at the completed, live, 3-d version of the water harp for the very first time. I felt the elation within the child in him and I also felt him working hard to resist the urge to run his own hand through the beams for the very first time, but he was mindful of the cameras. I leaned forward away from him momentarily and lifted my hand to do it for him so he could see it in action for the first time. I smiled as I instantly felt his understanding of the soft music as "our song" began to play. His satisfied grin grew even wider.

"It looks exactly like you drew it." He added in wonder as it finally became a reality for him in every way. His happiness at seeing it in person swept through me and the relief that I felt at that was *just beyond mind boggling...phenomenal!* It made me long for new vocabulary to describe it!!

"I knew you could pull it off! You will have to give me a personal, *private* guided tour of everything at a later date." He added with that familiar grin and a wink. Then his feelings changed in a flash, back to me. I literally rocked back on my heels a little when it first hit me, but I held onto his arms and stood my ground.

"*You*, on the other hand!" He said through heavy lids, those intense grey eyes staring unflinchingly at me from underneath. "*You* are making it hard for me to *breathe* right now! You are the most beautiful thing that I have ever *seen!*" He insisted vehemently. "Thank *God* I decided to come tonight!" He exclaimed unapologetically while looking me up and down in my special outfit.

I appreciated everything about it even more then, as his overwhelming desire washed right through every inch of me. At that moment I was certain that never in my entire life had it been more beneficial to don a dress! *Whoo!*

"It'll do." I agreed simply and then our lips finally connected and neither set was interested in flapping anymore. Not for a long while. His real, warm lips against mine! I could hardly believe it! When I remembered where we were again, I wondered if anyone had missed me yet. *Wow!* Then I remembered to breathe.

"Are they really all gone? You can't hear anyone around the area anymore?" I asked, hopefully. "I wonder how long I have before they send someone looking for me." I only half joked.

"Not *nearly* long enough for my tastes, I'm sure!" He answered heatedly. "I have to go. I don't want to chance being seen here. But I'd like to meet you later... Are you alone tonight?" He asked hopefully and I knew he meant Liliana.

I nodded. I was beyond excited to have Liliana there. The night was as much about her as it was me. But I had arranged for her to go home with my parents, rather than stay over with me since I knew that, contrary to what I would prefer, I'd likely be there quite late.

"*Good!*" He said, and his relief blasted through me like a cleansing summer thunder storm in the middle of a scorching heat wave! *Ahhhhhh! God* that felt good! Oh I had missed him *so* much, *dammit! Deep, deeeeep breaths... Whoa!* Dizzy, *verrrrrrry dizzy!*

Slow, *slooooow, deep breaths...* I smiled weakly as I laughed at myself.

"Go and enjoy the rest of your big night." He said with a chuckle at my usual antics. "Have a glass of champagne for me. I mean it." He smiled sincerely. "I'll be tied up until late anyway. I'll let myself in, if that's alright with you." He leaned in and kissed me again softly while he waited for an answer. I just nodded and kissed him back. I would ask him later about how he would actually do that. I had already determined that I would agree to just about anything to be with him again and that was before I ever believed it was an actual possibility!

"But if you don't mind... *Before I go...*" He stepped back. He slid his finger under the thin gold strands over my shoulder. Then he looked up and caught my eye again. "I have gone a long time on these old memories already. I could use a new mental snapshot to carry me through until then." He said softly. He slid his fingertips lightly down my arm then over the back of my hand. He flipped it up and lifted my palm to his lips and closed his eyes like it was the very fountain of life and he had been denied its' sustenance for *far* too long! I laughed at the absurdity of that image but it didn't seem to make it outside of my head, to the surface of my body. My face and lips apparently weren't interested in completing the physical actions necessary for laughing. Okay, whatever...

Wow! We had *really* missed each other! It was bordering on insanity already I knew, but I still loved it! Then he lifted my hand, brought it way up high and held it there, so I could give a slow, *just-barely-clothed* twirl in front of him. As I spun easily on the ball of my new and still slippery, sparkly sandals, I found myself smiling uncontrollably and remembering how much I had yearned to do exactly that just a few short hours ago. It had seemed a silly daydream at best at the time. I found myself wondering again how he always managed to do that. To bring every secret fantasy of mine to life. It really was too much!

He was enjoying it as much as I was though. For me, just feeling that was more important than taking the time to ask him how he did it. It was the best thing I had felt in *weeks!* I had to amend my statement again a minute later though, when his desire quickly followed. It washed right through me and ended squarely in my palms that were practically *pounding* by then from the onslaught of amazing sensations!

I opened my eyes again and stared up at him while he stared back down at me.

"*Damn* I've missed you, lady!" He said, barely coming close verbally to the intensity that he was feeling emotionally. That *I* could feel standing there next to him. Like a slow building earthquake, trembling just below the surface! It was all encompassing. Sorry, there really just aren't better words to describe the way it feels. Believe me I've searched my mental history. *Nada. Zip. Zilch.*

"Ditto." I answered him simply, knowing any words that I may come up with would be completely inadequate with the currently demolished state of my brain. I just stood, happily awash in it. Breathing deeply and forgetting where I was. He pulled me close again and stood back up straight against the wall, taking me up to his height with him. We simply held each other as tightly as we could for a moment, each of us enjoying the really good "*now.*" For about ten seconds, to be exact. Then his energy changed. He looked up quickly, startled. *Disappointed.* He looked at his watch, then back at me again.

"Nine minutes." He stated matter-of-factly. I looked up quizzically and he continued as he set me back down. "How long before they sent someone looking for you." He smiled.

"Oh!" Was all I had to offer in response. He chuckled then sighed in resignation. He pulled me close one more time while he buried his face in my neck. We held each other tightly again but very briefly. I breathed in his wonderfully familiar, clean, male scent as deeply as I could before he pulled back. He held my hand in his for as long as was possible then he let it drop and backed away, sinking slowly into the surrounding foliage and the darkness beyond.

"See you *soon!*" He promised quietly then disappeared.

Hfffmmmm! Phew! I took another deep cleansing breath and turned back toward the main trail and the approaching messenger.

Yup, I had been right all along. It was definitely going to be a long night!

Chapter 4

I could hear the trickle of the water cascading gently over the strings. I closed my eyes and listened to it as it played "*Overjoyed*" to me once more. I had put that one in just for us, the designer and the engineer. I smiled to myself at the comfort that it gave me when I heard it. I would take it where I could get it. I opened my eyes again as I started to sway slowly from side to side to the familiar rhythm. Just then I felt his presence behind me and my whole world lit up like someone had switched on the *sun!* Damn! I turned to look and he was really there! Not just a dream that time. *For real*! I could *feel* it!

Then I woke with a slight start… in my own bed… *dammit! Ugghhhh!* My heart sank. The room was dark. I wasn't sure at first why I had woken so suddenly. I had been quite happy where I was.

My heart was already beating fast but it still sped up as the realization set in that once again it had only been a dream. That however, was quickly followed just a half a second later by the surety that it *had* been real earlier! He really had been there… *and…* he was really there then, in my apartment *somewhere!* I couldn't see him, but I could *feel* him, and I knew suddenly that it had been that unmistakable energy that had awakened me! My heart skipped two beats then caught back up with itself as the certainty of that truth hit me full-on!

He was there! Oh thank *God!* I was glad that I was already lying down as that relief washed through me and short circuited every other function that I was normally capable of. I started to wonder if I would ever get control of my own body back from him. It was a hard thing to get used to. Not *bad* necessarily, just... *different.* I was about to lift my head off the pillow to try and figure out where he was exactly but as it turned out, it wasn't necessary. He was already close enough to stop me.

"*Shhhhh.* Don't get up." He whispered from behind me, where it sounded like he was crouched beside the bed. I was only too happy to comply while I tried to catch my breath as usual.

In the next second, I felt the feather light caress of his fingertips as they traveled down the side of my neck again, clearing a spot. *Oh my... holy... Whoooo!* I had missed his physical touch so much, that it felt almost *electric*, sending a current of pure pleasure running straight through me like white lightning! I was still in awe of that intensity! *Damn!!* His hand fell away and I immediately felt the loss, but only for a fraction of a second before the warmth of his lips replaced it. *Like in the dream*, and just like he had done earlier, picking up right where we'd left off. *Oh my...*

My eyes closed again as I breathed it in fully. I held it there, exalted momentarily in the singular sensation, never knowing when I would ever feel such a fabulous thing again. Then I felt his weight as he slid carefully into the bed behind me. My chest felt like it would burst from the joy of it! He was really there with me, *in my bed! Huuaaghhh, holy, shit! It was like an actual dream come true!*

I opened my eyes and I turned to see his face, in the place where I had imagined it a thousand times over the past long weeks. It was real that time though, pale white in the soft moonlight sneaking in through the half open blinds. I reached up and held that handsome face with one hand, just to be sure it was truly real and not my imagination. Seeing him there next to me, touching him, after only wishing for it for so long was almost indescribable!

It was like being left down at the bottom of a deep, dark well, waiting for a long, *long* time. Then having someone suddenly show up and throw you down an air tank and a ladder. The blasé' attitude that had been my constant companion as of late, was instantly gone, completely forgotten! But most importantly, there was *air* again! And it was *good.* Oh, it was *really, really* good!

Ahhhhhh! I took a few deep breaths of it before I even tried to speak.

"I waited up for you." I said, not in the mood to hide my impatience.

"I know. That's why *I* waited." He answered frustratingly. "We don't want it to look like there's anything *unusual* going on over here tonight." He added but I wasn't sure why. I looked up at him quizzically, wondering what it was he wasn't saying. Didn't want it to look that way to *whom*, exactly? I didn't have to wonder long though. His next sentence made it all too clear.

"They've had "eyes" on you here since I left." He whispered in my ear like it was nothing, while covering my neck with kisses again in between his words. My heart instantly started to beat faster again but not just for that one reason alone anymore. It was hard to hold onto rational thoughts as his lips wandered, and getting harder. The control that he had been holding onto so precariously earlier was *completely* gone, just like every *stitch* of his clothing. Once we had managed to be in the same place at the same time and *alone*, there was just no holding back physically, for either of us!

It was still shocking to me how very easily and how *un*-voluntarily my body would automatically assimilate with his! It was a natural movement, like swimming or breathing, a complete and totally efferent reflex.

His hand slid up my bare thigh, over the low-waist boy shorts covering my hip and then up my back, under my tank top. From there it traveled further up until he reached the base of my scalp where he slid his fingers under my hair and cradled the back of my head gently in his oversized hand. Our legs intertwined like vines until there was no space left between them. My left arm wound its way under his right and my hand reached over his side and up his back to flatten against his shoulder blade. We were like machine parts, or puzzle pieces, fitting themselves back together from memory as if we were specifically designed originally to work as a unit. It was truly *ludicrous!* And so completely *perfect, dammit!* As well as greatly, *greatly* missed! *Ahhhhhh!!!!!*

Meanwhile, through all of that I tried desperately to hold onto a train of thought long enough to respond to his little revelation.

"They ...*what!* They have?! I had no idea! *Jesus*, I *suck* at this!" I said a little louder then, pulling back some. I was exasperated with myself for letting him down so completely, by not really being that *super-hero/female spy* that he had once worriedly imagined me to be.

"I mean, I knew they would be watching me and my movements through things like credit card purchases for plane tickets and such. Why wouldn't they? It made perfect sense. If I traveled, it would probably be to go see you. But I'd still had no idea that it went to that type of extreme! I just thought they'd follow me if I left town. I never thought about the fact that they would have to know where I was all the time in order to know if and when I was leaving town in the first place! *Hah!* You'd have been better off if you *had* found some well-trained spy chick instead of me!" I stated, purposefully inflicting the self-punishment that that thought created!

A moment later I sighed, and tried to let some of the disappointment in my lack of perceptiveness out with it. That was an unusual one for me, to *not* pick something up. *Damn!* I had to admit then, that I really had been existing in somewhat of a fog. He was right there of course, wanting to rescue me from myself like he had never been gone.

"Don't be ridiculous." He offered generously. "How would you know?" He was just trying to be supportive but I didn't want him to do it. I didn't want him to bail me out. Not because I preferred to sulk. But because I knew that I still had to go without his help tomorrow, and the day after that. I couldn't afford to let my own defenses go just yet, however pitiful they were, and allow myself to rely too heavily on his assistance. It would be hard enough when he left again without knowingly making it harder. He tried again to calm me by emanating huge waves of reassurance as he gently stroked my cheek, but I held his hand still and stopped him, both physically and emotionally.

"Don't. Don't try to comfort me. *Please.* Just tell me what to do. What *not* to do! I refuse to be the weakest link in all of this and the one reason that everything falls apart!" I insisted. I was serious and he could tell but he refused to participate in my berating of myself. He was also smart enough to sense my unwillingness to be placated though, so instead he pulled back just slightly himself and waited patiently for me to calm down on my own. He knew I would, once the initial shock wore off. Of course he was right. I tried not to waste more time being annoyed by that too.

A moment later I took another deep breath and laid my cheek against his warm chest. Then I snuggled closer to him again. He mimicked me happily.

"How?" I asked simply. The *need-to-know* in me winning out as usual.

"They left a few small, but powerful cameras in the trees around the area before they went home that night. Jack eventually found them a few days later, but we've left them alone. At some point we may be able to use them to our own advantage. In the meantime at least we know what they see and don't see." He explained and what he said made sense, but it still bothered me that I had been left in the dark. I understood it completely, but that didn't mean that I agreed with it or that I liked it. He knew me well enough by then to know that I would find that objectionable and again, he continued to explain before I had a chance to form a complaint.

"I'm sorry that we didn't tell you, but it was important for you to be able to act naturally and do what you would normally do, so they wouldn't know we were on to them." He pulled back and tilted my chin up so he could look me in the eye again and his honesty washed through me as he spoke his next words. "And I didn't want to give you anything else to worry about. I'd given you enough already." He confessed with a sigh. He looked away for a minute and I could feel how upset he was at himself. When he looked back at me he voiced it like it was his deepest confession.

"I'm so sorry for *all* of this, Simone!" He insisted passionately. Being privy to the devastating level of regret roiling painfully in him just below the surface, it was easy enough to believe. "This situation is not exactly what I had in mind when I set out to convince you that you should be with me." He added with a sad smile and a shake of his head.

I felt what he had been going through every day that we were apart then and unbelievably but not surprisingly, it was far worse than anything I had suffered. He had more than enough emptiness and longing to match my own but he also had responsibility and guilt to add to his plate as well, at least in his own mind. I was fairly certain in that moment that he would take the whole thing back to spare me that pain if he could.

I had already decided that that wasn't a choice I would make though, even if it were really an option. I breathed it out slowly and tried to let it go. All I wanted then was to make him feel better. He'd already suffered much more than his fair share. I didn't like being the reason for his current pain.

"If you want to make it better, then you can tell me more about it. How much can they see? Wait. Let me close the blinds all the way." I said reflexively, starting to get up.

"No." He said holding me tightly to him. "Nothing unusual, remember?" He instructed slowly while sliding his leg up and down over mine. My brain turned to pure snow again momentarily but he was thankful for the reprieve and for my offer and he was in the mood to comply. His next words brought me back.

"They have the driveway covered at the street, everyone in or out of either place. One aimed into the woods, towards the entrance to the trails. One aimed at the back of Jack's place and another on the outbuildings. And one, aimed at your back deck." He finished and I could feel his anger at that but that wasn't all. He knew that I could also feel how much he wanted to fix it and how much it killed him that he couldn't, because I had finally figured out what he wasn't saying and it was the worst part.

"So they can see in here." I stated plainly, voicing what he wouldn't. My jaw literally dropped but I tucked my tongue tightly against my top teeth, trying not to overreact.

"*Hmpf.* That's probably the only *real* reason that I ever turned my car around!" He admitted humbly as his pent up longing poured freely through me. It was quickly followed by his joy at finally being there! Combined with my own, it was pretty overwhelming but I was still trying hard to pay attention. I breathed through it. It was important.

"So now what?" I asked, knowing there was absolutely no way he was going to get me to let go of him. They could go and get some popcorn of their own and enjoy the show for all I cared!

Of course, that wasn't really the issue. If they saw a man in my bed at all, they would surely know it was Ethan. Or at the very least they would *assume* that it was, and they would react accordingly either way.

They could not find him there. That was unacceptable. Both that and the possibility of them finding out that Jeremy was somewhere else, presumably alone and unprotected. I started to panic a little at just the thought of his leaving though. I looked up at him and felt his assurance very quickly, *thank God!* I didn't know what he had planned, but he obviously did have *something* planned, or I knew he wouldn't have come.

He slid his left leg out from underneath me and then backwards off the edge of the bed. He followed it with his left arm. Then he reached around me with his right leg and hooked it over both of mine. His right arm slipped over my waist, around my back and his fingers tucked under my ribcage. He looked me in the eye with clear intent and then pulled me with him as he slid us both off the bed in one silent backwards move.

He lowered us down carefully and I could feel a blanket underneath us when we reached the floor. It was too dark to see a color but I recognized the super-plush texture. I was sure it was the extra blanket from my bed for the cold winter months. I had used it once for Liliana on a chilly night when I had first moved in, but other than that, I knew it had been living tucked up in the top of my hall closet. It was a nice surprise to find it there, much better than the bare floor I thought, even with my recent obsessive cleaning spree. He reached back up and arranged some pillows that he'd had sitting beside the bed, into a shape vaguely resembling mine before he let the sheet fall.

When he finished his ministrations, I had to admit defeat. "Alright, so you make a better *'James Bond'* than I do. I think we've already established that though." I teased, in reference to a shared joke at my former antics once in a strikingly similar situation. I really was both surprised and amused though at his skill level with such a peculiar maneuver.

"Desperate times call for desperate measures!" He quipped with a trademark eyebrow wiggle in response.

Then he came back down with me and I realized that the blanket wasn't just for my comfort, as he pushed himself back up half way and we started to *move!* He used his bare hands on the hardwood floor on either side of us to easily slide our combined weight, stealthily across the room.

"The kitchen or the bathroom, Ma'am?" He asked graciously but with a wicked grin. I chuckled at first and then I realized something else.

"You've obviously given this some thought." I stated plainly as I tried to decide among the options. "I'm not sure." I admitted with another laugh. "I've never considered it myself."

"It's easy." He offered completely serious then. "Given the objects that we have available to hide behind in the apartment, which would be the kitchen island, and the floor space in the one room they can't see into, which would be the bathroom, it comes down to one simple question. Do you want it lying down, or standing up?"

My body was immediately burning embers at just the picture that his words created in my head! *Damn!!* Every nerve ending I possessed was pulsating from the sudden rush! *Ridiculous!* I searched my memory for another time that it had felt like, but there wasn't one. *Not a single one...*

It sent a storm of pleasure rushing through my body and it ended in a tornado, swirling through my palms where they currently rested flat against his chest. He looked down and the breath came rushing out of him for a change. I knew he was reveling in the light show that he had caused. He hadn't seen that particular phenomenon in a while and he was clearly as excited by it then, as he had been on that very first night.

Even though *I* couldn't see it firsthand and I never would, I *felt* it just as strongly secondhand a moment later, as his pleasure at it poured back through me. I searched my cloudy brain for an answer but the synapses absolutely refused to fire after that. There was nothing but the flashing bright white lights.

I reached deeper into my mind out of desperation and found an old and simple response that I could recycle, and held it in my brain just long enough to get it past my lips.

"Yes, please..."

Chapter 5

We made it to the bathroom doorway in a pile of tangled sweaty body parts. I hated to break the spell but I had too many questions still to stay quiet much longer. Long enough to catch our breath seemed okay though.

We had started in the kitchen. Since we were already horizontal to begin with it seemed like the logical choice. The area between the island and the lower cabinets was not as spacious as I would have liked it to be though. Or as *long* as *he* would have liked it to be, I thought amusingly while remembering his *mostly* successful attempts at keeping both his head and his legs behind the island at the same time. But we had made it work. Lord knows tight quarters weren't enough to stop us at that point!

The speed and strength with which we went after each other initially, though impressive, did nothing to tamp the flames. I expected us both to be completely spent afterwards. Instead, we were each content just to catch our breath and slide our way over to the bathroom where Ethan could finally straighten out and we could carry on. I was pleasantly surprised by just how happy I was to carry on *indefinitely*, but part of that joy came from the knowledge that I wasn't alone in that attitude. Although apparently I *was* alone in my immense amusement of his recurring leg cramp.

Once inside the bathroom he stood tall and stretched to his full height with a loud groan and a relieved expression. In there, that meant elbows on the ceiling, as I had once predicted. He didn't seem surprised by that though. As a matter of fact, he had managed the maneuver where he *just barely* fit without even looking up. I was duly impressed at first, but then I had to remind myself with a mental shake that he had actually *lived* there once. I was still in the process of absorbing that in small, random fits and spurts like that one.

He bent back down and reached out to lift me up off of the blanket, since by then we were far enough behind the screen at the head of the bed to stand in the bathroom doorway without being seen. I used his hands to pull myself up and happily gave my own body a long, welcome stretch as well. His overwhelming appreciation for that simple action came rushing through me instantly and his arms appeared around my waist at *almost* the exact same time! I just laughed at the still uncontrollable nature of it all. We had been apart for far too long to be satisfied easily.

Don't get me wrong, the pit stop in the kitchen had been *very* "satisfying" and I was *extremely* happy to be able to welcome that particular adjective back into my vernacular! But after all the time that we'd spent apart, it didn't even come close to being "*enough!*" It was going to take a lot longer than one night together to accomplish that!

He raised me up closer to his height, so that just my tip-toes were resting lightly on the top of his feet and he held me tight against the length of him. I wrapped my arms around his shoulders and laid my head up against his jawbone. We didn't move or say anything for a few minutes. We didn't need to. The contact was so fulfilling just by itself that we were both content to experience that one sensation alone for a while. It was my own insatiable curiosity that eventually won out over the perfectly silent moment.

"Nothing in here?" I asked, feeling the need to check. He shook his head once from side-to-side and I relaxed a little more as he loosened his hold and I slid back down to rest on my own two feet.

"I had Hank do an inside sweep on both places when we found the cameras outside." He informed me calmly. I pulled back and raised my eyebrows at my apparent lack of security but he just laughed. "Don't worry darlin'! No one's getting in here that didn't go through me." He assured me with that devious, confident smile.

"And how exactly is it that *you* get in and out of here, specifically?" I remembered to ask then. He gave a small chuckle, but didn't hold back.

"Through the garage. There is a number code for a small *not-so-visible* side door. No one can get into the garage without either a key or a code though. After that there is shall we say, an "*escape route*" that exits through the back of your closet and empties into a closet down in the garage. There is a key hidden at the bottom so it can be used in the reverse by those in the know, in the event of an emergency." He informed me with a wink. "I installed it back when I was living here. You know, my love of "*options*" and all." He said with another trademark eyebrow wiggle.

"Of course we've always had our own security cameras recording the entrances here and on the farm, but just the entrances. He added with a wink. "So while we can't stop them from spying on you at the moment unfortunately, we can stop them from getting in here, or at least make sure that we know about it if they do. And if *we* know about *that*, *you* will know about it too, I promise you!" He swore unnecessarily. He continued to reassure me anyway.

"Personally I have never, and wouldn't ever take advantage of that access without your knowledge unless it truly *was* an emergency." He said before I could even think my next thought much less argue it. It was so easy to move right past it because I instantly knew he spoke the truth. "So, like I said, there's no need for you to feel any less than totally secure here." He reiterated calmly. "Just try to keep the naked wandering to a minimum for the time being and everything will work out fine." He joked tightly.

What was really funny though was that I could feel how much he envied them. Not their current control over the situation or even their ability to watch me "wander naked," but simply their daily contact with me, even just visually. It was a funny thing to be jealous of but it was more than he had and he didn't try to hide how much that bothered him. I just grinned in response.

"Seriously though, I really didn't like keeping it from you, even if it was easy enough to do with you spending every waking moment at the jobsite." He both defended and accused at the same time. I just rolled my eyes. I *had* assumed that *Ethan* would keep tabs on things somehow, including me of course, so that part didn't bother me as much as "*big brothers*'" surveillance had. I knew Ethan's motives. They were based in thought of protection. Anderson's? *Yeah, not so much.* I sighed again and let it out.

"How *are* you?!" I finally asked for the first time. "How is Jeremy? And how is the plan coming to get him back home?" I added with a smirk. We both knew that I cared tremendously about Jeremy and that I would also help him in any way I could. He was a living, breathing example of what that time had been like in my own life. Ethan wasn't the only one whose difficult past had made him understand the need for a better future for others like us. I really wanted him to be okay. He deserved to be.

Aside from that, we all knew that when he came home, it also meant that Ethan could come home too. He knew exactly what I was asking.

"I'm fine." He grinned as he said it because we both knew that he was lying through his teeth, though he would never say so out loud. No, he would never let on how bad it was for him. That might incidentally make it harder for someone *else* and he would never knowingly do that. It just wasn't his style. Of course he would never say it, but he didn't really need to because that didn't stop me from *feeling* it just the same, and he *knew* that. I just grinned at him again and sighed.

"Jeremy's good." He added more seriously, answering my second question then, sort of. I was glad to see that *that* was the truth at least. I grinned at him then as he leaned back against the wall behind him before he continued.

"He's getting the hang of waiting to act until he can figure out exactly what it is he's seeing, and who he's seeing it in! But he still can't handle the idea yet of seeing something wrong in someone who doesn't know about it and *not* always acting on it. That part's hard for him, but I get that. I think we all do." He acquiesced quietly. "At least all of the *heights* that I work with do." He added simply and I remembered how hard that had been for me in the beginning.

"We all start out wanting to either make it go away, or if we can't, to try and fix everything we're exposed to. But that's just not really possible. He's starting to grasp the reality of it all, but he still has to learn the importance of careful consideration, on when to intervene and when to quietly walk away. We all have to come to terms with that concept to a certain extent if we want to maintain somewhat normal, private lives. People are people. No matter what our particular skill-set is, none of us are Superman and none of us can do it all, or do it all *alone!* It takes time and it takes patience to get a skill under control, especially a complex one." He sighed then. Again I thought about how hard all of that could be in the beginning but I was sure that as long as Jeremy had Ethan on his side he would eventually come around. He just had to, the alternative was too painful to even think about!

After that he closed his eyes and pulled me tight against him again. Then he rested his head on top of mine. I could feel how grateful he was just to be *there*, in the "*now.*" That was all he wanted to think about. His sadness at the reality of it all, finally answered my *real* question and it was not even remotely encouraging.

Dammit! Deep breaths… *in and out… Phhhhooaaoowww…* Before the scream in me could escape… *one… two… three deep breaths…*

He was refusing to dwell on it though, those fantastic compartmentalizing skills of his again. I wasn't sure whether to be angry or grateful, because I couldn't really argue with that perspective at the moment. However there was still too much that I would never dare to ask over the phone.

"Well, it's progress. I'll take it." I responded simply, trying to remain positive. Then I threw in something a little less stable. "Why do they want him so badly Ethan? Is it really just because of his skill? Do you think they already know exactly what it is?" I spit out bravely. These were certainly not the things that one usually discussed while naked, but my opportunities were few and far between to get answers. I couldn't afford to be picky.

He sighed again, realizing that my focus had truly been

diverted and decided to try and help me get past it, as quickly as possible. I grinned again at his motivation but held silent, waiting for his response.

"If they don't know then they must at least *suspect.*" He finally confided. "We know he has no other specific value to them to warrant such an aggressive pursuit. He's not "*sick*" anymore and he was never really a "*carrier*" of anything more dangerous than a previously known virus, although they would have everyone believe otherwise. That's all scare tactics. So we know there's no need for them to chase him down to '*quarantine*' him. Not *really*!" He added in an informants tone.

"Unless of course, their goal is to stop the spread of the *HgT* virus completely, and therefore the existence of new *heights* entirely." He proposed offhandedly. I wasn't sure how I felt about that possibility so I set it aside for later contemplation.

"He's smart sure. They'll know that from his public records. He's always been an excellent student. But he's not expected to design the next new atom bomb or anything. And we still haven't found any evidence of other known *heights* in his family line yet either that they could have been following to lead them to him, so we're fairly sure we can rule that out.

His skill is the only real motivation left that we know of to explain their aggression. It is *very* unusual and could certainly be very useful to someone who *did* want to take advantage of it. Let's suppose that they don't want to stop it, but rather just *control* it..." He supplied as an alternate possibility and I didn't feel much better about that scenario than I had the last one.

I understood that concept far too well though as I remembered how Anderson had tried to win Jeremy over once already by accusing Ethan of that very thing. I already knew that Ethan would never take advantage of someone just for their *height* abilities. He had spent long enough resisting every opportunity to do that very thing to have proven that to me already. He had no problem working *with* them though, side by side, towards a greater good for *all heights* in general. But that was because he recognized their value as individuals, not because he wanted to exploit them. It was a subtle distinction but it made all the difference in the world.

He would raise them up to a better place anytime he had the chance. Someone like Anderson, on the other hand, would have no problem seeing Jeremy as nothing more than a tool to be callously used and/or discarded in the pursuit of his own personal goals. Of that I was sure!

I had a quick flash then of what it would be like if Anderson *did* have someone like Jeremy on his payroll. *Yikes!* I realized that picking out new *heights* would be just like *window shopping* for him after that! *Way* too damn easy! Especially once he learned to decipher one type of *height* from another. What a "tool" he would be *indeed!* That realization gave me the biggest chill yet and *not* the good kind.

I was glad his skill was so uncommon then. Even if they didn't get their hands on Jeremy though, surly there had to be others out there with at least similar skills, somewhere. I knew they had to be thinking that as well. I wondered uselessly just how many cases they investigate before they find a skill they deem "useful." We could really be a dime a dozen, not even as remotely rare as I had always thought. Or it could be a one in a million scenario. I truly had no idea. I couldn't help thinking though, that if they really wanted that advantage, they would get it sooner or later, and that was scary in a whole other way.

Why did they want to know about every new *height* so badly anyway? What did they do with that particular information? So many questions ran through my head but I knew I couldn't ask them all. There wasn't time for that whole conversation. I did have to appreciate for just a moment though, that as smart as Ethan was, and as "*useful*" as his own particular skills were, how *very* lucky we all were that *he* was one of the good guys!

He had certainly endured enough abuse at the hands of the system *and* by those who were supposed to have "*loved and protected him*," to later justify turning against society as a whole. It made a perfect "*Movie of the Week*" quite frankly. But just the thought of an evil, tortured soul, loose in the world with Ethan's iron trap of a mind gave me an absolutely *icy* chill! Much worse than all the others had been! *Damn* my imagination sometimes!

That brought up a whole *other* reason that I hadn't even considered before that moment, that it was so important for him to do what he did to try and save those kids! He was not only saving them from their peers and families and what they were facing psychologically as well as physically, but he was also saving them *and all of society*, from what they could potentially *become* if they ended up being physically incredibly powerful, but emotionally damaged beyond repair!

It was far too much to consider thoroughly in the nude though, so I shook it off and slid up closer to his real life warmth. He was happy since he thought I was finally on board with his earlier attempt to just forget about all of it for a few minutes.

Suddenly I was. He finished his explanation, but I was barely listening anymore.

"Anyway, all we know for sure right now is that he has an annoying tendency to constantly know more than we think he does." He admitted and then he was quiet.

I laid my head down on top of his chest and gave a real sigh then. We stayed that way for another beat or two. Then I leaned back and reached up to run my hand through his thick hair and push the dark curls away from his forehead. It was noticeably longer than it had been when I saw him last, the thin lines around his eyes, a millimeter deeper.

"You must be *so* tired!" I insisted gently with a sympathetic tilt of my head, knowing it was probably a *huge* understatement and that it would undoubtedly remain unconfirmed. His response was as predicted a constrictive, purposeful silence. He didn't have to answer though. I could feel the wariness that gnawed at his bones. It was currently buried deep down under his desire and his excitement at finally being together. But it was there, just the same. I just looked at him feeling sorry about that, because I had no idea at all how to help him. "I wish you could *stay!*" I added hopelessly as I pulled myself up against his chest again.

"*Mmmm*, me too. *Believe* me!" He replied and I knew that he meant it in more ways than one. I knew that if he *could* stay, we would likely still be up for a very long time, but eventually he *would* sleep, dammit! That unfortunately wasn't an option for him at the moment though. He wouldn't take that chance. Nope, no rest for the wicked. Not yet.

"*Sing to me, Ethan!* Please!" I begged quietly then, wanting nothing more than to hear his singular voice and to escape the pain for a few blissful moments, both his and my own.

I felt a little selfish asking, but I had missed that just as much as every other part of his presence and the desire was suddenly greater than the shame that I felt for asking. I couldn't tell if he thought it was selfish or not. He was feeling too many things at once for me to decipher. Either way, he was quick to give me what I asked for. Anything within his power anyway.

Then I didn't know what he was feeling at all through my skills anymore, as his voice began to block it out, but he knew I felt it just as clearly through his choice of words.

"Here I am staring,
at your perfection,
in my arms,
so beautiful.

He began a familiar Maroon 5 song and I smiled as the pain melted away slightly, *his* share anyway. His voice was a lot deeper than Adam's was but the melody was still the same and the song choice was just too perfect, *again!* It immediately reminded me of the other time that he had done that to me at The Tavern. That song was now a permanent part of our history and I felt another "moment" coming on.

He continued to sing softly and the smooth and steady disruption in the airwaves that his voice caused, traveled across the space between us and carried blissfully through me as if I were nothing more substantial than a random fog. It filled every open space in my entire being. I closed my eyes and I let it in, welcomed it.

The sky is getting bright,
the stars are burning out.
Somebody,
slow it down.
This is waaay,
too hard,
'cause I know,
When the sun comes up,
I will leave.
This is myyy ,
last glance,
that will soon be mem-or-y.

I looked back up at him with a sad smile, knowing there was no escape from that truth, even with him singing. He stroked the hair from my face as he sang.

And when the day-light
comes I'll have to go.
But tonight I'm gonna hold you so close!
Cause in the daylight,
we'll be on our own.
So tonight I need to hold you so close.

At the end of that verse, he actually did just that as he sang the remaining "*ooh-whoa-oh's*" softly in my ear. Then he came back to face me and hung his forehead down on mine, giving in to the weight of the moment for once.

"I wish I could put you in my pocket and take you with me." He admitted somewhat hopelessly. We both knew it couldn't happen. It wasn't like him to let the sadness or his own personal needs take the forefront though, even for a moment and I was surprised by the passion behind it.

I couldn't blame him though. I also couldn't remember another time that he had done it. He always had to be so strong, for so many. When was it ever going to be okay for him to just be human like the rest of us and take care of *himself*? I reached up around his neck with both hands then and pulled his face even closer to mine.

I knew I didn't have the right words to fix everything that was wrong with the current situation, but I knew how to make him *feel* better. That at least, by the grace of all that was good, apparently *was* within my power and I would never dream of looking that miraculously generous gift horse in the mouth. Not when I could spend my time kissing his instead.

Sorry, that was *really* bad! I know. Unfortunately, that is the way my mind worked by then. And even though *I realize* how bad it sounds, I'm willing to take the heat for it. I really don't care. It's *that* good!

I didn't care anymore just then about security either, or plans, or even blankets. I just wanted to be as close to him as the laws of physics would allow. I stared up into his eyes and I could feel the same level of intensity coming back at me. I breathed it in entirely and let it enter me without restriction. Then I let it out and melted against his chest completely.

I really was lucky that he was as strong as he looked because otherwise I know I would have been spending an awful lot of time sprawled out on the floor. I knew as far as character traits went, it wasn't terribly attractive but he was the only one that had ever made me act that way so I explained to him that any weakness I exhibited was entirely and solely his fault. I refused to be embarrassed about something that I had absolutely no control over. Thankfully, he was cooperative.

"The list of things that I am 'responsible for' may be extremely *long already*, but I have no problem adding "making you feel like *that*!" He insisted in his easy charming manner.

He held me tight with one arm while he used the other to reach down and grab another foil square from the party pack box that he had left on the blanket. I'd laughed pretty hard at that when I first saw it. He explained at that point, that he had grabbed them on his way up through his old secret stairway where he'd tucked them away some time ago, for "*other*" types of emergencies. His only defense was the surety that the meager supply in his wallet was not going to cut it in that particular circumstance. As usual, I had to commend his foresight after the fact.

He lifted me back up then, which in the small room was not really optional. That lack of floor space and all. I wrapped my legs around his hips and held on to his shoulders while he turned around and grabbed one of my oversized fluffy bath towels off of the shelf behind us. Then he turned back and unfolded it to half its' size and put it down over the cold marble sink basin. I lifted my eyebrows in obvious doubt of the small wood vanity's adequacy for the job, but he just grinned and assured me it would be okay with two short sentences.

"It's fine. I built it." He said. He didn't use words to reassure me anymore after that, but he did it just the same. By the time he set me down on the nicely cushioned edge, I had no fears left. Screw it, I thought. If it collapsed, I knew he would catch me. *Hah!* That was a *worst-case-scenario* that I could personally live with.

I let one leg slip off of his hips at that thought and drop, but I held tight with the other foot and used it to pull him closer and just that fast, we were one entity again. Completely connected in ways that went beyond what I had always considered to be possible. It was still the most incredible thing that I had ever known, and the most fulfilling, even if I had no explanation for it. We were both very happy to be able to *stay* connected in that way for a while too, *for once.* We knew we didn't have tomorrow, but we had *all* the rest of that night! And we both intended to enjoy every *single* second of it!

The only regret that entered my mind after that was for my part in adding to his continued lack of sleep. But I also knew that sleep would never win out in him then, so I had to just accept that and let it go for the moment. I focused instead on experiencing the joy that we had missed so profoundly, on loving every part of him that I could reach and on breathing in all of him that I could, *while* I could. The feeling was mutual and very little time was wasted before the faint glow of dawn did finally start to creep in through the windows.

We had ended up back in the kitchen again by then, sitting on our blanket, having a snack. I had thrown my tank top and underwear back on, when he left me alone in the bathroom momentarily to go and get a head start on rummaging through the lower cabinets for sustenance. He however, hadn't bothered with clothes yet and I hadn't felt the need to suggest it.

We sat with our backs against the island and our legs crossed at the ankles. Only the soles of his feet made it all the way up against the cabinet doors opposite us though. Mine extended a mere three quarters of the way, and looked downright *dainty* next to his. *Hah!* That made me laugh, even if it was just to myself. There was a word that I wasn't used to associating with my own person.

I hadn't really noticed it before but I did then. *Hmpf.* Well I didn't *hate* it.

We relaxed there munching on some almonds and some pretzels while we chugged bottles of water tying to rehydrate. He was looking at me as we ate. A lot of what he felt, he didn't voice. He knew he didn't need to. I realized that I wasn't the only one who was noticing the changes that had occurred during his absence. While he was mostly just enjoying the fact that each of my parts currently existed in his basic vicinity, and taking that in rather joyously, he did have the occasional protest. Oddly enough, he protested the very thing I was just cheerfully discovering.

"*You've lost weight.*" He accused in a gentle but straightforward tone. "Here." He said as he handed me the bag of pretzels. "You've been working way too hard lately, you need to eat more. You can't survive with that kind of schedule on just the fruit and veggies that Shirley occasionally leaves for you." He said it sarcastically, but I could feel that he was mostly serious. "You're supposed to be taking care of all of this while I'm gone, remember?" He reminded me humorously while his eyes raked up and down my body. The humor didn't last though.

"I *know* hungry, Simone." He added solemnly, looking back up into my eyes. "It's not a good way to spend a lot of time. And I really don't like the thought of you experiencing it on a regular basis." He said, and I felt the sadness run through him. "There are other joys in life besides this." He insisted, referring to what we felt for each other. "Don't stop experiencing one for another, not *ever!*"

He insisted sincerely and I had to chuckle at how much sense that made, but again it was so much easier to say than to *do!*

Apparently he had been saving up a few things that he had been longing to say as well. *Hah!* I had to laugh again. I wasn't worried. I knew that giving up good food long term and getting too skinny was not a problem that I would *ever* have to worry about. That really was comical.

I'll admit that there are times when I'll ignore food in favor of other things, but they are always short lived and most often balanced out with alternating periods of shameless overindulgence. It was never a conscious thought, or taken to an unhealthy extreme in either direction. It was just an inner confidence that if I didn't have time for it then, I would *definitely* make up for it later!

I absolutely *love* food, but I try to remind myself not to stress too much if I miss out on a few things here and there occasionally. There is just too much amazing food available to us now 24/7 to try and experience every culinary opportunity that presents itself on a daily basis. I constantly had to remain cognizant of that to keep from scarfing down everything in sight! I really am *way* too much of a foodie to ever be away from it for what could *really* be considered "too long" though. It just wouldn't happen. Not by choice anyway.

I *had* been "*going without*" far too much, but it'd had nothing to do with my lack of *food!*

I *really* wasn't worried, but he looked down at me and held his ground mentally so I took the bag from him and happily added one of the pretzels to my mouth full of half-chewed almonds. He knew I was just humoring him but he didn't care. It made him happier to see me eat it.

Hmpf. If that's all it took, I thought cheerfully... I popped another into my mouth, as I smiled cooperatively up at him. That was easy. He smiled back, but again, it didn't last. I noticed why then as I realized that it was bright enough in the kitchen to see his face clearly. I knew only too well what that meant. Time to go.

Dammit! Our little stolen moment had been like a feast for someone who *was* starving, but it was almost over. I could feel the exact moment that he allowed that reality to re-enter our little bubble. I'd had to drink my water in order to get the pretzels down my throat after that.

I took a slow deep breath while I tried to readjust to the thought of him *not* being right next to me anymore. I felt that familiar, gutting sensation opening up inside myself and then I felt his searing pain come across my chest and roll over my own a heartbeat later. I closed my eyes tight and twisted my head to the side as I worked hard to contain both without crumbling into dust. I felt it all reach my palms in a deep, wrenching ache.

The next thing that I felt was the heat of his oversized palms tightly enveloping mine as he tried reflexively to banish what he saw there. I opened my eyes and stared up at him. *Damn!* Didn't I wish it were that easy? Yes Ma'am, and far too many times already! But alas...

He held them even tighter then in a momentary flash of hopelessness and he used them to pull me up and onto his lap. I settled over him and wrapped my arms around his neck while he wrapped his arms tightly around my ribcage. I wanted so much to be strong then. To be more of the kind of woman that he needed. In control, cool, more "*heroine*" and less "*damsel in distress.*" I didn't want to be just one more thing making it harder for him. One more person that he needed to rescue. I wanted to be stronger than that.

I pulled it off for a whole few seconds too, until I remembered again that I had no more work to get back to when he left. That reminder brought the pain to an unmanageable level, and the heart crushing truth spilled right out of me in spite of my best efforts to contain it.

"*Uggghhh!* This has to *end*, Ethan!" I insisted gripping handfuls of thick, dark curls in my fists. "One way or another. I want to be strong, I really do, but I don't know how much longer I can last!" I admitted completely abandoning my pride. I pulled back to look him in the eye but I held onto his neck for emphasis. "I forget how to fucking *breathe* right when you're away from me that long now!" I confessed heatedly. "It's not *normal* and it's your own damn fault!" I accused halfheartedly, even though I knew he already felt bad enough and making that guilt worse for him didn't really help me. I couldn't stop it from pouring out regardless.

"I don't know what you did to me Ethan, but it's not unlike the virus that changed my life forever. I may not understand it or how it works but I know for sure that whatever it is, you can't *undo* it!" He stared up into my eyes, quiet but with his thoughts going a mile-a-minute. He was contemplating a number of different things all at once. They all felt important but there were far too many, and they were moving way too fast for me to take them all in. Then I felt one emotion clearly. It was that extremely rare but very real fear again. He didn't respond right away. When he did I was surprised by what had apparently caused it.

"Would you, if you could?" He asked simply and with such an open and honest heart that I knew he deserved the same in return. Only I couldn't even speak at just the idea. My voice refused to participate. I shook my head no quietly, without a second thought. I felt his overwhelming relief rush through me and he reached up to pull my face down to his again.

I took a deep breath and when I felt strong enough to hold it together, I verbalized it.

"There is no *going back* with you now Ethan, and I can only survive where we are for so long. The only choice is to go *forward.* We *really* need to move forward!" The truth of that and how much I wanted it surprised me as usual. But we both knew he couldn't tell me what I wanted to hear. It still wasn't that easy. I wondered painfully if it ever would be.

"I'm working on it, *I promise* you!" He assured me while holding my cheek with one hand, which I knew was all he could honestly say. Then he pulled me tightly up against his chest again. I wouldn't have doubted the veracity of that statement even without the luxury of knowing it for sure. It only helped a little though. I sighed and we were quiet again after that. He pulled his knees up behind me and I leaned back and lay my head against his left thigh. I stared blankly up at the ceiling.

"I know you are." I continued like there hadn't been a pause. "But in case you haven't noticed, I have a number of strengths. Patience just isn't one of them." I tried to joke, but it was hard. "I've worked a lot on that one demon over the years but I haven't managed to conquer it yet." I informed him with a humble smile. He just grinned a half-ass grin in response. I felt his confidence radiating outward, that I was much stronger than I claimed to be. I wasn't sure I agreed, but it felt good. He stayed quiet as he ran his hands slowly through my hair that had been freed from its' bobby-pin prison hours ago, creating a silky blanket down over his shins and I closed my eyes. If I could have I would have purred...

How was I going to keep myself from thinking about him now? I couldn't help wondering desperately...

Eventually he sat up and pulled out his clothes that I recognized from earlier, from under the sink where he must have tucked them on his way in. Not surprisingly they were all neatly folded. I slid off of him so he could get dressed. Once he had his pants and his shoes on, we army crawled on our bellies over to the stairway and headed down before he stopped to put his shirt on at the bottom. He stretched his arms high over his head once we were hidden and vertical again'

"I'll have to remember to add '*the stairway*' to our list of options next time." He joked, but the thought of a "next time" made me both so happy and so sad at the same time, that I had to close my eyes and take another deep breath just to get past his innocent remark. Suddenly I was back to feeling horribly inadequate again in the "*tough-girlfriend*" department.

"Sorry." I reiterated sincerely, wishing I could at least hide it better. When I opened my eyes again I could see the pain in his face as easily as I could feel it. That was unusual for him and it just made it worse. I fell back on my old defenses and struggled to block it all out after that. To put the walls back up. Apparently I was going to need them a while longer. "Go." I insisted, putting my hand up to stop his attempt at comforting me again. "Call me when you get back, k?"

"K." He agreed. He wasn't happy about leaving, or my emotional dismissal, but he knew he couldn't really argue with either. He was better at acceptance than I was. He was even willing to accept that he had to go, but I could feel his unwillingness to leave it that way. Neither of us knew when we would see the other again next. I felt his determination a second before he pulled me close to him again. I wanted to resist but I didn't.

He leaned down over me and wrapped his arms tightly around my body with his chin tucked over my head. He just held me for a minute and let his incredibly strong emotions pour down over me. I didn't respond, but I didn't fight it either. I breathed it all in as deeply as I could. It was actually nice not to need the words.

After a long minute, he pulled back and leaned down to kiss me once more. I let him. I didn't kiss him back, I just tried to permanently imprint upon my brain the way his lips felt against mine …until they weren't anymore. Then I slowly opened my eyes.

"Hang in there hun.' Believe me I know how much this sucks!" He shared with a quick chuckle but I also felt his despair again, just the briefest flash. It was swiftly replaced by that familiar determination. "Just remember, this is only *temporary!*" He insisted fiercely.

I gave a weak but honest half smile at that as he backed up and let my hand go then retreated out my front door. He moved quickly over to a path that I hadn't ever noticed before in the woods to the left of my driveway. I had always just thought that whole area was impassable and blocked off, being completely covered in overgrown, evil, thorny rosebushes. I had certainly never tried to walk through them before. Those particular bushes were vicious and I had learned my lesson with roses long ago!

I just shook my head at being both shocked, and not at all surprised at the typically deceiving situation. I imagined from there he could pick up the trails around the bend and easily get back to his car parked on another road, much like we had done on the night that he had left, and all without being seen on the main road, in our driveway, or on the property. I continued to stare into the shadows long after he had crept silently through them lost in my own thoughts.

What now? I had to think for a minute… what day was it? Sunday? Yes. What would have been my "*day off*" anyway, I realized with just a hint of Mopey-Mary whispering in my ear that every day was "*my day off*" at that point. *Hmpf. Just shut the hell up Mary*, I thought defiantly, as I went back inside and closed the door. I *would* find other things to do. I just didn't know exactly what they were yet.

Usually, the lull in between jobs is a welcome time for me. I could rest, having completed whatever my latest obsession/project had been. I would usually also be flush in cash-flow again for a while like I was at the moment, so there was some breathing room there. Normally that would be the part where I would take my well-earned peace of mind and go find something fun that Liliana and I could do together. Or I would do something adventurous that I could cross off my bucket-list. But Liliana and I had just had our night together and then the opening and I wasn't due to have her again for days. Even then our time would be limited. Usually I could at least go visit her here and there during free time, but she had one thing after another lined up every day until Friday. All the windows in between her activities were so small that I knew it would be impossible to fit in anything more than a quick "Hello, how was your day/Good night I love you."

Besides her, all my current thoughts of adventure and excitement involved another starring character almost exclusively. He was the only who seemed equipped to fill that particular role, but unfortunately he was also the one person that I had zero access to. I didn't know what to even hope for at that point. I'd never been so sure about something before, that I was also so clueless about when it came to how to make it happen! I stood and I sighed a few more times before I crawled back up the stairs and into my little fishbowl. I slipped carefully back into bed while pulling the pillows off and sliding them underneath it at the same time. I left them tucked away there under my side of the bed for future use, then I made a big deal of sitting up and yawning like I had just woken up.

I got up and got some things from my drawers and went to go take a shower but it didn't take me long to realize that he had been right about that too. I already felt awkward and unsure of myself, and my movements were instantly less natural once I knew they were watching. I could see then why he hadn't wanted to tell me.

I really do suck at this! I thought again as I headed back to the bathroom, *alone* that time.

Chapter 6

All during my shower, thoughts of what I could do next ran through my head. Of course I could look for another job, but landscape design could be a tough business to work steadily in. Jobs tended to come around sporadically. Especially when you were an artist first and a landscaper second, that tended to narrow the field down considerably when it came to which jobs I was actually suited for or even interested in. Those jobs were often bigger though, like Wu Xing Gardens had been which helps to make up for a lot, but they also tended to be much fewer and further between. I knew the odds of my jumping right back into another one right away were slim to none and "*slim*" as of yet wasn't returning my calls. It would be awesome if it happened, but it was *highly* unlikely.

I thought about Liliana again and how school had ended while I was buried in my work at the Gardens. That had cheered me up some back then, thinking about how much time we'd have when I was done, but alas that dream was not to be a reality either. At Ben's strong urging, we had agreed to enroll her in a real, full-time summer camp program that she would be starting that very week. He was worried she would be bored for two whole months off with him working so much.

Again, I understood the reasoning, but I wasn't a big fan of the idea at first when he had mentioned it. I would have preferred to let her hang out on the farm with me and just chill, and I suggested it while reminding him that I currently had nothing but time. But Ben had reminded me of my own dad when that suggestion resulted in a long discussion about how it wasn't to her benefit to spend weeks at a time "*doing nothing.*" Then he had conveniently reminded me that my wide open schedule could change at a moment's notice. It was hard to argue with that, but I really *wanted* to. At least until I saw the place. That had completely deflated whatever wind was left in my sails.

The good news was that coincidentally enough the camp he suggested was actually right there in Pinegrove. It was called Juniper Glade. I knew it well, since I drove by the edge of what I like to mentally refer to as "*The Compound*" all the time. You could tell it was expensive because the place was obviously humongous yet they could afford to keep the general public from being able to see anything, *at all.* From the road all you could see was the sign at the entrance, a lot of trees and the back side of one very large garage. I knew that I was right in my original estimation though, when Ben told me what it normally cost, which was about what I paid in rent each month!

Ben had suggested it specifically because the owner Don was a dog lover who had seen him on the news and he had offered him a one-of-a-kind deal. He had offered Ben Liliana's membership at half price, so that meant a quarter of the price for each of us, and in return Ben had to agree to add regular house calls for his five dogs to his already tightly packed schedule, which of course he did. Ben got even longer hours than he had already been working out of the deal, but Liliana got something really awesome to be doing while he was busy. That made it worth it to him.

The bad news was that although I would get to see her more often during the rides that I would be giving her back home, a lot of the time that would be all and it wasn't nearly enough.

For that reason, I had still wanted to complain but once I saw it in person, I had nothing. The place was truly incredible! It had an Olympic sized swimming pool for laps, lessons and races, but there was also a whole wading depth water-park in addition to that.

They could play water volleyball and polo or they could just chase each other through the sprayers on hot days. There were also tennis courts and three different playgrounds, as well as a soccer field, softball field, baseball field, basketball court and a miniature golf course, all right there in that one spot. They weren't messing around!

They did arts and crafts too, and not just finger paints and paper bag puppets either. No they had jewelry making, papier mache, clay sculpting and many other things that even I would have had fun doing. Not to mention they had a leading nutritionist as a chef there and 100% of all the kid's snacks, meals and drinks were provided for them in that one price. It was like having 9-5 recess at an all-inclusive children's resort and no such thing had even *existed* when I was a kid!

After the tour I could never complain about her getting to go there. It was the absolute perfect place for a kid to spend the summer, if the parents could somehow pull it off financially, so with the deal we were getting we *would* have been crazy to say no!

She would have her cast on still in the beginning but that would come off a few weeks in. So she would have to avoid the water games for a while but there were more than enough arts and crafts options to keep her busy in the meantime. On top of all of that, I happened to know that Jonah would also be going there. That was the icing on the cake for her.

So even if I could have had her all to myself the whole time, I realized I probably still would have chosen to send her. I was sure that she was going to absolutely *love* it! But I on the other hand, was going to hate not having her all to myself like I had wanted, as quietly as I possibly could. That seemed to be my biggest job lately, learning to suffer in silence. *Grrrr…*

I would get a whole week with her at some point though. That date was still to be determined, but it was non-negotiable. It had been part of our original agreement, one full week for every six months away from *either* parent. Right now that was still me but during the divorce settlement we had agreed to revisit that topic again in another three months, unless something changed drastically in the meantime. I was already ready for it to change but it wasn't about me. It was about what was best for her and it always had been.

I couldn't help wondering sadly though, when *my* situation would ever be the *best* situation for *her*. I had to take a few more deep breaths then to keep Mistress Mary away but I managed it. I *really* was looking forward to my week!

It was up to me to tell him which week I wanted but I hadn't decided yet. There was so much going on and I didn't want anything to ruin my time with her. I wouldn't get a do over for a while and I couldn't bear to waste it. So like everything else in my life lately, that decision got put on hold until it could be better made. I refused to rush it and get it wrong.

I rinsed my hair while I thought about hanging around at my parents, but it would be pretty lonely there as well between the three different trips they had planned. With my father working at the University for the past twenty five years, summer had always been the best time for them to travel. They were going to be gone so much that particular summer that they had even made arrangements for the dog and the cat to go to a kennel while they were away, to save them all the planning and favor asking they would've needed to do otherwise. So, I didn't even have *that* to do to keep me busy, I lamented. *Damn!*

I thought of Vivianne next, as I got out and toweled off. She had finally returned to full staff and normal operations with the addition of Cindy, but I wondered how hard it would be to learn the art of tattooing anyway. It was just like drawing, only different, right? Then I wondered who on Earth I could actually *practice* on. *Hah!* Okay, so that was probably out.

I didn't think I could really work for Viv anyway, if I was going to be serious at all. Honestly, we'd kill each other in under a month. Our personalities were both too strong to be contained in one place for too long. No we were definitely friends who adored each other as long as we didn't spend extended periods of time in each other's personal space. I always say that every relationship has a reason why it works. Truth is, sometimes there's more than one. Sometimes there's many and the fact that we both not only realized that circumstance, but respected it, was yet another one of ours.

As I stood there contemplating my limited options, I suddenly realized that I had taken only undergarments to the bathroom with me out of habit. Unless I had company, I would usually come back out and get dressed next to my bed, where my bureau and the mirror were. I had the dilemma then about whether to go back to my room in nothing but my underwear to dress like I normally would, or to go try to find something in my closet and take it back into the bathroom to dress. That would be highly unusual for me though and it might make *someone* suspicious.

Ethan wasn't there anymore but I could still smell the faint scent of him in the room and it immediately reminded me what he had said about leaving the cameras alone in case we could use them to our advantage at some point. I really didn't want to blow that on the very first day that I knew about them for Christ's sake! *Jesus*! I had to at least be better than that! They would be used to seeing me dress by then already anyway, I reminded myself stubbornly. They were probably bored with it in fact. *Hmpf!*

Walking out there half naked however, was a lot harder to do when you actually *knew* for sure that some bastard somewhere was watching. I had already thought myself somewhat inadequate to handle the role of "*Bond-girl*" before, but I *was* his girlfriend at that point, or "significant other" or whatever the hell grownups called each other and *dammit*, I was planning on keeping it that way! I knew that in order to do that I would have to figure it all out somehow! *I could do it!*

In the end, I decided to just "*man-up*" so-to-speak and get it over with. I started with a deep breath but I let back it out slowly trying not to *look* specifically as if I had just geared myself up. Then I walked calmly back over to my dresser. I kept my breathing slow and even and I tried not to move too fast. It was harder than it looked though and my heart was racing just at the surety that I was not *entirely* alone. I was grateful then that I was at least in the habit of putting on my undergarments before coming out of the bathroom. I mean I did live in a house full of windows and sliding glass doors after all, so in a twisted way I was thankful again for *that!* But I wasn't used to having anyone looking *through* them!

I tried desperately to pick out something that I could put on right away without looking ridiculous for grabbing something completely inappropriate. Standing there in my skivvies in front of at least one stranger was not a pleasant experience for me though and it made it take longer for things like colors and fabrics to register in my brain past the questions like, "Are they looking at the cellulite on my ass?" and "*Shit*, is this bra see-through?"

I knew there were plenty of people out there who would eat that shit up, but personally I wasn't one of them. I myself liked my exposure of my private parts to remain just that, *private*, and strictly "*by-invitation-only.*"

I tried to think about Ethan then and our time together earlier, and how we had managed that in spite of their efforts, to distract myself from the current stress. That certainly got my mind off of *them*. I searched some more for something to wear, but I started to realize that most of the things left in my drawers were terribly out of season and I still hadn't bothered to change that. I'd been wearing almost nothing but work clothes for the past month so it hadn't really been a burning issue.

In the end modesty won out over comfort and I grabbed a pair of jeans just to put something on. I knew I would have to change eventually but it was still early and cool enough for the moment that I wouldn't die in them. I threw on a sleeveless t-shirt over that in an effort to balance it out a little. It was a work shirt but I didn't care. It was clean and I had no plans to go anywhere or do anything important anyway, I acknowledged confidently before the bitch in my head had a chance to snidely point it out. But there was something that I *could* do, I thought then with some relief and even a little bit of spiteful satisfaction.

Once I was dressed, I decided that in retribution for their little stolen peep-show, I would *bore* them to death! *Hah!* I slipped my feet into the pair of flip-flops by my dresser and I finally went to the closet to get the two large plastic bins that I used to store my off-season clothes. It freed up a lot of room in my drawers with the limited space, just by moving things out that I wouldn't touch for months anyway. At the moment though, due to my "all work, all the time" ethic, they still held my spring and summer clothes which I sorely needed.

I carried them over one at a time just to drag it out more, and dropped each one with a satisfying thud beside my bed. I tried not to spend too much time looking in my closet for the door that I had never seen before, but I did make out the split in the seams at the corners as I worked. It was well camouflaged and wasn't something that would ever have made me suspicious before, but knowing what I was looking for, it was possible to pick out. I smiled just slightly and then coughed to cover it up out of reflex and closed the double doors.

I spent the next two hours drinking coffee and sorting through clothes. Taking the heavy things out of my drawers and putting them in the newly emptied bins. It was boring even for me but at least for me it was necessary. I could only imagine how torturous it must be for the poor schlub/schlubs assigned to watch duty. *Hah!* I smiled to myself in secret satisfaction at that.

I made it through everything that I could do without actually trying anything on to see if it still fit, since I decided stubbornly that that was all the "*show*" the bastards were getting for one day. I didn't normally have to try a lot of stuff on each season anyway. I had finished growing long ago and my weight did not usually fluctuate by that much. But looking in the mirror at the way the jean's hung loosely on my hips, I had to admit then that I probably *was* five pounds thinner than last summer, maybe even ten if I was being *really* honest. Oh well, I would get to that later, I thought with an ironic laugh at the realization that he had been right after all. I just hadn't noticed.

I could see it then though, if I looked. In my smooth cheeks that were usually just a little too full, and my thighs that were stronger than ever but definitely a sleeker, more *defined* version than I was used to. It was a little surprising but certainly nothing drastic. I checked just to make sure that there were no spindly looking upper arms, no sharp collarbones protruding and screaming out for sustenance. No hipbones extending further than the hips. *Hah!* That made me laugh again. No, not even close. I was definitely still okay,

I confirmed once and for all and then I let it go.

Once I was finished with that task, I was out of ideas. I had already cleaned and dusted every surface and swept and vacuumed every corner last week, on the first day that I had been home with nothing else to do. I was glad then, for the fact that some idiot had had to sit through all of that too. I knew it wasn't particularly mature of me to think that way but I didn't care, for the moment the comical vision made me feel better.

I finally decided to just go outside and wander aimlessly for a while in the fresh air. I walked out the back sliders and down the stairs, but before I even reached the bottom I saw Jack and despite my previous intentions of solitude, I was instantly relieved. I headed over to where he was currently replacing a section of fence in the riding area.

"Hey Jack!" I called when I got close.

"Hey sugar, how's things?" He asked as congenially as ever but with a new, coconspirator's smirk. "Feeling any better today?" He asked with a teasing grin.

I knew for sure then that *he* knew that Ethan had been home, however briefly. It was his way of saying it without actually *saying it*. I had never remembered to ask Ethan what he had been busy with all night before he got to my place. Mostly I think, because deep down I knew he probably couldn't tell me. But it was obvious to me then that *Jack* knew.

He saw my grin and he also knew what I was thinking. Just as well as I knew his thoughts. It was tough not being able to really talk about it much, but it was a little easier just knowing that at least one person truly knew what I was going through, and understood. He chuckled again as he thought warmly about something. When he spoke up, I smiled at what it was.

"He looked a lot better today too." He confirmed, being uncharacteristically informative with an affectionate chuckle. I was instantly happier. That definitely made me feel better, but I was still a little surprised by his openness and instantly worried about our "*friends*" overhearing. I looked at Jack with wide questioning eyes and raised eyebrows while purposefully facing away from where I knew the cameras were.

"Don't worry, they can see us, but they can't hear us." He said while purposely facing the ground. "It's strictly video, no audio." He confirmed and I relaxed again with a sigh.

Then he handed me a hammer and some nails and held the next new board up as he directed me to nail it in. I was only too happy to oblige. We talked while we worked and it was really nice to have found a way to keep busy. It was almost like being on the jobsite with him again.

He had been a lot of fun to work with but extremely useful too. The man sure knew his stuff when it came to construction, which was only slightly surprising for a farmer. He worked the land first and foremost sure, but he also did everything else that came along with owning such a large amount of property. His personal skills obviously did not stop there. From working in mechanics to keep his equipment running, to matchmaking in his family, he did it all. *Hmpf.* I wondered then if I would ever know the full extent of his talents, but I felt the answer to that before I even asked the question and I smiled to myself. Good old mysterious Jack. Ethan was right about that as well, I decided then, curveballs did make life more fun.

Jack nailed his side in silently and I could feel him thinking about something that he longed for, but felt frustrated by at the same time. I waited to see whether he would share it with me or not. As it turns out, I was in luck.

"He's got a righteous mind and an iron will that boy, but he still needs occasional caring for too, just like the rest of us!" He insisted in a way that made me believe it was an ongoing argument between them. "He went so long without it that he falls back into lone soldier mode instinctually. It's his oldest defense mechanism and he's damn good at it!" He said with both frustration *and* a hint of pride I noticed. I was familiar with that confusing reaction to Ethan's purely reflexive selflessness.

"We try to fight that, and to remind him that people do care about him too. We struggle constantly to draw him in to a place where he knows what it's like to experience support and affection. But as you can imagine he's still somewhat resistant." He said sarcastically.

"Whenever it comes to letting himself get too close to people, or relying completely on others, he generally chooses to go the other way." He said looking down at the dirt. "Unfortunately he learned that response first." He stopped what he was doing and looked up at me then, feeling very relieved.

"You're one of the few I've ever seen him *not* do that with, outside of the family anyway. Like he thinks you might actually understand." I could feel how deep his feelings on that went. It was definitely a big deal in his eyes. I was even more grateful for the truth in that then. I decided to be generous in return and voice the reassurance that I knew, the *"father-figure"* in him was fishing for.

"I'd consider myself extremely lucky, if he were in my life on a regular basis at this point." I admitted freely. I could feel his relief but also his slight surprise at my open and uncharacteristic proclamation.

"You've had a change of heart then? Decided to participate in life again after all, eh?" He teased, knowing how shut off I had been when I first moved there barely five months ago. It was such a short period of time when I thought about it that way, but when I considered how much had changed in that time, it felt like *forever* ago!

"Well, I was trying to." I joked. "But yeah, things are definitely different now. Believe me I'm as surprised by that as you are." I added with a weak smile.

I had survived my divorce and learned how to be "*just* me" again for the majority of the time. That had been a lot tougher to pull off and so much less attractive in general as a mother. But I had somehow managed to adjust as much as anyone ever could to that currently challenging situation with Liliana, and I had at least learned to find the joy in the everydayness of it again in the meantime, regardless of the sucky circumstances. That had been a *huge* step for me, just having gotten past being so overwhelmed by the pain and that sense of loss that I couldn't feel the good things that were left. Thankfully that mentality at least was in the past. I never wanted to waste any of the good things that I was lucky enough to share with her.

We continued to get better every day at being a family again. A different kind of family then we had been before *sure*, but still a family. A strong one, made up of a lot of good people who loved each other regardless of any specific relationship status. It wasn't ideal, but I still considered us to be pretty lucky. It was hard, but I felt like we were making it work.

On top of that, I had found not just a *new* home for myself, but a *real* home, one that happened to exist in an incredibly beautiful and *peaceful* place that I was so very lucky to spend time in! One that even came with a whole second loving family full of exceptional people that not only accepted me, but truly cared for me and my Liliana like we had broken bread with them forever. That combination of good fortune occurring was already like lightning striking in the same place twice. I knew just how lucky we were to have ended up there. It had made all the difference in the world in our progress and I would never take that for granted.

Beyond that, being there had also led me to someone who had the ability to be a total block for my chaotic mind through his beautiful music, someone that gave me more personal peace than I would have ever dreamed possible. That was incredible all by itself. But on top of that he was also someone who had the ability to make me feel things I never, *ever* thought I'd feel, both physically *and* emotionally! Who shared with me terribly personal and incredibly important things about *myself* that I most likely would never have known otherwise. How could I even attempt to quantify the odds of that occurrence on top of everything else I had found there? It boggled the mind!!

I had to consider then that maybe Vivianne had been right that day on the deck, when she had dared to suggest that I was in *exactly* the right place. *Huh.* Damn her for being so smart and for knowing me so well. The current situation had the potential to be everything I had ever wanted but it all remained tantalizingly, just out of reach. It was frustrating to say the least. I sighed and tried to verbalize the strange place that we were in by then.

"I just wish that wasn't so hard to do, now that I actually

have a mind to do it." I confessed out loud at the end of my mental exercise, letting a little of that frustration show through. That was also uncharacteristic for me, but I was glad to be able to say it out loud for once, well sort of anyway.

"Don't you worry, sugar. I can tell how just much it's been weighing on both of you. Between that *specific* motivation, your combined intelligence and maybe just a little tap on the shoulder from Lady Luck, I'm sure you two will find a way to work it all out soon enough! Til' then though, you've just gotta keep doing what you're doing, because you're the only one who can." He instructed while handing me the next board to hold for him.

"I hope you're right Jack. I really do. But if not, at the very least, you'll have another set of hands to put to use here on the farm for a while. Whatever you need, mucking stalls, painting the barn, you name it. I owe you big-time for your participation in the Tree-fort Village anyway, since you won't let me pay you for your time." I was so grateful that he had held true to his word to help out, even though Ethan hadn't been able to because of course we had needed him even more then.

"Shit, you don't owe me nothing. I was happy to do that for the kids. That place is gonna give them joy for years to come!" He proclaimed with a giant, honest grin. "I'm happy I'll be able to say that I was a small part of that! Hope to have some grandchildren of my own to bring up there at some point soon enough and show it off to!" He professed as he thought about his own kids, most of whom I still hadn't even met yet.

"Well, thank you then. I couldn't have done it without you. Or your daughter! She was amazing by the way. You did a good job there, Jack." I added honestly. "She's the only one of your children that I've had the pleasure of meeting so far, but I'm willing to bet the rest are probably pretty okay as well." I offered with a wink.

"They do a parent proud, for the most part." He added with a warm smile. "You'll meet them all soon enough though, 'specially this time of year. They'll be rolling in and out now that the summer's almost over. Soon we'll be getting into the fall harvest with the apple picking and then it's right into pumpkins, both of which bring the whole family together. It's just too much to do without everyone's help. After that its right into the holidays and it gets downright crowded around here! Believe me it will make you appreciate the quiet times more than ever!" He insisted happily and his enthusiasm was contagious.

"It will be crazy 'round here, but I think you're ready for it." He said confidently and I could feel his sincerity, but also his boundless affection for the whole chaotic mess. He was *really* looking forward to it! His giddy anticipation made me laugh.

"I may need to meet them one at a time, if they're all as intense as the other Kent's I've met so far." I half joked. "But I'm sure one of them will get around to giving you some grand-babies real soon." I assured him sarcastically, knowing that in reality you couldn't really rush those things. They happened only when they were supposed to, and not a moment sooner. I am a firm believer in that. But personally, I wouldn't be the one to dissuade him. They were on their own there. I had my own familial stereotypes to destroy. I would leave them to theirs.

I wasn't worried though. It was obvious that Jack & Shirley's unconditional style of love and support would always outweigh any pressure their kids might ever feel. They were really good at putting the love first and the details later. Then I couldn't help thinking about Ethan again and how they had taken him in and shown him that same consideration. They were never obligated to do any of that for him, they just knew it was the right thing to do that no one else was going to do it and so they did it, consequences be damned. I remembered then that I had still never had a chance to thank him for that and I really thought that someone should.

"Speaking of "*happy to do it,*" *and* "*it's for the kids,*" and all that, there's something else that I wanted to thank you for. That's the way you and Shirley took Ethan in and loved him just as unconditionally as you do your own. Some people don't ever get to the point where they feel the need to take care of the children they created and deposited on this Earth, never mind someone else's! I don't understand it at all because I miss mine terribly every single day that we're apart, but I *know* that it happens! I've seen it! I've *felt* it secondhand, and I've also felt what that indifference can do to a tiny fragile heart looking for a lifeline!" I gave a shiver from head to toe to shake the feeling off. I hadn't liked it whenever I felt it and I didn't like remembering it.

"I know for a fact that some people will never even understand what it *means* to be compassionate towards another human being. Not only do you get it, but it's even more impressive to be that committed when it is someone else's child. That selflessness is something that he has in common with you both now. He really could be your son for all he takes after you." I ended with a smile. He was uncomfortable with all the praise but I wanted to make sure he understood it wasn't simple flattery.

"He is so lucky that you have that ability to recognize the good and the worthiness in someone that so many had already written off and forgotten. You took the time and the energy to hold a mirror up in front of him, so that he might finally see it for himself for the first time. *That also* takes a righteous and kind heart! *Hmpf.* You know he has one, but I think that's only because it takes one to know one!" I insisted with a crooked grin.

He was quiet but he smiled at my statement, feeling amused and waiting for me to catch on. I immediately wondered why. He just waited patiently and grinned. He finally had mercy on my perplexed look and let me in on the joke.

"Well I found you too in a way, didn't I?" He asked with a chuckle.

""Yeah, stuffing my face like a homeless person in the town diner!" I replied with a laugh of my own. But then I realized what he meant and I was shocked to think he would put me in the same category as someone like Ethan.

Sure, I had needed to be taken in at the time and... given a home that had a peacefulness that I desperately needed... and to be inspired to participate in living again... that did sound familiar, I had to admit. *Jesus!*

"*And* you are also able to recognize his kind and righteous heart, are you not?" He posed with a great satisfaction. "That doesn't just mean that you were as much in need as he was either, it means you were just as worthy, *if* you really believe any of what you just said about me." He proclaimed defiantly.

Huh. Hadn't thought about it like that... Why hadn't I thought about it like that before I spoke out loud? Typical Simone. Honesty first, contemplation second. Someday I would learn. Oh well, I didn't necessarily agree that it was the same thing but I realized that maybe I had even more to thank him for than I had originally thought. I just laughed again and shook my head a little, trying to grasp the entirety of that train of thought. There were just too many avenue's to explore though, so I decided to save it for contemplation during the vast empty spaces that I knew I would be looking to fill in the near future. Or maybe *someday* I could get Dr. J to just explain it all to me, I thought halfheartedly. I tried to shake it off and stay on track for the moment though.

"Okay, so thank you *again!*" I added sheepishly. "Look, I *know* it's easier to go through life sitting back quietly in the shadows, where you can judge everyone else's failures from a safe distance. Believe me I can be just as guilty of that as the next guy. Maybe it's even worse in my case because I *know* so much more, and yet I mostly spend my time trying desperately to ignore it all. I have no choice but to stifle a lot of it if I want to survive, I know that now and I know enough not to feel guilty for it anymore. But I also know now firsthand what courage and strength of character it takes to actually stand up and try to *fix* the things that you think are wrong! To actually try and make them better!" I said with a knowing smirk of my own.

"And I just wanted to say *thank you* to you for doing that and for everything that you all gave him, against popular opinion. It's truly commendable, and it changed everything for him! It would have taken him a lot longer to become the man that he is today without you and your unwavering family support. You were one of the first good things that ever happened to him!" I had to take a deep breath then just thinking about what he had been through as a child. I was still learning how to get past that darkness without letting it piss me off and I still only knew a small fraction of his nightmares. That truth just made it harder.

Jack nodded. I could feel his pain at that lost, tortured boy that he had found too, and his own deep desire to help and protect him came through, just as it must have been in the very beginning. He still felt that way and I understood it completely by then. I was grateful to him mostly just for choosing not to ignore it.

"He was a wreck, but that was just because of them. Underneath it all he was always a good egg. He would have been okay eventually, either way. I just got frustrated at how long it was taking and decided to help move it along." He replied with a modest chuckle.

"Well it's a good thing you did, 'cause just look at him today!" I said enthusiastically. "He is where he is because you cared enough to pick him up and kick him in the ass!" I added and I could feel both his surprise and his enjoyment at that.

"He told you about all that, huh?" He nodded to himself as he asked the question, obviously deciding that that meant something specific. I wasn't really sure what yet, but I knew it was meaningful. "Well, I may have been one of the first good things to ever happen to him." He agreed, then turned and squinted in the sunlight while he looked back up at me. He was more serious for a second. "But you're definitely one of the *best.* He's waited a long time for someone like you to come along. A woman who can not only see him for who he *really* is, but one who also has the capability to love him anyway!" He said slowly but clearly. He gave that a moment to sink in.

"He could have easily filled that space in his life long ago with any one of the beautiful woman who have thrown themselves at him over the years. And believe me when I say, there's been a lot!" He informed me with an eye-roll, not holding back. "But he never even considered it, not long-term. Not even once. Not before you." He assured me with more of that fatherly pride.

"He hung in there all this time, waiting patiently for *you!* And now you have to do the same. For *him*." He stated evenly. "I know you can handle it and you know damn well that he's worth it." He confirmed honestly knowing even without being an empath himself that I would never try to argue the truth of that simple statement.

"*Hmpf!* I know. I just wish that he accepted that so easily." I said not hiding my frustration. I had to look down at the ground again then as the sadness at even considering abandoning him washed through me. I shook my head while I responded quietly. "It would certainly be a lot less troublesome not to pursue this, believe me!" I said honestly. "But I don't really have a choice in the matter anymore. As far as giving up goes, it's just not in my nature." I said simply but honestly while giving my best attempt at a weak smile. He smiled back confident enough for both of us then, seeming pleased. Content for the moment, he moved on.

"Come on, *board me woman!*" He insisted loudly. I yelped in surprise and we both laughed. I was grateful to him again for snapping us both out of it.

As it turned out I would be grateful to him quite often over the next few weeks, for his company as well as his understanding, but mostly just for giving me so many things to do. As we made our way around the property day after day, moving from task to task, I finally found some of that sense of completion that I had been looking for in each little job that we crossed off of his honey-do list. They weren't life-altering tasks, but they were important in the day-to-day operations of the farm and that made them very satisfying in a very real way.

Therapy through manual labor, it had worked well for both of us in the past, and I was personally still a huge fan of it.

And despite my original sorrow at the idea, I was actually extremely grateful that Ethan's visits would become slightly more regular after that first one. I would wake to find him holding me every four or five days or so and I was beyond thrilled each time.

I had always been a notoriously light sleeper. You could just look at me sometimes and I would wake up. I had freaked out more than a few people at sleepovers as a teen, but then it probably had more to do with my fear of waking up with my arm in a bowl of water or with my face covered in graffiti than anything else.

Of course I would always "*feel*" a person approach even if I didn't hear them so it wasn't that hard to understand how it worked if you thought about it like that. Either way, hearing him entering my apartment was never what would rouse me. I'm not sure if he ever made a single sound. No, it was always his energy and his expanding joy at our close physical proximity that was the first sign of his presence for me. It would lure me out of whatever dream I had been having and I would never complain. It was a *great* way to wake up!

The arrangement was still dwelling well below the level of "*satisfactory*" but it was admittedly *worlds* better than the complete separation had been. I wasn't sure I could survive that again and he either agreed or had mercy on me. I wasn't exactly sure which but I didn't care anymore, I would take the close proximity to him wherever I could get at that point, whoever's sake it was for! I know, gag me with the dramatics and all that, right? I hear ya, really I do! But there was just no helping the fact that it was true, dammit all! I swear I'm just telling it like it is.

We didn't spend all of our time naked either, although that did account for a fair amount of it. We were both eager to have some of the other moments that we were missing too. So our visits usually consisted of soul-shaking sex, the latest important business including the question and answer period, a short rest period, which often included snack time, and then the teasing and laughter segment that I think I had missed the most. We kept it as light as we could before the heavy crept back in with the light of day. His visits were still too short, and too far between, but for the time being they would have to do. It was like bread and water. We could survive temporarily on the bare minimum if we had to. We would suffer, but we wouldn't starve.

I had wondered at his frequency one night in particular, after having only seen him two nights before. "I thought you were further away. It took you so long in the beginning to get settled!" He nodded, assuring me that I was right in my assumption.

"We've moved a lot since then." Was all he said about it, but it was enough. At least it made sense in my head, so I could file it away. Closer definitely equaled better in my book.

As it stood, it was at least tolerable. Anything we came up with was better than the former emptiness. I didn't know what the alternatives really were yet but I was still holding out hope that we would find one, somehow.

Or maybe, I thought wildly in a desperate plea for some of that golden childhood naivety to return to me, *maybe* if we held on long enough one would come find us. *Hmpf.* Wouldn't that be nice?

All I knew for sure then, was that something had to give, and *soon!*

Chapter 7

I tried my best to stay busy. I worked with Jack whenever there were things to do, *wherever* there were things to do. On the days that there was nothing left on the list, I found other ways to fill my time. I hiked quite a bit. So much in fact, that I had started to simply text my father when I was going, rather than blowing up his phone all day long.

He had never been a huge fan of texting but it worked and it was better than the alternative so he let it go. Being in a college environment for a living, he really did need to keep up with the latest technology anyway, and he knew that whether he liked it or not so he tried to be adult about it and embrace it.

When it was just too hot to hike, I had to find other things to do. Vivianne's day off was a moving target a lot of the time, but she tried to take it on Thursday whenever she could, so I took a chance one particularly boring Thursday and got lucky when I called her up.

"How 'bout a liquid lunch?" She offered and I was immediately on board.

"Sounds good! I'm on my way." I agreed with relief. I went into town and we met at our favorite Sports bar for Margarita's. I caught her up on my latest arrangement with Ethan over our first drink and was laughing hysterically at her responses by the time we reached our second. We decided then that we might want to add a little bit of solid food to absorb some of our "liquid lunch" and we ordered some fish tacos and a deep fried onion flower. It was terrible for us in the most awesome way and we devoured every bite as we got caught up.

She still didn't know all the specific details of his "*other*" side, and she had agreed that she didn't really need to necessarily. We had decided on a sort of "don't ask-*too much*/don't tell-*too much*" kind of approach where he was concerned. So she at least understood to some extent that he *had* one. oShe had already deemed him a "*good guy*" anyway. She was basically okay with trusting my judgment on people as a rule. Knowing my skills as well as she did, she had no problem with that part.

On the other side of that coin, Ethan knew that I didn't tell her anything too specific but that she *was* my main confidant. He understood that as well. He trusted me to know where the line was. It could be tricky sometimes, but it wasn't impossible. Especially since those weren't the kinds of details that she wanted to hear about anyway.

"So let me get this straight, he shows up in the middle of the night, bounces you off the walls for a while, but only the walls that the feds can't see, and then slips out before the sun comes up?" I just nodded my head and tried to hold in my laughter to keep from spitting my drink everywhere. "Damn! Where can I get me some of *that?!*" She demanded slapping the table *hard*, almost *entirely* serious! We're talking 97% here!

Although it was not even close to ideal in my book, Vivianne was already a champion of the situation. She had decided that it had officially become "*dangerous*" and "*adventurous*" and God help me the word "*romantic*" even got thrown around before our lunch was over!

I wasn't sure what I had been thinking, looking for support from her on that issue to begin with. With the newest development, she was even more on board than before. She just thought it was "*fully freakin' fantastic*" and "*way too cool*" and lots of other colorful terms for totally awesome! I found it very amusing, to say the least, but I still tried to talk her down a little. I really did.

"What about the other 48 to 192 hours in between his visits, that we're forced to spend apart?" I asked. She stared blankly back at me and I could tell that she couldn't quite grasp the concept of that as a negative. *Grrrrr.* I shook my head in disbelief but I had to laugh. Of course, that was just pure, classic Viv.

I had confessed my true feelings to her then just as I always do, at the same time that I admitted it for the first time out loud.

"God help me, but I really want all the in-between minutes too Viv. I not only *really* like him, genuinely as a person, but I feel better just being near him! Just physically having him there, in my general vicinity, is good in ways that I had never even thought possible for me." I sighed as it continued to pour out.

"I *really* miss the way he can hold a conversation with me without ever saying a word. Even as emotionally damaged as he is, he's still one of the best men that I have *ever* known!" I finished and she gave a decidedly sympathetic smile. She finally, truly felt bad for me. I laughed again, but it was quieter.

She was surprised by the softening of my attitude, but not as much as she would have been *before* my move to Pinegrove. She just hugged me and tried her best to be a supportive friend.

"Well good luck with that." She started encouragingly but then laughed. "Lunch is on me, since that's about the only thing here that I can help you with." She added laughing even louder at her own joke and my unfortunate situation. She shook her head.

"Sorry, hun. Not about the fantastic late night sex of course, that just makes me jealous, but for the annoying "*feelings*" part." She clarified with a screwed up face and a shimmy of disgust. I laughed and thanked her for her sympathy and for lunch, and we said goodbye but agreed to try to do it again the following week.

Of course I spent as much time as I could with Liliana, but even taking extra rides when I could steal them away from someone, and stopping by the house a little more often just to say hi whenever I was in town, still wasn't nearly enough to fill the size gaps that I currently had. I enjoyed what I could get though. We played car games like "punch buggy," "banana" and "pa-diddle" and sang our hearts out to the radio together as we searched for Volkswagen's, yellow cars and vehicles with only one headlight together.

My normal route, was the trip home. Someone from the city

would generally bring her up to day camp, since Liliana was already down there where they were. Then I would pick her up and bring her home most days, since I was already up here. It just made sense. Our parents were happy to pitch in as well, though that was still mostly his at the moment while mine were away so much. But they didn't mind. No one was in a hurry to give up their shift. All of them loved the ride up 95 as much as I did and they loved having Liliana to themselves for the half hour or so each time, so there were no complaints. We all wanted to have our turn.

Ben even had a turn once every other week, when he came up to make his "*routine*" house-call on Don's dogs, two of which were currently pregnant, one newly and one heavily. It was all a little crazy to keep straight at first between us all, but we finally managed to nail it down by email. It was harder to screw up once the schedule was there in black and white. And although we didn't have tons of time to do other things with her during the week, at least we did each get our own time with her.

It really does take a village to raise a child. You hear that all the time, and you know what? It's true dammit. It's a tremendous amount of work and you learn fast enough to take the *trusted* help where you can get it gratefully. But no one ever tells you that when you have a village full of helpers, you also have a village full of people that expect to *share* that child during the fun times too! That seems completely logical after the fact, but at first it had been a bit of a surprise.

I tried not to mind since I knew how lucky she was to have so many people in her life who loved her so much and wanted to spend time doing fun things with her. Not every kid had a Grammy and a Grand-Brad-Dad that wanted to take monthly trips to the zoo, and the Music Theatre, or a Nann that wanted to spend her day off at the butterfly garden, or a Grampy that wanted to take you golfing, or skating or to an art class. We all needed some of that attention in our lives though as children and it's definitely a good thing! Like everything else, it was all about the balance and I thought we were walking the tightrope fairly successfully as a family but it definitely spread her free time thinner than I had ever expected.

Some days I would get to keep her after day camp though, other than just my usual Friday's. We were still trying to keep to her schedule during the week. So even through the summer months that meant her being at home for dinner and her normal bedtime as much as possible. But on nights that we knew Ben would be working late and there were no grandparents available to fill in, I was more than happy to have to break the rules a little.

We'd have dinner out on the deck and go for a walk together, or we'd take a ride over to Stewart's and fight the mosquitoes for a spot in line to get ice cream. It didn't matter. It was all good summer fun and I treasured every moment of it that I got with her. I always wanted more, but I figured that I would always feel that way, no matter how old she got or how much time we spent together, so as usual I just tried to suck it up. I also tried not to keep her too long, too often on the other nights when I knew I had to bring her home early. She was still tired after her long day of activities at camp, and couldn't stay awake very long once she got there. That was especially true since she had gotten her cast off and added the water sports!

That had been both a happy and a sad day for me at the same time since I was happy the wrist was healed, but sad that I hadn't been able to be there for the actual removal. So many little things I missed, but they all felt big to me and I knew they did to her as well. I tried not to get too deep into that pain as I remembered seeing her afterwards.

She had come running up to me the next day at pickup, both arms waving freely, completely devoid of pink fiberglass. I had tried then too not to overreact and as I reached down to lift her up, I swallowed down the tears.

"Look mama! It's gone!" She exclaimed happily as she held her now healed arm out in front of her.

"That's great!" I said kissing it a few times playfully. "How's it feel?" I asked really wanting to *feel* her answer more than hear it. She was a lot like Ethan I realized when it came to her own pain, it was the one thing she most often wished she could hide. I had been instantly relieved by her answer though, when I could feel the truth in the words and in her mood.

"Really good! Like it never happened!" She insisted happily.

"Oh that's awesome sweetie!" I had been happy to hear that the last x-rays had shown that it had healed perfectly. It was just tough when he told me they were going to go in so early the next morning to have it off, almost as an afterthought.

I'd planned to be there when that happened, but he had gone ahead and booked it at 5:30 AM the following day to accommodate their schedules and that meant I would have to get up at 4:00 AM to make it there in time and Ben had made that sound ridiculous. He had also had assured me, that it was only going to take five minutes anyway, while the drive would take me over an hour and he had insisted that it truly wasn't necessary. I wanted to argue but it seemed petty and illogical after that so as usual, I had given in. I talked to her over the phone before she left and told her good luck but also that she wouldn't need it because it would be over so fast and she wouldn't feel a thing, and that I would see her later. As usual, it wasn't the easy choice but it seemed to be the right one. *Dramatic sigh...*

There was no holding her back after that in her activities though and that made me feel better! But it also made her very tired at the end of the day so I had to make a conscious effort not to be selfish and keep her until bedtime every night that I had her. I wanted to, but I knew that Ben was actually missing her a lot by then, too.

In light of that we had agreed to try and "*share*" that most precious time period, those few hours that existed after her day at Juniper but before she fell deeply asleep from exhaustion. I actually felt bad for him the few times that she was already out like a light just from the drive home on his nights. Those days he didn't see her at all.

For the first time I saw him having to deal a little with something similar to what I had been through when we first separated. There was a natural urge to be spiteful but I resisted it since I knew how hard it was for him already, even without my introducing that useless negativity.

I would never feel his emotions myself, like I did most other peoples, but in that particular situation I didn't need to. I had felt that separation anxiety firsthand and I knew how difficult it could be to wrap your heart around. But I also knew that he had to learn to deal with it eventually and he had to do it on his own, just like I had. Unfortunately he was learning lately that everything in life had a cost, even success.

Ben was going in a million different directions at the moment, but he had his head on straight for the most part, and I knew I didn't have to worry too much about him adjusting and not self-destructing. He just needed time. That was the other thing that worried me though, I didn't know how much more time we had.

At some point we still needed to talk about Liliana before her *heightening* became a real life issue. I would have loved to just wait it out and hope it wouldn't ever be necessary, but while that would be easier for us, it wouldn't help her get through it if it did happen. I couldn't risk that being any harder than I already knew it would be if that was in the cards for her. I also knew that it would be easier for him to handle it all, if I gave him time to get a grip on the latest changes first. I was just hoping I would be able to wait that long.

In the meantime, I took my turns and my visits, when I could get them and I tried to focus on something else and not how much I missed her the rest of the time. It definitely seemed to be a growing trend in my life, learning to live without the people that I missed the most, and I was *really* ready to turn that around! I just wished I had more ideas on how to do it. Until some came to me, I did the only other thing that I could, I kept moving.

I did spend a few of my evenings at The Tavern, even though that was only marginally better than being at home alone. At least there I could eat some dinner and absorb some human companionship, even if it was mostly vicariously through the groups of happy people socializing around me. I didn't mind. I would just borrow some of their upbeat energy while I quietly sipped my wine. Of course that only worked because *he* wasn't there singing.

I missed his music as much as his presence. You really couldn't separate the two in my eyes. And no matter how good the current musician was each night I was there, or how jubilant the crowd, I just couldn't find the same peace in their music that I always did with his. In the end, I still felt alone, even there, so eventually I would just embrace it and go home to actually *be* alone.

To my couch, and my TV, and my bed, where *every once in a while*, a phantom wave of pure joy would rush through and revitalize me! He never stayed long though. He was a perpetually temporary visitor and as much as I believed in what he was trying to do, I was getting to the end of my rope with that particular circumstance.

I had taken to staying up later and later each night, with no real work to tire me out during the day. I had no reason to rush out of bed in the morning either at the moment, so it didn't really matter. It had been a particularly bad week, with TruTV running a Forensic Files marathon every night. One episode would roll right into the next and before I knew it the sun would be coming up.

I knew it was a really bad habit to allow myself to fall into. But there was always that possibility that Ethan might show up lurking in the back of my mind, and that possibility however remote, always made it harder to fall asleep. *Just in case.* He never seemed to show up when I when I wanted him to the most though. Of course not, right? Even my somewhat informative dreams were very little help there. His plans would change so much and so fast that I rarely had time to decipher the hazy dreams before he would show up.

It was on that third Sunday after Ethan's first visit, at the end of my "*late-shift*" week that I woke once again to the sound of my ringing phone. "*Good* or *bad?*" my mind was quick to demand, searching for the appropriate response. I wasn't sure yet and I wasn't awake enough for it to be automatic.

I was really starting to like the sleeping later part. Waking up naturally, without an alarm, at whatever time I happened to be *done* sleeping. It was an interesting concept to me and a novelty that I had not experienced in quite a long time. Being a kid and going to school, having a regular day job and then having a child, had all required me to get up earlier than I would have liked for the last twenty something years or so without ever really giving it much thought. It's just what you do.

It seemed more natural at the moment though and even healthier, to wake up on my own and I found I *really* liked it. I did still occasionally feel a little guilty and/or out of sorts because of it though. You know, slightly *disconnected* from the "real world," *so-to-speak*. I was starting to wonder though, why the "*real world*" had to be someone else's interpretation of the perfect schedule. Why couldn't the *real* world be what *really* came naturally to each of us?

Unfortunately I already knew why, because the rest of the population was not completely onboard with sharing that new philosophy yet, at least not according to the feedback I'd gotten so far. It was changing, but not fast enough. I think that was mostly just because the great majority of people simply didn't have that option, and that made them slightly less apt to be happy for someone else who did.

I understood that perspective too and I didn't judge them for it. It was human nature. It was hard to be enthusiastic about someone else's success and happiness when you felt put upon, overworked and underappreciated on a daily basis, which the majority of the population did, and truly *was*. I totally get it. *And how the Hell do we fix that?* I wondered next... but anyway, I digress...

I sat up with a prominent wrinkle of confusion between my scrunched up brows. I looked up at the clock before I made a move to answer it. *Eh*, almost nine thirty, an hour at which I couldn't really bitch too much for being woken up. So I decided to pick it up, even though I didn't recognize the number, admittedly another weak moment in my drowsy state.

"Hello?" I answered in the form of a question.

"Hi! Simone?" A perky and somewhat familiar voice asked back.

"Yes." I confirmed and then waited.

"Hi! It's Marina Stavros, we met at the opening, at Wu Xing Gardens. Do you remember me?" She asked needlessly. No, I met celebrities every day I thought sarcastically, my usual half-awake petulance shining through.

"Yes, of course. How are you?" I said more congenially than I felt, not knowing what else to say.

"Good, good. Mr. Wu Xing gave me your number, I hope you don't mind." She said seeming sincere enough."

"No, that's fine." I said reflexively, even though I had no idea yet whether it really was or not.

"Listen, the reason that I'm calling is that I'd like to hire you for a job I have coming up if I can interest you. I know you must be *crazy* busy but I'm hoping I can tempt you away from whatever you're doing right now to get you to throw in a little charity work." She said half hopelessly and I tried to keep from laughing out loud.

"Gee, I might be able to squeeze it in. What'd you have in mind?" I asked, sounding mildly optimistic. Secretly though, I was gearing up for another regular haul up to New Hampshire and wondering if I really wanted to do that again right away. Oh well, I thought, work was work. If it was something that I could actually do, I certainly wouldn't turn it down. She surprised me with her next question though.

"Well, do you remember that little town in Mass that I was telling you I'm from? I'm sure it's totally out of your way, but I'm hoping that if I pamper you enough, I can convince you to spend some time in "Nowhere's-ville," U.S.A. this summer. Just for a couple of weeks! Because I am certain now that you are the *only* woman for this challenging job!"

She laughed but I could feel her enthusiastic insistence, even over the phone. I didn't know what it was yet, but whatever it was she sure was fired up about it! That was good. That kind of thing was contagious and I needed some of that good energy at that point, wherever it came from.

"Okay." I said. "How far out of the way are we talking?" I asked, afraid to even speculate. In my mind I was already thinking of places way out West like Belchertown. That particular little jewel was a beautiful, tiny little town just three short hours away, in the middle of the state. It had come up occasionally in my searches for a place because out there, $250,000 will buy you a five bedroom contemporary, one-family home with 4 full baths, and a kitchen stocked full of granite and stainless steel that had an acre and a half in the back yard. *Hah!* Whereas around *there*, I knew you couldn't even get a small condo in a town like Marblehead for that price. *Maybe* a one room studio, but certainly not a *nice* one! And *definitely* not one near the water! I was surprised form my mental musing once again though when she finally spit it out.

"It's a small town up in the woods near Boxford, called Pinegrove. I know, where is that, right? But don't worry, I can get you directions or better yet, I can send a car!" She offered and I did laugh then.

"*Seriously?!*" I asked with disbelief evident in my voice. She immediately took it the wrong way though.

"I know, I know, and believe me it's as rural as it sounds. But it's actually really pretty and it's extremely peaceful. It's the kind of town where nobody bothers the local celebrity newscaster, who happens to live next door, *or* even the occasional famous landscape designer!" She added as incentive.

"Well, I don't know if I can handle that kind of commute." I joked but again, it went right over her head. She was so sure that I would turn her down that she had come prepared to negotiate.

"Don't drive! Take the limo! You could just relax and catch up on your paperwork or your favorite TV shows while you travel! Whatever you need! The lap of luxury, I swear!" She offered quickly.

"Relax, will you? I'm kidding for Christ's sake!" I said then with another laugh. "It would take the car longer to get here than it would to deliver me."

"Huh?" She said, obviously confused by that. I laughed again.

"That's actually where I *live*." I finally told her without hiding my own surprise and I could instantly feel her disbelief as well.

"*What!* No *sir!* That's a riot! *Where?!*" She asked.

"I live over on Small Road, on Kent's Farm." I provided.

"Are you *kidding* me?!" That's like two streets over from my parents place on Clear View Road! I don't believe it! That's awesome! *You see?!* This is what I love about small towns." She said and laughed herself then. "It's fate! That's what it is!" She insisted, reiterating a quote that I had heard directed at me once before in my "quiet little town," and I knew then that it was truly meant to be.

Like every other job I'd ever had, I felt a specific calling. Not from a higher power or anything like that, there was just something that spoke to me personally somehow. I really needed that sense that I was meant to be somewhere, to push me over the edge into making a decision, especially when I was working on transforming a place. Since I already felt that there, I guess it was time to find out what the actual job was.

"Alright. I'm in. What's the deal?"

"Oh my God! Are you serious? Oh, you're going to love it!" She gushed excitedly. "I want to completely update and renovate the whole outdoor playground as well as the indoor and outdoor event areas of Breezey Memorial Park over on the edge of town! It's sorely in need of an overhaul and all new facilities in the main hall. But the place is a registered landmark and is run by the Conservation Committee as a registered historical property, so they have to go through months and months of meetings just to get approval to change a damn light bulb! I am *not* even kidding you!" She insisted with a sad laugh.

"Because every dollar spent there is "Public Conservation Fund" money, each and every expenditure must be voted on and approved by majority. It makes it a nightmare of epic proportions to try and get anything done!" She joked enthusiastically. "So the place is just sitting there corroding and going to waste. Whenever I'm in town and I drive by it, it makes me crazy! There is such potential there for it to be a great asset for the town, but nobody has the time or resources all by themselves to singlehandedly make it happen." She said with her exasperation over the matter clear. She sighed and began again.

"*But*, if the whole thing's done as a "gift" and the services are rendered as a collaborative "donation" to the city, then a ton of that red tape can be bypassed all together!" She finished and I felt that old familiar implied "*wah-lah*" moment in there.

Huh. Another job chock full of legal wrangling and committee approvals. Oh boy. Was I really ready to jump right back into *that* kind of mess again? I was hesitant of course, but I still had nothing better to do. That singular but incredibly potent fact was enough to convince me in the end. She wasn't done explaining yet though I could tell, so I waited while she continued.

"But for all I'm asking of you, I can't offer you much in the way of compensation, that's why I called it "*charity*" quite frankly, and was prepared to offer you the car as a perk. But the good news is that you won't have to do it all by yourself this time. I fully intend to get the locals involved too, a *lot* of them! Including the town Boy scouts because they happen to have a large group of teenagers looking to make Eagle Scout this year. The timing couldn't be more perfect!" She gushed.

"They need to complete community projects that encompass a total of 600-700 man-hours in order to achieve that goal! Most of them are well on their way and only need twenty or thirty hours to reach it. Lucky for them I have just the project to help them all fulfill that requirement once and for all!" She told me and I was blown away by the numbers.

"I also have a long list of local vendors and tradesmen that live and work here in town and are willing to donate goods and services to help see this project completed." She was getting more and more amped up as she went. It was easy to see how she had gotten so many people on board.

"I've actually been working on this for quite a while. I started out just wanting give back a little to my home town that had been so supportive of me while I was building my career. Now that I have enjoyed a little success and have some extra income and therefore some extra time, I wanted to pay them back in some way. But I wanted to find a way that wouldn't just be good today but would also make the towns future better too, the way it had helped to permanently improve mine. I know it sounds a little "movie of the week," but once I had the idea and began looking into it, I realized how hard it was to accomplish and why no one had ever done it before." She took another fortifying breath.

"By then I had talked to a lot of other people that had wanted to do it but couldn't and that finally gave me an idea! I liked the challenge in it and I can see that you are also not one to shy away from the impossible. Am I right?" I had to shake my head at that uncanny assessment. *Hah!* She had no idea.

"Um, you know that I don't really do "buildings" and interior spaces and such, right? I'm pretty much just an artist and designer who happens to like plants and using the great outdoors as my medium." I said humorously but honestly, wanting to be sure we were on the same page.

"I know, and that's perfect. Truly! We need to update the estate as a whole, but the more we meet and talk about this project, the more I come to realize that here at least, it really is all about the outdoor spaces. That is where the majority of the events and activities take place. Besides that, you won't be responsible for coming up with the schematics for the construction and electrical work and so forth. I just need you to come up with the overall plan for the space as a whole." She assured me logically.

"We can get all of the appropriate tradesmen involved along the way and they will handle the specifics and check for any potential contradictions themselves before we actually get started. We just need you to give us one cohesive theme that we can use to get the ball rolling in thirty different directions. After that, you will be able to focus on the exterior spaces while the rest of the workers split up and tackle the interior projects. We just need your creativity and your leadership skills." She explained and it made a little more sense to me then.

"Alright. That sounds slightly less insane." I agreed with a chuckle.

"Good. Here's the other thing though. Even with all the volunteers and donations, mine included, the budget will still be *super*-tight, like nonexistent. It's going to take a little miracle working. I'm not going to sugarcoat it." She hedged a bit. "But I've already seen what you can do with the odds stacked against you and it was nothing short of miraculous. If you can bring that fantasy place to life like you did at The Gardens, then surely you can resuscitate a once thriving park and formerly 'functional,' function hall." She joked but finished more seriously. "I have complete faith in your abilities." She insisted innocently.

I thought of Mr. Wu Xing for a minute and his formerly inexplicable faith in me. At least with Marina, I knew why she believed in me. Because she already knew that I wasn't afraid of the "impossible." I wondered for just a second if maybe she was actually an empath like me. Even with all my reading and personal experience, I had never met another empath just randomly in passing, at least not one outside the family. I tend to think that there just aren't many out there. It used to make me feel very alone, but it was starting to make me feel pretty special. I thought about Ethan again for another second and smiled before I snapped out of it.

No I was fairly certain that she wasn't an empath, I was sure I would have felt it bouncing back and forth like a mirrored hallway when we had met if that were the case. But it was easy for me to see why she had gone into the world of journalism, because I was sure then that she was what I would categorize ironically enough as a "*reporter*" in the most basic sense of the word. She had an undeniable itch, a completely *human* itch, to get behind the scenes of a situation and uncover the truths and '*report*' them back to the masses. Not everybody had the instinct or the ability to do that, and only half of those would do more than keep it to themselves after discovering the truth.

Not Marina, she was a reporter through and through and she had skillfully and surprisingly figured out what drove me to greatness if you will, whatever "greatness" meant for me personally anyway. It was that I was continually inspired by the "things that shouldn't be possible." Who knew if that was good or bad, it just *was*. I realized at that moment that I could look back on my life and see that theory repeated throughout, even currently. *Hmpf.* She'd had one more surprise left though and I could feel it coming just then, bringing my attention back to the conversation at hand.

"I should also tell you though, that I am planning on doing a story on the whole transformation, from beginning to end, so it's not a completely selfless act. I want to be honest about that from the beginning. Everyone else involved knows that as well, and has already signed off on it going in. I am going to do the renovations either way, whether the piece ever airs or not, but my goal is certainly to air it as long as the producers are on board with the finished piece. There, now you have it all. Still interested?" She asked excitedly and I couldn't help catching a little bit of her enthusiasm despite her obvious reservations.

"Yup! Count me in. Aside from the *on-camera* part, which I can tell you right now I will avoid as much as humanly possible, that actually sounds like the perfect way to top off my summer. Especially the "*local*" part! When do you want to get started?" I asked eagerly, already looking forward to the physical activity.

"Well, if you think you can swing it, I already have the two weeks after this coming weekend set aside. I know it's *really* short notice but the circumstances were unforeseeable. We got everyone to agree on a window of time months ago when schedules were somewhat malleable for so many people and it was *still* a logistical nightmare, so it would be almost impossible to change at this point! We were all ready to go when the original group that had agreed to oversee the project got called out of state on an important renovation. They're a major development firm with a ton of experience and were willing to manage this job pro bono like everyone else, so even though they had to put everything off until the last minute in order to fit it in, we were psyched!"

"Unfortunately they also have *uber*-important national jobs that take precedence over local volunteer work and I totally understand. They have a hotel they're overseeing in Vegas and they had been planning it for two years so when the timeline suddenly changed, they had to go with it. I know how it is, but I thought we were all done for sure! I knew there was no way we could "re-schedule" everyone involved and I couldn't get anyone who could replace them with so little time left! I had no idea what I was going to do until I remembered what you did at the Gardens. It took me a few days to get to a brave/desperate enough to ask you though." She admitted with a laugh.

"*So* if we stay on track with the original schedule, you would only have this week to take what we have to start with and come up with the final plans. Those plans will then have to be approved through the committee before we can start, but they had already promised to hurry the process along for once in order to meet the deadline." She informed me, her former frustration coming through once more. "It's mostly just so they can check for any blatant violations to the Conservation Commission's requirements. Barring any major issues there, we should be up and running twenty four hours after that." She said excitedly.

"We have everything else ready to go at a moment's notice at this point and you'd kind of have to run and jump on. Think you can handle that?" She asked with obvious fear at the possible answer and of course the competitive side of me was instantly peaked by the challenge. I realized then that she was counting on that too already, just a little. That made me smile to myself.

"How soon can you get me specs of the entire area and an *honest* budget?" I asked as a counter challenge.

"I can make a few calls and arrange all of that as soon as I hang up the phone with you! I was serious when I said we've been ready. The plan has been in the '*preparation*' stages for a long time now. I've just been itching to pull the trigger." She laughed at herself then. "I'm literally ready whenever you are!"

"Well alrighty then! *Bring it on.*" I insisted.

"Okay, you asked for it! Oh I can't thank you enough for agreeing to take this on! It won't be easy, but when all is said and done I promise you, you'll be glad you did, I just know it!" She insisted and we both hung up still laughing.

Huh, maybe Miss Celebrity newswoman wasn't so bad after all, I thought as I sighed and finally got out of bed.

I felt renewed then, like I could reach the air tank at least, if not necessarily the ladder. I decided to take advantage of it and go be around people while I was in a good frame of mind. I was sick of constantly struggling to keep my spirits up around the people who really knew me. They didn't necessarily buy the "I'm fine" bit as easily as the mere acquaintances did. It would be nice to get a visit in where I didn't feel like I was always on the defensive, especially since silence was usually my only available defense. I'd had enough of that already.

I showered and dressed quickly, having finally gotten somewhat used to my starring role in the "peep show chronicles." I iced my coffee, put it in a plastic to-go cup with a straw and grabbed a breakfast bar rather than stopping to eat since it was already halfway to lunchtime. I knew my parents were home in between trips and not due back at work for a few days so I called them on my way down so they couldn't talk me out of it.

"Hello?" My mother said as she picked up.

"Hey, Ma! Are you busy?" I asked right away.

"No, no. Just sitting here with your cousin Kari right now, having a nice cup of tea. What about you?" She inquired in return.

"On my way there actually. I was gonna stop down and say hello. Will Kari be there for a while?" I asked, suddenly excited about seeing her. She was the closest in age to myself of all the cousins and had always been my favorite "*partner in crime*" growing up, *pre*-Viv.

"As a matter of fact, I just talked her into staying for lunch." She answered happily.

"Awesome!" I replied, really feeling it for a change. "You guys mind if I invite myself too?" I asked not wanting to screw up any plans. I knew Kari was actually doing work for my mother and the hospital from time to time and they would meet on occasion to discuss business over lunch. She was quick to assure me that it was not one of those days however. She had just been passing by herself when she decided to stop in and I was more than welcome to join them. "The more the merrier!" She insisted.

"Alright, that's great. I'll see you in fifteen." I said and hung up feeling even more energized than before.

I took a deep breath and turned on the radio as Imagine Dragons' song "*Radioactive*" began to reverberate throughout the interior. The deep drum base mixed with the upbeat tempo was a perfect accompaniment for my newly invigorated mood and I immediately cranked it up and started to bob my head to the music.

I drove happily down "*95*," doing "*75*," tapping my thumb on the steering wheel, singing my heart out the entire way.

"I'm waking up,

I feel it in my bones,
Enough
to make my systems blow
Welcome to the new age,
to the new age
Welcome to the new age,
To the new age.
Whoah-ah-oo-uh-oh
Whoah-ah-oo-uh-oh
I'm
Radioactive,
Radioactive!

I sang with complete abandon and the ride flew by. It felt really good to have something to do again, both for the short term and the long term, to keep me from spending every moment focusing on things that were missing.

Chapter 8

When I got to my parents' house, my mother and Kari were sitting out on the front porch. In fact, it was so beautiful out that most of the neighboring porches had occupants as well. They were all engaged in various porch type activities like sipping, swinging and people watching. It was the norm around there for a beautiful morning in a neighborhood where everyone knew everyone and saw everything.

It was a big city for sure, but it was a tight-knit neighborhood where I had grown up and I knew who lived in each and every house. It was inevitable when you all lived right on top of each other. Not literally, since most of our neighborhood was made up of rare, large, single family homes, but in general within the city limits where things were mostly *thisclosetoeachother!* That closeness did breed a certain amount of unintended *familiarity.*

There was a full variety of ethnicities represented, but only a few of the sir names had changed on our street over the years, and the atmosphere continually remained the same. It was made up mostly of families like mine that had been in the same brick home for decades and stubbornly wanted to stay there for a few more. It was still pretty rare to see a new face around that particular area and it always freaked out the "originals' whenever it happened. Even with my issues, I was truly thankful for my childhood there in that highly sought after environment.

Of course I had been in just as much of a hurry to get out of there as everyone else, but not because I didn't absolutely love it, because I knew that no one really ever left for good. Everyone ended up back there, from time to time and then eventually, permanently for a lot of them as properties passed from one generation to the next. That was the beauty of it. I could leave for as long as I wanted to and it was easy because like Gen, I knew I could always come back and visit. I didn't know if I would ever want to "*move back*," even if they willed it to me someday, but I liked knowing it was there in the meantime. I was gaining a fondness for "*options.*"

It wasn't quite your "*Movie Night*" level of intimacy that we shared in our neighborhood. It was different from that. With such close quarters being the most constant common denominator in the city, respecting each other's space and privacy was absolutely crucial to any good "city-neighbor" relationship. Our idea of "close-knit" was more of an "*I saw someone crawl in your window so I called the cops for you.*" kind of thing. They would tell you this from the safety of their own home through an open window while you walked from your car to your front door. It was different, but that good 'ol, "*I've got your back*" mentality was there just the same.

I waved to the eighty-year-old Goozeman's on my way up the front walkway where they sat regally next door on their white wicker loveseat casting judgment on all who passed. I knew they would be the first to make a call if they saw anything amiss at our house, even if the person unexpectedly causing a ruckus was me! That day however, they actually waved back at me, deeming me momentarily worthy of their acknowledgement. That made my smile grow.

"The Goozeman's are feeling awfully generous today." My mother joked, as I climbed the few steps to the porch. "They waved at Kari too. I think they're getting soft in their old age." We all chuckled at that. I walked over and hugged my cousin where she sat on the long wooden bench that ran underneath the front windows. My father had built it when they first bought the house and it had graced the front porch for as long as I could remember.

"Kari baby!! How are you? My God, it's been too long!" I gushed in genuine excitement. She hugged me back just as happily.

We didn't have a very large extended family but we had a few characters that were colorful enough to make up for it. Kari was definitely one of them and also one of my personal favorites.

My mother Evelyn, or "Evie" as she was mostly known by, was the older of two girls. Her sister Joanna, or "Auntie Jo," as we always called her, had two children of her own. Her oldest was Andrew, who was 30 and married with three kids under five, and Kari, who was 27 like me. Our birthdays' were only ten days apart in mid-October and we had blissfully shared a party or two over the years as well as a great friendship.

My mothers' hair had always been a slightly wavy, soft medium brown with golden streaks mixed in to varying degrees depending on the time of year and her level of sun exposure. I had inherited that same hair for the most part, just in a slightly lighter shade of brown, and was generally grateful for its ease of care. But it could get boring at times.

Auntie Jo on the other hand, had always been more on the auburn side of the family brown, and while Andrew got the dominant brown gene alone, Kari had inherited her mother's share of the red and then some. I had always envied the richness and the vibrancy of her natural hair color just a little. When we were young we would spend hours braiding each-others hair or styling it in crazy ways just for fun, but hers had always looked cooler somehow. Back then hers was as long as mine still was. But as grownups we had both changed, just in different ways.

She'd cut her straight, shiny hair into an edgy angled bob years ago and it suited her completely. It was quite striking and truth be told I was still a little jealous of the uniqueness of it. Mostly though, I just loved that her firecracker personality had always matched her looks. We had gotten in an awful lot of trouble together growing up, but we'd managed to have so much fun in the process that there were still nothing but fond memories! Especially anytime all of the cousins stayed over together at Nann's house. We were allowed to sleep out on the second story screened in porch during the warm weather and we would stay up talking and playing games until the sun came up. Those were the most fun childhood memories of all the ones that I had!

"I'm great! How 'bout you, miss *celebrity* gardener?!" She teased. "I haven't been up there yet to see it in person, but I did see the piece on TV! It looked fantastic girl!" She said high-fiving me. "Really, like *super* cool!" She said honestly and the little girl in me that had always wanted to impress her couldn't help being happy that she really liked it.

"Thanks. It was a fun job to do, once we got past a few *minor* obstacles." I joked sarcastically.

"Yeah, your mother was telling me a little about the aquifer and the well and how that awesome water harp came to be! That's just crazy! But the solution was not only beautiful but truly *brilliant!* I mean, ku-*dos* sista'!" She said enthusiastically using our old slang term for each other. We weren't real "sisters," but since neither of us had one, and cousin seemed far too generic for our relationship, we had decided long ago that we would be each other's "sista's" instead. We even used to introduce each other that way for a while, just to confuse people. "This is my sista' Simone." She would say. "And this is my sista' Kari!" I would reply to a crowd of furrowed brows. Like I said, good fun. But she was my "sista'," the one I would have if I got to choose one anyway. No matter how much older we got or how far apart we grew, I didn't think that that would ever change.

Of course the part of me that felt that way was dying to tell her the whole story of how the water harp *really* came to be! I knew my mother couldn't have told her that part because she didn't *know* it. Very few people did. I found it very hard just then to resist the impulse to blurt the whole thing out once and for all. But I did, resist. I knew I had to.

Kari had been my original childhood "*confidant*," long before I'd ever met Viv, but we *had* grown apart quite a bit over the past ten years or so, as we each developed our own adult lives. In fact it was funny, hearing her calling *me* the celebrity.

I had gotten married, had a child, and went into art and landscape design. Couldn't be more boring, right? Wrong, because then I even took it one step further by fleeing to a quiet rural area, looking for some peace of mind! Of course it didn't end up being boring at *all* but that had been a complete surprise, not a plan!

Kari on the other hand, had gone completely in the other direction. When she graduated college she took a high powered job with a prominent advertising agency the very next day! She was obviously extremely good at it too, based on what I'd heard and read over the years and it showed in her lifestyle whenever I saw her. Her clothes were always the latest high-end trends and perfectly tailored to her perfect mannequin-like frame. Her car, a shiny silver convertible, was currently parked out front. She was also what I liked to call "a member of the lucky gene pool" since she was just like my mother who could eat anything she wanted and never gain a pound. Of course *that* gene couldn't find its' way into my DNA now could it? *Nooooo... Hmpf.*

Anyway, she had always been thin, but by sixteen she'd added tall to that as well and finished it off nicely at a "Heidi Klum" type of status when her chest finally filled out. It really wasn't fair but she was so genuine, that I didn't hold it against her. She was gorgeous but still totally single, and totally by choice. She already owned her own studio apartment downtown, *without* a co-signer, and of course her hair was still as sharply cut as ever.

I was perfectly happy myself, working in the sun in my boots and my jeans, wouldn't change it for the world, really. But I was acutely aware of the contrast in our lives and there was even more of a gap than there used to be. I was certainly not used to being the "*Hollywood*" one out of the two of us! That had always been her job. And as much as I still loved Kari and considered her my closest extended-family member, in the end that distance that existed between us by then kept me silent as far as confessing all went.

I had no doubt that my childhood secrets were safe with her, but my *adult* secrets on the other hand, were of a much more serious nature and I wasn't free to share them as easily as I would a schoolgirl crush. That was tough too, since I hadn't set out to have secrets at all, well any *more* of them anyway, and certainly never from family before. But I still had no regrets. I had always had to live a "life behind the scenes" so-to-speak to some extent. At least I came well trained for the job.

Hmpf. Maybe Ethan was about right too, I couldn't help thinking then. I felt like somewhat of a broken record admitting that yet again, and it was really shocking to me how often that was happening, but I realized it was probably true regardless. There probably wasn't anyone better suited for *him* than me. I not only already accepted the situation as daily life, but I was also pretty good by then at pulling off the charade that went along with it. It wasn't that hard to take it a step further to include him and his Camp in with it. I never imagined that I would meet someone like Ethan where it would become necessary to be even *more* secretive than I already was, but I also never imagined how completely worth it that effort could be.

No matter how hard it had been or would turn out to be to love him, I knew I wouldn't change it for the world. I would just find a way to deal.

I had never felt so sure about anything before. Even with Ben. I had loved him with my whole heart! *Hmpf. Still did* actually if I was going to be completely honest. There I said it. But I had never felt with absolute *certainty* that we were that "*one and only*" for each other. Not ever. As good as we were together, and we were good at times believe me, that one little detail had always nagged at me in the background. It was a nearly imperceptible detail at first that eventually became completely, totally unavoidable.

We had both *wanted* us to be! I had even believed for a short while that maybe we could *eventually* be that for each other! But it was always just a *hope* or a goal, something for us to attain to someday. It was a real possibility, but it was never a *given*, a certainty. Not like it was with Ethan, where it was something that I felt to the core of my bones! I still had no idea what the future would hold for us. That part was the unknown, but I was sure that as long as being with him was an option it was what I would choose. There really was no going back. I understood that much at least.

I snapped back to the present after that and answered. It felt like ten minutes had gone by in my mind but I knew in reality it had been more like ten seconds.

"We definitely ran into some roadblocks along the way, but

I was determined not to give up until we made it happen." I responded. "I say 'we' because I had a *lot* of help executing my design. It was based on dream that Liliana had told me about last year. You have no idea how amazing it was to be able to bring that dream to life for her." I insisted wistfully. I could tell that Kari agreed with that, she understood and I could feel her reliving our own adventurous childhood exploits for just a moment as she smiled.

"That was my driving force through it all. I worked hard every day too, but it took a lot of other people and a lot of specialized skill sets to pull it all together in the end. Thank God for my crew!" I gushed honestly.

"All this crazy publicity was just an unfortunate side effect, but at least it's been good for business." I said with a laugh. "I actually got another small local job this morning from a *real* local celebrity because of it, so there's *that!*" I added. "I couldn't be happier either, even though it will probably mean even more TV coverage in the end." I admitted, with an eye roll. "Oh well, good or bad we'll see. Its work though and I'll take it! *Woo hoo!*" I laughed again. And they laughed with me.

"How is Liliana? Kari asked then, shaking her head at my typical habit of getting a little sidetracked by my feelings. She had no way of knowing why I was so happy to potentially be back to work.

"I haven't seen her in so long! Surely she's in college by now right?" She joked as I worked to get the timing just right so I could sit down next to my mother in the hanging swing. I dropped in smoothly on the upswing and my mother grinned proudly at my success.

"She's awesome. Just got her cast off." I answered settling in. "She's getting so big you wouldn't even recognize her!" I said only exaggerating a little.

"It's true!" My mother quickly added in support. "You have no idea just how fast time can fly until you have children of your own!" She insisted looking back at me and I knew exactly what she meant then. It was really annoying actually, but it was also undeniably true. Kari on the other hand smiled her quirky signature smile and added her own view on the matter.

"Good! So then as long as I don't have children, I can keep time moving as slowly as possible, right? Plastic surgery is expensive these days. Preventative treatments are really where it's at." She quipped *mostly* serious. We all looked at each other then laughed again, we couldn't help it. I had missed the easy comradery that we had always shared. It was comforting to me to see that it was still there. My mother and I sat swinging slowly back and forth and Kari sat with her feet pulled up underneath her and we all enjoyed the beautiful day while we got caught up.

My mother explained her latest project at the hospital which was to raise enough money to expand the entire cardiology wing and bring everything up to the absolute latest technology possible. That was not going to be cheap.

The hospital where she had always worked was further into town than we usually went lately, especially for emergencies with the Northeastern Medical Center being so much closer. Besides that, Ben also had a few colleagues who worked there so it had just made sense for us to go there with Liliana when we needed to. St. Augustine's, where my mother had worked my whole life, was much bigger and better suited to caring for the masses. It was like a small city inside that place and she was the new manager and treasurer to a large group of its' hardest workers, the nurses.

My mother really loved her job and always had. Everyone who knew her knew that about her. It was a very large part of who she was, a woman whose strongest instinct had always been to help and care for people in need.

As newly promoted charge nurse, she was doing a lot less actual nursing and a lot more scheduling and managing, but her secondary role of fundraising planner was as busy and as demanding of her time as ever. She confessed that she had been a little depressed about getting away from the actual patient care at first. It didn't take her long though, to fill up her time with more of the things she was already doing.

"It became apparent pretty quickly that going to lunch meetings and networking dinners to ask for money that would benefit so many, instead of holding just one person's scalp together with your left hand while you tried to get their vitals with your right, was actually not all that bad of a tradeoff!" She admitted with a reluctant smile. She knew there needed to be good, skilled people out there to do it, but she had worked with and trained a lot of the women and men under her for many years by then, and she knew it was time to pass the torch and to trust in them. She understood where she could do the *most* good for the most people at that point with her experience and her social skills. It was serious business that she dealt with, but she still managed to keep us laughing a lot and often as she entertained us with her tales.

Kari took her turn expressing just how glad she was to be working more closely than ever with her favorite auntie in her new position and they talked briefly about some of their marketing ideas for new fundraising events. They were both very excited and I was glad they had each found something that they truly loved to do. I personally liked the idea of my mother not working quite so hard anymore and of her having more family around her. It made being farther away a little easier for me.

Eventually I was so relaxed that I decided there may never be a better time to tell my family about Ethan. *Whoa!* Of course, as soon as I considered it, the calm went away from me completely and my heart started pounding. But I knew I had to bring it up at some point and as far as my parents were concerned I was thinking then that a "divide and conquer" approach might not be a bad idea. I jumped in as quickly as I could without looking inappropriate, but before I could change my mind.

"So I sort of met someone." I started tentatively. They both went silent and looked up with sudden interest.

"Spill it!" Kari insisted then, suddenly sounding decidedly thirteen again.

"Yeah, what she said!" My mother seconded, sounding only slightly more mature. I raised my brows in amusement but suddenly felt like a deer in the headlights.

"It's *slightly* complicated..." I said, realizing once I had decided to talk about him, that I didn't really know where to start.

"Ut oh. Nothing good ever starts with '*It's complicated.*'"

Kari said warily, but with a teasing smile.

"No, that's where you're wrong." I replied calmly. "Because "*good*" is the one thing that I'm absolutely *sure* he is." I added. They both knew me well enough not to take that lightly. That was a big one out of the way.

"And...? What else?" My mother prompted. "I'm going to need a little more than that dear." She added sarcastically. I grinned at her subtle prodding.

"His name is Ethan Stone. He lives near me in Pinegrove, and he plays guitar and sings for the masses a few nights a week in a small restaurant there called The Tavern. Do you remember me mentioning my '*Magician*' Ma?" I asked her.

"*Hmmm.* I think so. That's the one whose music you liked because it was helping you get your work done, right?" She offered.

"*Hmpf.* Yeah. Only I didn't just '*like*' it, I found that it was a perfect block for me, and that is what kept me going back, in the *beginning* anyway." I chuckled to myself and they both gave me that look again. "I actually knew him for months before anything happened between us. I still had a divorce to finalize after all." I added with a sardonic flick of my eyebrows. "I couldn't even consider anything before that." I took a deep breath at that but I tried to get past it as quickly as possible. It was getting easier day-by-day, but it was still painful.

They noticed. My mom just gave me that, "*Awe honey.*" kind of sympathetic look with pursed lips and a tilted head, but Kari, who had not seen me since before all of that had happened, still felt the need to officially pay her respects.

"I was sorry to hear about all of that by the way. I was really surprised by the whole situation, but I was glad to hear about how you all got through it so respectably. I know it must really suck for you right now, but I think it's amazing what you're doing in the name of the 'greater good' for her. I can only imagine how hard that must be." She said with a sympathetic smile.

"Really, good for both of you guys though, for not going for the throat and tearing everything around you to pieces simply out of spite and anger. I've seen it enough already to reaffirm my personal belief in never wanting to get married at all. No offense!" She insisted, holding her hands up defensively. "But it's not for me. Sorry Auntie!" She added at the disapproving look my mother gave her, but she was used to it. She had always felt that way for some reason, even when we were little kids. I jumped in and tried to get back to my story to save her. It was an old reflex whenever that subject came up.

"Anyway, thankfully, he was patient and persistent and now I am really glad for that!" I just smiled in the end and they both stared at me.

"So when do we get to meet him?" My mother asked understandably.

"Well, unfortunately *that's* the complicated part. He had to go out of town unexpectedly to help a family member and I'm not sure when he'll be back. It's killing me right now actually, but I'm trying to be a mature adult about it and just focus on my work in the meantime." My mother and Kari both made eyes at me at that. I just laughed and went on. "I was succeeding too, at least mostly anyway, until the work ran out!" I laughed at myself more heartily then and of course they joined in. "Thank *God* for this new job!" I proclaimed a little too strongly as usual but they understood it completely that time.

Kari rolled toward us, laying down on the bench and resting her chin in her hands. "*Oooh*, cuz has got it bad, looks like!" She declared happily, again sounding more like my childhood cousin than a high profile ad exec.

"Yeah. *Hmpf*, it's pretty bad." I confirmed quietly as I turned to face my mother. "Remember when I was fourteen and I told you that I was *sure* that I would *never* find a guy to love if I constantly had to feel *all* of his feelings *all* the time?" I spoke freely since my cousin was obviously well aware of my special skills and had been for most of our lives.

"Well, for a while I thought maybe Ben was the answer to that, but we all know how *that* turned out." I allowed as I took a slow deep breath. "Now, all I know is that I could live forever on what I feel from Ethan, 24/7. If nothing else ever touched me again besides that, and what I feel *for* him, I would be okay with that. I have never been able to say that before about *any* man, whether I loved them completely or not!" I admitted sadly. They did not miss the importance of that statement. "He makes me feel things that I can't ever seem to get enough of, physically *and* emotionally!" I added and then laughed again.

"*Damn!*" Kari exclaimed but my mother was quiet. She knew what all that meant to me. She understood how unlikely I had been to ever make a statement like that. I was waiting for her reaction but she was still absorbing it. That was my mother, much like Ethan, she was never one to overreact too quickly. She was always very controlled in stressful or hectic situations. It was one of the qualities that made her so incredibly good at her job as a nurse. Even though she never got overly excited, it was a mistake to assume that she was overwhelmed. Much to the contrary, she didn't react to every single thing, but she missed *nothing*.

Every bit of information that flew at her during the storm was absorbed, carefully processed, and filed away for later. The questions and the harsh reality check would come, but she would take her time and do it properly, after she had organized her thoughts on the matter. Always. That was one thing I *tried* to emulate, the reflex to stop and assess, to find the smartest and the easiest way to win a fight before I engage in it. It wasn't always my first reflex but I'd been working on it for years.

"You'll let us know then… when he's back in town?" She prompted quietly. I just nodded. She nodded back while she held the stare between us, her mother's instinct on high alert. I had to smile again because I understood that instinct so well myself. I hugged her and then declared that I was going to starve to death on the front porch and give the Goozeman's the gossip of the day for sure when they saw the Medical examiner come to collect my body! At that thinly veiled threat my mother dutifully jumped up and dragged us inside to feed us lunch.

My dad it seemed, was on the golf course for the day but Kari and I had yelled hello to him from across the room like obnoxious children when he called to check in with my mother during our meal. I was sure she would fill him in on all of my "*news*" later on when he got home, so I would have somewhat of an icebreaker to help pave the way there. That was good.

My dad didn't get too involved in who I dated over the years, he was my dad after all and he didn't like to spend too much time thinking about that aspect of my life. I knew that and I tried to keep it simple for him. So I only bothered to bring home the ones that I was serious about to meet them. I could still count on one hand the times that it had occurred in my whole life, so he was grateful, but he didn't take it lightly when it happened. He knew I dated and enjoyed my life as much as any single gal. He ignored that for the most part. Only if I brought someone home, did he pay attention.

I was glad to have at least half of the news breaking over with, even though I could tell that my mother had not exactly accepted it as a done deal yet. That wouldn't happen until she'd had a chance to meet him herself, but at least someone in my family knew that he existed. It was a start, dammit. *Phew!*

I realized then with a grin, just how much I had been saying that lately! I was going to have to have a t-shirt made that said, "*Ethan was right*"... on one side, & "*Phew!*" on the other! It would save so much time!

On top of that excitement, Marina had also called during our lunch to say that she had put together a packet for me with everything that she had on the location and that it was on its' way over to my place as we spoke. I told her I wasn't there yet, but she agreed to have the messenger leave it on the back deck since I was fairly sure it wasn't supposed to rain.

About ten minutes later I was too worried to chance it and I quickly said my goodbyes. I excused myself, apologizing repeatedly to both of them for eating and running.

"I'll see you soon, I promise!" I assured my mother as she complained that our visit had been too short. I also promised that the next one would be longer then I made the trip back up 95 in a definite hurry, excited to devour the information and start working on a new design!

Chapter 9

The next morning I woke a little earlier, full of energy. I was excited to begin tackling the new project. I had looked it all over immediately when I got home the day before unable to resist the initial excitement, but the packet was a lot bigger than I had expected and after one quick read through of the whole mess, I had felt the need to step back and let it all settle in before I tried to make any decisions. It was a lot!

Of course, I would have to make a trip out to the site too, to get a feel for what was already there and to get a feel for the spirit of the place itself, as always. But in the meantime, I would try to nail down the basics of what needed improving at the very least I thought, diving in optimistically for the second time in as many days.

As I read through the finer details and looked further and further into the plans though, it seemed that just about *everything* needed updating! Nothing had been changed or renovated in decades! Not just years, but *decades!* There was an awful lot of ground to cover and a lot to accomplish in each area I realized. It was apparent right away that the place had a definite history to it though and I needed to renovate while being constantly conscious of not really "*changing*" anything *too* drastically. *Hmmm.* Challenging did not begin to cover it.

The place had an old soul, for sure. I could feel that just looking through the black and white photos of social gatherings from the past that were included in the pile for inspiration. It showed through in the bright, cheerful eyes of the original inhabitants and their guests.

The function hall or the "great hall" was attached to the main building which had been the original Breezey family home on the property, originally built in the "arts-n-craft's" bungalow style. In the background I could see the wood paneling in many of the rooms and the custom stonework inside and out. You could tell that the place had been beautiful in its' day, but in the current photos it was all very worn down and *very* specific and super hard to repair or replace while still maintaining the authenticity of the original craftsmanship. That issue was going to take some thought. Just which things to truly upgrade and which to keep original was a huge decision all by itself. I didn't want to take that too lightly. The only thing I was sure of at that point was that I wanted the intended quality and spirit of the property to shine through as much as possible in the end.

I was always a big fan of keeping true to the original design of a specific location or a time period when renovating anything, but it wasn't always possible to restore those things to their true beauty without losing what made them unique and beautiful to begin with. Especially things that had spent their life outdoors and in the unforgiving New England weather. In many cases, it just wasn't worth it fiscally. I understood that. Anytime it was even remotely possible though, it was *always* worth it in my book. The more I looked into the job the more I realized just how important it was going to be that I get that right! Aside from demolishing what existed and starting from scratch, which we had neither the time nor the money to do, we had to somehow match what was left that was usable, and bring the old and the new together in a cohesive way.

I looked at the photos some more, of the grounds and the surrounding water and the trails, and I thought about all the things that I would *like* to do in a perfect world. My mind wandered freely while I sipped my coffee. I was lost, deep into the rhythm of the ceiling fan, my thoughts and my one bouncing knee when my phone rang. I looked at it like it was a foreign thing for a beat. I picked it up only half paying attention. It was Jack.

"Hey Jack. What's up?" I asked as I answered it.

"What are you doing right now?" He asked back.

"A little work on a new project. Why?" I asked innocently, flipping it back to him once more.

"Good! It's nothing important." He joked. "Get your fanny down here! We've got family here and we're cooking out. Come and join us." He ordered. I could hear Gen yelling in the background that they needed another woman on their team and telling me to hurry up. Their team for "*what*" exactly, I had no idea, but she sounded happy and I was suddenly down for some of that energy at the very least, to help with my frustration.

I knew I didn't have a lot of time for the job in my hands, but I figured I had enough time for one last day off to recharge and mentally contemplate some of the bigger issues. I knew on paper it looked like a bad idea, but I knew that in reality it would actually be good for me and my process. It always was, but I was still getting used to the fact that I didn't have to explain myself to anyone. So I dreaded it initially on reflex, but a second later my current reality kicked in and I agreed without having to make excuses first.

"Alright, that sounds good actually." I also realized, as I rubbed my noisy stomach that I wasn't sure when I had eaten last anyway. It must have been some time ago I guessed by the sounds it was making. Thinking back, I was pretty sure it was yesterday's lunch at my parents' house, before the plans had showed up. That was probably not good. I really needed to stop doing that I thought, remembering Ethan's request that I "*take care of all of this*" and feeling a little guilty. I guess I really wasn't doing that if I couldn't even be bothered to remember mealtimes.

Eh, I copped out a little and blamed it on the heat. It always made me think about food less. Although the unintentional side-effect of fitting into all my old shorts from before I was pregnant with Liliana was actually quite beneficial, and I certainly wasn't going to complain about that! I honestly wasn't even sure why I had saved that stuff for so long, but I was glad that I had. It gave me lots of "*new*" things to wear without having to go out and shop and try things on. I'm sorry but any way you looked at that, it was a win in my book.

"Be outside in the next ten minutes or I'm coming up after you!" He insisted and I laughed.

"Yes sir! Can I bring anything, *Sir?*" I added for fun.

"Just your sassy little self, there missy. Unless you have Liliana, then bring her too." I could feel his smile even over the phone at the thought of seeing her. I knew the feeling.

"No, it's just me at the moment. But I'll be sure to bring my sass with me." I joked.

"Good! Don't think we'd recognize you without it." He said, getting in one more dig before he hung up. I just shook my head and chuckled to myself. Issues galore, but still so *very* lucky!

I finished reading the last page of the section I was on, then I put it all back into one neat pile. I got up to run a brush through my hair to at the very least, re-do my lazy-day ponytail. I slid my bare feet into my flip flops out of habit but then I remembered Gen's reference to a "team" that I had to assume belonged to an outdoor sport of some kind. I changed my mind and grabbed my new little gray slip on sneakers instead. The top was a wonderful mesh-like fabric that kept my feet from sweating if I did actually have to wear shoes in that heat and they also kept me from having to tie and untie, which I was always looking to get out of. That one trip just to go and get a few pairs of more summery shoes had been annoying, but thankfully was all that had been required to complete my summer wardrobe and it was well worth it. Even *I* could handle that.

I grabbed a six pack of Coors Light bottles from the fridge and put them in the little cooler that I kept tucked in the space beside it. I pushed the button on the door with my hand and held the lunchbox sized cooler under the spout while the ice poured down from the freezer to fill it up. Then I went and got a pair of sunglasses off my dresser and left through the back sliders. I had an overwhelming urge to wave to my ever watchful friends as I crossed the deck, but I channeled all of my maturity and I managed to resist it. I promise you it wasn't easy.

I walked down the deck stairs steering my thoughts back to the new job that I had been attempting to digest. I was feeling optimistic about it despite the challenges. I walked slowly with my cooler in my hand and all of the possibilities running through my head. I was thinking that if I could just get past the "historic" factor without ruining it, we could definitely make that place 150% more efficient and even more importantly, profit worthy for the town!

Of course, I was mostly excited about all of the different outdoor areas, though the thought of maintaining the many functions that those areas served throughout the seasons would be daunting to say the least. There used to be weddings, wine and art receptions, and concerts held there in the past, with hikes, fishing and kayaking, to balance it out. Those same areas were still popular even currently, for the trails, the fishing and leaf peeping in the fall. They would transform yet again in the winter and become perfect for snowshoeing and cross-country skiing. The whole front of the property was made up of a giant sloping field of grass called "Pope's Hill" and apparently it was the preferred location in the area for sledding and tubing.

Maintaining all of those uses and more, while bringing everything up to current standards was going to be a challenge for sure, but it didn't scare me away. Quite the opposite in fact and the wheels were still spinning in anticipation when the wiffle ball almost took my left ear off.

"*What the…?!*"

I decided to mentally join my surroundings then and not a moment too damn soon apparently! I finally looked up towards the wide green expanse in front of me and I saw a group of people that I had not previously noticed in my mental haze. I noticed them then though, especially Gen who was furthest away and currently doubled over in uncontrollable laughter. I looked over towards home base while the guilty party dropped the thin yellow plastic bat and ran towards first, shouting an apology.

"Sorry! My bad! You okay?" He asked breathlessly as he ran by on his way past second base, never breaking stride. "I am *so* sorry!" He laughed then too as he took in my expression on his way by. I was close enough that I was starting to feel it all. There was a lightness and a childlike amusement everywhere. The runner wasn't really sorry. A brunette woman ran by me to retrieve the ball from where it had finally landed. She threw it back to Gen trying to get the runner out at home base. I ducked and watched the play unfold. It was a good throw, but the runner was quick and he slid across the grass into home as Gen was still stretching to make the catch.

"Safe!" He shouted. "Seven-three! *Hah!*" He taunted. He popped back up and bounced back like a gymnast as he brushed the strip of botanical casualties off of his left hip.

"Next time I expect you to make that catch." Gen shouted to me in resignation.

"Uh yeah, sure thing. But only for you my dear." I said sarcastically, going over to hug her hello. The scoring run came over then and introduced himself to me. I already knew it had to be another one of Jack's kids just by the level of enjoyment they were both getting from trying to top each other. The fact that he was also blond and tall like Gen didn't hurt my hypothesis either, although where Gen had Jack's blue eyes, he obviously shared Shirley's brown. He had also inherited the same easy smile that each of the Kent's so far seemed to possess.

"Hey. Sorry about that." He reiterated with another chuckle, only slightly out of breath. He definitely still wasn't feeling all that bad about it though. He did seem sincere enough in his greeting however. "I'm Oscar. That's Beth." He added referring to the brunette player in the baseball hat, pink tank top and denim cutoffs that was waving to me from the pitcher's mound.

"Hi. Simone." I answered back. "And I'm fine, I think!" I joked while feeling around as if to check for missing parts. They all laughed and he made an attempt to explain himself a little bit better.

"Sorry, but its' 'guys against the girls.' That automatically makes you the enemy. I don't make the rules." He said backing away with his hands raised in the air.

"And in case you haven't noticed, we were down a player." Gen replied. "Which is the *only* reason that you are *currently* winning!" She said a little louder. He just laughed and tossed the bat to Jack.

"You could have three more players show up and you're still not gonna catch us." He taunted again, clearly enjoying himself. Jack approached the plate with a grin on his face that made it clear that he was enjoying it just as much. We had spent a lot of time together lately working really hard. So it was nice to let our hair down so-to-speak and spend some good 'ol "play" time together too. He was in his element, and he grinned hugely at me from home plate. He had on a weathered t-shirt and some old overalls that had been cut off at the knee, paired with his usual work boots. Somehow it said "summer casual" on him.

Gen crouched back down to play catcher and looked up at me.

"Good God woman, go cover the field!" She directed emphatically while Beth wound up for the next pitch. Jack stared at me also waiting.

"Alrighty then!" I agreed with a laugh, outnumbered. I walked over and put my cooler down by the paddock fence. I pulled one bottle out to take with me and cracked it open with a satisfying "*pssshhhhhttt.*" I took a long, cold swig off the top, slid it in the coozie and started off at a slow jog past Beth towards the outfield. I set the bottle down off to the side and just as I was about to turn around and say that I was ready, the ball whizzed past me again. By my right ear that time. *Mother...!*

I did turn then, lips pursed, shocked by the direct taunt and not bothering to hide it. Jack didn't pull any punches either though, as he hooted his pleasure at the dead on aim and started to run.

"Oh it is *on!*" I yelled still somewhat surprised at Jack's participation in such juvenile antics. He just laughed hysterically as he ran past second, surprising me with the speed he was capable of in those damn boots! I snapped to it once and for all then and ran for the ball, but I couldn't stop laughing either.

He made it home that time, and the celebrating was deafening! But the hooting and hollering stopped pretty fast when I caught the next two hits, consecutively. They'd had one out already apparently and that was enough to end the inning. My teammates were extremely supportive and the celebrating switched sides! It was really hysterical to watch how much they enjoyed competing against each other. It was a whole other level, but all purely good natured and *a shitload of fun!*

Travis was there too, rounding out the men's team. He was making his fair share of runs and plays but he wisely sat out a lot of the posturing and the smack-talk. He left that to the showier males of the group, like Oscar. He got his in though, from time to time.

I knew already that he was quick witted, but he wasn't the type that felt the need to jump on every opportunity that passed by. Sometimes just a look was good enough and the dig was simply implied. It was all he needed. I would feel the impact from the intended individual just the same. Especially when it was me!

Like when he had the ball and I was deciding whether to run for home or stay safe on third. He looked at me from deep in center field and said, "Go ahead… I think you can make it." *Hmpf*! I *almost* went too! After my late but eventual hesitation came the grin and the wink. *Son of a …*

I was slow to catch on to his dry humor at first and I had to keep checking his true feelings to see if he was serious or not. He would hold back his smile until the last possible second. Then his lip would curl up slightly on one side and laughter would erupt from all around. I grew to appreciate his humor more and more as the day wore on though. It was hard to know how to take him at first, but once I started to get him, I really liked him. He satisfied a basic need that was never guaranteed in my life. He made me laugh when I least expected it. That wasn't easy.

I wasn't really surprised that I liked him though. It made sense since I couldn't see Gen with someone that was either too timid to stand up for themselves any more than I could see her with someone who was a big bully. Travis' quiet, understated confidence suited her personality perfectly.

The way they kissed and whispered to each other in between taunts went a long way toward defining how they really felt about each other as well. They were okay with the space that existed between them temporarily and with being on opposite teams for fun. But they were just as comfortable with "*extremely close*" whenever the opportunity presented itself and that was admirable, I thought. I was still learning to deal properly with both extremes myself and not handling it nearly as smoothly. One more reason I was grateful for her friendship, I hoped maybe some of her more admirable qualities would rub off on me.

Shirley waved to me from the back patio then where I could see she was busily grilling and prepping food. She had an apron on over her shorts and she had things spread out over every available surface on the patio. There were oldies playing on the outdoor speakers and she was dancing around with her tongs in the air while she worked. She certainly seemed to be very happy doing what she was doing, and also just watching what we were doing, so I didn't have to ask why she wasn't playing. It felt like something that had been agreed upon long ago. And since no one tried to persuade her away from her tasks, I decided not to either. For the moment anyway.

I knew it would be in my nature to want to lure her out and get her to play with us at some point, if I ever got close enough to feel comfortable insisting, and if the opportunity ever presented itself. That was a lot of "*if's*" though, so I just filed it away in the "*to be dealt with at some unknown time in the future*" bin and moved on.

We ended up beating the guys 16-14, but I was actually a little disappointed when the game was over. It had been a lot of fun! That is when Travis spoke up in his gently reassuring voice.

"Don't you worry little lady, you haven't won anything yet. This is only game one of many that you will have to defeat us at if you ladies think you're going home with that trophy." He stated calmly, with a knowing smile. Suddenly I was confused.

"*Trophy?*" I asked almost afraid of the fierce determination I felt then from each one of them to possess it.

"It's nothing." Gen said being contradictorily casual. "Just the 'Kent Family Perpetual Award.'" She answered with a sardonic grin. "It's really just this ugly little banged up silver cup on a mangled wooden base that sits on the mantle in the dining room where it has been for as long as I can remember. No one even remembers what it was awarded for originally it's so old, but winning it now comes with some very important bragging rights." She informed me simply and I watched her eyes light up.

"*Ahhhh.*" I grinned. I understood then. It was just like my ongoing "*Sorry*" battle with Vivianne. Winning between us was one of those things that was amazing, but was never more than temporary. Always having the chance to win the title back when we lost it was the best part of the rivalry. We knew how to enjoy it while it lasted though and I could tell immediately that they all did too. I liked them even more then.

We moved quickly from Wiffle ball to croquet. I had always loved the game as a kid, but I hadn't played in so long that I was genuinely surprised to find that it was just as much fun as an adult. I also found that a mallet was a pretty handy thing to have around on occasion. Especially those occasions where grown men attempt to cheat and "accidentally" kick your ball a few feet away. It was fun and rather easy to threaten permanent shin damage with. It was also nice just to stand around and lean on in the afternoon sun in between turns, enjoying the comradery as we slowly sipped our beers.

Beth turned out to be as competitive as the rest of them and she seemed to fit right in with the family. I didn't pick up much off of her other than that though, not definitively anyway. Most of what she gave off was innocent enough feelings of drive and determination in the games, but it was all kind of fuzzy and dull.

Sometimes I would feel that when someone was trying really hard to hide things or bury them, but then some people I would just read that way in general. Everyone was slightly different. It wasn't about how well I was picking it up I had figured out over the years, but rather the strength of the individuals actual projection level that varied. For example I would never be able to "turn down" the potent feelings that came at me from Ethan. That's just how intense his feelings are. That kind of thing can never change completely.

I wasn't sure what the reason for it was in her case yet but it was obvious that she had built up a good rapport with Gen over the two years that she said her and Oscar had been dating. That went a long way with me because I knew Gen wouldn't befriend someone who was fake any more than she would date a jerk. I was sure of that much at least, but it was still another one of those times where the picture wasn't super clear. Thankfully I had those other puzzle pieces that I could use to try and get an overall image.

Not to mention that if someone was just one of those people with a fuzzy signal, it would be that way every time I saw them so eventually I *would* know for sure. One way or the other. For the time being I would give her the benefit of the doubt and consider her "innocent by association."

Oscar on the other hand was easy, he was a Kent through and through, no question of paternity there what-so-ever. He was polite and thoughtful to a "T," but also playful and teasing at the same time. For instance, he would bring Beth a new Michelob Ultra each time her bottle was near empty before she ever had to ask, but he would also go after her blue ball with an unrestrained vengeance, anytime he was poison and it was an option. She fully expected it too, the whole "no mercy" attitude fully applied, I could tell. She didn't shy away from it either. She continually embraced the challenge of it. That part of her intentions I could feel, no problem. It actually reminded me of me and Ethan a little.

I was sad for just a moment then that he and I weren't able to enjoy such a normal, fun day together but I didn't want to dwell on it. He *was* in my life and I was truly thankful for that, even if it wasn't quite "*fully*" at the moment. I mostly tried to just live in the present and I had been doing a pretty decent job of it I thought, so I attempted to keep it up and not to let the sadness get too deep. I was still pretty surprised the first time someone *else* brought it up though.

I simply wasn't prepared to have anyone ask me about him outright. It had been taboo for so long, just talking about him in general, since I was petrified of getting into a conversation with anyone who might ask me about where he was, or *why!* I was totally caught off guard by the innocent everyday-ness of it when Oscar put it to me.

"So when is Ethan coming back already?" He had asked me backhandedly while we picked up the balls. "And Mike too for that matter!" He addressed that one to the crowd in general. "I can't believe they're missing this slaughter! They're gonna be pissed!" He boasted about our loss in croquet. It was obvious that it had been no big deal at all to him to wonder aloud. I could feel that to him, Ethan was just another brother and he expected them both to be there. I noticed that Jack just bit his tongue, but he didn't disagree.

It had been so long since I had talked openly about Ethan to anyone that I had no idea what to even say at first. Then I reminded myself that they were his family. They were included in his bubble by proxy and they didn't think twice about discussing his personal life because they *were* his personal life and it was all fair game in their eyes. I found I liked that too.

I remembered Gen's similar attitude when I had first met her with Ethan by my side and I had watched them taunt and tease each other. I could feel how much fun they had been having that day, and I could feel that it was a regular thing. It was a "no holds-barred" kind of teasing, but only because they could rely on each other's' love and support so completely that they knew they could get away with it. I had been surprised at first by the level of sibling rivalry that existed between them, but then I was mostly glad for it. I decided I still was. It was good for him and highly amusing for me on occasion.

As usual you would think an hour had gone by while I pondered these things but in reality it takes a lot less time to think it as it does to explain it. But back in the real world I was aware that I really should say *something.* My response came to me naturally, but mostly as a defense.

"Definitely not in time to help *you* guys out!" I threw out over my shoulder. There was a great round of laughter that followed and thankfully after that, he let it go.

"Don't forget, by the time they get here, we'll have Sarah back from school' and then no one will be able to help you guys!" Gen boasted. It was the kind of thing that you assumed to be an empty threat made just for fun, but no one seemed inclined to argue with her. *Hmmm.*

"Sarah? Isn't she the youngest? Is she really that good?" I asked under my breath so only Gen could hear, surprised that the mere mention of the "*baby of the family*" had silenced the trash talk so thoroughly.

"*Oh yeah!* You just wait. Why do you think they're having so much fun now, while they can?" Gen both answered and taunted at the same time, getting louder as she went. There were grumbles all around, but still no major arguments. *Huh!* Well alrighty then! That sure was interesting! There was obviously more to that story but no one felt inclined to explain so I just raised my brows and let it go. A curveball for another day, I supposed… Oh boy, never a dull moment, I thought.

As we moved on to volleyball, my personal favorite of the activities, I grew a little more comfortable with hearing Ethan's name being tossed around out loud. I was really liking it actually.

It felt good to talk about him like he was any other regular person. Like he was a *real* person, who could maybe pull up unexpectedly and join the fun at any moment. I wasn't counting on that happening just then, but I was really missing that sense lately, that it was an actual possibility. It was feeling more and more like it was only his ghost that came to me in the dark of night. He was only partially there and only temporarily. Just enough to get by on. Never the full *homecoming*. Never the chance of anything *more…*

He felt more real to me when I was with them though, because he was real for them too. He had a sense of presence in all our lives, even when he wasn't there. I was definitely enjoying feeling that.

The simple truth was that the more people that discussed him, even if they *cussed* him, the more *present* he felt to me. It felt *good* and I wanted more of it! I was really glad then that Jack had called.

It gave me hope to know that Ethan had obviously led a fairly normal daily life with these people at one time and therein lied the possibility that it he could do so again at some point. *Hopefully soon*, I thought emphatically, for what felt like the millionth time!

"Don't worry, we'll have that trophy back by the end of the day, and those boys will know exactly who got their asses whooped!" Beth chimed in bringing my attention back around again like I was in a mental tennis match.

We could smell food by then though too and stomachs

began to growl, mine included so the bocce game was officially postponed until after dinner. We all started to walk up towards the back of the house where the wonderful smells were emanating from. Shirley came over to the edge of the patio and reached up to ring the dinner bell when she saw us all marching over. She just grinned and waited with her hands on her hips to greet us.

"I should've known." She said with a smile.

"We don't need no stinkin' bell woman, we have *noses!*" Jack insisted before reaching Shirley, holding her hips tight and kissing her soundly on the lips. We all agreed wholeheartedly and breathed it in more deeply through said noses on our way by. I laughed as each one of them made various "*mmming*" and "*ahhhing*" sounds in anticipation and I knew for sure that I was definitely in the right place.

People who knew how to really enjoy good food I'd found, had usually learned how to find the joy in life in general. Those were my kind of people. There was always more than enough anger, sadness, pain and jealousy to go around in the world, and let's face it, there always will be. People have to work continuously at finding the joy hidden deeply within all of that or we can easily lose sight of it all together. Myself especially. If that happens, often all hope and motivation to be positive in any way can go with it.

Given the constant influx of negativity that I experienced as part of daily life, I'd had to learn to combat that pretty early on to keep from drowning under it all. I knew I needed to keep the good coming in just as regularly in order to balance it all out. I was fairly good at it by then and mostly past the point where I felt guilty about it all the time, but it was still a lot easier to do when the people around me knew how to do it as well. It was such a small but *important* detail in a person's basic way of living, that specific attitude of truly appreciating every tiny wonderful thing! As I contemplated that some more I suddenly felt very lucky again that I even understood it at all. That was definitely a growing trend in my life though and I was starting to get used to it.

We made our way over and collected around a spread that was like a mid-summer Thanksgiving dinner! They had a picnic style table that was made of wood with the traditional attached benches and all, but it was circular, rather than rectangular and it was a *lot* bigger than usual, big enough to easily seat ten or twelve people in fact! In the center of the table was a large lazy Susan that was filled with platters of BBQ chicken, steak tips, burgers, and hot dogs. There was also a bowl of roasted vegetables full to over flowing with zucchini, summer squash, asparagus and artichoke hearts which made me think of Liliana with a smile.

I was still missing her way too much, especially since she hadn't even needed a ride home that day. She had skipped camp to spend the day at a friends' birthday party. But I would have her with me the next day and looking forward to that made me feel better, as always. I knew I would also see her at least one extra day during the following week while she was off from camp, we just had to figure out which day. All I knew for sure so far was that it wouldn't be on day one of my new job. In the meantime, I was suddenly starving!

As we filled our plates the middle began to turn and I oohed and ahhed myself as seasoned grilled potato wedges and broccoli slaw appeared in front of me alongside a beautiful green salad. Food could never make up for my missing Liliana's company either, but it *did* at least tend to make me feel better in the meantime, same as anyone else. It *is* called "*comfort*" food for a reason and as I've established, I'm smart enough to take it where I can get it.

Oscar brought out a round of ice cold beers for everyone, and after passing them out, we ate like we had been lost at sea for days! I for one felt relieved not to have to try and act like a proper lady and be super-polite. I was much happier fork-fighting over the darkest charred steak tip with the pinkest center. *Yummm!!* That was between Oscar and myself, but being the gentleman and "*host*" that he was raised to be, he reluctantly offered it to me.

Of course rather than play the "no, no, you take it" game that he had so clearly been expecting, I happily accepted his offer and popped it in my mouth in one bite. The crowd got a good laugh out of that as well, including Oscar. He was mischievous, but completely open and honest and beyond easy for me to read. It was clear that he didn't hide much from anyone though so that wasn't surprising. Besides being open, he was also a ton of fun.

Eventually, we all had our fill and we sat and groaned for a while until the lights came on and the bugs came out. That was as long as we could sit still if we were going to stay outside. I wasn't the only one who thought so either I noticed, as people started to slap themselves and fidget restlessly.

"Alright! Let's do this!" Travis shouted as he tossed the little white pallino ball up in the air. I knew then why they had left that game for last, as in the settling dusk the little ball started to glow bright green. I looked over and noticed that half the balls in the pile where we had left them to go eat shared that neon shade, while the other half glowed a bright blue. It immediately reminded me of The Tree-fort village and that made me smile. "We have a few of our own *glowing* things around this neck of the woods!" He joked to an appreciative crowd. "Unless you girls are ready to just admit defeat." He offered backhandedly.

"*Never!*" Beth, Gen and I all shouted as one and every one of us fell over laughing again. A few minutes after that, we got our shit together and we all got up to help Shirley clean up. Then we took turns with the can of bug spray and ten minutes later we were back out on the lawn tossing glowing bocce balls around in nothing but tiki torchlight. I had thought of Ethan again of course, when Jack started to light them, but after one long deep breath, it made me smile rather than frown for once.

Shirley sat with a glass of wine in her lawn chair with a front row seat to the festivities. We were all tied up for number of games won at that point and we'd decided it would be the "best two out of three" in bocce for the win.

It started out a total man fest, with them expertly knocking our balls out of scoring range and kissing the pallino left and right. But the girls hung in there and eventually started to pick up the pace, smoothly rolling in one point after another. By the end, we walked away with the last two games *and* the all-important victory! The boys, still venting about their undeserved luck, went to retrieve the "cup."

It was carried out of the house with such pomp and circumstance that you would have thought it held the ashes of a loved one! The "boys" came up and presented the cup to us "girls," as the rightful winners. It was a dented, tarnished silver cup on a scratched up wooden block base. There were no engraving plates left on it, just holes where you could tell they had once gone, and the word "Champs" hand-painted in their place.

We held it up and fake screamed, cheered and took pictures with it on our phones like it was the Stanley Cup! Then Oscar reached over and filled it with his beer and we each took turns drinking from it ceremoniously and hysterically. Then it was rinsed with a water bottle, wiped clean and returned by the "cup-handlers" to its place of honor back on the farmhouse mantle. That was the deal.

It was okay. There was never any doubt I was already sure, of who was currently in possession of the cup. It was intense and awesome and I couldn't be happier to have become a part of the tradition. It was just one more Pinegrove gem for me to be grateful for.

Things quieted down after that and Travis and Oscar worked to get the fire going in the big cinderblock pit on the back patio. In five minutes we were sitting mesmerized by the flames. It was such a nice night that no one was in a hurry to go inside, not even me and so I pushed the work thoughts back just a little while longer.

We finished our drinks and we talked, but mostly about nothing as we sat contentedly and slowly poked at the fire with our long wooden skewers. Once their job of holding marshmallows had been fulfilled, their fate was simply to become a sweet smelling addition to the hypnotizing fire. It reminded me of family camping trips from my childhood and I sat momentarily thinking about how I couldn't wait to bring Liliana over for the next one.

"Happy thoughts?" Gen asked, surprising me. I hadn't realized until that moment that I was smiling.

"Yeah. Just thinking about how much Liliana is gonna love this stuff and you guys. I hope you all don't mind, but I've already self-invited both of us to the next one in my head." I confessed with a grin. They all laughed.

"Well I'll be here all weekend and I can't wait to meet her tomorrow." Oscar said. "From what my dad has said she's a lot of fun. Very *adventurous!* No fear." He added complimentarily. "Sounds like me as a kid." He claimed proudly with a wink.

"Sounds like you now." Travis added dryly in his typical style and we all laughed some more.

"No fear is a good thing, as long as it's kept on track by a sharp brain." He insisted. "Luckily for me, I have control over both." He boasted with his usual cocky grin as he tapped on his temple and the laughter continued.

"Well I haven't had a chance to spend any time with her yet either but I know we're all looking forward to it. We need some little ones around here." Gen said looking at Jack and Shirley. "So they can take the pressure off of *us* for a while." She added slyly to Travis, Oscar and Beth. Everyone seemed to agree with that quite readily.

"Yes!" Travis agreed.

"Absolutely!' Beth seconded almost simultaneously. Jack was the last to respond but put the discussion to rest on his own terms.

"I for one am so glad to see that I brought my children up right and that you all aren't fighting over who will get to have the families "first" grandchild. You know it warms this old heart that you would never act so petty as to rush something so important, just because the first one is sure to be completely spoiled rotten. We will be first time grandparents after all. But I'm sure that once we get at least one under our belt, we'll get it under control. I just know the rest of you will understand if he or she already owns everything we have by then." He finished sweetly. How he said it with a straight face was beyond me but the laughter from all of us after that one, even Shirley, drowned everything else out for a while.

It was the perfect way to end the day and even walking back up the steps to my apartment alone afterwards, I couldn't help smiling. I was *really* glad that I had decided to go out and spend the day with them. I was even happier that they had let me!

I knew it the most important thing that Jack had ever given Ethan as well. That feeling of support and joy. That sense of belonging. You know, that feeling of being "*home!*" That in turn, was what Ethan worked so hard to try and give back to the people that he helped. I couldn't help thinking, how lucky it was for the rest of the world, that he'd had such a good teacher.

Surely that couldn't have been an accident. Angels again or *heightened* intervention that time? *Hmmm...* I didn't know but I felt sure it had to be something *non-coincidental* in the major scheme of things. I would have to remember to ask Dr. J what he thought about that one too someday I decided, *whenever* I happened to see him again.

I smiled to myself once more at that small victory for the good side though as I locked the doors. I ignored the pile of papers for a little while longer. The time to play and relax had helped me to recharge mentally, so I just needed a few good hours of sleep to recharge physically and I would be ready to attack it. I took a quick shower and came out in my shorts and tank top and slid straight into bed. I reached up to switch off the light and silently wished the current watchman goodnight.

Chapter 10

I was up fairly early the next day in spite of our late night fire. The building anticipation made it too hard to sleep. My body was still tired, but my mind just wouldn't let up and I could only roll over and squeeze my eyes shut so many times before I had to admit defeat.

I finally got up around seven thirty and I got dressed with barely a thought for my audience for once. At least something was getting easier I acknowledged, trying to look at the bright side as usual. I headed out onto the deck and dropped the packet from Marina along with my sketchbook and supplies onto the table.

There would be no lounging at The Tavern for a couple of months, leisurely sketching while sipping cocktails. Things needed to happen even faster for my new job than they had on the last one. That was okay though. I didn't mind the tight deadline. I was properly motivated since there was no time left to procrastinate. I didn't need to worry about cutting down the working time any more than I already had! My mental health day had taken care of that!

I had another trick up my sleeve that I knew would help though, *greatly.* It was something so small, yet it had given me such an advantage already. I picked up the remote and aimed it at the CD player inside. I hit play and Ethan's deep voice filled the space and every last one of my nerve endings at the same time. *Ahhhhhhhh....* You have no idea what a relief that can be! I'm still working on the words for that...

I sighed deeply and decided to just dive right in. I started with what I knew we could change, both inside and out. I thought that maybe I would be able to back into the rest of the less obvious choices from there. Although my job was mostly to focus on the outside, I was also responsible for the design as a whole. That was new for me. But since there would be as many as fifty local tradesmen donating their services along with a hundred or so other volunteers working on various projects, I would have plenty of experienced help. I just had to keep the overall design and style cohesive throughout the property. I understood the idea behind it, but having the physical stack in front of me brutally illustrated the sheer scope of it. I had sincere doubts about actually pulling it off as I sat and stared at it at first.

I refused to give up that easily though. I flipped back to the beginning of the stack of schematics that each tradesman had presented in the proposal round for each area and I started again. I got a few steps in on each one, but that seemed to be as far as I could go in any one direction. At each dead end, I would back track patiently and start again, but I just kept getting stuck. There were still too many by-laws and regulations that I had to research before I could make most of the important decisions about materials and style and I realized after about an hour that I wasn't really getting anywhere at all. I tried not to get frustrated, but it was hard. *Really* hard!

Of course it would have been easier to have each worker involved there with me throughout the actual planning stages to answer questions, but every one of them had come in and made their prospective plan for their own part on their own time over the course of the past year. Just thinking about the logistics of trying to schedule a new meeting with all fifty something of them in a three to four day span made my abdomen knot, never mind the amount of emotional baggage that would come along with meeting that many people. *Hmmmm.* I needed options.

I though back then on one of the most important lessons I had learned so far in the pursuit of success in *any* business venture, as I remembered another pearl that I had gotten from my ever-wise father. That was to "*Never let a good contact go. You never know when you may need them again.*" I decided that I might already have all the tools I needed to get through the latest disaster after all. I just needed to utilize them. I picked up the phone and called my latest and greatest asset. She answered on the second ring.

"Hey Simone, what's up?" Gen asked casually.

"Hi. I hope I didn't catch you at a bad time." I offered sincerely.

"No, it's fine. I can eat and talk if you don't mind my chewing in your ear." She offered in between bites. I looked up to see that it was actually lunchtime. *Geeze*, I'd done it again. I hadn't even bothered to eat breakfast. I wasn't worried though, not after everything I had eaten at the cookout the night before. I wasn't even really surprised that I still wasn't hungry after all that!

"Everything okay?" She asked then and for a moment I felt her real worry. I knew instantly who it was for and quickly jumped to correct it.

"Oh yeah. No, "*everything's*" fine." I assured her. "Well at least as "fine" as it was yesterday, anyway." I added sarcastically. "It's just that I may be in need of your unique talents again already, believe it or not. You don't actually have like, *other clients* or anything, do you?" I joked.

"No, no, in fact I was bored to death and I was just getting ready to head to the beach for the day." She joked. "Hah! *Not!*" She said laughing. "Troubles on the new job front already?" She asked.

Although I had mentioned during our chat at the fire that I had gotten a small local job, I hadn't elaborated at all at the time because I still hadn't had time to look through it all myself enough yet at that point.

"No, but I'd like to keep it that way this time around. This one has to move real fast, big surprise right?" I joked. "There is no room what-so-ever for "*issues*" this time though and I'm not exactly up on the laws governing Pinegrove's "historical landmarks." I don't think I have time to learn them and still get the plans done fast enough to pull this one off either. It's a big, *big* job! The whole thing's being done pro bono for the town, my part included and a lot of people are coming together at once to try and make it happen. I really don't want to let them all down, but I honestly think I may have bitten off more than I can chew this time. Are you noticing a trend with me yet?" I asked sarcastically before she could comment.

"*Definitely!*" She agreed with the humor in her voice evident as it mixed with a surprising amount of admiration.

"*Anyway...*" I continued, smiling myself. "Any chance your free to help out in the next day or so? Or maybe recommend someone who's qualified to help that may want to jump in on this? Maybe someone looking for a charity write off perhaps?" I added with a hopeless laugh in the end.

"Is this by any chance Breezey Park we're talking about?" She asked, her interest suddenly piqued.

"Yes, why? Is that good or bad?" I asked warily in return.

"Good, I think. I've been hearing vague stories about plans to update that place for some time now but nothing has ever come of it to my knowledge." She informed me.

"Well it's about to, once and for all, *if* I can get an executable plan down on paper in time before we miss our window with the contractors. Care to help me accomplish that?" I asked with one eye closed in fear of her answer. I was sure it would be too small and too tedious a cause to attract her attention that time around, but I felt it made sense to at least ask her first. Maybe like Jack, she could at least point me in the right direction.

"I know it's not as exciting as unexpectedly uncovered aquifers, and court battles with cocky little khaki wearing know-it-alls." I joked. "But it should also be a lot easier to accomplish." I offered with another chuckle. Turns out I was wrong though, about her not being excited by it at least. She completely surprised me with her enthusiasm!

"*Hell* yeah! I'd love to help get that old place fixed up! Man! We used to go sledding up there every winter on Pope's hill, and we'd fish all summer long on Johnson's Pond. I haven't been up there in a long time now though. Last couple events I went to there just made me sad to see the condition it was in and that was years ago! It hasn't been much more than an eyesore for most of the last decade or so now. But it *could* be fantastic! Not to mention a great asset to the town, *if* it were run properly." I could tell that she was getting fired up and I just let her go.

"Even just to have it as an option for an event venue again would be huge, there are so few located here in town. All the other options around here are at least a twenty minute drive away. That's not the end of the world, but it'd sure be nice to finally see some of the revenue generated by *our* own towns' baby showers, birthdays and weddings, actually go back into *our* own town for once, instead of it always going out, you know?" She asked sounding as passionate and as educated on the matter as ever.

Gen was one of those rare people that not only understood the need for being a caretaker and nurturer to our planet, but she also understood that good, smart, and *productive* business practices were the only way to ensure there would be a way to support that lifestyle. Breezey could easily be that kind of a place. I knew exactly what she meant, as mostly average as I had been at my few business classes, I understood that concept completely.

Places like that meant more than just a one-time hall rental fee for the town. They meant that sure, but they also meant local caterers would also get more work, and local florists' jobs would increase as well. It meant there would be extra earning possibilities for the police officers and volunteer firefighters from town, in the form of details required to keep the peace and direct traffic during big events. And that the local limousine company could maybe afford to run another car and the town could afford to hire local landscapers to maintain the property and make it even more appealing to rent. It was a big circle of paying it forward but it benefitted everybody in the end. Not by *growing* the town. Just by sustaining and more efficiently utilizing and *supporting* the good parts that already existed.

That in turn insured a future for the town as a whole without having to sacrifice what made it great in the first place. It worked in so many ways that probably only Dr. J could see them all at once, I thought with a slight smile.

"I know exactly what you mean. You've got to help me make sure we get it right, and sooner rather than later!" I insisted then.

"I can meet you at The Tavern tomorrow night at 5:30. That's the earliest I can get back out there, but I will give you 'til closing. That's the best I can do on such short notice, for this week anyway. Besides being swamped here, I really need to sleep in my own damn bed! And I don't mean my old full-size bed in my bedroom at the farm, as grateful as I am that it still exists there for me from time to time. I *mean* the king size one in my spacious townhome that happens to also have *Travis* in it!" She said laughingly.

"I totally understand! That's awesome, and I'll take it!" I said agreeably. "Thank you, Gen! You know I say that so much lately, that I'm beginning to wonder how I ever used to get any work done without you!" I said only half-kidding.

"Well working with you so far has been anything but dull! I'll give you that! But I'm actually really excited that this is finally going to get done!" She threw in and I could tell she was already looking forward to it.

After we hung up I felt a lot better about the situation but I remained at somewhat of a standstill and I could feel the clock ticking, so I decided to go and spend the day at the site until it was time to pick up Liliana from day-camp. I still needed to get a feel for the place. That was important and it was time to get it done.

The heat had been relentless the past two weeks and that day was no different. I packed everything back up and brought it inside, knowing how quickly afternoon thunderstorms could pop up in that heat. I traded my flip flops for some socks and hiking shoes and tied my hair back in a loose braid. I texted my dad, grabbed my keys, my digital camera, and two bottles of water instead of one and headed out.

The drive across town was as calming as ever. I would take those long, beautifully wooded back roads over crowded, high-speed thoroughfares with their streetlights every fifty yards any day of the week. I did like to go fast, but more than that I liked not having to stop and go the whole time. Even if it was a steady 40 instead of 70, it was so nice to just *go*... to be able to just *drive*...

I opened the moon-roof and all the windows rather than cranking the AC and simply enjoyed the summer air blowing through the car. The temperature was so warm that it felt like a silk blanket as it caressed my skin, even at a fairly decent speed with everything all the way open, and it smelled like my childhood. It was especially easy to enjoy with my hair tied back, knowing that it wouldn't blow in my eyes and temporarily blind me while I was driving.

My first instinct was to press play and listen to Ethan's CD, but I resisted it. It was a favorite of mine for car rides and times when I needed to block out the outside world, but for the moment the plan was to let the outside in. I decided to stay open to that concept on the way over, so the arrival wouldn't be too jarring when I turned the music off. His music in particular was just too good at blocking. Besides that, I wanted to feel the surrounding areas as I approached. A homestead of any kind was inextricably linked to its' surroundings. I would not make the mistake of underestimating that reality, no matter how obscure.

I switched on the radio instead and was rewarded when Dobie Gray's "*Drift Away*" came on.

"*Sweet!*" I shouted to no one as I cranked it up and sang along.

"Gimmie the beat boys,
and free my soul.
I wanna get lost
in your rock and roll
and drift awaaa-ii-aaaaaay…"

I sang with teenage-like abandon at the top of my lungs and thoroughly enjoyed every chorus. That song was followed up by Lenny Kravitz singing about that illustrious "*American Woman*" and after that came the Eagles with one of my all-time favorites that represented another side, "*Witchy Woman.*" The songs were uplifting but not necessarily good blockers. It was perfect but in spite of that circumstance, I still hadn't felt much on the approach besides the usual untouched wilderness of the area, even as I passed the few other houses leading up to the property.

By the time I turned off the main road and onto the Breezey Park property, I felt as if I was the only one around for miles! I was still feeling completely positive though, at least inside *myself*, so I could be certain that any negativity I picked up was external.

I turned down the radio as I drove slowly down the long skinny lane, taking it all in. I had to go slow to navigate all the ruts and potholes. The pavement had risen up and separated in many places with the heat of summer versus the cold of winter and from the looks of it, had not been repaired or even patched in a *very* long time.

I looked up at the weeping willows that unlike the ones at The Tree-fort Village were not only pale green and real, but also ancient and massive! Their untrimmed branches gently swept the roof of the car and the windows as I passed. The sound reminded me of the car wash at first, but my next thought about the accompanying insect life was not as pleasing. I tried to watch for falling ticks, just because my brain always went directly to the absolute scariest of places. Of course I knew the likelihood of my actually seeing one kamikaze down was probably slim to none. That realization made me long for Ethan's presence for the eighteen millionth time! His skills really did come in handy. I had a can of bug spray in my car that I had planned to use when I got there, but I was starting to wish that I had *pre*-applied. If only my dreams were that good, I thought with a chuckle.

It opened up again after the willows and I could see lots of other trees to my left where the woods started and what must be Johnson's Pond not too far beyond that. To my right I saw a parking lot and I pulled in. It was as faded and broken as the entrance road had been and any lines that may have been there originally were long gone.

From my window I could see the main building that sat at the top of the hill above the large, empty lot. It was so dilapidated that it almost looked haunted. I knew better than to judge something like that based solely on looks though. If there *were* any residual spirit energies there, I would feel them *long* before I would see anything to confirm it with visually. And yes, there are residual "*energies*" so-to-speak stuck in lots of places, but that's another story for another time. I didn't want to think about that stuff while I was there alone. I was really hoping it wouldn't come up. I wasn't ready for that part yet anyway and I would never go tour a place with so much history all alone. I just wouldn't.

There were instructions in the packet that Marina had sent me about who to contact when I needed the keys to get inside, a Mr. Jameson, but I wasn't ready for that yet. I wanted to start outside first, on the property that gave the home its' *heartbeat* so-to-speak. Every man-made structure was exactly what some human had intended it to be. Always. But *property*, land, chunks of Earth governed by fickle Mother Nature had their own ideas about how they should be and would revert to that ideal rather swiftly if left alone. I was fairly certain that the place had been left to its' own devices more than long enough for it to have fully recovered its' "natural" state. *That* was what I wanted to see and to *feel*, first and foremost.

I stepped out of my car and liberally applied the aforementioned bug spray. Then I put on another layer on top of that in an attempt to ward off my "heebie-jeebies." It worked, but only a little. I threw the can in the back seat and I grabbed one of the water bottles. I didn't bother locking the car but I did take the keys with me. I clipped them onto my belt loop by the carabiner clip and slid the strap to my small digital camera over my wrist. Then I dragged my forearm across my forehead to wipe off the sweat that had already accumulated there during my meager preparations.

Whoo! It was gonna be a hot one for sure! I crossed the lot and stopped to do a wide, slow circle so I could take in my surroundings and pick a direction to start off in. I took a deep breath, spun, and on the exhale ended up facing the woods and the water. I didn't go against the magnetic forces aiming me, but rather obediently headed directly into the woods in front of me. Luckily I was at least pointing in the direction of an old trail.

I stepped onto the path where it opened up tauntingly at the edge of the crumbling asphalt. The tall, dry grass crunching and crackling beneath my feet as I passed was the only protest to my intrusion. I stepped over the low rock wall a few feet in and proceeded further into the woods. They were thin enough there to see the water through them once you entered and I immediately headed in that direction.

I looked up into the canopy at the impressive height of the thin but aspiring trees while I walked and was rewarded with the sight of a great blue heron gliding majestically by. I was struck speechless by how big it was, and how casually it passed over me while still managing to be *so* incredibly graceful! Then I quickly looked back at the path after I tripped and almost fell. I thought about how *un*graceful that particular stunt was while I laughed to myself. If you were going to bird watch, it was best to do it sitting or at the very least, *standing still.*

The path wound around the trees a few more times before it reached a small hill that led down to the pond. I stood at the top and looked down. The trees were shading my eyes from the sun but it was bouncing off the open water like a thousand tiny mirrors. As I stared a mother duck came swimming into view, her babies following dutifully behind her. They quacked in my direction as they swam but that was all the notice they paid me. The whole scene was beautiful and peaceful and I felt only good vibes coming at me. I lifted my camera and pushed the tiny silver button. I heard the familiar "*ting*" as it powered up. I raised it up to aim it at the scene in front of me, trying to capture the beauty that my eyes could see as much as an inanimate object was able to. I took a few shots from each equally impressive angle and then I kept moving, as did they. The trail eventually reached down by the waters' edge and curved to the right to follow along and so I did the same.

Just as I turned the next bend, a pair of deer picked up their heads at my unexpected intrusion on their lunch. It was clear that they had not seen any humans there in a long time by their matching, shocked expressions. I tried to raise my camera as slowly as humanly possible to get a picture before they ran, but they still bolted like lighting at my very first twitch. I clicked wildly as they made their escape, spastically leaping more than running in an instinct as old as time that told them not to let me get a hold of their hind legs.

They had no idea how beautiful I thought they were, but I knew that others shaped like me would love to take advantage of their trust to shoot them and eat them and mount the remains, so I didn't mind their fear. It knew it was a far healthier reaction for them. It may keep them alive to chew leaves another day. Run, Bambi run.

After a while, the path curved right again and eventually it came out onto the bottom of what I knew from the sheer size of it, had to be Pope's Hill, the sledding area. From there I could walk out across the flat plain back to the main road on my left, hike up the mountainous "hill" in front of me, or take another trail back into the woods on my right. Since I had already witnessed and disrupted my fair share of wildlife in the woods, and I came from the road to begin with, I decided to go up instead. With the humidity steadily building and a few heavy looking clouds rolling in I got about halfway there before I started regretting that decision.

"*Phew!! Goddamn!!*" I didn't hold back since only the squirrels and the birds were there to bear witness. I could go slower I knew, but once I started up I was inexplicably anxious to reach the top. The sweat was beginning to pour down my forehead and run down my neck into my cleavage where I knew it would pool in my bra and leave me feeling like I was wearing a wet bathing suit under my shirt. I could also feel it dripping steadily down the small of my back and into places south of that. I had stopped caring about twenty yards back. I felt my thighs burning and my calves get tighter and tighter as I got higher and higher. I pushed on until I reached the top, triumphantly. There I finally took about ten good, deep breaths with my hands on my knees before I stood straight again and climbed up onto the old, faded picnic table triumphantly to enjoy the view that I had worked so hard for.

"*Whooo!*" I would have to remember that trail the next time I needed to lose a few pounds, I thought sarcastically. That wasn't really an issue just then ironically enough, so I put it out of my mind and I enjoyed the view from the top of the hill as well as the slight breeze that I could feel up there. Even with the dark clouds on one side, the view was beautiful.

As I looked down to the bottom I got a definite sense of the excitement of catapulting yourself in that direction, headfirst, on a fast moving sled with the icy wind on your cheeks! I could just hear the "*whoops*" of laughter as they went! I sat and I smiled as I pictured it. *Felt* it. I would have loved this place as a kid, I thought wistfully.

My dad used to take me to the same place that we had hiked, to go sledding. There was a huge hill out in front back then called "Page's Hill," very similar to the one I was standing on, where we would fly down and climb back up relentlessly until we almost froze to death! In the summer we would stand at the top after our hike and my dad would point out all the places around the city that we knew.

"See that, big green tower?" He would ask. I would nod my ponytailed head once I found it. "Follow that to the right until you see the red house. You got it?" I would nod again. "Now look right below that, that blue spot is grandma's house." He would inform me with great delight at my surprise.

"Wow!"

"And you see that yellow square right over there to the right of that? That's your old nursery school." He would tell me. I was always in awe that places that looked so big in person, could appear so tiny from up there. But that was all completely gone by then. My grandparents were also gone, on both sides sadly, and the blue spot had been sold to a lovely young couple over ten years ago. But I couldn't help feeling just a little bit sad that *they* would never get to see it from up there like that, like *we* had!

Breezey Park however, I thought with stubborn optimism, was still there. That was the biggest battle won already. The town had done the right thing by buying it and therefore at least preserving it. It needed work for sure, but it wasn't too late for it to be saved for future generations to enjoy. Even if I couldn't go back and do it for my own childhood places, I was at least happy to be doing it there. At least they would still exist *somewhere*. That was something and something was always better than nothing.

I took my camera out again and took a handful of shots of the view in every direction. Then I took another deep breath and hopped off of the table to start back down the trail. Just as I turned toward the trail though, I saw a car pass in my peripheral vision and I stopped, looked back. It was one of the unmistakable and interchangeable grey sedans that was supposed to be "undercover" and yet practically *screamed* "Federal Tail!" I sighed at the predictability, but I was *pissed* at the intrusion. The car slowed, but never stopped and eventually passed on by.

"*Uggghhh!!!*" I trotted down the trail, letting gravity help me gain speed as well as burn off some of my anger. I knew it didn't do me any good, but that didn't stop it from existing, although that would be nice. I was getting better and better at letting it go though. *Deep breath...*

The trail dumped me back into the parking lot where I had started, but on the other side. I walked across the uneven pavement half expecting the grey sedan to come rolling up the long lane, but it stayed as quiet as ever.

The trail had taken me in a big circle around the property, and had been very beneficial but there was still a lot of ground left to cover. Since the annoying creepers chose not to invade my time in the space after all, and the rain was still holding off, I decided to keep going. I still really wanted to explore all the areas in the middle. Like the giant, dark and wild looking gazebo that was still just *barely* standing over in the center of the grassy area beyond the parking lot. Talk about looking *haunted!* It looked downright *possessed!*

As I approached I could see that there were branches from a neighboring tree among other things growing all around, over and through it in nature's subtle but pervasive battle to reclaim the space. Nature was currently winning. The gazebo wasn't giving up without a fight though. The closer I got the more detail I could make out on the wood that crossed the distance between supports. It was intricately carved and it was beautiful where it wasn't covered completely by branches or moss.

I reached the opening and tucked my head inside, under the gnarly overgrowth. It was darkening slightly outside with the clouds, but it was even darker inside. There was just enough light for me to see that the floor was rotted out almost completely in the center.

The dilapidated interior was a daunting a sight. At the same time though, I recognized something so intimate and beautiful about the way that the vines and the branches invaded and filled the now forbidden space, that I was instantly more attracted to it. I twisted around the branches for a good five minutes just trying to make my way inside but with my first few victorious steps the floor began to creak beneath my feet. It was obvious that entering further would be riskier than it was worth at the moment

I finally admitted defeat in really getting deep inside but I settled on the next best thing. I took out my camera again and reached as far as I could with my arm extended. I started to snap pictures from every angle that I could, including the ones that I couldn't get to on foot. I abandoned the idea of exploring it further for the time being, but deeply inspired, I vowed to return to that issue first to see that particular place brought back to life. It would be hard work but it would be *fantastic* when it was done, *if* it could be done, I just *knew it!!*

The overall mood that I had gotten from the property as a whole, I came to realize in the end of my travels around the structures, was a sense of knowing patience. There was a feeling that it was just "waiting," like every square inch of the place knew that it had a higher potential, but it was content to rest until the time came that it was ready to be reached again. I didn't know how to get there yet, but I felt strongly that the land was onboard. And since the site apparently would not be fighting us that time around, I felt sure that we would get there even faster. Granted, it sounds ridiculous, but I knew it with 100% certainty.

There was a memory there built into the hills, of the exuberant living that once took place on a daily basis. And there was a desire still waiting patiently within the land, for that life to return and to bring that positive energy back with it! It fed the land and vice versa, just like at Jack's place. That was suddenly very clear to me. That was the way it was supposed to work. Don't ask me how I knew that, I just did.

I was willing to bet that the Kent's knew it too, that it was the love and the life that they all brought to the land that made it so fertile. They sowed the seeds of care and diligence and they reaped the rewards which gave them personal satisfaction. That joy coming off of them in turn, fed the living, thriving things that grew around them with that positive energy and it was win-win. All living things need *more* than food and water! *This* I also know for sure!

That circle of life was represented everywhere there. It was that grain of truth that we all recognized, that perpetuated the faith in the desire to give in order to receive. It was a lot of deep thoughts, for an empty stretch of property, but it inspired rather than dissuaded them. I just tried to breathe it all in and to process and remember as much of it as I could.

Eventually I made my way back to the lot and my car, still avoiding the buildings themselves completely. It was getting even darker despite the fact that it was only late afternoon, but I had gotten what I wanted there and I was happy to be on my way at that point. I had a lot of ideas swimming around in my head and only a short time to get some of them down on paper before it was time to get Liliana.

I dropped heavily into my seat and reached for the second water bottle. I finished half of it before I took a breath. I took a few napkins out of the console to wipe the sweat off of my face one last time, and then I texted my dad that I was heading home.

I started the car and cranked the AC while I put the windows up and closed the moon roof to keep the cool air in and the hot air and *the insect population* out! As I pulled back onto the main road, I looked behind me in my rearview mirror, half expecting to see the grey sedan following but of course the road was quiet and empty, as least as far as I could see.

It didn't *feel* empty necessarily. I sighed but didn't let it worry me. I wasn't sure if I was getting tired of it, or used to it and I wasn't sure which was worse. Complacency could be *especially* dangerous. Just then there was a loud crack of thunder and a few seconds later the sky opened up. I was relieved by the timing at least.

Oh well, I thought resignedly. We all had a job to do and I was going to ignore them doing theirs and just focus on doing mine.

Chapter 11

I worked inside on the island to the hypnotic sound of the driving rain until I had just enough time left to make the trip to Juniper. I was excited because Ben had a late business meeting to discuss the possibility of taking on a few partners and I knew I was going to have her overnight. I packed everything back up as quickly as I could and by the time I headed out the door the rain had stopped and the sun was beaming brightly once again.

As I drove, I marveled at the way the water rose from the hot asphalt as newly formed steam and surrendered back into the atmosphere almost as fast as it had come down from it! The foliage were all dark and shiny on the trees and in the grass but the sunlight glinting off of each droplet promised to take care of that just as quickly. Meanwhile the roots of all the trees and plants drank it in hungrily from underneath and dried the ground as well. I was having a hard time finding barely a puddle left anywhere. It had been a loud and heavy storm and it was already as if it had never happened.

Luckily, with the bad weather having passed, I could time trips like that almost down to the minute, since there was never much in the way of "traffic" in Pinegrove. It was basically just a simple equation. (Speed limit) X (distance). I was the last car to pull into the pickup line, but I was on time. *Phew!*

I was extremely relieved to be getting my feet wet in the decision making process for the design and it had been hard to make myself stop once I started. It was a still a very small amount of progress but at least it *was* progress and that was more than I could say for how well "diving right in" had gone. I was excited to get back to it too but one of the few things that could take my attention away from work was on her way over to my car and I was much more excited about that!

It was still hard to deal with how much I missed her when we were apart but I really didn't expect that part to ever change. It wouldn't matter how old she got either I realized then, child or adult I would always want her near me and in my life as much as possible!

I know it's completely morbid, but some days when I feel the sadness of our situation start to overwhelm me, I think about the poor people whose children are missing or even worse, the ones' who have died, and it reminds me to be grateful that I still had her in my life at *all!* Like I said, I know it's horrible but it's tough to get to a place in my head where our current situation actually looks like something to be thankful for! The truth of the matter is though, there are far too many *real* scenarios out there to pull from and unfortunately I knew that all too well.

I managed to shake myself out of it before she hopped in the car. She hugged me hard on her way into her seat and I felt everything else melt away within the warmth of her strong little arms.

"Have I told you lately that you are the best daughter ever?" I asked innocently and her smile lit up the whole car.

"I'm your *only* daughter mama!" She said while she laughed.

"That's doesn't mean you're can't be the best." I assured her with a tickle and she laughed some more. It really was all I needed, at least for the moment. I waved cheerfully to the program director as we pulled away.

I decided then that I wasn't in the mood to cook. It was just too hot. So we stopped off at Nikko's Beef & Pizza on the way home and ordered two junior beef's, three-way, with a side of onion rings. I tried not to eat fast food too often but when I did, a roast beef sandwich was one of my all-time favorites! Liliana was taking after me there as well and she was as excited as always when I suggested it. In fact she seemed to have inherited my love for food in general and I was glad for that at least. It really was about the little joys in life and being able to enjoy them. That was key to overall happiness.

We took our white paper bags with us along with our soda's and ate out on the deck, both of us *mmmm-ing* simultaneously as barbeque sauce mixed with mayo ran slowly through our fingers. Yup, you could definitely tell we were related, I thought with a smile. I just silently hoped that there was enough "Ben" in there too, to balance out all the "me" that she had obviously gotten.

"What are we going to do after dinner, mama?" She asked in between bites and I could feel her excitement at all the possibilities running through her mind. Some days she came out of camp exhausted and although I would be disappointed, I knew it would be a quiet night. But after being cooped up all afternoon because of the rain, she was full of energy and ready for anything. I grinned at her enthusiasm.

Well I know a few people over at the farm that are anxious to meet you if you're up to it." I informed her.

"Really? Who?" she asked obviously intrigued.

"Let's see, tonight there's Jack's son Oscar and his girlfriend Beth. He's the youngest of Jack' two sons." I informed her.

"There are a lot more of them who also want to meet you, but they haven't all come home for harvest season yet." I explained. She could tell from my anticipatory attitude that they were people she would want to meet.

"Okay, sounds like fun!" She answered enthusiastically. I was glad to see that neither being around lots of new people, or large crowds seemed to bother her still and I was relieved. But with her next birthday closing in and examples of her "*awareness*" growing on a fairly steady basis, I had to admit to being a little surprised by that. I was also a tiny bit hopeful too that maybe that meant something better for her, maybe she was *different*. Mostly though I was just surprised, if I was being honest with myself.

Still, the more I noticed it the more I thought about it and the more I thought about it the more I noticed, that she only seemed to experience it when she wanted to, when it appeared to be useful or convenient. Other times it didn't show up at all. Could that really be a thing?

Hmmm. I thought optimistically, what if nature really had figured out a way to genetically improve upon my situation the next time around? *Hmpf*, wouldn't that be nice, I added in doubt of the possibility of something so far-fetched. But who knew?

Come on mama!" She shouted, pulling me back literally and figuratively. Then she heard a distinct noise and she looked excitedly up toward the farmhouse. "I hear a dog!" She declared with the same excitement that some people reserve for things like Bigfoot, or the Easter bunny!

"Oh! That's who I'm forgetting." I said teasingly. "That must be Rufus." I added with a smile. He belongs to Beth and Oscar. They said they might bring him today but I didn't want to get your hopes up until I knew for sure. Come on. Let's go meet him." I said standing up and wrapping all the mess up in the wax papers and stuffing it all into one bag. I wiped the table with the few remaining napkins and went inside to throw away the trash. Liliana followed me and we both washed our hands, then headed back outside and down the steps to the grass.

Beth was the first to see us coming and wave but Rufus beat her to us in three giant strides that closed the remaining distance. That was to be expected when your legs were as long as his were though, and you had four of them to boot. I was just as excited to see that they had brought their Great Dane with them as Liliana was. I had made Beth promise that she would after everything she had told me about him at the last cookout, and I could see right away that they hadn't exaggerated one bit.

He had the traditional coloring of a harlequin with the stark white fur punctuated with various black ink spots. He was absolutely beautiful but definitely one of the biggest Danes I had ever seen for sure! Talk about genetics! He looked to me like what you would get if you bred a white stallion with a Dalmatian!

I had always loved Great Danes growing up and I suspected that it was at least partly because they were the closest thing to a horse that a "city girl" was ever going to get. I never had one, but I had always wanted one.

Beth had already assured me that he was a big giant softy

and that he was excellent with kids so I wasn't worried about that. I was mostly looking forward to seeing Liliana's reaction to him instead. She loved animals and had obviously seen and played with an awful lot of them over the years at Ben's office, but she was still too young in his eyes, to be responsible for owning one yet. He was of the mind that *too much* responsibility, leveled on them at *too early* an age in their development can have lifelong detrimental effects.

I had thought of Ethan and a few of his quirks like the OCD with cleaning and organization and even though those weren't horrible things necessarily, I knew he had a point. I also knew he wouldn't be able to hold her off too much longer, but in the meantime I really thought that she would enjoy a doggie play-date!

I could already feel his overwhelming sweetness as he got closer. It wasn't the same with animals as it was with people. There wasn't a whole "*conversation*" so-to-speak of emotions to pick up, just a general overall state of mind, which with animals was usually pretty obvious anyway. I mean if a dog wasn't happy about your presence, generally speaking you were aware! Cats on the other hand could be a little trickier, but that was a train of thought for another day.

The general mood I picked up from the oversized puppy as he bounded towards the new people was pure joy and liveliness.

I watched Liliana squeal with absolute delight, as Rufus reached her location and started to lick her face wildly. At her height she couldn't really do much to stop him and he was smart enough to take advantage of that for as long as possible. I suspected he was also enjoying a little residual barbeque sauce at the same time. She just hugged his neck and giggled hysterically, loving every minute of it.

Eventually Beth caught up to Rufus and after letting him get in his initial licks, called him off easily as she made her way over to hug me hello.

'Rufus, *heel!*" She commanded in a casual tone and he immediately sat back on his haunches and began to pant happily. Liliana wiped off her face with her arm and a laughing "yuck!" then went back to patting a much calmer Rufus. Meanwhile he tried to keep the licking to a minimum of short, sneaky bursts in between Beth's knowing glances.

Well the non-human meetings had gone well, so I figured it was time to move on to the human-human introductions.

"Liliana, this is Beth." I said as she went over to say hi and pet Rufus with her. Then Oscar came running out and whistled piercingly just before he threw a ball as far as he could, which was shockingly far! Rufus responded immediately by bolting after it. Oscar walked over to us while he waited and shook Liliana's hand hello.

"Sorry. He's been inside too long. He just needs to run off some of that energy for a few minutes and he'll be fine." He assured her with his charming grin.

"And this is the one and only Oscar." I said rolling my eyes while Beth chuckled. "You too will have lots of fun together, I'm sure!" I added with a grin.

"It's a pleasure to meet you my lady." He said bowing regally in front of her. Liliana chuckled, amused by his good-humor and I could feel right then that they were already connecting on that child-like, fun-loving level and were fast on their way to becoming friends. It was an instant recognition of kindred spirits.

Everything was basically dry again by then so we started to walk just to let Rufus run off some energy while we enjoyed the fresh evening air and the fact that it was the beginning of the weekend. We talked about how I was going to see Gen the next night, but that unfortunately it wouldn't be in time for Liliana to meet her that weekend. Hopefully the next.

"I haven't seen her much either lately." Beth agreed. "She's always so busy! It's a good thing though. It's what she's always wanted to do. It's about time that the rest of the world started to see that she's so good at it and utilize her passions. She really needs to be out there fighting the good fight!" She allowed with a charging fist to illustrate her point. "I do miss her lately though. I really hope we'll all at least be here again next weekend." She added a little melancholy, but I could tell that she immediately thought better of complaining when she remembered how much I was still missing someone else.

"Sorry." She said with a regretful shake of her head. "I definitely shouldn't complain. I know how much harder it would be if it was Oscar that I wasn't seeing for such long stretches." She admitted quietly to me but with a wince.

"It's okay." I replied easily. "It's not your fault so you don't have to apologize. I certainly know what you mean though, on both counts!" I agreed. I gave her a sideways hug while we walked. "I am happy to say that I will be "utilizing" her skills again on this new job so it's win-win there. She gets to help fight the good fight and I have an excuse to see her!" I joked with a grin and a high five. "I'll tell Gen you said hello and that you miss her." I added making her feel better.

Meanwhile Oscar tossed the ball around and Rufus chased it. He was so excited for the game that it enticed us all to play. We all ran around playing in the grass, Rufus happily chasing the ball and people alike. We each enjoyed the opportunity to act like children for a while in the summer air, but Beth and I were the first to tire out. Liliana and Rufus however, were still bounding around full of energy so Oscar took one for the team and went back out into the field to play catch/fetch with them some more while we sat on the sideline and watched them and the sunset.

Of course I could tell quite easily that he was having just as much fun as they were so I didn't feel too bad about leaving him on his own. I noticed that Beth didn't either. We sat and leaned back on our elbows chewing grass and laughing at the "kids" as they ran around falling all over each other. Then they switched to having races to the ball. Oscar had to keep throwing it further and further for it to be any kind of challenge for them.

He gave Liliana a head start each time, *a big one*, since Rufus could run so much faster. He would tell Rufus to sit by his side while Liliana jogged way out. When she reached the grain silos at the edge of the barn, Oscar would throw the ball over the silos, freeing Rufus to take chase. Even with the impressive distance it was pretty close each time which one would be triumphant as they raced to the other side, but both were having the time of their lives regardless. Every once and a while they would roll around and wrestle for it while Oscar waited.

It was pretty far just to reach the silos from where we were. I was sure I could never throw that far, even with my half-decent arm. Between the distance and the wrangling, it took them a while to bring it back. That gave us time to chat in between tosses. It was nice. We talked about the last band that had played at The Tavern, and the new menu items that the Chef was trying out lately in between throws. A few tosses later Oscar mentioned Jack's latest adoption and we were all enthralled by the sad story.

"You know we're getting another horse, right?" He started out with. I had heard the important points of the story, but not the details.

"Yes, but that's about all so far." I answered.

"The shelter where the horses are now sent out a packet to every horse farmer in the eastern part of the country looking for places to take them in. If I know Pops, he's definitely going to take one in, if he can swing it, maybe more. If there's one thing he can't resist, it's an innocent soul in need of a home." He said with a wink. I did not need convincing on the subject and I smiled knowingly in return.

"Where are they from again?" I asked trying to remember the few details that Jack had mentioned.

"Down south, somewhere in the Carolina's. They seized like fifty horses from some asshole who was neglecting them terribly! Some of them to *death*!" He said shaking his head in disgust. "He took in every animal he could get his hands on, but he only fed and cared for the one's he saw potential income in. The rest were sold off for 'illegal purposes' or simply left to starve to death in their stalls. Some of them actually ate the wood off the walls! I saw some of the pictures in the packet and it was horrific! I'm telling you, you don't even want to see them! That shit will break your heart!" He declared and none of us was in a mood to disagree. We sat quietly with our somber thoughts for a minute or two before I realized it was too quiet, and that it had been for too long.

"Is it just me being overly protective, or have they been gone a while?" I asked somewhat afraid of the answer. Beth and I both sat up and listened intently then and as Oscar's head snapped in the direction that they had taken. He gave a quick whistle but there was no response. I tried not to panic but every hair on the back of my neck was suddenly standing on edge!

I knew sometimes that could just be due to the initial scare, a wake-up call type of moment that is completely terrifying for a split-second but is then taken back like a sick prank, when the worry is revealed to be unfounded. The fear is very real in that second though, and only fate could decide which way it would go at that crucial point. It was that lack of control during that one horrible heartbeat that I hated the most.

A mere few seconds had gone by while I processed all of this and we all held our breath as we waited to be "pranked." I reached out empathically, trying to feel her but I thought something had to be blocking her. It was as if she had disappeared, but I *refused* to believe that could have happened that fast! And without me feeling it. There had to be another explanation! But what? I tried again to pick up some sort of a clue! The only answer however was an eerie, continuing silence. I was sure I was overreacting, but that was as much as the mother in me could take on faith.

I popped up and started over there thinking they must be just beyond sight where they were rolling around on the other side of the silos. Beth and Oscar were already reassuring me as I got up.

"I'm sure they're just lying the grass where we can't see them, finally too tuckered out to come right back." Oscar insisted with a lazy grin as he watched me go. I could tell that he purposely waited to react, thinking it would turn out okay if he didn't lend energy to the possibility that it might not be. That was fine. I just needed to be sure.

I kept going towards the silos, staring at the furthest spot I could see as I came around the other side, certain that they would appear in my line of vision at some point. But as I reached the other side all I saw was empty grass and the trees in the distance and I still didn't feel much more. The pit of my stomach dropped out at that point and every worse-case-scenario instantly started to run through my head!

Did they run too far, end up lost in the woods? Was there someone in the woods, Fed or otherwise, just waiting for a chance to steal an unattended little girl? Could they really have gotten far enough away that fast? Would someone really do that?! Could someone really have incapacitated that "big old dog" in some way in order to get away quietly? It seemed ridiculous at best but I still didn't know where they could be! I thought frantically as I began to spin in every direction, scanning desperately for a clue. I was about to scream out her name and pray for a response when I heard Rufus bark.

I spun around on my heel again but looked up that time to see his tail wagging at the top of the section of regular stairs that twisted up the outside of the silos and just past my sight. Thank God! I thought, sure that Liliana must be up there on the stairs with him. I was relieved and furious at her at the same time as I ran back towards the bottom rung on the far side. The fear in me at her being in such a scary spot grew on my way up the rickety, open planked stairs, and those belonged to the first set, the "*easy*" ones. I still wasn't feeling her yet and that was strange but I was getting madder as I went and I wondered if that had something to do with it. I tried to calm down at that thought but kept going and searching as fast as I could.

Once I rounded the bend and reached the top my heart stopped again at the sight that awaited me. The stairway I was on ended at the small platform where Rufus stood at attention, with his front paws on the set of metal rungs that extended the rest of the way up and over the top. Liliana was not there on the stairs with him after all, but I could finally *feel* her and she *was* there! My heart started to pound then at the scenario that that pointed to.

"Liliana!" I did yell then as I stood on the platform next to Rufus, still surprised that it was empty besides the dog. Then I heard it. The sound made my heart start pounding again but in relief! It was a small, quiet sound but I knew for sure that it was definitely her when I heard the tiny, "*Mama?*" in response. I knew where she was then, but that was of little relief since my fears had been confirmed when the response came from *inside*!

Once I heard that I bolted into action. "Down Rufus!" I commanded and he listened immediately. I wanted to run up to the half-open sliding doorway that I could see, but the higher I got on the bars the sketchier it got. I was suddenly acutely aware, after one particularly scary slip, that if I fell off I wasn't going to be much help to her. I took a deep breath and tried to calm down again but to keep moving quickly, just *carefully*!

"Liliana, I'm coming! Just hang on sweetie!" I said in reflex as a manner of speaking. She responded again but I could feel right away that she took it more literally.

"I am mama. But can you hurry?" She had meant it literally too and desperation was the clearest emotion in her response!

Oh shit!

My heart almost stopped at the implications I felt in that. I remembered all the stories that Jack had told us about accidents in grain silos and how common they were. Apparently they were the highest cause of agricultural deaths. Who knew? I myself would have guessed "tractor accidents" but I was mentally begging forgiveness for my ignorance and hoping that we would not be adding to that horrifying statistic in penance for my sins of ignorance! It was at that point I finally had the presence of mind to call for backup.

"*Oscar! Beth!*" I yelled in their general direction as loud as I could. "Come quick!"

I finally reached the small doorway and my heart stopped again as I peered down to see her standing inside. She was holding onto a wooden beam that extended out in front of her just near enough for her to reach. She was over by the far wall and about three yards down from the entryway. Nine feet had never looked so terrifying in all my life! She was holding onto the beam with both hands up as high as she could reach. She was frozen there, looking tiny and afraid in the shadows.

"Oh my God Liliana I'm coming! Just stay *right* there!" I commanded desperately. I don't know where I thought she would go but I was petrified to even take my eyes off of her in the dimly lit space.

"Don't worry. I can't really." She answered and her anxiety

was increasing my own by the second. "My feet are kind of… *stuck*." She said, and she was really confused by that. "I'm sorry mama. I fell. I thought it was just a regular floor when I got up and that I could just walk across it to get the ball, but on the way back my feet started to sink and I was scared because I didn't know why, so I stopped. I'm holding on as tight as I can but I don't know what will happen if I let go. I was going to climb back up but I can't now." She looked up at me again. "I'm so sorry mama. I didn't mean to fall in." She admitted feeling incredibly guiltily.

"It's okay baby. I know you didn't." I assured her as my heart broke at the heavy remorse I could feel from her over the situation. "Just *don't* move and it will all be fine! Okay?" I coaxed carefully.

"*Tell* me she's not in there! *Simone?!*" I heard Oscar demand from the ground.

"*Sorry, can't do that!*" I shouted as I leaned back. There was an appropriate amount of urgency in my voice, but I was still trying to keep the panic from it for Liliana's sake.

"*Shit!*" I heard him exclaim in response, but he too tried to keep it to a quiet condemnation. I could hear his steps as they sounded on the treads and they were fast, but oddly I felt almost no vibrations as he started up after us.

"Don't worry. I've got it." I assured him. "She says her feet are stuck. I'm just going to climb down and pull her out." I yelled back to Oscar as a courtesy, thinking there was no way I could wait for him to get all the way up there.

"*NO!!!*" He shouted up, immediately and effectively stopping me dead in my tracks! Literally two seconds later he surprised me as he came up next to me at the top. I was shocked at how fast he had flown up there!

"She must've crossed over an air pocket. That can happen when the grains start to dry and shrink, but stick in place. Air pockets form in between the layers and if you fall in one you can cause a cyclone effect end up underneath the entire the load in a matter of seconds." He said it quickly as he climbed the metal rungs, and only loud enough for me to hear. He started unhooking a mass of straps and ropes that I hadn't seen. It was attached to a pulley system that was tucked up inside the roof of the silos.

"That is why you *never* get in there without a harness on. Ever!" He instructed calmly, but effectively scolding me as he put first one leg through the apparatus, then the other. "And you *never* go in without someone else standing outside watching and anchoring." He added to me and to Liliana as he handed me the other end of the rope after he untied it from the peg.

"Are you sure? I can go! I don't mind." I insisted. "I'd prefer it actually." I added really wanting to be in motion. He shook his head and didn't waste a single second arguing.

"No! I know what I'm doing. That will save time, and not put *both* of you at risk! *Jesus*, Ethan would friggen' *kill* me!" He mumbled sarcastically under his breath while lowering himself down through the opening. He was joking and trying to break the tension as usual but I could feel the real fear in there at that possibility as well and it surprised me just for a fraction of a second.

"Now I'm going to go down the rungs on the inside wall nice and slowly. I don't want to disturb the floor that she's standing on until I absolutely have to. Once I let go of the side, you hold that rope *tight*!" He instructed and I could feel the importance in that. "Understand?" He checked. I nodded.

After that he passed beneath the lip of the opening and I couldn't see him anymore. At that point I could only hear him, but I could also feel him and that was important. His concentration on his task and his determination that this end quickly and in a favorable manner echoed mine, so I felt a little better while trying to wait patiently on the landing if I lived it vicariously through him in the meantime. Not a lot better, but a little. I just focused on his emotions and tried to remember to breathe as he went.

He was also focused, like a laser, but he still joked casually with her as he ascended. It was for her sake and I could feel that it was helping. I listened to him as he tried to keep from scaring her with the risks of the situation. A panicked reaction on her part could turn that floor into quicksand and I knew I would dive in right after her if that happened. Then there would be two bodies at the bottom of that pile for him to fish out! I tried my hardest just to keep breathing and not to think about it anymore than necessary. I certainly didn't want to do anything to bring it on, even mentally!

I closed my eyes and wrapped the rope around my hand an extra time on each side just to reinforce my hold. *Deep breaths…*I focused on what Oscar was feeling and saying again.

"So only half his size and you figured out a way to outsmart Rufus, huh?" He asked her casually.

"No." She giggled and my heart clenched. "He's actually pretty good at stairs. He didn't stop until he reached the towel bar ones." She provided honestly. "The ball was on the door on top of the roof so I thought I had it for sure. All I had to do was climb two more steps that he couldn't climb with his big giant paws." She explained confidently. She had momentarily forgotten her predicament and he was getting closer by the second. He kept her talking.

"I'm surprised he didn't try to follow you!" He insisted with a laugh. "He's not always smart when it comes to choosing his own good over his impulses." He added meaningfully. She missed the implication, but I definitely did not.

"I thought he was going to! It felt like he would for a minute." She replied surprising us both, and a separate part of my brain that wasn't freaking out registered that too. "He could practically just stand up and reach it with his mouth, and he even tried once!" She narrated proudly. "So I had to grab it quick. I had it too, but I slipped when the door slid open and I fell inside." I heard her say guiltily. He was silently thanking God it had been full at the time!! She remembered where she was by that point in the story but thankfully he was almost to her by then.

I pulled in some slack and climbed a few rungs until I could see him again, where the edge of the grain met the wall. He had gone down the outside level and around in her direction as far as he could along the outside edge before looking up at me and giving the thumbs up.

My heart leapt into my throat and I held the rope with all my strength. I climbed back down to the platform so I could spread my feet and lean back into it. I knew the situation probably gave me added strength, but I was still praying that I would have enough weight, leverage, and physical muscle to hold them both! It was the opposite of the kind of thing I usually wished for but I didn't have time to reflect on that.

I felt the tension increase and pull on me as he let go, but it wasn't nearly as heavy as I had expected. In fact it was entirely manageable. I looked up at the intricate pulley system and realized that a lot of the weight was obviously redistributed among the multiple connection points. He would have known that when he chose our roles, I realized. I breathed a little deeper then. Just one breath but it felt good. I had needed it.

I couldn't see them anymore from where I was, but I could still make out the feelings and the sounds. I felt the change in tension as he reached as far as he could, and again the moment that he added her weight to his own. I held on as tight as I could and tried not to fall off the small platform in relief. Beth came up behind me just then and held me around the waist with her left hand, and held the rope with me with her right. She apparently wasn't one for scaling silos in a single bound like her boyfriend or her dog, but in the end she did have impeccable timing!

"Thank you!" I said but she blew it off. She knew it wasn't necessary physically. It was mostly just a show of moral support.

"Don't worry. He's got her. She's perfectly safe now. You can go ahead and breathe." She added with a laugh. I did let out a gust of air, but I refused to let go of the rope or move until I saw them with my own eyes.

Liliana's blonde hair poked through the opening first. I pulled the slack in again and went up to pull her out. She slipped over the edge and I felt her weight against my right side where I held her, on the "right" side of the silos again, and a wave of relief washed over my whole body! I held her tightly with one arm as I climbed back down to the platform and put her down. I dropped down with her and hugged her for a few seconds, holding her as close as I could and giving thanks *that* I still could!

"Jesus you scared me!" I let out then. "Please don't ever do that to me again! You almost gave mommy a heart attack!" I said exasperated but still smiling. I really didn't have it in me to scold her any more than that just then, but I needed her to at least know how serious it had been!

Oscar popped out next and returned the harness and supporting rope to their corresponding pegs inside. Then he slid the door closed and climbed down the metal rungs. He landed on our platform with a thud, startling us all.

"Okay! Apparently it's time to talk 'silos safety!'" He announced and we all laughed, practically giddy once the threat had passed. "You too Rufus!" He said pointing to the dog that was still waiting on the stairs. "Everyone, down! Pull up a patch of grass." He commanded.

We all laughed but we did what we were told and went to sit in the grass. I sat and pulled Liliana onto my lap so I could hold her close while Oscar proceeded to explain all about silos, what they were used for and the dangers inherently involved. For once she didn't protest or try to slide off my lap. She was just as content as I was for the time being to be held. It was hot out and the extra body heat didn't take long to make us both sticky, but I didn't care and I could tell that she didn't either, for the moment. I obviously never wanted anything scary to happen with her, but I had to acknowledge that there was always a "heightened" sense of being alive anytime there was a very real brush with death! We both held on a little tighter and we were much more grateful for that than annoyed.

Oscar told us stories about silos a lot bigger than theirs and some even smaller. He explained about how it used to be before the harness systems were installed and how hundreds of farmers and their helpers would perish each year in senseless accidents without them and a few simple safety measures in place.

"The real danger comes when you are trying to unload from the chute on the bottom and gravity refuses to do the work for you. Some crops are wetter than others and when they dry they can stick in place. The answer has always been to get your most nimble worker, usually also the youngest and most inexperienced, to climb on top and rake it out and push it down. Lots of times, that works out just fine. But there are always those rare times when the unexpected happens. Like when an air pocket has formed, like we saw here today, and a worker falls through."

"Depending on the size of the pocket, he can be up to his knees in seconds, or worse! The amount of weight involved in even shallow depths, can take an incredible amount of time and manpower to move by hand. It's certainly not ideal if you're trying to free someone. That's why it's not done that way in the first place. So *that's* where the real danger comes in." He instructed solemnly.

"When someone gets trapped above, and the men below finally get the flow moving, unknowingly setting off a collapse underneath them. It's like being in an hourglass filled with quicksand when that happens." He said referencing the term that I had heard Jack use. It was obvious that that kind of vision resonated and stuck in everyone's psyche so it was a great teaching tool. You weren't likely to forget that.

He let that thought sink in with each of us for a second, but not too long. He knew he didn't want to create *nightmares* per se, just a healthy respect for the danger. On that note he clarified our situation.

"Thankfully Liliana was not in that kind of danger today, because all the chutes and augers below were closed and shut down tight, so there was no chance of anything moving out from under her. *But* there always remains the danger of the isolated air pocket. Thankfully the one she stumbled into was tiny, but we never know how big they are until *after!*" He said, letting that sink in for a moment as well.

"Still, all silos can be 100% perfectly safe, if you have safety rules in place, *and* you follow them! *So*!

"I am changing Rule #1 to; we ***never*** climb on or go in the silos without direct permission from a senior Kent, for ANY reason! Ever!" He made his eyes big and intense for that one to give it weight. "Got it?" He asked seriously. We all nodded. "Say it!" He shouted and we jumped, but then complied. I could feel, dimly, that Beth had been through this scenario before but that she was tolerating it once again for our benefit.

"Rule #2; you ***never*** go in the silos without a harness on.

Say it!" He instructed. We all repeated what he had said again in a haphazard fashion. He was happy enough with that and moved on.

"Rule #3; we ***never*** go in the silos without someone knowing, usually said Kent who gave permission, standing right there to watch, listen, and hold said rope." He stared at us and made a prompting motion with his hands until we all tried to repeat that, chuckling a little more with the varied success on that one.

"Rule #4; only Rules #1 - 3 matter! *Say it. Learn it. Live it!*" He said, finally laughing himself. Once the danger had passed and he'd had his say, I could feel him sensing that it was safe to revert back into his playful, irascible self. He didn't like having to be the hard guy, but I knew then that he could be when he had to be and I respected him a little more for it.

I just grinned as he fell back in the grass next to us. That was like an unspoken command to Rufus that the serious time was over, so he too jumped in the pile and starting licking, well... everyone.

"Guess I'll have to get you a new ball." He joked as he pet Rufus.

"Why?" Liliana asked innocently as she pulled his out of her pocket. "His is right here." She said as she threw it for him and he followed it like she was his new Queen. Oscar stared, jaw slack, clearly surprised!

"*Hah*! Of course it is!" He said triumphantly as proud of her as if she were truly related. He fell back again and laughed some more then looked over at me and Beth. "Why were we so worried about her exactly?" He asked sarcastically. I had to laugh too because I certainly knew what he meant, both empathically *and* personally. She still threw me for a loop all the time and she was only 5 and 3/4 years old. I could barely wait to see what the future would hold for her!

After our excitement we slowly made our way back to the patio for a fire. Usually Liliana would stay close to me after any kind of unsettling situation. I had to smile though as I noticed that since our momentous cuddle on the lawn, she had been staying closer to Oscar instead. That was fine with me though. Learning right away that she could rely on the Kent's was a lesson that I was okay with.

As usual I hated how we got there, but not the end result.

Everyone was finally worn out by then by the day's events as a whole, but happy with the way things had turned out so spirits were high while we sat around the fire pit telling jokes. Jack was not so happy at first, but he was better once we had a chance to fill him in on how quickly Oscar had saved the day!

"Huh, thought we had more time for that one. Won't make that mistake again." He muttered half under his breath. "You tell them the rules?" He asked skeptically while he thought about it some more.

"Yes, sir!" Oscar answered dutifully, but with that ever playful smile and wink at us.

"You all recite 'em back?" He asked us sternly, not ready to let us off the hook just yet.

"Yes sir!" We all answered as one.

"Hm. Well alright then, I guess we're good here." He declared and we all went back to laughing like we were children who had gotten off without a punishment. None of us wanted to dwell in that scary place where we had *almost* been any longer than necessary.

Jack lit a fire and Shirley brought out the fixing's for us to make s'mores while I slipped to the edge of the patio to make a phone call. I didn't want to do it but I knew how Ben would take the news of what had happened and I didn't want it coming to him from anyone else. I figured that he was still out to dinner but he took the call anyway, probably worried something had happened. That thought dropped my spirits a little but I wanted to get it over with as quickly as possible. I cut right to the chase and started with, "I just want you to know right off the bat that everyone's fine."

I summed up the story as fast as I could, quickly getting to the part where Oscar knew exactly what to do because there were proper safety features in place. He was still angry at first at the thought of her being so vulnerable and of course questioned me for the fiftieth time about whether the farm was really a safe place for her to be spending time. I had expected that.

I reassured him *again*, that it was the safety precautions

installed there that had kept it from being a very different story and that was the most he could ask for.

"She could have climbed a tree to that height in the same amount of time and been in no less danger Ben. You know that. Life doesn't come with guarantees." I said with the insinuation crystal clear.

It was tempting for him to want to place blame but it was fairly obvious that no one had done anything that warranted it. Eventually he came around when I pointed out that no one ever expected her to climb up there by herself, least of all me! He had to agree that he was surprised by her bravery as well and somehow that made him just a tiny bit more reasonable. That and the added fact that he knew just how "unexpected" some situations could be, of course. He insisted that he would have a talk with her the next day about personal safety and common sense, but I made him promise not to punish or berate her about the "silos incident," as it would become known from then on.

"Trust me, she feels bad enough at the embarrassing chaos she knows she caused!" I assured him.

"Good! That's good. Hopefully she won't do anything like that ever again! Let me talk to her please." He asked in the end and I walked over and purposely held it out to her where I knew they both could hear me.

"Daddy's glad you're okay. He just wants to say hi." I said simply as I handed it over.

They talked for a while and I felt her initial trepidation, but it melted away as he spoke to her. I didn't know what he said but I could feel that she was relieved and she excitedly told him a few details of her escapade and how Oscar was like Superman only on a rope! He didn't keep her long. I heard her say, "Okay, I love you too daddy." Then she came over and handed me back my phone.

"Daddy's not mad." She told me and the relief in her innocent, little girl eyes made me actually want to thank him for once.

We got back to enjoying the beautiful summer night after that sitting by the fire and it helped to un-do some of the residual negativity we had been feeling from earlier.

I sat and watched Liliana play, throwing the glowing pallino to Rufus when it finally got too dark to use his own ball. She was staying *very* close as instructed, but she was feeling lighthearted and carefree still and I was *extremely* relieved by that. Thankfully, she didn't seem to have been overly traumatized by her ordeal at all. She was acting and feeling exactly the same as before the "silos incident," aside from her newfound fondness for Oscar. *Hmpf.*

I remembered what I had felt earlier about them becoming fast friends and knew then that I had been right. Of course I'd had no idea about the impending danger that would facilitate that bonding so efficiently! I mean, that part would have been a nice thing to have foreseen if you were going to "*foresee*" things, don't you think?! I posed angrily in my head to no one at the unpredictability of my gifts. It definitely had its downside sometimes.

Of course then I thought about that and realized that if I had seen it, I would have surely stopped it and for better or for worse, they're relationship would forever be cemented. Maybe that was exactly why I *couldn't* see everything. Maybe I wasn't meant to. Maybe someday I would understand it all, I told myself as I watched my marshmallow burn to a crisp.

The Kent's in residence snapped me out of it when they stood and gave a little speech about how safety always comes first on the farm, then training, then practice, and then safety again. But once you had that down there was still one very important element that they couldn't teach, and that was bravery. After the speech Oscar pulled the cup from behind his back and they awarded it to a shocked Liliana with great pageantry for her bravery. He filled it with a half a can of grape soda and she drank it happily while and we all sat around the fire and clapped.

She was feeling silly but she still thought it was great fun. She laughed at herself too but she finished it then gave a bow and did a little dance before she giggled again. Everyone was laughing just as hard as she was by then and we all felt like one big family by the end of the night. Yay! My families liked each other, I thought with a silliness that kept me young, at least in my mind.

Eventually it quieted down and we got up to thank everyone and hug them all goodnight. We walked back without a flashlight, even though Shirley had offered us one. We simply didn't need it with the moonlight at near full blast. There wasn't a cloud in the sky anymore and I looked at my smartphone along the path to see that it had cooled to a perfect 76 degrees. We walked casually, hand-in-hand and I looked down at her just as she smiled up at me thoughtfully. It all came together with the day that we'd had to create a poignant moment that I knew neither of us would ever forget. The scares, the reliefs, the joys, the newfound friends and the memories made. All outlined and capped off by the crisp, clean moonlight, at the end of a surreal day. Deep breathes were in order.

We had lost some of the everydayness between us, sure. But we still had our special moments and I knew that it was more important to keep that alive between us than to try and cling uselessly to the inconsequential. With that realization I finally understood that we were more successful in our current relationship then I had given us credit for. I was relieved as I realized that things were in a better place than I had thought.

It reminded me of another life-changing moment that had occurred under a similarly bright moon and I smiled. It was hard not having him there to hold me through all of life's little crisis's, but I was still incredibly grateful for his existence in general. I just wished silently as we went inside and went to bed, that he was currently "existing" a whole lot *closer* to me.

I woke up early the next morning to bring her to camp, yet she was still up before me and she was coloring.

"What'cha drawing doodle-bug?" I asked as I made for the coffee pot.

"It's a picture of my friends here at the farm to show Daddy!" She declared happily. "I know he might still be a little bit upset about yesterday and I don't want him to say I can't come here anymore." She added innocently, like it was a real possibility. I wasn't quite so cavalier about that proposition, but I wasn't going to take it out on her.

"Don't you worry about that, sweetheart." I assured her

calmly. That's not just up to him. I'm still your mother and you're as safe here as you are anywhere else! Even your own home!" I couldn't help pointing out as I shook her now healed arm lightly in illustration. She giggled and I could tell that she felt a little better after my confident statement.

I did wonder then what kind of things he said to her though, when I wasn't around. I could picture it being things like, "*We'll give this a shot pumpkin, but if it doesn't go well, we may have to do things differently from here on out.*" or something along those lines. I tried not to let those negative thoughts ruin my mood or our day though. I sighed deeply, finally really glad that we weren't married anymore.

I looked down at her picture and it made all the difference in the world in lifting my mood. She had drawn herself sitting on the fence next to me. I was sure of that because she always drew me with the same long straight brown lines for hair. Jack was standing next to us in his boots and overalls with his hat on, and Cookie was standing in between them. She had Shirley next to me with a flower in her hair, holding a plate of cookies.

Down on the ground in front of me sat Beth with her short black hair and Rufus taking up her entire lap. Then there was Oscar, in front of Liliana, on one knee. He looked as if he was being her step stool to get on Cookie, treating her like a princess. I was sure it was Oscar because of the blonde hair and the fact that his smile was almost as big as his head! It was amusing on so many levels but I was also in awe of all the details she had incorporated. I couldn't help being proud that she had obviously inherited some of my artistic ability along with the other stuff.

Mostly though it was shocking how well she had fought her case without using any grown up words at all. Everyone looked completely wholesome and helpful and I was proud of her whether he got it or not, but I hoped for both our sakes that he *would* get it, and that he would take what she was telling him to heart.

"It's beautiful honey! When did you get so good?" I asked completely serious.

"We get to draw a lot at camp!" She answered casually. "We have a really good art teacher and a lot of times if they are having a sports day I choose to take the art class instead. At first it was because of my cast, but I really started to like them." She said casually, but I could feel how deeply she felt that! "We do fun things in there!" She added excitedly as she colored the grass around the pictorial version of us. "I'll have a bunch of cool things to show you when camp ends, mama. I can't wait!" She added and her enthusiasm was all I needed to push me over the edge.

I knew I was very lucky to have such an awesome kid in my life but every once and a while she reminded me just how awesome she really was. At the moment I was feeling particularly grateful.

"Who want's pancakes?" I asked and she immediately cheered.

"*Meeee!!!*"

"Alrighty! Blueberry, chocolate chip, or plain?" I offered as I started to get things out of the cabinets. I could feel her having a hard time deciding so I made it easy for her.

"Tell you what! I'll make all three!" I shouted and she cheered again.

"Yayyy!"

Breakfast was wonderful and blissfully uneventful! We sat and enjoyed our pancakes together as we watched SpongeBob. After that we cleaned up and packed her stuff. We had a little bit of time before we had to leave but we decided to save the rest of the outdoor adventures for next time and just relax while she finished her picture. She showed me proudly when she was done. She had added Ben into the scene by then. He was sitting in his car, waving. I wasn't sure if that would help or hurt her case but I wasn't about to say so.

"I'm sure he's going to love it, but if he doesn't understand what it means, you have him call me and I'll explain it to him. Okay?" I offered and she nodded.

Once I dropped her off and got back home I went straight back to the packet. I kept my phone close in case either Ben or Liliana needed to call me. But with the silence there, I found the quiet space to focus on my work. There was still a vast amount of decisions that I couldn't make yet, and it was still way too early to meet Gen, but

I was excited about the vibe I had gotten from the grounds and I continued on with that until my neck got too stiff to look down anymore.

Then I leaned back and reached up to rub it as much as I could while I twisted it back and forth. It was officially all I could do in that one sitting but it had felt good. I mean, except for the stiff neck. *Mentally* it had felt good!

I jumped up and put everything away. Then ran to change, excited not just for the progress that I was eagerly anticipating, but also just to see Gen again. It had been years since I had made a *for-real* "new friend" and I had to chuckle at how excited I was to see her.

I was missing some parts of my life lately for sure, desperately! But other parts were decidedly more fulfilling than usual and that was something else to adapt to. But I did and while my life was less than perfect at the moment, at least there was enough of a balance to get me through the day. I could never take that for granted.

In my eagerness, I was ready an hour early but I couldn't sit still anymore so I just left early rather than sitting around waiting.

I headed straight to my favorite spot to meet Gen.

Chapter 12

I took the scenic route, partly because I really loved the scenery but also to kill some time. I still got to The Tavern early so instead of asking to be seated right away, I waited for my usual table to open up. They all knew me well enough by then to know what I wanted when I showed up there anyway. I didn't usually have to ask anymore.

I knew it wasn't really a good idea to be so predictable, even just in general. But try as I might to avoid it, truth is I am a creature of habit. When I find something that works, I'm pretty loyal to it. That applied to more than just geography but it was one of those instances that a familiar spot was the best spot for me for so many reasons that I would risk being easy to find in order to stay in it. I needed a little security and comfort just then.

I felt that way about a number of things that I knew I should know better about. But being both human and occasionally just plain stubborn like everybody else, I still choose to do them anyway about ninety percent of the time. There were a few times though that I ended up regretting it and that turned out to be one of them.

I was just taking my first sip of my wine, as one of the young men that waited tables when Dani wasn't there walked away. I knew from the black nametag with the white letters that his name was "Joshua" and from our few conversations that he did *not* like to be called "Josh!" That was about it. He was never chatty like Dani but he was fast and he always got my order right, so I would never hold that against him. He was also always pretty neutral on the emotional scale whenever I saw him there, all business. Lord knows that worked for me. I was quite content to take my drink with nothing but a nod and a smile and let him go about his business. I had my own business to attend to once Gen got there anyway and I was very excited to get to that, but in the meantime I was perfectly happy with just the company that Kendall Jackson had to offer.

So I was definitely not thrilled when I felt someone come up behind me and stand at my shoulder waiting to be noticed. I was particularly unhappy that I was already sure before I turned around that it wasn't Gen or any other female. The masculine quality to the energy was strong and it was the first thing to hit me. I sat still and considered how long I might be able to ignore them and wondered if I did, if they would simply go away. But as I began to feel the invading energy more clearly, I knew it wasn't gonna happen. I was sure then which male it was *specifically* and I almost jumped out of my skin when that particular surety sunk in!

Anderson! Dammit! *Shit!* I maintained my frozen physical state a second longer while I tried to compose myself enough mentally to turn around. *Apparently I wasn't the only one running out of patience!*

"Good evening, Miss Harrington." I heard from behind me. Yup, impatience was currently the driving force there, no doubt! Would that be good or bad for me, I wondered. I still wasn't ready to talk to him face-to-face, but oh well because there he was, dammit.

"Mind if I sit down? I promise I'm not here to press charges, at least not at the moment." He coaxed slyly as he stepped forward and finally made eye contact. "I'd really just like to talk to you if I could." He insisted in his best "*Federal Agent Negotiator*" voice. I wasn't buying it though. He had an agenda for sure. I could feel that plain as day. I just wasn't sure what it was yet.

"Why don't you shoot me an email instead?" I suggested

sarcastically. "Simoneharrington@gmail.com" I provided with a broad smile. He accommodated me and my joke with a quick humorless grin. Then he sat down in the booth across from me anyway.

"Sorry, but I don't really have time for that Miss Harrington." He added tiredly. "And if you care at all about anyone besides yourself, and I think that maybe you do, a very small someone in particular that you are fighting for right now, then you'll hear me out." He challenged. His intent, clearly a play on my protectiveness as a mother, made it crystal clear that he knew one thing about me for sure. My daughters' well-being was priority number one. He was already betting that it was something he could use to try and manipulate me.

I ground my teeth together while I mulled over the risk factor of each available response, but I couldn't help wondering what the Hell he could possibly have to say that he thought I would be interested in! Why was he so confident that I would sit there and listen to him? Was he just underestimating me? Or was I still underestimating him? *Hmmm, careful Simone...* I reminded myself silently. I knew that either one could prove to be catastrophic! I was still considering it all at lightning speed in my head, petrified of making a wrong move. He was definitely a pain in the ass, but he was a *smart* pain in the ass! I would do well to remember that.

"I care about lots of people Agent Anderson, how 'bout you?" I returned trying not to give anything away, but also wanting to feel his response more than hear it.

"Many, *many* more than you would like to give me credit for, Miss Harrington." He declared and somehow it didn't feel like a lie. That confused me a little. Again, *hmmm.*

"Sure, but only the '*right*' people, I bet." I threw out at him. "The ones who do your bidding or go along quietly and don't ask too many questions, right? The rest are simply expendable?" I demanded.

"No, Simone. You've got me all wrong. You're so used to relying on what you *feel* that you have begun to ignore most of what you already know to be true and half of what you see and hear." He threw back giving away even more of his intimate knowledge about me. *Hmpf*, good to know, I thought. He didn't wait for a rebuttal. I could tell that he thought his honesty would go a long way in garnering my trust. Yeah, not so much, but nice try buddy.

"I actually care about the general welfare of *all* the people that I serve, which is every single American citizen, *including* you!" He stated boldly as the waiter walked by and dropped off an icy bottle of foreign beer that I hadn't seen him order along with a glass. Anderson ignored the glass and picked up the sweating bottle to take a long drink. Looking relieved, he sat back and continued to sip for a minute while I mentally digested. I wanted to be disgusted at his use of patriotism to further his underhanded cause, but again it didn't *feel* like an outright lie. And again, I was confused by that.

What the hell did that mean? I knew he was trying to influence and coerce me. I would not make the mistake of forgetting that, but it seemed to be more concern and anxiousness that fueled his weariness, rather than an angry or aggressive energy, like it had been during our last encounter. The only thing currently keeping me in my seat was that confusion and the desire to figure it all out. The problem was that I was pretty sure he knew that, and I had to assume he was using *that* to his advantage as well. But did that make him wrong, or bad? Not necessarily, not that alone anyways. That was even scarier.

He was supposed to be the bad guy. He was supposed to try and manipulate us to further his own agenda. I expected that. I wanted to deny him anything he requested and refuse to encourage his conversation just based on that knowledge and my experiences with him alone. So why did everything he had to say feel sincere? Why was the desire to get more out of him, stronger than the desire to get up and leave? I had to assume that he wanted it that way.

He had finally admitted that he was in fact aware of my *gift*, although not much more, so that must mean he at least knew how it worked. *He had also inadvertently confirmed that he knew such things existed!* So was he forcing those feelings, just to throw me off, to fool or confuse me? If he was, he was damn good at it because I couldn't detect a seam anywhere in the fabric of his tale. *Dammit.* I hadn't counted on that!

I'd always assumed that when I did finally run into him again, he would declare his position clearly as the enemy, just like last time, and I would defend myself and the other innocent's against him. It was a no-brainer. The new *"caring nice guy"* angle was not something that I had been prepared to battle against. Now what? I wondered as I stared blankly at the exit.

Even as I felt my mind protest the bad idea of talking to him, I felt my resolve to keep it black and white give way a little. There was a part of me that felt that *need-to-know* so deeply that it overrode the sensible side, time and again. It was turning out to be another one of those times.

I thought again about the random talk of a cure that he had thrown around at Jeremy too. I had pushed that to the back of my mind, where it could sit without infecting my other thoughts, but I hadn't forgotten about it. How could I? There was still a deep curiosity there I realized, whether I liked it or not.

"What is it that you want, Agent Anderson?" I finally asked going against my better judgment. My goal then was just to keep him the one talking as much as possible.

"I know you want me to be the bad guy here Simone." He provided in a deep and quiet voice as he put his half empty bottle back down on the table. "But I promise you, I'm not." He said plainly, voicing my worst fears aloud and coming off sincerely again. That alone was more frightening than I ever could have imagined!

Only for a moment though as I reminded myself that it just meant that he *believed* it to be true, not that it *was* necessarily. *Careful…*

"I'm just a guy, trying to do his job. You know that job where I'm supposed to 'protect and serve.'" He added as a reminder. "I know you think that's what you're doing too but believe me, it's *not!* All you're doing is endangering more and more people, by avoiding the very people that are qualified to help in a situation like this. Neither of you has the training or even the understanding to deal with the things that I get paid to deal with, and that's the way it's *supposed* to be!" He explained logically.

"Our government spends a lot of time and money properly educating and equipping certain *specific* eligible men and women to efficiently and properly protect its people from harm, all *types* of harm, so that it's citizens re not left to helplessly fend for themselves, whether they are aware of it or not." He said with confidence.

"Not every country can say that, but here in America we are extremely lucky to have that as our reality. It's no small endeavor I assure you but it is a noble intention Miss Harrington, and one that we take as seriously as a protective parent would." He explained using that angle once again. "Not the self-serving plan of some evil underground organization that's out to hurt you, like some would prefer for you to believe. That is the first thing that you need to reevaluate if nothing else! I'll give you a minute to go ahead and rethink it." He added with a slight smile while he went back to downing his beer.

I stared up at him sitting there in his standard grey suit and tie, *really* looked at him. I opened up even more then and *felt* him too, as deeply as I could, trying to get past the easily offered outer layer. I was willing to listen to his tale, but I was staying on high alert. I didn't however intend to follow script and do as I was told, so I spoke up instead.

"I love my country Agent Anderson, and I'm as patriotic as the next guy." I confirmed, thinking that was safe enough. "But I'm not naive enough to believe that the government doesn't occasionally resort to inserting its' own private agenda in order to maintain a '*greater good*' from time to time. I'm quite sure that there are far too many instances where '*by any means necessary*' comes into play in a job like yours. Let's not pretend that we live in a child's fantasy land Agent Anderson." I said hoping to get past his smooth talk once and for all.

"Fair enough." He agreed. "I'm prepared to be completely honest if you are." He challenged smoothly with another grin. I would know if he was or not anyway, but he had no way to be sure that I was. I also knew now that *he* knew that, so I wasn't stupid enough to trust or accept any such deal. It was a "*non-negotiable*" aspect. Nice try though, I thought again with a cheeky grin.

"I have no reason to be otherwise." I offered in my most innocent voice, in direct contradiction to my thoughts. He chuckled lightly.

"Look, I know you're in contact with Mr. Stone, *somehow*. I'll give you both credit, I still can't figure out how you're pulling it off yet, but I know that you are, and *eventually* I will figure it out!" He assured me intently.

"Instead of waiting for that to happen, I'm starting to think that it would be better for all parties involved if you could just talk some sense into him." He said finally putting his cards on the table. I was fine with him doing that. I had no intention of doing any such thing myself.

"I have no idea what you're talking about, Agent Anderson." I said pleasantly, but completely poker-faced. He just smiled knowingly at my denial. I smiled back. He wasn't remotely convinced by that but that was okay. I had given him nothing new and that was my only concern at the moment. His frustration was beginning to show more and more. He shook his head in annoyance but I could feel that he had expected no less from me. That was flattering I supposed, in a backhanded sort of way. Maybe I was getting better at this stuff after all, I thought momentarily. He kept on trudging steadily towards his point, whatever that was.

"This has gone on long enough. I've been very patient and I think extremely generous, in letting so many known accomplices to a federal crime go unprosecuted. That is not because I don't have enough against them to arrest them all either, quite the contrary. It is strictly out of my desire not to cripple this miniscule town by incarcerating nearly 40% of its population that I'm holding off. I could change my mind at any time if I wanted to though, *believe me!* You have to trust me when I say, that's really not my goal here Miss Harrington. My objective is to preserve the safety of the citizens that I protect, *not* to destroy them!" He took a deep breath and another long sip of his beer.

I noticed then that he really did look tired and like he had needed a shower and a shave two and a half days ago. I could feel it more clearly then. The battle was taking its toll on him as well, physically and mentally. We were not alone in our suffering it seemed. The petty side of me wanted to be glad and truth be told, *was* just a little. I really did try to be the bigger person whenever I could but I was only human and I couldn't ignore or forget the past torturous weeks. I also didn't want to feel sorry for him, but I couldn't help that either and I had to admit that I didn't like *that* any better!

I didn't want to accept what I was getting at face value, but I knew he couldn't fake what I was feeling and it was a far cry from what I had felt the last time we'd talked. The anger and fierce determination that had all but defined our last encounter as I sped past him, seemed to have been replaced by a sense of sadness almost, and a weariness. I didn't trust that it would last, though. Anyone could get tired. I also had to wonder how much of that was only allowed to surface specifically for my benefit, to further his cause. As genuine as his attitude appeared to be, I had to at least consider that he was only letting me see it to up his credibility level and I tried to remember to tread lightly.

I still wondered briefly if something had changed, or if I was just suddenly being allowed to see a different side. Right at that moment, it was the persistent weariness that was most prominent in his energy. It lasted for the next few minutes but even as I sat and pondered it, it began to change. I felt the "*good cop*" fade out and the "*bad cop*" tag in.

"But you *are* all keeping me from doing my job right now, and that has gone on long enough." He said slowly... Suddenly his strength was back, full force. "I'm here tonight to tell *you*, Miss Harrington, so you can in turn tell *him*, however it is that you manage to do that..." He added with a humorless "*Jack Nicholson*" kind of grin. "That my patience is running out!" The sagging spirit was completely gone then, replaced with a raw energy that had grown out of desperation and I knew from experience how unpredictable, and therefore dangerous that could be.

"He doesn't need to risk adding more charges than he's already facing to the list. He doesn't need to endanger any more well-meaning citizens than he already has." He added and I knew that one in particular was directed at me personally.

"He just needs to relinquish custody of the patient before this goes any further. Tell him that for me, would you please? For your sake, and your families' sake, as well as the sake of every other innocent bystander in this hardworking little town. His time is running out. He needs to stop hiding behind so many innocent people and do the right thing. Before more *serious* measures have to be taken. Trust me, you all do not want that!" He finished without wavering and the threat was *exceedingly* clear!

He had the power to make all our lives a living hell. No question. He tipped the bottle upside down to finish the last half inch of amber liquid then he placed the empty bottle on the table along with a fifty dollar bill and he stood to leave.

"Have dinner on me. Take some time to think about what I said and what the smartest course of action is here, for *everyone* involved. But not too much time." He warned. "I don't know what I'll do if I find myself starting off another week in this town! If it gets to that point, I'm telling you I won't be responsible for the resulting town-wide fallout, he will." He warned menacingly.

He walked away on that note and worries for every person that I cared about began flying through my head. Jack and his family, all the locals who had stood up for him and tried to help. Would they all be punished, lose their jobs, their homes, for the decisions of a well-meaning few? Could Ethan really live with that? Could *I*?

And how could I hope to spend more time with Liliana if I was constantly afraid for her safety whenever she was in my care? How was I supposed to go forward and not backwards in my relationship with her while this situation was hanging over my head? He had all but asked me that very question outright.

How was I going to spend the next two weeks immersed in the new job like it would require, if I was looking over my shoulder the whole time, or even worse, if I lost 35% of my workforce halfway through?! I had no doubt that he would follow through on his threats if it came to that. He was offering his version of an olive branch, which was the path of least resistance, with the least amount of casualties that still led to what *he* considered to be the inevitable conclusion, our surrender. The desire to do that the easy way didn't necessarily make him a bad guy though.

As I sat considering that, I realized that his unpredictability was truly becoming his most dangerous trait. Once I had put someone in a mental category, I liked for them to stay there but he was proving to be harder than normal to categorize. I was still sure that he couldn't really be "the *good* guy" though. I had no doubts about who "the good guy" was. But I had to at least consider that maybe Anderson was a *"half-relentless/half-decent, just-slightly-misguided*, guy."

Who knew? It really was all relative to your point of view I supposed. I would never let on that he had swayed my opinion of him in any way. I knew better than to give him that advantage. But while I could choose not to acknowledge it, I couldn't *un*-feel it. *Dammit!!*

If I wasn't so completely sure of Ethan and *his* motives, I would probably have been absolutely petrified by that revelation. As it was though, it just confused matters more. They couldn't *both* be the good guy, right? So how did I find out all that I was still missing? How can you protect everyone, without sacrificing anyone? I knew there were reasons for the decisions that the government occasionally had to make. Sometimes good ones, sometimes not, but I got it. I was starting to understand all too well how difficult it could be to enforce situations that you cannot fully explain with anything other than a "*trust me, it's for your own good.*" But that didn't mean that it was okay to let it all go without ever questioning any of it either. I was well aware of the need to keep that mighty imbalance of power constantly in check. Simply having more information and using that information to your own advantage, didn't necessarily make a person *right*.

I also knew that Ethan was as honest with me as he possibly could be, but that there was still a lot that he purposely didn't tell me, that he *couldn't* tell me, simply for my own safety. I understood, but it made it hard for me to defend a position that I rarely ever saw in action firsthand. I knew that essentially he was right to do what he had vowed to do to help, but I couldn't personally vouch for every situation that he engaged in while in pursuit of that goal, just the righteousness of the intent and the worthiness of the end result. Was that really any better than what Anderson did? It certainly felt like it was and I definitely wanted it to be, but he had a way of making me question it and that drove me crazy! *Damn* him!

I was still trying to wrap my head around it all when Gen dropped into the bench that Anderson had vacated only moments before and I was so engrossed in my thoughts that I had actually forgotten for a moment that she was even coming!

"Hi!" She said as she plopped a big stack of books on the table. "I brought some light reading material." She joked before she noticed my expression. As she did though, she stopped smiling. "Hey, everything okay?" She asked warily, worried again and unfortunately for good cause that time.

"I think so." I answered just as nervously. "But according to Anderson, who was kind enough to drop in for a cocktail just a few moments ago, the current tranquility may be short lived." I informed her with the appropriate amount of dread. I stared forward blankly in an attempt to avoid her eyes and the truth of my own statements.

"He was here? He talked to you?" She asked quietly while glancing around the room looking to see who else may have noticed.

"Oh yeah!" I confirmed, giving up on denial and looking her in the eye then. "Sat right down and told me how very understanding he's been, but how all of that kindness is officially about to expire. Wanted me to let *him* know." I added with meaningful eyes. I could feel that she understood.

"What did you tell him?" She asked simply and straight to the point, the lawyer in her emerging as usual in sticky situations.

"Nothing. I kept to the basics." I assured her. She looked up at me and held my gaze for a second during her texting until she was convinced, then nodded approval.

"Is that …?" I asked cryptically, my eyes dropping down to her moving thumbs. I couldn't help wondering if she actually had a direct number for Ethan. I tried not to be jealous, but if she did I needed to know. Once delivered, what he did with the information would be up to him, but I *would* make sure that the message got to him one way or another and I never knew when I would see him next.

"No." She answered sadly and I wasn't sure if I was disappointed or relieved that I wasn't the only one in the dark. I could feel that her sadness wasn't just for herself though. She also felt sad at the knowledge that I didn't have it either. I wasn't sure if that made me feel better or worse. I took a breath and tried to let it go.

She saw my expression and reassured me as much as she could by jotting down a quick note on her napkin. She pushed it over in front of me so I could see it. It said. "I'll tell dad - he'll get word to E." After I read it she pulled it back, tore it up into tiny pieces and stuffed them into my ignored water glass where they proceeded to return to the pulp they had originally started out as. Then she smiled and pulled down the first book.

"Alright, you ready? Let's get to work!" She stated with a perfectly unaffected smile. It definitely ran in the family...

Chapter 13

Once we got past the shock of my unexpected visitor, we pulled ourselves together and got to work on the plans. What else could we do? At least the work took my mind off of the turmoil for the time being, as usual.

I got out the stack of blueprints, schematics and maps and I went through each section with her. As I did, she looked up the codes and ordinances associated with each area. We slowly started to fill in all of the missing pieces and as we went and we ticked things off the list one at a time. Gradually, throughout dinner and then coffee, the pile of plans that were done was growing and the pile of unfinished ones kept shrinking. At one point, while I was filling in the last of the details on a wheelchair ramp that we were adding, I heard Gen chuckle slightly to herself.

"*Hmpf. I should've known…*" She mumbled.

"What's that?" I asked looking up from my task, giving her the other half of my attention. I could feel her amusement and her contemplation of something.

"Oh nothing, just thinking about how much I love our little town and all these people who want to pitch in and make it better. I really am amazed by the sheer volume of volunteers, but I guess I shouldn't be." She answered with a wistful smile.

She wasn't being *dis*honest, she knew better than that, but I could tell that she *was* holding something back. I had no idea what, but I sensed something of a romantic nature and I wondered if maybe she'd had a past relationship with one of the private contractors on the list that she didn't want to discuss. It was a feasible theory since every single one of them were local. Oh well, if that was the case, I was content to let her keep it to herself. We could talk old boyfriends another time.

We kept going. She gave me until closing like she had promised and somehow by the time Joshua was bussing tables and tallying his tips we had miraculously gone through the whole pile.

There were still decisions left to be made and lots of work left for me to do filling in and fine tuning before I handed the plans back to the committee for approval and then eventually onto the individual contractors. But all of that was up to me at that point, and it was all stuff that I knew I could handle.

"Make sure your bill reflects some overtime for the late hour." I insisted as I stood to hug her goodbye.

"Nah, consider it my official *'professional'* contribution to the project." She insisted in return.

"What?!" Are you serious? You don't have to do that! I'm paying for this myself." I argued. "It's not coming out of the budget for the project so you don't have to worry." I insisted, but she didn't budge.

"I really want to. Don't *you* worry! It actually *is* a good write off for me." She joked and in the end I gave up with a heavy sigh.

"Alright then at least let me get this." I insisted calling a truce and grabbing the bill. She wanted to argue but she knew better than to try and win both. "Thank you so much! For *everything!*" I added triumphantly as I hugged her tighter. She hugged me back, full of understanding.

"Don't worry about it, seriously. Just focus on what you have to do and everything else will work itself out." She insisted one last time before she left. I wanted to believe that was possible. I really did.

I dropped the bill down on the fifty that I hadn't touched since Anderson had left it there, and threw three twenties on top of that. I wanted to make sure that most of that fifty just went into the tip. I certainly didn't want his money.

I gathered everything up and drove home on auto-pilot. I

left the radio on, but I didn't pay any attention to it. There was too much in my head already for anything else to fit. Just when I thought I had things even remotely figured out, everything went and changed again! Anderson had just effectively tossed the deck into the air *fifty-two-pickup* style and I had no idea where the cards would fall. I decided then that I had been wrong in my earlier assessment. It wasn't getting easier.

I parked in my usual spot and climbed the stairs with legs that felt too heavy to lift. I dropped my stuff on the island and let out a huge sigh.

"*Don't scream.*" I heard softly from my bathroom, just before Ethan stuck his head out of the doorway.

"*Holy…F…!!*" I exclaimed, cutting myself off mid-swear with a pounding heart. Thank *God* he had at least warned me! I'm sure I *would* have screamed at the top of my lungs otherwise! Instead, I closed my eyes, stood still and held my palms flat on the countertop while I took a few huge, deep breaths. When I felt my heart start to beat normally again I looked back at him. He was completely unfazed.

"I heard you've had an eventful couple of days." He said putting it mildly. "Why don't you come and tell me about it." He invited casually with his arm extended towards me. I could feel his desire to hold me from there, both for my sake and for his own. He hadn't been able to offer me his comfort earlier, but he was offering it then and I didn't need much coaxing to want to be nearer to it. As the feelings that I had been missing so profoundly swept through me, I let out another huge sigh, that time in relief.

I was still a little dizzy from the adrenaline rush of being so surprised and I half walked, half floated over to the bathroom doorway behind that blessed screen, to the one place where we could hold each other freely! It was so incredibly hard to wait to see him in between visits, I could barely describe it adequately. But in the name of balance, it was an equally intense relief whenever he randomly showed up! Like *ten* Christmas mornings in one!

I know I've used that reference before where he is concerned but I just can't think of a better comparison to capture that purest feeling of true joy! It really is the kind of thing you usually only feel as a wide-eyed child. When you can still believe in fairytales and magic! Generally by the time you've made it to adulthood you've seen and learned too much about the real world to be *dazzled* like that anymore. Somehow that was not the case where he was concerned though. He could *dazzle* me without breaking a sweat every time and I just wanted to revel in that! I had missed it *so* much!

Once inside the bathroom he pulled me close and as usual, our first few minutes were spent in a silent, grateful embrace. Before long though, I let out another heavy sigh. I pulled back and looked up at him.

"I need a shower." I announced exhaustedly. I reached up and wearily ran my hand through my hair to pull it away from my face and sighed again. "Join me." I invited. He just growled deep in his throat in response and started to remove clothing, mine as well as his own. I let him handle that while I reached over and turned the water on. We didn't bother to wait for it to warm up. Once we were both undressed, we got in. It was still quite hot and humid out and the tepid stream felt pretty damn good.

I stood in the tub and I leaned back in his arms as the spray poured down onto my neck and chest and I let the water drown it all out a little. He started by rubbing my shoulders and I thought I might pass out from how good it felt! I let out another deep sigh. I don't know how many that was by then. I had lost count.

"How's Liliana?" He asked quietly beside my ear. I knew that he would already know that she was okay physically, and that he meant emotionally.

"She's actually really good." I answered both slightly surprised but also honestly. "Thanks to Oscar. If he hadn't been there to stop me I would have jumped right in after her and things may not have ended so happily." I felt his silent, internal response to such a situation and it was *quite* dramatic! He was full of fear, anger, and a *deep* guilt at not being able to be there himself to keep us both safe. I took a few deep breaths while he reigned it in and then I tried to reassure him that he had left us in good hands.

"Thankfully, he was *right* there, and he knew what to do.

He ignored my panicked outbursts and had her out of there in no time! Of course it still felt like forever to me, but that's no one else's fault. I've never been a big one for being on the sidelines. But I will be forever grateful to him for his quick thinking and his cool head." I laughed then. "Until we got down. Then he made us learn and recite the safety rules like a boot camp instructor!" I could feel that Ethan was still feeling a lot of regret over the situation but he had to laugh at that.

"*Good.* Say it. Learn it. Live it!" He added seriously echoing what Oscar had said and I had to smile.

"Yeah, yeah, no arguments here. I'm just glad we got another chance to learn it the right way instead of the *hard* way." I admitted honestly feeling both grateful and exhausted. I sighed deeply again after letting that one go. He hugged his arms tighter around me for a minute trying to absorb and wipe away what he couldn't change. His desire to make me feel better alone though, did just that.

"All's well that ends well, *thank God!*" I said wanting to get past that particular negativity. "She really seems to be totally fine though. I'm not entirely sure how, but I'm not complaining. Although she may be just a touch too attached to Oscar at the moment." I joked as I rolled my eyes. "Since Beth seems to be pretty well adjusted, I won't worry about that just yet." I added. "One problem at a time." I said sarcastically. I sighed again moving on mentally to the next one.

"I'm sorry. I'm really trying not to be a total Debbie Downer, but having Anderson show up at The Tavern earlier, after the day I had yesterday, just capped it off!" I said with a humorless laugh.

"I get it. When it rains it pours, right?" He asked beside my ear again with a slight chuckle as the water poured down on us both.

"*Mmm hmm.*" I confirmed. Anderson says 'Hi.' by the way." I added backhandedly. "Spent a fair amount of time trying to convince me that he's not the bad guy here. That he really just wants to help. Sound familiar?" I asked with a flick of my eyebrows as I turned around to face him.

"*Mmmm.* Always divide and conquer with him." He bit off, allowing a little anger to show through for a change. I took that in and continued.

"What he really wanted, was for *me* to tell *you*, '*somehow…*'" I said with an eyebrow wiggle and a sly grin of my own. "That you need to turn Jeremy and yourself in and *soon*! Otherwise his extremely generous patience in not arresting half the local population is going to expire and he will not be responsible for the town-wide carnage that ensues." I informed him plainly.

"That's not exactly verbatim, but I think you get the gist." I sighed again. "So *now* what?" I asked wearily as I laid myself against his solid frame once more, resting my cheek on his chest. The thought of it all being over "*soon*" was more than a little appealing to me, I had to admit. But of course that all depended greatly on *how* it ended!

He sighed deeply himself but didn't speak right away. That was not surprising since I knew full well by then that he would never talk just to fill the silence. I was used to that already. I was still surprised though when he took the shampoo and poured some in his hands and started to wash my hair!

He massaged the lather gently through my scalp with his fingertips, making small, slow circles from my forehead to the nape of my neck. Then he worked it all the way down through the ends while I continued to rest languidly against him. He picked up the removable shower head, tipped my chin up just slightly, and carefully rinsed it all out. Next he took the conditioner and after spreading it in his hands, he gently massaged it through from scalp to tip once more. I breathed slow and deep while he rinsed it one last time. It was the most luxurious thing that I had ever felt without having to leave someone a tip and I smiled up at him when he was done.

"Way to change the subject." I teased, but he just smiled in return. He reached for the soap then and began to fill a loofah with its lather. He handed that loofah to me and repeated the process on a second loofah for himself. Don't ask me why, but I always seemed to have at least three or four of them hanging around at a time. Honestly, it was probably mostly for the happiness that the color combinations gave me. Either way I had them and I was glad for that as we spent the next few minutes "*exfoliating*" each other quite thoroughly.

It really *was* a good way to change the subject. We stuck to that task alone for the most part of the next ten minutes or so, but we were definitely a little more thorough in some areas than others. He took the shower head down again and sprayed us both off after our "painting with lather" session, then set it back in its' cradle.

Then he reached for the soap again and my razor and sat down on the edge of the tub. I had no idea what he was thinking until he pulled my left leg up and rested my foot on his knee. He worked up a new lather in his hands, then he began to slowly apply it from my ankle, up my calf and higher, over my thigh. I had to laugh then.

"*Seriously?* This is my life now? I go from total deprivation to utter *decadence*? This can't be for real Ethan. You have to stop!" I insisted, thinking it wouldn't be good to get too used to that kind of lavish spoiling.

"Don't worry." He assured me. "I have an ulterior motive, so it's not *completely* selfless." He admitted with a wicked grin and for the first time since he had reached out to me in the doorway, I felt him give the heat free reign. It made its' way through me unrestricted and as my heart pounded violently against my ribs I wondered at the sudden intensity. My breath abandoned my chest as usual, leaving me to gasp helplessly for replacement air while I considered it. *Whoa*!

"I've been thinking about something lately." He admitted aloud then, very calmly. "Stop me whenever you want." He instructed as he started going even higher up my inner thigh with the bar of soap.

"*Ahhhh*... I see." I said with a knowing grin as his hand slid even higher. I knew what he was so excited about then at least. I was aware that people currently did a lot more "*grooming*" in that area than just shaving their bikini line. Having been married through the years when such things had become popular, and a complete non-participant for some time after that, I hadn't bothered to keep up with the latest trends. I honestly hadn't even considered it.

But I could feel the way *he* felt about it! Once I kept myself from falling over the side of the tub, that excitement suddenly convinced me that it might be a worthwhile experiment, at least temporarily. I just smiled and held my breath. He took that for what it was and he got to work. He started at my ankle again with the razor and made his way up my calf slowly, gently. He was doing a really good job and I was happy to assume that his skill level was simply the result of years spent shaving his face. If not, I decided that I didn't want to know. He made it up to my thigh and I started to wonder nervously if I should stop him after all, but as many times as the words passed through my mind, they never made that crossover from mental thought to verbal protest.

I had no idea how far he intended to go, but I figured that whatever happened, even if I hated it, it would grow back. His desire ramped up another *thousand* or so notches with the first stroke of the razor over that most *delicate* of areas and it was officially too late to turn back. That left me free to stop fighting the current of indecision and just commit to experiencing it fully instead.

Another wave of his excitement washed over me and I dove in mentally on the rise and decided to just ride it out. It was always an amazing challenge with his unusually strong feelings anyway, but that time it was much more of a bull-ride than I was used to, alternately wild and tame.

That was due to how seriously he was taking his task. His unflappable control came back out repeatedly to reign in the excitement while he worked. Over and over I felt the intense heat of the scorching fire, then the alternating calm as it would come flooding in to tamp the flames, allowing him to maintain his steady hand throughout his ministrations.

I took slow, deep breaths through it all and I watched fascinated as he *very* carefully sculpted a masterpiece. At least that's what you would think he was doing just based on the concentration level. I was pretty glad for that focus though. I did *not* want to have to explain a mishap of that nature in the E.R. I thought in a momentary panic while he put one foot down and picked up the other. I would have to leave the entire *state* after something like that!

He was careful though and he was *thorough!* By the time he finished, both of my legs were perfectly smooth from top to bottom, as was the entire *under*side of my "*bikini*" area. The remaining patch left in the front was a perfectly shaped inverted triangle. I was grateful for that since I had no desire to look completely pre-pubescent. I was quite relieved that he obviously didn't want me to either. He left just enough for it to be perfectly clear that I was a fully grown woman.

"Nice work." I complimented honestly while looking down at it. I moved around a little in an awkward fashion getting used to the new *super-naked* feel of it. It was different for sure, but not necessarily in a *bad* way. I wondered then if the same attitude applied to his grooming or if it was another one of those *double-standard* kind of things, so I backed up a step to blatantly check it out.

He knew right away what I was thinking and he was happy to spread out and oblige me with a better view. I had seen enough of him to know that I had no complaints with the hardware, but taking a moment to appreciate the detailing for the first time *specifically*, I could see that he was a steady hand at it for a reason. I pursed my lips and nodded at the area that, while not completely bald on him, was cleaned up nicely with the surrounding areas tightly trimmed. It only reinforced my previous approval status.

"Again, I have to say, *I'm a fan.*" I offered pleasantly surprised.

"I am truly a man of many talents." He teased with that wicked grin and we both laughed.

The heat abated a bit for the moment but that was okay. It was really nice just having him there, teasing me. It helped me to decompress in ways that I still didn't even understand. His presence worked magic for me like no one else's, whether he was singing or not. There was just no denying that. I had missed my magician, for sure, I thought with a grin at my old, oddly appropriate nickname for him.

He stood up and we both rinsed off again and then he shut

the water off. He reached out and grabbed us each a towel and we wrapped ourselves up in them. I stepped over the edge of the tub and then sat back down on the side. I wanted to stay in that mental space where things were light and fun but it was really hard to maintain with all that was hanging over our heads. He looked down at me.

"You okay?" He asked seriously and I didn't bother to hold back.

"I'm worried Ethan. What's going to happen to all of those people that just wanted to help? What's going to happen to Jack, or Dr. J, and Gen? Will they lose clients when they are dragged through court, guilty until proven innocent in the public eye? What about their families? What's going to happen to Jeremy if they get a hold of him? What about this job that I'm supposed to be committed to for the next two weeks? How can I do that now? How can I *not* do that now?" I begged and he just listened, wisely sensing that I just needed to unload.

"What about Liliana? My first thought when I couldn't find her was that someone, maybe some frustrated agent looking for a new angle against us had taken her. I don't want to have to think that way, but I *do* and I hate it! How am I going to keep her safe if I'm not sure it's safe for her to be here with me? How could I keep her away when she loves it here so much and I want her here more than anything? Will I have to give up even more time with her than I already have in order to keep her from harm's way? I will, if it becomes necessary, but how will I ever explain that to her, or to *Ben* who's always ready to assume the worst?" I questioned.

"I have all of this swimming around in my head now on top of everything else! And I know that you want to tell me that all of that is going to be okay, but even if that were somehow true, it still only solves half of my problem. Because besides all of that, I'm mostly worried about how you're going to handle it all. What are *you* going to *do*, to try and protect everyone else Ethan? Because I know for sure that you will do *something!*" I stood up in front of him.

"*Ethan.*" I said holding his face in my hands for a change.

"What's going to happen to *you?* You think that part doesn't matter, but you're wrong! You're *wrong…*" I finished passionately, staring up at him with my heart in my eyes.

He didn't speak. I could feel everything though, everything he wasn't saying. He was worried too, and he was determined that he would do whatever he had to do, to protect them all *and* me, first and foremost. It was exactly what I had expected.

"I don't know what I'm going to do yet." He finally answered, honestly as usual. "But I promise you that I will figure it all out before it's too late. Neither you, or anyone else here has to worry." He assured me with his normal confidence and that ever-pleasant smile firmly in place. He knew he was alone there at the moment though.

"Seriously Simone. Don't worry about me." He requested. He looked down at me again and I could feel his deep desire to make everything right without his inevitable resulting punishment affecting me. "*Please!*" He added more desperately, as he closed his eyes and rested his forehead on mine. He knew he couldn't save everyone from being hurt if the repercussions he faced in order to do that ended up hurting *me.* That would only allow him to help everyone *but* me, and I could tell that that was unacceptable to him. You'd think that would've made me feel better, but it didn't. I knew it just meant that I made it even harder on him.

I sighed and squeezed my own eyes shut against the pain that I felt seeping from him even though I also felt his deepest wish that it wouldn't. It wasn't something he could control, not then, not with me.

"Sorry. There's nothing I can do about that Ethan. Some things just aren't optional, you know?" I said with a wink, being my stubborn self. "I *care* what happens to you! It *will* affect me, whether I want it to or not! I'm just going to have to learn to deal with that, and so are you." I said again really wishing I could do more to ease his pain, just like I knew he wished he could do more to ease mine. That was love right there though I realized, in its' purest form. It was that true, deepest desire to make life better for another person in any way possible, regardless of the personal cost. Only neither of us could accept a personal cost without it affecting the other. In our case it was a real bitch of a catch 22!

I dropped my towel and I leaned myself up against him. I wrapped my arms around his neck as I stretched up to my tip toes in an attempt to reach his lips with my own. He didn't like my statement but he still leaned down to help me in my endeavor. He was okay with fulfilling *that* particular desire.

"In the meantime, I would really like to spend some time appreciating you in every possible way, while I have the chance!" I whispered against his cheek. His response was quick and it took me out at the knees as usual! Fortunately he knew enough at that point to hold tight around my waist as the ripple hit me. I held on even tighter to his neck and my lips blindly found the pulse in his throat just above the Adams' apple that was currently bobbing up and down in an attempt to swallow his own wave of pain. We melted to the floor.

Ethan stretched his legs straight out in front of him, filling up the entire space. I bent my knees as I ascended and ended up draped over his lap. He reached into the closet where we kept the almost empty "*party pack*" and I raised myself up to allow him access. When he was done I settled back down. I looked him in the eye again, the desire from both of us pouring freely through me. As it reached my hands I raised them up, spread my fingers wide and ran them through his hair on both sides at the same time. He closed his eyes.

"I should cut this for you." I offered, typically off topic.

"Can you?" He asked, opening one eye. He was genuinely surprised and intrigued as usual and I still loved that. I nodded. "Next time it will be my turn to play barber." I stated with a wicked grin and he smiled.

"*...and today's curveball is...*" He whispered with a slow shake of his head and a smile. Then he pulled me down to him again and nibbled on my lower lip. I forgot everything else for a long time after that. Sometime later I do remember him admiring his handiwork while I was doing all of the *real* work! But I didn't mind because I was admiring the results of it as well! I had to admit that the new, *incredibly* smooth sensation was strange, but definitely *ve-*

heeeerry nice!

"*Whoa! Huh*, who knew?" I wondered aloud as a shiver visibly ran through me. He cleared his throat and grinned mischievously while his brows bounced up and down at that. I felt his enjoyment as strongly as I could see it.

"Oh. *Hmpf... ...right.*" I allowed with an easy smile. "*Hmmm*, good call!" I confirmed giving credit where credit was due but I didn't stop to discuss it any further. I could feel him agree wholeheartedly.

The ride on his emotions after that was even wilder than it had been earlier! I just tried to remember to hold on. It surpassed every amusement park ride that I had ever known in its exhilaration level, so I had no more clever comparisons there!

The situation was still less than ideal, and I might need an extra oxygen tank handy to get through it, but I could not think of one thing *more* worth being breathless for!

Chapter 14

Thursday morning I finally met with the caretaker Daniel, and spent the day going through the entire sight in person. We met early and I had completed my first actual walk through of all of the interior spaces by 9:00 AM. Daniel was a fairly small guy, a few inches shorter than me even, but he had a perfectly proportionate body. He had a small head and a compact round jaw that matched his miniature, taut, tanned calves. From top to bottom he was just all-around petite, like he had stopped growing somewhere around thirteen and had been the same size ever since.

Although it was clear that he was not thirteen, he did have a pleasant, young looking face that went along with the body and he still had all of his thick, shiny hair which was mostly still as brown as his kind eyes. I knew that he had been married for some forty odd years to his high school sweetheart because Marina thought it was a fantastic and important fact and had shared it when she was telling me about him originally.

I could already tell that he wasn't the kind of guy that yearned for what he didn't have. He struck me immediately as someone who was always focused on being grateful for what he *did* have. That attitude had obviously given him many years of true happiness and I had wondered as we talked why more people didn't live that way.

He had taken me on a tour through each building on the property as he casually explained its history to me. By early afternoon I learned that the property covered over forty seven acres in total, although the majority of that was there within the hill. He told me about how it was the first settlement in the area since the Indians and how it began with the textile mills that sprang up along the creek which ran from Johnson's pond down to the Merrimack River.

"Those mills were originally run by an extremely affluent gentleman from the Vail family from over in Haverhill, but would later become the property of the Breezey family. It was 1873 when Arthur Breezey, one of five children who grew up in Charlestown, Mass., first began working for the owner of the mills by pure chance and circumstance. Some say it was fate." He narrated proudly and I tried to hide the chills that ran through my body.

"He was already commuting up from the city to work as a clerk in the Haverhill post office and had recently switched over to a better position as a clerk in a wholesale glass and crockery store. He would ride the train back and forth every day and it was during one such commute that he happened to sit across from one Ezekiel James Madison Vail. He had so sufficiently impressed the refined gentleman by the end of that infamous ride, that he was rewarded with the offer of a position as his personal carriage driver on the spot. Being the shrewd business man that he always was, he took it on the spot. He was later brought up here to live and work in South Pinegrove." He informed me proudly. The history lesson continued as we strolled.

"Arthur was an ambitious man but also an honest and extremely hard working man so he continued to advance through the company just as quickly, learning everything he could about the industry along the way. He was leading a very successful life by the time he met and married Lara in 1883. They went on to have three children together, a son they named Arthur Vail, and twin daughters, Malory Paulette and Lara Jacine." He just kept on walking as he talked but it tickled me the way he could recite their full names with such ease, like they were family to him. It was obvious that telling that story was something that he enjoyed and would happily do a lot more of if he got the chance. I just grinned and followed him. If they ever decided to hire a tour guide, I knew who it should be.

"When the original owner of the mills died in 1881, Arthur

was placed in charge of the company and awarded a substantial salary. He worked tirelessly in that position for eleven years before he finally managed to purchase the company with a relative of the owner, Benjamin Vail as his partner. It was just over a decade after that, that he bought his partner out and became the sole proprietor." There was a quiet pride emanating from Daniel as he stood silently smiling up at the "proprietor's" massive likeness in oil that hung in the great hall where we had stopped. I waited quietly and let him have his moment. After a beat or two he started walking again.

"He was a notorious workaholic but he was also an avid outdoorsman who liked to play just as hard. He preferring hunting and camping over relaxing on a beach somewhere during his free time. He first built a home in the city near his parents. It was huge and built *"in the very best manner possible"* for that day-and-age." He shared using air quotes. "It covered six city lots and was designed to fit of a man of his newly acquired stature. It wasn't long however, before he added the bungalow here in Pinegrove as a *"daily"* residence that suited him a lot better. It also allowed him to finally avoid the tedious commute back and forth. He wanted his family to be able to enjoy it too, at least during the summer months." He explained over his shoulder.

"His built his home on the edge of this property, which at that time was being used by a local dairy." He added turning back towards me as we walked. We passed through the original living room and dining room that were right out of a museum with the stonework on the fireplace and the surrounding deeply stained handcrafted paneling that covered all the interior walls. The furniture in the room was not really as old as the building but it *looked* like it was as it was obviously all handpicked to reflect the period. They were solid pieces made of roughhewn wood and classic colored heavy-weight fabrics. The kind that could have come from the textile mills back then.

"He built his arts and crafts style bungalow, high up on the hill here to take advantage of the cooler summer breezes." He told me leading me in through the long screened in porch. "He even went so far as to utilize many of the mill workers during the slower months to complete the construction as fast as possible." He added smiling.

"The arts and crafts movement of the time was fed by the desire to go against the excesses of the Victorian era and to get back to basics. This home made a nice contradiction to the pomp and circumstance of their 'official' home in the city." He provided, and I could easily understand what he meant as I took in the small size of the rooms and appreciated the simplicity of the beautiful woodwork. It reminded me again of the task of trying to restore someone else's craftsmanship but I chose not to think about that challenge at the moment.

"This home, like others of this style, was designed using natural materials like exposed wood and stonework to fit in with the land around them." He said with an obvious interest and knowledge on the topic. As he explained about the original craftsmanship we stopped in the dining room and I felt as if I were in the very heart of the building, protected by other rooms on all sides. That would be "home base" there, I decided then. We moved on but I had to take a few looks back as we left the older sections of the building and entered the newer additions.

"Lara actually liked it here so much that they began to stay here with the children as long as the seasons would allow. They even added a second cottage for the in laws so they could have extended visits with their grandchildren during their stays. The grounds around the cottages were further developed by that time with the addition of a tennis court and various flower gardens. Lara herself cultivated the most amazing sunflowers here! They feature prominently in the background of a lot of the old photos." He grinned while peering out one of the many windows at the unruly gardens in their current disarray. I could almost see it as it had once been, just as I knew he could.

As we walked he told me about how the mills saw their years of great success, at one point even being responsible for providing blankets for the Union soldiers during the civil war. "Over time however their machines became outdated and the fabrics that they produced grew less desirable than the newer softer fabrics that were coming out and eventually they were all closed down." He said matter-of-factly.

"Arthur passed away at seventy two. He had been sick for some time before that. After his passing, the family sold the property here and moved back into the main house in the city full-time. The property changed hands a number of times after that in the 1950's before it was eventually sold to a group of Italian catholic nuns who, recognized the peacefulness of the area. They planned to create a novitiate for young Italian women considering the church as an avocation." He informed me. I was a little surprised by that but it was believable there, for sure.

"Unfortunately for them, the reputation of The States during the turbulent 60's made it hard to convince Italian woman that it was a peaceful place to travel to for this purpose." He laughed at that and I could feel him remembering that time in his own life but he didn't elaborate. He moved on.

"While they were searching for a new mission they agreed to use the property to help out a group of local women in dire straights. Specifically a group of special needs women who had been locked away in a mental hospital in Danvers for most of their days, simply because no one knew what else to do with them for one reason or another. Some of these women had spent their entire lives there until it was finally, mercifully closed down. That unfortunately left them even worse off than they were before though as they went from being tortured, used and abused, to being completely helpless, neglected and homeless. The nuns had officially found their mission." He said with a smile as if he was personally proud of them. That sad story immediately reminded me of a similar one but I shook that off too, as fast as I could.

"Anyway, over the next thirty five years the nuns added this whole "*East Wing*" onto the main building and converted some of these larger rooms here into dormitories for the women and the summer camp programs that they later added as well." He explained as we passed through the long hallway and I could almost feel the comradery of those women as we went. "Eventually they also added a pool, a large vegetable garden and yet another separate cottage where visiting priests could be housed." He pointed to the small cottage to the left as we walked outside.

"The local children have always naturally flocked to the big hill out front for sledding, even back then." He said gesturing towards the hill that I had stood atop just days ago. "The sisters never discouraged them but invited them instead. Because of that it was nicknamed "*Pope's Hill*" by the children, which it still is today." He finished with a smile. I could feel how much he enjoyed telling the story and I could see why. It was the story that went along with all of the good feelings that I had picked up there. It was a *good* story.

"The disabled women, distraught families and young campers escaping the oppressive heat of the city, all knew a time full of peace and healing while they stayed there. It was that feeling that the sisters knew existed originally that they had always intended to share, and they eventually did fulfill that purpose. Inevitably though, the needs of that group of women who had started it all, became to be too much in their elderly years to be properly cared for by the nuns anymore. A few had already passed of old age and the rest finally had to be placed in qualified medical facilities to finish out their days." He added sadly.

"After that the nuns decided it was time to sell the property and use that profit to fund their next mission from God, whatever that would turn out to be. By then the property was quite impressive and the town was eager to take possession of it. It wasn't an easy acquisition however, since by the 1990's the property was valued at $954,000! The town simply could not afford that."

"It took over two years to negotiate and raise the funds necessary to buy this place for the town but they finally pulled it off with only $160,000 of that money actually coming out of the town's own pockets. The rest was either donated from various sources or raised at specific events. But the largest donation in the end was made by the remaining living Breezey family members themselves in their last will and testament. Their donation came with only one request. That was that the property would be permanently renamed Breezey Park after the man who first saw the potential in the property for more that industry and settled there. Given their part in the town's history already it was an easy decision. A deal was finally struck, hands clasped, ink slashed across parchment." He said somewhat dramatically, enjoying his tale. That was just fine though, so was I.

"In the town's hands the property thrived at first with the promise of so many great things being touted as future possibilities. But without someone experienced to fix it up and run it properly, and with every single decision or expenditure requiring a full committee meeting, things quickly fell to the wayside and energies along with attentions slowly went elsewhere. It was one of the best collective ideas the town had ever had, but with no plan in place for the follow-through, it lost momentum." He finished with a resigned acceptance and a shrug of his small shoulders. Marina had been absolutely right about that it seemed, in that everything just took way too long to accomplish for any one person to stick it out on a regular basis.

Even with all of the history and the living that the place had witnessed over the years, he told me that he was and had been the only person doing any type of maintenance at all to the place for the last four years. I could see why that bothered everyone so much. According to him his duties lately had consisted simply of plowing the main road in the winter, turning the water on and off to keep pipes from freezing, and mowing the lawn just around the main buildings to maintain access. They were the things of bare necessity and not much more.

We had wrapped up our tour and I had shook his hand and thanked him earnestly for all his help. His insight had been invaluable to me and I told him so. Then I rushed home to eagerly finish up the remaining plans. By dinnertime they were all completed for the estate as a whole. I had them couriered back to Marina so she could get them to the Conservation Committee A.S.A.P. for approval.

When I got back I was exhausted so I used the time while I waited to hear back from her to check out mentally for the night. I slept deeply and stubbornly until I felt recharged enough physically to open my eyes.

I knew I had needed it but I was still frazzled when I woke later than I would have liked on Friday. I immediately checked my phone with one eye and flew out of bed when I saw the message that I had been waiting for was there! *It was a go!*

I threw on the first items of clothing that I could reach and grabbed the plans and stuffed them in my leather case. I had already separated everything by job, and I just needed to get it all copied and sent off, piece by piece, to all of the appropriate contractors. I headed out to my local "office supply" store and had it all reproduced, separated and ready to hand deliver by lunchtime. Then I took my first deep breath in days!

The plans for the new roof on the main building as well as the gazebo were off to ABC Roofing. Plans for the new bathrooms in the function hall were on their way to Burnett & Sons Plumbing right over on Rt. 97, as were the plans for the outdoor fountain and the new locker rooms that would be built downstairs to facilitate both the exercise classes and the weddings that we hoped they would host again in the future.

There were separate spec's with the details about which areas of the main house were too rotted away to be saved, where there was structural damage that needed to be gutted and rebuilt. That category included the main building as well as many of the other structures on the property and was one of the biggest piles. That oversized stack had gone off to the Rock Construction Company in one of the biggest envelopes the store had.

The long list of which windows were to be replaced, along with the specific dimensions for each one, went into a slightly smaller envelope and was sent off to a local artisan whose business was called Affordable Restorations. He was not only right in town, but he had also promised to reproduce the original period designs exactly. That was already invaluable but the fact that he was donating the custom vintage windows along with the installation, put it over the top.

The list went on and on, but once all of the dividing and addressing was done, I left and still managed to get to Juniper a few minutes early to pick up Liliana. We stopped at the market on the way home and made it in and out without going down a single interior isle. We went around the perimeter of the store once and we were done! It was perfect.

Back to my place I made us a real dinner of chicken parm

and salad and I turned a sub roll into the perfect garlic bread for us to share with a little garlic butter and a sprinkle of fresh oregano. We sat quietly and ate and enjoyed the peace and quiet for a while after the excitement of her last visit.

We stayed with the calm and quiet theme since I could tell it was one of those days when she was completely tuckered out from camp. We watched her new favorite movie "Meet the Robinsons" then called it an early night. There was generally that small hope in the back of my mind as my head hit the pillow that Ethan would show up and join me, but I knew that would never be the case on a Friday so I let it go faster than I usually did. I slept great while dreaming about it though, even though that's all it was.

By Saturday morning I had received the confirmation that all the packets had been delivered and I was immensely relieved. With that accomplished every contractor had the weekend to make sure they had the necessary supplies on their individual job list before we got started on Monday. Most of what ended up in the final plan they had pre-planned for themselves anyway, so I knew it shouldn't be too challenging for any one, but for the moment it was in their hands.

On that note, I had my own ordering/gathering to attend to for the outdoor areas that I was working on, but since my parts wouldn't start until day three, I knew I had enough time to spend the morning at the riding paddock with Liliana as she began to reacquaint herself with Cookie. Judging by how happily the horse pranced around and the way she nudged her with her nose repeatedly, I started to think that maybe Jack hadn't been entirely kidding when he said how much she missed Liliana. After they got their affection in, she walked her around the paddock for a while, occasionally stopping to feed her a slice of apple.

After a half hour or so, Liliana finally felt ready to hop back on and they rode around together for the last half hour until it was time to bring her home.

When I got back home I sat at the island with my laptop and ate a sandwich while I ordered everything that I would need. I had left myself the rest of the day to get it done but it had turned out to be easier than I had expected. It was partially because my job supplies were actually limited to plants and such that time around, and partly because Liliana had requested a specific color that had already given me my theme. That made it easier to narrow my choices down and by 3:30 I was done and back to doing nothing but waiting so I decided to go for a walk.

It was too hot but I was too bored to care. It just made me move slower. Despite that I was still back by 5:30, not knowing what to do with myself. I showered and even dried my hair just to kill a little more time. Then I grilled a chicken breast and some asparagus for dinner and ate it while I got caught up on the latest episodes of my favorite true crime shows. That took me well into the night and I went to bed with the usual hopes of a visit, but the next thing I knew, it was morning. At least being up late helped me to sleep late on Sunday and I was happy that it was almost noon already. Every little bit helped when all you had was time.

I cleaned the apartment again but that didn't take as long as I would have liked either. I paced. A lot. I stared out the windows, mentally trying to avoid the cameras without knowing exactly where they were. I walked the orchard and saw all the apples that were beginning to turn red. I thought about what Ethan may have come up with to save everyone, and if he'd pull it off. I cringed. I shook myself out of that mode and didn't allow it to come back. I washed my car. I even vacuumed it and did the windows too! I cooked again, but it was only pasta with a mushroom sauce, so it didn't take long. I was so hungry by then that it didn't take long to eat either. I sighed. A lot. I turned the TV back on and click, click, clicked.

At about 8:00 I finally gave up on the TV and went to bed. I tossed around a lot, but I didn't dream so thankfully I still felt rested. I was so happy that it was finally time to start when I woke up that I practically flew out of bed! It was still *super* early, but I didn't even bother to try and get back to sleep. I knew it would be pointless. Instead I jumped in the shower and then threw on my work clothes in the dim morning light without even remembering my audience for once, I was so excited.

Driving over I tried not to focus on the fact I still had no idea what was going to happen with Anderson. Until that changed in some way I had to just continue forward. I hadn't heard from or seen Ethan since I had told him so I had no choice but to wait to find out what he would do along with everybody else.

Thankfully, I had no time to waste worrying about it. I had to keep moving. A lot of people had each dedicated a certain amount of man hours to their part of the job, but they all had regular, bill-paying jobs and schedules to keep outside of that. If we didn't plan it out just right, we could end up missing someone's small window of availability all together and have say, a playground full of PVC piping and plumbers who didn't have another free day until the fall.

That was a very real possibility and it was nerve-wracking to say the least. Especially with Anderson's newest angle threatening to punch holes all over the all-important schedule. And it certainly didn't help my nerves any that the whole process was going to be filmed either! Every misstep or outright disaster would be preserved forever for prosperity. That thought gave me the *least* amount of comfort, especially with a possible appearance from Anderson looming largely in the cards!

I shook it off again and did what I had done for the past two days, I focused on the work. It was all I could do. I had to stay productive. Being the control freak that I am, I had entered everything onto my laptop when I finished it and created a spreadsheet with a chart of every plan for every area. Then I color-coded the whole thing to make it easier to grasp visually as a whole. I started with what things would get done by whom, and then I numbered them all as to what order they would need to get done in. It had taken me more than a few hours to do it, but when I finally finished I had felt a lot calmer and I knew that it had been well worth the effort.

From that chart I extrapolated a schedule that listed every task, from miniscule to gargantuan, and ordered them from the first day of work to the last. Everyone had a hard copy of the master plan along with the detailed plans for their own parts and each had received and approved their personal section of the schedule.

If it wasn't on there, then it wasn't going to happen because the schedule accounted for every single minute of every day for the next two weeks. It even included plans for the few groups that would be working overnight shifts, like the ones refinishing the original hardwood floors. The schedule was *that* tight!

It was going to be the key to a successful outcome there, whether I was around to personally enforce it or not. I had made it close to fool-proof though so if someone else did have to step in and take over, they would be able to follow it easily enough and things should stay on track. Well, provided a giant chunk of our workforce didn't all go away at the same time that I did. I wasn't really sure *what* we would do then.

Since all of the services being rendered were also being donated, I couldn't see any way to set up "back-ups" to replace them all on a moments' notice, should we need to. There was just no budget for something like that. But until that particular disaster struck, I couldn't afford to spend time on it. All we could do I thought resignedly to myself, was stick to the schedule as long as it was possible.

I rested my hand on it where it currently sat in my case on the seat next to me along with my own parts of the plans, and I embraced the fact that for the foreseeable future it was going to be both my warden and my new best friend.

I took a deep cleansing breath and then I gathered everything up and climbed out of my car. I stood and stared up at the run-down structure. *Day one*, it begins, I thought. It was petrifying but also exhilarating at the same time. That was always the scariest and the most exciting part. The very beginning when the desired result is nothing more than a vague concept, a plan, a faint wish that exists only in your head. Where that risky leap of faith was still required in order to make it from where you were currently standing, to where you hoped to end up.

It was always inspiring to me and invigorating as well, but the fear remained just the same, whether it was my first job or my fiftieth. I inhaled deeply once more, as deeply as I could, then I let it out heavily and began my journey up the row of cement steps toward the main building.

I looked down at my feet as I went, concentrating on the oversized steps. Each one was its' own square platform that led you up to the next, and each step was placed slightly askew from the previous one creating a gentle curve up the side of the hill. I took my time and tried to remain focused on judging the odd distance between them correctly and on that "first day" energy. I made sure to ignore Mary as she whispered in my ear that it could also turn out to be the "*last day*," on the job, or any other. I knew it may be true but I refused to stop and consider it. Those musings simply did me no good.

I took a few deep breaths and worked to remain neutral as I climbed. The higher I got though the more the sense of history began to filter through me, reminding me of what I had felt in the gazebo. The joy, the laughter, the excitement of the good times. I clung to that and paid even closer attention as I combed it for any blatant negativity. Just like last time though, I found none.

I wanted to always be aware of the history there, but most of all I wanted to make sure to renovate in a way that would be useful to the present. It was important to keep my focus on that goal because old impulses could unduly influence me if I wasn't careful and prove useless to current needs. So I was listening, but consciously filtering.

I reached the last step and I turned back to take in the view from the top of the hill. I could see past the lot all the way out to the main road, and through the thinnest section of the woods behind the lot all the way up to Johnson's Pond. I just stood and took it all in. It was still hot but thankfully that day hot meant low-eighties and not high-nineties. It was actually a nice break and almost felt cool. Of course it's all relative.

The only other car pulling in the lot so far was Daniel's, the friendly, knowledgeable caretaker. He was back there that morning to give me my temporary set of keys and I found I was looking forward to seeing him again. He was a kind and nurturing soul and I didn't dread his presence at all empathically which was nice, but I knew it would take him a few minutes to reach my location so I used the time to absorb my surroundings a little more.

There was a certain sense of accomplishment just in standing at the top looking down, I noticed first off. I was sure then that that was a big part of why the property stood way up there where it did to begin with, besides having better "*air flow*." It was that "king-of-the-mountain" syndrome that I felt the most from that vantage point, I realized happily. I smiled at that and tried to stay optimistic.

I saw Daniel approaching then and I remembered feeling his initial curiosity about me as he had wondered why I would want to take on such a job in the first place. He didn't know me as well as Marina did yet, I thought with a chuckle to myself, itching to get started. She wasn't due for another couple of hours but I didn't intend to wait.

"Good morning Miss Harrington." He said congenially as he approached.

"Morning." I replied.

"Right this way." He said waving his deeply tanned hand in the direction of the main entrance as he prepared to lead me the last few steps. On the way, I decided to learn a little more about the only other person that had been putting energy into the place recently, since the previous day all we had talked about was the property.

"So how long have you lived in Pinegrove Daniel?" I asked curiously.

"Oh, all my life! I grew up here, born and raised!" He proclaimed proudly. "Right down the road from here actually." He said pointing in the direction that I had come from. "Parents still live there in fact. My own place is a few streets away now." He added with a humble smile. It was neither a boast nor something he would hide. Pinegrove was simply "*home*" to him, nothing more nothing less. I remembered seeing a few rather nice homes along the main road though leading up to the property, that I knew had to be quite old just due to the distances between them.

Modern day construction was something else, a totally different mindset. Thankfully that was somewhat less prevalent around there, but in most places now a days, if they could find a way to make it stand up in the space between two objects, they would build it. That area however was not only in a town that didn't adhere to that philosophy, but was also on one of those older roads that still had some woods or fields separating each of the large properties like the Kent's, and Breezey Park. I was glad then that his family owned one of those grand places and that he seemed to have the same type of care for the town that I already did. That *so* many did, I was realizing more and more that there really were good reasons for that.

I would wonder sometimes, at the loyalty that people show to a group or a place, but not there. Not anymore. It was quite clear by then how people felt about that town, and *why*.

Everyone who was lucky enough to live there knew it and acknowledged it, and no one wanted it to change.

Chapter 15

Marina showed up a short time later around seven, and her camera crew's van pulled in roughly thirty seconds behind her. I was sitting under the giant oak tree out in front of the great hall by then, enjoying the shade and the breeze while I waited for everyone else to arrive. I looked down the hill and watched as the film crew began to unload their equipment. Lights, microphones and cords, oh my!

There were only three guys but they seemed to have it all down to a science I noticed, when they were connected and set up for their first shot of the day in less than five minutes. They were aiming the cameras at the sun that was still rising behind the trees, where you could just make out the reflections off of the water in the distance. The serenity of that one scene struck me as a really good depiction of what the place was about. That made me feel like maybe they knew what they were doing, which made me relax just a fraction more. I sincerely hoped they would get it right, *and that I would appear in it as little as humanly possible!*

They spent a few minutes there, focused on Marina as she began by talking about the long history of the property that I had so recently learned myself, and finished by explaining what they hoped to accomplish. She was as polished and professional looking as always, even though she wasn't dressed in her normal "newswoman" attire. She was wearing a much more casual outfit of dark blue denim shorts that came to just above her knees with a short sleeve, red, white and blue plaid button down shirt. She finished it off with a pair of white tube socks that were pushed down to the tops of her work boots, that while obviously brand new, fit her well and nicely completed her "construction worker" look. Her hair was in a low, no-nonsense bun but still looked perfect. I could just make out her clear voice as it carried across the stillness of the early morning air and I could tell that she was approaching the explanation for her attire. I leaned against the tree to my left, just to be absolutely sure that I was out of any shot they may try to get of the great hall, and listened.

"You may be wondering about my choice of outfits for today." She allowed looking down at herself and then back to the camera. "Well, although I certainly spend my fair share of time in the hustle bustle of the city with wardrobe and stylists at my beck and call, *this* is where I grew up. This is the *real* me." She admitted humbly.

"It's the perfect place whenever I need to get away from it all, but it's more than just a getaway, its *home*. And like so many other residents of this unassuming town, I will do anything that I can to help keep it the same beautiful, peaceful place that we have all grown to love. No matter how much time I spend in the land of make believe, I need to know that I can always come back to this reality and find my true peace. I know that doesn't exist everywhere but I've found it here and like so many others, I refuse to take it for granted or to give it up without a fight." She said with a serious look.

"Don't get me wrong though, I'm well aware that you can't just stop time, and that you have to embrace change and growth to survive. But that doesn't have to mean new high-rise apartment buildings, or even a new neighborhood of Mc Mansions going up every other month where miles and miles of farmland used to be! That would only overtax this small towns resources and eventually destroy what we would strive to save in the first place.

Thankfully that is not the only option. The solution can be something as simple, but as powerful as investing time and care into preserving an existing good thing. Sometimes it means getting together every resident there that feels not only like they *should* pitch in, but like they can't wait to! Invite them to participate in the processes required to get the results that they say they want for their town. Instead of just blaming the next guy and asking "Why didn't anyone do anything?" long after things fall apart, give them the opportunity to take responsibility for the future they want to see and make it happen!" She said enthusiastically. They may surprise you!

"Of course we all know that it can be a lot harder to do than to say and sometimes it takes a lot more time and effort to restore and preserve what we already have, than it does to just bulldoze over everything and start fresh, I know. That approach won't work for what we have here though. To understand why, you have to know the mentality of this small, but caring town and its' hardworking people." She shared with a knowing smile.

"You have to realize that it's not about a "quick fix. It's about the viability of a solution long term. It's about recognizing the true value in the rare natural open spaces that still exist, but also about attempting to retain and celebrate the history of our little town instead of repeatedly allowing it be lost to time and industrialization." She was as enthusiastic in her speech as any newscaster would be, but it was easy to tell that she really believed everything that she was saying and I couldn't help but agree.

"It's about being the kind of people who take an extra minute or two to think of a solution that honors that concept in a way that can prove useful to us today. That attitude aims to ensure that places like this one not only thrive now, but for the next generation as well. We should care about what we are leaving for them. Sounds simple enough right? So why is this whole concept such a rare occurrence?" She looked up at the main building then and the camera followed her. I didn't think they could see me, but I was still glad that I had moved over.

"It sure doesn't look like much right now, but this place has a heart and a soul that has served this town in one way or another for *decades* and it waits patiently for resuscitation so it can do that once more. It's not only worth it, but I assure you it's time." She said with admiration clear in her voice. "I am not the only one who thinks so either." She added, looking back at the camera again for emphasis.

"That is why we are here, *all* of us! Over *a hundred and fifty of us* have stepped up and volunteered to come together over the next two weeks to help in one way or another to renovate this entire property, from top to bottom, inside and out! Then we will simply hand it back to the town, a viable, self-sustainable, *valuable*, functioning asset!" She proclaimed proudly.

"There are plumbers, builders, electricians, designers, painters, plasterer's, decorators, landscapers and roofers, just to name a few of the vocations that are represented on this project. There are also lawyers, printers, truck drivers, restaurant owners, banks and countless other businesses that have contributed *somehow* along the way to us getting *here!* Believe me the list goes on and on. That alone is astounding to me in its' own right. But what makes this group even more unusual, is the fact that every single one of them lives or works right here, in this town, *and* that every single one of them has agreed to do their work on this joint endeavor 100% free of charge!" She gave a moment for effect there along with a perfect "can you believe that?" stare.

"They will get absolutely nothing out of it monetarily, but that's not what's important and they all know that. The truth is that everyone involved will in fact benefit from whatever success is achieved here, in one way or another. Not only will they get to experience the joy of the community coming together in a profound way, and believe me that is something that everyone here *will* remember, but they will also get to feel the pride and the deep satisfaction of a job well done. Then in the long run, they will reap the rewards in the form of the future jobs and benefits that this place will have to offer everyone in town. It all comes back around in the end, isn't that what they say?" She turned and looked back at the camera again then.

"Now how often do you hear about something like this happening?" She asked honestly, but appropriately sad. "Again I ask, why is this notion so unusual? Why is this not happening in every town across the country? Each community doing whatever it can to help maintain and improve its' own existing assets." She was a pro at what she did for sure, and I noticed that again as she gave that just a moment to fester before she continued.

"So surely by now you've guessed why I am dressed this

way. Because I'm not here *just* to cover this story, I'm a participant as well." She revealed with her patented smile. "And while I can offer no master skills in any particular field, I am hard working and always willing to learn something new. In that vein, I have vowed to help in whatever capacity I can be most useful, even if that means I'm hauling trash. I honestly don't mind. Besides whatever meager assistance I can contribute here, I fully intend to bring this story to the people, because it sure is nice to hear a little good news every once and a while now, isn't it?" She asked and again, I nodded my head. It was basically the reason that I almost never watched the news anymore.

"Either way, I couldn't be prouder to be here and to be a part of something so amazing. So let's get to work!" She finished with a huge smile and then bounded up the big cement stairs as the shot followed her then ended.

I waited an appropriate amount of time after I saw the cameraman drop the camera down before I gave her a slow clap about half way up, alerting her to my presence. She grinned up at me and took a mock bow. Her crew was taking their time going over the angles for the next few shots, multiple arms waving randomly in the air in various directions while she climbed.

"Damn, that's a lot of stairs! I had almost forgotten that part!" She joked and huffed a bit before coming over to hug me hello. "Good morning! Have you been here long?" She asked. I could feel her excitement bubbling over and I knew it really wasn't just a story to her. It *was* going to be a good story, hell I'd watch it, but I could tell how much she meant what she'd said. She really couldn't wait to get started. I was still walking the tightrope between giddiness and dread myself, but I tried to let her attitude become contagious and tip me more in that direction. It was almost working.

"Not long, just over an hour." I answered. "It was perfect, actually. It was just long enough for Daniel to come and give me the keys and one last tour of the fuse boxes and heating ducts and such." I said.

"Ah, I see. He's "Daniel" already, huh? That didn't take long." She joked understandingly as we started to walk towards the main entrance together. She was making it easy to like her so far as well. I was silently hoping that trend would hold since we would be spending an awful lot of time together over the next two weeks. Well, *hopefully* anyway!

"Yeah, he insisted." I confessed with a laugh and she nodded in understanding.

"He really is just the sweetest thing, isn't he?" She added being as honest as usual. "His wife is too. I just love them both to pieces." She gushed.

"He sure is easy to talk to and he was just full of information about the property! The fact that there are people like him who have not only stayed here year after year, but that still care about the area the way he does, just makes me want to do this even more." I admitted, finally starting to feel a little better in spite of the odds against us.

"I just hope we can pull it off without any major disasters, 'knock on wood.'" I added with a rap of my knuckles against the doorframe as we passed through it. She looked back at me and I could feel she was surprised by my actions. I decided to explain in the simplest way possible.

"I don't believe in every superstition out there, and I think that belief is key really when it comes to things like that. But that one particular worry holds enough weight with me for some reason that I just don't chance it. 'You don't tug on Superman's cape, you don't spit into the wind, you don't pull the mask off the ol' Lone Ranger' *and you don't go around tempting fate by spelling out your worst case scenarios unless you want someone to hear you and make them happen.*" I joked and we both laughed at that. "Okay, it doesn't rhyme with the original Jim Croce lyrics, but it's still a really good philosophy to live by." Marina shook her head and laughed but she also gave her own knock on the way by for good measure.

We entered through the main hall and continued down the corridor beyond to the original, old fashioned dining room where I had already set everything up. I had added two modern, industrial sized freestanding air conditioning units to the previously antiquated décor but in the end the contradiction worked perfectly. Command central was ready. I had the all-important schedule tacked up on the wall and it extended all the way from the ceiling to the chair rail.

"It sure looks worse when you put it that way." She joked, eyeing the length of the document up and down. "Are you sure this is only two weeks?" She asked, mostly being sarcastic but not entirely.

"Yup. Starting in *three… two… one!* I responded looking at my watch and we both laughed again, albeit more nervously that time. "No, but in all seriousness, the first workers are due to arrive on site in about thirty minutes, the second a half hour after that, and the third and fourth and fifth twenty minutes later. It's going to start off with a bang and it's going to stay that way pretty much all the way through, if we're lucky. After that we should gain a crew every time we lose one, which will keep us in a fairly steady state of chaos, I'm sure!" I added hopefully. "Are you ready for this?" I asked, really wondering how she would fare if she did have to take over mid-way through the storm.

"As I'll ever be." She insisted with a reservation that I could feel. "You?" She asked in return looking for encouragement and I wished that my response was as automatic as hers had been or even as optimistic. I hid it well enough though.

"Ready." I assured her calmly and with much more confidence than I actually felt, for her sake.

We started to go over the all-important schedule together one item at a time. I showed her how the colored text connected with the corresponding areas on the main map. It was tacked up right next to the schedule covering the other two thirds of that wall. It showed where on the property anyone and everyone should be at any given time. All you had to do was look up what job they were working on and then find the area that shared that color and *wha-la*, there they would be! Well, at least in theory anyway.

Again, I had really been a coordinator more than lead designer. There were enough of those already and my main goal had simply been to keep it as organized as possible. I really hoped that my efforts would prove worth the hours spent. She seemed to follow it all easy enough though and that gave me just a fraction more confidence. No matter what happened, they didn't *really* need me from there on out. Whatever consequences I may encounter, they would survive without me and the work would go on. Knowing that, I relaxed another notch and tried to just go with the flow.

The day just kept unfolding, one task at a time, and fairly smoothly. All I could think as the hours passed was, "Yes, *but for how much longer*?" I wanted to believe that it would be that turbulence free from start to finish, but it was just too... *Hmmm...*, I thought as I considered even in my head, what I could say without jinxing us. *...uneventful?* Yes, I supposed that worked. It was too *uneventful*. I wasn't counting on that at all and it threw me off, both physically and mentally. But again, I tried to go with it, hoping I was just being pessimistic as was my habit.

We got all the way through to lunch without a hitch and the relief for the amazingly positive start was palpable within the crowd. People started to laugh and joke a little more with some of that original apprehension of the unknown having gone away. Some even tapped into the true spirit of the place and just laid out in the grass to enjoy their breaks in the sunshine, I noticed through the windows. People were also realizing en masse around the property, that a lot of things weren't as bad as they had originally seemed. In fact, as it turned out a lot of the changes would be merely cosmetic. For the most part, the place just needed a good "sprucing up" so-to-speak and it was finally going to get it.

The overall atmosphere was optimistic around me and I was extremely grateful to have that to draw on. With my own work outside still two days off I spent most of the day hiding inside, away from the majority of the crowds and holding down the coordinating side of the work that I had agreed to take on.

As crews came in and out of command central to check in or give status updates, I noticed only upbeat energy. Alongside that was a feeling not unlike the one you get on a holiday, when the whole extended family shows up in one place at the same time. It was like a busy hive on a sunny day. There was a great, buzzing energy and it was being generated by all the people who knew each other around town getting to work together on one job, many of them for the first time. There was genuine giddiness and a sense of homecoming in the air for some of them that hadn't worked together since trade school. That energy lifted the spirits of everyone who came in contact with it, not just me for a change.

More came through with good news than with bad, and a few had come because they had finished their jobs early and already wanted to volunteer to help out somewhere else! It really was funny how addictive that rush that you get from giving back can become.

Overall though the tone had remained mostly upbeat and optimistic all day, so I was caught off guard when Marina came through around three and looked up at me with a definite worry weighing down her brow. She had changed the whole atmosphere of the room in under a second. I could feel it and see it.

"What?" I asked completely petrified of the answer but still hiding it beautifully, for the moment. The only consolation that I could come up with was that at least the likelihood of someone having accidentally uncovered an unknown aquifer there *had* to be slim! That would be like lightning striking twice on the same person but in two different places! Surely not even karma, even on her bitchiest day, could possibly be that cruel! At least I *hoped* she couldn't with a confidence that was shaky at best.

"*Ummm...* It's nothing really. Don't freak out." She requested with a nervous smile, causing me to inch even closer to completely freaking out.

"Too late. Spill it." I demanded wanting to just rip the Band-Aid off fast. I was always one to pick the "bad news" first, whenever given the option between the two. What does that say about me, do you suppose? *Anyway...*

"Well it's just that the foreman for the construction workers is asking for you. Says he's confused about the part of the plan to repair the floor in the gazebo. He thinks the whole thing should just be ripped out and replaced." She rolled her eyes and I felt her exasperation at that attitude.

"I didn't go inside, I was too afraid." She said with her hands held up in defense as she looked down at her shoes. "So I have no idea how much damage may have already been done before they thought to get approval to make changes." She admitted reluctantly.

"I'm sorry, I tried to explain about the craftsmanship that went into that original work and how we had really wanted to preserve that, in that piece in particular. But he just kept insisting that it wasn't possible." I could feel her own worry as she explained.

"Now I know I started this whole mess, and I'll do whatever I can to help because I really do love this place. But when it comes right down to it, I'm still just a journalist, so this is where I have to call in the professionals and in this case, that would be you. Personally, I have no idea how to deal with disagreeable employees. I'm usually on the other end of those kinds of negotiations." She admitted with a guilty lopsided grin.

"So I was thinking maybe you could just take a walk over there and calmly but *firmly* explain to him why he should do it your way, if it's not already too late. You know, in the name of keeping things moving." She suggested hopefully.

All I could think then was that I knew things had been going too smoothly, dammit! Something always had to come along and create a few bumps. I hated thinking that way but it was that balance thing again and I could always feel when it was leaning too far to one side. Just then I could also feel her real desire for me to take charge wafting across the room while I contemplated my options. I wasn't as excited about the idea myself but unfortunately I knew it did fall under the category of the job that I had signed up for.

"Fine." I said with a resigned huff. "I'll take this one, but you're getting the next one, I swear!" I insisted heatedly. She was more than pleased with that arrangement. I took another deep breath and let it out before I made a single move to leave my little insulated, wood covered sanctuary. Alright, truth be told, I took two deep breaths. One just wasn't enough. I had been pretty content there, safely ensconced behind the barrier of the four surrounding walls and the rooms beyond.

I geared myself up to leave it all as I walked out through the antique archways. I passed through into the living room and onto the long porch. I squinted at the sunlight burning through the windows. I hadn't been holed up in there *that* long but mentally it felt like about a week. I exited the squeaky wooden door and walked out into the full sunlight for the first time in almost five hours. It was hotter by then but still not brutal. I took a moment to adjust to it as I breathed it in. I let it fill me and I welcomed it as it warmed me, and began to melt away the slight chill left on the surface of my skin from having been in the AC for so long. I tried to keep my energy high as I headed over towards the gazebo, where I knew the troublemaker was working, or more accurately, *not* working. *Grrrr....*

On the way over I thought about how I had pessimistically anticipated a certain amount of head butting during the project. It was not only inevitable but completely expected on a job with so many "*Chiefs*" and so few "*Indians,*" as one of my old teachers used to be fond of saying, but I had thought that we might get at least a few days in before the acrimony started to emerge. *Hmpf!* Oh well, people were people after all and it wasn't really surprising, just disappointing. The only real shock was the speed with which it had occurred.

I'd had experience dealing with strong personalities throughout my recent years of being the "boss" on jobs, and I had been forced to step in on far too many occasions already between arguing craftsman who each thought their opinion was not just the right one, but the *only* one. In some cases, it was true, in others not so much. But they were all necessary in one way or another for what they could contribute to the cumulative success of a project as a whole and the key was always not to lose either one. In the end, it came down to making sure that each and every worker/craftsman felt understood, appreciated and respected. I knew, as an artist myself, how far that went towards reaching an ultimate goal as a unit. Mutual respect was paramount. I got that. I could handle that, in theory.

It was just going to be a lot harder to do that there with *so* many artists in such a small space and squeezed into such a tight time frame. I knew all along that it would be trickier under those circumstances. I had been mentally prepared for it. Well, at least I thought I had. It was always easier "in theory" than it was in, *not-so-cooperative-gosh-darn-it-annoying* real life though.

As I approached the front of the gazebo I stopped for a few seconds to gather my fortitude. There were a handful of men in typical construction gear lounging around outside. I noticed none of them appeared to be working though and they all looked away and started to disperse in different directions as they noticed me.

Greeeaaaat! That was just what I needed, to alienate the company that would be doing the majority of the work there, and on the very first day no less! *Uhhhhggg!!*

I kept going, more determined than ever then, not to let it get out of hand, especially since I wasn't necessarily going to be around to try and keep it under control after the first day. The original platform had been completely cleared of broken branches and debris, making it possible for me to climb the steps. As I did, I was amazed to see that the floor not only remained intact but that it had already been patched and expertly sanded as well. You could see the new sections easily where the wood was still bare, new against old. It was an intricately woven, irregular pattern, much like the tree that had created it. The workmanship however was seamless and I was sure it would be impossible to detect once it was all re-stained. It was absolutely *beautiful!*

I knelt down on one knee and ran my hand flat over the place where the two edges met for confirmation and it was perfectly smooth, just as I had expected. I spun around looking up at the top half of the gazebo and was in awe of what had been done. All the branches that had grown through had been left alone but the walls and ceiling beams had been repaired around them as if the whole structure had been built that way originally. It was something that I would have loved to have thought of and it made me smile in pure delight. Even more surprising than that though, I was finally realizing, was the fact that I was completely alone.

Huh? Where was the obstinate foreman? Why would he start an argument with Marina if he had already done what we had asked and done it perfectly? It didn't make any sense and I hated that.

"What do you think?" Ethan asked then from outside.

"*Whuuuuhhh!!* Oh! *Huh?!*" I stammered, out loud as I looked up and out and found him sitting under a tree behind the gazebo. It *was* Ethan! I couldn't believe at first how thoroughly he could still surprise me! *Jesus Christ!*

He was far enough away that I hadn't felt him before I saw him for once. But he really was there! In a public place, in broad daylight! *What the...?!* That did not want to sink in, my brain kept trying to reject it as wrong. It wasn't a trick though I was sure, as his enjoyment of my expression came rushing across the distance and soared through me. Yup, there was no mistaking *that!* He was walking over to me slowly and calmly as if it was absolutely nothing out of the ordinary. *Hah!* Didn't I wish!

"Don't you like it?" He asked teasingly as he neared the steps. I still couldn't answer him though. My mind was too busy currently searching for too many other answers already, to take in any new requests. I just continued to stare at him as he slowly climbed the three steps to join me on the new platform. He stopped about fifteen feet away from me and waited patiently for me to catch up.

The wheels were turning so fast in my mind that I was really surprised that there wasn't smoke coming out of my ears! Why was he there? What was he doing? Where was Jeremy? Was it because of Anderson's threat? *Anderson!!* Shit! Where the hell was Anderson?!! I wondered worriedly. I looked all around us nervously but oddly, I didn't see anyone but Ethan. Where the hell had everyone gone? But I couldn't hold onto that new question either. I was too busy wondering what all of that, had to do with him being there? Try as I might, my mind couldn't sort through the possible answers and find one that fit. What did finally click though, was that he *was* there! Standing right in front of me! My next reaction was automatic.

I spanned the distance in three strides and leapt into his arms! He caught me around the waist and spun me half way around to absorb some of the impact as he laughed. I hugged him tight for a second more then pulled back to look at his face as he put me back down. He was extremely relieved that I had finally come around.

"What are you *doing* here?! I asked urgently but softly. He answered me easily as usual.

"I'm pitching in, like everybody else." He said simply like it made perfect sense but I could tell that he was enjoying playing with me, still way too relaxed for my comfort level. After a moment of having his fun though, he decided to be merciful and explain.

"My company had agreed to donate this work long before I knew I would be *'out of town'* when it came time to do it." He stated. "Or that *you'd* end up agreeing to oversee it." He added with a smile. I could feel his happiness at that development but I tried to focus.

"Your "*company?*" I asked, obviously confused. "Which company would that be?" I asked, doubtful that I would miss such a thing, even in my extremely hurried state. "Talk about curve balls!" I added, trying desperately to figure it all out. He just smiled understandingly and I could feel how glad he was that I was feeling some of that for a change. I gave a sarcastic grin back in defiance and he laughed out loud.

"'*Rock*' Construction Company." He answered with his own mischievous grin. "I had to come up with a company name for the haphazard group of people that I threw together to help me build my house, in order to get insurance and building permits and so forth. I was ready by then to have a roof over my head that was really my own for the first time. So as you can imagine I was eager to get the work done as fast as possible." He admitted with a wink.

"All the reputable companies had waiting lists that were six months to a year, long and most of those wouldn't even return my calls. But there were a lot of qualified, unemployed workers hanging around town who needed steady paying jobs, just like I had not so long before that. So I pulled as many of them as I could find together and slapped a name on us all in the beginning just to serve that original purpose. Some of those initial choices turned out to be bad decisions, but good learning experiences." He said with a laugh and a wink, feeling humble.

"In the end though, it mostly turned out to be a great collaboration of talented people who just happened to be in the right place at the right time and some long lasting work relationships have grown out of it." He added with a smile.

"It's a little bigger now than it was then, I admit." He threw in with a quick raise of his eyebrows. "But it still has a lot of that same group of honest, hardworking guys at its core and the same good intentions as always, whatever we work on together." He said proudly.

"I originally wanted to use my family name, but I knew that was not always the best idea with some of the work that we do." He allowed with a guilty grin. "And besides that, '*Stone*' was already pretty much dragged through the mud, used up and burned into the ground around here anyway. So I simply chose a synonym instead. It's *almost* the same." He finished with a shrug.

"The surprises never cease." I stated calmly while shaking my head slowly back and forth. One of these days we really have to swap full bio's." I joked in awe.

"*Nah.*" He argued. "Its way more fun this way." He added with another eyebrow wiggle as a full wave of enjoyment flowed freely from him. "Normally though, in rare situations like this one, where the timing is *unfavorable*, I would have just sent a crew in my place which I had been planning to do. But I have to say, this turned out to be the perfect opportunity at the perfect time to reintegrate Jeremy safely, and to take the heat off of everybody else." He finished with a self-satisfied smile.

"I would have told you about all of this, especially given your position here." He added and I could feel his pride in there for me as well. *Wow!* Nice. I was almost ready to forgive him after I felt that, *almost*.

"I swear. It wasn't one of those things that I needed to keep from you. It's just that it truly all came together at the very last minute and by then I thought it might be more fun to just enjoy the surprises while they last." He grinned a half grin at me again then. "You have to admit, you were *very* surprised!" His amusement made me laugh whether I wanted to or not. He was aware of that too and he checked to see how I really felt when I stopped. "Are you mad?" He asked with a sheepish smile.

"*Hmpf!* I don't know yet. Give me a minute. I'm still not quite up to speed here. Not that I'm not *thrilled* to see you, you know I can't hope to hide that! But I still don't understand. Why here? How does this help?" I asked, still somewhat confused. "I know it would be a great experience for him, if he's really got his new skills under control enough to handle a highly populated situation like this, but how will it help him get back home?" I challenged. "What about Anderson?" I added, my voice getting a little higher with each question.

"Well, the biggest risk right now is that Jeremy will disappear and they will get away with it because either 'A,' no one will want to get involved out of fear, or 'B,' no one will even care because they've painted him as a troubled, possibly suicidal teen with 'unresolved medical issues' in his own community. It puts the balance in their favor. They know that. They will use that." He assured me calmly.

"So, we make sure that his 'community' first of all, knows that he is not sick, or troubled. And secondly, that he is full of life, loves his family and would *never* run away *or* try to hurt himself! That's important. We also need to make sure that people see that it's safe to associate with him and his family again without fear of repercussions, legally *or* medically. Then, we need to make sure that he's notable enough throughout all of this, to a wide enough range of people, that they can't possibly act against him and still hope to stay under the radar, which I know is probably the only thing more important to them right now than me and Jeremy." He explained and that at least made sense.

"That objective to keep this from the general public never changes with them. It's the one thing that remains steady no matter which *'Agent Anderson'* we run into. Only the faces change." He said and I could feel him looking back mentally on past *"Jeremy's" as well.*

"As much as we can't figure out, like why they spend so much time keeping track of heights, or what they hope to get out of it, we do know that they don't want to go public with it all any more than we do, although I'm sure it's for different reasons.

They may change their minds at some point, if it somehow works in their favor. I can't ever rule that out. But for right now I don't see it helping them, and they don't do anything that doesn't benefit them in some way. *Always* remember that!" He said intently and I was starting to get it.

"He went a little rogue last time at the farm which I'll admit, surprised me but only a little because I know now that that's exactly what it was about. It was his ace in the hole that I thought he wouldn't go there in a public place and he used that assumption to his advantage. But even that was only on a very small, local scale. I think he weighed the gain greater than the risk that one time, knowing how closed-mouthed a small town like this can be, especially when you threaten them with arrest! But it's not their usual M.O. and I don't expect a repeat performance anytime soon, especially since it didn't work out so well for him in the end." He added with a half-smile while he thought back on that night for a second or two.

I felt him switch his attention back to the present a moment later like someone had flipped a switch. His emotional vibrations were that sharp for me. I still hadn't fully adjusted to it, at least not to the point where it became so familiar that it didn't jolt me anymore. Maybe I never would. Maybe I didn't want to, I mused silently until he spoke again.

"I know it won't necessarily guarantee that they won't come after him." He admitted and I could feel the small amount of remaining fear. "But it will certainly make it a lot harder for them. Shift the balance back in our favor a little, maybe give us all a little *breathing* room again!" He added vehemently while staring down at me with a deep desire flaring brightly in his eyes. I just closed mine as it washed over me secondhand.

"Anderson's too smart. He won't go that route again right now, especially not on a national scale. I know it's a bit of a gamble, but I am betting the odds and I really hope my hunch is right because I know that we can't hide him forever, believe me!" He said looking down at me. "It's just not a good solution, for *anyone!*" He said resignedly pulling me gently against his chest again. "We needed a real solution, not just a temporary one. That is why I needed time to get it right. This plan should work!" He finished with a humble but positive attitude.

I rested there, happily, for a beat or two trying to absorb

what he was telling me. I was almost afraid to believe it. As soon as the elation at his statement began to develop, the doubt came rushing in and blocked the parade route that the relief would travel. That had become quite common for me. The recently appointed defensive guards that had been protecting my heart weren't prepared to lay down their weapons just yet. Not without specific confirmation.

I leaned back and looked up at him. "So you're *home*, to stay, as of right now! Is that what you're telling me?" I asked specifically, looking up at him. I needed to clarify that before I let the dam go completely because once the guards let that wall down, I wasn't going to get the emotional floodwaters back. They had been pent up in there for way too long. He nodded his head intently above me and I wanted to rejoice, but I could feel that there were addendums to that still. I waited precariously for the balance weight.

"Yes, I'm home, but how long I'll be "staying" remains to be seen. I can't deny there's still the possibility of a short stay at *their* 'camp' at some point in the very near future." He admitted with a shrug. He tried to laugh it off but I knew it was for show so he stopped trying and just grinned painfully at me again. I wished for a moment then that he really was a magician and he could fix everything with a wave of his magic guitar.

"I don't know what Anderson's next move will be yet, only what my response will be to each possible scenario." He explained further. "He played a "force." I have no choice but to respond. The next move will be his." His grin died away a little I noticed as he contemplated all the possible outcomes. They were certainly not *all* "good." He didn't let it stop him though, as usual. He took a breath and finished explaining.

"I'm sure they can come up with more than enough to arrest me if they decide to so it's really a matter of whether Anderson wants to act on it now or wait for a more opportune time. Hopefully, I've taken away enough of the present benefits for him to at least temporarily abandon the idea. But even if he does arrest me, just for the satisfaction which would surprise me, we're pretty sure they won't be able to hold me long. Not until I'm convicted anyway."

That nonchalant comment did not get by me without leaving a permanent mark. I could even barely consider the size of the hole that hit had made in my armor without gasping so I decided not to. I breathed deeply through it and let it go. He went right past it as well, making it easier for me of course. *Holy...! ...breathe...*

"The rest we can talk about later, okay?" He requested with a slight glance around us at our very public location and I understood. As I looked around us I noticed that people were starting to drift back over.

"Then I'm not mad. Not only will you be home, but you'll be *here*, where I will be practically living for the next two weeks! I can't think of a better way to get through this." I said honestly. It was almost comical to me how much I had originally feared that "we" mentality, since by then it gave me such strength to imagine that it might actually exist. He understood and appreciated the shift in my attitude as well.

I was still worried and I still had a thousand other questions, but I realized then that it at least meant the hiding was finally over! Like *really* over! I didn't know the details yet or how it would go down but I couldn't stop the relief then from *finally* beginning to run through me! I tried really hard to keep my breathing even as the realization spread like a physical thing! It was a lightness that was beyond normal sensations.

I was so overwhelmed with joy then that regardless of the building audience, I reached up and ran my hand through his hair and around to the nape of his neck. He smiled even bigger at my unlikely behavior but didn't plan to try and stop me. That was crystal clear. I thought it was funny that he would think I would care at that point. I on the other hand, knew myself better than that and joy overrode embarrassment in my book, that time and every time truth be told. I didn't care who was watching anymore!

I held onto him and pulled him down so that I could kiss him. As his lips landed on mine I was smart enough to treasure every second because I had no idea what would happen next. I could still feel that same sentiment present in him so I knew that even he was worried for once. I wasn't sure how we were going to handle the fallout yet but I knew we really would handle it much better together than apart. That fact finally gave me peace instead of palpitations.

People were approaching and we could hear them beginning to whistle and cheer a little, but for once in my life, I truly didn't care. I kissed him until I felt that the hovering wave was almost ready to crest and come crashing down on us. *That* was the line! Then I knew it was time to take a step back and find my breath again. I still wasn't into letting it go *that* far in front of a crowd, no matter how happy I was to see him!

I had waited days and sometimes weeks at a time recently for his company and his touch. I was a pro at delayed gratification by that point. I knew I could wait a few hours for the work day to end. After what we'd been through already, that seemed ridiculously easy in comparison.

I pulled back and we both sighed deeply that time. The applause erupted fully then and I shook my head slightly in amusement more than embarrassment. I laid my forehead gently on his chest again in defeat and the crowd enjoyed that as well.

"Is this how you're going to handle all of our 'relations' issues?" Marina asked sarcastically as she climbed the steps towards us. Her camera crew stayed behind, enjoying being a part of the audience for once as that got another good laugh. People started to notice that there was something to notice, so more people noticed them noticing and headed over themselves. I just chuckled low in my throat at the shocked faces.

Oh well, nothing left to hide now. I picked up my head, stepped back, took his hand in mine and made a slight curtsy and they all clapped and hooted some more while I rolled my eyes.

"Thank you, thank you very much. Crisis averted! You can all relax." I said to the crowd in general. Then I answered Marina. "I got this one. The next one is yours, remember?" I joked and the crowd enjoyed that just as much. So much so, that a few other workers throughout the audience pretended to have "issues" for her to handle. She just shook her head and laughed with them.

"Alright people, show's over! We are on a very tight deadline here. So let me just take *one* second, while I have you all

..." I said with another eye-roll. "...to say how truly impressed I've been so far with the way you all have worked together and the results that I have seen already are beyond spectacular! Thank you all so much for being a part of this on behalf of Marina who put it all together and the whole town! Just keep up the good work! I can't ask for more!" I said in the end and everyone gave another small round of applause there. I waited a beat.

"Now, having said that, and please don't take this the wrong way, but I really need you all to get back to work! Like *now!*" I shouted playfully. "Seriously people, have you seen the schedule?!" I added with a chuckle. "*Go!* Vamoose!" I said with a few loud claps to give it an extra jolting effect. They stared to break away then and shake their own heads as they went away laughing, but at least they went. "You guys are amazing!" I threw in encouragingly even though I knew they didn't really need it. They were all making moves by then to head back to wherever they had come from. Well, almost all of them.

"Ethan Stone! I should have known you would have a hand in this fiasco. Somehow you always do." Marina said with a sly grin as she walked over and hugged him. I noticed that she was also surprised by his appearance, but pleasantly so. I wasn't sure what that meant yet. I may have been jealous if I couldn't feel exactly what they both felt when she was pressed so tightly up against him. Lucky for me, I did. And that was amusement, mischief and friendship, *old* friendship. *Someone's certainly enjoying serving up his own curveballs today*, I thought as I grinned at them.

"Now I know why you sent a guy I didn't know to do your dirty work! *You*, I wouldn't have taken any shit from!" She added, again with a familiar sort of attitude. I tried to determine then where their friendship had originated from, whether it was just from growing up in the same small town and going to the same school, or if was it from spending time together at "*Camp.*" I considered it silently while they ribbed each other. When she pulled back and turned to me I still wasn't sure.

"Simone, I had no idea that you were mixed up with this troublemaker." She had him pegged alright, even though I knew she thought she was kidding. Maybe it was just school then.

"Yes, I spent a lot of time at The Tavern when I first moved here, still do actually, and his music drew me to him like a moth to the flame." I partially explained, purposefully making light of the situation.

"*Hmpf.* If only if had been that easy!" He whispered walking up behind me once more and I chuckled too. *God*, it felt good to laugh again! I had to take stock of how amazing it was even though it was such a simple thing. I leaned into him and rubbed my face on his chest in pure contentment.

"Well this will take some time for me to mentally digest." Marina said out of one side of her mouth, the surprise still evident in her voice along with a certain amount of amusement. "But in the meantime, I believe that we have a segment to film. Right? I received a message that instructed me to meet my next '*very special interviewee*' down here." She said with a wink. "Thank God it's not really some disgruntled employee with an attitude and a bone to pick with management! Are you ready?" She asked him then and I looked up at him surprised.

"Yes, but it's not me that you are going to interview." He informed her.

"It's not?" She asked, clearly confused.

"No. Follow me." He instructed Marina as he headed back out of the almost finished gazebo, pulling me along beside him. I still wasn't sure about their connection but I noticed that she listened to him without question. I at least I had an idea of what was happening that time, so I just went with it but I couldn't help but wonder at her blind faith.

"Nice work." I finally complimented getting distracted by the craftsmanship once more on the way by.

"So you *do* like it!" He teased at my just getting around to answering that question.

"It's perfect." I said softly, looking up at him. I could feel his relief and satisfaction at my answer. "But we already know that I'm a big fan of your work." I said with a sly grin referring to things that I knew only he would understand. He wiggled his eyebrows and smiled, but otherwise kept silent. He knew that I could feel his response, even though he couldn't voice it at the moment. Oh, how I had missed that non-verbal communication that we shared! There was so much that I could still barely even imagine getting to experience on a daily basis. But I had never been more ready to try!

I held his hand tighter and he squeezed mine back in response. It was so simple and *sooooo* nice! *Damn!* I tried to keep my breaths slow and steady so I wouldn't get dizzy while we were walking. Yeah, that was all I needed! I figured one embarrassing spectacle a day was enough.

Jesus! Slow… Easy… whoooo!

Chapter 16

We walked over to where the very beginning of the outdoor work was taking place behind the main building, by the edge of what used to be the small children's playground. At the moment that mostly just meant clearing out everything that was over grown, but of course that was almost everything. It was back breaking and tedious work and best suited to the young at heart, literally! We didn't need a fifty-something-year-old landscaper having a heart attack after five hours of pulling weeds and hacking away at vines! Teenagers on the other hand, always had energy to spare. We had a perfect match on hand, the scouts and their machetes. Thank goodness!

Their plan was to be on site every day of the project from start to finish in order to log enough community service hours to qualify for Eagle status, but that one project was going to take up most of if not all of day one. I was even more grateful then for their sake, that it wasn't ninety five out anymore and I hoped that the bearable weather would hold. It *was* early August after all. We were getting very lucky at the moment. Marina waved to her lounging camera crew on our way by the parking lot and they collected their gear and fell in behind us.

"So this will just be a teaser segment." She explained to me, suddenly sounding a lot more knowledgeable about what was going on. "The first of three. It will go out on tonight's evening news, to promote the upcoming special I'm planning. These short stories will give the viewer's something to follow and a reason to check back over the next few weeks while we're actually finishing the renovations and doing the post-production editing. The producers just *love* that kind of hook!" She admitted rolling her eyes. "It will give you a *very* public platform that you can use should you need to make someone very special, very '*visible.*'" She added and then I knew for sure. She was definitely a fellow "camper." I also had no doubt then, that if Ethan hadn't shown up and made it known that we were together, I would never have known that. *Hmpf!* The day was just full of surprises.

I smiled slowly at her but I didn't get anything super weird or overly intense from her then any more than I ever had, so I still wasn't sure if it was her or a family member that had led to her association. I just knew for sure, that she *was* an "*associate*" of our fine camp, somehow.

Hmpf… Did I just say "*our*" fine camp? *Hah!* I did, didn't I? Well, it was only to myself so it didn't really count, but still. *That didn't take long, did it?*

I realized then that it reminded me of when Liliana first came into our lives. Before she was born, we couldn't even imagine what it would be like to be parents! It was like being told you will host an alien being for the next eighteen years. But as soon as we met her, we instantly forgot everything about what life had been like before her. Likewise, I realized that I already couldn't imagine *not* being involved in the camp in some way. That seemed to be the case for everyone who learned about it though. At least from what I had seen so far. It was no wonder Ethan was so careful who he told about it.

He looked back and grinned at us both then addressed Marina. "You should go ahead and get set up. We don't have much time left. I'll bring him over." She gave a quick nod and walked over to talk to her crew. I glanced back at the group of seven teenage boys that had already made it three-quarters of the way across the park and had just reached the giant, rusting swing-set structure. They were sitting on the ground and celebrating that accomplishment by taking a water break.

I noticed Jeremy then for the first time, sitting right in the thick of it all, laughing and pushing one of the other boys in response to something he had said. His hair was a little longer, like Ethan's, and his skin was light pink from the days' work in the hot sun. His eyes were bright and bag free though, like he had gotten back to sleeping on a regular basis and his mood seemed to match that of his peers once more. He looked and acted just like every other teenage boy there and I had to work hard to keep the emotion that I felt at that from boiling over and making me cry in front of everyone. Even though I had nothing to do with it, I felt like a proud hawk whose baby bird had left the nest. I took a few more slow breaths before I spoke. Then I turned to Ethan.

"He's doing really well, huh?!" I asked, letting the relief show. He nodded back at me with a humble grin and agreed.

"Yeah. He's really gotten a good handle on it lately. I knew it was all about the proper motivation for him." He said smiling in Jeremy's direction. Then he looked back at me. "But I got the source wrong at first." He admitted with a good-hearted chuckle. "I thought it would be the hormones that would keep him working the hardest. But in the end more than anything else, he *really* just wanted to come *home*." He said quietly and I knew that we *all* understood that desire unequivocally. I nodded.

"He's come a long way and in a short amount of time. He didn't have a lot of choice, but he handled it better than most people would have. Honestly, I'm impressed." He said feeling that pride again, only for Jeremy that time. As that feeling washed over me it made me proud again but for both of them. I knew there was a reason that I had no problem helping Ethan in his *not-always-perfectly-above-board* quest to help *heights* in need, and I knew for sure that I was looking at one really good one.

At his core Jeremy was a *really* good kid who in spite of all his potential, almost ended up with nothing. The transformation from *norm* to *height* threatened to take it all away. In the end though, he became a greater man than he had started out as. That struggle had made him into who he was and who he would always be first and foremost, a humble but incredibly powerful *height!*

I could see then how special that made him, in ways that I would never have been able to appreciate before. I also knew that the reason he had managed to navigate and survive that transition so tactfully, to be there that day participating in that amazing cause, was because of the help and protection that Ethan's "*organization*" had provided him. I couldn't find fault with that, knowing what I knew. That was all I personally had control over. Everyone else had to decide for themselves, should they ever get the chance, but I had no reservations left what-so-ever when it came to being involved and helping in that aspect. It was just something that had become part of my life. I couldn't know that it existed and not *assist* in some way.

I realized at that moment that with or without Ethan, I would always want to help other *heights*. Especially since I knew so few others could. I had no qualms about maintaining their privacy either. It really wasn't all that different for me than my life "*before.*" I had always had to be discrete with certain issues in the past. It was just a matter of adding a few more actors to a newly expanded charade. I could handle that.

"I'll be right back." Ethan said bringing me out of my head. He jogged over to Jeremy, high-fiving a few of the kids on the way by. He approached the area where Jeremy sat and offered him a hand. Jeremy reached up to take it and stood, taking his water bottle with him in his other hand. I saw Ethan talking to him and then he looked over and waved at me excitedly. I could feel his eagerness to have me witness his improvement and I was happy to oblige. They came back over at a pace that was more befitting of a teenager who was way too cool to run, or even jog too fast but he hugged me unashamedly when he finally reached me.

"I sure have missed you!" I said being both supportive and honest as we stood back looking at each other up close. "You look awesome!" I said, my own pride for him taking center stage.

"Thanks. I'm feeling pretty good, I have to say." He offered with a grateful confidence. "It's really good to be back." He added even more earnestly. He wanted to stay somewhat cool about it but I could feel how deeply he meant that in particular. It was true that that motivation had been *everything* for him. I could feel it. I was a little more accepting of our own tortuous separation then, just knowing that it had done him so much good. Not a *lot* more accepting mind you, but definitely a little. Let's just say it felt less like "*wasted*" time after learning that at least.

It had been hard though and it was only slightly less painful to recall, so I did what I had been doing for weeks and I purposefully focused on the good parts that we had experienced in between. I grinned silently as my mind continued to wander through the happy side of those thoughts.

"Hey did you know her colors change with her mood?" Jeremy asked Ethan innocently, taking me completely off guard. He was looking perplexed as he was obviously quietly observing things so few people would ever see. Ethan and I shared a grin at that reminder that we weren't entirely alone there at the moment. I gave a brow raise and a sideways grin as I self-consciously slid my hands in my back pockets. Meanwhile Ethan answered him.

"*Hmpf.* Yeah. I've noticed." He agreed simply with a smile he couldn't hide. Thankfully Jeremy seemed to miss the implications and he continued to try and explain.

"I mean, there's usually some slight variations, but nothing like that! It's weird, right?" He asked looking for confirmation from his teacher. "Is it because she's an empath? Is it the strength of her emotion that gives it such vibrancy?" He added as the wheels started to turn. When Ethan just nodded, I could feel some things falling into place for him. He was still not entirely believing what he was learning though. Not at first. "Her emotions are really *that* much stronger! *Damn*!" He finished with an awed look.

He was a smart kid, and one who'd recently had a crash course in *heightism* so it wasn't *that* surprising that he had finally figured me out, but I was still trying to adjust to the thought of mine and Ethan's secret dialogue not being entirely secret anymore and it was strange. I got over the initial shock just enough to respond.

"Welcome to my world." I said with a grin.

"Alright, let's try to focus on one thing at a time right now." Ethan suggested, effectively redirecting the conversation back to the task at hand.

"K." Jeremy agreed. He smiled apologetically at me for speaking as though I wasn't there as he tried to refocus.

You ready?" Ethan asked. "Just like we talked about now, nothing too complicated, nothing fancy." He reminded Jeremy as he regained his attention. "Keep it simple and stick to the truth as much as possible, it makes it easier to remember later. She'll lead you in to everything we want to cover, you just have to act and answer naturally. You got this!" He reassured Jeremy calmly as I saw him take a deep breath. I felt his adolescent anxiety running through me and mixing in with my own. He looked at me and I gave him and encouraging smile and a nod anyway.

"Go break some teenage hearts." I said making him laugh and we were all a little more relaxed after that.

"Yeah, alright." He agreed acting shy again, but much calmer. He looked over towards Marina and her crew and I could feel the intensity when he focused his stare on them. It was somewhat familiar in sensation to the way Ethan's stares felt, but still distinctly different. Very easy to distinguish from what I was used to. He did manage it nice and discretely though I noticed, before he got too close. It was much better in the "*control*" department than he had been before and I couldn't help being impressed. That really *was* quick!

I grinned at Ethan knowing he would be aware of it too. He grinned back and I felt his satisfaction in Jeremy's control level mix with mine. Marina and her crew must've checked out, because after that short assessment he picked up his chin and his pace and headed over to where they were getting ready. They shook hands with him when he arrived at the pair of director's chairs that they had set up in front of a backdrop to act as their "mobile" interview stage. Jeremy pulled himself up into the chair opposite Marina and they talked quietly for a few minutes while the cameramen checked the lighting and sound quality.

I could feel her kindly but confidently assuring him as she explained the angle that the interview would take. He nodded a lot and his own confidence stayed steady so I relaxed a little too.

I looked back at Ethan and we grinned privately at each other, aghast at Jeremy's surprising mention of my "color variations." He was still the only other person who had ever spoken about it out loud besides Ethan. It actually made me feel more embarrassed than the kiss in the gazebo had! Like I had gotten caught with my pants down. It was weird after having had it as such a private thing for so long. The truth was that it was only private between myself and any present visually gifted *heights*! Who knew I'd ever meet more than one?! As I thought about it I realized there were likely to be many, especially in our company! I sighed and we shook it off, but we were both thinking that we would have to keep that in mind for the future.

Ethan tilted his head then towards a picnic table behind us and I followed him over there where we sat down together to watch. Then he took out his phone and holding it facing the "stage," he began to video tape the proceedings. I scrunched my brow at the peculiar action, but I knew him well enough to know there had to be a reason for it.

The real camera's lights went on again and a few seconds later one of them pointed at Marina. She started to speak, perfectly on cue.

"Day one. The work is officially under way. No turning back now!" She said with an excited smile. "So what better time to start meeting a few of the inspiring individuals involved in this amazing venture. One group in particular that we are lucky enough to have here, are the local Boy scouts. Now I'll take a boy scout as a helper on a project any day of the week just on principal, but these aren't even just any old scouts. No, we are lucky enough to have this project fall on a year when not just one, or even two, but *five* senior scouts are hoping to reach the rank of 'Eagle Scout' and let me tell you, that's no small feat! Lucky for us, in order to accomplish that goal, they need to complete a community service project with an unimaginable amount of man-hours, and boy did we have the project for them!" She said with an exuberance that only a journalist could pull off.

"They are all, *every one of them*, fine examples of what you would want your own son, nephew or neighbor to be like. Not perfect by any means, just basically all around *good* kids. They have to be to have gotten where they are today. But one scout in particular has overcome *extreme* adversity to be here." She said, her voice taking on a more somber tone.

"He was a regularly awarded student, a record breaking athlete who from what I hear, enjoyed his fair share of attention from the female teenage population of this town!" She added with a knowing grin. "For all intents and purposes, he was a young man with a very bright future ahead of him. He was one of those dream kids who did everything right, and still he almost lost it all. I happen to know that he's one of the *most* grateful to be here today! Let's meet Jeremy Hoffman." She said turning to Jeremy as I imagined the scene expanding to include him.

"Hey Jeremy, it's really great to meet you!" She said enthusiastically.

"It's very nice to meet *you!*" He said both politely but also with a humorous amount of male appreciation in his eyes. That got a chuckle from the small crowd. Marina just smiled graciously, accustomed to taking compliments.

"So tell me Jeremy exactly what happened to you to threaten life as you know it so completely, and how are you doing now, today?" She probed gently and then crossed her legs so she could rest her elbow on her knee and her chin on the heel of her hand, appearing to be in deep concern over his answer.

"Well one minute, things were pretty much perfect just like you said, I was living my life and being a kid, you know? Going to school and hanging out with my friends. The next thing I knew I was in the hospital, so sick that I couldn't even stand up. It was pretty terrible." He finished with a nod.

"No one knew what was wrong with me at first. It took them a while to figure it out and meanwhile I just kept getting sicker and sicker. It was really tricky because no one thinks of West Nile Virus so much in New England in the dead of winter. But we'd had a really warm stretch and my friends and I took advantage of the nice weather to go hike up to the old swimming hole. No one's really gone swimming over there since like the 1800's or something 'cause of like pollution and stuff and now it's mostly just a giant swamp, but it's a great place to fish and catch frogs." He explained naturally.

"Anyway, you never expect to get bit by mosquitoes around

here in February, so you don't exactly think to wear bug spray, you know what I mean?" He asked with a nonchalant shrug of his teenage shoulders. "Unfortunately, the mosquitoes don't exactly have a calendar. If it warms up enough, they hatch. If they hatch, they feed, simple as that." He said sounding much older than his years.

"That must have been very scary for you." She said with a look of fear all her own. "I hear your fever at one point reached *104.5 degrees!* That's not your every-day kind of sick." She said, dread evident in her voice.

"Yeah. Um, that's what I hear anyway. I mostly slept through a lot of that. See, only about 1% of the people who contract West Nile will ever develop the really serious type of neurological illness from it like I did, but out of those people, up to like 10% of them will actually die from it." He said and I could feel the reality of that for him from his words alone. The west Nile part wasn't exactly true in his case, but the rest was accurate enough just the same.

"Once it got real bad, they kinda' knocked me out so I could rest and heal and hopefully find enough strength within me to get over it. They didn't really know if I would or not, but they had done all they could. They told my parents that too, straight out. I overheard them talking about it before I went to sleep." He admitted with a loud swallow and I could feel how that little truth had really affected him from where I sat. *Ouch!* He kept going though. He had already survived that part.

"I was mostly just worried about my mom then. I had never been that sick before and I knew deep down that I might really, actually die. It was scary, but all I could think was that I didn't want something that bad to happen to *her*, you know?" He admitted looking up at Marina for just a brief, honest moment. He looked back down at his hands in his lap and swallowed again before he continued. "She didn't deserve that. She didn't do anything wrong. She was a good mom, you know? I just couldn't stand the thought of her ever being hurt that much!" He said as he choked up just for a brief second before he pulled it together again. He was doing better than I was at the moment!

"I have a lot of little brothers and sisters at home and they really need her, you know?" He reiterated again in his teenage vernacular. I felt my heart break for him just as I felt everyone else's within earshot do the same. I knew it was powerful stuff. If it were possible, I knew I would feel all the hearts breaking around the country while it aired, but thank God it wasn't*!*

He took a deep breath and he brightened enough to finish his tale then. "I did come out of it though, after almost a week! Only when I woke up, I was still confused, and scared, and a real long way from '*back to normal.*' I really wanted to be, but it took me a few more weeks to even start to feel like myself again." He admitted sheepishly.

"I tried to go out and pretend that I was fine, but I really wasn't. Not yet. I was mostly just weak and tired a lot in the beginning, you know, like short tempered because I just didn't have the energy that a teenager like me used to take for granted. It made me angry at first that I couldn't do everything I wanted to right away." He added, looking down at the floor. I knew that part of his story would cover his outburst at Movie night nicely. "But it got steadily better and better." He explained with another shrug as he picked back up another notch.

"Then after a while, I got past that too. I was really lucky that my real friends were still there, waiting for me to come back around." He admitted with a warm, shy smile. "Once I got back on my feet, it was like I never left. I can't even tell you how happy I am to be here now with my fellow scouts, perfectly healthy, working on our Eagle project together for the town, after not even being sure that I would live through the night at one point. It's hard to explain but it's pretty awesome." He said with a one shouldered shrug and smiled.

"Maybe after college I'll know big enough words to describe it better, but all I can say now is that being that close to death changed things for me. It made me more aware of everything that I still want out of life!" He said and his excitement for the future was clear. Another big goal accomplished.

The things he was discussing were lessons that were very *large* for a fifteen year old to grasp, but it was obvious that he had not only lived them, but that he had truly learned them. It hadn't been easy, but just like Ethan's trials had made him the strong man he was today, so too had Jeremy's journey left a stronger, wiser young man in its' wake. It was annoying to see how that worked, but it *did* work. There was no denying that. I thought of Liliana again and my stomach tightened.

"Little things that I used to take for granted, I appreciate now in ways that I never had time for before I got sick. It taught me a lot about how lucky we are just for each day." He said as his eyes lit up and I could feel that they weren't just words. He really felt that way. My chest filled with pride and affection more and more as he spoke so honestly. He was really starting to perk up, almost at the end of his story, and I breathed it in with a half-smile at his quiet confidence.

"I'm really feeling great now, you know? Back to 100% and I'm glad to be moving past all of that. It was tough but I survived and I've earned the right to put it all behind me, so that's what I'm doing. Fortunately for me, life goes on. Now I'm just looking forward to making Eagle Scout, finishing high school and thinking about college, same as the rest of my friends. That's more than enough." He ended with a smile so charming that I was sure he had learned it from watching Ethan.

I looked back at Ethan then and saw him touch his screen to stop the recording. I looked up at him next to me on the bench and I could feel that he was pretty pleased. *Hmpf.* I was too. He really had done a good job of working with Jeremy during their time alone. I smiled up at him, my pride showing just as clearly.

"You did *good.*" I said simply but honestly and I could feel it as it started coming back around again. His uneasiness told me just how uncomfortable he still was with praise, but his pleasure at my approval hit me soon after that and it was beyond fulfilling. I tried not to get lost in it so I could pay attention to the wrap up, but I was as helpless as ever in the face of his pleasure and I missed most of the end despite my good intentions. The next thing that I knew, I was tearing my eyes away from Ethan's just as Marina was shaking Jeremy's hand and thanking him for doing such a great job.

Jeremy gave us a quick satisfied look with his head tipped in our direction, then he walked back over to where his friends were. He was bathed in an adorable blush but was also exuding a grand sense of accomplishment that was entirely brand new. I looked back at Ethan again and saw him adding a text to the video and then he hit send. He set his phone down on the table and looked up at me.

"Where did that just go?" I asked, trying to catch up.

"Straight to my buddy Anderson in direct response to his '*warning*.'" He answered with a satisfied half grin. "I'm so glad he left me his card. I don't want him to have to wait for the evening news, but I do want him to know what's going to be on it." He said with an eyebrow wiggle. "I expect it won't take long for him to respond to my offer." He added.

"Offer?" I asked, not bothering to hide my dread at the prospect.

"*Mmmmm.* To give him access to all of the results from Jeremy's testing, the *real* ones." He looked at me for added emphasis. "But not to Jeremy himself. He's been through enough. And that's only if he agrees to leave Jeremy alone after that completely *and* not to prosecute anyone else in town that was involved, *all present company* included." He said with a wink. "If I'm right, he wants the information more than he wants to gain possession, of any of us. And I don't think Jeremy will be at as big of a risk from him anymore after today, even with the results. But we'll have to wait and see how it all plays out." He explained only mildly concerned.

"Of course his attitude can always change. We're not discounting that possibility at all." He added on as an allowance. "But it should at least get us through this day, so we stand a chance of dealing with that some other day." I noticed that his confidence remained steady regardless of the odds. I wanted to feel the same but I wasn't quite there yet.

"Do you think he'll really do that? Just take the info and walk away? That sure would be nice but I'm sorry I don't trust it, especially knowing what they're going to find." I admitted still worrying about every other possible outcome.

"That's okay. They already know. They're just looking for

confirmation and if that gains us all our freedom it's a small concession since we're not really giving them anything. One way or another, it *will* all work out. We just have to take it one step at a time." He insisted. I felt his usual comforting waves washing over me then in an attempt to physically reassure me. I sat for a moment and let it happen. I closed my eyes while I breathed it in. As usual, I was hesitant to rely too heavily on it, especially given the lesson in separation and patience that we had so recently learned, but it was exactly what I needed at the moment and I had missed it so much that I couldn't resist the fact that it was actually available. I didn't really want to. I figured I'd earned that one. We sat that way in silence for a few minutes, blocking everything else out.

Then I heard the reverberation on the picnic table as his phone alerted to let him know he had a message. We both turned to look as the screen lit up in tandem to the sound. We stared at it for a few seconds like it was a venomous snake writhing on the table.

Jeremy walked back over and came up next to us. He noticed where our attention was focused, looked up and asked intently. "Is that him? Did it work?" I could feel the apprehension rippling off of him and it made me even more uneasy, regardless of Ethan's best efforts.

Ethan picked it up and swiped the screen. He didn't make us wait long before he nodded. He likes the video." He said raising one eyebrow. "He wants to meet tonight, with *both* of us." He added quietly, surprisingly enough while looking back up at *me!*

Huh? Well that was certainly interesting. What was I, his best bud now or something? That was all I needed. But then I remembered the old adage regarding what distance to keep your enemy's at and I decided maybe I should go along after all. "See what I could see," so-to-speak.

"Fine. When?" I asked Ethan and he hesitated as I felt both his reservation and his reluctant pride as they rushed through me at the same time.

"We meet at The Pines at 9:00, my dear Lara." He teased, in reference to the female heroine, but there was no real humor in his voice that time, only acceptance.

Chapter 17

As we made our way slowly down the curving, dirt road my apprehension grew. I focused on the cloud of naturally occurring soft, superfine yellow sand that rose up around us to distract myself. I remembered hearing Jack refer to it once as "*Pinegrove Gold*" due to its' high quality and high demand in the market. At the moment it was just as valuable to me as a beautiful distraction.

I looked away from the ground and my gaze swept up to the tops of the towering pine trees beside us as we crept past and I at least understood the reason for the name of the place then, if not necessarily the reason that I was there. My anxiety had ebbed and flowed a hundred different times since accepting the unexpected invitation. What did he want with me? *Hmpf.* It was all well and good to act tough on the spot, but it's another thing all together to maintain it throughout the moments that follow! It was all just way too *real*!

I was doing a fair job of allowing the scenery to take my mind off of it though. I knew the old race track had been redone to house the town's baseball and softball fields a long time ago. I couldn't help wishing that we were simply there to play a game of ball. I tried to take slow deep breaths and reminded myself that Anderson could have arrested me at any time over the last month if he really wanted to. I'm sure he could get me on an 'obstruction of justice' charge or something similar easily enough, but he hadn't. That fact was inescapable and I knew that Ethan had to be right about where his motivation truly derived from. We weren't important to him other than as a way to get to Jeremy. If we gave him everything he could ever want to know about Jeremy, then there would be nothing left to gain from us and based on theory at least, from Jeremy himself. It was a scary risk but I had to admit it made sense. *If* all he wanted was the knowledge.

If not, we probably only had as long as it took for him to be sure that Jeremy was potentially as powerful as he had suspected. That should take him at least a little while to sort out though and hopefully by then it would be too late to simply steal him away quietly. Marina had done a great job with that.

All of that should have helped me to stay calm a lot more than it actually did. Even if we weren't the main target, I knew that didn't make us *safe* necessarily. In my experience being a pawn was never the best option in any major battle. If you were going to go into a battle at all, ideally you wanted to be in a better position than *that.* Everyone knew that pawns were expendable.

That was what had me so worried that I kept forgetting to breathe. Ethan on the other hand was as calm, cool and collected as always. I gave his demeanor some serious consideration for a minute and decided that it was an even better distraction. Especially since I knew most psychological professionals would completely mistake his calm attitude and wrongly label him "*emotionally detached.*" They would never believe the depth of the pain and understanding in his powerful feelings. Because they would never accept that he was self-disciplined enough to keep so much contained *and* remain calm! *Hmpf.* But I knew better!

He wasn't broken. A little damaged sure, aren't we all? But definitely not broken. In all of his own struggles, they had never managed to break him. I knew that to be 100% true, but of course that's just me. He really is *that* strong when it comes to putting logic before emotions, and it isn't a symptom of some psychosis. He has that ability simply because he never had a choice.

Like then, he would do what he needed to do for now, and deal with the feelings later, somewhere in the dead of night I suspected, when the remainder of the world was resting. It was still hard, but his inner strength never let him dwell on it. I was still mostly envious of that part. The only thing I picked up from him at that moment other than that calm was his faint worry for me, but even that he kept mostly buried. Although that was *also* for my sake.

It was just more proof that he wasn't completely removed from the ability to feel compassion, but again, it was only proof to me and I didn't need it. I was already certain that he was one of the most *compassionate* men I had ever known, and I had *really* "known" just about every man who had ever crossed my path! I tried to focus on that as much as I could. It definitely helped.

I refused to let myself get sidetracked by him completely though, whether he would have preferred me to or not. I really needed to stay on guard while trying carefully not to panic. It was a super-fine line and I was doing my absolute best tightrope walker impression. *Arms wide... ...deep steady breaths... ...just keep moving...*

With that analogy playing out in my head, I gave a sigh and calmed down another micrometer. I returned my focus to the "*now.*" He gave me a sideways look and a half smile in response to my accomplishment without his assistance. I smiled back a little, pleased myself with my success but it was still shaky.

I switched to listening to the crunching beneath the tires as we crept along just fast enough for the cloud not to overtake us. At least I told myself it was just the dust cloud that kept us approaching so cautiously. For the moment it worked. *Deep breath...*I closed my eyes and the sound calmed me that much more. I didn't open them again until we finally slowed to a crawl.

We didn't stop completely until we rolled up to the furthest set of fenced off bases and dugouts. There we could easily see the infamous grey sedan parked in the furthest spot, behind the "home" team's dugout. So we stopped on the "away" side, leaving room for a quick getaway if necessary. I was really hoping that those types of heroics *wouldn't* turn out to be necessary that time around though. I'd had enough excitement the last time we all got together to hold me over for a while!

Ethan pulled past the spot, then backed in and shut off the

car. He took the flash drive full of Jeremy's medical information off of his key ring and clipped it onto his belt loop. He smiled over at me. "Ready?" he asked. And just because he had asked, I suddenly wasn't sure.

"*Uhhhh*... I think so?" I answered finally, hardly convincing anyone. He took my hand and waited for me to look him in the eye. I knew he would wait all day so I didn't bother to try and ignore him. I looked up at him with my resignation equally unhidden and he squeezed my hand tighter while his assurance washed over me. I stopped fighting it for a moment then and absorbed as much as I could.

All the while I knew I was also going to need to rely on some fortitude of my own. If I was really going to be a soldier in the fight for the future good of *heights* and all that, yada, yada, yada... *(so dramatic, I know)* I really was going to have to toughen up some, I decided stubbornly. Once Ethan's generous energy was neutral again, I sat still a moment longer, feeling just my own determination and the fresh air, testing my strength to maintain it. On top of what he had already given me, it felt really good. When I felt my calm return, I held it for a few beats and let the new, clean energy fill what little space remained. *I could do this...*

"Let's go." I said without reservation then. "*I* want to go home *too!*" I added vehemently.

He understood my cryptic statement immediately but his surprise at the intensity of my conviction actually froze him for half a second. That made me smile and sit a little taller. I squeezed his hand that time and then I turned, opened my door and got out. He recovered quickly and followed suit. We reached the front of the car and we rejoined hands in the dark, completely still, warm air. We walked past the metal bleachers and through the squeaky gate in the chain link fence.

It was dark on the infield without the big overhead lights that would normally be on during a night game, but the clear sky gave us just enough moonlight to see our way. The outfield was barren and quiet except for the bats and the fireflies that we could make out chasing each other in the distance. Still, Ethan knew as well as I did that we were not alone. I hadn't seen Anderson yet but I could definitely *feel* him!

"Beautiful night for a game." He called out suddenly from the shadows at the far end of the dugout on our left. I jumped a little at the sound but I hoped that Ethan was the only one who noticed that weakness, as he squeezed my hand again in a subtle attempt to steady me. We made a slightly wider swath to our right than we had originally intended and stopped just past the pitcher's mound, closer to the shortstop than home base. Ethan answered him.

"Sure is. Who's up first?" He asked in return like we were back on the farm, all there for a friendly game of Whiffle Ball. In the serene setting, surrounded by the soaring pines on three sides and the river on the fourth, covered in a warm black velvety blanket full of stars, it was easy enough to believe that's all it was. A game. It was surreal like a dream, but much more dangerous. Still I tried to focus more on the illusion than the reality to keep me calm. Whatever worked, I thought desperately.

Anderson stood and walked out of the dugout as he slowly tossed a baseball up into the air and caught it with the same hand. "I believe that would be me, after your recent grand-slam with the *home*-video on the nightly news." He offered clearly not expecting any protest. "Nice quality, by the way. Remind me to compare cell phone features with you sometime." He threw in casually. It was super relaxed but far from genuine. He stopped once he got to home plate and I for one was grateful for the remaining distance. I'm not sure what advantage I thought it gave us really, but as long as I didn't think too hard about it, it helped. I wasn't in a nit-picky mood.

That distance was close enough for me to know that he was feeling anxious too, so at least I knew I wasn't alone. But I wasn't sure if his was due to the stress of the situation or his excitement at what he hoped to gain so I didn't take too much comfort in it. We did appear to be alone otherwise though, which was part of the agreement, and I tried to let that reassure me. At least it was two against one, right?

"I'm glad you liked it." Ethan answered easily with his trademark grin. "It was our own take on 'reality TV.' You know, based on real events, but slightly scripted and edited for maximum viewing effect." I could feel that Anderson was actually amused by that as well and he smiled back in spite of his aggravation and his own weariness.

"*Ahhhh*, yes. That is a very popular genre these days, isn't it?" He agreed. "West Nile, huh? Smart! It makes perfect sense, doesn't it?" He continued not afraid to give praise where it was due. I could feel that he actually was impressed by the details. "I may use that one myself in the future." He added, his tone and the atmosphere changing ever so slightly. It was extremely subtle but I felt it and I squeezed Ethan's hand again imperceptibly to make sure that he felt it too.

"What about you, Stone? Will you be saving that one for reuse in your own repertoire? Surely you are not stupid enough to be responsible for *all* the "*unspecific-interference*" that fellow agents have run into in this area in the past, are you?" He baited. "I've already given you way more credit than that and I'd hate to have to rethink my entire opinion of you." He added as a warning while he began to pace around the batters' box.

"I can't help wondering." He stopped and looked up at us. "Are our paths going to cross again in the future on another case of '*West Nile Virus*' Stone?" He asked and it was obvious what he meant. Someone back at headquarters had obviously been poking around and started putting two and two together. I didn't feel like he knew for sure, but he had enough to give him a hunch. I could feel that much with ease.

"Well I can't imagine a scenario where that would happen, but I know better now than to ever say 'never.'" He answered with a shrug and a convincing amount of innocence and amusement at the idea. "But c'mon, let's be serious. I'm a musician, not a doctor! I just happen to live in a small town with the same bunch of people that I've known all my life. I'm just trying to help my buddy's kid get through a tough spot and you were in the way of that. Sorry 'bout all that, but it's really nothing personal." He added with a charming smile. Nobody was buying it necessarily but it was passing the time peaceably so far and I thought that that may be enough. Then he turned his attention my way and my stomach dropped. I had been waiting for it but I still wasn't prepared.

"What about you, Miss Harrington?" I felt his attention focus on me then like a laser and I stopped breathing all together while I waited to hear what he wanted. "You've just recently relocated to this area. So where exactly does *your* fierce protection level in all of this stem from, exactly? I just have to ask, you understand. Why are you even here? Not now, but in general?" He asked innocently, like it was an afterthought. But I could feel a distinct curiosity there that was as intense as it had been before. He knew who and *what* I was by then, at least on paper, but he still couldn't figure out why I was *there! B*esides as Ethan's occasional girlfriend, how did I fit in? It bothered him not being sure but I was okay with that. I was still working to figure it all out myself. Why should I help him catch up?

"Besides you personally inviting me?" I asked flippantly. "No specific reason, just the 'right place at the right time' I suppose." I supplied with a nonchalant shrug. I tried to keep it as convincing as I could without crossing into blatantly "*making false statements.*" Nobody was buying that either necessarily, but it was all I had to offer on the subject so he tried another tactic.

"*Really?* I mean given all that you've got going for you personally, with your burgeoning career, your supportive, *prominent* family, and such a beautiful young daughter that you are trying to see more of. I just don't understand why you would risk all of that to voluntarily get tangled up in situations like this one, in a little town that you just randomly moved to a few months back. It's not the kind of thing an intelligent person would choose to do and as far as I can tell, and you seem to be a smart enough lady." He allowed.

"So I wonder if maybe you think you've found a place to '*belong*,' because you think you share something in common with these people." He added sarcastically, like the notion was ridiculous. "It's very naive of you to think it's all that simple, but at least I could understand that." He stated outright with a laugh and it dawned on me then finally. That was it. That was why I was there. That asshole was still hoping that I would be the softest and most vulnerable of the group and therefore hopefully the *weakest* link!

I knew he wouldn't understand it, even if I had the inclination to explain, so I was glad then that I didn't. I could feel Ethan's desire for me to be careful but I didn't need it. I had more than enough "intelligence" of my own to keep me quiet and confident.

I simply shrugged. "You would never understand." I challenged. He wasn't intimidated by that though.

"No? I might surprise you, you know. You really shouldn't rely on *intuition* for *all* of your information gathering. You can miss a lot of important facts that way. You have to be very careful." He warned cryptically. "There are a lot of people out there that can very easily manipulate skills like yours if you're not careful. Did you know that?" He asked in a warning tone while he paced again. That tid-bit was unexpected but I refused to be baited by it. I knew his tactics too well by then.

"I know that you think you're doing the right thing and that in turn gives you strength Simone. I get it. I wonder though, how you would feel, if you found out that what you were doing *wasn't* necessarily the right thing." He threw out casually. He stared at me after that and waited a long beat hoping I would crack.

Hmpf. Not today, Anderson. I thought with a new conviction. Not after everything we'd already been through to get there. We were almost *'home!'* I could almost *taste* it! He was *not* going to take it away from us at the last second! I was *not* going to let that happen and it was certainly *not* going to happen because of *me!* I stared back, my resolve nothing less than concrete. He waited a few seconds more but finally had to acknowledge the impasse. He was annoyed but not terribly surprised and he moved on. He looked back over at Ethan and I took a long, slow, clandestine breath in acute relief.

"So what is it that you have brought me, Stone? That I am supposed to accept in exchange for half this towns' freedom, including your own?" He asked disbelievingly. Ethan held up the flash drive that he had removed from his belt loop.

"This! If all you really want is to make sure that he's in no way dangerous or communicable than we're willing to share that proof with you. This should be all you need. It's is a copy of all Jeremy's medical records and test results for the past six months." He said confidently. Anderson didn't look impressed however. He actually chuckled a little and shook his head.

"You're going to have to do better than that Stone." He threw back just as confidently. "We've had access to that information since the beginning. There's nothing in there that we want." He informed us with a grin. "It may have been too soon for the results that we were looking for to show up when that testing was done. These things can take time to develop. We need to do our own tests in order to be certain what we're dealing with before he can be completely cleared." He insisted deviously and I was instantly worried but Ethan wasn't.

"He has been retested, recently. And while you've had access to *someone's* records, I can assure you that they weren't Jeremy's!" Ethan replied with a chuckle of his own. Anderson was the worried one then, but he wasn't convinced yet so Ethan continued to explain.

"When I went to pick up a copy of his records for the family one day as a favor, my buddy there had some trouble finding them at first. Then he realized that someone had accidentally switched his patient number. Turns out that everything that they had on file under his name, really belonged to someone else. Their cases were so similar that no one noticed! Boy did we have a good laugh about that once we finally figured it out!" He supplied with a razor sharp smile. "*That's* what *you* have and have had since day one!" He added nonchalantly. He paused while that sank in before continuing.

"'Cause you know what we did, just for fun? We left it that way on purpose, just to see how long it would take the hospital staff to find and fix its mistake. Call it small-town quality control." He finished with a very satisfied smile at the change in Anderson's expression. "This right here, I promise you, is the only copy of Jeremy's real records you will ever get a shot at and it's a time-sensitive offer." He insisted while waving the flash drive. His argument suddenly held a lot more weight without him admitting to any crimes, I noticed.

"I can tell you that yes, some of the results on here are

somewhat unusual. And while the good doctor's here couldn't make sense of everything they found, we *are* all sure, without a doubt, that nothing they found was still harmful in any way to Jeremy or to anyone around him. He's not sick anymore and he is in no way communicable." I could feel Anderson's wariness to swallow the whole scenario being presented to him, especially Ethan's innocence in it all, but I also felt his recognition of the little bits of truth in Ethan's remarks. And when his anticipation absolutely *raced* at Ethan's mention of "*unusual things*" I knew we were on the right track.

"He's completely fine now. Whatever else this tells you, if you can make any sense of it at all, I know that it will tell you *that* and I need you to agree to leave it that way, once and for all!" Ethan insisted emphatically without ever raising his voice. "You can take this pile of random information. You can study it, dissect it, add it to your data files or whatever it is you need to do!" He offered stubbornly, pretending complete naiveté. "But this is all you get! If you take this you have to agree to let *him* get back to just being a damn kid! That's all he wants and that's all any of us in this town want *for* him. Just finish your information gathering expedition once and for all, and leave us all alone! That's the deal."

As he finished his little speech he slid a switch with his thumb. I had never seen a flash drive with a switch like that before but he made its' function clear very quickly. It was insurance. *We were* still sitting ducks after all. That "two-against-one" impression could always turn out to be nothing more than that, an impression.

"You have ten seconds to decide before I release this kill switch that will render the data permanently irretrievable! And I'm gonna need it in writing within that time, signed, witnessed by me and sealed with your saliva." He instructed pulling an official looking contract out of his back pocket.

"If you say no, you won't *ever* get the information in my hand any other way, nor will you ever see Jeremy again, I promise you that." He insisted and I could feel his 100% honesty in that even if Anderson couldn't. He backed it up most effectively for him though. "You can go back on your word and arrest us if you want to but this is a small town Anderson. People can be hard to find and files can be *'re-lost'* or even *'accidentally'* deleted from the system entirely because key employees spent the night distracted, worrying about their friends and family that they never heard back from." He suggested innocently in a calm, relaxed voice. He was finished then. I could feel that that was all of his cards on the table. I just silently prayed that it would be enough. He was asking an awful lot. I was glad that he wasn't giving him enough time to find a way around it.

"*Ten... nine... eight...*" He began the countdown.

I could feel how much Anderson despised being backed into a corner but I could also feel his reluctant acceptance creeping up to the surface too. He wanted what we had! He knew he was still winning as long as we really *had* what we said we did. He just hated that it was Ethan that was calling the shots. I knew that was part of Ethan's tactic though, to keep Anderson feeling like he was walking away the victor and that he was only giving up face and not real power or key goals.

Ethan stood at a cocky stance waiting, as if he had no understanding at all of how much danger he was in. But the fact that Anderson was annoyed by that, also kept him from thinking too hard about it. I knew it was all part of the plan. We had talked about that. Even if we hadn't had the time to prepare in advance for a change I would have felt it all, and I would've wondered why he was acting so out of character. Then I would have had to puzzle it all out, quickly trying to catch up. It was so much nicer to actually be in the loop for a change. It seemed our plan was working too because then I could feel that he wanted to get it over with as much as we did! I sighed just slightly in relief but I knew that Ethan felt it. I *felt* him feel it. We stood waiting for another beat, but that was all.

"Let's see it" He called out. He raised his arm and started doing the one handed clap towards himself in mid-air, motioning for Ethan to come forward with the flash drive. Anderson kicked home plate away, leaned down and pulled a sleek laptop out from under the sand as we began to walk over and slowly close the gap between us. "I always like to keep my hands free, just in case." He offered in a falsely jovial manner while he unzipped the plastic bag protecting it and threw it aside. He opened the super-light ultra-book and held it out. Ethan plugged the flash drive into the USB port but he didn't let it go, nor did he take his thumb off of the switch.

"You can't copy this until I let this button go, and if I fall without switching the secret release button first, it will self-delete, so don't bother." Ethan warned with an innocent wiggle of his brows, playing it off as a fluke. "My buddy doesn't mess around! Don't ask me how it works but he's the top guy in IT down there and he's like a magician with these things." He added acting duly impressed. I tried not to laugh at the fact that my Magician had just secretly called himself a "*magician.*" I was definitely tickled by it but I was smart enough to keep it to myself.

We all watched as the drive popped up on his screen and the files began to auto-extract one at a time. The documents began to layer one on top of each other, window after window, after window. There were many and they came up quickly. Anderson's eyes were fast though and I felt his joy register as he locked onto recognizable bits and pieces as they flew by. He was happy. *Those* were the results that he had been expecting to find! He was feeling self-righteous vindication at finally seeing the proof once and for all! I looked back at Ethan and gave the slightest nod. He understood.

"Do we have a deal?" He asked outright, his playfulness suddenly gone. Anderson looked at Ethan, then at me and finally back at the screen again. I could feel him weighing out each desire one last time. He really wanted to arrest us once and for all, just for the satisfaction of it. But thankfully and luckily for us, he wanted what he saw on the computer screen more.

"Deal." He agreed and tore the paper from Ethan's other hand. He scribbled a quick signature on it then held it out to Ethan. Once he signed his name Anderson took it back and folded it, then he put it in the attached envelope. He licked the gummed edge, pressed it closed and angrily slapped it against Ethan's chest. I knew all it really did was buy us time, but I sighed loudly anyway. I just couldn't hold that one back!

Ethan moved his thumb up and down twice, then took it off of the button while keeping his hand on the flash drive. Anderson quickly typed in the commands necessary to copy the material. When he was satisfied that he had it all saved not once but twice, and instantly emailed off somewhere, he nodded to Ethan who removed the drive and clipped it back onto his key ring.

Anderson closed the sleek laptop and tucked it under his arm. I could feel it clear as day then. He was done with us, at least for the moment. He had what he wanted and just like the patrons on opening night at the Gardens, his interest was already elsewhere. He made one last remark before departing, letting his aggravation at being manipulated show.

"I hope for both your sakes that our paths *never* cross again after tonight!" He warned with a pointed finger. Then he turned and headed back into the darkness. We heard his car door close. His headlights cut across the field and we were momentarily blinded after having adjusted so thoroughly to the dark. Then the beam swept sharply to the left and we could see again. A second later the overly bright light was gone and so was he. All that remained were the spots in our eyes, the discarded plastic bag on the infield and the billowing yellow dust cloud on the road.

Was that it? Was it really over? Could that even be possible? After everything we'd been through, could it really be that easy? I turned to look at Ethan for confirmation. He smiled a very satisfied smile down at me as his happiness at the turnout rolled off of him and tumbled through me.

"I can't believe he's gone. I mean, seriously? Is this *real?*" I asked softly in the renewed silence. I was afraid of the answer, afraid that I would wake up and it would all turn out to be another dream. He reached down and stroked my cheek gently and his smile grew. He was quick to reassure me for once.

"Yes. *This is real!* I told you that hell was only *temporary!*" He insisted happily with a sideways grin. I leaned in and rested against his chest for a beat or two while I let the truth of that sink in.

"I've never been so happy to say '*you were right*' to anyone before in my whole life!" I admitted still in awe that we were really and truly free citizens again in every sense of the word! I pulled back and looked up at him. "Don't get too used to that though." I warned jovially. I couldn't help it, the relief made me practically giddy. He just chuckled.

"Let's go get our most recent Camp graduate and bring him back home for good!" He said and his relief at that surpassed my own. I took another deep, "I-can't-believe-this-is-real" breath and then I took his hand.

He sent the others at Camp a quick text once we got back in the car to let them know the plan had been successful and that we were on our way back. Then he started the engine and the wave of elation that I was riding was like a magic carpet that left me feeling like I was floating high above my seat as we drove away. Never in my life had I felt more awake or more aware of every single molecule around me! I sat in awe of how I felt for most of the ride.

We had left Jeremy there at Camp with Dr. J, Hank and Roxy during the negotiations, with instructions on what to do if things went south. It was still the safest place for him as long as he was in town and not being actively pursued, but it was only supposed to be temporary that time. We knew that by the end of the night we would either have to give the order for them to go, maybe for good, or we'd be able to bring him back home once and for all. Camp was just to be a holding pad until we knew which.

Jeremy's family knew what the plan was and while they waited to hear from us one way or the other, they were home. Probably watching the evening newscast of the special replay again and again I guessed, trying to ease their anxiety. Ethan decided however, not to text them with the news. I smiled because I could instantly feel his plan and I was onboard that time. He sure did like his surprises. Then again, so did I.

We met Jeremy and the others at camp and were greeted by hoots and hollers, hugs, and high fives all around as we got out. We celebrated appropriately but not at length. It was still somewhat surreal to be so happy in our little bubble there in *height-land*, so far removed from the rest of reality.

Once we had thanked each person for their help and cracked a few jokes, taking advantage of the giddy atmosphere, we hugged everyone goodbye for the time being and loaded Jeremy and all his stuff back up into the SUV. The three of us drove off still waving and headed to the Hoffman's humble abode for a surprise late night visit/delivery.

We pulled up and the house was quiet. It was also dark but for the random flashing lights from the TV glowing through the living room windows. He killed the headlights as we pulled up and then the engine. We rolled quietly to a stop and we got out, closing our doors as quietly as possible. Jeremy had to cover his mouth with his hand to keep from laughing out as we quickly unloaded everything and made our way up to the door. Ethan just stared at him with a wide-eyed grin when we were ready and he pulled it together. He really had come a long way from the lost kid that we had talked to that first night there. I grinned happily as I thought about it and he smiled back, seeming to understand. He was so much wiser than his years at that point that I had to shake my head.

Jeremy reached behind the shutter of the window next to the front door and pulled out a key. It must be a local thing, I thought with an exasperated grin at Ethan. He grinned back without apology. Jeremy however, was oblivious to our exchange and turned the key as quietly as he could in the lock. Then he slowly swung the door open and we could see his parents, sitting in separate reclining chairs but holding hands across the space in between. The scene was silhouetted nicely in the light of the evening news.

They had the story featuring Breezy Park and Jeremy DVR'd and they were in fact playing it back again, just as I had predicted. It was an easy assumption though because I knew I would be doing the exact same thing.

When the real thing walked up behind them though, they instantly flew from their chairs and burst into tears of relief! They knew what it meant for him to be there. The uncontrollable laughter started to mix in with the tears then. It was far too overwhelming for me to hope to contain and I was instantly right there with them, tears of joy streaming down my cheeks. Ethan was more controlled than the rest of us as always, but I could feel his joy and his deep satisfaction at the outcome quite clearly, whether he gushed outwardly or not. He did turn and wink at me though, in acknowledgement of our shared moment. My smile grew even wider.

It didn't take long for little ears to search out the sound of their role models voice and to spy on us from the top of the stairs. When their hopes were confirmed by what they saw, they came charging down in an uncontrollable parade of cheering chaos with all three dogs nipping at their heels! My smile was starting to hurt it was so big by then. Ethan grabbed me around the waist to pull me closer to him for protection as all five of Jeremy's younger siblings ran up and joined us in a giant group hug.

After a few minutes Jeremy let go and pulled back to look at all of us. He embraced his parents again, with one arm around each one's shoulders and then he looked up at us.

"Thank you." He said simply but sincerely to Ethan. I could feel how truly happy he was right then to be home but I knew that everyone else there could feel it just as easily as me. He took his arm off of his father's shoulders and extended it to shake Ethan's hand. Ethan shook his in return that time instead of hugging him again. It was clear that Ethan didn't consider him a *kid* anymore, but an equal.

The message between us was simpler and he did let his mother go to hug me one last time, quickly but sincerely. I noticed that neither Pete nor Helena thought it was weird or inappropriate. They just felt like I was extended family at that point and I was pretty happy with that. It finally felt legitimate by then.

Eventually we separated ourselves out of the pack and said goodnight, leaving them to reconnect as a family without our interference for the first time so many weeks. I noticed that everyone present was excited about that situation too, each for their own reasons.

As we stepped back outside into the stillness, he closed the door and looked down at me in complete seriousness. I felt his intensity wash over me before he said the words.

"Now let's get *you* home!" He offered happily and sweeter words I had not heard in a long, *long* time!

We raced straight back to my place. There I nearly reached the limit of my physical capacity for joy just from the slow, intentional, almost *ritualistic* closing of the blinds! Every... last... *one of them!* I was sure that by the next day the cameras would be long gone and it wouldn't matter anymore but it was still *extremely* satisfying that one time! We each started on one side and met in the middle. There weren't many things that equaled that enjoyment level in my book!

I tried to come up with an analogy but what came to mind were mostly inappropriate things like finally getting to pee after having to hold it through hours of torturous stop and go, Fourth of July traffic. That may not be the most romantic analogy but it did best illustrate my point. It was the kind of thing where you had to suffer an incredibly torturous hardship, one you previously couldn't even *conceive* of. Then prolong it for an extended period of time where every second you think you can't possibly take anymore, then you may be able to *truly* appreciate the pure and powerful relief that eventually follows when the suffering finally ends. You get it now, right? See.

Personally, I understood that depth of feeling all too well, even without the cringe-worthy physical analogy. But that was not the "*norm*" and actually, I really was glad about that. I didn't feel the need to spread the knowledge of bad the feelings around so much. I was content to keep as much of that to myself as I could. There were enough of those emotions out there already. But we had survived the torturous part and miraculously made it to that *life changing kind of good* feeling, and I was reveling in the relief without reservation for once, completely, as the last... shutter... *shut!*

Uuaahhhhhh...

The rest of the night was spent on a higher plain completely devoid of clothing and words, one where sleep and nourishment were neither required nor considered for a long, *long* time. Just knowing that sleep was an actual option at some point for once was more than enough to keep us putting it off for quite a while. We fed off of each other's intensity and it was self-perpetuating like a rechargeable battery that could continuously power itself off of its' own energy *while* expending it.

The most amazing thing of all was lying there together

afterwards in a sprawling contented pile as the sun came up without him making a single move to run off for once. Instead we laid side-by-side, staring at each other with our worn out half-smiles as we finally surrendered and waited blissfully for sleep to take us.

I refused to be the first to let go though. I needed to *see* him fall asleep and know that he really would! To believe that he really *could* before I could let go myself. Once his lids dropped and stayed down for more than thirty seconds *(yes, I counted)* I gave just one last *huge*, tired smile then sighed deeply and slipped off the edge myself. We didn't sleep very long but it was still the best few hours of sleep that I have ever gotten in my life!

It was hard to explain and definitely another first for me. *Hmpf. Never a shortage of firsts…* But it was incredibly fulfilling and also something else that I could very easily get used to.

Chapter 18

I still can't believe you're really here! Sitting on the deck wrapped around me like every day simplicities such as this are completely normal and not just *very* recently, highly unattainable." I said trying to explain how unreal it felt to just sit calmly in the open and do nothing with him.

"Well get used to it." He instructed playfully. "I like it here, and as long as I can get away with it, *next to you* is where I'm planning to be for the foreseeable future." He said warmly over my shoulder.

We had woken fairly early still full of good energy despite barely sleeping. Ethan had texted Jack just to check in and make sure nothing new had "developed" overnight.

"So far so good." He'd quickly replied. *Phew…* for the moment anyway… It was obvious that Jack had been awake as well, since he answered so fast and once he knew we were up he stopped up with Shirley bearing banana nut muffins and coffee. It was perfect actually, especially since the remaining Kent's currently in residence were all still fast asleep. I wasn't ready to share him that fully just yet.

Jack and Shirley were as happy to see him home as I was and they each hugged him in greeting. They weren't quick, "hello" hugs either, but the long, "*it feels so good to hold you in the flesh again*" kind and being near that had made me feel even better than I already did! We sat around the kitchen island and talked for a few minutes while we ate but they didn't stay long. Everyone knew we both needed to be at Breezy eventually, but I was glad that I had told

Marina not to expect us until after lunch, *if* things went well!

We were both wearing shorts and tank tops since we hadn't dressed for work yet. After they left, we sat nestled together the long way on my bench staring into the woods. We didn't have to shy away from the perfection of the spot anymore, as we had received confirmation from Jack earlier that "*someone*" had been by to collect the cameras already, before we ever had to tip our hand and have Hank remove them.

I was still worried about what they were going to do, *eventually*, about Jeremy and what they finally knew for sure about him. I also wondered when they would become interested enough in Ethan's interest in all of that, for their interest in *him* to change. I had to admit with a mix of honesty and dread that the same probably went for myself at that point. But in the meantime, I planned to enjoy the peace and quiet while it lasted. I knew better than to waste it!

It was really strange though to be so free and unrestricted again. I realized just how quickly I had become accustomed to living a life in hiding when I was with him. Thankfully it was finally time to learn how to just be "*normal*" with him. Or at least as close to that as either of us would ever come anyway, I thought to myself with a grin.

"It's a whole new reality for me too." He admitted, pulling my hair back on one side so he could see my face. "But I think I can find a way to get used to having you pressed up against me on a daily basis." He said as he rubbed his scruff covered cheek carefully against mine.

He hugged his arms tighter around my shoulders where I sat comfortably between his knees. "What about you?" He asked bravely while he crossed his ankles over mine and used his legs to pull me even closer. "Do you think you can really handle this, having me wrapped around you on a full-time basis?" He asked teasingly, at least at first.

"I mean I'm not moving in or anything, but I'm not planning on sleeping *alone* again anytime soon either!" He growled into my ear with his usual amount of intensity. "I've had enough of that to last me for a while." He added wholeheartedly. He grew a little more serious after that and let his worry show through, just for a minute. "I know originally you wanted to maintain a certain amount of space. Do you still feel that way?"

He retained that playful edge to his voice, but I could feel that his curiosity was just as real as his apprehension when it came to what my answer would be. I could also feel that it was one of those rare times that he was just like the rest of us and would have preferred to be able to hide that worry from me.

He'd perfected the art of playing it cool long ago, like we all try to do to varying success, in order to avoid being overly vulnerable in our relationships. He knew he couldn't do that with me though and while he mostly accepted it far too easily, there were rare moments like that one where he found it less than desirable just like everybody else.

Hmpf. *Good!*

I was actually a little relieved by that. It certainly didn't make me think any less of him, but it did make him seem just a bit more *human* for once, less *super*-human. I really liked getting a glimpse of that every once in a while.

Even that though was only possible because of my *heightened* empath ability! And while naturally I was grateful for it sometimes, I had always wrestled with that particular circumstance when it came to my relationships. I'd mostly insisted over the years, that I would've preferred to live without that advantage in that one area, if only I could! And as much as I had meant that for the most part in the past, I had to admit that I was actually pretty happy about the circumstances when it came to being with Ethan. In fact I could never hope to deny that anymore with any kind of a straight face.

I knew though, that at least it worked both ways for the first time, and likewise I'd had to accept *his* built-in ability to see way too much of me at every turn in exchange. In the end, it all seemed fair enough. The "laying one's self bare" part of our relationship appeared to be evenly balanced out between us and I knew that at that point in life I really couldn't ask for more than that. I turned halfway around in my nest of arms and legs so I could look at him fully.

"I've strongly avoided even the *idea* of getting involved again for some time now truth be told, because I was just *done* trying to convince myself that it was really possible for me! It all just started to seem like such a waste of time! I really believed that if I couldn't make it work with someone as perfect as Ben than it must really be me." I said honestly as I laughed at myself. "I mean, who was I kidding, right? *Seriously*, who wants to love someone that can't give you any privacy, *ever?!* I mean, *I* wouldn't!" I said vehemently, being painfully honest. I stopped and took a deep breath but he just gave a small chuckle and I could feel his lack of desire to back me up on that. I didn't understand that still, but I wanted to.

"*Why*, Ethan? Why is it not a problem for you? I still don't get it. Can you explain to me *how* it's possible that you are really so okay with my skills? No other man ever has been before, *ever*! No matter how much I *wanted* them to be or how hard they *tried* to be! And I have to admit, it's really hard for me to trust what I don't understand." I confessed with just a hint of that familiar fear in my eyes.

"It's simple." He answered with a nonchalant shrug. "Think about it for a minute." He instructed with his normal patience for explanations. He retained his trademark smile, but I could feel him gearing up to reveal his own painful truth. That surprised me a little. I couldn't think of what one might have to do with the other. See? Sometimes *knowing* things only leads to more questions.

"For a good part of my life I was forced to spend all of my time with a woman who refused to ever even acknowledge the *existence* of my feelings! Which I can honestly say, she did *perfectly!* Aside from my physical birth, I know for a *fact* that my pain never once touched that woman. *Not ever.*" He said plainly. "She was the antithesis of love."

"Then there is the fact that most of the people I interact with outside of Camp have already judged and sentenced me before I even get through hello. They all think they know who I am, whichever one of the misguided impressions of me they've settled on over the years. *Hmpf.* They never stop to notice who I *really* am.

Most aren't even capable. I've learned to accept that, even use it to my distinct advantage." He added with a wink. "But I've also learned to detect the few that are different." He said quietly and I wished I didn't immediately understand but my own experiences had taught me exactly what that was like unfortunately. He finished up his explanation then, making way more sense than I had ever expected him to.

"So is it really a huge surprise that later in life I would fall hopelessly in love with the one woman on Earth that I happen to know for sure, sees the real me? Can you think of a better match for me than someone who can't ever even *hope* to ignore my feelings, but instead *feels* each one of them as if they were *truly* her own?!" He asked with a lopsided grin. "I mean what more could I possibly ask for Simone?" He added humbly. "And yet you have *so-ho* much more to offer!" He added strongly, shaking his head. "*So* much more..."

I realized then that he was actually trying to tamp down his true joy at the situation to keep me from thinking that he was gloating. *Gloating!* I was absolutely *stunned!* I was just shaking my head back and forth in shock and my chin hit the proverbial floor as the simplicity of that concept knocked me flat. I had never even *considered* it from that perspective before. *Ever.* Huh.

He truly *doesn't hate that I can feel all of his feelings! He* loves *the fact that I feel all of his feelings! Loves it... Hmpf.* Wow...

Then it registered that he'd said he was *in love* with me!

...!!!

I wanted to pick my chin up off the floor just so that I could drop it again! I wasn't sure which revelation was more surprising then. Thankfully he could tell that I was on overload with those two small, but figuratively *huge* pieces of information and he took pity on me as usual, in his own charming way of course.

He leaned in and kissed me until I forgot not only what we were talking about, but where I was.

At some point I realized though, while I tried to catch my

breath, that in true Ethan fashion he had not only saved me from myself and complete mental overload, but he had also saved me from having to respond. I did wonder then in my shameful but acute relief, if it was out of chivalry or out of fear of what my response might be. I wished then that I had been paying closer attention.

Apparently I still wasn't done reassuring yet. I was even more certain of my answer than ever at that point and I went back to trying to explain it to him.

"Look, I know I'm not Lara Croft, or Heidi Klum, or even Martha Stewart dammit! But you know what? That's alright. When it comes right down to it, I know who I am *inside*, and at this point in my life I just strive to be the best *'me'* I can manage. I've finally come to terms with the fact that that's all I've got. And at the end of the day, it's enough. I'm okay with 'me.'" I assured him with a quietly confident smile. "*Really* I am, truly and completely! I couldn't always say that before, but I've finally reached that place within myself." I reached up between us and ran the tip of one finger lightly across his bottom lip, just because it looked so inviting that I couldn't stop myself, *and because for once I didn't have to stop myself!* Then I tried to focus again so I could finish my thought.

"I just never thought I would find anyone *else* who could honestly say the same thing, and since I will always have the added gift of knowing what's true and what's a lie, it's not something someone could ever fake." I added with a painful half-smile. "I wasn't pessimistic, I just knew my odds, and they weren't good, let me tell you!" I insisted humorously but honestly. Then I reached up and touched his face.

"Yet in spite of all of that, here you are. You're very real existence thoroughly surprised me Ethan." I admitted with another quiet laugh.

"My decision to remain unattached was the right one at the time, it was the responsible choice, based on knowledge and experience. It never came from a place of anger or fear. And I can also honestly say that I most likely would have never wavered from that opinion if you hadn't come along. But you *did*! Against incredible odds, you did! And you changed *everything!*" I finished letting my full admiration shine through my eyes for once. He smiled a very satisfied smile.

"I get that." He said being more than agreeable. "You already know that I felt much the same way. I was certainly never out there looking to pull an innocent woman and her equally innocent child into all of this! But looking or not, *hmpf*, there you were! Even using every ounce of will that I possess, as disciplined as I like to think I am, I simply could not resist you indefinitely!" He stared at me and I felt so much of that initial roller coaster of emotions go through him as he remembered it all, that it was easy to relive it right along with him. I knew then that I wouldn't change a second of it, even if I could.

"I never know what to expect where you're concerned, Ethan. Everything about being with you is so completely different from anything else I've ever known. I have no point of reference for comparison. I just know that it feels more '*right*' than I've ever had the pleasure of experiencing otherwise." I could feel his brightness at that lifting him up and taking me with it.

"I've known love, don't get me wrong. You know on paper, I've had at least a handful of decent relationships, and at one point I supposedly had everything that everyone always said I was *supposed* to want. With Ben I had all the things that were *supposed* to make me happy! Even that one rare man whose feelings would *never* bombard me like everyone else's always had." I explained inadvertently filling him on that little tid-bit for the first time. I felt his surprise and his *deep* interest in that information, both professionally and personally, but I didn't stop to expand on it. It was not the point.

"But even with everything I had, deep down I still felt a little lost, my heart was never 100% satisfied even though my head said everything was great. Most of the time I still just felt *alone!*" I admitted guiltily. "Not all the time obviously, but at important moments, you know, the times where you notice it the most. I never knew what it was that was missing Ethan. It took me a long time to even admit to myself that something was. But it was undeniable in the long run." I provided with a shrug.

"I understand what was missing now, and I'm more than ready to try living life *with* it on a regular basis instead and see how that works out." I chuckled and he grinned. "I don't really know *how* to do that yet." I admitted humbly. "But like always, I'm hoping that I'll figure it out as I go." I added. He was pretty pleased with my long and drawn out, but affirmative answer.

I leaned up for another kiss. I was still adjusting to the fact that I could kiss him whenever I wanted to. That was still blowing my mind on an almost hourly basis. I wasn't sure if he would be more annoyed than pleased by my overt affection at some point, but so far I had felt nothing but enjoyment during and after any such advances. I was glad too because I could definitely get used to that as well!

I had given him a lot to think about, but he knew that I would feel his responses, so he didn't bother to voice them all. He simply worked through it and moved on. "Don't worry darlin,' we'll just make it up as we go until we find what works for us, okay?" He offered being his ever generous and charming self.

"K." I answered simply as I climbed up onto his lap and settled down facing him. He looked at me and was silent for a few moments. I could feel him considering something for a while before he spoke up.

"I know we'll both be at Breezey all afternoon, but I doubt we'll see too much of each other today. "He said, knowing what was on the roster for the day. "And later I *have* to go to work at The Tavern. I've been gone far too long and I need to check in." He said.

"New *heights* tend to just show up there unannounced from time to time, especially when they're really desperate. I don't always know when they're coming. There's not always an announcement or a prior personal recommendation in situations like that. Sometimes they come based solely on a rumor that they've heard somewhere once and choose to act upon simply because they've run out of other options."

"If they come a few times looking for help in that state of mind, and find no one, then they eventually go away thinking that it was just a stupid fantasy and that they should never be naive enough to believe in such things again in the future. It can have lifelong effects on their ability to trust and accept outside help. Word of that would get around too. You already know how important it is not to feel like you're all alone." He reminded me and I could feel how him worry about anyone leaving there feeling like that.

"I know it sounds dramatic, but I really do try not to go too long without being there, just in case. Honestly, that is my full time job, *most* of the time. I have determined over the years that it is truly the one spot where I am most useful, spotting the *heights* who've come in looking for help." He said, shrugging his shoulders in humility. "But the reason that I'm telling you all of this is that I feel I must re-state my case for how invaluable *your* assistance would be to my team as a time saver in the whole '*pre-screening*' process." He added shamelessly. He wasn't beating around the bush anymore.

"*Come with me!*" He requested in a quiet voice but the wealth of meaning behind that simple request flooded through me. I knew then, what he had been contemplating so carefully before. I could tell immediately that he was asking me to come partly because he simply wanted to be near me. I got that. But aside from that I knew he also meant it as a serious business proposition, an invitation for me to become fully involved with him in *height* "receiving" so-to-speak, "part of the team." It was a big deal and I didn't take it lightly in the least, but I still didn't have to think about it long.

I knew I wanted to be a good mother to Liliana more than anything, but beyond that helping *heights* was something that I knew I would always want to do with my life. It felt the same as becoming a nurse in the emergency room to me, like my mother had done. It would occasionally be hard sure, and it obviously required a lot of commitment and personal sacrifice. But it was good and it was necessary, and it was important that there were good people out there doing it. I really did want to help. Maybe even just in the one small way that only *I* could. Maybe at the end of the day that too, was enough.

I had other things that I wanted out of my life, I would never claim to be nearly as selfless as he was, but I did want to help by then just as much as he did. It just felt right to me in the same way that being with him felt right, and I didn't need to question either one any further. That was actually highly unusual for me since I always tended to over think everything. For whatever reason, it was a complete no-brainer for me, a done deal already in my heart.

"Alright." I replied. "I'm in, but with a 'right to rescission' clause, just in case ever I need out for Liliana's sake." I added on. As sure as I felt about my decision, it was an automatic, maternal reflex for me. He laughed at my typical need to always keep one foot on the ground for her and I just shrugged my shoulders.

"Again I have to say, anytime sweetheart. The option to 'exit stage left' is always open to you. Shit, you can take the bike if you ever need to. You know where it is and the keys are always in it. I trust you and your judgment completely. If I didn't, I wouldn't be asking what I'm asking." He offered without further argument.

"Oh, *the bike!*" I enthused with a wistful yearning. "Oh man! We should take it out again sometime soon!" I suggested. "That sure was a nice ride!" I added, remembering that night with a joyful look on my face.

"*It sure was!*" He agreed looking down at me. I could tell that he was remembering things from that night as well, but I knew that his memories were obviously from much *later* that night, as a searing wave of heat rippled through me instantly relighting still smoldering embers deep inside. "The bike ride was nice too though." He added with a huge grin. I laughed as I shook my head.

He stood then, like I was nothing more than a linen napkin over his lap, and held me around my hips as he walked us back inside. We only had another hour or so before we had to be at Breezey but it was more than enough time to turn the world upside-down all over again. All I could think afterwards was, "*Hmpf*, I'm supposed to get used to *that?*" Yeah, okay. *That might happen!* Maybe someday...

We took turns showering since it was actually more efficient time-wise. We knew if we got in there together, we would end up getting sidetracked again and having it take longer instead of it being faster. Besides, I had my new grooming routine to add to my list of usual tasks and the extra elbow room made that much easier to accomplish. I still wasn't quite the pro at it that he was, but I was already getting used to it so I had to get used to keeping it up. It was better if I could do that without having to avoid a mishap brought on by an accidentally bumped elbow.

After our showers we were both starving but it was getting late so I grabbed some leftover pizza from the fridge and tossed it under the broiler while I cut up some of the veggies from the bowl on my island that Shirley always seemed to keep full. That particular day it was cucumbers, Roma tomatoes, green bell peppers and some romaine lettuce so I whipped up a quick and simple salad. I grabbed some butter garlic croutons from the cabinet and some ranch dressing from the fridge and took the now sizzling pizza out on my way back to the island where I set everything down. We were sitting and eating in under ten minutes. It was the perfect amount of food and we ate in perfect silence. Then we cleaned up and headed off to the jobsite. Together. *Hmpf.* Wow.

That was new in and of itself and it made me smile to finally be moving forward, however late or limited. It was progress and it actually felt really *good!*

Chapter 19

We arrived to find that the day at the jobsite so far had been blissfully uneventful. Well, at least as uneventful as a whole town working together on one project could be anyway. But there were no more surprises or problems for Marina to report when we arrived at command central early that afternoon, just updates on which projects were finished and who was still onsite and I for one was thrilled with the lack of excitement.

After greeting us with a shared relief at the plan's success and at the fact that we were still around, Marina went back to the notes that she was working on at the table. Ethan and I went over and stood looking at the charts on the wall as I pointed out the remaining projects on the schedule for the day. Ethan perused the map and gave a last minute run through of the plans for the kitchen demo he and his crew were due to start work on at 2:00. Thankfully things were apparently running right on time, schedule-wise.

Marina sat quietly but I noticed her staring at us once or twice when I glanced over during our casual discussion of the details. I was listening to him and answering at all the appropriate times, but all the while I was thinking about how nice it was to finally be on the jobsite together. I was remembering my original anticipation when I thought we would be working on the water harp together at the gardens. Sadly that had never come to pass, but we were finally together there and so far it felt just as good as I had anticipated. Even though I knew we would be in separate locations all day, we would both be *there*, in the same place for once and just that alone was *huge* for us! Standing there with him, discussing schedules and budgets was so simple and yet so satisfying that it made me feel things that were usually reserved for more rewarding activities. I liked it but I found I wasn't the only one.

I could feel Ethan's joy plain as day too. It was more straightforward and uncomplicated than mine but even that wasn't the entirety of it. I could feel it coming at me from across the room as well. That was a little more surprising but it was a *nice* surprise. Marina felt joy for him too and the new and unexpected circumstances between us and it was clear to me at that point that she really was a good friend to him. She noticed my attention and smiled. Then she shook her head, still in shock by the ridiculousness of it all and she got up to leave.

"Alright, you two seem to have everything under control here." She joked. "I on the other hand, have a segment to shoot. I'll see you later." She threw back with a smirk as she stacked up all her folders and hurried out. I could hardly complain since that was basically her job in the whole thing, especially after what her "filming" had done for us already, but it did seem a little abrupt. I wasn't the only one who noticed either.

Ethan looked at me with a furrowed brow, waiting for an explanation of whatever he had missed. I just shrugged my shoulders. "It wasn't anything huge. She's just still adjusting to seeing you act so... *domesticated.*" I joked. "But she's really happy for you." I added. "How long have you two known each other?" I asked then, since we had a moment alone.

"Oh I've known Marina since we were kids." He answered with a warm smile and I could feel him remembering their shared past fondly. "We rode the bus together all through school. We never dated or anything like that." He informed me backhandedly with a half-smile, knowing that particular information would interest me. I couldn't help being relieved, even as I tried to pretend that it was inconsequential. He just grinned at me again and generously moved past it.

"She was always involved in the school plays and on the school newspaper, that kind of thing. Anything vocal really. So everyone in school knew her, or at least *of* her." His giddy stroll down memory lane took a left turn then and I felt the ugliness that covered most of his old memories creep in.

"For a while when I was young, I fantasized that she might be in a position to help me." He admitted through a wave of that old darkness. As usual, he didn't loiter there. He kept moving through it and then past it and I sighed. "She really wanted to help me too! Of course my mother was a lot smarter than two naive fifth graders so we were never successful in any of our various endeavors to expose her, but we did eventually end up with some hilarious 'failed attempt' videos and being really close friends." He finished with a more confident grin.

He was quiet for a minute but I could feel the deep level of trust he felt with her. It was nice not to feel threatened by that. Instead I found comfort in it, the same way that I was relieved by feeling his families love for him. I was comforted by the fact that there were others whose instinct was also to protect him if and when I wasn't there to do it. It was a weird thing to think about but it made me feel better just the same. He wasn't done yet though and his next sentence helped me to better understand.

"She promised me when we officially gave up after one particularly dismal attempt, that someday, when she was all 'grown up' and adults couldn't take advantage of us anymore, she would find a way to *really* help me!" He smiled brilliantly then, since we all knew that she had already lived up to that promise *at least* once just recently. I shared his warm glow then and we enjoyed it in silence for a while.

I looked at the clock and thought about another special visitor that I was expecting on site that day. Since Liliana had the week off from camp, she had asked if she could volunteer too at "*mommy's new workplace*" on one of those days. I had explained all about my new job to them and Ben was eager to check the place out himself. I hadn't known at the time how things were going to turn out with Anderson's deadline looming, so I agreed on a plan for "day two" just to put it off until after whatever was going to happen, had happened, and simply hoped for the best. I was extremely glad in the end not to have had to cancel after all!

My next thought, was that it was as good a time as any for Ethan to finally meet Ben. *Phew!* That idea was not exactly a welcome one either but it had to happen sometime, right? *Slow, deep breaths...*

"Come on. Walk out with me and you can say hello before you get to work." I offered. He knew full well though that it was more than Liliana that he would be "*saying hello*" to. I had talked to him about it already too. He didn't shy away from the awkward situation though. He was dreading it on one level sure, but on another he had a brand new curiosity about Ben due to my recent revelation, that was hard for him to ignore.

He looked back at me and held his hand out. His determination began to fill me, but there was enough room left over to fit my admiration for his relentless fearlessness in tackling whatever life threw at him. I had no idea how he did it, time after time but I found it to be one of his most prominent traits. Of course that's what made it so easy for so many to constantly rely on him. Like a sturdy wall with a good solid foundation, you simply expect it to be there to support you. And like any good, sturdy wall, his goal in life was to never let anyone down.

We walked through the interior rooms and stopped in the kitchen on the way by so he could check in with his crew. They all shook hands and slapped each other on the shoulder and expressed great relief at still having him available to do some actual work! He agreed it was a relief and said he would return to do just that within the next half hour, then he left them with instructions on what to start on in the meantime.

After that we walked up and into the Great Hall and left through the front entrance. We looked down the hill as we came through the double doors into the sunshine and were just in time to see Ben pulling into the lot below. I tightened my hold on his hand in silent support. He grinned appreciatively and I felt his calm settle in. We ascended the stairs together and started across the lot. It was nice to feel it knowing that for once it was for himself more than for my benefit.

Ben shut the engine off and got out just as Liliana burst from the backdoor of his new Acura. It was a lot nicer than his last car and even slightly used, I knew it cost a small fortune. But with as busy as he'd been lately I was fairly sure he could afford it so I chose not to bring it up, especially since it really wasn't any of my business anymore, not as long as Liliana had half of everything that she needed first. After that he could buy a spot on the shuttle to the moon.

"Hi mama!" She yelled as she ran up to me with her arms flung wide. I let go of Ethan's hand and lifted her up in a bear hug. It always felt so good to hold her warm little body against mine that I wished for just a second that she was smaller again so I could get away with not putting her back down.

"Hi!" I answered laughing at her exuberance. She reminded me of myself just then and for better or for worse, I had to smile.

I'd texted Ben that morning, when I was finally sure that I'd be able to make it, and let him know that Ethan would be there too. I didn't want to blindside him with that. That certainly wouldn't help our situation any. Liliana looked over at Ethan who stood smiling by my side. She waved silently to him with a warm smile like she had just seen him last a few hours ago.

"Hey there Liliana. How are you? It's been a while, huh? You been enjoying your summer so far?" He asked all at once. He sounded like he was just trying to be polite but I knew he really cared about her answer. He didn't know her well enough yet to *really* miss her like I always did, but I could feel how much he genuinely *liked* her.

"Yeah. Camp is awesome!" She offered honestly and he gave me a discreet half smile at the innocent but ironic reference.

"Yeah, I always liked camp too!" He agreed with a brilliant smile as we all turned our attention to Ben. He was off that day as well and would only be attending to Don's dogs while he was in town, so he had ditched his usual Dockers and button-down shirt for a more casual look of cargo shorts, a t-shirt and old work boots. He was keeping his blond hair cut a lot shorter too but despite his attempt to look more professional, it just made him look even younger than he really was. He removed his sunglasses and tucked them onto his belt loop as he walked over.

We kept going in that direction as well until we met him half way. I had to relinquish my hold on Liliana then as she straightened her legs and arched her back to slide down off my hip. Oh well, it had been good while it lasted and that was longer than usual lately. She was already basically too big to be picked up anymore but I was holding onto that one as long as I could get away with it. I would never be the one to say no more. I would piggy back her around fully grown and still be happy just to be next to her if I could. It didn't matter to me, but I knew that someday it would to her. Until then...

He reached us with a congenial smile on his face but as usual I had no way of knowing whether it was real or forced with Ben. I decided to assume it was genuine until proven otherwise.

I could feel Ethan's natural inquisitiveness next to me, as he quietly assessed every nuance of his newest possible adversary. I could even feel it when his stare intensified into that very *specific* assessment without turning to confirm it visually. Then I wondered immediately what he had found, knowing that Ben was at the very least, "*unusual.*" I had to turn and look then for visual confirmation of what I was picking up.

He caught my eye and gave a very discreet but surprised side-to-side shake of his head, silently answering my unasked question. Again, it was so nice not to need the words. I found I was relieved, but also surprised, truth be told. Ben had never been your everyday, run-of-the-mill guy so I wouldn't have been surprised had he turned out to be *some* sort of *height*. Apparently though, that was not the explanation in his case.

Ethan went back to his evaluation after that and a short time later I felt a hot rush of *fierce* but typically well controlled jealousy flash past. I wasn't sure what thought had sparked it specifically but I felt it plain as day. I cocked my head at him, a little surprised at that rare moment of personal weakness. I could see that he wasn't proud of it but again he knew he couldn't hide it. He lifted one shoulder and one eyebrow as an open admission, but offered no defense. Whatever it was it had been powerful, but he had already tucked it safely away. *Hmmm…*

I was not nor would I ever be one of those beaten down and pathologically lonely women that blindly mistook possessiveness for love, but the thought of Ethan with any other woman made me feel much the same way so in that one instance at least, I understood and I chose to let it go. As long as it was only an emotion and not an action, I couldn't blame him.

I just smiled and shook my head ever so slightly because *I* knew for sure that no matter how much I loved Ben it didn't matter, we knew that we would never really be able to make each other *truly* happy. It had taken us some time to reach that conclusion, but we had both come to grips with that unavoidable truth by then. It was just Ethan's turn to learn it. I decided I would allow him the time to catch up. If he still had issues after that then we would have a real problem, but I was fairly confident that it wouldn't be the case. I decided to see if I could help it along.

I walked up and hugged Ben hello, not bothering to hold back on the casual affection I hoped we'd always show each other. We would never be each other's soulmate but that didn't mean we had to be enemies. We would always share a child and I wanted the lines to be clear right from the start. I wasn't lying awake at night, pining for Ben anymore, but I treasured the good relationship we shared for the sake of our daughter. I would never jeopardize that merely to facilitate someone else's ego.

I acted based solely on those beliefs and not my fear of what his reaction would be. It was tough to do but I felt it was the right choice. I could feel his stare behind me and I waited for the green eyed monster to make a repeat performance, but it never came. Thankfully, what I felt instead was respect for me and my integrity in a tough situation. As his response came flooding across my chest I was admittedly relieved. It was tempered by an underlying, strained patience but I would take it! I pulled back and introduced them.

"Ben, I'd like you to meet my friend Ethan." I said looking back at him with obvious pride in my eyes. "Ethan this is my ex-husband, Ben." I added just ripping the next Band-Aid right off. It was still a little strange to say "ex-husband" but I knew I would get used to that in time too, just like the rest of it.

Ethan came forward and shook Ben's hand. He was dressed in his work jeans and an old t-shirt but I knew he made a pretty formidable impression anyway just being clean and neat from not having started the work day yet. Still, his humble attire helped to take the pressure down a half a notch and since I didn't want Ben to feel overwhelmed, in the end I think it helped the situation. It seemed our timing in choosing when they should meet was perfect in at least that one small way so far. That little assurance made me feel a just a tad bit better moving forward.

"It's nice to meet you." Ben responded politely. His true first impression was also a guess, but again he seemed sincere enough.

"Likewise." Ethan answered and stepped back to stand beside me again. It was subtle but no one missed the implication. Liliana chose that moment to speak up again.

"Are you going to be working at the big house up on the hill?" She asked Ethan. "We're going to be helping mama in the garden!" She explained enthusiastically.

"You are? That's great!" He responded wholeheartedly. "Well my crew and I are working in the kitchen in the main house today. We're going to be fixing a floor and tearing out a whole wall!" He explained just as excitedly.

"Coooool!" She responded wide eyed and duly impressed.

"So what are you guys going to be doing out here, Ben?" Ethan asked. It sounded innocent enough but I heard the slight underlying challenge in there as clearly as I felt it. I knew Ben wasn't one to engage in senseless posturing any more than Ethan normally seemed to be, but he would want to impress Liliana as much if not more than Ethan had with his answer just because he was her dad and therefore naturally wanted to be the most impressive man in her eyes. Some things you didn't need to be an empath to understand.

"We're going to help Simone tear out all these old dead vines and bushes out here." He explained waving toward the overgrown front lawn. "Then we'll replant some more appropriate hedges that will actually thrive here long term and give the area some cleaner definition. After that we're adding some perennials that will spread each year. Liliana got to choose the color scheme. You want to tell him what you picked?" He asked looking down at her, getting her even more excited. Her answer was quick and confident.

"Purple flowers!" She enthused. "Millions and millions of purple flowers!" She said while twirling in a circle, arms held wide. After five perfect spins she stopped short and didn't appear to be affected at all. She just kept on talking without even the hint of a wobble. "This whole hill is going to be purple!" She added with obvious pride. She was truly looking forward to it as much as I always did and that made me really happy. Her green thumb technically could have come from either one of us. I didn't care about taking credit for it. I just rejoiced in the fact that she had one. It was one of the more rewarding pastimes in life in so many ways and it was nice to know that I would always share that with her at the very least.

It was clear that Ben was also happy with her response. I knew it gave him a sense of security on such unfamiliar turf to have Liliana skipping so happily by his side, excited to spend the afternoon working with her daddy doing something they both loved.

We had really been surprised in the beginning and even a little sad sometimes truth be told, at the vast amount of time that we had been expected to share her with everyone. We had always appreciated our quiet family times together whenever we could get them. It wasn't exactly the same between me and Ben anymore, but I knew we both still felt that way where she was concerned.

"That sounds great! For a vet it sure sounds like you have a lot of experience in landscaping." Ethan stated conversationally as we strolled. Again he sounded sincere enough but I could feel the slight challenge in there as well.

"*Huh!* Yeah, about ten years actually." He replied somewhat defensively. "I guess Simone never mentioned it, but that's actually how I got through Vet school. In fact, I'm the one who helped Simone get her hands dirty to begin with." Ben informed him jokingly but not without pride while we walked along the bottom of the hill. I tried to keep my grin to myself. Of course he would want Ethan to know that. I didn't blame him. I knew that if he had been standing there with a beautiful woman by his side, I would want to be wearing all of my credentials on my sleeve too.

"What about you? I had heard you were a singer in the local pub." Ben threw back with a little attitude of his own. "I'm a little surprised to see you here tearing out walls." He added. I was really hoping that things wouldn't escalate in that direction and Ethan was mostly on board with that attitude I could tell. He just nodded and smiled back at Ben.

"That is primarily my full time job, yes. But that still leaves my days free for various other endeavors like a little side work in construction among other things." He offered leaving himself a perfect way to explain away other future vocations, I noticed. Ben just nodded back silently as we walked taking that in.

Ethan was more than secure enough in his own masculinity to escape the constant need to prove it. He was still human though, and like it or not Ben's connection to me put him firmly on the opposite side to a certain extent, but he wasn't looking to dwell on it God love him. Instead he chose to be magnanimous about it by acknowledging the underlying rivalry, but then leaving it alone. I got it but I certainly didn't intend to encourage it either so I tried to steer the conversation away from that frame of mind as quickly as possible. Those kind of competitive instincts were of little use in a collaborative situation like we had there at Breezy, and even less helpful where our personal relations were concerned.

"I wasn't even due to start work on this part until tomorrow but they've made such amazing progress so fast, that the surrounding areas were all cleared out and finished up early. Since I have a few extra pairs of hands, one well trained pair in particular," I added purposely. "I'm actually really excited to get started! Everything seems to be coming in ahead of schedule, 'knock on wood.'" I threw in as I rapped my knuckles on a tree stump that we passed. "And I'm more than happy to try and stay on trend." I said reflexively not wanting Ethan to read too much into it, either Ben's presence or my excitement.

"Yeah, that's awesome! The more the merrier, right?" Ethan offered. He meant it too to a certain extent, which made me smile. That really was the point there after all, but there was definitely a fair amount of "*sucking-it-up*" swirling around in there with it. I could tell that he felt the social weight to be a good "host," since it was his hometowns' project and as always he was fully prepared to properly represent. Of course he would think that way, right? But I was still relieved and I was ready to move on before he changed his mind.

"Come on sweetie. Before we get started, I want to show you the old playground!" I said directly to Liliana. "It's already well on its way to becoming the *new* playground!" I informed her excitedly.

"You guys go on ahead. I'm going to go grab my tools and stuff out of the trunk. It was nice meeting you Ethan." Ben said with a wave as he dismissed us temporarily and started back towards his car.

"You too." Ethan agreed and I had to grin. "Just holler if you guys need anything." He added honestly. Ben agreed with a nod then waved again before turning fully and walking away. Ethan turned back to me with a sigh of relief. I leaned up to show my gratitude with a kiss. He obliged me by leaning down to receive it.

"Thank you." I said simply but sincerely summing it up well enough.

"Your quite welcome, Simone. It's the *least* I can do!" He added thinking heavily for just a quick second on all we had experienced in the past weeks. I closed my eyes at the strain and the suffering that I remembered all too well and breathed deeply when it passed. He was right. It was good to be there and a momentary discomfort was a small concession for the peace that we had finally found. I held his eyes and smiled back. "Alright, well I'm going to get to work myself." He said then. "You guys have fun though, okay? He suggested with a half grin. "I'll see you later Liliana!" He said distracting her momentarily from the butterfly she was trying to catch.

"Okay, bye!" She said with a wave before running after it once again. He squeezed my hand and let free a storm of really *good* emotions then. They poured over me and immediately washed away all of the thoughts from the past, even if only temporarily. It all balanced out, somehow. It was astounding but entirely clear to me then that his elation was actually bright enough to balance out *all* of that unpleasantness, for both of us! *Hmpf.* Wow. He grinned happily at my improved mood, then turned and headed back up the hill.

"Come on." I said to Liliana and we went in the opposite direction towards the park. When we reached the top we walked around behind the great hall and her smile spread wide at the sight of the swing set. It was one of the tallest inverted V's I had ever seen and just the *thought* of going all the way over on it like I had always dreamed of doing as a kid made my stomach flip! She looked up at me with that unspoken question exploding off of her.

I nodded at her knowing it had been re-chained, oiled and declared fully functional yesterday. It was really good news that we were able to salvage it, rather than having to try and replace such a unique thing. She ran over and hopped onto the new flexible black rubber seat and began to pump her little legs back and forth, as hard as she could. I followed over there watching her. She had still barely gotten to the halfway point when I reached her, so I gave her a great big push to help her out. She squealed in delight and soared through the air streaming nearly liquid ribbons of pure joy as she went! It was amazing! I pulled the feelings in and let them back out in a big cleansing sigh and then I took the seat next to her. I walked backwards as far as I could within the confines of the supporting chains and then I lifted my feet, shifting my weight to the seat and soared high into the air after her.

My ponytail flew out behind me and I stared up at my boots as they swung up in front of the sun and the puffy white clouds. I delighted in her peals of her laughter as she passed me on the return swing and I leaned into the next swoop with all of my weight. The sun flashed in between my knees that time and I was struck again by just how large the monstrosity really was! I slowed a little then, after the fear of flying across the meadow in a hip fracturing arc passed through my mind. When I reached "gently swaying" I turned in my seat instead to watch her fly by in wild childhood abandon, blond tendrils sailing through the air.

It was a thing of absolute beauty and I was stunned into stillness. As I waited for her to slow down to a stop, I thought about the next hurtle I had to face for her and I knew that it was time. I had to find a way to prepare somewhat, somehow, for what may come. I didn't want anything to ever take that happiness away from her. I *would* find a way to keep that from happening! I vowed silently. Whatever I had to do, I would do. That much I was sure of. Once she'd had enough she finally jumped off into the sand with her humongous smile stretching from ear to ear. That was all I had ever wanted for her, from that very first minute that she had become a reality. Just to know that she's happy. I took her hand and we headed back down the hill to join Ben.

The underlying heaviness made the walk back down a lot slower though. It wasn't about Ben and Ethan getting along that time. It was even more important than that. It was about her future. I was full of dread at the fact that I could no longer put off sharing the information that I had with her father. He needed to know. He *deserved* to know! But how would he take it? That was where the dread came from.

I knew Ben. There was no way that he was going to accept all of the *height* stuff easily, especially not where she was concerned! He would fight it all the way and I knew from experience how he could be when he felt threatened. His defenses went into overdrive then and I knew the thought of anything hurting her would make him feel incredibly threatened. I had been trying to fortify my strength to the point where I felt ready to battle that, but I knew I couldn't afford to wait any longer. Ready or not, time was running out. *I could feel it.*

It had taken weeks of tireless debate and irrefutable proof way back when, before he had accepted and eventually believed in my own empath abilities. It had been both fun and exhausting at the time trying to convince him. I expected it would be much the same doing it again, but without the fun part. I still had hope that he would come around by the time we needed to handle it in real life though. It wouldn't be easy, especially since he *had* decided in the end that his life was better off *without* those abilities in it. But I had to try once more to make him understand. Not for my sake anymore, that was officially a lost cause, but for hers.

I couldn't help but wonder though, in my moments of self-torture, if he would eventually feel that way about his own daughter someday. Would he decide that he was better off without her in his life too, should she in fact turn out to be a *height* like me? I couldn't even imagine that honestly, but then I'd never imagined *our* current situation becoming a real possibility either. It made complete sense much later, but at the time it was inconceivable.

The thing is, with all I've seen and learned, I have no choice but to remain a realist. That being the case, I had to consider everything, even that.

Whatever the outcome would be though, it was time to deal with it. I wouldn't tell him there, that was out of the question. But it would have to be soon, especially since I no longer had the major life distraction of Ethan being gone to personally use as an excuse for avoiding it anymore.

I would set a date for that discussion at the very least while he was there. That decision didn't help me lift my feet any higher or faster though. Big surprise, right?

Chapter 20

The rest of the day surprisingly went as smoothly as the first half had production-wise. The other work crews on site made great progress as well and had very few reasons to seek me out, which made completing my own tasks even easier. That was an interesting turn of events though, to have Ben present on a job where I was in charge for a change. The few times I did stop, to answer questions for the roofers or to direct the satellite dish installers to the appropriate spot, I definitely noticed Ben *noticing.*

Of course I couldn't feel his reaction, but his unusually generous smile told me that for once he was actually proud of me and maybe even a little impressed. He had already told me that he saw the TV spot on the Garden's and he thought I had done an amazing job. Of course Liliana had told him all about it, endlessly in fact the next day from what I heard. I had to admit though that it was pretty cool to finally get some credit for a few of my strengths in his eyes. *It was about damn time!* I couldn't help shouting in my head with a long overdue sense of satisfaction. A day late and a dollar short, but whatever.

In spite of my mental reservations Ben and I had gotten a lot more done than I ever anticipated. I'd forgotten just how well we worked together. Even without the nonverbal communication between us that my skills would normally afford me, we always knew where the other person was on the list of tasks and what they were going to do next based solely on old established work habits. It made the job flow that much faster.

Liliana was actually quite helpful too. She easily spent as much time dancing around the area as she did gardening, since I had set the portable speaker for my mp3 player in the middle of the hill instead of working with headphones for a change, for their sake. I had a lot of other music mixed in with Ethan's and I didn't think anyone would notice. As it turned out I was right and even if she didn't *need* it necessarily, she had enjoyed the music immensely while we worked. I secretly hoped that it would always be just a pleasing *option* for her.

She still found plenty of time to complete her equally important tasks of moving small rocks, and pulling weeds in between theatrical spins. By the time we stopped for a water break around 3:00, the whole area was clear of anything that was dead or just growing in the completely wrong place.

As we sat resting and sharing the snack that they had brought of goldfish crackers, string cheese and juice boxes from the little cooler, the truck from the nursery arrived. It was full to overflowing with all of the purple flowers and everything else that I had ordered.

Their arrival signaled the end of our break and we got up to help unload. Once that was done we worked side-by-side, straight through the late afternoon hours with Liliana setting the seedlings out in neat and even rows ahead of us. We worked like a well-oiled machine together, planting row after row until the last black plastic tray was empty.

It quieted everything else around me and I lost myself for a while in the familiar rhythm. We moved across the property, going from left to right and top to bottom as we progressed and we ended up back down by the far corner of the parking lot when we finished. I realized looking up for the first time as I sat back on the grass, that I had to give Ethan credit for not "*stopping by*" even once to check on us throughout the day. That was the way it should be of course but I knew that I probably wouldn't have been as disciplined if the roles were reversed, especially after the length of time we'd spent apart recently.

I know I make myself sound like a horrible person sometimes and alright, honestly I'm not really *that* horrible. I'm actually a kind-hearted person who tends to gets taken advantage of more often than not. But regardless of the failings of others, I still try to be as brutally honest with *myself* as I can be in the name of non-hypocrisy! Most of the time though, that just means looking for the worst in myself and exaggerating it out of proportion to make it easier to see and fix. I've learned to accept that I'm a work in progress, but self-awareness is imperative for that improvement to take place. So just ignore me if I seem to be a little overly self-critical on occasion. It's all part of the process.

I tried to refocus while Ben and I sat in the grass, exhausted and watched as the rest of the day crews packed up and cleared out. While they headed down the long entry road, the evening crews were pulling up, everyone waving to each other as they passed. It was a warm and comforting kind of atmosphere, especially nice for me, and I relaxed for a few minutes in appreciation of it all. I was glad that that was the first real impression Ben was getting of my new hometown. It was a good representation of what I loved about it. He also saw how happy Liliana was too and how many people there already knew her and couldn't wait to say hello to her. I could tell that finally helped him to relax a hair himself. All together it was enough to make me happy for the moment.

I leaned back on my arms and sighed contentedly while the late day sun burned through the trees and reddened my cheeks one shade deeper. My damp ponytail fell behind me and off of my neck and I felt the light breeze cool the damp skin underneath. Ben sat quietly next to me doing the same, except for the hair thing. We were dirty and covered in sweat from the work but I had no regrets. It had felt really good to me to be back at it again. I would be sore in 24 hours, but I knew from experience that it would get easier as the days went on. I glanced over at Ben, who was looking as relaxed as I felt and it seemed like a "now or never" kind of moment so I took it.

"This was really great Ben. Thanks for bringing her up." I said looking over at Liliana where she was squatting, finishing her last task for the day of placing a handful of special rocks in a circle around one of the few remaining miniature trees. She was taking it very seriously, placing each one in just the right way. It made me smile. "And thanks for helping!" I added wholeheartedly looking back at him. "I can't believe how much we got done!" I said honestly.

"It looks pretty good." He said with raised brows, giving a fair assessment. "It *felt* pretty good too actually!" He admitted looking back at me. "I should be thanking you. I haven't made time to do this work in a while and I've really missed it." I could *hear* the longing in his voice even if I couldn't feel it.

"Well anytime you need a fix, feel free to call me!" I joked and we both laughed. Of course we both also knew that he wouldn't have a day off again anytime soon, but it was a nice thought. I took a deep breath and dove in on the high note.

"So I was wondering if you had just a little more free time maybe one night this week, so we could get together and talk." I asked tentatively. He could sense my change in mood and he looked back at me with suspicion in his eyes. Well *that* didn't take long, I thought resignedly.

"What's wrong with right now?" He asked warily. I sighed again.

"Look, I don't want to freak you out, but it's about Liliana and it's potentially very serious. I'm going to need some uninterrupted time with you to get through it all." I looked down at my feet and avoided eye contact as he absorbed that. I could feel his stare if not his reaction, even without seeing it. We both knew what he was thinking about. Something we had always dreaded most. That slim chance that she would be *too much* like me. The hardest part was that if she was, it was only the tip of the iceberg.

"*What the hell, Simone!* What are you talking about? You can't just say something like that and then not tell me what you mean! Weren't we were going to be better than that to each other?" He complained. "Have you felt something that I should know about or not?" He demanded fearfully. I knew he would feel that way, and I had known it would be hard to mention it without explaining, but I had to start somewhere. Better to let some of the initial resentment wear off before I gave him a whole new reason to resent me I decided, maintaining my silence for a beat. *Deep breath…*

"I'm sorry, Ben. I really am. I've been trying to find the best way to do this for some time now and unfortunately I'm no closer to a good solution than I was before, so I figured it was time to just get on with it regardless. But I really can't do that here, not now. How 'bout tomorrow night?" I offered. "I can come down and meet you after work." He seemed like he would rather argue about it some more and I began gearing myself up for a disaster. He surprised me though. I don't know if it was exhaustion or just a sense that he wasn't going to win that one, but for whatever reason, he acquiesced.

"Fine, come by the office tomorrow night. We close at seven but I'll be there until at least eight thirty or nine." I looked up in surprise and he took that opportunity to stare into my eyes as if he might see the answer there and save himself the wait. I recovered quickly though and stared back plainly while I answered him.

"K." I agreed simply. I sighed deeply again, having gotten through step one at least and I stood up. I brushed some of the dirt off of my backside while I waited for him to get up and do the same and then we started to quietly collect tools.

I stacked mine neatly off to the side to replace in my toolkit later then I turned to help Ben. As we finished loading the trunk with all of his and Liliana's things I could finally feel a faint ripple of that familiar and welcome intensity wash through me. I took a deep breath full of it and let it out slowly, savoring it a little. Ethan wasn't close, but he was *closer* than he had been all day. I glanced around discreetly but didn't see the instigator of said feelings anywhere. Liliana came over and jumped up on me to hug me goodbye and I forgot about it momentarily. I reacted just in time to save myself a knee to the gut and laughed as I lifted her up into a bear hug.

"Alright my little tree squirrel, you be a good girl for daddy, okay?" I instructed and she nodded. "And enjoy the rest of your week off! I'll see you again in a few days but you're going to be super busy with all the grandparents fighting over you until then!" I added and her smile grew in anticipation. I could feel just how special that made her feel and I loved it. It made up for the moments that I missed out on a little, knowing that at least the other people with her enjoyed them as much as I did. "I'm so glad we got to spend today together first!" I gushed honestly.

"Me too mama! It was so much fun and we really rocked out that garden!" She said mimicking perfectly what she had heard from one of the passing workers earlier. Of course I burst out laughing and she just giggled back. The phrase had rolled off of her tongue so effortlessly that I couldn't help the vision of her in a few short years, when she would actually *be* old enough to say things like that for real. I was both looking forward to those moments of shared laughter and panicked by the thought of how fast we would be there for just a split second, wanting to slow it down. Love really is totally irrational.

"We sure did honey!" I answered, keeping the rest to myself. "You were especially helpful today! That tree looks perfect now." I told her while nodding down at the miniature Japanese maple and its' beautiful new border. "I couldn't have done it any better!" I told her honestly and I could feel her brighten at my praise. "I'll see you on Friday, okay?" I said as I put her down.

"Okay mama! We're going to the Aquarium tomorrow!" She shouted excitedly.

"I know! I'm jealous! If I didn't have to work I would come with you! Will you take lots of pictures for me?" I asked and she agreed happily. I bent down and gave her one more hug and a kiss then she ran over and got in the car. Ben stood by her open door waiting silently. When she was buckled in he closed the door then turned back to look at me one last time.

"I'll see you tomorrow night." He reiterated without hiding his dread and gave a half-hearted wave. I nodded and waved back as he got in and started it up. I continued to wave to Liliana in the back window, as he pulled out of the lot and headed down the long driveway. When I couldn't see the car or her little arm anymore, I dropped my own arm, sighed deeply and started back up the hill to check on everything else.

By the time I reached the top however, I had located the source of the intensity that I had felt before, and allowed myself to be sidetracked by it momentarily instead. Ethan was sitting at the same picnic table that we had shared the previous day, taking a break of his own when I found him. He was eating a couple of the power bars that we had stocked command central with and washing them down with a bottle of water. I walked over and stood near his leg and I instantly felt a smidge better just being close to him. I would normally have tried to hide it or to downplay the intensity of the relief I felt being next to him, to retain some semblance of pride. But I noticed that he instantly felt the same way and he made no moves to hide it, so I decided not to either. Who was I kidding? I let some of the stress out in another sigh then but it came out a lot louder than I had intended. He chuckled.

"Everything okay?" He asked with a supportive half-smile. I sighed again before I answered.

"Yeah. For the moment anyway." I answered sarcastically. He looked up at me and I could feel his genuine interest in what had me so worried.

"I finally told Ben that we needed to talk. I'm going to meet him tomorrow night at his office to try and explain all of this *heightening* stuff to him before it's too late to give him any kind of a head start on processing it all." I informed him with a meaningful look. I sighed deeply one last time after I got that out. "Any advice?" I asked in the end being partly sarcastic and partly hopeful. He immediately understood my mood. He'd been in my position many, *many* times already and I was sure that it was probably still just as hard for him every single time.

He took my hand and pulled me down onto the bench next to him. "Come, sit. I think it's time for you to tell me a little more about your somewhat *unusual* custody arrangement." His reluctance to ask was obvious but it was also unavoidable. "I'm sorry. I didn't want to pry before, or to rub salt in obviously still festering wounds. But the details could be really important now, especially if he turns out to be '*unreceptive*' to what you have to say." He added with a meaningful look of his own. "Unfortunately that's not uncommon although I wish I could say that it was." He finished quietly. I understood, but I wished I could say that I didn't.

"Before you tell him *anything* Simone, we need to be

prepared!" As usual, not so much as a twitch from him.

"For what?" I asked fearfully.

"For *anything*!" He answered honestly and it did nothing to calm me, but of course that was not his intention for once. It wasn't meant to be a reassurance that time around, it was a clear warning. I took it with the appropriate amount of dread.

"I'm guessing that your decision to let her stay with him full time had a lot to do with your *'emotional issues.'*" He offered with a half-smile making hand quotes in the air. "Am I right? I'm sure you were probably thinking something along the lines of, 'if you love her, you had to do it that way because it was the best thing for her.' How am I doing so far?" He asked tauntingly. He didn't wait for confirmation. He didn't have to.

"I know I'm right because I can tell that it kills you on a daily basis, and I can't see you agreeing to it any other way or for any other reason. You're much too strong a fighter to ever have just given up on something that is obviously so important to you. I know that much for sure already." He smirked at me and I immediately knew what he meant.

"But if there's more to it than that Simone, if he has something over you that I'm not aware of, if there's anything *else*... you need to tell me *now*!" He explained intently. I understood his point easily enough but was thankful for once that it was the only thing that had ever really come between us. I shook my head.

"No. That's it. Or at least the basics anyway." I answered not bothering to hide the painful truth anymore. "Giving her up..." I started then stopped to clear the sob that instantly appeared in my throat. I swallowed it quickly and tried again.

"It was the last thing that I ever wanted to do and I never could have imagined things turning out the way they did as I sat there holding her in my arms every day. *Never!* Even just trying to consider the possibility in an imagined "worst-case-scenario" was beyond difficult. I could never really wrap my head around it. *Hmpf.* But eventually, when we had exhausted every other single possible scenario, and it got to the point where it really looked like the *best* viable option, I was in *shock!*" I sighed again trying to hold it all in.

"I just kept arguing with every issue that he brought up, insisting that I could make it all work somehow... But there were just too many things that I knew I couldn't do properly on my own, with her or *for* her that she still needed to be able to rely on her parents for at five years old. It got to the point where I just couldn't argue anymore. There were no arguments left that supported me being her one and only, full-time parent." I admitted quietly. Even at that moment, they were still some of the hardest words I had ever had to speak out loud.

"I didn't want to force her to grow up suffering the consequences for *my* 'gifts.' I had missed out enough for it already as a kid, but I never wanted her to! Whether she had similar issues someday or not. I just couldn't let that happen. It wouldn't have been fair to keep her all to myself and force her to share that hardship with me full time when she had other, *better* options available to her." I explained with my own pain and disappointment more than obvious. I looked him in the eye then and spoke my next truth partly just because I needed to say it out loud.

"If I was all she had, then believe me I would have and would *still* gladly do my absolute best every single day for the rest of my life to give her the best possible life I could, and no one would ever be able to stop me!" I insisted heartily. Then I softened in resignation. "But I'm *not* all she has! And she deserves everything that he can give her that I can't. That's all there is to it" I said quietly.

"She has a father who loves her, completely! I have zero fears for her well-being when she is in his care. He's a *good* father and he was more than willing to take on parenting her full time!" I added honestly. "I was actually really lucky to be able to say that, in spite of the circumstances. And at the end of the day, even my absolute best still comes in a distant second to what he has to offer, *for right now*." I allowed. "I know that. I don't *like* that! But I had to accept that." I took a deep breath and let it out along with the futility of fighting it.

I had worked hard at being able to embrace that pain and move through it. If I had to find a silver lining in the current situation I would have to say that it at least forced me to improve upon my coping skills. It was a fortunate side effect of an unfortunate situation, but it was progress, and it always helped to focus on the bright side wherever I could find it. *Deep breath…*

"I just couldn't justify taking that away from both of them only to save *myself* the heartbreak. How could I make two people suffer when there was another option available where just one person was left to suffer instead? In the end it really came down to simple math." I finished feigning nonchalance, before the sob fought its' way back up. I let it out that time. It was too much to hold in anymore after that. I turned away for a minute until I got it under control again but I didn't try to deny the pain its release. I wanted it out of me. I was better at dealing with that pain by then, but it was never going to be "*easy.*"

A few minutes later I looked back at him as he sat patiently waiting. He didn't urge me to try and stifle my feelings, nor did he try to talk me out of feeling them. He just gently stroked my back and waited for me to work through them and that was more beneficial than I could have ever imagined. After a few minutes I took a deep breath in and let it out with a huff.

"I basically put off leaving for as long as I could just to avoid it, but I knew eventually that even that wouldn't be good for her. I didn't want her to grow up in a home like that, where you're aware that your family members were only present because staying was easier than leaving. A cold home where there is no love, or happiness, just a stark and heavy sense of responsibility, and disappointment." I looked at him and saw the firsthand knowledge of such a situation register on his face. He knew exactly what I was talking about, and he knew that I was right. Unfortunately for both of us, *right* is *always* harder! But of course that's why so few people ever choose and follow through with it. I'm not judging when I say that either by the way, just stating a fact that I am unfortunately all too aware of.

"Yes, it killed me. It still kills me. But I knew that if I gave her just a little more time to be an innocent, happy child, and used that same time to personally step back and get a better grip on myself, then I wouldn't have to lose her completely in order for her to turn out healthy and happy. I just had to let go a little, for a little while." I said with a last rogue tear escaping. I brushed it away. "I convinced myself that as long as she came through it all okay, then I would be fine too, *eventually.*" *Hmpf.* I looked at him again with a new understanding for that part of his story. "I guess we do have that in common after all, that tenacity when it comes to holding on for '*eventually!*'" He gave a warm half smile in appreciation.

"*Thank God!*" He added gratefully as he caressed my cheek.

"I'm still not giving up. I will find a way to make it work at some point. Until then..." I trailed off.

"You are a lot stronger than you give yourself credit for Simone. I have no problem giving credit where credit is due. You did what you had to, even though it wasn't the easy thing. You live with the pain and the stigma of your choices every day because you know they're the right ones. You should be proud of that instead of constantly feeling guilty for it. I know that concept seems foreign to you but I wish you would at least consider it from time to time." He offered generously then he kissed me out of genuine appreciation.

I could still feel his sadness as he took in the whole situation. I gave a weak smile back at that. I felt a little stronger again and I finished up my recitation.

"Anyway, what we have is only a temporary agreement. It's more of a 'legal' *understanding.* We have promised to revisit it periodically and to tweak it as necessary but we also agreed not to flip-flop constantly, especially when it comes to any changes in physical custody unless or until such changes are expected to be long term. We don't want her to feel like she's being pulled back and forth." I didn't pause to explain there because I knew he understood that hell as well.

"At some point though, when it makes sense for her, I know her and I will be together again full-time, like we're *supposed* to be! I do believe that and I don't want to do anything to jeopardize that. I can't let her get even farther away from me. It's too much." I sighed deeply again trying to mimic his ability to get back to the now. I had to focus on the future. That was what mattered at that point. *Pfhoooooohh!* I let it all out.

"So, legally?" He prompted wanting to know more of the specifics.

"Legally we have "joint custody," 50/50 as far as any major legal or medical decisions go, but it's stated that he has current *physical* custody and that she will stay in that house and at her current school, etc. Neither of us can travel with her without the others direct consent and any deviation from the current schedule needs to be discussed and approved by both parties in advance." I said trying to remember all the important points.

"For the most part it just means that we've agreed to try and cooperate and to act like adults who care mutually about their daughter. So far that has worked out really well and I'm actually pretty proud of that." I admitted feeling a little better again. "Unfortunately, I can't deny that a lot of that success has been due to my constant willingness to get thrown under the bus for the sake of keeping the peace. Personally, I don't care. I know it's worth it in the long run. But I'm not so confident that he will be as willing to do the same when his turn finally comes." I said with raised brows and a sad, slow shake of my head. "And it will, someday." I stated unequivocally. "That much I know."

He looked at me intently and I could feel him diving into dangerous waters mentally. "Tell me Simone, what if he's not willing to cooperate with you after this? What will you do then?" He asked bravely, voicing things I didn't even dare to think about. I looked up at him but stayed quiet for a few more seconds, considering it.

"I honestly don't know." I admitted letting the fear show a little for once. "All I can say for sure is that I will always try to do whatever's best for her, in any situation. I know that noncommittal vagueness seems fairly typical of me at this point, but I truly believe that some decisions just can't be made until you face them. I don't know what else to say." I added.

"You're right of course. Always much smarter than you give yourself credit for too." He complimented with a half grin. "Most people would have given an adamant answer, one way or the other, but at least fifty percent of the time I find that that answer changes completely when it comes to fruition in real life. You *never* really know what you're capable of, until you have no choice but to find out." He agreed solemnly staring back at me. I could feel his contemplation of many different situations. They came at me so fast that I didn't have time to dwell on any of them but none of them were good.

"There are a number of traps and pitfalls to avoid here. The most important thing is not to let any of those possibilities catch you completely off guard if you can help it." He stated smartly. "You need to have a plan "B," Simone, *and* a plan "C for each scenario," just to be on the safe side. Options are always good." He gave a reassuring wink at that. Then he reached up and slid his hand under my hair and gently pulled me forward so he could kiss me again. "I don't want to see you get hurt anymore. That's gone on long enough. You deserve to be happy too you know." He informed me seriously and I had to laugh. Out loud. My reaction surprised him of course.

"I'll believe that if *you* will!" I teased back and he grinned again, the whole thing that time.

"We're quite a pair, huh?" He joked with a laugh and a shake of his head. "But seriously, if you explain all of this to him and he doesn't understand, we will need to have a plan of action ready. If she gets sick and he tries to keep it from you, or to keep *her* from you and your '*wacky*' ideas, what are you going to do? I've seen what people go through when they understand the process firsthand and then aren't able to be physically present when it occurs in another loved one." I noticed that he didn't include himself in that group mentally but he still understood how important it was to *most* parents.

"It can be torture for both the parent and the child to be separated at a time like that and I know *neither* of us wants to see that happen here! You're going to need to know what your options are, *all* of them." He pointed out.

It was hard to consider, part of why I'd put it off for so long obviously, but he was right. I felt the truth swirling around in there with the pain and the fear. That's where the truth often lives I have found, in the places that you'd rather not look. Boom! There it is.

Every time.

"I guess I should talk to my lawyer. Get some clearer answers." I said giving in.

"That's a good place to start." He said with a nod. "Do it today or early tomorrow. Get everything you can in writing, and remember to keep copies in multiple places." He instructed, his experience with such things shining through and scaring me just a little bit more.

"Ben seemed like a nice enough guy Simone, and I really hope it stays that way. I do. But never underestimate how low people will go in the midst of a custody battle if things get ugly. Think about how much you love her and how hard you would fight for her!" He insisted vehemently. "We already know he feels the same way so I think our top priority in this case, is to avoid that fight at all costs. You two have been right about that all along. But if we can't…" He trailed off and I felt those less desirable options swirling around in the air again. There was no need to voice them between us.

"You should make a mental list of the absolute worst things that he knows about you, and then you have to assume that if it comes down to it, he'll use every one of them against you. Don't let him knock the wind out of your sails by surprising you with that. It carries too much momentum. Count on him hitting below the belt. Have a defense ready for any attack. Always stay one step ahead and you'll be fine." He instructed and then he leaned his forehead on mine.

"In the meantime, you have to try not to worry so much." He advised earnestly while stroking my cheek. It would have been a ludicrous request if not for his calm washing over me like a soft blanket. "I'll be here to help you in every way that I can. In any way that you ask me to." He clarified. I knew he was offering us the full protection of the Camp and everything that went along with it. That reality scared me a little though and I really hoped that I would never need it. But with what we were facing, I couldn't deny that it made me feel better just knowing it was an option.

It was good advice, the part about not worrying, but I had

no idea if I could pull it off or not, even with his help. I sighed again and he could tell that I'd had enough for the moment. He pulled me in close and hugged me tight.

There were so many questions floating around in my head then and so few answers still. It made me laugh out loud when I thought of trying to explain it all to someone else coherently, when I still had so much left to discover for myself. Hell, *about* myself! Ethan was curious then where my thoughts had led me so I shook my head and I told him.

"I can't believe that I need to suddenly act the authority on this subject in such an important conversation, and I don't even know half the answers to the questions that he's bound to ask! But at some point, soon, I really *would* like to explore the subject further. A *lot* further! Especially the part about what my options are for finally finding some of those specific answers about myself once and for all." I told him seriously. He started back intently, actively listening and focusing on not projecting his excitement on me in order to let me finish.

"There still hasn't exactly been time for that to be my top concern yet in all of this, but I am definitely excited about the possibilities I now know exist to explore that further. I have to admit that opportunity is a big draw for me. That curiosity is an itch that has always demanded to be scratched. I still wonder in the quiet moments late at night for example, if there are really things that you can do to help me find some of those answers? If there are, then I think that's an important step that I need to take, because those answers won't just benefit me anymore. I'm thinking that it might be the best place to start in helping Liliana as well." I postured.

"I mean the more we know about my own genetically *heightened* background, the better idea we will have of what to expect in her to some degree, right? I know we'll still have to account for possible deviations like every other inherited characteristic but I figure it can't hurt to have a starting point." I admitted nervously but logically.

He nodded. "No, you're right. I'll set something up as soon as I can and I'll let you know when, okay?" He offered. I nodded in return, extremely grateful but even more nervous once it was a real plan and no longer just a notion in my head. Was that really going to happen? Was I really going to finally get real, official answers to the questions that had plagued me my whole life? I wanted to get excited but it was too much to digest all at once and it was still way too soon to believe it so I beat the excitement back down until it sat quietly in the background again, waiting.

We were both silent for a while after that. It felt good just to be together and I wanted that energy to fill me before I had to face anything else. He held me happily enjoying the momentary peace as well for a while before he eventually spoke up again.

"Come on. Let's get out of here and go get cleaned up for our 'night shift.'" He suggested reminding me that I had agreed to go to The Tavern with him. I would have preferred to just go home at that point, shower and go to bed. But since he wouldn't be there with me for a while, and I didn't want to be alone with my obsessive thoughts at the moment, I decided I could wait. The thought of listening to his music live again immediately lifted my spirits anyway and I was suddenly on board.

"I'm starting to see why you never sleep." I joked as he pulled me up after him.

Chapter 21

When we arrived at The Tavern he drove around to the back side of the building and pulled smoothly into the spot closest to the back door. It was obviously "his spot" judging by the way his tires fit the ruts so perfectly. It was pretty mundane stuff, especially compared to our overly dramatic lives as of late, but it was my first time seeing it from that point of view, *his* point of view and my brain still needed to add that to the new list of "*normal's*" that it was busy formulating.

I realized at that moment how often I felt more alive with him doing everyday things, than I had even doing remarkable things without him. It was an interesting observation to me and like so many other little epiphanies where he was concerned, I wasn't sure if it was good or bad necessarily. Either way it was undeniably true and that *was* surprising.

He took my hand as we came around the car and we went in through the door marked "Employees only." It was amusing to watch him use a key from his actual key-ring for once to open a lock. He just flashed those beautiful white teeth at me and held the door as I ducked underneath his arm.

We walked slowly through the large, darkened backstage area maneuvering carefully around chairs, instruments and sheet music stands until we came out into the restaurant through a door beside the stage. Right away I noticed the change in atmosphere. There was attention being paid to someone coming in with Ethan that way, and I could pick out the ones who noticed quite easily from the ones who could have cared less.

Among the dozen or so employees currently milling about preparing for their shift, there were four in the "*I care*" category. There was the bartender Mario, who I had met once or twice but very rarely talked to, since I always sat in a booth. He had done a fine job of ignoring me all along and I had always appreciated that, but I noticed that he noticed me then. Outwardly he remained neutral but inwardly I could feel his assessment side working overtime. I left him to it.

Beside him was a gentleman that was obviously a cook, judging from the white apron that he always sported around his waist whenever he wandered by. He was in his fifties or so with a slightly rounded midsection and what was left of his graying hair was close cropped. I hadn't seen him as many times over the past months since he'd spent the majority of his time in the kitchen, but he always reminded me of "Mel" from that old show "Mel's Diner" whenever I did see him. He was currently out of his domain, standing at the bar and staring right at me. I could feel the mental "*Huh?*" from across the room.

They weren't the only ones contributing to it though, so that may have been a factor as well. There were at least two other sets of eyes trained on me as we entered. One of those remaining sets belonged to a guy in a handyman type of uniform who was on a ladder, working on a speaker up in the far corner of the room. I didn't remember having seen him before at all and as much as I didn't like or generally *need* to rely on stereotypes, I couldn't help but notice that he didn't really *look* like a handy man. He struck me as a little too young and able-bodied to have settled into such an *uneventful* profession already. There was a strong vitality about him that I could feel from across the room. It was obvious that he was a lot more than a handy man.

As quickly as I had him figured out, he seemed to do the same with me. I could feel his surprise at the rarity of the situation when he flicked a questioning look over at Ethan for confirmation. That was not lost on me. But I also felt his quick but complete acceptance after the ever so subtle nod from Ethan indicating that I "*checked-out.*" He seemed satisfied, mentally dismissed us and was the first to go back to his own work. *Sweet!* I really wished then that everyone else was as easy as he was.

Ethan smiled down at me for just a second, knowing that I had felt the whole thing and kept walking confidently across the floor. I was with him up to that point, but the fourth pair of eyes threw me for a loop, I'll admit.

They were the most unnerving of all based simply on the surprise factor. They belonged to Dani, and as well as I had thought I knew her, I realized that I hadn't ever noticed her in direct relation to Ethan before that moment. Her focus had always been either on me or on the other patrons in the crowd whenever I had interacted with her. I'd never observed her when her attention was focused solely on him, as surprising as that seemed to me then. It was pretty intense at that moment though! I had to assume then that it was something she intentionally put out of her mind on a regular basis, whether or not she knew that anyone else would ever be able to notice it, but I had no guesses as to *why* someone would do that.

It was truly surprising and even thinking back purposefully on our interactions I couldn't remember anything that stood out in my memory that should have tipped me off. He just always did his thing and she had always done hers.

She'd always been happy to answer questions about Ethan regarding his music or his hours. At the time it had just felt like the normal amount of promotion you would expect from someone who was not only working for the establishment that had hired the artist, but who was also a real fan. I figured she would have to be to want to work there and listen to his music all the time, right? I had never noticed her *possessiveness* towards him though! Not until the moment that she saw us walk across the room together hand in hand. Boy, I felt it then without a doubt. *Yikes!*

Well *that* was unfortunate! I had really liked Dani too, I thought with some sense of that balance weight I always worried about finally rearing its' ugly head. I really didn't want to hurt her, but I could tell then that it was going to be inevitable. She had very real, very *deep* feelings for him, and... She. Was. *Pissed!!*

Great!!! I gripped his hand tighter and pulled back a little.

His eyebrows crumpled in question at my hesitance.

I looked over to the kitchen door where Dani stood glaring at us and then back at Ethan. He instantly understood. He slowed our pace for a half a second, but he didn't stop. He sighed heavily and led us over there.

"Dani. How are you?" He asked politely. She had no choice but to respond in kind or risk showing that she was upset.

"Fine, fine, thanks." She answered quickly, obviously surprised to be signaled out. "It's been a little crazy around here. You know, busy though, so that's good right? You?" She rambled and I started to wish I could make it less awkward for her. Apparently I wasn't alone in that impulse. I quickly realized that I wasn't the only one Ethan felt the need to rescue on occasion.

"Good." He said calmly. "Glad to be back. I definitely miss this place when I'm gone too long." He said with a disarming smile. "Thank you for keeping things running so smoothly around here in the meantime, but then I had no doubt that you would. You always do." He finished with a genuine sense of gratitude and I could feel her warming up under his attention and starting to forget her anger already. I looked away to hide the humorous shake of my head. Her inability to hold her anger in the face of his charm was a very familiar phenomenon to me and I decided that it was probably a good time for me to say hello.

"Hey Dani. How's it going?" I asked bringing her attention back to me and I felt the hit immediately as she noticed the fact that he was still holding my hand. Her amnesia receded some at that realization and I felt her jealousy full force once again. To her credit though, she hid it well.

"Hey there Simone! Well this is certainly a surprise!" She stated simply, trying to play it cool and keep her inner turmoil *inside.* Of course she had no idea that it was a futile endeavor.

"Yeah. It kind of was to us too." I joked, playing along. I was trying really hard to keep it light but the air in the room felt about as light as a led blanket.

"Okay well anyway, welcome back. I guess I'd better get back to stocking the service station. Those napkins aren't going to roll themselves!" She joked uncomfortably as she began to back away.

"Thanks Dani." He said again as she finally slipped away into the kitchen. I let out a loud breath as I looked back up at Ethan.

"Is this going to get easier at some point?" I asked exasperated by the new and strange confrontation.

"Don't know. Guess we'll find out together." He said simply with a quick shrug and his usual content smile.

"That, I have to admit, was completely unexpected. I had absolutely *no* idea!" I told him and he knew that my admission was more than just your average busy, self-involved person not noticing. For me not to have picked that up before was downright strange. "Did you know?" I couldn't help asking, although I had to admit to being fearful of the answer.

"Yes." He said without hesitation, as honest as always. I was a little disappointed at first but he wasn't done so I decided to hear him out.

"Well, suspected as much anyway. Once I was fairly sure that I wasn't simply imagining things, the random personal questions, switching shifts to be here when I'm here, the thinly veiled stare full of longing from across the room..." He explained with an exasperated raise of his brows. "I thought a lot about whether it was a good idea to have her continue working here or not. But she's never made any declarations to me or anyone here or anywhere else in town about being interested in me. In fact she's never acted on it in any way what-so-ever, and so far, it has never affected her ability to do her job." He said with a shrug.

"So since I couldn't *prove* it you have to understand, aside from asking her outright which can be tricky for an 'employer,' I had no real reason to let her go. I still don't!" He ended with another shrug which was a lot for him. "It honestly hasn't been an issue until *right* now." He explained and I knew that it was the truth of course. He looked back at me warily then.

"That bad? *Really?*" He asked, his head cocked to the side like it simply didn't compute. It was painfully obvious that he still wasn't totally convinced for some reason. He was thinking that it didn't feel right.

"*Mmmmm. If her desire to keep you to herself was equal to her physical strength, she would've dropped an oven on me where I stood.*" I confirmed quietly but definitively, immediately dashing his hopes of minimizing it all.

We walked away from the area where my usual booth was and towards the elevated table nearest the stage instead. It was in the farthest corner of the room and it had a wraparound bench that was raised up a few steps higher than the surrounding dance floor and tables. He would sit up there sometimes and go through sheet music or grab a bite in between sets. Every now and then it would be occupied by a few of his "*out of town friends*" or those I now knew to be his "family members" but most often it sat empty.

I had never had any desire to wander over there before myself, so far from my usual comfort zone. I was pleasantly surprised though as we climbed up and sat down, at how comfortable the more lightly padded wooden bench was and how great the view was from that vantage point. I was sure it was no accident. I liked it immediately. It made me feel safer with my back to the wall and a second exit to my right. I don't know why I'm like that, I'm just like that. Maybe it's because I was fated to end up in a life where that kind of thing mattered. Who knows, maybe it's a package deal that fate gives you as a gift at birth? I chuckled at that notion, but only in my head before the seriousness of the situation put a damper on it.

"I wonder why she works so hard at keeping it to herself." I mused aloud. "Why not just go after you after all this time? I mean surely she could have gotten another job by now if you meant that much to her, couldn't she?" I asked curiously. "I don't get it." I admitted with a furrowed brow. It was an "*unknown*" and I could never let those go, even when I *wanted* to.

"How long has she been here and how much does she know about what really goes on here?" I asked quietly then, trying to place her in some sort of mental category successfully. Is she a *height?*" I asked outright. I wasn't sure if he would answer me, or if that somehow violated one of the "*privacy*" policies. He was straightforward and unfazed though, so that was good at least.

"She's been here for almost two years, she knows nothing about us and no, she's a *norm.* She knows I meet people here sometimes, but they're all *"old friends," "extended family"* or *"adoring fans"* as far as she knows." He provided. "She's just an honest to goodness hardworking employee and I really *need* that for this place to work! I rely on the people who are employed here to keep the place going, completely separate from the constant chaos of camp *and* without too much interference from me. I know where my strengths and weaknesses lie." He admitted easily with a charming grin. "In that vein, the *norms* far outnumber the *heights* here, by about seven to one actually." He threw in with a smile. A quick bit of math in my head told me that there were only roughly 3-4 *heights* max working at The Tavern and I knew he was one of them. So was I *#4* of "3 or 4?" Or did that make me #5? I wondered distractedly.

"Dani fits the bill for what I need here very well, in all respects. She's not married and has no kids. In fact, she has no family around here at all that I know of. That was my only qualm in hiring her in the beginning, that she had no local references of any kind. But she had just moved here, so I gave her a chance. That detached availability has turned out to be her best asset in that she has the freedom to change her hours at a moments' notice if I ask her to, and believe me I *do!* And with her skill set she can basically run this place whenever I need to be away. She's actually really great at her job." He allowed with another casual shrug and I was only slightly annoyed by his obvious level of affection for her. I took comfort in the fact that it didn't come close to matching hers for him.

I placed my elbows on the table and my chin on my fists and sat quietly in thought for a minute contemplating it all. He didn't let it go on for long however, before he distracted me from myself. He reached around my hips and slid my whole body closer to him. I looked up and smiled while he leaned in for a kiss. I didn't bother to resist him. I laid my lips softly on his as they approached and enjoyed the contact for a long moment before I backed off. *What a day!*

My next thought though, was that it was one thing to unknowingly shock Dani with our announcement, but it was another thing all together to sit there and flaunt it in her face once I knew that it was an issue for her. I wasn't that mean, nor was I a glutton for punishment!

I pulled back and stared plainly into his eyes and he understood my hesitation without the words. It was nice that it worked both ways occasionally. He didn't even pretend to agree with my worry though.

"Ut uh." He said right away, shaking his head back and forth. "I won't hide anymore. I'm all done with that where you are concerned." He stated unequivocally. "*Especially* here!" I for one had no arguments with that once I thought about it that way.

"Fine." I leaned in and kissed him once more just to prove it. "But I'd keep an eye on that if I were you." I said not bothering to hide my foreboding.

"Noted." He agreed simply. "I'm going to go check in real quick in the kitchen. Can I bring you a drink on the way back?" He offered.

Mmmmm, yeah. A glass of wine would be fantastic, thanks." I answered.

"Red or white?" He asked next.

"*Ummmm*, white please." I decided.

"K. Be right back." He informed me. He kissed me again then nibbled on my lower lip a few times before he pulled away reluctantly and slid out of the booth. I sat back and took in my surroundings from the new vantage point for a few minutes while I waited. I could see everything that was always behind my back before. The entrance, the hostess station and the back half of the dining room that was furthest away from the stage where it was quieter. I had never spent any time over there but it looked just as nice as the rest of the place.

That is where I saw Dani again a moment later, when she came out and started putting paper placemats on the tables. I sighed deeply and considered the potential outcomes of the situation. For the most part they weren't encouraging. I decided then that it may be better to just face it head on and get it over with, woman to woman. Hell it was worth a shot, right? I thought optimistically as I slid out of the booth and hopped down. I started over to her.

I knew that she was aware of my presence behind her because I could feel her tension skyrocket as I got closer. She pretended to be unaware though. I cleared my throat and she turned to look at me, annoyed that her plan to avoid me was being overruled.

"Hey Dani? Hi." I said with a friendly smile. It was not returned. She just glared at me again so I kept going. "I just want you to know that I would never intentionally come between another couple. I'm just not "*that*" girl." I gave a laugh that was also not returned. *Ooookay!*

"But I also want to point out that that's not really what happened here, even though you're kind of acting like it is for some reason. I am sorry though, if this hurt you in any way, I really am. That was never my intention, but we *are* together and it would be great if that wasn't going to be an issue here!" I said trying my best to be diplomatic. I really should have known better though. Love was anything but diplomatic, especially unrequited love. She managed to find a laugh for that no problem.

"*Hah!* Don't flatter yourself, honey." She responded with a cold chuckle. "You're just the flavor of the month! Ethan doesn't *do* 'permanent!'" She insisted with a dismissive shake of her head and even though there was humor in her voice, there was venom in her thoughts on the subject. She only half believed her own statement where I was concerned though and I could tell that was what bothered her the most. It was definitely a side of her that I had not seen before. She didn't stop there.

"He'll be over you and onto the next chippy before that spot on the bench cools off from your lovely ass cheeks!" She finished with another laugh at my expense as she walked away without a backward glance.

Well, that could have gone better, I thought despondently as I walked back over to the raised banquette. Oh well, I'd tried. I sat back down just as Ethan came out with my drink. *Yay!* I took it and sipped it twice before I set it down.

"You okay?' He asked with an amused half smile, obviously

detecting my change in mood. I was saved from a long explanation when three members of the covering band came in through the backstage entrance and started setting up equipment behind Ethan's chair.

"Fine." I assured him pleasantly, but I contradicted it by taking another long sip. He just gave a soft laugh and then a kiss to match, before he headed over to the stage. He had told me that instead of canceling the band they had lined up for the evening originally, he had decided they would sit in and play together. He walked over and they all started shaking hands.

Their name was "Southern Comfort" and I knew that it was more for the southern rock music that they were known for than the alcohol. I'd heard them a couple of times while he was gone and had liked them a lot. They were a little heavier on the rock n' roll than Ethan's usual set list but I had really appreciated that at the time. They chatted and joked with each other for a few minutes then got down to business.

Ethan picked up his electric guitar that was leaning against the amp and spent the next few minutes tuning up. I felt the shift in atmosphere as he mentally switched hats.

Ahhhh... I had really missed my Magician while he was away, I thought with an appreciative smile to myself. I saw him speak something softly to the others and they all nodded vigorously in agreement.

I saw Mario open the door out of the corner of my eye and people started to slowly file in just as they started their first song. It was a classic and it made me smile harder as they began the familiar intro.

Carry on my wayward son
There'll be peace when you are done
Lay your weary head to re-eesst
Don't you cry no more!

Then it was just Ethan's soulful voice cutting across the room.

Once I rose above the noise and confusion
Just to get a glimpse beyond this illusion
I was soaring ever higher
But I flew too high

He looked over at me intermittently as he sang and I felt his conversation to me in it even without the *height* help.

Though my eyes could see I still was a blind man
Though my mind could think I still was a mad man
I hear the voices when I'm dreaming
I can hear them say!

As usual he sang as if the words were all his own and an image of him waking from a dead sleep in an instant flew through my mind. The existence of that one demon was particularly clear to me by then just from knowing him, I didn't need to feel it from *him* anymore in order to *feel* it.

Carry on my wayward son
There'll be peace when you are done
Lay your weary head to re...eeesst
Don't you cry no more!

If only... Someday... I thought.

Masquerading as a man with a reason
My charade is the event of the season
And if I claim to be a wise man, well
It surely means that I don't know

It was amusing to me just how greatly skewed his own humble opinion of himself really was. I had to remind myself though in his defense, that at least it was skewed in the right direction. There were so many reasons that he could really be a complete egotistic ass if he had a mind to, but it made me laugh to even try and picture him behaving that way. He had *plenty* of self-confidence sure, that was *not* an issue! *Hmpf.* It wasn't the same thing at all. He just wasn't one to focus on the past for long periods of time, neither its' pain nor its' successes.

On a stormy sea of moving emotion
Tossed about I'm like a ship on the ocean
I set a course for winds of fortune
But I hear the voices say!

Carry on my wayward son
There'll be peace when you are done
Lay your weary head to rest
Don't you cry no more
No!

Carry on,
you will always remember!

As he sang that line I could see the slight momentary change in his expression as the ugly memories obviously passed through his mind, though it was quick. I was amazed at how much I could still read from him even with his music's total blocking ability, once I took the time to notice. By the next line he was smiling at me meaningfully again.

Carry on,
nothing equals the splendor!

Now your life's no longer eeemmpty
... surely heaven waits foooor you!

I sat and smiled back at him, happy to finish on that note and as part of his present reality. They finished up the last round of the chorus and the crowd clapped, reminding me then that we weren't alone even though it felt that way.

He looked over at me as the last vibration on his guitar strings faded away and I could feel every last bit of his being still reverberating through the room. From the child that he had survived being, to the teen who eventually grew into a strength that was even greater than his ever-increasing size, all the way to the man that he became who was deserving and maybe even finally ready to know some sort of peace and happiness in his own life.

I had to stop and thank God that I was finally ready to share that sentiment with him, if we could just figure out *how*! The only thing that I could think of that would be worse than not being together at that point, would be being together, but not both wanting the same thing. That thought was soul wrenching and unfortunately, instantly reminded me of Dani's predicament.

I shook that off as fast as I could because I knew that as inconceivable as it seemed, it really wasn't that unusual. It scared the crap out of me to even think of wanting someone the way I wanted Ethan, who didn't feel the same in return! It was one of those things that hurt physically to even *imagine*! In spite of all that we had been through already, I knew we really *were* very lucky! I understood what Dr. J had meant in the very beginning, and I knew by then that he really was as smart as he seemed!

As I silently comtemplated all of this, they went right into the next song, a more upbeat classic from ZZTop. I could tell immediately that that one was purely for the crowds' entertainment. They seemed to appreciate it and so did I. I tapped my toe on the step and my thumb on my glass throughout the whole thing. They played three more rock classics after that before he took his first break and came back over to sit with me. The band headed over to the bar to say hello to the bartender who was apparently an old friend of theirs.

He was hungry again by then and once he mentioned it, so was I. Both craving a little protein, we decided to share a plate of Buffalo wings but he ran into the kitchen and got them rather than having Dani come and wait on us. I thought that was a smart choice, never being a big fan of saliva sauce myself.

The wings were great, and I already knew I loved the blue cheese dressing, so I was momentarily a very happy girl. The fact that I was getting to spend the evening in his company made everything about it even better. Other than catching the occasional uncomfortable stare from Dani as I licked my fingers, I thought my first night *"on the job"* so-to-speak was going fairly well. Then I happened to look up in between bites and I had to rethink my mental assessment. It had been such a long day already but I realized then that it was about to get a lot longer.

"Ut oh. *Here we go!*" I said as Oscar fell through the door in a fit of raucous laughter. Beth and Gen followed close behind him, but in a much more mature fashion, both shaking their heads and rolling their eyes at whatever inappropriate joke he had made. Apparently the bus was not done unloading though because they kept coming. Next through the door was Travis, and he was with another man that I'd never met. They were deep in serious conversation, completely oblivious to the antics of the others. I had known they wouldn't be put off for long but that didn't mean that I was prepared for them to show up all at once!

I tried to take it all in slowly and retain the calm I had been enjoying but it was difficult as they made straight for us at an alarming speed. I was afraid I would be rendered speechless by all the energy hitting me at once as they approached. It was filling me even as I considered it! It was strong, but I realized right off the bat that it was *surprisingly* more than bearable, it was actually pretty great! I was filling up with a pulsating excitement and an acute relief at Ethan's homecoming that I more than understood! The closer they got to me though, the more I felt their collective joy and I was smiling so hard already that I was sure I looked like a complete idiot. I tried *really* hard to stop.

"Wow! They sure are an energetic bunch, aren't they?" I said through my teeth, attempting to make light of it. Ethan was smiling just as hard at their approach I noticed, but he pulled it back for just a breath when he looked down at my *crazy-happy* expression. He ran his fingers slowly through my hair in a calming manner and as a show of emotional support. When that hand reached the nape of my neck, he held me tight and pulled me closer until my forehead touched his.

"You've stood up to life's craziest curveballs, the fierceness of my *personal* demons, and Federal foes that you shouldn't even know exist! I'm pretty sure you can handle drinks with my family." He insisted with his own wave of encouragement and calm temporarily outweighing the impending storm. The strength of his desire to reassure me was temporarily keeping it all at bay. I was relieved as my expression returned to that of a semi-normal human again.

"Thanks." I said as I smiled a much more controlled smile up at him in gratitude. By the time I looked back out toward the crowd again, they had already arrived at our location and they started to pile into the booth one at a time. Gen slid in first on Ethan's side and hugged him tightly. Then she punched him again for leaving and we all laughed. Oscar and Beth got in on my side but that didn't stop him from getting his affection in. He just stood and reached over me to give his own version of a hug by bumping shoulders with Ethan while they slapped each other on the back. I just laughed from my tenuous position beneath the abdomen tent.

"That's okay! Don't let me get in your way!" I joked. That got another round of appreciative laughter from the crowd as he hugged me next more earnestly and laughed even harder. Things started to settle down a little after that. Travis and the new guy made their way up to the opposite side of the table, after pulling some tall stools over from where they rested against the far wall. They slid on and one at a time, clasped hands with Ethan over the table. It was a two-handed shake that portrayed a wealth of history between the participants. They were glad to have him back. *Almost* as glad as I was! I could feel it too but I barely needed to.

I could tell just from the level of affection alone that the newcomer had to be another Kent. The brown hair threw me off at first, but the accompanying blue eyes were the same brilliant shade that Gen also shared with their father. I realized then that Jack's hair had obviously not always been silver. I could easily see it having once been the same soft shade of brown.

"Simone, this is Mike, the second eldest of Jack's brood." Ethan said as an introduction. He shook my hand then. Not like he had Ethan's, but still in a warm and inviting way.

"Hello Simone." He said in a voice that was kind but also authoritative without any conscious effort on his part. It was obvious to me right away in the way he spoke and even the way he held himself that although he wasn't the oldest, he was a dependable "second-in-command," the family voice of reason.

"It's nice to finally meet you." He said as if I was somehow responsible for not making that happen sooner. I just raised my brows in amusement and shook his hand.

"Likewise." I agreed. "I am making my way slowly but surely through the family. I can only handle meeting so many Kent's at a time!" I joked in my defense and that got another round of appreciation from the table. He seemed to enjoy that unmerciful honesty even though he tried to hide it. It annoyed me a little that he was playing so hard to get when things were finally going so well with everyone else. But the more I felt him out, the more realized that he and I were probably more alike than I would want to admit. After that, I felt pretty sure we'd be okay, eventually.

Dani came over then and took orders from everyone. I couldn't help noticing that her hostility level was still pretty high, but again she showed no outward signs of it, so I let it go. I felt bad though, that she was clearly taking her anger at me out on his family. That didn't sit well with me. She could be mad at me all she wanted, I could take it. But they didn't deserve it and the misdirected hostility kind of pissed me off, I had to admit. I realized that I was grinding my teeth together from absorbing it all by the time she walked away. Ethan had been engrossed in conversation with Travis momentarily and I didn't think he noticed. That unfortunately had left Gen's attention free though.

"You alright?" She asked quietly with a little nudge. I nodded. "What was that all about?" She wondered out loud with a nod in Dani's direction. I was glad then that I wasn't the only one who had noticed it. I let out a chest full of air before I answered.

"Oh you know the usual. Unrequited love, misplaced aggression, all that good stuff and I'll tell ya, it was all news to me!" I admitted with wide eyes for emphasis. Gen and I had never spent an extended period of time discussing my personal issues, but she had indicated to me that she was *aware* of them long ago, presumably just like all of Jack's kids would be. Being "family" appeared to be the only "in" one needed to be privy to any and all info around the farm. I was okay with that policy though. I got it. I felt safe enough with that particular family and their security level already as a group not to fear for my secrets. Like the people at Camp, they knew all about my situation, but for the most part, they just didn't bring it up. That worked for me.

"Huh." Was all she said for a while but I could feel the analytical wheels turning inside her head at that new development. I still felt pretty much the same way so I left her to it and went back to my drink. I grabbed it with both hands and pulled it towards me to save it from all of the arms flying around. It was all I had left momentarily since Oscar and Mike had already cleaned our platter of remaining wings. It didn't take long though for Dani to return with the drinks and more trays of food. She left just as quickly as she arrived and with the same amount of chit chat as before, none. No blatant hostility, no snide looks, just an indifference that I certainly wasn't used to. I let out another long sigh but it was much too loud for anyone to notice.

Ethan reached up and took one of my hands off of my glass and clasped it in his. Then he tucked them both under the table on his warm thigh, all without ever looking away from his current conversation with Travis. I stood corrected. *He* had noticed. I smiled and laid my head on his shoulder for a brief moment in appreciation and closed my eyes. The noise of his boisterous family over the crowd was deafening but for once it didn't bother me. It couldn't stifle our silent conversation. I found that it overrode everything else. I looked up at him as I straightened and he grinned over his shoulder at me. For that one moment, it felt like we were the only two people in the room. It was during that stolen moment of peaceful bliss that I had my next eye-opening realization.

It dawned on me then at least partly how it was that he was a block for me. I understood that it wasn't anything he consciously *did.* And though there was definitely a quality to his voice that was like no other for sure, it was more about his energy that was just *so* much stronger than everyone else's, that pushed what would be a moderate advantage well into the extroidinary range. To the point that it completely blocked all the dimmer energy out. That just happened to work beautifully for someone like me.

It's similar to how some people broadcast out so weakly that I can barely read them. Like that unassuming kid that you barely notice is in the room for instance. You can talk to someone else for ten minutes and then be like, "Oh damn Lou, I didn't even realize you were there!" But part of why you don't notice them is because you don't *feel* them, because *everyone* is empathic to some degree. I didn't invent that, like Ethan I just ran to a whole new level with it. Now that's not to say that the "Lou's" of the world aren't passionate about things, because they most certainly *are*! They just keep it close to the vest. It's always a well-kept secret, and a surprise when you later hear, "We were all *so* shocked!" or "He was always such a *quiet* guy." Yeah, not really. He was just a non-projecter.

Then there are those people who you could never *not* notice were there! They're not always just the loudest ones in the room either, although sometimes that can certainly be the case. They're the ones who absolutely *light up* the place when they walk in, sometimes without saying a word, simply because they give off such a powerful energy! You know who I mean when I say that, I'm sure! We all know at least a few of these people. We all *feel* that elevated mood around someone! People don't necessarily realize it but they *need* that good energy to feed their own and we will all naturally gravitate towards a person like this for what we pick up when we're around them.

That was the difference between Ethan and the general population for me, his already naturally intense, but then *heightened* energy! I still didn't understand why his energy was so strong or why when he was singing it was even that much stronger! But I realized that even just sitting there next to me quietly, I could *feel* him much more intensely than I could anyone else in the room.

Of course then I wondered typically, if another empath, should I ever meet one, would feel him the same way that I did or if it was strictly some sort of electrical amplification that only occurred between him and I. That led me to ponder so many other things that I eventually had to shake my head to clear it all. He turned and smiled at me and my usual "antics" with his usual "amused patience," but didn't ask me to explain.

We went back to our respective conversations until a few minutes later when the band members came over to say hello to everyone on their way back to the stage to begin the next set. There were more hugs and handshakes all around as the group and the laughter continued to grow. Apparently they were all old school friends as well. I was quiet through most of their catching up, aside from the introductions, just trying to manage the overflow until they got it all out of their systems. After that, they each headed back over to the stage.

Ethan squeezed my hand then got up to follow. I watched him as he sauntered back over there. The crowd outside our table had grown as well over the last hour or so and the room was almost half full by then, pretty busy for a weeknight. I got the feeling that when Ethan was back in town, word got around quick.

He was in his usual uniform of dark hip hugging denim and a soft, dark grey, vintage looking tee with his usual matte black leather riding boots. I smiled to myself since I knew then that there was actually a motorcycle to go with them. I still hadn't had a chance to cut his hair yet and the unruly mop only made him look more rugged and therefore even sexier. He probably *hated* it, I allowed then with a silent grin.

As the various emotions towards him began to filter through me from around the room I realized that I wasn't far off on the general consensus of his appearance. There was a definite shared appreciation echoing back at me as he took his seat. I looked around and noticed the other handful of women in the room that were currently noticing him too. I smiled in complete understanding. Luckily for me, that was one thing I was pretty sure I didn't need to worry about.

It should have bothered me that so many women were sexually attracted to him, but it didn't. Not at all! I actually laughed and it felt really good to finally let that petty insecurity go completely. I knew he could never be swayed by that kind of casual attention at that point, so it really wasn't a temptation for him at all. I felt that rare "*lucky*" thing again, that I could know that as certainly as I did.

Of course *they* couldn't know that. They would keep coming back every night to eat and drink and admire, and never be any wiser to the futility of lusting after him. He had entertained that attention in the past for fun I knew, and they probably did too, but I could never hold that against him. It was the past and things were very different for him at that point. It made it easy for me to process it and let it go. Especially since Dani wasn't one of those admirers at the moment. He looked down at his guitar and started to play a "Lynard Skynard" song and the background noise all faded away again. *Ahhhhhhh....*

I started to think that I could easily see myself spending most of my free time there with him without too much coercion on his part. Aside from Dani's occasional hostility, the peacefulness I felt there was something that I'd already grown accustomed to. Unfortunately, it was so comforting that it kept me from feeling the intentions of the approaching inquisitor.

"So tell me how it is that you're planning to fix him, in order to succeed where all others have failed." Mike challenged me bluntly as he slid unexpectedly into Ethan's empty spot. He was grinning slightly and raised his eyebrows at me in jest, trying to play it off as a joking confidence between friends. But even with the music blocking I knew what it really was. I sidestepped the noose that he had laid out for me so carefully and just grinned back at him.

"Now why would I want to go and 'fix' him?" I asked grinning. When I like him just fine the way he is." At that he burst into an honest laughter. I grinned and raised my own brows back at him. I laughed myself for just a second and then I looked back out at Ethan. "I'm just planning to love him, that's all I've got so far." Then I looked Mike in the eye again. "I'll have to make the rest up as we go." That was actually far more honest than I had planned to be, but I could tell by his expression that at least I had passed his little "*test.*" He pursed his lips and nodded at me, clearly somewhat surprised.

Apparently that was another tactic that ran in the family, I thought with a chuckle as I remembered my run in with Jack that day in the diner that had led to my getting my apartment. Which I realized then, had led to everything *else* that had eventually led me there! *Damn!* My mind spun for just a second at the dizzying concept of the whole sequence from beginning to end! Was all of that meant to be, just for Ethan and I to end up together?! In that particular time and place? It was an intensely interesting question but one I had no real answer for so I chose to let that go as well, for the sake of my own sanity if nothing else. Unanswerable questions were traditionally my least favorite.

"Don't listen to anything he says." Gen offered in support as she came back from the ladies room with Beth. She saw my expression and mistakenly assumed it was from my run in with her brother. She sat down next to me again and Beth slid in after her. Mike eyed us each meaningfully one last time before he mentally dismissed us and returned to go sit on his stool and face the stage. "He's a cynic to the end. Entirely unreformable!" Gen insisted loudly in my direction over the music, with only a touch of humor. I let the mind blowing thoughts go and tried to focus on the present conversation again. "He'll get on board eventually, you just have to give that one some time." She insisted calmly. "He just takes a little more convincing than your average person." She said sarcastically.

"*Hah!* I know the type." I replied dryly. Beth spoke up then too.

"Listen to her on this one!" She insisted and I could see the "*Been there, done that.*" look in her eyes even if I couldn't feel her feelings as clearly. She was still heavily muted in that aspect but I was getting used to it. It was actually reassuring to me to know that it hadn't changed.

Gen separated a beer bottle for herself from the newest group of beverages recently left in the center of the table by the ever stoic Dani, and then liberated the new and full wine glass as well and slid it my way. I took it gratefully, with the sincere hope that no part of her anatomy had found its way inside. I was thinking as I sipped that if it had, hopefully the alcohol would kill anything left behind.

I let it all go then and clinked my glass against theirs in celebration of all of us simply being present at the moment to celebrate. We all drank to that. I looked at Gen and I could feel us both remembering the last time that we had been there in comparison. We both silently appreciated how much of an improvement it was and how quickly we could be back there again. They *all* felt that way to some extent though I realized.

It really did help, being with other people who truly understood what it was like to love him, and to miss him at the same time that we respected him for what he was doing! It gave a sense of reality to the entirely unreal world of *heights* and all that it entailed. That appreciation boiled over and poured out of me then.

"Thank God for you guys!" I exclaimed wholeheartedly. They smiled in return with instant understanding. "I don't know what I would do without you guys to talk to sometimes." I explained and I could feel that they both understood what I meant.

It was reassuring to have people in your life that understood your problems and were supportive when things seemed at their worst. I was lucky enough to have a select few in my inner circle in life already who qualified for that distinction but the Kent's were included in that exclusive group too as far as I was concerned. I wanted them to understand what a big deal that was for me but I wasn't sure how to explain it properly. I looked up at Gen and Beth and searched for the correct words but they just laughed at my struggle.

"Don't worry." Beth assured me with a knowing grin. "We get it." She insisted. "Yes, your beau over there is the ringleader of this operation, but at some point we *all* 'chose' to become involved, in one way or another and we *all* decided to take the associated risks and to make those sacrifices because we believe just as passionately in what he's trying to do as he does." She leaned in then, placing here hands over mine and spoke intently. "You are *not* alone!" She insisted with a grin. It was funny how in the end it always came down to that one reassurance making all the difference in the world. Gen raised her glass to that and we all clinked again.

As I sipped I glanced over at Ethan and caught him looking back at us. It was obvious how happy it made him to see me connecting so well with the only people that he had ever considered family.

That was a big deal for him and when he finished one song and paused briefly before the next, I felt the weight of it hit me from where I sat. His unconditional love for them enveloped the room like a tent securely covering them all. His love for me however, was a smoldering heat burning brightly in the center of that comfort zone that lent a vibrancy and a glowing warmth to all that surrounded it.

Sitting there feeling those two different but positive waves begin to meld together made me proud to be responsible for the resulting atmosphere and I was more than happy to share it. Happy to be a part of that feeling, however it came about. There are *countless* things I *have* to feel, very few that I actually want to feel! That was a perfect example though of those rare, but wonderful feelings that kept me going through the hardest of times.

Every day would not be so good. We knew that already. We had just lived through the counter-balance to the current joy so we didn't need to be told that there *was* a balance to maintain, and the joy that our connection created generated quite the deficit. There was no way to ignore that fact. That would always have to be made up for somewhere.

At that thought I had my second epiphany of the night as I realized, in a very abstract way, why connections like the one that Ethan and I shared were *not* a dime a dozen. They couldn't be. It would be disastrous! The sheer amount of hardship it would take to balance out the highs of every single connection if they were all as intense as ours would be beyond staggering! It would be constant highs and lows every day, all day just to try and keep the balance between the two poles. It would be completely exhausting for everyone involved! It made sense that there needed to be a lot more *middle-of-the-road* mixed in there in order to keep things on an even keel. There is a comfort level somewhere in there for everyone. Extremes in general are certainly, understandably a lot harder to maintain long-term. I tried not to let that particular truth terrify me.

Then MoMare whispered snidely from the dark recesses where I had left her. "*How lucky do you feel now huh, when you look at it like that? How long do you think this can possibly last?*" She asked tauntingly.

I refused to let her pessimism bait me though. I was getting too strong by then to give her that kind of power over me anymore. I accepted that it was not the norm to be as intense as we were, but I also knew that *we* were certainly not the "norm" either, so it wasn't quite as surprising or unsettling as it would have been otherwise. That perspective was slightly easier for me to live with.

It was still a question as to how we would balance it all out from then on, especially if it was truly going to exist on a daily basis. I had no clue yet how we could maintain that, but I felt certain that working with him, his family and the Camp was a really great place to start.

Chapter 22

The next day at Breezey was another whirlwind of productivity and positivity similar to the previous ones and before I knew it, it was over and time to head down to Ben's office. The momentum that the job was picking up was awesome. My anticipation of the coming task however, was not.

The ride down 95 was long, but not long enough to calm my nerves. It was after 7:30 already and I knew Ben would have closed up shop for the day, but that didn't make me feel any better since seeing his staff wasn't what I was nervous about. It was the fact that Ben's innate inability to ever just "go with the flow" was a big part of why we had eventually separated and I didn't know how much that had changed since then, if at all.

I'd personally never had a choice but to go wherever the external flow took me, regularly. And no matter how understanding we tried to be of each other's position, it was really hard to be a "team" when we were continually on different sides. It was no one's fault, so there was no one to blame specifically but it sure made things difficult. I spent a lot of time just defending myself and my spontaneity back then. I finally realized however, that it was something else I wasn't really sorry for, and I grew tired of apologizing all the time just because it didn't work for *him*. That didn't automatically make it *bad* or make it wrong for me to be that way, it just made me *wrong for him.*

Anyway, that constant disparity had always made it hard for us to talk about things sometimes. Things like politics, music or what was the best way to get in or out of the city from a given location. We could never agree on simple things like that. Our minds were just on different wavelengths when it came to that stuff. We generally agreed on the big things though, you know the important stuff like how to raise our child, or whether it was better to rent or own, so the hard decisions in our relationship were actually easier for us. It was just those pesky little day-to-day things that had always tripped us up, dammit.

I used to wonder worriedly how we ever even ended up together and he would always joke that "opposites attract!" My response was always something like, "Yeah, sometimes uncontrollably and until they smash together and destroy each other, like matter and anti-matter!" *Hmpf.* We always laughed it off but sadly that distance between us and our point of views' on things had become even greater and more apparent over time rather than less. I was really hoping as I drove, that by that point firsthand experience and wisdom had closed that gap a little. Still, I wasn't holding my breath.

I parked and went around to the back door that I was happy to find he'd left unlocked for me. That was always how I had gotten in after hours before and the reflex was familiar and automatic. I entered and walked down the same pale blue hallway that I'd passed through a million times before, my flat leather sandals making a soft clapping noise on the tile all the way down to his office at the end. It was all so familiar and yet bizarre to me since it was no longer a part of my day-to-day reality.

I gave a soft rap on the slightly ajar door out of respect for that new distance and he called to me to come in. I took a deep breath and pushed the heavy wooden door open. *I could do this! For Liliana!*

Ben was sitting at his desk writing in a file. He held his index finger on his left hand up to me as he finished writing something with his right. Then he put finger and his pen down and looked up.

"Hey, thanks for coming down. Come on in and have a seat." He said motioning toward his shiny brown leather sofa. I sat down heavily, ignoring the noise it made and he came around his desk to sit beside me. “So what’s up? What’s with all the dramatics, Simone?” He asked getting right to the point as always and setting a no-nonsense tone that made me sigh in dread of the coming conversation. I drew a complete blank momentarily when I tried to consider where on Earth to start. I had run through it over and over in my head on the way down and yet it didn’t help at all when it came time to finally spit it out.

“Are we alone? I asked looking around, feeling the need to make sure before I started.

“Yeah. Everyone else left over an hour ago.” He assured me with a suspicious look. “*Why?!*” He asked impatiently.

“Alright, there’s no point in pussy-footing around this anymore so I’m just going to plow straight through it, forgive me if I throw a lot at you at once. I promise I’ll answer questions afterwards, at least the best I can.” I assured him. I took another deep breath and dove in.

“So I know we said we wouldn’t impose assumptions on Liliana turning out like me, and I know you’d like nothing more than to have it never come up again. You also know that I would be completely happy to go along with that. But I think I’ve seen enough evidence lately to be sure that we are not going to get off that easily.” I gave that a moment to sink in while I thought of a way to explain that it could be just the first step in a whole mountain of issues yet to climb.

He stared back at me unflinchingly, but silent. He wasn’t ready to respond yet. That would make it real and he hadn’t heard enough to convince him yet. I knew that just by knowing him and his stubborn ways. I understood and I took advantage of his silence. I kept going.

“No, I’m not 100% certain yet but I feel like I should keep you in the loop, especially since that’s not even really the worst of it anymore.” I sighed heavily at that and he could no longer remain quiet.

“What are you talking about? What could be worse than that?” He asked automatically. I didn’t wince visibly, but I did close my eyes momentarily when the unintentional stab sliced deep into that old wound. I took a slow breath and reminded myself that he wasn't the one I needed to please anymore. After that I opened my eyes and let it go.

"Listen, you already know that I'm more than just your average every-day empath, right? Well as I'm finding out there's a very specific reason for that that I never knew about before, one that only a select group of people who have that reason in common actually know about." I saw his increasingly suspicious look at that and I knew I needed to keep going fast. A short explanation for that implied secrecy would go a long way towards him paying attention from there on out so I threw a quick one in.

"When it comes to other people's prejudices and fears it's just better that way for all involved. I'm apparently not the only one who feels safer keeping it to themselves." I said plainly. That I could tell he believed easily enough.

"Anyway, the reason that I'm trying so hard to explain it all to *you* is that I believe there's a very good chance that someday Liliana may find herself in this select group as well. So being the responsible co-parent that I am, I thought that you should know about it beforehand. Believe me, it would be a lot easier to keep all of this to myself where you and *many* others are concerned, and for the most part I still *intend* to do just that! I know how hard it is for some people to even understand this stuff, never mind accept it as a part of everyday life." I gave him a look that conveyed my disappointment in him for a change, instead of it being the other way around, since it *was in fact* a reality whether he accepted it or not. He was surprised enough by that attitude to return to silence.

"I didn't want to believe it all myself at first and you know how open minded *I* am." I reminded him. "So *I know* this isn't going to be easy for you Ben. But eventually I did have to admit that it all made sense and I'm hoping you will be able to as well. It took me a while to come to terms with it and I expect you'll feel pretty much the same way, *at first*. That's why I felt this couldn't wait any longer. I wanted you to have a chance to digest all of this and to deal with the possibility that there may be a very *different* future for her than the one that we had in mind, *before* it can come to pass and catch us all off guard." I sighed again and waited for him to process that.

He screwed up his face again like he was annoyed at me for the fact that he had to deal with stuff of that nature at all. It had always been that way. In the beginning he had felt privileged, and special that I had shared my "*private circumstances*" with him. But eventually I think he saw it as more of a curse. I was pretty sure he wished he could go back in time and "*not know*" it by the end. I was used to that attitude but I was really tired of feeling guilty and solely responsible for it all. Maybe someday I hoped silently, what I was sharing with him would help him to understand that it was *not* all my fault, and that these things existed in the world *in spite* of me, not *because* of me. It was a hope, but again I wouldn't hold my breath.

"I don't need you to agree to anything right now Ben. I just need you to hear me out because if it happens, we're going to have enough to deal with without having to go through this initial shock phase with you at the same time. I'm trying to help us out here by maybe giving us a head start, at least with that so we'll be ready to deal with the *height* factor when the time comes, if it ever does. But *if* it does, we are going to need to be strong for her and united in our goals to do what's best for her. I know that I can't expect you to make those decisions properly and responsibly without knowing all the facts. But once you do, you *will* do what's best for her. I'm counting on that Ben." I admitted letting my desperation show just a little. "We need to be on the same page before anything happens."

"Before *what* happens?! Jesus Christ Simone! What the hell are you talking about?" He finally demanded impatiently. I looked up again and held his gaze.

"Her possible *heightening.*" I said flat out. He just stared at me like he was suddenly scared for my sanity. I wasn't surprised. I sighed and tried to back track a little.

"Look, I'm an empath. I always was an empath and I always will be. That parts just who I am, and I think there's definitely at least a trace of that in her as well. It comes and goes with her still in a way that I haven't figured out yet, but it's something that she was born with, like green eyes or blonde hair and whether it ends up being a dominant trait in her or a recessive one, she *has* inherited it to some degree. That part's nonnegotiable and only extraordinary in a very normal, understandable kind of way." I took a breath.

"What may or may not come *after* that is extraordinary in a much more unusual way and that's the part that I'm worried about." He still just looked confused and I remembered that look very well from my initial meeting with Ethan when I had been the one trying to comprehend such things. I knew by then though that it was a process and that I had to let it happen at his pace. I gave that a moment to sink in before I continued.

"My abilities were very different when I was younger Ben, simpler. Not nearly as intense as they are now. It was the change that occurred in me around seven years old that made the difference between who I was then and who I am now. That change occurred when I got sick. *Really* sick." I added meaningfully looking up at him again. He scrunched his brow but still didn't interrupt.

"It's funny, because it's really just a simple virus when you come right down to it, and everyone gets it at some point like any other bug that's going around. But it's not just a sore throat, sniffly kind of virus. It's a lot more serious than that. No one knows yet where it originated from or how long it has existed specifically, but it can be traced back at least a handful of generations for sure." I told him trying to keep the details simple and as vague as possible for the time being until I knew how he was going to react.

"There's some speculation that it may have been manufactured by the government itself and unleashed on the population as some sort of experiment." I added cautiously. He was not immediately receptive. "You can roll your eyes at that all you want." I commented at his annoying response. "But unfortunately our government *has* been known to experiment on its' own people, that's a fact Ben. You know I'm no conspiracy theorist and I don't like talking about things like that happening anymore that you do, but it doesn't change the fact that they're true. I have no idea if there's any truth to it this time around yet or not, but I do know that they *are* aware of it and they are keeping track of who it affects and how, for whatever reason." Again he looked at me like I was telling him the sky was polka-dotted.

"Something else I know for sure is that they don't like it when everyday citizens get too nosy or too educated about it either, or when they get in their way while they're investigating a case. Most people know nothing about all of this and they like it that way. Whether it's to keep us in the dark so they can use us as guinea pigs or if it's to protect us I don't know. But I do know that they work hard to keep it out of the public eye." I informed him honestly thinking I would just get the worst part out there. He dropped his jaw and just stared back at me for a few seconds before he responded.

"The *government* Simone, *really?* He asked skeptically. I was expecting it though so it was easier to deal with that time around. I just kept going with as much explanation as I could give him.

"Where it came from, whether it was Mother Nature or some mad scientist's laboratory doesn't matter. The fact remains that it *does* exist. Some people only get a little sick and get over it without ever thinking anything of it. They just think they've had a really bad bug or the flu. Life goes on again as usual afterwards and they're never any wiser. Their name gets checked off on a list somewhere unbeknownst to them as someone who is unaffected, a "*norm*" and life goes on." I said matter-of-factly.

"But it affects *some* of us *very* differently! People like me who have some unusual element that sets them apart just slightly to begin with. In people like that apparently the virus reacts with that element much more vigorously and they in turn get a *lot* sicker! Like *life threateningly ill!*" I said with a serious look. He looked sick himself when I said that so I could tell that he understood my fear.

"If and when they finally pull through it, they come out quite different on the other side and whatever set them apart to begin with becomes *much* more intense, permanently '*heightened.*' That is the difference between me and any other run-of-the-mill empath. I have since learned that somewhere along the line the '*height*' box was checked off on my chart, as I am in fact a *heightened* empath. So of course therein lies the genetic possibility that Liliana may turn out to be some sort of a *height* as well." I finished quietly and I gave that a moment to sink in.

"I'm still learning about what all of this stuff really means for the big picture but common knowledge or not, it definitely does *exist.* I've already seen enough examples *besides* myself, to believe that completely and I know firsthand how difficult an adjustment it can be when someone goes through it. I don't want our Liliana to face that situation confused, scared and alone, not if I can help it and I'm finally learning that maybe I *can!* To make it easier at the very least!"

I took another slow breath and closed my eyes for a beat to calm myself. I knew the more worked up I got, the less seriously he took me as a rule. I had to get back into an old mindset to remember that.

"We need to be prepared." I said calmly as I looked up at him again. He shook his head in a wet dog manner like he could simply deny the words entry. His shocked expression was wearing off some but instead of responding, he got quieter as I could see it starting to make sense in his medical mind. I gave him another few minutes to mentally digest. Finally he made an attempt to respond but it was weak. Again, I knew the feeling all too well without ever having to be able to read his.

"I don't even know what to say Simone. I don't know what you *want* me to say." He insisted helplessly.

"I know. I get it. I do. It will take some time for all of this to settle. I'm still working on that myself, believe me! But I needed to start somewhere and I was afraid that I was waiting too long. You know, you really scared me when you called to tell me that she'd been sick. I had just found out about all of this then and I wasn't ready to deal with her going through it yet. I admit that's why I was a little *too* freaked out that day at the hospital. I was really glad that it turned out to be a false alarm and I still am, but it was a wakeup call for me that I had to tell you *soon*! I was hopeful that we'd be better off dealing with it together, as a team, if it happens. I still am. I need you to be on board and to take this seriously, while we still have time." He just stared at me again and his face asked "*How?*"

"Look, I really hope it never becomes an issue. I hope this

whole conversation turns out to be a *huge* waste of both our time! I *really* do! Maybe she won't ever come in contact with the *Hgt* virus. Maybe she won't react to it as strongly as some of us do. Maybe her skills are such a small part of her that it will never interfere with her life or her happiness in any noticeable way! Maybe all of this will never matter at all. That would be fine with me still, *believe me!*" I said calming down again a little bit. "But I just couldn't run the risk of her being left in the lurch when she needs us most, simply because I was too afraid to deal with the possibility of the alternative!" I insisted honestly. I looked him in the eye again. "And you can't either Ben." I added in my most serious tone.

"So who else knows about all of this? Obviously this Ethan guy, who else? What does all of this even have to do with him?" He asked suspiciously. *Great, here we go.* I thought dismally. I could tell that he was hunting for the king of the wacko's so he could behead him and therefore discredit the whole village in one fail swoop. I needed to take away his sword.

"Yes. It was Ethan who told me. But he's not crazy Ben, and he's not alone. There are others, many other respectable, intelligent professionals that I have personally met. People who have dealt with it in their own families, who have gone on to try and help others, just like Ethan has." I argued.

"Respectable professionals huh, really, like who? Anyone who'll be willing to meet me face-to-face and give me some actual medical documentation of this so-called 'virus' or its aftereffects?" He asked logically but annoyingly.

"Yes and no." I said and sighed heavily. "Those people and things do indeed exist, but it doesn't work that way. They're not going to come forward and talk to you about it or just hand over proof of things that they also work tirelessly and selflessly to keep from becoming public knowledge. That's the only thing we all have in common right now, is the belief that this is all better dealt with privately. A *height* needs that protection and anonymity most in order to live a normal life sometimes, at least in the beginning while they learn to adapt. These people take great personal risks in order to safeguard the *heights* they help." I tried to explain. "It's a very big deal to them!"

"How convenient." He said sarcastically. I sighed again.

"I know." I agreed despondently with an ironic grin. "I told you this would be hard, but you know that *I know* the difference between the truth and a lie when I hear it, right? You have to at least trust in that by now." I insisted reasonably. He stared defiantly at me but didn't argue.

"What difference does all of this make anyway? If she's sick we'll bring her to the doctor and get her treated, just like we've always done. Or are you going to tell me you don't believe in traditional medicine anymore now too?" He accused looking for a foe to fight *somewhere* that would keep it all from being real.

"Of course not! Don't be ridiculous please." I answered even more calmly than before to counteract his pessimism. "But there's a good chance that they won't know any more than the fact that she has a bad virus. They can only do so much. How we respond to the extraneous symptoms that may arise from that virus could affect her disposition for the rest of her life! Uneducated professionals often have no idea what to do in those kinds of "unknown" situations. The kids become guinea pigs at best! Misdiagnosis can be as damaging in the long run as no diagnosis and that is often all they have to offer! You may be a vet but you're still a doctor yourself and you should still be able to understand what I'm telling you." I implored reasonably.

"It's different every time for every person. She will need people around her that understand that and can determine what the proper treatment is. We owe it to her to get that for her and that's not something you do on the "local provider network" Ben. It's just not! Maybe someday." I added sadly. "You don't even know how lucky we are to have these avenues available to us when so many never did or never will!" I took a breath and went on.

"These people do exist and for that very reason. Of course she will see a real medical doctor, but be prepared for the fact that it may not be enough! Truly though, that's not even the part that I expect her to have the most trouble with, she's a strong healthy kid. I think she'll get through that as well as possible." I said with a sad resignation. "It's the *'after'* that's really the most difficult, when the fever goes away and everyone leaves you alone and life is supposed to go back to normal. Except that it never does Ben. Not *ever.*" I looked up at him sadly for a minute and I knew he understood that at the very least from knowing me and my struggles. Well maybe he didn't understand it, but he at least knew that it was a real thing.

"*That's* what Ethan does! He helps people through the *'after.'*" I explained with quiet admiration. "I wish I had known him back when I was struggling daily, and I'm glad that Liliana will have options that I did not, if and when she should need them." I added honestly. His face still belied nothing but indecision but that was okay, for the time being. It was as well as I had expected it all to go. I stood up.

"You should go home now." I said evenly. "Don't try to do any more work tonight. Just go and sleep on all of this and call me tomorrow with your questions. I will do my best to answer as much as I can. In the meantime *please* understand that I need you to keep all of this to yourself for now, at least until you can make an informed decision. For all of our sakes, including hers. Okay? And trust me when I say that I am only putting you through this because I want what's best for our daughter and I know *for sure* that you do too!"

He looked numb but he nodded slightly in agreement. If it wasn't about her we wouldn't even still be having a conversation, I was sure of that. But I could also tell then that that was all I was going to get for the night. He was on overload and I was familiar enough with that condition to know that he needed time more than anything else that I could give him then.

"You alright?" I asked wanting to make sure before I left him alone. He nodded again, only slightly more vigorously than the last time, but it was just enough to convince me. He looked up at me briefly then went back to staring at the floor, deep in thought. I was a little less convinced after that. "You sure?" I prodded. Again he nodded. I decided that it was probably as good as it was going to get. "Okay, then I'll talk to you tomorrow." I assured him. I gave him a quick hug and he used one arm to absentmindedly hug me back. Then I stood and I slipped out quietly the way I had come in.

I exited the air conditioned building and felt the warm evening air sweep over my bare skin. It felt good, like a warm blanket. There was an instant wave of relief and a weightlessness that spoke of oxygen deprivation. When the dizziness passed I looked over towards my car and saw the sun beginning to set behind it and create a beautiful wash of reds, pinks and yellows. I stood there staring for just a moment. I took a deep breath in and finally let all the pent up emotion back out with it. *Phew!*

At least that part was done! Step one. It wasn't a huge accomplishment in and of itself, but it was one less thing on my plate full of worries and a *big* step in the journey towards our collective "happily ever after." I was sure of that. Although if acceptance was the light at the end of the tunnel, I still couldn't see even a faint glow of it reflected on his face yet. I remained hopeful though that we would get there. I wasn't ready to give up on that yet.

I started the car and opened all the windows and the moon roof to let the beautiful breeze blow through the vehicle while I texted Ethan.

:} Went as well as I could've hoped. Fingers crossed. Headed home now.

The return message was quick and simple.

☺

I smiled back at the silly graphic on my screen even though I knew neither he nor it could see me, then I put my phone away and pulled out of the parking lot. I couldn't help noticing then, how very different the trip home felt from the trip there.

That comfortable old familiarity that had been my companion on the way down wasn't the primary atmosphere between me and Ben anymore. What would happen from that point on was a complete unknown and I could still feel the loftiness of that loss of gravity as I drove off into our new and uncertain future. I acknowledged it but there was little about it that I could change or control anymore so I tried to just breathe my way through it the best I could.

It was slower going home for some reason but it didn't matter to me at the moment. I just cruised along behind the traffic until I got off the highway and back into Pinegrove. From there I breathed a little easier as always. I enjoyed the lush greenery of the back roads and all that I knew they concealed as I traveled them until I reached the farm, appreciating them in ways I really never could have before living there.

I pulled into my sanctuary and down my private driveway and a smile instantly sprang to my face as I noticed Ethan standing there leaning against his car in the setting sun. It was parked right *beside* my usual spot. I was on an endorphin high as I pulled in beside him and got out, at how amazing it felt to have him there waiting for me to arrive home, right out in the open like that! *Damn!* There were joys in life, and then there were *joys!*

That was a new kind of happiness for me and it was bigger than my body was used to but I was working hard to embrace it. My smile still hit earlobes as I got out of the car but that was okay because so did his, so I didn't even bother to try and hide it. I just walked over and fell against the solid, warm surface of his body as he opened his arms to envelope me.

It was like existing on pure oxygen and it made me feel like I was consuming a meal, just being that close to him. I felt full and complete in ways that I had never even dreamt about before. I had been in a constant state of wonder ever since he had come home, and the awe at the joy of that reality had not even begun to wear off yet.

Hmpf. Not even close.

It was a little disorienting though, I had to admit. I still felt like I was floating a lot of the time at the idea of finally being able to spend so much time together and I knew I couldn't walk around on a cloud forever. But I was thinking that a just little while longer sure would be nice. I needed the time to find my way through all the newness.

"Now what?" I asked looking up, honestly not sure. After

the last couple of days I couldn't seem to even imagine what came next. As it turns out, I didn't have to imagine it though and that was the absolute best part.

"Next, you give me that haircut that you promised." He stated matter-of-factly as he ran his hand through his still too long, ridiculously sexy hair to pull it out of his face. I looked up and cocked my jaw to one side with a grin as I recalled the memory where that promise lived. He winked. "Then we make some dinner. I'm thinking pasta." He added thoughtfully as we walked hand in hand up to the door. "Then we go to bed." He said simply. "No work tonight." He promised with a whisper in my ear and never had anything so simple made me feel so amazing!

"I think we could both benefit from a quiet night at home." He insisted with waves of desire and contentment pouring off of him.

"*Man* does that sound good!" I agreed easily as we headed up the stairs together.

Chapter 23

The next few evenings on the farm were chaotic but enjoyable, especially with so many Kent's around. Ethan and I were still busy during the day with Breezey and would be for the next week and a half, but we helped out on our free evenings whenever we could. It was more hard work added to our already long and physical day jobs but it was undeniably fun, picking corn, bailing hay and driving tractors back and forth to haul it all in. The fresh air combined with the good company made the tasks rejuvenating rather than taxing. Especially when you added in all the laughter.

Without the pain and the distance taking up so much space in our lives, there was finally room for the everyday, for simple nothingness and for wonderful things like *comedy!* I had begun to realize just how funny Ethan was when no one's life was in immediate danger! He made me laugh so hard sometimes that I was starting to think he should moonlight as a comedian!

Of course, so few people were ever allowed to see that side of him that I knew that he'd be hard pressed to put enough of an audience together to make a living at it, but anyway… Put him together with Oscar, Mike and Travis for even just a half an hour and I would have a stitch in my side from laughing every time! It was just so nice to finally get to be an *actual* "couple." To become more …*real.* Less "Invisible Super-hero and Wanna-Be-Bond-girl" and more just plain old, "*Ethan and Simone.*" *Hmpf.* I had wondered what that would be like for so long and the truth was that so far it was pretty freakin' phenomenal!

Liliana had finally gotten to meet the rest of them, when I picked her up from camp and brought her back to the farm that Thursday for dinner, fresh picked watermelon and a fire. It was just as easy going and natural as the day she had met Oscar and Beth, just minus the drama!

It was still funny to me how easily they all got along just like long lost cousins at one of our family reunions. Between Travis making flowers disappear and pulling coins out of her ears, and Gen, Beth, and I playing badminton with her amidst glass-shattering squeals of delight, it was as simple as pie to get her to love them all as much as I did! The boys had the next game when Jack and Ethan showed up and we sat, eating freeze-pops in the grass hooting and hollering at every amazing swing!

The Kent's really were a great group of people though so I wasn't that surprised that both Liliana and I already felt as comfortable with them as Ethan did. Of course I hadn't met Sarah yet and Mike and I still had our issues and the occasional "difference of opinion" from time to time, so it wasn't all doves & roses. He had showed up while we were sitting around the fire and was as sweet as molasses when introduced to Liliana. Not in a fake, condescending way either, but genuinely so. Me however, he mostly continued to ignore. That was fine though.

It was becoming very clear to me by then, that despite the current distance between them in their daily lives, Mike was obviously the closest friend to Ethan of all the siblings. He was annoying but he was mostly just being protective, and only *slightly* possessive. I understood and could forgive that, even if it was a pain in the ass. Most of his needling throughout the night had been in good fun anyway and I would never admit it but I actually kind of liked the way he kept me on my toes. Of course so did everyone else!

I knew he wasn't convinced yet that I really understood, accepted and loved Ethan as much as I did, as much as *they* did. It was definitely frustrating at first, but after a while I decided that he could take as long as he needed to, to realize that I wasn't going anywhere or using him for anything. As long as he didn't interfere with things between us in the meantime, I was done trying to convince him. I had much more important things to worry about still. Like *everything else*.

The rest of our lives were still moving in every direction at once so it was nice to be falling into somewhat of a semi-relaxed rhythm there, especially between me and Ethan. It wasn't exactly the untouchable peace that I had been fantasizing about, not yet, but it was a huge improvement over what we'd had before so I would never dream of complaining.

We would wake up to start our day together at whichever of our places we had ended up at, generally intertwined with each other in some fashion. Sometimes we would unwind and get moving after the first sound of the alarm, when we needed to set one. More often though we would become willing victims of that close proximity, choosing to get even closer rather than to separate. Neither of us really minded the delay, it just meant a slightly later start. Either way, as early as we were often up, we were always at Breezey by 8:00 AM when we needed to be.

We had also found much to my delight, that we enjoyed almost all of the same foods, making mealtime decisions blissfully easy. There was never any arguing or pouting because someone had to settle for what the other person wanted. It was just a matter of figuring out what we were in the mood for, or what was fresh that day. Not to mention that basically anything I took the time to prepare for him, he was grateful for. I could have served him warmed over road pizza and he would have accepted it with genuine appreciation as long as I took the time to plate it for him. I tried not to let that fact affect my self-confidence as a chef though, since I was pretty sure that most of what I made for him was at least marginally better than road pizza.

On top of his authentic joy at whatever I served him, when I cooked, he cleaned up. That apparently was the deal. But there were just as many days that he cooked and I cleaned up, and when he cooked a meal for us, he didn't half-ass it. He cooked it *well!* That was another pleasantly surprising part of the new arrangement, I found. I wasn't just taking care of him, we were actually taking care of each other. It was only slightly different from how my relationships had always been in the past, but it was different enough for me to notice and to decide that I *really liked* it.

The only nights that Ethan and I were spending apart by then, were the ones that Liliana stayed over. I was always thrilled whenever that happened whether it was a regular visit or a last minute change of plans, and I would never say no to an opportunity. He knew that and would never even want me to, much less *ask* me to, but it *was* somewhat of a bummer for him because it meant he was on his own for the night whenever it happened.

It was still an either/or kind of situation for me where they were concerned, at least for the time being, but he never complained about that either. He knew how much my time with her meant to me and he was always genuinely happy that I felt that way. That was one of the things I liked best about him. One of the things that had surprised me the most in the beginning, and one of the things that convinced me that maybe I *could* really have a life with him where I had once thought that completely impossible.

Sleeping was already tough for me without him by then though and I missed him just as much as I missed her when he couldn't be there, just in a *very* different way! The thing that was so hard for me then, was that I was always missing *someone.* Of course that was still nothing compared to his side of the situation so I would never complain about that either. At least I knew I *would* sleep, albeit poorly.

Ethan slept poorly at best a lot of the time. He just accepted it as the way it was. Most nights he was happy to lay beside me while I slept anyway, and at least rest his body. But there were many times when the restlessness would get to be too much even for that. I would wake to find him gone from the bed, doing crunches or pushups out on the deck where he hoped he wouldn't bother me, or gone altogether on a run. He started to leave me notes after the first morning I mentioned that I had woken up and looked for him, always so considerate. But even in his happiest of places, he still only got a few hours of sleep each night and I knew that was his "best case scenario" so I really hated having to take it away from him.

Sadly, I knew for a fact that he slept rarely, *if at all* on the nights that we spent apart, since unfortunately for him he couldn't really be anything but completely honest with me about it afterwards. That knowledge always made it a lot harder for me than simply missing his presence. As usual, I could tell that he would hide it if he could, just to spare me the guilt. Of course we both knew that wasn't really possible. There was dissatisfaction and there was frustration but mostly there was just reluctant acceptance, on both our parts.

The up side was that whenever we missed each other that much, it just made us that much crazier to see each other the next night and that was always kind of fun I had to admit, if only to myself. He also would tend to sleep the best of all on those days, *afterwards*, so there was that to be grateful for too. I really did try to dwell on the bright side of it all as much as possible. I knew from experience how much easier that made things!

Most of the time though, even with all that we were up against, things were surprisingly good, especially the waking hours! While we waited in our somewhat nervous limbo for whatever Ben's reaction to her possible new reality would be, we just tried to enjoy the calmness and the quiet that the interim afforded us. The peacefulness was reenergizing on a soul-deep level, but the calm also finally made room for thoughts about our future and what might come next to exist.

Without the daily stress that we had been living with before, there was actually time to think of those other things that I had set aside for "later." I drifted off on many an occasion while working at Breezey, in bed with him at night somewhere between sex, sleep, and late-night wandering, or randomly during mindless repetitive tasks on the farm. Wondering about where we went from there and other important things, like what exactly *did* Ethan want from his future? He already had an awful lot on his plate. Did he really even have the option of wanting more? Another few days had passed before those questions finally wiggled their way down past my lips.

I'd had Liliana unexpectedly the night before that when Ben had gotten called back into work. We still hadn't spoken directly since the night in his office and again he had only texted me to say he was going to be tied up too late for me to bring her home. So I had happily kept her with me overnight and unfortunately that had left Ethan odd man out. Of course Ben knew that too but I tried to convince myself that that wasn't why he was doing it so often.

Ethan had told me that he planned to spend the night at his place, catching up on some paperwork and getting in a workout. I called him the next morning after I dropped Liliana off at Juniper and asked him if he'd slept at all. He'd let a casual "*nah*" roll of his tongue, like it was a completely trivial thing. I sighed, sad for the circumstances, but he was as upbeat as ever.

"But since I got so much work done last night, and got in a good long run, I'm glad we have the morning off from Breezey because I'm planning on taking a nice long *nap* real soon!" He added slyly.

"Oh really, when?" I asked just to make him give me specifics so I would know that he wasn't "*stretching the truth*" trying to make me feel better.

"What time can you be at my place?" He asked back candidly instead. I shook my head and laughed.

"See you in ten minutes." I replied and hung up still smiling as I put the pedal to the metal.

We hadn't really "slept" then either, but I for one was certainly left feeling *refreshed*! If he was tired it was less than usual because it didn't show at all at the moment. I relaxed a hair more knowing that.

We laid there naked in the blazing mid-morning sun, stretched to our full lengths on a blanket in the reasonable privacy of his back/front deck. We were still catching our breath when I couldn't help returning mentally to the one question that had haunted me most in the past few days as he had casually tossed Liliana on his back and playfully hauled her around the farm.

I laid there enjoying the aftereffects of electricity still zinging through my body periodically and thought to myself that it might be the best time I would ever have, between the current circumstances and the calmness of life surrounding us, to bring it up. Just to get it out there and find out once and for all where he stood on the subject. What the future held for us would be determined largely by whether or not we wanted the same things. I still had no idea if that was the case or not. It was important information though and it was time for answers to those questions, whatever they were.

I looked over at him, laid out with his arms thrown wide, palms up. They reached past the blankets edge so that the back of his knuckles rested against the red stained deck, but the heat of it against his skin didn't faze him. I stared fascinated as his abdomen went concave from his hip bones all the way up to his ribcage before it extended again and continued alternately in rapid succession, working to replenish his oxygen levels. His skin was still covered with a thin layer of sweat from our recent activities, and since I didn't say it out loud, I allowed myself to admit that it actually *glistened* in the sunlight.

Sooo ridiculous, for Christ's sake! I thought again as I tried to focus. It was an important topic and I didn't know how long it would be before I got another chance or the nerve to ask him about it again. Once I'd had time to think about it again my curiosity had become pretty powerful and it was gaining strength daily! I took a few slow, deep breaths and finally just went for it.

"So what about you Ethan, do you ever want children of your own someday?" I threw out bluntly before I could chicken out.

His head snapped toward me immediately so I knew he took my question as seriously as I did. A lot of very different, very *strong*, emotions passed through him at once so I still had no idea what he thought about it. He just stared at me for a long minute continuing to breathe deeply as the parade of varying emotions passed. I waited patiently, going against my own nature as long as possible until he finally spoke.

"I don't know." He admitted, his verbal answer so far still as frustratingly non-informative as his wild emotions. Then he gave a great huff and looked up at the sky. He folded his arms and stacked his hands beneath his head. "A part of me does." He said contemplatively before he took a few more, deep but slower breaths. *One... two... three...* I tried not to count them but it helped to keep the anxiety busy while I waited.

"I think it must be an amazing thing, to have a child of your own flesh and blood. Someone who will grow up to look like you and act like you. Someone who will *love* you and share not only your genetics but your passions in life." I could feel how strongly he felt about those things and I was surprised.

"*Hmpf.* I can really only imagine a scenario like that though." He gave one last huge exhalation. "I don't have a lot of personal experience to go on or a lot of firsthand knowledge on how one does that properly." He added with a self-deprecating laugh.

"It makes a little more sense if there are two fairly decent, fairly stable people who are really committed to being there to raise and support a child for the long haul. But that's hard to say these days and even harder to actually do, *I know!*" He allowed referring to my currently difficult parenting status. "And for someone in my situation it would be even harder, let's face it! I don't know if that would really be fair to anyone." He admitted with a shoulder shrug like it was an irrefutable absolute.

"That and so *many* other issues make it hard for me to say whether it's really feasible or not. It may be that it's just not in the cards for me." He informed me calmly. He didn't hem and haw or stumble through his statement, but I could feel his genuine sadness at it. It was deep and I was surprised by that. I was also surprised to feel the same way by the end. It *was* sad that it was so hard for him to even want something so simple and so fundamental.

"I don't know if my circumstances could ever really be ideal enough to consciously and responsibly decide to bring a child into it. But I can tell you that if I ever do have one, it *will* be because I *consciously decided* to and not because of simple carelessness, I promise you that!" He said just as calmly but with the same amount of conviction.

I knew there were lots of people out there who were "surprised" by the arrival of a child, myself included. But I also know a good number of them were and still are quite happy about it, not everyone of course, but plenty. I had zero regrets about my own "surprise" but I knew his parents did not fall into that category so I understood where that attitude came from and I wasn't personally offended by it.

He just meant that if it ever happened for him, he wanted it to be *intentional.* There was nothing wrong with that. I thought about it then and while I had always been grateful for his being so considerate with such a delicate topic, I was suddenly *blown away* by the fact that I had never had to *ask* him to use protection when we were together, *ever!* Not... even... once! *Hmpf.* Wow. He smiled, brightening again considerably and tried to laugh it off a little.

"It's not good for our future as a species for everyone to be procreating so recklessly and without forethought anyway. There are already enough people out there doing it that shouldn't be." He joked. It didn't last though. There was something more still, something specific. I could feel it but I didn't know what it was exactly. I waited but I didn't have to wait long. He took a breath and dove straight into the next wave. He didn't hold back from me and my question once I had put it out there.

"On top of all that, what if my father was right Simone, and not just an asshole? I mean I think I understand his stance now anyway, knowing what he did. I'm sure his motivation for preventing the situation was probably more selfish in nature than mine today, but his goal was still simply to keep this cycle from perpetuating!" He insisted with a shrug of his shoulders.

"And so the question becomes, what if you are an actual caring, intelligent person who knows what the odds are for any possible offspring you may create to have a *heightened* future? Do you knowingly go forth and procreate anyway without feeling guilty for condemning another innocent child to this life? Is it a curse or a gift that we're passing on? Are they a blessing or a scourge to the world?" He asked bluntly to the universe at large. "We still don't even know!" He argued logically. I had to admit that I didn't know the answer any more than he did. I was still working that one out.

He rolled over to lay on his side and bent an elbow to

support his head on one hand. He looked down at me and held me with his stare. "What about you?" He asked outright in return, with a lift of his chin. "Tell me this. Would you go back and change having had Liliana if you could? Knowing as we do now, the likelihood that she will suffer the same fate as us?"

He didn't flinch when he put it to me, but *I* did. I was annoyed that he had managed to turn it around on me so completely but I understood what he meant, once I had to actually consider it myself. It was certainly a lot to think about.

I had no idea what I would do if I had really thought about it first myself. I hadn't had any of that information, or even a conscious decision regarding the timing previous to getting pregnant with Liliana. We had gotten married so quickly and found out so soon after that she was coming, that it had become a reality before it ever had a chance to be a discussion. What *would* I do, had I known back then all that he had taught me*? Hmmm.*

I stared up at the perfect aqua blue sky while I thought about it, *really* thought about it. Would I give up every joy and happiness that she had ever brought me and everyone else, to save her from having to face a life full of these types of difficulties? Would I deny Ben the daughter that had changed everything for him just by being born in order to spare him the hardship, frustration and helplessness he's sure to experience later on? Would I deny her every wonderful and memorable experience that goes along with being alive, to save her every hardship she would ever face for being different?

After long, honest and painful consideration my answer was hard won, but my conviction was absolute.

"*No.*" I assured him confidently ending the few minutes of contemplative silence. Never!" I looked back at him as I rolled over onto my right side to face him. "And I'm personally *extremely* glad that your father didn't get his way either!" I growled then at just the *thought* of him *not* existing! *Yeowzer!! (Yes, that's a word! Sort of...close enough.)*

"I know firsthand how hard it is to even *think* of someone you love suffering, believe me! But we all have to learn how to get through some of that pain in our lifetimes Ethan. Everyone will experience some amount of suffering at some point. No matter what form it takes. No one is exempt from that, *height* or *norm!* I believe that. Overcoming those struggles in our lives is what makes us *whole* in the end!" I insisted. He just looked at me and listened but I could easily feel that he still wasn't convinced.

"Look, I think we all know now that you can't be truly appreciative of the good times, without having fought through the bad times to get there! I wish it wasn't so, I know we both do! I also wish that people could just inherently understand the true beauty in all of the small everyday joys, without having to lose them first to see it. But people are just funny like that. The lessons hardest won are usually the ones that stick and mold us into the smarter, stronger people that we are supposed to become." I insisted.

"Sometimes the harder a person fights to get there, the better the person they are when they arrive!" I said with a smirk and raised eyebrows referring to his personal story." He smiled back a little at that point of view.

"Who are *we*, to decide that these amazing people that are just waiting patiently to come after us, should never get the chance to slay their own dragons or fulfill their own destinies, because it may be hard for them or painful for us? I mean no one has a guarantee that their child won't ever have to face any adversity Ethan. We're not really *that* different." I reminded him.

"And if we aren't willing to give birth to these special children, they will eventually just show up somewhere else. If they are truly meant to exist, I believe they will, somewhere. Who knows if those parents will be as equipped to deal with it as we are?" I challenged logically and I could tell that that was a new perspective for him. I felt him finally settle down another notch and I smiled. I raised myself up, pushed him flat and kneeled down over him.

"Listen, my parents weren't perfect and I don't mean to always make them seem like they are, but that is something else I have to give them credit for. They understood that they had to be able to let go and trust me to fight my own demons or else I would never be able to survive in the real world without them. They could try to prepare me and always be there to support me, but they knew they couldn't *stop* me from going out into the world and trying to make it mine, in my own way! We all have to learn to let our children do that, whatever they will face in the process. It's hard, I'm not going to lie! But no, I wouldn't keep them from existing just to save myself *or* them the extra work in their case. I still think it's worth it." I finished quietly with a shrug as I leaned down to graze my lips across his.

"Let's face it, you basically have to be willing to let your heart get up and walk away from you, in order to be a parent in the first place! No matter what else you may ever be up against, that is always going to be the hardest part. Never let anyone tell you differently!" I insisted, letting him in on a painful truth. "But you can't let that stop you from living life, sharing life, or giving life. As terribly "*Hallmark*" as I know that sounds!" I admitted with a self-deprecating laugh. "That's *one* thing I know for sure!" I said as I kissed him once more then sat back up to look down at him.

"So no, it probably won't be easy. *Hmpf.* But I get the distinct impression that it's not really supposed to be, for any of us!" I finished confidently. He was quietly contemplative still at that point but not for long. He came back strong and turned it around on me once again.

"So you're saying that you would consider having another child, with *me?* Two *known heights.*" He challenged outright once more, taking some of the smugness off of my face before it ever got too comfortable being there. "Is that why you're asking Simone?" He didn't even blink while he waited for my answer.

I on the other hand almost choked on nothing but air! *Deep breaths...* I tried not to overreact to his question but it set off the million other questions I already had in my head like fireworks! I waited a beat before I tried to speak.

"I was asking because I had absolutely no idea how *you* felt about it. Not because I was sure how *I* felt about it!" I half-joked in defense. I took another fortifying breath and kept going with what I was feeling right then, just letting honesty be my guide through the unknown.

"But yes, now that you mention it I *would*, if the situation were right." I said with another honest shrug. "I think you'd make an excellent father Ethan, I really do." I added seriously.

"Look, I don't know for sure if I will ever have more kids or not but if I do, I know it would probably have to be fairly soon in order for it to make sense for me. And since I don't see myself 'procreating' with anybody else in that short a time frame, it would probably pretty much, have to be with you, I guess." I said with a smirk. I noticed first surprise, then elation and finally amusement from one end of my statement to the other. I grinned then leaned in close again.

"If that ever turned out to be the case, I would personally consider myself very lucky to bear a child of yours Ethan, *height* or otherwise." I proclaimed simply but honestly staring him in the eye with a shoulder shrug of my own.

It was only one sentence but I could feel the impact that it had on him and it was *astounding*! It was as if a thousand different tumblers to an overly complicated lock had just suddenly fallen into place at once. Whatever my statement had unlocked, I couldn't see it on his face, but I could *feel* it taking a first long, deep breath of its' own and he *knew* it too! He kept silent though and I could see that he wasn't ready to acknowledge it yet, so I finished with my thought as though a building hadn't just fallen down around us.

"Although aside from that remote possibility, I really don't see it happening for me and well honestly, that would be okay too." I admitted in the end without defense sitting upright again. I had surprised even myself with my declaration but I said it because it was the truth and there was really no reason to hide it at that point.

He was still far from decided himself but he was so thrilled by *my* position on the issue that he had begun to rethink a lot of things he never thought he would. He was surprised not just by the shock of my statement but also by the intensity of the feelings that had surfaced in himself once I gave him something completely new to consider. Maybe even hope for.

I watched as it continued to swirl behind his eyes for a while and I breathed through each varying wave of emotion as it passed over and through me. I could feel his excitement slowly growing for something that he had never let himself yearn for before, even as he worked hard to backpedal and keep that from happening in habitual self-preservation.

He was extremely leery of changing his longstanding position, and I understood why, but I could feel him at least playing with the idea. *Hmpf.* It was a start. I hadn't allowed myself to *really* consider it before either but I couldn't deny that our talk had ignited an excitement deep inside of me as well. I didn't know what would come of it if anything but I was quite happy to have real "possibilities" for a future between us finally exist, whatever they may be!

We sat quietly like that in thought for some time before the intensity overtook both of us and he reached up to pull me down to him once more.

I went along willingly. I figured regardless of whether we ever did it for real or not, practicing in the meantime hurt no one.

Chapter 24

Beyond our newly developing personal life, we had our new shared Camp responsibilities, on top of whatever else we took on at the farm, *after* our day at Breezey! Mostly that just meant spending a few evenings a week at The Tavern though and I honestly had no problem with that. Especially once Dani seemed to have come to some sort of mental acceptance with the situation.

It was a pretty sudden turnaround, which was unexpected and took me off guard at first. But she was much more cordial and less, "full of *seething rage*" the next time we saw her, and even less so the time after that. By then she had simply become *detached*. It was definitely a little weird to feel nothing but emptiness where there had been such a passionate *rage* before, so I really couldn't just let it go, but it was another huge improvement so I determined to take it and move on until I had a real reason not to.

Ethan seemed to agree with that attitude since it was pretty much what he had been doing in that area already. It was only temporary I knew, but it was still a relief because I really did like being there. It was definitely worth putting in the extra hours to me to be able to meet the ever-widening range of fascinating people who came through there on a regular basis, *heights* and *norms* alike! Once I was privy to the "guest list," The Tavern was a whole new, exciting and informative world!

Just in that first week alone there were countless instances to support that statement! Sometimes they came in looking for help in getting from point A to point B, both logistically and morally. It was difficult to say which was harder, and they relied heavily on his experience for guidance in both. Some were merely relaying messages or updates on past campers as they passed through town. Those encounters consisted of a lot of high fives, hug/pats and short, stunted sentences.

"How'd it go?"

"Perfect."

"Everyone on time?"

"Yep."

"Good, good. Sit, have a drink."

"Thanks."

The conversations were simple, to the point. No extra words thrown in. Ethan was a big utilizer of modern technology but he still believed wholeheartedly in the only form of communication that leaves no physical trail, face to face. I learned right away that he was a very important link in the passing of sensitive information along a highly guarded chain of trusted humans. They had created their own "live intranet" so-to-speak.

There were other nights when they came just looking for advice on how to handle a current, *difficult* situation with a new *height* somewhere else. That's when I started to realize that the "organization" as he referred to it, was a lot bigger than I had previously thought, that it was obviously a lot bigger than just *him* and our little town of Pinegrove! Apparently we were just "home base."

It made sense since he couldn't personally see, treat, and help every *height*, in every town, and every state, every day! I mean obviously! Why hadn't I realized that before? He wasn't Superman after all, but he might as well have been to them. He never turned away anyone he thought he could and/or should help. Each deserving individual got what they needed in some way, at some point, either there or at some carefully arranged future date. The deserving ones he couldn't reach personally were given a way to contact a specific, trusted connection closer to them.

Occasionally he would simply hand someone a stack of

money on their way through, or the keys to a very expensive car equipped with bullet proof windows and turbo engines for quick getaways. Other days I watched as they discretely came in bearing similar things that they in turn left with him. *Valuable* things, placed casually in his possession like a simple offering to a gracious host. Planes, boats and automobiles alike. Yes *planes!*

I understood then what he had meant about "putting everything that was donated back into the camp," and how he could always be so generous and yet so "prepared" for every circumstance. The influx was extremely impressive and fairly regular! I admit it was much more than I had ever really grasped before. It made me proud of what they had accomplished, but it also made the stakes that much higher.

I knew that was a big part of why Ethan kept such a low profile through it all. That cover was important if he was going to pull off that kind of activity long term. He got it and he was okay with it. Even with all that had passed through his hands by then, he had still never flaunted any of that power, or ever once used a resource in his possession frivolously. Not that I ever saw anyway. That was not what was important in all of that and he knew it inherently.

In the end, it almost always still came down to him spending time talking to them one-on-one, and showing them that they were not alone. Perpetuating that camaraderie that we all believed in and relied so heavily upon. (Notice I said "*we*" already.) That was a predominant theme in almost every meeting though because it was so incredibly important to each individual and to the organization's overall success as a whole, that everyone involved felt like they were part of something bigger than themselves, something *important* that they wanted to protect! That attitude was contagious and it served their purpose well.

The most fascinating part for me though was still all the different abilities that I was learning about from night to night, both through conversation and through firsthand meetings.

Like the Albanian gentleman who had come in with his brother and his uncle. I was still amazed just thinking about it! He was a quiet, dark haired gentleman in his fifties, and apparently he could pick up the presence of metals on or near a person's body to the point that he was basically a human metal detector! He could immediately tell you not only who was packing a gun, or a knife, but how many and where they were hidden! That was a very unusual, but highly *useful* skill to say the least. It had made him extremely *valuable* in his home country but it had also made him a prime target. Even with the vast wealth that he eventually earned from his job in "protection," he'd had an *extremely* difficult time getting out. From the gist of it I figured out that he didn't "exist" in his country anymore, and that Ethan had helped him with that, hence their long-surviving connection.

I tried to be discreet as I was learning the ropes and to respect each individual's privacy as much as I could. I knew I would appreciate the same if the roles were reversed so it made sense to me. Most knew that I was a *height* of some sort too and therefore safe to talk in front of, as evidenced merely by the fact that I sat there next to Ethan at his table. But very few were privy to what I could do specifically. I had already learned long ago that it wasn't something that was appropriate to share with everyone right off the bat, even in those circles, so I stuck to that philosophy. It was a mutually respected private matter unless a *height* was willing to share voluntarily.

I was still curious about him though and I had no idea where a skill like his would have originated from physically. That particular time my curiosity got the better of me as usual. Eventually I had to ask. I wasn't sure if I would get an answer or not and I knew I couldn't complain if I didn't. But I figured there was only one way to find out and since I already knew nothing, I had nothing to lose.

He was one of the more open ones thankfully and allowed Ethan to explain it for him, in better English than he could, he had admitted jokingly. Once given permission, Ethan went on to say that for him it was partially an intellectual skill, meaning it stemmed from a certain part of his brain that we as humans don't usually access, but that it was combined with a very specific sense of smell and an overall general physical sensitivity to certain materials in the air. Like their presence physically irritated him. So much so that it ended up being almost a full body experience for him in the end.

That, Ethan explained, is how he saw his *height* colors, all over his whole body. They were just more vivid in specific areas like his head, nose and chest, but it could change locations, with different materials affecting some areas more than others. It was the kind of thing that made sense when you understood it.

"When you don't have that inside track to the personal explanations, variations like that can be very confusing for me." He shared.

"They make it hard for me to try and categorize people based on sight alone." He added honestly. "I always know they're doing something in a *heightened* manner, I just don't know what!" He smiled at me and I could feel him remembering his frustration at not being able to categorize *me* at first. I was very familiar with that particular frustration though and I smiled back knowingly. "Just another reason that we are such a good team." He said with a very satisfied smile and I had no problem agreeing with that either.

It was that very type of information that made it so exciting for me to keep going back night after night and I knew that as long as I kept going, that would never change. Besides that, we really did work well together and we continually figured out more and more instances where that was the case as we went along.

Like when Ethan knew the anxious twenty-something that was over by the bar was a *height* and a total newbie, desperately looking for help. But all that he could be sure of on his own, was that his gift was an intellectual one as his colors surrounded his head. He couldn't read the large group of *norm's* that he had come in with so easily. Was it a trap? He was always leery of those with so many "*Anderson's*" out there. Was the unknowing *height* just bait? Maybe they were there to support him, or maybe they were completely clueless to his situation? These were important distinctions when it came to how Ethan would handle things and it took time to figure those things out, usually anyway.

For me though, it was actually quite easy to sit and tell him about each person in their group as we talked quietly in between his sets.

"The older guy is feeling very protective. I'm thinking definitely a brother, or at the very least a real close cousin. He's on edge like he doesn't understand why they're here in the middle of nowhere, but he *suspects* some sort of wacky, *voo-doo* connection." I said with a laugh. "And he doesn't like it."

"The two guys next to him are the classic best friends, the other '*two stooges*' if you will and they're trying really hard to be strong for their buddy. So I'm guessing they probably know exactly why they're really here and they think they're gonna act as his back-up." I laughed a little then at the sad situation. "I don't think either one would be much good against the brother though if it comes to that. His energy is much stronger than both of theirs put together." I sipped my wine as I talked and tried to be discreet.

"The brunette is his lover but I would say only recently so. It's still all '*new and exciting.*'" I told him with a wink and a grin and then I felt that particular emotion come back to me tenfold! I laughed but tried to keep on track so I could finish my assessment before his break was over.

Phfoooo... I let it out and tried to refocus. "She seems to have no idea what's going on with him past his boxers though and is actually checking out the brother from time to time. She's considering upgrading." I added with an eye-roll.

Armed with that information he knew that he would help the boy but not there. He would use a distraction to slip him a phone number to reach him at later, *privately.* He would get what he had come there for while his party would be none the wiser. The fight that they'd all anticipated with one emotion or another could be avoided all together. That was always the preferable option when it was available.

The newbie had held the door for the others as they filed out at the end of the night, some relieved, some disappointed and some just thinking it a waste of time. His head was tilted discretely down towards the floor as he smiled slyly at Ethan. Then he followed his group out, invaluable phone number tucked safely in his back pocket.

Ethan had just looked at me then grinning and I had felt his relief at how fast we had gotten to that next step by working together and at what a natural collaboration it had been between us. Night after night, he was feeling more and more grateful for my presence and my help and I had to keep reminding him constantly how much I was getting out of it as well. As we sat one night after closing in our booth, finishing our drinks, I tried to convince him by reminding him of all of this.

"My thirst for information on this subject, now that I know it *exists*, is basically insatiable Ethan!" I insisted.

"Even if we weren't together anymore for some reason, I can't think of one mind you and I don't want to try but just say *if*, you would still have to work really hard to keep me away from here at this point." I admitted honestly with a shrug and I was glad that he was relieved rather than upset by my stance. "There is just so much here for me to experience and to learn! You don't understand how enticing that is to me!" I insisted heatedly.

"I want to know everything that I can about the other *heights* out there so that I can help them and others to come, just like you all do. But it will also help *me* to be the best parent possible to my daughter! Whether that is just by improving upon my own situation for her sake through my education, or if I end up gaining information to help improve *her* situation someday! Either way it's all invaluable to me." I insisted honestly.

"Don't you see? We are already facing enough obstacles in our quest to give her the best life possible. I will take and utilize any advantage that I can get to even things back out a little." I assured him. "Even the most innocent of encounters here can turn out to be huge learning experiences for me and I absolutely *love* that! I *need* that!" He smiled and I felt his understanding so I took a breath and drank my beer while I thought back on a few other examples.

Like the night that the beautiful black woman with the practically shaved blonde hair and the giant pale green eyes had showed up at our stage-side table. She had come over without hesitation and introduced herself to me while Ethan was performing. Her name was Felina and I thought it was as pretty as she was. I invited her to sit and she told me that she had decided on a whim to stop in to see Ethan on her way into the city for business. She lived six hours south of there and didn't get up to visit very often, she had explained.

She told me that she was married and that they currently had their second child on the way. As she spoke she absentmindedly slid one hand protectively over her small but noticeably rounded midsection. She hadn't seen Ethan in over seven years she'd told me conversationally, but credited how well she was doing with being the reason for not needing to see him, at least not in person. She then credited Ethan with being the reason she was doing so well.

Ethan's smile had lit the corners of the room as he waved to her when he saw her there. I felt his unexpected, overwhelming happiness at her presence and I knew then that her visit was even more special than the others. He eventually came and sat with us during his next break and I had mostly listened as they got caught up.

She went on to tell us that her husband was also someone that Ethan had helped, years ago and how it was that *extremely discreet* realization between the two of them through their local connections that had brought them together originally. So she had Ethan to thank for that as well, she added backhandedly.

Her skill, which she had told me about voluntarily thankfully since I never would have guessed it, was also an intellectual one but it stopped there for her. She was a straight up math whiz. She had always been good at it in grade school but not much else, especially not making friends. One winter in high school though, everything had changed. She got really sick for a few months in a row with one thing right after another. It seemed like if something was going around, then she caught it. It turned out to be a very bad winter that led to a very good development though. After missing weeks upon weeks of school, and thinking she would surely flunk out, she came back and worked so hard to make up for it, that she shot to the top of the class solving problems that she hadn't even been present to learn the methods for!

It was not only fun but extremely uplifting to hear her talk about it. About finally being important to her school as the star of their math team and how they worked hard to help her pass her sophomore year despite the excessive number of absences. She radiated happiness when she talked about having the respect of her peers for the first time ever after having been dismissed as nothing worth paying attention to for so long. She spoke about how freeing it was to have the "popular" kids finally say hi to you when you had so many new *real* friends by then that you truly didn't even care anymore.

My own school days hadn't been that bad but I still knew exactly what she meant. I think that we all start out a little overwhelmed and nervous in the beginning of our social careers. Somewhere along the line, and it's different for everyone, we all eventually find our place, that one spot where we feel that we belong. That is when life really starts to get good, when you get to that place where you not only figure out who you are, but you're finally okay with it. It was great to hear her talk about how she had gotten there and about how Ethan had helped.

"Like the night I met Felina!" I burst out with. "That story alone had been worth spending the entire week here for." I insisted still arguing my case, as if he had been privy to my thought process. I smiled thinking back on it some more.

During her conversation with Ethan I had learned that she was a very well paid accountant for a *very* successful company. She was also a happily married, soon to be mother of two. Most importantly of all though, she had a full life where it wasn't necessary for her to hide her *heightened* skills. That was *huge* and it had to be really nice, I thought wistfully. I was trying sincerely not to be jealous of something that was so simple and yet so profound at the same time. I knew that every *height* skill had its' own advantages and drawbacks, but I had to admire her particular circumstances. I was really happy for her, happy that she existed at all. She was living proof that a *height* could embrace being a *height* fully and still have a happy and successful life. It was nice to know that it was at least possible so I was grateful to her for that, in and of itself.

She told us that in her spare time she volunteered to tutor

students struggling in math. She was obviously in high demand as far as tutors went, especially since she refused to charge for her services. With the technology where it was then, it was possible to connect by Skype or any number of other online services, even ones that could translate her instructions into other languages. That made her client list virtually endless!

That in turn, made her potentially very powerful. At least in certain circles. But rather than take advantage of the situation financially or for personal recognition, she chose to use it to help other *heights* instead. Whenever they were referred to her, either through Ethan or through one of the local connections in her area, she always gave them top priority in scheduling. She went out of her way to give back in a way that only she could and the world was a better place for it. I was inspired by her story and I admired her a great deal by the end of that evening.

"Do you see what I'm saying?" I had asked him. "By the end of my first week of helping out, I knew how lucky I was to be here with all of these people. But most of all I'm lucky to be sitting here next to you every night that I can!" I held his face in my hands and looked him in the eye. "And there is no place that I would rather be." I finished quite convincingly, hopefully for the last time. I backed it up with a kiss and thankfully that seemed to be the end of that particular worry from him. I was glad because I had really meant every word I'd said.

Later that night though, we had both laid awake in bed in the dark with our own thoughts. I contemplated the fact that he was fully aware that she was a *height*, knowingly having a baby with another *height*, her second actually! Yet he hadn't commented on that. I remembered the soft curve of her belly and wondered curiously myself what the outcome of that union would be. Her husband's skill, she had told me herself while Ethan smiled silently, was completely different from hers in that it was a purely physical one. He was apparently *very* strong.

"He'd had the virus when he was thirteen and every muscle in his body had cramped up in endless rounds of painful spasms for days before the fever finally broke. He had been unable to walk, stand or even sit up during the viruses course. Once he recovered from that his strength, at first entirely depleted, began to increase a little more each day until it was obvious that something was going on. One day he would crush a glass while washing it, and the next he would break the doorknob off the door while trying to open it! At first his family was relieved at his recovery, but eventually it had become clear that something had changed, drastically! They had taken him to see a handful of specialists but they were all equally baffled by his condition and his continually increasing strength. Thankfully, not too long after that he had found his way to Ethan and the good doctors at the Camp." She'd explained.

"There he finally got some answers about what had really happened to him, which I believe helped him more than anything else. Then he got some much needed help with where to go from there. He had to relearn everything physical all over again in order to keep his circumstances under wraps and attempt to blend back in with the rest of the *norms*. They taught him how to do that." She confided.

"Later in life there were other things he had to learn, like how to be a *very* careful but equally *thorough* lover." She smiled slyly. "*I* taught him *that*!" She threw in with a wink and a grin. I had smiled as I looked down at her waistline and agreed that they had obviously found a way to make it work. "I can say without a doubt though that the Camp saved his life that first day so that I would later have the chance to be a part of it. For *that* I am beyond thankful to Ethan and everyone at Camp all over again." She'd said quietly with a warm smile aimed in his direction.

So of course I laid there wondering how nature would combine those elements for them when mixing the two original DNA strands together to make one new one. What was the sum of a *computation master* and a *human Hercules?* An overly muscular brain, perhaps? Would that be good or bad? *Hmpf.* Maybe their son would grow up being able to chop through wood with his bare hands while instantly calculating the number of pieces it would break into! *Hah!* Okay, I was tired by then and starting to get silly I'll admit, but there was really no way of knowing and it was a lot of fun to play with the possibilities, at least in my head. In real life I knew it was a lot scarier to actually try and live among those variables. Not impossible, but definitely harder.

Obviously they couldn't be the first *height/height* couple and surly they wouldn't be the last, but they were the first ones that I personally knew of that were procreating! That was a big deal to me for obvious reasons to say the least and I could never resist the urge to ponder such things.

They had one child together already that she had gushed about and shown us pictures of. He was darker skinned, like her husband but he shared her pale green eyes. That was already an impressive feat in genes. On top of that, he was absolutely adorable! He was literally perfect and just looked like a perfectly normal toddler, but of course he was barely three years old and it was still a mystery to everyone just what the future would hold for him *or* his sibling. I sighed at that much broader thought.

Of course wandering down that path of random scenarios eventually segued into thinking about my own situation with Ethan again. It was inevitable.

I noticed that he had been genuinely happy for Felina and I had felt no worries from either of them regarding her pregnancy but he still hadn't given me any of his own emotions on the subject at the time. I wasn't sure which of the many possible reasons specifically was responsible for him keeping his own feelings separate, but I could feel quite clearly that he was.

Before too long he had sensed that I was getting myself worked up again about *something.* Even in the dark he could tell, just by my breathing pattern which should have been slow and even by then but wasn't even close.

He rolled towards me and reached around my waist. Then he slid me gently across the smooth sheets until I rested firmly against him. I was pretty tired at that point so I just let it all go. I breathed in nothing but his scent and eventually I fell deeply and peacefully asleep.

Chapter 25

With all the changes happening and all that we had on our plates, it was as busy and as chaotic as you would imagine but that still wasn't enough apparently because it didn't mean that the rest of the world stopped knocking. In spite of all that we were already balancing, life went on around us. My parents were part of that life and they were done being put off.

I was nervous at first when my mother called early that Sunday morning to say that she'd heard Ethan was back in town and she was wondering when they would finally get to meet him. Apparently I had her afternoon with Liliana to thank for that. After hearing that though, frankly I was surprised at her show of patience in having waited *that* long!

I had just seen Liliana the night before and other than missing Ethan, it had been blissfully uneventful. Just nice, quiet peaceful time with my daughter. Walking, cooking together, coloring, watching movies and even sleeping in until 8:00AM! It was wonderful but she had never bothered to mention the fact that she had talked to her grandparents about Ethan. *Hah*! Surprise!

I was tempted to try and put it off further at first, just to have him to myself a little longer, but the more I thought about it the more I started to lean the other way. I really wanted them to meet him for themselves *before* Ben could even think about trying to poison them against him. I knew he hadn't talked to them in the past week either, as both sets of grandparents had tag-teamed their activities and my parents had only met with his parents and not him. Ben had stayed out of the loop completely for once, "so he could catch up on some work" supposedly. I was relieved by that circumstance, even though I knew the real reason for it. I was nervous about the prolonged silence, but I knew it wouldn't last forever and regardless of the outcome, I figured it would be foolish of me not to take advantage of that time while I had it.

My parents loved and supported me but they loved Ben too and they were trying to be as fair-minded and as cooperative as I was in keeping the whole family "*together*" after the divorce. It was just better for everyone if we all got along. I got it. I was even glad that they got it so well, but it was not the best time for them to go being his best friend. I really needed to have them on my side!

My parents had always been my most dependable back up whenever I needed it and I *really* needed it just then. No matter what life had thrown at me that was the one advantage that no one could ever take away from me before, and I wasn't planning on giving it away with the China and the living room set.

The fact remained, that as accommodating as they could be towards polite society when they needed to be, *they had also raised ME*, a *heightened* empath! No matter how conservatively they lived their lives, they were undeniably among the small group of informed people that knew without a doubt that these things existed. They had learned that the hard way a long time ago.

That meant that I would not have to waste time convincing them of anything and that they could already relate on a level that others would be hard pressed to understand. Certain "*others*" especially! With that prospect currently facing me I needed their understanding more than ever.

I was also strengthened by the certainty that they would do anything they could to help their granddaughter. They loved me as much as I loved them and as a daughter I was very lucky, but their love for her as their only grandchild was something else all-together! People tell you it will be like that, but when you actually see it its mind blowing at times! But I really had no problem with it. I loved her a little bit more than everyone else too.

Their support of me had been the very foundation for every other strength I'd ever gained and when that support had extended to her it had doubled, rather than being cut in half. Towards both of us, it was unconditional. I needed that just then and I was counting on it when I decided to invite them up.

"Sure! Why don't you guys come for dinner tonight?" I heard the words come out of my mouth before I was sure I should say them. Ethan's eyes snapped open on the pillow next to me at that, then grew to twice their size in surprise. I just shrugged back at him and waited for her answer. It was short notice but once I decided to do it, I didn't want to have time to back out. Maybe they wouldn't be able to make it, I thought hopefully at first. Then God help me, I immediately worried that they wouldn't be able to make it. She saved me from myself by answering quickly.

"Actually we'd love to dear! For once we didn't have any plans. We were just trying to decide on a restaurant for this evening but this will be so much better!" She exclaimed happily. I was instantly both relieved and a nervous wreck!

'How's 6:30 sound?" I asked trying to calculate how much time I would need to prepare. Another week would have been better but whatever, I thought with a mental laugh. In a few hours was good too.

"Perfect! We'll see you then honey!" She added.

They were going to love him, I just knew it! They *had* to! *Ahhhhh! What had I gotten myself into?!*

I hung up with that question repeating in my head. It carried on during my shower and throughout our breakfast. We both had that weekend day off from Breezey. Since so many other contractors only had their weekends free to do their work on the side, I had left those days on the schedule for those who had needed them most. Thankfully that weekend that didn't include Ethan or myself. Besides that, Ethan didn't usually play at The Tavern on Sunday nights so we were off the hook there. Since pitching in at the farm was strictly voluntary, that left us free to focus solely on the upcoming dinner date once Ethan texted Jack and let him know our plans for the day. All of that made it seem a little more doable. At least in theory anyway.

I tried to breathe and to distract myself as much as possible in the meantime. I made myself dizzy a few times in the process, but I managed to keep it together. Ethan ended up being very accommodating in that endeavor by being a fantastic "*distraction.*" That killed a few of the late morning hours anyway. That was denial mode. After that I went into preparation mode, which was really just *cleaning* mode.

I cranked up the radio, grabbed my supplies and started at the front entrance on the stairs. By the time I picked my head up again I found myself at the far wall. Another hour and a half had gone by and everything right up to and including the closet was spotless. Ethan had helped as much as I would let him and he did a good job too, but by then even his patience had worn out and he'd had enough.

"Will you stop already?" He shouted as he pulled me down into his lap where he sat watching me from the bed. "If the place is any cleaner they'll be afraid to sit down!" He declared and I had to laugh.

I looked back then and saw it as a whole. I know I tend to repeat myself, but let's just say he wasn't *wrong.* My parents knew me and my habits. They knew that when I was tied up in too many *mentally absorbing* activities at once, as I was known to be, I could occasionally let domestic things slip a little. Never permanently, or to the level that a "*home organizer*" ever needed to be called in or anything. Believe me, I've seen the shows and that inevitability scares the holy hell out of me! I could never let it get *that* far! But it would go far enough occasionally that at some point I would suddenly look up and go, "Alright, I can't put this off anymore because I can't *stand* it anymore! And then I would physically and mentally "*clean house*" until I felt brand new again. Sometimes the whole process was only metaphorical but more often it would carry over into the literal as well and be readily apparent in my living space.

They would take one look at the place and know exactly where my head was at, I realized with a laugh at my own expense. But I knew it was a good place, an honest and refreshing place and that they would know that too. It was a sign of issues coming full circle for me so-to-speak. The realization that they knew me well enough for the atmosphere to speak volumes actually made breathing a little easier. The motivation for the impulse actually made sense to me then but I tried not to think too hard about it. I just sighed, happy that it was done.

Ethan had mainly just sat on the periphery and chuckled at my neurosis, undaunted by the "meet-the-parent's" that awaited him. I could tell that he viewed it predominantly as an unprecedented opportunity to learn more about me and therefore was actually looking forward to it. *Of course.* If he was nervous at all it was nervous anticipation and my actions were a perfect distraction for him. That made me smile at his good fortune but roll my eyes at my own typically less satisfying situation.

"Alright, you're right. I think I'm done here. I suppose I can't avoid the next task any longer." I admitted with one last spectacular sigh." Let's do it." I said standing up.

"Are we jumping off the Merrimack Bridge?" He asked dramatically with a sarcastic grin at my foreboding.

"Worse, driving over it to the plaza on the other side. You know how I feel about the supermarket." I answered woefully. He just chuckled.

"What were you thinking of making?" He asked casually.

"For my parents? That's easy. All I need is a couple of good steaks to assure that dinner is a success." I answered simply. "That, any green vegetable and a baked potato and we're golden. Probably some ice cream for dessert just as insurance." I added, musing out loud. "Although I'll have to get mint chocolate chip and maple walnut to keep everyone happy. It's a small price to pay." I joked in spite of my nerves.

"I'm on it." He replied without hesitation. "Why don't you go take a nice long bath and try to take it down a notch?" He suggested with a grin and I practically melted at just the idea.

"Oh my God, *are you serious?!*" I asked flabbergasted and not ready to trust the fabulousness of it yet.

"Entirely. I have a few errands to run anyway. Let me take one dreaded task off of your plate for you while I'm at it, okay? It's the least I can do to try and make this easier for you. Especially since

I never had to go through any of this myself, not even with Jack and Shirley, since you had already taken care of that for me before we met." He joked with a wink in the end.

After that he offered to run the bath for me while I made him a short grocery list. He came out and grabbed his keys from the bowl then came and took the list from me.

"Are you sure that's all you need?" He asked cooperatively after scanning it.

"That's it. Everything else I have here. Oh, unless you want to pick up a nice bottle of red wine." I added, thankful that he had asked. "You are truly the best! I don't know how to thank you for this!" I gushed holding his face so I could kiss it. He was quick with a response.

"Yes you do. Later." He joked again. I laughed as I rolled my eyes at his typical sense of humor. A short time after that I rolled them again in disbelief at my momentary good fortune as I slid into the warm, foamy tub. *Ahhhhhh...*

I laid there happily luxuriating in the escapism that it offered until despite the warm weather, the water finally went too cold to stay in it anymore. Oh well, it had been *really* good while it lasted and it had taken the edge off of my nerves, just a little.

I gave one last cleansing sigh and decided at that point that it was time to face the rest of my day *and* my future. I knew that once my parents met Ethan, it would all be really, *really* real! All of it! No turning back after that into denial or my own private fantasy land again if things didn't work out. Nope, the only way to go from there was forward and we were truly traveling in that direction. From that point on it was just a matter of where we would end up. *Slow, deep breaths...*

I got out and dried off, then got dressed in my room enjoying the fact that I could do that again freely. I picked out a pair of comfortable denim shorts and paired them with my new favorite metallic printed cotton tee specifically because it looked sort of dressy, even though it was so soft that I could sleep in it. I pulled a brush through my hair and pulled it up into a high, neat pony tail. I added a pair of silver hoop earrings and a modest amount of makeup to make me feel a little bit more put together and confident. Then I pulled on my leather sandals to finish off the respectable but still casual look. I glanced sideways into the mirror and then I sighed again. I was as ready as I was going to get.

I went to the kitchen and tried to keep busy while I watched the time slowly tick by. I carefully selected some veggies from the bowl to make into a salad and seriously pondered the various ingredients from the pantry that I would use in the marinade for the steaks. Both of those things killed a little more time but the music on the other hand, was an easy and quick decision. I simply hit play and Ethan's soothing voice rang out through the speakers and instantly calmed me. Between that and the mindless chopping, I was in a much better frame of mind by the time he came back with the rest of the things that I needed.

He had obviously gone home somewhere during his travels since he too was freshly showered, shaved and sharply dressed. I had to stop momentarily and appreciate how handsome he looked in his nice shorts, short sleeve button down linen shirt and sandals. It was the perfect mix of understated class, and laid-back vacationer. I gave a whistle of appreciation.

"You look like a politician on sabbatical! *It's perfect!*" I declared happily.

"I'm glad you approve." He said agreeably. "You are looking particularly lovely yourself my dear. It seems like the bath agreed with you. That's good." He said as he leaned down and kissed me. He added a half-smile and an eye roll at my music choice when his voice rang out in the silence from behind us. I just smiled defenselessly.

He hadn't offered explanations about what else he'd had to do and I didn't ask. He respected that I needed time to deal with my demons on my own sometimes, before I could tackle them head on. I gave him that same space and consideration in return so that he could deal with his own issues, demon-related or otherwise. I didn't need to know every detail of every situation that he was involved with in order to trust him. That was *really* nice too, I'm not gonna lie. We were able to have that space between us comfortably, without any suspicion mucking it up.

He dropped the bags on the island and we unloaded them together. His happiness at the improvement in my mood made his mood even better in turn. I thanked him then, for the space and for the understanding that he had shown. He smiled and laid his forehead down on mine in a brief appreciation of our understanding of *each other*. I smiled back, pretty pleased so far with our *forward* progress.

"Can you start the grill for me?' I asked.

"Sure. I have a few calls to make anyway. Enjoy your music." He said with a smirk and a roll of his eyes on his way out. His bashfulness in the audience of his own voice was comical and went a long way in explaining why he had never given me a CD before, when he was around.

I was quite happy to do as he had suggested though as I unwrapped the beautiful fillets that he had brought me and placed them on a plate. Then I started combining ingredients in my favorite mug. First I poured in some extra virgin olive oil and some Worcestershire sauce. I always laughed whenever anyone tried to say that on that cooking show with that guy named "*Guy*" that visits restaurant kitchens all over the country. It's extremely easy to say if you grew up in New England hearing it spoken properly all the time like I did, but it never ceases to amaze me the endless ways that they can butcher it across the nation. However you say it though, I would seldom marinade a steak without it, even a really good one.

To that I added a few splashes of a well-aged balsamic vinegar, a light sprinkle of garlic powder, onion powder, and mustard powder and just a dash of smoked paprika to the mix. I whisked it all up and poured it over the steaks. Then I sprinkled them liberally with sea salt and some fresh-cracked black pepper. I flipped them over and repeated the process with the salt and pepper on the other side then I left them to marinade. I washed my hands and then the perfect looking green beans that he had picked out, then I snapped off the ends. I put them in my stainless steel steamer and put that into a pot with a little water underneath. I sprinkled them with sea salt as well and put the lid on.

As I worked and sang along quite happily with the eclectic mix of songs on my treasured CD, I couldn't help thinking back to not so long ago when it was all I had. How quickly we forget sometimes, I thought with a much weaker smile. *Hmpf*, especially when remembering was so very painful. But I would never forget the thoughtfulness that he showed in gifting it to me, nor would I ever forget the lyrics or the melodies that had carried me through so many lonely hours. I would find joy in those songs forever after that. Their place had been imprinted in my heart and in my brain and I was grateful that they existed. I would always have them to *enjoy*, but I was *really* glad that I didn't *need* them on a daily basis anymore. Finally being on the other side of that situation made life *much* more tolerable!

While enjoying the moment in that place of happiness and generosity, my mind wandered unexpectedly to whether anyone else would ever get to enjoy a whole CD of his music like that, or if it was just me. That made me feel incredibly special, but not happy. I thought the world could really use a CD like his and I wished silently that he had any intention of sharing it with them, but I knew it would most likely never happen.

With all of the change taking place already lately, I was fairly sure that particular adjustment to his lifestyle was highly unlikely to occur. Our upcoming dinner on the other hand, did have the potential to make a *major* difference in our collective "before" and "after" and I was really hopeful that it would turn out to be a change for the better, for everyone involved.

I loved my parents and I would always be close to them so obviously for me to be successful with any man, he would have to get along with them and vice versa. It was really the only option. I could never live a life divided the way that some families do. "My family" for this holiday, "your family" for that one. That separation always bothers me when I see it. It just doesn't make sense to me. There's just one family. You're either in it or you're out. Otherwise how do you separate it? Where do you draw the line? Families grow and you have to continuously expand your heart and your mind and embrace that. That's just life, if you're lucky anyway!

Growing up, our individual families were small, so we always made even more of a point to get together for all of the holidays and each other's big events. It was that, "It's okay if your immediate family's tiny because we are all one *big* happy family" attitude that had always made every event feel so special. Being an only child myself, I had always thought it was a good philosophy to live by. To this day and especially with my divorce from Ben, I am still a fan of the one big happy family motto and at some point, Ethan would have to pass that test with the rest of my family in order for us to have a future together. Might as well just get it over with, right?

I didn't have any real worries there though, not with the way that he had adopted the Kent's as family so completely. I just needed to give my parents a chance to see that about him. I knew he understood that family is not always where you come from, sometimes it's where you find it in your life. That concept was not a problem for him. So why was I so worried? I decided to be honest with myself.

I took a deep breath and then I realized that it was mostly about what their attitude towards the *height* stuff was going to be. I knew I would tell them sooner rather than later if not that very night. I had no need to hide things like that from them, just to find the right time. Since all that related directly to him though and his lifelong goals, I knew it would dictate what feelings they would associate with him by default, good or bad. So their feelings on the matter were a really important point for me, because I knew the two would always be connected.

I was as anxious as you could imagine at the thought of talking to them about it, but for once that wasn't the only emotion or even necessarily the dominant one. In spite of my worries, I was also excited. Like *really* excited! After all, we had shared many years when it was just the three of us, desperately looking for answers. Endless, exhausting days, and countless sleepless nights, begging for answers from the universe because that was our only resource.

I finally *had* some of those answers and I was about to share that information with them! That was a circumstance that I had not been sure would ever come to pass and that little girl in me was eager to see it through!

I still had a long way to go to comprehend it all myself but I could not deny that I was looking forward to telling them what I had learned so far. Just the fact that I had information to tell them at all was no small feat in a family made up of a college professor and a head nurse! I was really eager to see, hear and *feel* their responses to all that I had to share!

The knife slipped then, off the side of the onion and into my thumb, thankfully catching the nail in my absentmindedness and not the skin. It brought me immediately back to the task at hand as I jumped and pulled my hand back in reaction. I took a deep breath and checked the tomatoes for unwanted fingernail slices. Then I inspected the nail itself. When I was sure there was none missing, just split, I sighed again. I ripped off the damaged piece of nail and threw it in the trash, then I tried to focus on slicing the cucumber and not my fingers. I laughed at myself as Ethan came back in and walked up to the island.

"What else I can do?" He asked as he stole a slice of carrot.

"You can have a beer." I instructed with a head tilt toward the fridge. "I'm serious" I added at his perplexed look. "I think the alcohol will help relax everyone and my father has a rule about never being the first one to have a drink in his hand at any gathering." I admitted with a sideways smile. "I know he'll be more than happy to join you though, if you are already having one." I informed him with a wink.

"I can handle that!" He answered cheerfully. I was glad that I already happened to have some Sam Adams Summer Ale on hand which I knew both Ethan *and* my father liked. *Bonus*! I opened the wine that he had brought me and grabbed two glasses. I filled one and left the other one out for my mother.

After that Ethan came and helped me finish up the salad and by the time that was done I heard my cellphone chime to alert me that I had a text. My head snapped up at the sound. My father was working really hard at getting fluent in the art and he had insisted on an "all-text" form of communication lately. I took a deep breath and smiled up at him without even looking at my phone.

"They're here." I said with a nervous smile.

Chapter 26

Ethan knew that I was anxious, but he also knew that there wasn't any fear that time around. He didn't need to worry about "protecting me" or "rescuing me" or even keeping me calm for once. I just needed him to stand beside me and be himself and I knew it would all turn out fine. He had some nervous energy of his own as the moment approached, but still no desire to try and get out of it. He maintained his anticipation and excitement in spite of it with very little effort. He was still happy to do it "for me."

"Thank you." I said simply but honestly. I felt his sudden appreciation in return, about a second before he crushed me against his chest and kissed me, *hard!*

I closed my eyes and tried to breathe through his overwhelming expression of feeling. The room began to spin and I started to forget why I had wanted him to stop. I melted into him, grateful for the warmth and strength with which he held me. Then he pulled back and smiled at me.

"Alright. Let's do this!" He stated encouragingly and I looked around, trying to remember where we were. When it came flooding back, I tried to breathe deeply again without passing out.

"Okay!" I said humorously, trying to get back on track. "Thanks for *that!*" I added jokingly. He just grinned impishly at me. Then both of our heads snapped up as we heard the car doors close.

We looked wide-eyed at each other for about a second then quickly ran down to greet them in the driveway. I hugged each of them as they walked over to us. I was happy to see that they had dressed casually as well and that my mother had flats on that would make walking across the gravel much easier than if she'd had her traditional heels on, especially since I hadn't thought to tell her about that part. So far so good.

"Mom, dad, this is Ethan." I said officially making the introductions. He shook my mother's hand first and then my father's. They were very polite, as always but I had to work hard not to smile at my mother's first reaction when he approached her. To her credit she did not take the step back that I had, even though I felt how much she also wanted to. She was definitely tougher than me but that was no surprise. Her initial involuntary weariness didn't last either. He made direct eye contact when he greeted her and his smile was warm and genuine. I could feel both her notice and her appreciation of those things right away.

"Mrs. Harrington. Mr. Harrington. It is an honor to meet you both. I have heard so many good things about you that I feel as if I already know you." He finished and by then my mother's smile was just as genuine.

"Oh in that case I'm sure you only got half the story." She quipped in response and we all laughed. It was a good start. *Breathe!* Whoo! *Okay...*

"Come on up. Let me show you guys my place, finally! I can't believe that it has taken you this long to get up here!" I exclaimed as we started walking.

"Or, it has taken you this long to *invite* us." My mother came back with quickly and we both grinned.

"Alright, I'll take half the blame if you will." I offered.

"That sounds fair honey." My dad answered to both of us, ending the argument before it could start. Then we reached the top of the stairs and they were both silent as they took it in. Ethan and I grinned at each other as we came up behind them. We were familiar with the sense of awe that the place could give you the first time you saw it from that vantage point. Until you were used to it, it could be thoroughly overwhelming. We waited patiently while they gaped in awe. Eventually my mother managed to speak.

"It's everything you said it was, that's for sure! It's absolutely gorgeous honey!" She gushed honestly.

"Ethan here actually had something to do with that, well the inside anyway. The Kent's are like family to him. They took him in as a teen and he fixed this place up for them and their children in return. He was even lucky enough to live in it himself for a while before he rebuilt his own house down the street." I provided.

"Oh? You're a carpenter Ethan?" My dad asked.

"An occasional one, yes sir. You?" He asked in return, conveniently making it about him instead.

"Also occasional." He answered with a nod. "I teach over at the University full time, but I tinker in my woodshop a little whenever I can. I'm a big supporter of our local tradesmen when it comes to the big stuff though." He added humbly. "I know my limits."

"Well you did a remarkable job." My mother complimented as she tried to absorb it all. "It really is beautiful, and such a beautiful spot!" She gushed looking out at the view. "That alone makes it a dream place before you even get to the inside, which is like something out of a magazine!" She added as she did the "wow" twirl. I just grinned and breathed a little deeper in the knowledge that their original reaction to the place matched my own. Then came the insightful and questioning "mom" comment that I had been expecting.

"*And so clean!*" She praised with a knowing look back over one shoulder. I just grinned and kept silent. See? *Mommy knows everything.* There is a reason that these sayings exist.

"Thank you. Ethan replied humbly trying to deflect a little. "But I did not accomplish this singlehandedly by any means. I had a lot of help in executing my vision for this place." He added looking around at the details reminiscently. I noticed my parents noticing how personal it was for him and I decided to side-track that direction of thought for the moment. It was too soon to get into all of that just yet.

"I'll take you guys for a walk after dinner and show you around the property." I offered just a little bit too enthusiastically.

"You will *not* believe the size of the pumpkins they have already!" I gushed.

"That sounds perfect, hun." My mother agreed cooperatively, as we walked over to the island. She was willing to be waylaid, at least temporarily.

"In the meantime, I was just having a glass of wine. Can I get you one mom?" I asked politely, hoping I hid the desperation in my voice from her.

"Oh, I take it back. *That* sounds perfect!" She joked. "A glass of wine, a nice dinner with the two of you, then a walk on this gorgeous property." She sighed wistfully as she took the glass and had a sip. I breathed a little more deeply, let my guard down for just a second. Of course that's when she hit me. "I'm so glad that I decided to call you this morning." She added with just a slight twist of perfectly placed guilt.

"Me too, mom." I added honestly, ignoring the taunt. "I've thought about you guys a lot recently and I've been wanting to talk to you but we've been so busy at Breezey and helping out here since Ethan got back that the time has just flown by! It's been one thing after another, you know?" I challenged with a knowing look.

No one in our family was a stranger to occasional drama or unexpected circumstances from time to time, including my loving *norm* parents. I had been a very understanding child growing up of all that their busy and important lives had entailed. All I expected was the same in return. I held my wine glass up and she clinked it against her own with a smile that spoke of a truce.

"I do dear. That's why I'm really glad it worked out." She offered diplomatically.

"Well I think I hear one of the ice cold Sam's in the fridge calling my name. Can I get you one Mr. Harrington?" Ethan asked perfectly nonchalantly.

"Sure, why not." He decided happily. Thanks and please, call me Seth, and this is Evie." He suggested. His slight, but perceptible softening made me take my first deep breath. I knew it was still only on a "polite/superficial" level but for the moment I would take it.

Ethan went to grab them a couple of beers and I went and

got the potatoes that I had pre-nuked slightly to make them soften faster on the grill. I wrapped each one in a square of aluminum foil with a pat of butter and a liberal sprinkle of sea salt and fresh-cracked black pepper while my mother told me about how her latest project at the hospital was going. She and Kari were working together on a weekly basis by then and I loved hearing about it.

"I can't tell you how nice it is to be able to give the business to a highly qualified, *deserving* family member to begin with, but getting to see her on a regular basis on top of that is such a nice bonus! That gets harder and harder to do as you all get older and go off in so many different directions." She lamented. I just nodded because I knew she was right. I was already learning that the hard way, much, *much* too soon! *Anyway...* I shook it off and tried to focus on the family that I was lucky enough to have there with me at the moment. I didn't take any of that for granted anymore.

"I'm so glad that you're finding your new position so fulfilling. It's good that you're not pulling such long hours anymore too, but it sounds like you're still inspired by what you're doing. I think it's nearly impossible to be successful at even the simplest thing if your hearts not really in it, so they're very lucky to have you both." I insisted seriously.

"Thank you sweetie. Luckily for me, I think they know that after all these years." She added with a sideways smile. "In fact, if they had their way I'd be signing a contract for another thirty!" She confided with an eye-roll. "But believe me I'm not *that* crazy!" She joked as we started to load up things to bring outside. "I have a husband, daughter *and* a granddaughter to consider these days! That's all much more important!" She added cheerfully, taking the plate of potatoes.

"That's right! Wouldn't want to miss a minute of spoiling her now would we?" I replied sarcastically. She didn't care. She had no guilt where Liliana was concerned.

"Absolutely not! It's our duty and our right as grandparents!" She insisted with a wink at my dad. I noticed that he didn't even consider arguing. He just nodded and grinned in support as he opened the door for us.

I smiled back at Ethan as he grabbed the salad while I carried the tray with the plate of steaks and the pot of beans outside to start grilling. Everyone followed me out onto the deck with a food item or a door in one hand and their drink in the other. It was a beautifully balmy evening with a wonderful breeze and there was no better place to spend it. I was always happier when it was nice out, but especially since it kept us all from being crowded inside at the island.

"I thought Simone said you worked as a singer?" My father asked as they sat down at the table that I had pre-set. I could tell that the wheels had been turning and he was finally ready to ask a few questions of his own.

"Yes sir, a few nights a week at a restaurant that I own here in town." He answered smoothly. Of course he would *start* with that information with *them*, I thought with a begrudging grin. He grinned slyly back at me and kept going.

"The place basically runs itself and they can't fire me so I'm happy to say that I'll always have that outlet. I don't really consider that "*work*" though, more like my life's passion." He added with an honest smile. I had to hide my grin at not only the basic admission but also the secondary truth revealed in that as well. He really was honest almost all the time when he spoke, whenever he could be, he was just selectively creative with his choice of words.

It was smart and it obviously made it easier for him not to have to make up and remember lies. He was extremely skilled at only telling people what they needed to know. I tried to remind myself again, to have some patience with all of that myself. It really wouldn't be a good idea to hit them with years' worth of info all at once. That would not help our situation. No, I had to learn how to take it slow once and for all. One revelation at a time. I could handle it! *In... out...*

"So you are a carpenter/singer/restaurant owner? Do I have that right?" My father asked, obviously a little surprised by the combination.

"*Hmpf*, yes sir, among other things." He added with a laugh. "Let's just say I'm more of an entrepreneur than a 'one act' kind of guy. I'm always looking to learn new things and to expand my base of knowledge. You never know what skills may come in handy someday." He added cryptically but honestly. Again I tried to hide my smile as I turned to place the steaks on the grill. Even though the sizzling when they hit the pre-heated racks was loud enough to temporarily drown out the conversation, I could still *feel* how pleased my father was by that attitude and it immediately reminded me of his philosophies for me growing up.

"Neither knowledge nor experience will ever make you '*less*' prepared." He announced, proudly agreeing wholeheartedly like he was reading my mind. He had always said that, and it basically meant that any opportunity to learn something new was a good one. Boy did I have an opportunity for *him* coming up! I thought to myself, trying to hold the excitement in. I sincerely hoped he would still feel that way then! *Deep breaths...*

I liked that they had that in common though and thankfully, so did my father. That would work for the moment. My mother was the tougher case for once as she knew that this relationship was different than any other I'd ever had, from the few small but important details I had already given her. She was hyper focusing on that at the moment and she didn't take any of it lightly, no matter how good he looked on paper.

I had to grin again at her inherent protectiveness. She had watched me go through enough pain and she would do her damnedest to stop it from recurring in the future if she could. Of course she *couldn't*, so it was ridiculous but also completely understandable at the same time.

I knew what that was like by then. I wanted to laugh that she was still so adamant that she would keep that from happening, even though I was hardly a little girl anymore, but it obviously didn't matter. Apparently the desire to shelter one's offspring from pain did not fade with age. When I thought about Liliana in that context it made perfect sense to me, so I couldn't hold it against her anymore.

Phew! Do you see what it's like to live in my head! With this overactive barometer weighing in all the time? On everything? Hah! Ex-haus-ting! Anyway...

Dinner was ready soon after that and we all dove in

appreciatively. My mother was a master at social graces yet still managed to expertly insert some very pertinent questions into the conversation in between bites.

"*Mmmm!* This steak is cooked perfectly honey!" She complimented happily. As I smiled at her praise she slipped one in. "So how long have you lived here in Pinegrove Ethan?" She asked conversationally. I would have worried at her known level of verbal manipulation with anybody else, but not with him. It was nice to be able to relax and know that he would hold his own without my help. He'd had way too much experience in "*dealing with the parents*" in general already to be slipped up easily. I sat back and crossed my legs and balanced my wine glass on top of one knee while I watched it unfold.

"Basically always. Part of the time I spent across town with my mother. The rest of the time I was down the street from here with my father, on the property where I live now. It belonged to my grandfather originally and I inherited it a while back. Other than my time spent living here on the farm in between, that's pretty much my whole life in a nutshell." He supplied with an honest shrug. Of course the *geography* portion of his life story was the *only* simple part, but again they didn't need to know that yet.

"Any plans to go and "see the world?" She asked in response to his "small town boy" story. I could feel the "*Are you going to run away again on a regular basis because you're still searching for yourself?*" question that was really in there and I gave her a sideways, closed-mouthed smile when no one else was looking. She just gave wide eyes back and innocently mouthed, "*What?*" as she waited patiently for his response. He was too quick to fall for that either though.

"Oh I see plenty of the world right here, I assure you ma'am! One thing I have learned is, if the world has something to show you, it will find you wherever you are." He insisted with a laugh. We all joined in then at his quick and entertaining response, even though he and I both knew he really wasn't joking. Some of the most amazing people in the world sought him out there in little ol' Pinegrove, and on a regular basis. Of course my parents had no idea about that part yet either. I just sipped my wine and rolled my eyes. My father smiled up at the puffy clouds but my mother caught it.

There was another unspoken question then but it was more of a, "*What am I still missing??*" kind of thing. She knew already that there was more going on than met the eye and she wanted to know what it was. There really are some things that you just cannot hide from a mother. I have come to accept that.

I'm not gonna' lie, I have used that knowledge to my benefit in raising Liliana from time to time, now that I'm on the other side. I presently also had her convinced that "mommy knows everything." Of course *her* mommy sort of does, but that's not the point. She doesn't know enough about the rest of the world to understand that or question any of it, and so she accepts entirely for the time being that my skills with her are endowed to me simply because I am "mommy" and "mommy knows everything!" I was smart enough to use that advantage while it lasted to keep her out of trouble, and I also knew that my mother was smart enough to do the same. It definitely wasn't a *height* thing, it was a *parent* thing.

"So Ethan, never been married? No children?" She asked bluntly but still "conversationally" enough.

"No ma'am. I've mostly focused on my work up until now." He answered, still being entirely honest. Much more than they knew.

"Really? So what's changed?" She challenged with feigned innocence. His answer however, was quick and confident.

"Everything. All because of one very simple thing." He added, looking over at me with a happy grin. He wiped his face with his napkin and placed it on the table. Then he leaned in on his elbows and looked back at my mother again. "I've never known anyone like Simone before. She came along and changed everything." He finished still with that ever-present smile, though the seriousness of his statement was not lost on them. I could feel their surprise but also their understanding at his position.

"Yes, we know the feeling." My mother agreed sweetly with a sense of amusement at their shared experience, like she had been waiting for someone to say that to her all along. I could feel an even greater understanding dawning in her about the reality of "us" after that. It was quiet for a few beats but my father saved us that time too.

"So I think I'm ready for that walk now." He suggested and my mother immediately seconded it. Ethan and I each nodded agreeably with a sigh of relief. We all stood up and gave a stretch. I told my parents to finish their drinks while Ethan helped me to clean up. On the way back out I saw my parents looking picturesque, leaning side-by-side on the railing with the beautiful scenery behind them and I was inspired to bring my camera. I grabbed it from the bowl and snapped a shot of them without them knowing, then I slipped the strap around my wrist.

After that we all made our way down the back stairs and onto the lawn. There were sighs all around. It felt good to move after such a satisfying, but filling meal! The fact that it was a gorgeous evening just put it over the top. We noticed Jack and Oscar then by the hayloft so we went over to say hello.

"'Bout time you all made it up here!" Jack insisted with a firm handshake to my father. "Welcome!" He added heartily as he hugged my mother.

"Good to see you again Jack, Oscar." My dad replied feeling just as welcoming, emotionally.

"You too." They both agreed.

Ethan grinned at me then whispered in my ear. "See, I didn't even have to introduce our parents." He joked with a smile in reference to how easily he had gotten off. I gave a sarcastic, half-smile back at him as he half hug-patted Oscar hello. I was thinking that I was actually really happy that something in his life had been easy because of me, even if it was merely coincidental.

"I understand now why my daughter is so happy here." My father added bringing my attention back to them. "She doesn't get home nearly enough but at least now we know why!" He joked wistfully. "And I almost can't say that I blame her!" He added complimentarily looking around us. "*Almost*." He added to me with a wink.

"Well I can't speak for the tenants property, the law is fairly clear on that unfortunately." Jack revealed with a tilt of his head and a coconspirators grin. "But you're welcome to stop by the *farmhouse* anytime you like!" He finished with a wink and a hearty laugh. "My parents and Ethan joined him. I just rolled my eyes.

"Please! Don't encourage them!" I begged Jack. They already have enough weight in the guilt department without help!" I added defensively.

"Are you kidding me? Keep it coming! We'll take all the help we can get!" My mother insisted making us all laugh again.

"Well this place sure puts our humble garden to shame." My father allowed with a friendly smile.

"Oh I doubt that. This girl right here has a pretty mean green thumb. She had to get that from somewhere!" He insisted playfully.

"Well maybe she got half from each of us and it made one whole *real* gardener in the end." My mother joked, mimicking things that I usually think about. I guess I knew where I got that from. *Hmpf.*

"What do you guys grow?" Oscar asked. "If it's anything we know, we may be able to give you some helpful tips." He offered politely. "Sometimes it's as simple as adjusting the soil components."

After a few minutes of swapping secrets we explained that we were showing them around and walking off our dinner at the same time.

"Oh, you've gotta take them over to see the pumpkins!" Oscar insisted.

"Gonna' be prize-winners at the fair this year for sure!" Jack stated confidently.

"We were planning on starting there as a matter-of-fact!" I assured them both.

"Ethan be sure to take them the around the cornfield so you can use the footbridge to cross over the stream. It's pretty high right now. It will be easier and it's just plain prettier that way this time of day." He said with his usual warmth.

"Yes sir." Ethan answered respectfully.

"Your property is beautiful and I can't wait to see more of it. Thank you, for *everything*." My mother said meaningfully to Jack as she hugged him again. Jack just smiled back but I could feel that they understood each other inherently. She was thanking him for more than just being a good landlord.

"You're most welcome! *It's our pleasure!*" He replied. Again I just rolled my eyes at how quickly and predictably my parents had gotten in tight with my new extended family. It was weird at first, but it made perfect sense if you remembered our families' philosophy. When it came to discreet, caring, supportive people that you could really count on, it was always "the more the merrier" with us. My parents knew that the Kent's treated me and Liliana like family already, so they automatically treated the Kent's like family in return.

I smiled then and shook my head. What're you gonna do? Things could be worse right? Yes. *So much* worse. I was happy they were getting along so far based on their own merit too, and not just for our sakes. That was what gave me the most confidence. They were the people who knew us best and if they not only liked each other, but also thought that we were good for each other, it would go a long way toward easing both our minds. It didn't guarantee the future by any stretch, but the families' acceptance was one really good thing to start out with on the "*pro*" side. I mean *huge*. I knew we would *each* sleep better at night if we had that.

We walked down the street side of the property sticking to the path between the cornfield and the road. We could see the sun starting to set just over the tops of the stalks. Jack was right about how pretty it was and I was glad that I had brought my camera. It was warm but not sweltering and the mosquitoes hadn't come out in full force yet so the timing really was perfect to dawdle and take a few shots of the sunset and the company. My parents were pros and happily posed at all the right moments. They were also thrilled when I showed them the one I had taken on the deck and I had promised to print and frame it for them.

We walked single file until we reached the stream. My dad helped my mother across the small bridge then he took my hand to help me but he kept it when the trail widened on the other side. We let Ethan pass us and fell in behind him and my mother as they chatted. Those two walking off alone made me more nervous than anything else had so far, but there was no subtle way to put a stop to it so I bit my tongue. I could feel his excited anticipation and his amusement at my worry, so of course my worry grew. *Oh boy…*

My father and I were silent for a few more yards while I was paying attention to the atmosphere ahead of us. It was mostly still just teasing and inquisitiveness on both parts, so I tried to stop focusing on them and focus on my father instead. We had never needed idle talk to pass the time between us, but walking was a good time to talk about important things when there was a need. The background activity would often free my mind up somewhat and allow me to concentrate more thoroughly on his words. He knew that and like myself, had not been afraid to take advantage of it over the years when he really wanted my attention. That evening was no different.

"So it seems that he agrees wholeheartedly with what your mom told me *you* felt. That's all very nice and fairly impressive even." He offered kindly. "But tell me, does he *know* yet?" He asked quietly but without hesitation. There was no need to hem and haw about that between us. We both knew that no relationship was a done deal for me until they really knew what they were dealing with.

It had always been a huge ordeal to decide when to tell someone that I really liked. Right off the bat before you could get attached but also before you knew if you could trust them? Or later, when you knew there was a good enough reason to go through it and you felt safe sharing it but you run the risk of them hating you for not telling them sooner. There really *wasn't* a good time and until that moment of 100% honesty, there was no way to know if it was real or if they would eventually bolt. My dad was traditionally not interested in getting personally involved with anyone until they had passed that particular hurdle. I didn't blame him. I looked up at him and caught his eyes, then gave a half-smile and a nod.

"Yeah. But before you look at me like that, it's not because I told him." I quickly threw in, my hands held in the air. "*Hmpf.* He told me." I answered cryptically.

"Interesting. How did he know? Who told him, Jack?" He asked logically. My parents both knew that Jack knew, and I realized that Jack most likely would have told him at some point, him being part of the family and all. But with Ethan's *height* skills Jack had never *needed* to tell him. He knew that about me before he knew anything else. I turned my attention away from his muscular backside once again and back towards my father as I attempted to explain, *at least partially* to start off with.

"No. No one told him. No one had to. That's the thing with him because that's where his own abilities come in." I informed him with a flick of my brows and a grin at his surprise. "You know I try to be 'selective' about who I share such intimate information with like a good girl." I added with a sarcastic smirk. "But it was never even an option with him because he can actually see traces of whatever genetic anomaly exists in us that makes us the way we are." I said with a flick of my brows at his reaction. I tried to keep going before he had time to form questions.

"I was pretty pissed about that intrusion in the beginning, I'm not gonna lie." I added with a secret smile for the other set of ears that I knew were listening. I thought I saw his head bow and his shoulders raise just slightly, as he appeared to stifle a chuckle. In response to which conversation though, I had no idea.

"But eventually I realized that it was the best thing that could've ever happened to me because it took that whole issue out of the equation for once. There was never any question about whether he could handle my abilities or not because he knew about things like that long before he ever knew about *me!* For the first time ever *I* didn't have to be the one to introduce that element into someone's life, and wait with bated breath to see how they would take it. He already lived in a world where those things existed and he welcomed me in." I explained wistfully.

"For once it wasn't about that element *first and foremost*, it was just about us, which was enough believe me!" I added honestly. I was quiet for a bit after that but I could feel when his inquisitiveness began to go on overload. As a lifelong proponent of continued education, his curiosity was no surprise. I had expected it. I imagined that was where I got *that* part from. I tried to feed that need somewhat before it became too much to contain, just enough to keep him temporarily satisfied since I knew we were almost at our destination. *Small doses.*

"As it turns out, my situation is not quite as exceptional as we have always believed. We knew that it existed in other's in our family, but I now know that there are also other families like that besides ours and many other variations on what we experienced that are all connected!" I felt the shock of that sink in as he stared at me without speaking.

"Ethan's family for instance, is a lot like ours. Well, in that one respect anyway." I quickly corrected. "Other than that, our families couldn't be more opposite but that's why he has the Kent's for family now." He walked a little slower as he started to process what I was *almost* telling him. I was trying to remember to pace myself and not blurt everything out at once but it was really hard! Especially with my dad.

It was his job in his eyes, to worry about and prevent me from getting into things that I shouldn't. Getting serious about someone whose whole life was focused around the very issues he had always tried to teach me to minimize for my own safety, was a definite "*shouldn't*" in his book and I could feel his reservations building based on that factor. That was going to take some work. I wasn't worried yet though because even though he had been prepared not to like him as an option for me as soon as he heard that, it was still obvious to me that he did. He had been much more impressed by Ethan in person than he had wanted to be. I knew the feeling and I just hoped he would focus more on that and go from there.

"I'm still just learning about the big picture of it all and we'll talk a lot more about that as I learn more, I promise you!" I insisted while grabbing his hand and swinging it back and forth in an attempt to physically keep the conversation moving.

"There is so much that I am eager to tell you both already! But for now, I'd really just like you guys to get to know him first, the real him, like I have. Not 'Ethan the Singer/Business Owner/Professional Student/Builder/Farm Hand/Champion of *Heights* etc.'" I couldn't help throwing that last one in even though he wouldn't know what it meant yet. I figured it couldn't hurt to get him used to the sound of the word.

"For right now, I just want you to know 'Ethan,' both of you. The rest we'll get to later, I promise. Okay?" He looked back and I could feel the wheels turning but he wasn't upset, not yet. So far he was still mostly just *super*-curious and cautious. It was still far better than Ben's reaction had been though so I would take it for the time being.

"Alright." He agreed simply as he nodded. "We'll go with that for right now. But we definitely have more to talk about, and not after such a long hiatus like last time either. *Soon!*" He insisted in a way that assured me he wouldn't be ignored on that subject. He didn't put his foot down so-to-speak very often, but when he did, he *always* meant it!

"Deal!" I agreed and caught back up to Ethan and my mother just as I heard her surprised, "*Oh my!*" ring out across the field of pumpkins.

"They really are *humongous* aren't they?! I thought you meant like *jack-o-lantern* big. I've never even *seen* a pumpkin of this size before!" She exclaimed. "That one over there's the size of a baby hippo!" She added with an incredulous laugh. "What does Jack use for fertilizer for Christ's sake?" She asked half in shock and half kidding. "I don't remember that being on his list of tips!" She declared in awe.

I just laughed at that. "*Hmpf*. I tell you what it is, it's the love that he sews into every inch of this soil, I swear! Seems like there's something growing out of control somewhere here year round. I used to marvel at it all the time too, but now a days I just try to enjoy it and to give back as much as I can in return. It feels really good. I totally get it now." I said in the end with a shrug. I could feel my parents' slight surprise at my poetic insight, even while I felt that they both pretty much agreed with the concept.

We walked around the field for a while, weaving through the rows. We posed on and next to some of the most amazing specimens while admiring the many different shapes and colors. It felt good to be out and to move but it was a lot of fun too. At least until the mosquitoes started to outnumber us. At that point we surrendered and decided to head back.

My parents walked ahead of us on the trail, hand-in-hand. I could sense the "We *really* have to talk later!" atmosphere between them but that didn't surprise me. What did surprise me was the fact that neither of them felt any urgency about it. That spoke of slow but eventual acceptance to me and I sighed deeply as we strolled behind them. I reached my hand out then for Ethan's and he took it, happy that I no longer had a worry for who saw. His grin was quick and full of satisfaction at that.

Back at my place, I offered my parents one more drink and some bug spray. My mother declined the drink, but gladly accepted the bug spray! My father was open to both. It was a little better higher up and we all agreed that the open air felt really nice so we decided to tough it out. I lit some citronella candles that I set all around us, then I lit two more for in between us. One I set on top of the table, and one I set underneath it to protect our ankles. We sat pretty comfortably after that. So much so that the questions started up again, only I noticed they were less "inquisitor" type questions, and more the, "I'd like to actually know more about you" kind. My father started that round off.

"So did you go to school around here Ethan?" He asked.

"I did. I went to the district high school, and then it was just a quick jump to the community college the next town over. But I've taken a lot of classes there over the years and I've received my degrees in business, engineering and music so far." He was matter-of-fact about it, not bragging at all but I could tell that my father was impressed. He still didn't entirely want to be, but like it or not that had taken him off guard.

It was a lot easier to dismiss some stereotypical kind of guy, for the usual reasons. Unfortunately for him, Ethan didn't fit any of those molds so far, and I already knew that he was never going to. He clearly had not been expecting a "backwoods-restaurateur-singer-scholar," with *skills of his own* to present himself as a modern day suitor! But I could tell that he was actually pleased to know that he was like me, *and* so successful! That part he couldn't help but admire a little and I totally got that too. It instantly reminded me of Felina again but I shook it off and tried to mentally stay on topic.

"It's a real low profile school as far as notoriety goes, but academically it has a lot to offer and it's been really great for me. I'm always taking one thing or another, to this day. I just finished a course in photography last month and I am starting one on German next semester." He informed us all, surprising me just as much as everyone else.

"Oh? What's the German for?" My father asked curiously.

"Who knows?" Ethan answered with a smirk and a shrug and I think my father fell a little in love with him just then, I swear! He was making it *waaaay* too easy! My mother was silent, taking it all in and keeping perfect mental notes, but I could feel that he was really starting to grow on her as well. Wow.

"So I guess the only thing left is to have you play something for us." My dad challenged in a playful way as he sat back contentedly with his freshly cracked beer.

"Sure." He answered happily. I went and got ice cream for everyone and a water for my mother while Ethan went and got his guitar. He took two big bites of his ice cream then put the bowl down on the table. He accommodated them by agreeing to play for us all while we ate, but just one song he insisted, since *his* ice cream was melting. They laughed but accepted the deal.

He played "*I don't Dance*" by Lee Brice, for us and it was ridiculously perfect. He may as well have just said out loud, "This is how important your daughter is to me and I'm not going to hide that from anyone anymore, not even you." I'd heard the song on the country stations a few times but I had never heard him play it before, didn't even know that he knew it. It was a nice surprise when he started out, soft and mellow.

I don't Dance
I'll never settle down
That's what I always thought
Yeah, I was that kind of man
Just ask anyone

I don't dance, but here I am

Spinning you round and round in circles
It' ain't my style, but I don't care
I'd do anything with you anywhere
Yes, you got me in the palm of your hand
"Cause I don't dance.

It was a metaphor for all the things he never let himself have before and even though the lyrics were so simple, they conveyed a very big message. It was profound but he still smiled gently as he sang it.

Love's never come my way
I've never been this far
'Cause you took these two left feet
And waltzed away with my heart

No I don't dance, but here I am
Spinning you round and round in circles
It ain't my style, but I don't care
I'd do anything with you anywhere
Yes, you got me in the palm of your hand, girl
'Cause I don't dance...

It was soft and deep and as usual I felt his heart in every line as he sang one more round of the chorus. He cut it a little short, probably due to the demise of his dessert, but I could have sat there listening to it all night. I clapped when he finished and I was not alone.

Thankfully it seemed like my parents felt the same way. In spite of his sweet, but *not-so-hidden* declaration, *(apparently something we were still doing)* they were enjoying the song as much as I was. At least as far as I could tell with him singing, which was also nice. I had sat there staring off and thinking about that among other things, lost in my own head until Ethan finished. When the clapping stopped he asked my mother what was so funny, wondering what he had missed.

I wondered too then and looked over to find both of my parents grinning. Their answer told me that apparently I was not alone in my bliss.

"It's just nice to be able to sit here and enjoy a private moment between my husband and myself while she is present and know that she's not subject to it! *Hah!* Where were you when she was younger? We could have used you then!" She joked playfully then thought better of it. "Oh never mind. You were just a kid then too weren't you? Anyway. The song was beautiful. Thank you." She complimented with a knowing look, then she sat back and sipped her water with a grin.

"It is very peaceful here, isn't it?" She stated happily. "I'm starting to see the appeal." She allowed generously in my direction, meaning more than just the scenery and we all knew it! I felt Ethan's joy absolutely skyrocket at her near open acceptance. Mine quickly followed.

At that point I yawned and sat up. Things had already gone way better than I had expected and on that note I was ready to call it a night while we were ahead. People seemed to take the hint, *all* of them.

One by one, everyone gave a tired, satisfied stretch. Ethan expertly secured their immanent departure by suggesting "a shot of brandy for the road" to my dad, after my mother had promised that she was driving. I didn't know where it came from but it was perfect, especially the opportunity to bring up "being on the road."

He happily accepted and when Ethan came back from the kitchen he had the bottle and two shot glasses. They toasted to "learning new things" with a sardonic grin and they drank. After that we walked down to the car where there were hugs and handshakes all around.

"It was very nice meeting you Ethan." My mother said intently but honestly. I could feel how comfortable she felt with him by then which spoke the loudest. "I can't wait to talk with you *more*." She added with a wink and he nodded acquiescence.

"Agreed." He promised with a grin of anticipation. Oh boy,

I still wasn't comfortable with that yet, I thought with more than a little foreboding.

"It's been a pleasant surprise, shall we say for now." My dad offered with an extended hand. He was still teetering between reflexive denial and acceptance but I was okay with that for the time being. Ethan was too.

"I can accept that." He answered happily. "It's been a pleasure to meet you both."

"Good night. I love you guys. Drive safe okay?" I said out of habit while I hugged them. My dad smiled at the "to and fro" of our father-daughter dance. By then he was feeling the weight of the new and different circumstance almost as much as my mother had been earlier. I knew it was scary for him and I could understand it better than I wanted to.

As a mother you struggle every day of forever to maintain the balance between caring and smothering, but as a father of a daughter you eventually have to completely relinquish control over the most precious and most vulnerable thing in your universe and you have no choice but to let it happen. Hence the reason that I didn't put him through it very often. He wasn't avoiding it anymore though. He knew it was a big deal for me and therefore it was a big deal for him. I could feel that he was on the path toward acceptance but he had a ways to go yet. I silently hoped that nothing would come along and knock him off course before he arrived at the intended destination.

"Good night. I love you too sweetie." He said simply, then he opened my mother's door.

"Love you. Call me tomorrow, okay?" My mother called over the roof of the car as she got in.

"Okay, I will. I promise." I assured her with a shake of my head at her excitement. He closed her door then went around and got in the passenger's side. We waved as they pulled out.

When I heard the last vestiges of tire on gravel signaling their departure from the driveway, I let out the breath that I felt like I'd been holding since I woke that morning to the sound of my ringing phone! *Pheeeeeew!*

"Wow! Thank God that's over!" I said as I climbed back up the stairs. I walked straight over and fell back dramatically on the bed. "One more dreaded task off the 'to Do' list!" I declared with apparent relief.

"What are you talking about?" He asked following me. "That was awesome!' He argued happily. "I *love* them, and you know they love me!" He bragged rightfully with a huge grin as he playfully dove in next to me. I knew that he had expected to like them based on everything that I had told him about them so far, but I really had focused mostly on just the good parts for the sake of each story at the time. It could be very different when you met someone for yourself in person, and had your own hurdles to get over. He grew serious then and I could feel that there was more.

"It felt really good to be honest with them, and for the most part to be *myself* and have them accept me anyway. You don't know what that means to me Simone!" He insisted heartily. "How much I appreciate them already just for that ability, and for teaching it to *you*." He added more quietly.

"Actually I do." I said with a smile. "And of course they like you. How could they not?" I asked teasingly. "You are an amazing human specimen after all." I said jokingly, but with an appropriate amount of praise. "And now it is time to reward you properly for all your efforts." I whispered in his ear.

"Ooh, I like the sound of that!" He replied quite happily.

Chapter 27

The overall trend continued on the jobsite and the work at Breezey went by in its' own blur of activity. By the middle of that week it was already wrapping up. As each job had been completed, we crossed it off the master list. Drawing that first line across the first completed job had been immensely satisfying! But by that morning we were so far into the list that we had to squat down to cross the remaining one's off. It was starting to look like we would really, *truly* finish early! Wow.

It was the complete opposite of what I usually experienced on jobs of that size, but with so many people working together so cohesively, the work was practically doing itself! Even when the work would unexpectedly end up being doubled on a job, the crew would double just as fast! It was like riding a speeding open-air train every day, the wind blowing your hair back as you tried to hold on it was going so fast, but I was abosolutely *loving* it!

It was also still somewhat shocking, but wonderful when Ethan and I would get up and head in together each morning. I had to remind myself daily that that part was only temporary because I knew that also wouldn't be hard to get used to. But I was smart enough to consciously enjoy it while it lasted. I still took no moments with him for granted.

It was really nice having Jeremy there every day too, and not as a "camper." He was just another Eagle Scout candidate there putting in his volunteer hours. His parents dropped him off every morning and picked him up every night, just like all the other scouts that didn't have a license yet and it made me smile at the simple joy they exhibited to be doing it. I loved showing up in time to see his younger siblings all hassling him lovingly from every window of the family minivan as he disembarked. It filled me with an immeasurable joy to see them as a cohesive family unit once again. It was even nicer seeing him act, not as a *norm* but at least "normal" again!

Half the time I spent at Breezey, I was admiring him from afar handling and enjoying everyday situations with his friends, being silly and carefree. It was so nice to see him pull that off that I just wanted to follow him around all day and spy on him.

I knew that by the time the job was done there, he would be fully reintegrated back into his own life and that we would see a whole lot less of him. I was really glad that that had turned out to be the case but I wouldn't deny that I was going to miss having him around. Of course Ethan and Pete were friends, who were even more like family than before, he reminded me. Ethan also mentioned that they weren't going anywhere and that we could visit him anytime we wanted to. It helped, but I understood what it meant to be a teenager with a bright future. He would be very busy for the next handful of years. It was good news and I was glad but I was still trying to absorb as much of his new disposition firsthand as I could, *while* I could.

I realized then that that was something else that Ethan and the others must have to deal with a lot, getting attached to the *heights* that they help. To some extent, I assume it's unavoidable. I mean if you didn't care, then you wouldn't help, *right?* But part of helping sometimes, was letting go when your work was done. *Hmpf.* It sucked but I got it.

I just tried my best not to be overly intrusive in my admiration. Since I had so many workers checking in and asking questions, keeping busy and away from him enough to avoid being obnoxious was actually pretty easy.

The constant flow of contractors in and out was visibly slowing though. The list of items left not yet covered in pencil lines, was dwindling down to almost nothing. I had to kneel by then to even read them. It felt good, both to stretch and to be so close to being done. I was *completely* ready for it that time around. Ready to celebrate with everyone else and to get on to whatever came next for Ethan and myself.

Marina stood next to me, quietly reflecting on everything it had taken to get where we were and feeling pretty relieved that it was all finally coming true. I was really proud of her for taking it all on in the first place and I felt lucky to have been a part of it, just like everybody else. In that spirit we had a big cookout planned for the weekend so we could get them all together one last time and thank everyone. She put her arm around my shoulder when I stood as she looked at the list from top to bottom again with me to check it over one last time. We were just waiting for the last few groups to finish up and it would be official.

"We really did it, didn't we?" She asked with a grin.

"It was mostly you, but yes, I think it's safe to say at this point. Two more crews to check out and it's a wrap!" I agreed excitedly.

"I just have one last interview to do, and my work here is done as well. Then it's all up to editing." She said with a satisfied sigh. She turned and looked at me then and I felt it. "Are you ready?" She asked with a smirk.

I had figured it was coming at some point but I was starting to hope that I'd been wrong. No such luck apparently. "*Ugggghhh.* I don't know Marina. Is that *really* necessary?" I asked in return truly hoping to avoid more publicity. She knew what I meant though and why, so I knew I could trust her not to air anything that would hurt us. That actually took a lot of the pressure off.

"Well you *are* technically the "Foreman" on the job and it would look weird if you didn't appear in the story *at all.*" She reminded me. She also promised on her career to keep my participation short and sweet, so I finally agreed.

She was true to her word, but of course that was only after a short non-negotiable trip to the van to see the "hair and makeup" people. I had to laugh but I'd reminded myself then that it *would* end up on TV at some point, even if it was at 3:00 am in the morning. That made me laugh even more, because then there was actually a good chance that Ethan would see it! I was also pretty sure my family would TiVo it at the very least once they heard that it existed so I gave in for a second time.

"I must be tired at this point." I joked with a shake of my head. We laughed and the two women there laughed with us at my obvious reluctance.

Thankfully it wasn't anything too dramatic. They re-combed my ponytail, after applying some styling cream and a wonderfully smelling shine serum. Then they swabbed the sweat and dirt off of my face with some makeup removing wipes and applied a light moisturizer mixed with a tinted sunscreen for which I was actually grateful. They used very little "makeup" in the process which I was also thankful for. It was really just a brush of mascara and a touch of lip gloss for shine. I didn't look different, just better. I hugged the two nice women and thanked them for their help. Then I hurried back out across the newly paved and painted parking lot and up the hill to get it over with.

The interview itself was quick like she had promised but she still managed to get me emotional in that short amount of time as we sat in the newly finished sunflower garden. We had replanted it in its' original spot in honor of Lara Breezey, wife of the original inhabitant, and it had turned out to be my favorite spot. They were only three feet tall when we transplanted them there, but by the fall you wouldn't be able to see over the top of them and it made me smile like I imagined she had once, decades ago.

I wouldn't see the finished product of Marina's special until everyone else did when we all watched the debut at the cookout in a few days. Until then I was done too and with the last contractor pulling out as we finished up our interview, so was everyone else. Breezey Memorial Park was done!

Marina and I hugged tightly and then went our separate ways. Once I was temporaraliy alone in the lot I stood and looked back up the hill at what we had all worked so hard on. It appeared brand new but still authentic to its era at the same time. It was warm and cozy but still fresh and vibrant, *alive*, as if it had just been built! I felt then that we had truly pulled it off. I could already hear the laughter of the next generation of families that would, stay, play and celebrate there and so much more. I was filled with a sense that what we had brought back to life was *good* and it would be a new bright spot in the community for all to share. It was as if I could hear the cheers ringing through the trees, from the past and the future at the same time, it was that clear to me! I sighed deeply in relief as I stood and absorbed it all. Before long I felt another pleasant sensation wash through me, from a very familiar and welcome source and I knew I wasn't alone anymore.

Thirty seconds after the first sensation had hit me, Ethan walked up behind me. He wrapped his arms around my waist and nuzzled my neck. "Another job well done, boss." He said looking up at the finished product with me. I beamed because I knew that even though it was unquestionably the result of many, many people, his praise for my part in it all was 100% honest and not just sweet talk. That meant the most to me.

"Thanks. It is good, isn't it? I'm just glad I got to be a part of it. Marina was right. This was an amazing experience." I reiterated as we stood looking up and taking it all in. The halls exterior was freshly painted and shone bright white with the newly installed landscape lighting that was just starting to turn on all over the grounds as the sun set past the trees. It all looked like a picture from the past. Only rather than being cold, sparse and black and white, it was newly transformed to an incredibly colorful, well lit, lush and inviting place again! Like one of those oddly real-looking puzzles with the paintings by Thomas Kinkade. It was *living* again and it was beautiful! Just in the way that the original artisans had intended it to be. That made me the happiest. That was basically my plan in its entirety, restore rather than replace everywhere that it was possible.

The original woodwork throughout the interiors had been stripped of their many layers of paint, sanded, stained and recoated in polyurethane until it radiated a beautiful shine that could be seen through the windows. The walls that were painted originally had received a fresh coat of paint, brightening everything to its original soft cotton white. All of the appliances in the main building as well as the outbuildings had been updated to modern high efficiency models, as well as all the furnaces and water heaters. But every place that the original craftsman design was still relevant and viable, it remained. It had just received a much needed facelift by many expert, caring hands.

It would be its own attraction from there on out, with its history so proudly and so functionally displayed. There were full color plaques that Marina had had sublimated by a local graphic artist that hung in every area. Each one depicted that areas' original history along with beautiful, full-color illustrations of the restoration process for future inspiration. They were as pleasing aesthetically as they would be educational and entertaining to visitors.

The main hall had gotten its hardwood floors refinished on the dance floor and the stage, and a new deep water blue, Berber carpet on the upper dining level. The chandeliers were restrung and any missing crystals were replaced. Once they were all polished up they sparkled in a way that was not only astonishing, but truly stunning! The giant oil portrait of Arthur Breezey even got a more impressive replacement antique frame and was rehung in the newly expanded entrance. It had its own explanatory color plaque, dedicated lighting and a high-backed, long wooden bench placed underneath.

From that spot you could sit and look out the windows beside the double doors to watch for your ride, or you could simply escape the excitement of the crowded, overheated hall for a minute. I could see it all so clearly in my mind already.

The other rooms and outbuildings all got new plumbing and updated electrical as well. Besides the property-wide update to modern codes, they all received a fresh coat of paint inside and out, as well as new rugs, bed linins and curtains all carefully selected to match the original style. A few even got new roofs but most were actually in good shape. Structurally, almost all of the various buildings were still sound which I attributed to good craftsmanship to begin with. I had wanted to maintain that as much as possible and I really think in the end that we had accomplished that goal as well. I knew the townspeople were going to be really happy with it and really proud to show it off.

The grounds were no different for me. I knew I wanted them to be usable and relevant to the present, but I still found it easy to follow the footprints of the past in deciding what would go where and why. Most of the areas had a designated use already and I didn't see any reason to change anything that worked as is. Everything else, we tore out entirely.

Ben really had been a big help in replacing a lot of the things that needed to go out in front, Liliana too. I was thrilled with how the grounds near the entrance had turned out. But that was only one fifth of the property that I'd had to transform. Some areas were more challenging for sure, like the overgrown playground that we couldn't even *see* at first! Once uncovered and rebuilt, the playground with its equipment that was so old in design that it was "new" again, was sure to awe and easily entertain the next few generations of children.

My favorite thing in that category was the amazing whirly bird that I'd had built from my childhood memories of something similar we used to ride a few times a year at my cousins house. I had loved it and I had never seen another one like it since.

It held six people at a time in a crisscrossed, circular, triple see-saw formation made of metal bars. Each spot around the outer edge of the circle had its own "bicycle-type" seat with a set of handle bars. There were footrests too but unlike a bike, they were also in front of the person, directly underneath the handlebars. When the person stood up the handlebars and the foot bars would separate while the bars stretched like a giant pair of scissors. When you did this, the whole thing would start to spin on its axis like a giant top. Each movement up or down added to the momentum. When all four people would pump their bars at the same time, it would continue to spin faster and faster until the weakest one either threw up or finally begged the others to stop!

It was crazy but it was the most fun I ever remembered having on a piece of playground equipment and I knew I wanted to resurrect it there for future generations to enjoy. It was an incredible find, to learn that we had a local metalsmith who could build it for me in time! I wasn't sure what era it came from originally, but it happened to blend nicely with the feeling that I was going for. All together with that, the restored towering swing-set, and the mountainous jungle-gym with monkey bars and ropes to climb, it was more than enough to physically entertain children for hours at a time.

As for the landscaping, I just knew I wanted it to look timeless. In that endeavor we had edged the entire outside of the fence that surrounded the park with a wildflower garden so that there would be something new blooming there three quarters of the year. Inside the fence there was a 6' wide cement track that extended the circumference for walking or biking. In the center there was a grassy area for summersaulting and cartwheels on one side, and that famous "Pinegrove Gold" surrounding the equipment to cushion any falls on the other. The end result was such a picture perfect park for that property that I truly couldn't have been happier.

The hiking trails we left mostly untouched other than to clear the naturally occurring debris from years of disuse and remark them. The scouts proved invaluable in that endeavor as well and in two and a half days with their know-how and their spray cans, they made quick work of what had the potential to be a long drawn out job. Then there were a handful of small trees that had sprouted up on Pope's Hill over the last few years. A local botanist carefully removed and relocated them to the forest to avoid future sledding accidents. That was about the extent of the grounds work there.

We did make one major change however by adding a small automatic rope lift to make getting back up a little easier in the future. Not *too* easy and not in a way that took all of the fun out of it mind you, you still had to hold on while it pulled your weight uphill, but it was enough to take the edge off so that you could get in a full day of sledding or tubing. It was another addition that was purely for fun alone, but I felt that that had always been the hills' purpose anyway and I didn't want to change that, I was happy just to add to it.

There were more changes in the other areas, like the lower lawn with the formerly overgrown willows that had been expertly trimmed. They still had their grand, sweeping branches, but they no longer brushed the newly laid pavement or the top of your car. They were cut back just enough to reveal the period appropriate black iron light posts that we had added in between them up and down both sides. Where it was dark and foreboding before, the whole entryway was currently awash in a golden glow. That led you straight to the parking lot on one side and then the gazebo that we had "*liberated*" beyond that.

It looked completely new with the surrounding and invading trees all removed so that the it was an unthreatened, freestanding, medieval looking structure when we were done. The branches that would remain forever entwined were cut, supported and lacquered where they wove in and out of the roof to match the beautiful floor. It had a very ancient, fantasy like quality to it and I had let it take me in that direction in that one area without restriction.

I really liked that both parts of its' past were equally represented there, both the high times proudly displayed in highly decorative wood carvings, and the quiet times when it had sat idle and became one with its' surrounding nature. Its full history was proudly displayed.

I had added landscape lighting all around the outside and angled it up towards the intricate ceiling to add to the dreamlike effect. On top of that, I went with alternating pink and blue lights since the regulations weren't as strict outside as they were inside and they made the whole thing that much more romantic. It wasn't disturbingly off par with everything else to the point that it looked completely misplaced, it was just different enough to easily hold the distinction of being a very *special* spot. I could already hear the proposals and feel the high hopes of anxious prom dates from where I stood.

I turned and smiled contentedly at Ethan and sighed deeply again one more time,

"We're done here. Let's go home." I suggested contentedly. He just smiled and took my hand as he led me quite happily back to his car. I got in and rolled down the window. Then I looked back on the property with a satisfied smile as he drove us down the long road to the street. The willows appeared to be waving goodbye in the evening breeze as we passed.

It had been a great job and I had really enjoyed the

experience. It had also been a major turning point for Ethan and I and I would never forget that. But I was *really* glad that it was done and that I could finally detach from all of that craziness long enough to catch my breath.

I really needed to take a moment to reflect on our newly combined day-to-day. That was still challenging enough all by itself.

Chapter 28

Since we'd finished early at Breezey, we unexpectedly had the next two days off before the final celebration happening on Saturday. We took all of Thursday to just rest up and relax our weary bodies and neither of us had any regrets about that. It was a wonderfully lazy day full of lounging, snacking and comfortable sex. By Thursday night we were ready to get out for a while so we went to The Tavern for a bit. It was just as exciting and enlightening as always, but we did make it a point not to stay too late.

The next day was Friday and my usual night with Liliana. I was starting to feel the end of the summer season nearing though and I wasn't ready to call it a wrap on her summer as a five year old yet. I had already arranged to have her an extra night so that she could attend the opening at Breezey with me on Saturday, but I also managed with surprisingly little resistance from Ben, to pick her up early Friday morning too so we could have the whole day to spend at the beach.

It wasn't always the easiest place for me, even though I loved it, but I knew that she loved it too and I wanted to focus on that before it was too cold to matter. I had sent one last text that night to let him know what time I would be there in the morning and not surprisingly she had come outside with her little rolling suitcase right when I pulled up. He hadn't come out, but simply waved from the doorway where he watched to make sure she made it safely to the car. I knew it was to her though and not to me so I didn't bother to wave back.

Everywhere else, things were going so unbelievably well that it scared me, literally. Of course there always had to be a balance weight somewhere and right then it was clearly, predominantly Ben, so at least it wasn't too hard to find. It was just killing me that his personal stubbornness was still making *my* personal life so very hard. That was one thing I really *had* hoped to put an end to with that exuberant lawyer's fee. It was making me antsy but everyone else around me was urging me to let it be for the time being, even my parents.

I had called my mother the day after our dinner like I had promised and we had talked in a little more detail about Ethan and what role he played in our little secret world of extraordinary people. I also told her a little bit more about what made those people so extraordinary in the first place. I explained what *heights* were and how the HgT virus was responsible. I described the whole process as much as I understood it. My mother was quiet during my tale but I could feel it immediately when she remembered exactly which virus I was referring to in myself. I could feel her recall that fretful night with me in the E.R. strongly, even over the phone. She was silent for a while after that as she put it all together and it began to make sense.

"I've actually seen that box on certain medical forms over the years, now that you mention it. We were never taught about it specifically in school and I was ashamed to admit that I didn't know what it stood for when I was young. But in my defense newly updated diseases and tests are being added to, and deleted from the forms all the time, so things that you've never seen before will occasionally pop up here and there. A lot of them are specifically for certain departments or their specialists. " She offered honestly.

"Everyone in the hospital has questions about those things now and then or jokingly ignores something foreign because it's so new that the rest of us don't know what it's for. We even have a code name for them at St. Augustine's, we call them "BAWE's." 'Boxes added without explanation.' 'Yeah, just skip down past the BAWE's section,' people would say when trying to direct new interns. Eventually I just got used to that." She admitted thinking back.

"When you're as busy as we are and you don't have a reason to further investigate one new box out of a hundred, something that simple and seemingly inconsequential never becomes anything more than a new acronym on a sheet. The majority of the staff will never learn every single one, simply because they will never need to." She was quiet for another minute but I could still feel the wheels turning so-to-speak so I waited.

"*Hmmm.* I'll certainly have to pay more attention to things like that from now on." She declared. "There are so many, now that I think of it specifically…" She added trailing off.

"All these years in medicine and I can still occasionally feel like that young student who thought she would never figure it all out. This would be one of those times." She admitted with a short laugh.

I worked to reign her focus in. Once I knew she grasped the basis for the concept of *heights* in general, I went on to explain as much as I could about how Ethan had devoted his life to helping them without telling her everything at once.

"He knows how hard these things can be to live with because he experienced that same hell firsthand. That provides him with a unique perspective on how to best help others struggling in similar ways. It means a lot to him to be able to give back, now that he's managed to grow past it, and he uses every resource at his disposal to further the cause for a better future for *all heights*." I finally spit out. I knew how dramatic it sounded but I couldn't think of a better way to sum it all up.

My mother was feeling slightly patient with my flair in describing my latest escapade, but I could tell that it was partly because she was still doing so much digesting. I understood that all too well.

She knew me better than anyone though, and she knew that even things that appeared to be nothing to others, could *be* a very big deal for me! She also knew I was attracted to, well the impossible like Marina had pointed out, and she didn't doubt the enormity of what I was claiming to have stumbled upon. Even though she sometimes had to take things I said with a grain of salt, acknowledging the core of truth, but removing the dramatic emotional surroundings, the things I was telling her *really* were that big for once! It was a whole new concept for why my life was the way it was, and it was also very real. That was going to take some time to settle. I understood that too. I tried to push on while keeping the dramatics to a minimum.

"I know it's a lot, but he's never done anything for me to hold against him. It's a very noble calling for him to have devoted his life to and his selflessness is contagious. So much so, that he has acquired quite an impressive team of talented, caring people to help him in that endeavor. Very intelligent, skilled, but most of all *discreet* people! And I am proud to say that I am one of those people now too." I was a little worried about how "cult-*ish*" I knew it all could sound at first and I was quick to try and expand upon that desire before I lost her completely.

"Seeing what Ethan does made me realize that I've never taken the time to think about or to try and help other young and confused empath's looking for a place in the world." I shared honestly. "Something I had desperately wished for myself back then." I reminded her though it wasn't necessary. I could feel her remembering how lost I had been for a while.

"Now that I'm a little older and better established, I find that I really want to be there to help others with that. To be that person that I had wished existed. I think I've found a way to make her exist after all." I said with a world of meaning and I knew that none of it was lost on her. "The better I get at it, the more I have to share with someone else facing the same obstacles. But that's only part of it." I stated honestly.

"There's also the very good chance that one day the person I will help the most will be my own daughter." I said putting it out there once and for all. That revelation held a world of meaning for her in particular, being someone who had definitely "*Been there done that!*" with her own daughter that she loved so much. It was hard and I knew she knew that better than anyone else ever could! I also knew she heard the catch in my voice when I said it out loud.

I could feel instantly that she didn't want me to suffer like she had. She wanted better for me, naturally. Of course the desire does not make it a reality and I had known all of that already. I pushed past it.

"On that note, I've recently tried to have this talk with Ben, to help him to prepare, because I felt like it was only fair that I share something so important with him. *Hmpf*. I don't think he's handling it all as well as you already are though. Of course we've always known that this stuff is hard for him, and I'll admit it would be a lot for anyone, so I'm really trying to be patient, but we also know how *that* goes." I joked sarcastically. She did her "all-knowing mom" thing again and waited for the rest.

"I'm still really scared of what his reaction will eventually be, but in the meantime I'll take all the training I can get." I said. She was silent but I could practically *hear* the wheels turning!

It was a lot but the nurse in her was quick to understand Ethan's stance and his life choices. Thankfully she was also someone who could appreciate that point of view, but I could tell that she still worried about me getting too caught up in something so all-encompassing, and in a weird motherly way, she also worried about my needs getting left behind in all of that. They were both old worries for her where I was concerned. But a moment later, she reached the end of the thought and then she was worried for Liliana too. That part was new.

"I know your father and I were away from you more than we would have liked to be while you were growing up. But what you'll start to see more and more as you both become more successful, is that's how it is if you want a successful career so that you can comfortably and reliably take care of your family. If you actually want both of those things out of life, you learn very quickly that you will always have to give up some of one, to fulfill the other. You try to balance it all the best you can, but when something needs to be done in either area, you have no choice but to do it, regardless of the personal consequences from the other side."

I knew what she meant and I knew that Ethan's loyalties to the Camp were absolute, but I knew his loyalties to me were just as strong already, and that was more than enough to comfort me. She wasn't quite there yet though.

"I already feel guilty that we couldn't do more to help you with those struggles when you were young, but I would feel even worse if I thought that we inadvertently trained you to expect less from your loved ones for the rest of your life! We did the best we could at the time and told ourselves that it was okay because the good we did then in our work, would make life better for *you* later on, when you needed braces, counseling, and college, and someday a wedding and a family of your own! So we worked hard and made sacrifices, but that was because we wanted to insure that it would be better for you now than it was then. I can't help wondering, with all that he's taken on, can he give you better than that? Because I know you have a hard time believing it sometimes sweetie, but you deserve that. You really do!" She insisted lovingly.

It was a very logical question. One that I had already asked myself many times but I had accepted by then that all I could go on there was faith in the way I knew he felt about me. I knew *absolutely* that being apart was just as difficult for him as it was for me. That was all the assurance that I needed and certainly more than I'd ever had before.

"Honestly, I'm not sure yet how we'll balance it all out, but truth be told I'd be more than happy with a tie between Camp and myself." I laughed lightly as I said it but I knew it was true. "Seriously. I know he will always be committed to that cause, 100% heart and soul. It's who he is and I would never want to make him change that even if I thought I could. But he can't take care of everyone else forever and never take care of himself, or ever let anyone else take care of him! Even a shooting star burns out eventually with nothing there to fuel it." I said sadly.

"In that vein I do believe he needs me as much as I need him and that I can make his life better as well by being in it, which inadvertently helps his causes. As it turns out I may be the *only* one that actually fits into his life in a way that truly works. He's certainly the only one that ever fit properly into mine." I admitted honestly.

"There will have to be some changes and some adjustments made along the way, on *both* sides! We're aware of that. At the moment though, I know we both really want it to work so hopefully we'll find a way. Honestly, who knows? My visions of the future are still as shaky as ever." I admitted jokingly and we had both laughed at that. "But I do see him in it. That's the one thing that is finally crystal clear." I added confidently.

"Yes, I see that as well." My mother agreed with a reluctant sigh. "That's fairly irrefutable at this point. I still want what's best for you though. I can't help it, I'm a mother. As such, I also know that it's already way too late for my opinion." She laughed again knowingly at that." But for what it's worth, I really do like him and the more I learn about him, the more that feeling is reinforced. But that doesn't mean I have decided whether or not he's really good for *you*. I still plan to spend a *lot* more time talking with him in the future, about all this *height* business!" She informed me bravely. "But I know that won't change how you two feel about each other and that makes me happy for you!" She said quietly which made it even more heartwarming.

"So for the moment I'm okay with Ethan, we'll take that as we go, but you have to give Ben a little more time. Trust me, I know what it's like to be the proud parent of a perfectly normal little girl and then have that suddenly taken away from you. It's not easy to accept. *It takes time!*" She insisted knowingly.

"You understand what it means to love a child now, so you know how that feels but you have the added advantage of having lived through it, so you also know that it will eventually be okay. Ben doesn't have that firsthand knowledge for reassurance. All he has right now are the fears that exist on the *other side* of knowing. You're going to have to give him time to get to where you are and to do that he has to go through it. Don't push him if you don't have to." She advised and having her give me the same advice as Ethan had made it a little easier to try and accept. Even so, I could feel us going backwards with each day that passed in silence and I *hated* it!

I tried to take it in, acknowledge it for a moment to let my subconscious know that it wasn't being ignored, and then let it go with a deep sigh, like I had been doing every day since our talk. Viv had had enough by that point and spoke up from the back seat of my car where she sat beside Liliana.

"Girl you better get it all out before we get there! I haven't had a beach day in weeks! Mopey Mary shows her face on that sand and I'm telling you right now I will drag her sorry butt down to the water and throw her into the biggest wave I see!" She declared lovingly in what I knew was not an empty threat.

Chapter 29

"I'll have help too, right?" She asked a giggling Liliana who high-fived her in response. Then she looked back at me. "You got me?!" She asked smiling at me in the rearview mirror. I just grinned back.

"Mopey Mary?" Ethan asked with a curious smirk from the front passenger seat.

"*Hmpf.* Yeah that's how I have been known to jokingly refer to my darker half on occasion." I admitted with a guilty smile. "I didn't always want to take credit for the things that foreign, overly strong feelings would make me do or say, so she became my alter-ego/scapegoat. You know, the party officially responsible for any negative outbursts that might escape on their own. I didn't always have a say or a lot of control over when things like that would happen back then and it was fun to have something to joke about, even at my own expense. Thankfully though, she doesn't make too many appearances these days." I added with a wistful smile at each one of the occupants in the car.

"*Hmpf.* Guess I'm not the only one with issues, huh?" He joked teasingly. I smiled. "God no, not even close!" I agreed wholeheartedly with a self-deprecating laugh. He gave a surprised, but genuine chortle in response to that, still not convinced that my "*crazy*" came anywhere close to his "*crazy.*" I didn't know if I wanted to win that argument or lose it so I let it go.

"Don't worry, I said to Viv and the car in general. "MoMare

wouldn't dare show her face on a day like today! It honestly could not *be* a better beach day!" I declared happily while turning up the radio, determined to make it true. We all sang along to Florida/Georgia Line's "*Baby you a song*" with wild abandon while we looked out our windows appreciating the beautiful day in a way that easily gave strength to my statement. I felt a little better then too as each of their own growing levels of positivity filtered in and through me and added to mine. I would take that all day long!

"*Baby you a song and you make me wanna' roll my windows down, and cruise...*"

We did just that down 113 as it wound along with the windows and the moon-roof open, just singing and bopping our heads until we hit the highway. I put the windows up then, temporarily but left the moon-roof open for air. We weren't on 95 long enough for it to bother us. We pulled off a couple of exits later in Salisbury, opened everything back up and continued to bop our heads through a series of lefts and rights until we reached Beach Road.

It instantly brought back memories from my youth of driving that familiar strip a million times with friends and family over the years. If there was a playback reel it would be a steady stream of every type of vehicle that I had ever driven there in, each representing a different time in my life, financially, or a different boyfriend. From the station wagons of my youth, to the Mustang with T-roofs that I bought and the muscle cars of my boyfriends throughout in my teens, all the way to the "luxury" family sedan that I was currently in. It was as varied as any rock video could ever aspire to be but the only thing that was different from beginning to end I realized as I thought back was me, my clothes, and my transportation. As for the strip itself, not much had changed at all.

We had a lot of choices for beaches within driving distance, both north and south but they were all very different. The right choice depended on what you were in the mood for. Fried clams, ice cream and rock collecting? Devereaux Beach in Marblehead was the number one place for that, although they really don't encourage you to take the amazing rocks that make up 80% of the beach home with you. Kite flying and tanning? Definitely Nahant Beach. You want hiking, rock climbing and old creepy underground barracks to explore in between swims? Winter Island in Salem was your beach of choice for the day. For a pure North Shore beach in its most natural state, including local wildlife, there was Crane's Beach in Ipswich, as long as it wasn't greenhead season anyway. But Salisbury Beach had always been a popular choice for me for encompassing so many desires at once.

You could easily be there for twelve hours and not run out of things to do! You had your beautiful soft sandy beach on the State Reservation for the day time, and the Midway for water parks and endless fast food choices if you got bored. You could ride go-karts, and then the water slides all afternoon. Then there were the restaurants, bars and arcade parlors that lit up the night and invited you in for a drink and a game of Keno or dinner at an elegant restaurant overlooking the surf. After that, you could go next door and join the line dancing to the live band out on the huge upper-deck. It was pretty all-encompassing. We weren't there for the whole kit-and-caboodle that time around though, we were just there for the sand and the sunshine.

We turned off the main drag and pulled down the long reservation road toward the beach and away from the games and excitement, behind the other thirty or so cars trying to do the same thing on such a gorgeous summer day. I was picking up a lot of overheated, impatient grumpiness at the traffic, but I didn't hold onto it. I refused to let their anger ruin my day or my companions.' Of course then I started in with my own neurotic thoughts. Like the one about having to leave a place like that in any kind of a hurry with a crowd of pedestrians and cars that large and only one way in or out. It almost sent me into a panic attack in my seat!

I knew I had no reason to have to worry about that at the moment for once having at least Liliana and Ethan with me so I knew they weren't in danger somewhere else where I wouldn't be able to reach them quickly. Viv I hardly ever worried about honestly either way. I generally felt bad for anyone who tried to screw with her actually. My parents I tended not to worry about too much either since they were both so healthy and were almost always in the direct vicinity of the best help available if they ever needed it. Ben was no longer my concern but he was surrounded by medical professionals as well regardless. Ethan and Liliana weren't my only concern, but generally they were my biggest worries from day-to-day. So I decided rationally that as long as they were safe there with me then everything would be just fine...*!*

I realized then that my insane rationalizing just made it all seem even scarier so I stopped. *Hah*! There you go, just another little joyful snapshot of what it's like living inside my head sometimes! *Anyway*... Viv saw me in the rearview mirror, recognized the momentary look of fear in my eyes. Unfortunately she knew me well enough to know when to check in on me.

"I *mean* it." She warned one last time and I believed her. Ethan just grinned with his head laid back casually against the headrest. Then he reached over and rested his hand over mine. He stroked the inside of my wrist slowly back and forth with the pad of his thumb and the sensation not only calmed me down, it made me want to *purr*! I just took deep breaths instead and listened to the music as we crept down the road one painful, microscopic inch at a time.

Mercifully ten minutes later the teenage girl in the bikini top, cutoff dungarees and flip-flops cheerfully took our money then handed us a small, plain pink ticket with a star shape punched out of it. I had to smile that such a simplistic system to thwart trickery was still utilized. Or that it was really even necessary, I mean come on. I was happy to pay the ten bucks just for the luxury of the nearby bathrooms that were always well stocked with dry toilette paper, never mind a place to park the car! For a whole makeshift family group to enjoy the day at the beach, I thought it was *very* fairly priced! It baffled me that some people would go to such great lengths to avoid paying it.

As I thought about how much it was worth it just to have the bath houses, I pulled up and parked beside one, making pit-stops on the way in and out with a young child super easy. Also because it would make the car easier to find later on among the miles long sea of blistering windshields when we came back sun-bleached and tired.

We piled out and Viv and I took Liliana up for the first of those stops while Ethan unloaded all the various chairs, bags, coolers and our trusty beach umbrella. When we came back a few minutes later we all took what we could carry, including Liliana who took all of her own buckets and shovels in an oversized beach basket and wore her towel all rolled up with its back pack straps. Ethan easily took the cooler and whatever else Viv and I couldn't.

We headed across the vast steamy lot and up the long faded wooden causeway. We shuffled along going from sand over pavement to sand over wood planks. That eventually led us over the dunes and down to the soft beach where it was finally *all* sand. The blissful ocean breeze as we crested the hill was incredibly refreshing, then I saw the size of the crowd and I faltered again for just a heartbeat. That was it though. I sucked in a big breath full of all the excitement coming at me and resolved to power through.

"How about that spot over there?" Ethan suggested quickly pointing towards an empty space in the middle of the beach. It was *right* in the middle of the crowd but I knew from experience that it was also close enough to the water for your feet not to burn the whole way there and far enough away that we wouldn't have to keep moving our stuff backwards to escape the incoming tide. By the time it reached that spot, I knew we'd be home eating dinner.

"Works for me. What do you two think?" I asked Viv and Liliana, choking back the negatives.

"Perfect!" She declared while Liliana cheered and they immediately headed over to claim it. We dropped our piles of stuff that made it look like we were going to camp there for the night and started to set everything up. The umbrella was something that I had never bothered with before, always having loved my time in the sun, but it was necessary for Liliana with her fair hair and skin. She could not sit in the burning rays glaring off the open water all day, even with SPF 100! Not even the tan she had by that point from being outside at camp all summer could protect her from that kind of exposure. She would burn up like an ant under a magnifying glass.

First and foremost, I didn't want her being uncomfortable or possibly damaging her skin, but beyond that I knew Ben would surely read me the riot act if that happened! It just wasn't worth any of those possible consequences.

Once we had our chairs set up and Liliana laid out her blanket sized towel in front of all three of us, I pounded the umbrella into the sand on the right hand side and then opened it, giving her a sunny half of her blanket and a shady half for later. I had slathered her up with a waterproof sunscreen before we left to avoid the inadvertent sand exfoliation you end up with when you apply on the beach. It would be a different story when it came time to reapply later but I had learned enough by then to take at least one the easy way.

When Liliana was settled and digging away happily in the sand with her menagerie of buckets, I sat back in my own chair. I took the water bottle that Ethan handed me and took a sip before I set it in the cup holder on the arm of my chair. He handed another one to Viv, then he went to sit on the blanket and help Liliana with her construction. I had to smile at his own reluctance to bare his entire body to the mid-day sun when he decided to keep his long sleeve surf shirt on over his board shorts, baring for the most part only gorgeous cheekbones, hands and shins.

Viv on the other hand, pulled her tank-dress off with zero inhibitions then plopped back in nothing but her tini-bikini to bake properly in the mid-day sun. She plugged her phone into the portable speaker that she had brought and set it up on top of the cooler. Then she adjusted her shades while the "Eagles" began to play and we both sighed.

The seagulls flew by overhead and called out to each other in the distance as it all blended in with the sound of the waves and began to soothe my frazzled nerves. Mary didn't have a chance at that point. Our problems still existed, but they couldn't follow us there. It was too bright, too peaceful and there was too much fresh air in constant movement for anything negative to stick for very long. I sighed and closed my eyes wondering why it had taken me all summer to get there. But I wondered that every time I was at the beach.

Growing up close to the beach makes it easy to thoroughly enjoy it throughout your life, but it also makes it unbelievably easy to take it for granted. You know the old, "*Don't have time today but that's okay, it's not like it won't be there tomorrow...*" syndrome. I mean it's not like the beach is going anywhere. Right?" But the time does pass by and I do miss it. Like my visits with Viv, I just forget about it until I'm back there again.

I took off my own t-shirt and shorts to reveal my usual modest one-piece. It wasn't the sexiest thing on the beach but even on the thinner side like I was those days, it still made me comfortable enough that I didn't feel the need to hide anything, rolls, stretchmarks or otherwise. That made it the perfect choice.

I laid there feeling the sun warm every inch of my exposed skin and I exalted in it. The vitamin D was almost palpable as it entered my bloodstream, fortifying me like a magic balm. I was focusing on the rays of light that I could not only feel, but see as a bright red curtain through my closed lids. With the constant ocean breeze blowing across my skin to keep me cool, the pure contentment that I felt from Liliana, and the current surrounding sensations, I was one happy girl! I knew a state of bliss would be hard to maintain long-term in a crowd that size but I was smart enough to take what I could get.

I listened to his laugh mixed in with hers as they discussed the proper etiquette of castle building. It made me so happy that I found myself smiling as well.

"Well that's better I suppose, but it's still kind of annoying." Vivianne said pointing it out as only a good friend would. "You could try to dial it back a hair, I mean we *are* in public." She said, pretending to be aghast at the idea of my being so openly enamored.

"Sorry, I really thought I was doing a better job of that these days. It's not easy you know!" I insisted heatedly.

"Yes! I know! Stop rubbing it in" She demanded playfully. "By the way, does he have a brother?" She added quietly. We both laughed and Liliana ignored us but I caught a quick sideways grin under one raised brow from Ethan. I gave a sly half-grin back when she wasn't looking but tried not to encourage him any more than that.

"So how are things at the shop?" I asked curiously, trying to change the subject. "Cindy seems to be working out pretty well at least." Viv smirked at my transparency, but she answered me anyway.

"She is amazing! She is super talented, but she doesn't walk around acting like it! It's extremely refreshing! She truly enjoys her work and she spreads that positivity all around the shop. I love it! I'm *so* glad I hired her! Business has gone up 20%!" She reported happily. I could feel her genuine contentment with the situation so I moved on.

"That's awesome! I'm so glad it worked out for the better in the end. Everything happens for a reason, right?" I added reassuringly.

"*Mmm.*" She answered non-committedly from behind closed lids.

"So how about the other position that you were looking to fill? Any new prospects there?" I asked hopefully.

"None what-so-ever." She answered quickly and without emotion. "Unfortunately for me, all the good candidates exist inside a novel or on the silver screen. The real life prospects are all a lot less impressive, or *taken*." She added snidely. She wasn't truly depressed about it yet though, just temporarily resigned. If she gave up all together, then I would know she needed me to step in. Until then I knew all I could do was to try and support her like she always did me.

"Don't worry, amazing people can turn up when you least expect it." I reassured her still form as I shared another secret smile with Ethan.

I closed my eyes and listened to the amazing but entirely real version of the "beach" soundtrack that appears on almost every *natural sound's* CD. The seagulls calling out the best picnics to each other. The music playing softly and reminding me of my favorite summer days from my teens. The wind moving steadily over my body and every other obstacle in its path, singing its' own song as it went. The laughter and playfulness erupting all around us. The waves crashing slowly but methodically against the sand behind it all. I laid there and I soaked it in with every breath.

I had a modest SPF level sunscreen on myself, but I would always be a sun lover. I tried to be fairly responsible throughout the years, especially at work and I really hoped I wouldn't pay too high a price for it later. But I would always be happiest outside with the sun pouring down on me. It was my ultimate happy place. Even there though, it didn't take me long to get restless in my chair. After a half hour or so, I flipped over, but then also turned end-to-end to face Ethan and Liliana so I could watch them work.

"If we build this wall up high enough, we can run a moat all the way around!" Ethan suggested excitedly.

"Yeah!" Liliana quickly agreed. "Oh and we can make a bridge across here!"

"I love it!" He agreed as they worked. I watched happily feeling even more content than before but I still couldn't stay still for much longer. I gave up on the "relaxing" and the "tanning" and went to help with the building instead.

"You guys are crazy, you need the blue bucket to make proper turrets." I insisted as I pulled it out of the bottom of the almost empty beach bag.

"Ooh! That's perfect! You've been holding out on me?" He accused Liliana playfully. She giggled.

"I forgot about that one!" She insisted innocently, her smile lighting up the beach even brighter.

"I'll get started on this side while you guys finish the bridge, then I'll let you do that side while I start bringing the water for the moat." I offered already looking forward to the exercise. It was a lot easier to take a crowd that size in a refreshing place like the beach but it was still a lot of energy, even if it was good energy! I had always loved the beach but I had never been good at sitting still on a crowded one for very long, no matter how much I *wanted* to!

Ethan gave me another sideways grin in understanding. I thought about that circumstance as I patted the sides smooth. It helped a great deal I found, just to have someone present who really understood what it was like for me and how hard I worked to make it look easy. If I succeeded, then I didn't appear to have anything to complain about. That was the non-gratifying catch. It was a private struggle that I wasn't used to getting credit for, but feeling that acknowledgement from him was settling in a way that I wasn't used to. The best part of that was just not having to feel defensive. For once a defense wasn't necessary. Yeah, I can't even express how nice that is!

It was exhilarating to experience my situation from a completely new perspective. It didn't make it easier necessarily, but more tolerable. I still found I had a lot of energy to expend though so I started making water runs to fill the moat. When that was done along with the castle as a whole, we celebrated and took pictures on our phones before the wind and the tide could wash all our work away. Then we went down to the water to rinse off and cool off at the same time.

"Have fun." Vivianne replied calmly at our declaration as she flipped over and changed the music to the scorpions and completely tuned us out.

Liliana loved the water but at her size she was still content to simply sit and play in the shallow waves at the water's edge. We sat knee deep in the water with her, rolling and laughing as the waves pushed us around. She never acted afraid of the deeper water, but she had yet to ask to go out there. As a mother I was pretty happy with that circumstance since she was much less likely to be in danger right next to me, there on the sand. I knew all too well how quickly things could go awry in just a few short minutes apart in hip deep water with these currents and I wasn't ready for that kind of risk yet.

I always had to acknowledge that as a parent but I tried not to stifle her, or to be that mother that never lets their child play or *live* for fear of them getting hurt. Honestly, I tried hard! Still, I would never purposely push her out of a situation where she was safer voluntarily. I was open-minded but I wasn't stupid.

After an hour or so of that, I suggested we go back up for a drink and a bite to eat. Liliana suddenly realized that she was "*starving*," and wholeheartedly agreed.

Even Vivianne roused herself long enough to share a

sandwich and a can of soda. I took the opportunity of stillness to quickly reapply Liliana's sunscreen as well as my own, then passed the wipes around so we could all clean our hands. Then we attacked!

Ethan and I had made tuna, ham and cheese and chicken salad sandwiches, then we cut them all in half so we could all have some of each if we wanted to. We had also packed individual sized bags of chips to avoid arguments and the inevitable sand in the bottom of the big bags. We had put the pickles, grapes, carrots and apples in plastic containers and once we had our sandwiches and drinks I put them on top of the cooler to make them easy to get at.

We ate in silence, each of us contentedly taking in the scenery while chewing. Every few minutes we would trade containers or grab a new sandwich half and then it was silent again. When we were done we put it all back into the cooler, greatly disappointing the seagulls nearby. As they sauntered off angrily to scope out their next meal elsewhere, I suggested my next favorite thing to do on the beach.

"Who wants to help me dig a hole?!" I asked enthusiastically.

"Me!" Liliana yelled just as excited.

Ethan just looked at me questioningly again with raised brows at my suggestion.

"Didn't you ever just want to see how big a hole you could dig in the sand? It's fun!" I insisted looking only slightly crazy. I giggled then too. He wasn't judging, just curious. He understood my need to do *something* physical with how much I was filtering in a situation like that. I could feel him thinking hard about other ways that he could help. At first I thought it was really sweet.

Then I realized just how *wrong* I was. All of his top ideas on how to help me expend excess energy had nothing at all to do with being *sweet* and everything to do with being naughty, very, *very* naughty!

I took a long, slow, deep breath and then I shook it off. I laughed as we collected our shovels and buckets. Then we wandered around a little until we picked a good empty place to begin digging. We only debated it for a minute before we settled in and got started. I grinned back at him about thirty feet back up the beach where he sat quietly on the blanket.

He relaxed with his arms behind his head and watched us for a while as we worked. Eventually, my plan to avoid the crowd backfired as usual though, as our slightly *un*usual activities always ended up drawing a crowd. Unfortunately, when you dig a six foot hole in the middle of the beach, people notice.

The parents look quizzically, snobbishly, wondering what the point of it is, but they keep their distance and their critiques just above a noticeable whisper. The children however, never care what the reason for the hole is. They just always want to get closer to it. Liliana had coincidentally made a lot of friends in similar situations, on similar beaches over the years. I figured that couldn't be a bad thing.

Of course Ethan was paying attention as well. I tried to be modest and aware of the fact that I only had a bathing suit on when I bent over, but digging was physical work and you tend to forget about how you look while doing it. Until I started to feel it, coming back at me while he watched. It hit the pit of my stomach and made me want to sit down for just a minute. I didn't give in though. Instead I stood tall and took a breather while I grinned up the beach at him. He grinned back but stayed put.

We were about three feet down and five feet wide when Viv noticed not only the crowd gathering, but the handsome, ring-less dads that had accumulated as well. The situation had piqued her interest at that point and she finally came down to help. Unfortunately only so many people fit in the hole at the same time and Liliana was still having too much fun with her new friends to get bored yet. So I decided to forfeit my spot and attempted to climb carefully up the wall without sending it crumbling beneath me and on top of Liliana and Viv or the two other two little helpers that we had accumulated.

The sand began to slide under my hands and I was about to willingly fall back in and try again when a rather large hand caught mine and held me firm, then pulled me out without a single moments' hesitation. I caught the edge of the precipice with my bare foot and held on. Thankfully the ground beneath me also held. As I stood up tall on the same level as the crowd again, the storm of surrounding emotions came rushing back and hit me all at once! It was mostly pleasant, just more curious in nature than before, but it was still an *awesome* sized wave! I breathed it in and held tight for a moment while it rolled straight through me.

The breeze washed through me too though and as always, it helped a little. After that I mostly just felt Ethan again where he stood holding my hand and it was a huge relief. His blocking ability really did go beyond his singing. I loved the way the dominance of his feelings whenever he felt something really strongly, acted like a space filler to block out almost everything else. He pulled me up against him, and held me tight around the waist with both arms. I sighed not once, but twice. It was the perfect rescue from the hole and from the crowd.

He grinned then and his intense look spoke volumes. But his feelings simultaneously washed through me like an electrical fire and that all but spelled it out for me so the look, while intense and entirely enjoyable, was superfluous at that point. He had me at 'hey your fire, meet my fire." It was mental, physical and chemical at the same time and it was amazing and ridiculous and still not getting old in the least! He leaned down and his soft, warm lips brushed mine. *Damn*!

My sand covered body rubbed mercilessly against his then in the most discreet way humanly possible. Apparently it still wasn't discreet enough though.

""You two should go for another swim and 'rinse off.'" Vivianne suggested with her usual dry humor. "We're good here." I could feel what she thankfully wasn't saying in front of the crowd.

"*Mmmm*. I probably should rinse off." I said agreeably to Ethan as I ran my hand up and through his close cropped hair. The new cut was extra short to combat the dead of summer heat and it looked even sexier on him than the long hair had. *Damn!* I tried to focus again. There were one or two whistles on the beach from the more 'educated' of the lookers on, but it wasn't enough notice for us to care.

"Let's go." Ethan agreed, looking *more than* hot and ready,

God help me! I was starting to think that it wasn't a good idea to entertain such playfulness on a "family outing" when Viv spoke up again.

"Don't worry. Lil' and I have got this thing all wrapped up." She assured me with a wink. "As soon as we hit water, we'll start filling it back in! It's like a science experiment!" She insisted. I just rolled my eyes but didn't make any more of a public spectacle out of it.

"Alright. Be right back." I said to Liliana as we started off down towards the water.

As we reached the edge of the waves that we had lounged in earlier, it was even warmer and it felt really good. That instinctually made us venture in past the water's edge that time. But it was a trick, because the deeper you got the colder it got! I knew from experience though, that the only way to get used to it was not to fight it but to just keep going and get the shock over with all at once. When I got about hip deep I did just that. I took a deep breath and braced myself. Then I dove into the next wave.

"*Pwuoaaahhh!!*" I shouted in a particularly unladylike way when I came back up. He laughed but followed my lead, although he did it in a much smoother manner as he simply laid down in the water and started to swim out. I shook my head at his cavalier attitude since I could *feel* just how shocking it was for him as well! Again he felt it for sure, he just didn't react outwardly. I liked knowing that he really was human though, just like the rest of us, especially when I knew I was the *only* one who knew. I can't lie, I had no choice but to be impressed by his control. It was just the kind of thing that held a lot of weight in my world.

I myself did a few more energetic, spastic dives under water in an attempt to get my blood flowing and speed up the acclimation process. When the shivering stopped and I started to feel half as comfortable as he looked, I trusted myself enough to swim after him.

By the time I reached him we were a good fifty yards from the beach and it was blissfully quiet, both literally and emotionally. He swam over to me and wrapped one arm around my waist while the other worked with his legs to keep us afloat. I wrapped my legs around his hips and used both of my arms to keep my side up. The sun was beaming in the perfect, cloudless sky and in the silence of the waves, it felt like we were the only two people there. Unfortunately that was both good and bad. The good part was obvious, the bad part was that it made me want things I shouldn't want when I knew we weren't *really* alone!

He was feeling the same thing but he had less of an issue with it. He kissed me slowly while we bopped up and down with the motion of the waves. Both sensations were incredibly relaxing and hypnotic. I reveled in it happily for a while until I felt the heat rising to the point that I couldn't feel the temperature of the water anymore. He slid one hand down over my hip and then easily in through the side of my bathing suit. His palm felt like a propane heater under the chilly water and as it found its' way over one chilled cheek and up underneath me. I closed my eyes and sighed loudly at the intense pleasure of it.

"*Mmmmm.* That feels too good, like *way* too good!" I shared honestly before I laid my head back in the water, trying to cool off a little. But I don't think it's a good idea to start something that we can't finish right now." I informed him with some disappointment. He just smiled slyly back at that and I could feel the "*dare me, please!*" in there.

"I won't make love to you out here. That would be inappropriate, and easily distinguishable, even from a distance." He insisted logically as we drifted slowly back and forth with the moving water. "I could however, take a moment to manually bring you to climax while I have you all to myself. Help you expend some of that extra mental energy in a much more efficient and pleasurable way." He offered totally serious. "I can guarantee that you will feel a lot better." He insisted slyly. "And I promise that I will keep you above water throughout and float your slack body safely back to shore afterwards, right before I kick your ass at ladder-ball." He grinned in the end just for show.

"You're absolutely crazy. You know that don't you?" I asked with a grin.

"*Hmpf.* Why? What's crazy about wanting to make you feel

better? You deserve that and if can deliver it, why wouldn't I want to?" He asked and then growled in a way that somehow made it sound totally reasonable. "I meant what I said about there being many joys in life Simone and I want you to experience them all! If one joy helps you to more fully experience another, where's the harm in that?" He asked tauntingly while swishing us around in a circle with his beating limbs.

"Life is short Simone, you have to stop ignoring it as it passes you by thinking that maybe the next experience will be one you will be able to *fully* enjoy. You don't know that there will always *be* a next one!" He argued heatedly. "Life is meant to be lived. We each have to live it in our own way, but we all have to live it! Even you." He insisted quietly as he pulled me closer. "And I will happily do whatever I can to help facilitate that." He promised without hesitance as he kissed my neck.

Then he made his way back up to my lips and kissed me deeply and I was truly floating, in every sense of the word. We both knew that his offer was a serious one, but as soon as I looked back at him, we both knew that I wasn't going to accept it.

"Thank you. But no thank you." I answered with a happy smile. I get it, I do. And you're right, I know. You're *alllways* right dammit!" I allowed jokingly. "I'm trying to learn not to hold that against you." I added with a smirk.

"I agree with you that life is meant to be lived and enjoyed. I've always known that. But that didn't always stop me from hiding from it on occasion anyway, it's true. Life wasn't always worth the struggle that came along with it." I admitted with a shrug.

"I've worked hard though on getting to a place where I can do that, live life and really enjoy it. I'm ready to live a life that is full of peace and free of guilt for expecting happiness of my own, and I'm starting to think that if I can do that, that it might be worth it after all. I'm happy to say that I'm a lot closer to that than I ever used to be. I'm actually glad that I met you now and not five years ago." I said aloud as I realized myself just how true that was. "I'm glad I am who I am now and that you're who you are right now as well. You make my life better in so many incomparable ways." I said as I swished my arms slowly through the water.

"But I can't keep letting you handle the hard parts *for* me all the time. I need to finish my own personal journey of learning to cope with my own stuff, and I need to do that on my own, *first*. I really feel as though I'm almost there." I added humorously. I felt his understanding and admiration for that attitude.

"When I do finally feel confident enough in my ability to cope on my own, then I will be in a better place to share myself fully with others and I will be able to accept any and all help much more gratefully, especially yours! Don't think for a second that I don't appreciate you and your efforts on my behalf and the security that your strength adds to my life, because I do! In ways that I know I can't adequately put into words!" I insisted.

"But it's important that I don't rely *solely* on that. Better to enjoy it as a perk, than to *need* it to survive! Know what I mean?" I asked openly.

"Completely." He answered simply. He was relieved that I wasn't turning him down out of shame, guilt or fear and he was proud of me for that. I can't even explain the difference it makes being with someone who *truly* gets you. I could feel his pride for me and he knew that so he didn't bother to voice that part. He did finally voice something else that he was feeling though.

"Do you have any idea how much I love you for things like that?" He asked just as openly in return. He didn't even blink, he just stared happily into my eyes and my next words came easily.

"I'm guessing maybe half as much as I love you for actually understanding it!" I offered. It wasn't the first time his feelings had been verbalized, but it was the first time that I'd felt safe enough to confirm that I was just as foolish as he was. His smile grew to epic proportions with my declaration and I could feel his emotions going back in an unsafe direction again. I smiled back and tried to get the situation under control.

"But really, thank you for the offer." I whispered softly then made a suggestion of my own as I separated myself from him and righted my suit. "I have another idea. How 'bout we swim off *our* excessive energy?" I suggested knowing he needed it as much as I did by then. "I'll race you back!" I yelled as I dove into the next wave and headed with it towards the shore. He laughed out loud then dove in after me.

I was no slouch in the water, when I had my wits about me anyway, but his strokes were still twice the length of mine. As we raced back to the shore, the lead changed hands multiple times although I suspect that was more due to sportsmanship than anything else.

Eventually we reached the sand. Of course his feet reached it long before mine did which gave him another distinct advantage. We both ran up with the incoming waves laughing hysterically. When the water was at our knees he gave a last minute sprint up the beach. Even if I wasn't laughing so hard I would have had no hope of catching him and we both knew that.

So okay, he beat me of course, but not by much. He made sure of that out of consideration for my feelings. It was just enough for it to be uncontestably official. His raised his fists in celebration and made the mock cheer sound of an imagined crowd while he danced around in a circle. I laughed even harder at that and happily collapsed on the beach beside him.

Viv and Liliana waved to us, from their half-filled in hole in the sand. We sat on the shoreline catching our breath and we waved back. They had filled the hole back up halfway already, and there were a chain of giggling children with buckets running back and forth filling the rest with water. Vivianne had lost her group of male admirers, but she didn't seem to mind. She was sitting with Liliana and two other kids on the edge of the hole on a towel with their feet dangling in it like it was a mini spa bath.

"Come on. Let' go help." I suggested getting up. "That should be just enough to do us both in completely. All we'll care about after that is a good nights' sleep." I added optimistically, in reference to our next couple of nights apart. He just growled at that thought but I ignored it as I reached down to pull him up.

Chapter 30

I turned the knob on the grill until I heard the "*click, click, click*" followed by the satisfying *whoosh* of the flames as they caught. I moved across and turned the other three knobs on and down to medium/low then closed the lid to let it heat up. I followed a similar procedure with the next three grills that various people had brought and set up side by side for us to use. That done, I turned and smiled to myself as I looked back into the crowd.

I saw where Ethan and Liliana had gone to right away. They were sitting in the folding chairs that we had set up in the shade under the giant oak trees, blowing bubbles for the other young kids to chase while they waited for the show to start. That wouldn't be until later though and he had agreed to "entertain" her for a while when my hosting duties started to be more tedious for her than fun.

By the time we had all got to Breezey, there were already helpers starting to set up and we had jumped right in. She had been happy with that for a while, putting out table cloths and paper plates and opening up all the little umbrella nets that would go over the food to keep the bees and the flies away. After an hour or so though, I could feel that her excitement was more for the park and the other kids she started to see arriving, than it was on hanging out helping mom. I had mercy on her and suggested that she help Ethan who was currently showing the kids how to use the pile of bubble stuff that we had brought for them. She had jumped up and cheered in response.

She was officially no longer the least bit leary of him. By then he was already well established as "mister fun!"

"Thank you mama!" She gushed. Then she kissed me and she was off. Ethan looked up and smiled when he saw her coming over. Then he immediately looked at me to make sure that I knew that. I smiled and nodded back at him and he was satisfied. I watched her until she arrived where he was a short distance away. I noticed that he did too. When she got there he handed her one of the crazy looking bubble wands and her face lit up.

There were huge round wands that made the really big bubbles, and long wands with multiple holes that made a whole row of bubbles all at once. There was even one the size of a hula hoop that the kids could stand in and lift to make a giant bubble around them! Of course that was a little harder to do than it was to say, but they were all having a lot of fun trying.

I could feel her contentment from where I was while she enjoyed the activity immensely and I wasn't surprised by the innocent simplicity of it. I was surprised however, by the level to which his feelings matched hers.

I thought I would feel more of a placating attitude from him, or even just a sweet but temporary patience which was quite normal for adults when they were dealing with children, especially ones that weren't theirs. But that was not the case at all. I was pleasantly surprised to find that he was genuinely enjoying their time together just as much as she was. His thoughts weren't on how long he had to stay there or when he could do something more adult instead, they held just as much contentment as hers did to simply blow bubbles and create fun for the others. I knew he faced enough of the real world on a daily basis to appreciate the quiet moments when he got them. It made me smile on the inside, in ways that I still didn't quite have words for. I know, you're probably getting sick of hearing that but I'm honestly still trying to digest it and the mental repetition helps me process. Sorry.

What I saw and felt also renewed my belief that he *would* make a great father and I truly hoped that he would get to fulfill that desire someday, even if it wasn't in the present or with me. I was surprised to find that I really meant that too. Whether it happened between us or not, I still hoped he would know that kind of love at some point in his life. He deserved to and a child deserved to be loved the way I knew he would love one if he ever got the chance. I smiled and left them to it while I went back inside the kitchen to help finish prepping the food and gathering tools.

I turned up the little portable radio in the kitchen and took out the huge stainless steel trays of donated "Laurie Burger" patties from the fridge. I set them out on the long counter to make it easier for the volunteer chefs to grab once the grills were ready. I was trying to make it as easy as possible for them, short of leaving the raw beef out in the hot sun. The same went for the big boxes of hotdogs and I got those next and put them beside the burgers. It was still early so I knew there was no need to rush. The plan was to cook as people wandered around and admired the finished renovations. There was already a good sized crowd and there were pictures flashing in every direction as craftsman of every field proudly showed family members and colleagues around their personal contributions, both inside and out.

My phone chimed then and I pulled it out to see who it was. It was a text from Ethan.

The real playmates have arrived.

I knew he was referring to Jonah, Emma and Paul. She was always happy whenever Jonah was around in general and when they learned that their friends from camp, siblings Emma and Paul would be there too, they were both beyond excited on the phone. It was seriously the cutest thing ever hearing them gush to each other about the upcoming opportunity to see each other outside of camp! I'd had a smile from ear to ear, but I had kept silent while they talked.

Ethan's next text had been a question.

Jeremy's taking sibs and others up to park. Lil and co. want to go with. That ok?

I had no problem with that so it was an easy response.

Sure. Thanks for checking.

It felt really good to have more kids around for her sake and I was pretty happy to see her so happy to be there. Heck, and to *be* so happy myself at the same time! It had been a while since that had happened concurrently and it didn't go unnoticed. I definitely acknowledged it and gave a silent thanks before I went back to my arduous search for utensils.

Once the food was ready and people were seated with their plates, the special would begin on the big screen set up out in the middle of Pope's Hill. It faced back up to the top so that everyone could sit staggered on the hill and have a perfect view like a natural outdoor amphitheater. Everyone was spreading blankets on the grass and little ones had been repeatedly rolling down the hill and running back up it trying to burn off some of their energy. It reminded me of movie night, on a much bigger scale. I smiled to myself at all the good feelings I had picked up already.

Though it meant I would have to leave that sanctuary eventually, I thought it was a great idea for the viewing given the size of the crowd that had turned out. It was a private celebration for just the volunteers who had worked on the job and their immediate families but it still felt like the whole town was there! It seriously had to be close to 75%! It would have been far too crowded inside for *my* personal comfort, even in the great hall. So I was glad that Marina had settled on an open-air venue instead. It had cooled down to a much more comfortable 78 degrees with a light breeze and would be a perfect evening for it.

I heard someone coming in through the back hallway just as I bent to grab the plastic silverware from the bottom drawer. As usual, I recognized Ethan's familiar warmth long before he came up behind me. He rinsed the bubble residue from his hands and wiped them on the towel hanging next to the sink. Then he walked over to where I was and slid his clean hands over my hips and up my sides where he ended up making small, wonderful circles on my lower back with his thumbs. I groaned in appreciation for a few seconds before I straightened up to lean back against him and his hands slid up to rub my shoulders instead.

"So how can I help you in here, so I can get you out there?" He asked with a grin as his body contacted fully with mine. I closed my eyes and just soaked up the good feelings and his warmth as I leaned into him. I was getting better at accepting that it was really an everyday thing and that he wasn't going to just run off a moment later every time he was near me, but it still didn't come automatically yet. I opened my eyes and answered him.

"Actually, you can help me find the things on this list. There are a million drawers and cabinets in here now, thanks to you." I added sarcastically. "If I have to check them all myself I might be in here all day!" I half-threatened, and half-joked. I really was impressed with his handiwork though in transforming the room into an incredibly functional, yet historically inspired, modern kitchen.

"Yes, you'd just love to have that excuse, wouldn't you? Well I'm sorry but that's not happening." He insisted with a grin. "I'll help you. Let me see." He insisted gesturing for the list. He quickly scanned it and handed it back to me. Then he started opening drawers and cabinet doors with me. As we wandered around the kitchen together, my mind wandered as well.

The latest round of domestic bliss was more than I had dared to hope for and I wasn't too proud to admit that it mostly scared the shit out of me! I'm not gonna lie. Having him there was really nice and it made me *really* happy so of course it was *really* hard to fully accept. Besides my daughter, I hadn't wanted anything or anyone that badly in a *long* time!

As much as I had tried to avoid all of the emotional entanglement originally, once I was actually tangled in it, I knew I wouldn't trade it for anything. It finally felt right in ways that I never thought it would. I wanted life to stay just like it was between us right then, but my mind was always looking for the catch that would screw it all up, that damn "*balance weight*" again. There were so many places in our life that it could be dangling besides Ben, just waiting to drop.

The brutally honest truth is that the more you *have*, the more you have to *lose!* I had learned that inconvenient lesson very early on with my hard-won, but precarious peace of mind that on some days, still managed to elude me. Loving Ben so fully then losing him anyway had reinforced that belief even more, but giving birth to Liliana had solidified it.

I loved her so completely, that just the thought of her being in pain or in any danger *ever*, was enough to send me into a full blown panic attack if I let it take me over! I had never really relayed to Ethan the true depth of it, but leaving her had felt like what I imagined it was like to have to hack off a limb in order to escape certain death!

That's honestly the only way I can explain the true *wrongness* of how it felt. It was once a completely ludicrous proposition that at some point became the preferable choice over the only other available alternative, which in our case was letting her be hurt by our separation any more than necessary. Better to hurt myself in ways previously *inconceivable* than to let that become a reality for her! It was the scariest thing I had ever known up to that point.

I knew no one could really ever separate us permanently, that was impossible, but the pain of losing the everyday with her had still taught me things that I wished I'd never learned! Things like, as long as she was okay, I could survive almost anything, *temporarily.* I was a stronger person for it but the road to where I was had been long and shall we say...*unpleasant?*

But somehow he had managed to up the ante on me once again, by giving me that type of daily normalcy, a real sense of completeness that I had begun to believe would never exist for me and that was scary enough to make my knees go week, only not in the *good* way for once!

He was finally present in all the small everyday things that I had fantasized about, and in new and humongous ways that I hadn't even dreamt about! With Liliana there with us as well a lot of the time, I truly couldn't ask for anything more. Tell me that wouldn't scare the shit out of you! *Come on!* I'm afraid to even say it all out loud most days! *Jesus! Deep breaths…* Anyway…

Things with Ben were definitely still strained, so there was always that to keep me grounded at the very least. He had yet to agree with or deny the possibility of what I had shared with him, since he still had yet to respond at all. I could only guess that he was trying to find out more about it on his own, being the exemplary student that he always was.

He also very rarely ever took what I said at face value without corroborating proof, always assuming that I was far too emotional to ever be completely unbiased in any situation. It was deeply insulting in subtle ways that he never quite understood for some reason, but I was long since used to that as well.

I tried not to worry too much, I didn't think he would get very far that way. At least I hoped he wouldn't. I had made a few late night attempts myself in the interim just to see, but I had not managed to turn up much of anything that was useful. I hoped he would fare similarly. In the meantime all I could do was wait out his stubborn existence in limbo. I was still trying really hard to be patient but we all know how good I am with that by now at least, right? Like it or not though, I *was* getting better.

I was pretty proud of myself for the growth that I had made in that area recently, but a part of me still wanted desperately to shake him and make him tell me what the hell he was thinking once and for all! Truthfully though, I was far too afraid of what his answer might be, to be the one to force it out of him. I had no choice but to wait and see which way he went with it first. Ethan was still adamant as well that I not push him and I was trying to take his seasoned advice the best I could. For the moment I figured that no news was good news.

Aside from the pink elephant in the room, things between us were bearable, especially since we weren't really talking. He was still keeping his cool about Ethan though, for the moment at least and I was really hoping it would last. I really needed it to last! I had to work hard to keep myself from hyperventilating sometimes when I thought about it all too much.

I wasn't sure which was worse, not having Ethan around at

all and spending all my time wishing that I did, or having him there and constantly spending every minute wondering when or how I was going to lose him again! Sometimes even to the point of completely forgetting how to enjoy the "*now*" dammit!

At that point I fantasized about a life together that someone couldn't come along and pull out from under us like the proverbial carpet. I didn't know if that was really even a possibility though. I started to think that if I spent enough time dwelling on it, maybe I would invent a way. *Hmpf*, or maybe I would go insane. You know, either way...

He had learned to recognize that now familiar look of borderline panic in my eyes as well as Viv, if not better. He came back over to check a drawer near me, caught my expression and reached out to pull me back.

"Hey. You okay?" He asked, coming around the counter and turning me to face him. I sighed deeply before I answered.

"Yeah. I'm still trying to get used to the idea that this is all real and that you're really here. And that you're going to be able to *stay!*" I said with a smile."I really want to relax and enjoy it, but I keep waiting for Lucy to pull the football away and laugh maniacally in my face. You know what I mean?" I joked as I pulled his face closer just so I could touch it against my own. "I'm sorry. I can't help it." I admitted.

"*Hmpf!*" It was his turn to laugh. "I know exactly what you mean, but I'm not leaving again anytime soon! Not by *choice*, anyway." He added with his hands up defensively. He shook his head just to back it up. "I'm serious Simone. I've already informed the others that alternative arrangements will have to be made if that becomes a necessity again, because our former policy doesn't work for me anymore. We've always respected a person's right to put their own family and loved ones first. I'm no different except that I've never really had anyone holding me here before. Not like I do now. I'll never abandon a *height* in need as long as there's anything I can do to avoid it, and if you don't know that about me then you should." He said seriously. "But I'll never abandon *you* like that again either! I promise you! You are just as important to me now." He stated unequivocally.

He pulled me close against his body and wrapped his arms around my shoulders, swaying comfortingly from side to side. "As long as you still want me here, this is where I'll be." He loosened his arms around me and pulled back to face me once again.

"You can count on that much at least!" He insisted and of course I could feel his sincerity coming through loud and clear and that was the most comforting part of all.

So I knew for sure that he meant what he said, but it was still going to take time for me to get used to the idea that fate would play along. I had to laugh at myself that I needed him to be in my life so badly. I hadn't even *wanted* such a thing a couple of short months ago, yet it had become my absolute peace on Earth. *Damn*, life sure was funny sometimes.

"Aha!" He proclaimed looking over my shoulder. He went around me to open a wide drawer, then triumphantly pulled out the extra-long tongs, the last item on our list. He placed them on the sheet tray that I had loaded all the other utensils on and turned back with a challenging smile.

"Alright, I think that's all we need for right now." I answered with a smirk. "Would you mind taking this stuff out to the grilling area for me? I asked as I gave him a small push back towards the doors. "I'm fine here now. I'm just going to open all the rolls and put them in this basket and then I'll be out. I think I can handle that alone." I joked reassuringly

"Fine, I'll go. But if you're not out there in the next twenty minutes, I'm coming back for you." He warned and of course there was zero doubt in either of us regarding his sincerity that time either. I just laughed and gave him another gentle push.

I tried to focus on one thing at a time. For the immediate future I just had to get through the day. It was a great overall mood and a fun atmosphere which, like the beach, obviously made it much better and much easier to face the fact that I did have to go out there at some point. It was just a LOT of energy to funnel for the second time in as many days and I knew from experience that it would be exhausting. I was proud of myself for not missing any of it though and I was prepared to fully enjoy it. I was simply trying to pace myself.

I really was looking forward to all of it though and that was new for me too. *Big* changes! *Phew!* It was pretty sure that it was all for the better, I just had to survive them!

I made my way outside eventually, when I couldn't put it off any longer and I started to think I was taking long enough for Ethan to actually come back looking for me. I got the volunteer chefs all set up with everything they needed and then I started to wander around. I saw Ethan by the storage shed helping Daniel bring out some more folding chairs for the handful of people that were too old, too dressy, or too pregnant to sit directly on the hill. He smiled when he saw me, obviously pleased that I had kept my word. I grinned back as they turned to make another trip.

Daniel had been helping out since day one when he had showed up to hand over the keys. He just didn't work on specific jobs. Instead he stayed constantly on the periphery. If someone needed an obscure tool that they didn't have on their truck, he would scoot off to one of the various toolsheds and miraculously come back with it. Whenever a big job came up, like unloading the new support beams that required many extra sets of hands, his were right there to pitch in. I knew he was also giving four of the local tradesmen rides back and forth so that they too could participate in the renovation.

By keeping himself from being booked into any specific jobs, he remained available wherever he was needed, whatever he was needed for. That made his presence there as invaluable in the past two weeks as it had been over the last five years. Even without lifting a hammer, I knew he was one of the happiest to see that day come to pass and I was fully enjoying *feeling* him enjoy the celebration. He'd earned it.

Since I was on my own for the time being, I continued to roam aimlessly and watch other people doing the same. We all wandered around while the food cooked, that well-seasoned barbeque smell intoxicating in the summer air. Between that and the giddy atmosphere, it was like strolling around the county fair with its' various aromas and attractions. People stopped off at the new park and watched in awe as the children quickly figured out the new/old equipment.

They meandered in and out of the cottages and planned what week of the year it would be best to rent one or talked about how they could "put the in-laws up there for the weekend of the wedding." Most people entered the main building through the great hall and gawked at all of the improvements there, especially the new gymnasium and dressing/locker rooms that we had added downstairs.

It had been the claustrophobic, basement rec room to craft fairs and AA meetings of the past, but it was another area where we had made some fairly drastic changes.

Gone was the low-hanging, smoke stained drop ceiling. It had been replaced with new darkly stained beams made from three separate pieces of wood that left the inside of the square hollow. We used that space to enclose all of the wiring, plumbing and heating and painted everything else around them white, opening the whole area up immensely. The room was much more spacious feeling after that. The old linoleum was replaced with a new hardwood floor that would allow it to act not only as craft fair area but also as a basketball court or a yoga studio when necessary.

The most exciting part though was the new locker rooms that we had built into the back part of the room, with the men on one side and the women on the other. They met in the middle where the steam room, sauna and whirlpool tub were all installed. It was a very luxurious place to unwind after a workout or in preparation of a special event. The walls were all hand painted by three teenage artists from the local Art Association. They were done in a mural of blue skies emerald waters, and surrounding lush islands. It was the perfect fantasy for the interior space since there were no windows for reality to intrude through so one's imagination was free to take over. Between the steam floating around your ankles and the artificial bird and insect sounds on the surround-sound system, it was practically a fully immersive virtual experience!

We'd had a lot of fun with that area since it was brand new

to begin with. That left us free to set the precedence for it right from the beginning. In fact one of my favorite overall qualities about the remodel as a whole, was that combination of new and old. It was obvious from the shocked looks and the ear to ear smiles that I witnessed when I passed through, that people were enjoying our efforts there most of all.

Eventually a loud air horn sounded off, signaling that the food was ready and people started to mosey back toward the tables to get in line and grab a plate. I stopped by the park to get Liliana and met Ethan on the way back. Liliana had been so excited that she couldn't stop talking about it. I was tickled by it but not at all surprised. Nor was I surprised to find that the whirly bird ride had been her favorite, just like it had always been mine. Something else we obviously shared genetically since I knew not everyone enjoyed or could even *handle* being spun around at such great velocity. It also reminded me of what Ethan had said about how great it must be to share interests, traits and passions with someone and I knew that he was right, even if he hadn't experienced it firsthand yet. Somehow he still understood. He and I just listened intently to her tales of wonder and grinned at each other on the walk over to the food tables.

We filled our plates up, cafeteria style with burgers, dogs and the various pot-luck sides that had been brought for us to choose from. There were so many options though that it made choosing really hard! Thankfully the limited space available on our 9" heavy duty disposable plates made narrowing it down to the top three or four choices a little easier.

Once we had each filled our plates to capacity and added the appropriate condiments, we grabbed napkins and a can of lemonade from the big barrel and found our seats on our blanket at the top of the hill. Marina came over with her plate and sat next to me. Liliana sat in front of us. Ethan waited until everyone else was settled then sat on the opposite side.

We began to devour our selections excitedly while, critiquing and comparing our choices as we watched the sun set over the trees. Eventually we finished, dusk settled and colors finally started to flicker on the screen. Marina picked up her plate and quietly excused herself at that point. We waved a silent goodbye.

The scene opened up on a beautiful sunrise through the trees over Johnson's Pond and I remembered the shoot from that first day with a smile as I moved my plate aside. The camera panned down and landed on Marina, talking about the amazing history of the place and getting everyone fired up. I also remembered that speech from day one. Of course everyone else was seeing it for the first time, along with the creative editing, music and effects that had been added since, and I could feel how invested they all were emotionally and how proud they all were to be there by the end of that very first segment.

By the time she looked away from us on screen and up towards the hill to "*get to work*," everybody present was ready to volunteer all over again!

I watched the way the crowd reacted to the all of the different emotional stories with sympathy, comradery and unconditional support as I felt it all wash through me. I watched their faces light up when they recognized each other, and then *themselves* on the screen for the first time! Jeremy in particular was shy when his segment came on, but I was close enough to tell that he wasn't afraid anymore. There was a newfound acceptance in him by that point that gave him a quiet strength. He listened with everyone else as the onscreen Jeremy told the "public version" of his story. The crowd erupted in applause when his smile faded out onscreen and he stood and took a mock bow as he laughed.

I could feel both his and Ethan's amusement at how close to reality it was for him to play the "actor" in that piece. It was very enlightening in ways I had never gotten to experience before being both "behind the scenes" and "*behind*-behind the scenes" of that as well! I was starting to think that at least in certain situations, maybe all that TV stuff wasn't so bad after all. When you had some sort of control over it, it was actually kind of fun.

A short while later my segment came on the screen and I had to rethink that opinion. I cringed and put my arm up over my eyes while I laughed. "Oh no!"

Ethan laughed too but he didn't let me hide. He playfully held both my arms behind me at the elbows, then he pulled me up into his lap to watch it with him. I sighed and laid my head down on his shoulder and watched it through one eye. Liliana just giggled up at us. Marina's perfectly beautiful face filled the screen as she asked her first question.

"So how do you feel now that it's over? *'Fait au complet?'*" She added with dramatic flair. I gave a sideways smile before I answered.

"I feel good. Really, it's a huge relief to have gotten through such a big job so fast, but as it turns out it was such an awesome job to be on every day that I am actually going to miss it. I'm sure I won't have another one like it for a long time!" I admitted honestly and a little sadly. "The camaraderie on this job was unprecedented in my personal experience. It was a collaboration the likes of which I had never seen before and certainly never had a chance to be a part of! But you were the driving force for that, so the kudos really go out to you!" I insisted with a grin. She was quick to laugh that off.

"I just got a bunch of people together. They all did the work and what amazing work they did!" She added wistfully. "But you, you took a job guiding all those people that many others had merely laughed at due to the sheer scope of it, not to mention the miniscule time frame and resources, and you made it look effortless. I don't know how you do that exactly but thank God that you do because you pulled it off!" She insisted with an off-camera smirk, getting me back a little.

"It was easy, really! Everyone showed up here ready to rock it out and that energy remained intact throughout! So much so, that we even came in a few days early! I mean come on! Even without experience in this industry, you have to know that's saying something right there! That is very rarely *ever* the case, I assure you! A job running long? *Totally!* Happens every day. But coming in early? *Pffft! Almost never!*" I insisted with a laugh and the infamous '4th wall' was instantly broken as every contractor standing around watching the interview could be heard laughing and agreeing with me. Marina looked back at the camera with wide eyes, sharing the moment awkwardly with the audience for a beat. Then she turned back to me on screen.

"Well I personally just want to say thank you for taking my call." She joked at first and we all laughed again. Then she got more serious and I knew what was coming. I buried my face on Ethan's chest and he chuckled low in his throat but he left me be that time.

"And thank you for bringing the ball of positive energy that is uniquely you to this job, and sharing it with everyone here! It was also contagious and it was the best kind of bug one can catch. You brought not only a magnificently laid out game plan of a fabulous overall design, but also the mental fortitude to pull so many craftsman together and to see it through to the end, no matter what! My gratitude for all you have done here is yours forever." She finished emotionally, a catch in her voice at the end. The camera panned back to me at that point and caught me tearing up amidst the sunflowers. I cringed again.

"I'm honored that I was lucky enough to be in the right place at the right time." I said simply, trying to hold the emotion of it all back. I remembered how angry I had been at her at the time for getting all mushy on me, especially *on camera!* But I knew she really meant it so I tried *hard* to forgive her. I still couldn't bear to watch it though and I buried my face deeper into his shirt waiting for the screen to fade to black. It was silent for a minute and I could feel that same rush of emotion coming at me from all around as everyone got caught up in the segment. Those were the kinds of emotional tidal waves that could be *especially* devastating for me!

I tried to just breathe through it, used to dealing with it internally. But then I felt his calm flow through me as his hand came up to gently rub my back. It made it that much easier for me to ride it out.

As I straightened just a hair taller and took another deep breath, I thought about how lucky I was for the millionth time that day. Eventually the atmosphere began to pick up again as the special ended with a video tour of the property as it was "*after*," accompanied by some mercifully upbeat music. I watched with everyone else then until it came to rest on the sunflowers once more in the setting sunlight. As the music faded out, the screen went black and the ending text faded in. It said, "*Coming soon, to a town near you!*" It was meant to be inspirational to the viewers across the nation but it worked on the local ones just the same. As the screen faded to solid black that time, the clapping started.

A few seconds later everyone stood whistled and cheered for what seemed like a very long time and I took advantage of every second of it to calm and reenergize myself. It lasted a few blissful minutes before they quieted down and started to collect themselves and their belongings. The outdoor lights came on then all around us and slowly people began to stand and make their way up the hill.

Back up at the top people mingled by the barrels in the waning twilight disposing of their plates and then wandered over to the dessert table that Marina had set out during the show. The brightly colored strings of lights that she'd hung all around the tables drew the crowd like moths to a flame. Since she'd already seen the whole special finished, she had logically volunteered to cover dessert duty while we all watched it. Ethan, Liliana and I had taken our time joining the throng since were already sitting near the top of the hill and we didn't have as far to go. Eventually we got up and moseyed over.

There was an awesome assortment of delicious looking pastries, cookies and pies to choose from, but they all seemed to pale in comparison to the beautiful cupcakes that were decorated to look like real flowers. They were so vivid and lifelike, they were almost too gorgeous to eat. In the end though, the cupcakes with their creamy looking frosting and decorative but edible leaves, were just too attractive to resist. All three of us grabbed a different "flower" off of the table and then we headed over to the gazebo to savor them slowly. I really loved it there and I wanted to spend a little more time there before we left. Ethan was quite agreeable.

Liliana however, got sidetracked halfway there, which was also becoming quite common. Jeremy had come by again with all the little ones explaining that he had promised to take them up to the park one last time before they went home. Of course when she saw all her old friends and her new ones going too, Liliana wanted to go with. I smiled at Jeremy for being so patient with them all and there was a deep understanding in his eyes that was so much older than his years. He chuckled and gave a half grin but I could feel how humble he was for what he had received and how grateful he was already to be able to give back, in any small way. It was crazy for someone so young to get it so completely and yet in him it made perfect sense.

"Thanks. We'll come grab her on our way out in a little bit." I told him.

"No hurry. I'll be up there for a while." He assured us with an eye-roll and another sideways grin. I could feel how content he was to be back with his siblings and the time spent amusing them was a joy for him at that point. Eventually things would level back out again but everyone seemed to be enjoying the situation in the meantime. We both laughed then waved as we watched them make their way up the hill like some grade school field trip.

I watched them for a few minutes as they traversed through the crowd and noticed Jeremy's small, extra-intense stares from time to time, but only because I knew what to look for. They were much more subtle by then. He had come such a long way. I smiled at Ethan who had waited patiently for me to have my moment and then we walked the rest of the way over to the majestic looking gazebo.

We went inside and sat down on the railing side-by-side. It was such a peaceful and magical place that it really was one of my favorite spots. There were a few other people there already but they were far enough away that it still felt private. We started to slowly peel back the paper and nibble our cupcakes as I talked excitedly about how I couldn't wait to come back and take a series of photos there throughout the seasons. The cupcakes were surprisingly as delicious as they were beautiful but even that could not distract the photographer in me that was so motivated by the natural beauty, from babbling. He was both amused and inspired by my enthusiasm and he finished most of his by the time I stopped talking.

That was only because I suddenly saw a familiar but unexpected face in the mix behind him, and my enthusiasm for being there quickly went away.

Ben?

I realized right away that he looked at the end of his rope as dread began to spread through me. My mind didn't want to accept the fact that he had waited all that time only to show up at that worst possible moment! He was searching the crowd and he didn't look happy. My first instinct was the fear that he was there to try and take Liliana from me for some reason and I was gearing up for a huge scene, but he surprised me again. He spotted us in the gazebo and immediately looked like he had found what he was searching for. He made a beeline right for us. Ut oh.

I was shocked to see him there at first but then I remembered that as a volunteer on the job, even for one day, he would have received an email with all of the relevant info. *Right...* It made sense then but it didn't make me any happier.

As he made his way over to us through the throngs of people I groaned. He looked like he'd spent his night off having a drink or two and a personal pity-party. His eternally perfect hair was tousled and his clothes looked like they had made their original appearance the day before. He had clearly worked himself into quite a tizzy. He walked straight up to us ignoring everyone else he passed. Thankfully *most* of them ignored him in return. He was a man on a mission. He stopped at the bottom of the stairs and called out.

"Ethan Stone. You and I need to talk." He said simply. What the...? That was the most surprising part. He gestured for Ethan to come outside the gazebo with a crook of his finger and then walked off toward the woods expecting Ethan and *only* Ethan to follow.

Ethan looked at me, clearly shocked by the request but he hid it as beautifully as always. I could feel his silent reassurance that "flipping out" a little at some point was completely normal, and he had told me how that was different for everybody. He felt sure that he could handle it.

"Don't worry. I'll just go and see what part of this he needs help with and I'll talk him down. Why don't you go and hang with Jeremy and Liliana for a few, finish eating your cupcake." He suggested in a calming, but slightly protective way. I looked down at it then like it was a lump of dirt and could think of only a few things that I wanted less at that point. One of them being the current situation. He stood and leaned down to kiss me lightly and tried to reassure me one more time. "It'll be fine. Don't worry." Then he headed off into the dark woods in the same direction that Ben had taken.

I wanted to believe him but I was still reasonably nervous. I looked back wide eyed and wary with my thumbnail jammed in my teeth in a vain attempt to contain my frustration.

I walked out of the empty gazebo and dropped the suddenly nauseating cupcake into the nearest trash barrel. Then I headed up the hill towards the park. Partly because Ethan had suggested it, and partly because I instinctually wanted to be closer to Liliana. Just to make sure that she was safe and far away from *whatever* that was, until it was over. I was as oblivious to the crowd then as Ben had been so Marina actually surprised me when she commented in a confidants' tone from right beside me.

"*The ex?*" She guessed with a sympathetic half-smile, nodding towards Ethan's path as he walked off into the darkness beyond our vision. I jumped slightly at first then sighed and nodded grudgingly. We walked up to the top of the hill until we reached the area just outside the park, where I could still see down to the bottom. I stopped there. Marina was surprised at first but looked both ways, down the hill at the view of the path where the men had gone, and beside us where Liliana played happily with the other kids. She smiled back at me then in complete understanding.

We sat on a bench there on the crest of the hill and made small talk while the kids climbed along the jungle gym. I did my best to keep my cool and hold my patience but it started to seem like an eternity and I still had no idea what the hell was even going on! I had no idea what was going through Ben's head or what he had finally decided that had him so upset. I was probably most annoyed that he hadn't even bothered to fill me in first before he went off starting trouble over it! *Grrrr!* The longer I waited, the more pissed off I started to get.

I was tired of trying to keep it all together for everyone else's sake all the time, making sure above all else to never cause a scene or bring unwanted attention upon myself! I was tired of trying to make everyone else happy, just so they would leave me be, when no one was ever that worried about *my* happiness at the end of the day! It was very frustrating when all you wanted was a peaceful life and all you ever got was chaos all the time! I started to breathe heavier as I worked myself up over it. Marina finally spoke up when she saw my nostrils begin to flare.

"Are you gonna be alright?" She asked with a smile and a friendly jab to the ribs in an attempt to break the tension.

I took a deep breath and practiced my calming techniques. I reminded myself that involving all of the townspeople in my private affairs *wouldn't* make them more tolerable. Of that *one* fact I was unfortunately certain, so I pulled it together and laughed at myself a little. "Sure, just give me a minute, or a *decade.*" I joked.

"I'm sure it's not easy, going through a divorce. My parents split up too, when I was sixteen and I know it was tough for us for a while. They just weren't themselves during that whole mess, not for a few years really, but we were a stubborn bunch. Eventually, things settled down and they both returned to normal again, except they were much happier by then, separately. It was actually pretty nice once we got there." She looked at me and smiled sympathetically. "You'll get there too, eventually. If anyone is going to come equipped to help you handle a tough situation delicately and efficiently, it's Ethan." She assured me supportively. I nodded. That seemed to be a reasonable assumption.

"Thanks, I hope so. I didn't come from divorced parents myself, neither did Ben oddly enough for our generation." I admitted with an ironic laugh of my own. "So we don't have that particular skill-set in our arsenal necessarily, but we're learning as we go and we've been trying really hard to keep it civil, contrary to what tonight would suggest!" I laughed again but it was even less humorous that time. "Unfortunately, intentions only go so far. Where we stand at the moment remains to be seen." I added resolutely and then we were both quiet again for a while, just watching the kids as they played.

Liliana and her friends got their next turn on the whirly bird and I watched, a rogue smile tickling the edge of my lips in anticipation as they began to pick up speed. She laughed and held on tight as they spun in pure childhood abandon and I felt it slap into me over and over again as it radiated outward in fast, spiraling waves! They were loving it, and for a brief moment, so was I. It didn't last though.

Just a minute later, Marina and I turned to the sound of Ben thrashing down the path and out of the woods alone. Even from that distance, we both noticed. Luckily it didn't seem like too many other people did. I stood up reflexively. He looked around for a minute, obviously searching, then he looked up the hill in my direction. Our eyes met and he immediately started up.

He held my stare the whole way up the hill but caught me off guard when he walked right past me without ever stopping or looking away. He went straight up to the playground fence and called to Liliana. That was bad.

"Come on, sweetie. Change of plans, you're going to come home with me tonight instead." He said calmly to her. So I had been right in my original fear after all, I realized with a sinking in my chest. Another nightmare come to life. She looked disappointed but I could feel that she was afraid to argue, not knowing the reason for the sudden change. He looked back at me, blatantly challenging me to contradict him for some reason still unbeknownst to me.

"What are you doing Ben? What's going on? *Talk to me!*" I insisted trying to catch up. I still had no idea what was bothering him but nearby onlookers were already beginning to pay closer attention in an effort of their own to find out. Marina got up and walked over to where some other parents loitered by the fence to give us some space and maybe distract a few of them for us at the same time. It was a small gesture but I appreciated it. Jeremy went over and stood near a few of his friends on the inside of the fence. I could feel that he intended to stay in eyesight of us, just in case I needed help. It was sweet but just another reason that I definitely couldn't let it come to that. I tried to take a slow breath before I spoke.

I looked back at Ben where he stood in front of me. He just ignored my questions and continued to glare at me while Liliana slowly came around the fence and took his outstretched hand. "You can't do this Ben. I have rights." I challenged right back, albeit quietly.

"Oh yeah? You know exactly what I'm doing and why. Do you really want me to announce it? Because *I will!*" He threatened, clearly not afraid to up the ante in his agitated state.

I tried to remember to keep breathing and to think before acting but it was all happening too fast. Even though the crowd had dispersed to a certain distance, their attention was even more focused on us than before. I was trying to decide if I should grab her up and face his wrath publically, since I knew he would never *physically* take her from me. Or if remaining frozen where I stood and letting him have his way for the moment so that we could deal with it later, *privately*, was a better response. I was temporarily torn between the two.

As they walked past me though I snapped out of it. I calmly grabbed Liliana's hand to stop her. He glared back at me again but my look of immovable determination portrayed my lack of patience nicely and he wisely backed off for a second while I knelt down to say good night.

Regardless of my rights or my anger with him at the moment, one thing made my mind up for me like it always did. I knew I didn't want to see Liliana upset by her parents making even more of a scene than we already had, so I knew I had to let her go for the moment, *again*. It pissed me off even more that I knew the only reason he actually stopped and waited was because he was so sure of that instinct in me.

He knew I would try to avoid a scene at all costs, that I never wanted to rock the boat unnecessarily, even more so right then than usual. He counted on that predictability. As long as he acted crazy first, I would have to play the sane one. One of us had to, to keep things in check, at least from her perspective. He knew that and he was using it to his distinct advantage. I realized then sadly that Ethan had been right about that aspect as well. It was a cheap cheat and it pissed me off but I knew I couldn't show it, not there. Not then. So cheap or not, it still worked.

I hugged her tight and whispered in her ear that it was alright for one night. "No one's mad at you and you didn't do anything wrong, okay?" I assured her. "Daddy and I just need to work something out but that's between us and I don't want to do that here. So why don't you go ahead and go home with Daddy for tonight and we will have our extra night together one day next week instead." I promised looking up at Ben with unbendable determination clear on my face. "Don't worry about anything in the meantime, okay?" I requested since her concern for both of us was stronger than her own disappointment at the moment.

She nodded but her wariness was far from gone and that bothered me the most. I was so mad at him then that I almost changed my mind on the spot. Before I could act on the impulse, I gave her a long reassuring hug and a kiss goodbye. That made her feel at least a little bit better. It was all I could do at the moment, but it helped. I stood up then and stared at Ben while I took a deep breath, trying to contain it all. He reached down and she took his hand again. Then he turned on his heel, tightened his jaw and walked away.

I was standing there completely dumbfounded for a few beats after he left. It was like being carjacked by the police. You knew you had been wronged but when it was by someone that was supposed to be the good guy, what could you do about it? Those *options* that Ethan had made me look into earlier made a lot more sense then. There weren't a lot of them though and it wouldn't be easy to exercise any of them either, so I really wasn't encouraged much by what I had found out. My main goal had still been to somehow keep the peace. *Yeah, no problem……that was going swell…*

I was so cold at that moment standing alone on that hill that it suddenly felt like the middle of February to me rather than August.

Ben sped down the long entrance road and pulled out onto the street with a small but noticeable squeal of burning rubber. I was relieved to see that only a few heads turned at the unexpected noise. I couldn't stand the suspense anymore. I got up and waved to Jeremy and Marina from across the park. They gave a sad "*I'm sorry I had to see that*" face and waved back. I was sorry too.

I took a deep breath and headed down the hill and across the lot, towards the path. By the time I entered the woods, the darkness in front of me was all consuming. The woods appeared to be nothing but a vast, black, empty stillness. I knew that wasn't really the case though. I knew they were very much still inhabited. I certainly didn't need to *see* him in order to find him in the dark. His emotions burned as fiercely as a wildfire. I could simply *feel* my way!

I approached slowly, sensing that he had intended to cool off some more before talking to me. *Ohhh*, that was not a good sign, I thought dismally. *What the hell had happened?!* I walked over to the nearest tree and leaned on the low hanging branch while I tried to gear myself up for whatever had caused our latest catastrophe. I stared up at the moon through the trees, putting off the inevitable for a few more beats. He stood facing away from me and held the branches of a neighboring tree so tightly that I had real fear for their future viability.

I could feel the levels of barely controlled anger, protectiveness, and most of all frustration rushing off of him in one jumbled stream. It coursed through me and it did little to comfort my already tumultuous emotions. I waited as patiently as I could for him to speak but when he finally turned to face me, I was afraid of what he would say. I let go of the branch and stood square on my feet when I felt it coming. He didn't make me work for it for once. As soon as he felt okay to talk he looked me right in the eye and let loose.

"He asked me flat out if I was going to help you hide her from him if he doesn't play along, if and when she gets sick." He informed me while still staring unflinchingly.

"*Ahhhhh.*" I said with a heavy sense of sudden understanding. "Well at least I get it now!" I declared angrily as I sank down onto a nearby rock. He looked back at me and waited for me to explain my outburst.

"He took her home with him." I provided angrily. He sighed, obviously even more disappointed. "He's clearly just trying to make a point. I could have fought him on it, but he knows how much I've always hated to make a scene and with this latest revelation, he knows that's truer now than ever before! He wasn't afraid to take advantage of that fact in order to get what he wanted either. You were right about that." I informed him with my frustration barely contained. I sighed in disappointment and Ethan picked up the conversation, thinking out loud.

"I don't know exactly what he managed to dig up on me or *heights* in general, but something definitely spooked him. Maybe he's just been hearing things around town about this mess with Jeremy. I don't know, *but I will find out.*" He promised angrily.

"I tried myself from different accounts and through different search engines." I shared trying to be helpful. "I googled everything that I could think of. I didn't find much that was of any use at all! I don't get it!" I shouted exasperatedly. He took that in and nodded.

"There's not a lot to find." He insisted. "I know there are a few unflattering reports out there though that have leaked from individuals that we've "saved" *heights from* over the years! They tend to give us the worst reviews." He joked humorlessly. "We have people who check the net and all the social media sites daily, working hard to keep it clean of our *activities*, but information moves fast these days. Just like us, once information shows up anywhere, someone else can copy it. Even if you delete it afterwards once that happens it's too late. It still exists, *somewhere.*" He shrugged his shoulders helplessly and I could feel that he wished he could control that particular weakness more. I didn't hold it against him though. I knew there was no way to stop information from traveling at the speed of optic light, even *mis*-information! In fact that often traveled even faster!

"The trick is in convincing people which sources to believe." He continued practically reading my mind as always. "The few statements I've been shown over the last few years that badmouthed *heights* in general were built on just enough truth to make the tale hold water with troubled family members or friends. But they were otherwise horribly skewed, widely biased and entirely one-sided. We assume they are also probably largely planted by the government agents themselves in their ongoing efforts to discredit others in their fight against them. Again, depending on which sources you believe."

He added sardonically.

"In the end whatever the source, it's information just the same and it's out there for anyone who manages to look hard enough, anytime we don't catch it first. We do our best, but there will always be something that gets missed or something new that gets added tomorrow." He said resignedly. "Unfortunately, struggling family members are always the first to search out that false info."

"People like Anderson know the difference between the crack pots and the honest folks crying out for help. They know which stories to check into and what to ignore as complete hyperbole. They've been at this for a long time. We're starting to catch up. But regular people like Ben can't know the difference between the outrageous lies and the slightly stretched truths any more than he knows up from down right now. That's when bad information is the *most* dangerous!" He said looking back up at me intently again. Anything he finds in his current frantic state of mind, he's going to believe lock, stock and barrel, especially if it helps him to demonize or discredit this new and unpleasant truth." He said without holding back. Then he really let me have it.

"Although we both know that he's not even really that far off base on this one." He admitted honestly. "That was the hardest part of all this time around." He stared at me openly and I remembered that straightforward look from the time that we had discussed Jeremy's few possible fates.

"Our intentions are never to be malicious or predatory in any way and we don't separate families unnecessarily." He explained honestly. "That is never our goal. You know that. But since our priority is always to put the *height* and their needs and their personal safety first, there also always remains the chance that it could come to that. I decided that it would be a bad idea to lie to him about that Simone. That won't work in this case." He didn't flinch or look away when he told me that part.

"I wouldn't swear to him that it wasn't a real possibility and he got pretty pissed to say the least." He chuckled but it was cold and I could feel how seriously he was taking that new revelation as he looked me in the eye.

"I swear I didn't try to antagonize him!" He assured me. "Normally I would do whatever is necessary to placate the anxious *norm's* and just worry about settling things down around the *height* for a while first and foremost. But this time a temporary fix wouldn't have worked." He explained. I could feel how sure of that he was but I still didn't understand why yet. Thankfully he continued to explain.

"Anything could happen with Liliana still and we don't know when, but we do know that he's not going anywhere. Whatever happens, he is going to be present for it. As long as you are a part of my life, then he will be too. I have to deal with that fact realistically. Since I'm not planning on an immediate future without you in it, I felt it was smarter to just accept his presence and deal with it accordingly by being honest with him right off the bat." He explained and it started to make sense. "Unfortunately, honesty is harder. He doesn't want to hear the truth right now, but it will be better for him and *all* of us in the long run." He added.

I knew what a skilled liar he could be when he needed to be but I also knew that he was right, and that it wouldn't matter. Ben would certainly stick around long enough to find out the truth and there would be no going back and repairing the rift once Ethan had been made out to be a liar in his eyes. It would be too little, too late for Ben to rethink his opinion of him after that. I could see it all quite clearly. Ethan was right. Better for him to offer up an unpleasant *truth* now and still have hope that by at least by having been honest, he would be trusted to be honest in the future, when it mattered. I didn't necessarily need Ben to like him, but I did need Ben to *trust* him. *We* needed Ben to trust him. And for that, honesty was key. It was brutal, but it was key.

"I don't know what his next move will be now but I know that it'll be a defensive one. And I'm sorry but it will be bigger than taking her home early on 'your night.'" He insisted meaningfully. "I know what he's going through right now. He's scared. He feels like he's losing control over someone he cares an awful lot about and he's not going to take that lying down. I wouldn't either. I get it. So we are going to have to be very careful for a while now because he's likely to strike out at any opportunity in his present state of mind. He'll be thinking that the best defense against the unknown will be a good offense. I can't predict what he'll do, but trust me when I tell you that he's going to do *something*. Most likely it will be some sort of scenario to try and undermine us and/or your reputation in general, just because that will make him feel safer. All we can do in the meantime is try to be prepared." He stared at me intently again.

"I'm so sorry Simone. It was not my intention to make this harder for you. I'm afraid I still owe you an apology because even though I really had no choice, that's exactly what I've done." His confession had me thinking back on my conversation with Marina from earlier. Maybe he wasn't necessarily going to make my transition easier after all. *Hmpf.* I still couldn't fault though him for knowing what would work, eventually. He was only human, and I knew he had done the right thing. I knew it because just like always, it was so damn hard. He wanted to make it better, I knew that. Unfortunately for him it just wasn't going to be easy. I could tell that he had already come to terms with that. He was waiting for me to catch up.

"We have to be ready now for whatever comes next. *You* have to be ready for whatever comes next." He insisted unequivocally.

I stood there and looked back up at him, comprehending his meaning completely. My head meanwhile felt separate from my body and my hands and feet were totally numb.

I could not lose her completely. I could not survive that. It was simply not an option. Ethan was right about me in that respect as well because that is the one thing that *I* would also never take lying down. I would give up *some* things if I had to, to make life better for her, but separating us entirely would never be better for her and I would never agree to that. I would fight until my dying breath to be a part of her life.

But Ben knew that too, of that I was also sure. So what *would* he do to try and stop me? The possibilities that flew through my head all seemed ridiculously far-fetched but I knew that sadly they were all within the realm of possibility once he deemed himself officially on the "other side."

I stared off into the stars as I pondered the possible new future with Ethan that I had barely begun to see glimpses of. It was beyond amazing and I wanted that in my life too, truly! But did that mean that I could handle the circumstance that came with it, or that I was ready for what came next? It was a good question but I was still waiting for a good answer.

It didn't matter whether I had one or not though. Life didn't ever simply "*pause*" itself and wait patiently while people adjusted to its manipulations. It went right on with all of its' former plans and continued to push and pull us all in as many different directions as it wanted to, or as it *needed* to, to fulfill its own purpose.

I couldn't help thinking though, that if we ever finished the quilt work of life blending that I was constantly dreaming of, with all of the amazing people involved, the finished product had the potential to be a truly beautiful thing!

As I returned mentally to the current stressful and downright scary reality, I wondered seriously if that was something that I would ever see come to pass.

Chapter 31

I had tried to call Ben repeatedly over the remainder of the weekend once we'd all had a chance to calm down a little, but it had gone straight to voicemail every time. I wasn't surprised by that but I *was* annoyed. I refused to leave a message or to text him about something so important, and he would know that so he had effectively cut off all communication.

I thought about going over there and trying to get him to see the reasoning behind Ethan's stance but I was fairly sure no good would come from discussing it further until he had at least come to terms with the whole *height* situation in general, which I still wasn't convinced he had done. Beyond that, he then needed time to process the latest revelation and decide how he was going to handle it. I knew that, but I can't say the wait wasn't killing me! It was like Déjà vu, *here we go again...*

Find out something life changing, deicide as a good person to tell Ben, beat down the fear and anxiety to finally accomplish it. Then wait in tortured silence for his next unpredictable reaction. First with me, then with Ethan. It was becoming a regular thing and I didn't like the pattern. It always ended with me requiring a patience that I still didn't fully possess.

I tried in earnest to use what newly acquired strength I had gained in that area to keep things in perspective in the meantime, but that mostly just meant that I spent a lot of time walking around sighing and growling under my breath. By late Monday afternoon Ethan had had enough of silently watching me suffer.

"Come on." He said resignedly pulling me up off the couch. "Let's go get a burger and a beer. We need a change of scenery!" He insisted and although my heart wasn't in it, I couldn't argue that it sounded better than what we were currently doing.

"I don't know about the burger, but I'll take the beer." I half-agreed as I followed him to the top of the stairs where we both slid our sandal's on and headed out.

He drove to the Tavern and parked in back. We went inside and sat at his table so we wouldn't have to wait for mine. I scanned the room as was my habit by then looking for hostile natives, in other words Dani. Ethan caught my searching glance and answered my unasked question.

"She's not on tonight." He said easily. He gave a wink at my expression of feigned denial as he went to get us our beers. I sighed in relief, knowing I could at least enjoy my meal that I was suddenly, *miraculously* in the mood for.

I hadn't eaten much since the "incident" at Breezey and I knew that was half the reason that Ethan had suggested the "change of scenery," to one where the food always smelled so wonderful. He wasn't always as smart as he thought he was necessarily when trying to "influence" me, but he was certainly sweet. I laughed to myself though when I thought of him hearing me refer to him as "*sweet.*" *Hmpf.* That would get a chuckle out of him for sure!

A moment later he appeared carrying two beers then returned to the kitchen only to come back with the burgers a few minutes later. "Okay, they're not Laurie burgers, she couldn't make enough to keep up with what we go through here a week unfortunately, believe me I checked." He said with a laugh. "But chef does a pretty good job. I won't enter any competitions against her mind you, but when a Laurie Burger's not available, I'm pretty happy to come here for one. Check it out. Let me know what you think. Your opinion means a lot to me." He said sincerely as he slid one plate over in front of me.

It was served open faced, which I personally liked so the lettuce didn't wilt on the way over to my table, but that's just me. It was covered in melted cheese that was both orange and white. There were a lot of potential combinations there that would make me happy. It was accompanied by a mound of golden brown hand-cut fries, that fancier places liked to call "pom frites," and they proudly took up the other half of the plate.

It looked picture perfect and it smelled heavenly so I decided at that point to let my taste buds be the judge. I placed just a few rings of purple onion on top of the cheese. I know it's a "*red*" onion but let's face it, its purple and I was in the mood to call a spade a spade. Over that I stacked the fat, ripe tomato slice onto which I sprinkled a little salt. Then I topped that with the still fluffy green-leaf lettuce. I slathered a little of the mayo on the top bun and pressed it down.

I picked it up and looked up to see Ethan watching me with barely contained anticipation. I grinned, flicked my brows and took a bite, managing to get the whole thing in my mouth with just a little bit of wiggling. He laughed at my gusto and I smiled back at first but then the flavors hit me and my eyes rolled back in pure bliss!

"Wow! Yeah, not bad at all!" I agreed wholeheartedly through a mouthful of food. "My burger buds will definitely not go unsatisfied in this town, one way or the other!" I declared happily as I chewed. He was very pleased by that. Both by the fact that his cooks burger measured up, since he knew I would never lie about such a thing, and by the fact that that I was eating enthusiastically again. He tried to hide that part from me underneath the rest of it, or at least not put it out there right up front, but I knew that he knew that I knew his motives. *Phew!*

He just grinned and dove into his own burger at that point and we ate in contented quiet, the only sound the chatter in the background and the soft music of the jukebox.

We were so enthralled in our meal and our own mental conversation that neither one of us noticed Dani until she was half way over to our table.

"Well, I wasn't expecting to see you here, but now that I

think about it, it's kind of perfect." She stated cryptically startling us both, which was *really* rare! My last bite stuck in my throat as she stood there glaring at Ethan and left me thinking that I may never let my guard down again! I had no idea what was going on but I could tell that she had made a decision and I felt like it was *big!* I was instantly worried that whatever it was, it didn't bode well for us. It didn't take her long to make that decision crystal clear.

"Here." She said coldly, slapping an envelope down on the table. Ethan didn't touch it at first. Only stared down at it and waited.

She was annoyed by that, but not enough to ruin her excitement completely. "I was going to leave these for you but I find there is some satisfaction in handing them to you in person." She allowed. "Consider yourself served, *boss*." She said sarcastically.

"I'm officially suing you Ethan Stone, for half of everything that you inherited from *our* grandfather, Augustus Stone." She stated flatly like it wasn't life changing to both of them. "And half of everything that you have acquired since then using that money." She added as an afterthought like it was simply his share of the lunch check.

I could feel the shock set in and the sense of gravity leave his body. I was familiar with the phenomenon, but not when sensing it in *him*! I held tight to his hand and tried to somehow physically anchor him, and to convey the sense of peace that he always imparted on me in similar times of great stress. I wasn't as good at it as he was though and it sucked, but I refused to give up trying. I held his hand tighter and spoke the obvious question for him.

"What are you talking about Dani?" It was the question I was feeling from him the most so I went with the simple bits to start off.

"I'm talking about The Tavern, the long list of Stone family properties, as well as the "*additional assets*" that I have found but can't quite explain just yet, *everything*!" She said in the end happily.

I could feel the wheels turning in Ethan's mind so fast that that old adage about seeing smoke come out of his ears seemed completely plausible to me! He picked up the envelope then and opened it. I noticed that she immediately smiled. We all knew what that meant but for whatever reason, he stopped fighting it.

I looked over his shoulder and saw that the reason for the suit was listed as the fact that she was supposedly his "biological half-sister" on his father's side, "Joseph Stone's *daughter*!" And therefore legally entitled to half of the Stone Family inheritance!

Um, *Bomb... - ...shell*! Whhhhhaat?!

I could feel that Ethan was in a similar state and trying desperately to digest what he was reading and what she was saying, but apparently it was his turn to experience some of that "overload" that had become so very popular in my world lately. Dani took that opportunity to finally have her say.

"He may never show his face back here to fight you on that clean sweep of an inheritance that you pulled off, but *I* sure will!" She insisted with conviction. "My mother certainly didn't want to talk about Joe very often, but she did tell me exactly who my father was. There was never any secret there. There didn't need to be because she had told me from the very beginning that my daddy hadn't wanted kids, ever. But she had wanted me, so she left him and never told him. She always said that I could try to find him anytime I wanted, but that he would only tell me the same thing she had. Since he never tried to see me or talk to me even once in all my life, I figured she was telling the truth." She admitted logically. I could tell quite easily though how much that had hurt her. Ethan was less stunned, more interested at that point, so he didn't interrupt her.

"I had a lot of time to myself growing up, with no siblings and only one parent who worked two jobs for as long as I could remember, to find out everything I could about him. And about his *son*, the only child he knew about or ever laid claim to." She shared as her jealousy became glaringly apparent once more. "At least you had his name. And for better or for worse, you had him in your life growing up. He was a real person who existed for you! For a long time I thought you had it all! I carry just as much of his blood in my veins but I never had any of those things." She shared sadly.

"I know I shouldn't have let it bother me, but as a child, those feelings are not necessarily rational. But don't worry. It didn't last too long since it became exceedingly clear once I got old enough to start doing some *real* digging, that my mother was right. He hadn't wanted you either." She threw out casually with a cruel laugh.

"Yeah, it wasn't too hard to find out how much that first born son had suffered at the hands of the system and his classically neglectful parents in the end, since it's all a matter of public record. So maybe you didn't have it so much better than me after all. That made me made me feel better for a little while, I'm not going to lie." She admitted looking wistfully up at the ceiling.

"Then, for like a minute I actually started to feel bad for you. Even started to think that maybe we were more alike than I had thought after all, that maybe we could be some kind of family to each other." She trailed off in the end when she said that and it was clear to me that that had been her real goal at some point long ago, before it all changed to rage. *That* was where her resentment came from! *Aha*!

"Then of course came the stories of how you ended up on top all over again when you inherited *everything* from another family member that I'll never get to meet, good old grandpa Stone." That's when I knew there was actually something to *inherit*! Because Lord knows there is absolutely *nothing* of any value in Joe's name! Never was, never will be." She confirmed with a harsh laugh and I felt the jealousy again.

"So you had a tough childhood. So what. You weren't alone mister!" She declared angrily with laser-focus eyes, never realizing how many meanings those words took on. "Look what you have now." She insisted. Again I could feel her jealousy, but I could feel her admiration too. She secretly knew how hard he worked and how selfless he was. That knowledge was warring with her internally throughout her tirade.

"Anyway, I already did the DNA test. All I was waiting for were the results." She insisted coldly and I knew that was a lie. She had been dragging her feet, hoping for a different outcome for some time. I wasn't sure what exactly or why, but that much was clear. She tried to play it off. "These things are incredibly slow unfortunately if you haven't murdered anyone or anything." She tossed out sarcastically. Ethan wasn't quite so stoic after that though.

"You did what? You ran a DNA test on me? How?" He asked immediately afraid of what she may have given out and to *whom*!

"Yes. I did." She answered bravely. "I won't say that it was easy. For a small town dude, you sure are *way* too careful about leaving personal things lying about, but I eventually found a way." She provided slyly.

"I had my mother send me her DNA sample in a kit that I provided, to eliminate my maternal DNA. Of course providing my kit was easy-peasy. Yours took a little longer. But perseverance paid off and I finally got it, and proof that you are the person who provided the sample." She added with a satisfied, child-like smile.

"Now it's all about the results, which are 99.999% conclusive and will stand up in any court in this country *'bro.'* And those results state quite clearly that I share a paternal link with you that proves once and for all that I *am* in fact a Stone, and that as such, half of all of this is rightfully mine!" She said looking up and all around us.

"We can do this the hard way, or the easy way, but one way or the other I promise you, we *are* doing this!" She insisted heatedly. Then she was suddenly quiet again.

"It's about time for *my* happy ending!" She declared full of pent up emotion, then she turned and walked out the door.

As we both sat in stunned silence thinking about what had just happened, it all started to finally make sense to me. The sense of longing, and wanting to *"belong."* Even the possessiveness and the jealousy that she had directed towards his family, which I had mistakenly thought was misplaced, made perfect sense when you realized that she considered herself a sibling and wanted to be a part of the comradery that she saw him share with them. It was never about being jealous of me romantically, and taking it out on them. It was about me being the final straw when it came to him having relationships with everyone but his one true *relation*, his own sister!

Of course he never knew he *had* a sister, so it was hardly his fault, but one could understand then at least where her emotional motivation had been coming from.

It made me want to go find her and hug her and tell her that yes, life sucks sometimes, but that it would be okay. That it wasn't her fault he didn't know her and that it wasn't his fault either. If they took the time to talk, I knew they would be able to work it all out, but of course she didn't give me or him that chance. I wasn't foolish enough to think she'd listen at the moment either. *Ugghhhh!!* Not again... That was also a recurring theme lately. *Sigh.*

It was funny how easy it was to see the resemblance between them, once the truth had been pointed out. I *never* would have simply guessed at it before! It wasn't the kind of thing that I could tell just by knowing people. *Thank God!* I could just imagine the amount of people who would request a free and easy paternity test if that were the case! But knowing what I did then about them both, certain things did stand out. Like the dark, silky curls and the intense look that could slice a heart in half, as well as the smile that could raise you up on a cloud!

Of course I wondered then if they had more in common than looks, having come from the same *height* father, but I thought back to our earlier conversations about her and was pretty sure that wasn't the case.

"You said she's a *norm*, right?" I asked looking for clarification. Ethan still hadn't spoken much yet himself. His emotions were running through him at a mile a minute.

"Yes. *Hmmm*. That's interesting, but it's not that unusual. If it's all even true, although it's not a hard story to believe." He stated simply before getting lost in his thoughts again. I was familiar with the scenario though so I didn't hold it against him. I just went back to my own internal pondering while I waited for him to finish processing.

Of course, all siblings are different individuals, each a direct result of a slightly different combination of the same starting pool of genes. People rolled those dice with countless genetic sides every time they came together to create a new one. Obviously you can expect that siblings, creations from similar starting pools, would share some traits, but not all. They weren't identical after all. *And* I reminded myself, they were only *half*-siblings at best.

I started to wonder then on a side note, how many more children my parents would have had to have, to get another one like me. The possibilities were staggering. Could be hundreds, could be one. *Truly*! DNA was funny like that. It was completely rational and entirely random at the same time.

We paid our bill and went straight home after that. It was a silent, but emotion-filled ride! We climbed the stairs hand-in-hand and went straight to bed. We stripped down to our underwear and I threw on a tank top then fell into bed. We simply held each other tightly without speaking or taking it any further. It felt good. Lying together like that in the stillness and serenity of my bed there on the farm was a safe place like no other, for both of us. We each felt it separately, but together it was even greater.

It was a closeness that was much more intimate than sex. Even though sex with him had introduced me to a closeness that I hadn't known previously, it was more than that. It wasn't about that wonderful and mindless release that we found so easily and so fully with each other that made life more tolerable in general, rather it was about the complete mind*ful*ness that we shared subconsciously on multiple levels. It was refreshing in its ease and the amount of strength that we each received from it.

I rested against him at times, and held his head in my lap and stroked his hair during others. He enveloped me completely with his limbs for a while, wanting to be as close to me as he could get. Later when we got too hot, I draped mine freely over his while we enjoyed the cool breeze of the fan.

It was a very long, and restless silent night, but that unspoken comfort had been exactly what we needed. In the end it was enough to get us through it.

Chapter 32

After the completely unexpected "Dani" fiasco, I was happy to try and ignore the situation with Ben for another day just to try and catch our breath in between blows. Ethan had been in research mode all morning trying to find out all he could about Dani's claims which kept him fully occupied. I completely understood and tried to help in any and every way possible. But in the end he really just needed time to get the ball rolling and I was most helpful to him just then by letting him do what he needed to do. I was fine with that too, but unfortunately it left me free to obsess about my own issues and my patience didn't last the whole day.

By lunchtime I'd officially had enough. I grabbed the phone one last time and decided right then and there that if he didn't pick up that time, I was going over there. I was tempted to continue to use the drama with Dani as an excuse to ignore it all, but I knew I shouldn't let one unexpected situation keep me from resolving another. It was a cop out at best, let's be honest.

It would be nice if life only threw things at us one at a time, but for some damn reason that was just never the way it worked. Besides, I thought optimistically, maybe I could resolve at least one thing and take that off our plate to make the rest slightly easier to focus on. Wouldn't that be nice? Just the existence of the possibility gave me strength.

It was as if he had felt my determination telepathically because he picked up on the second ring. I was incredibly relieved at first that he was *finally* going to talk to me, but it didn't take him long make his intentions clear once and for all and then I wished he hadn't.

"Hi!" I'd said at first, clearly surprised that he'd answered.

"What do you want?" He asked bluntly without any formal pleasantries. I ignored his initial attitude and tried to start things out on a better note than that.

"I'm glad you've finally calmed down enough that we can talk civilly." I said giving him the benefit of the doubt. "We have a lot to discuss, but I wanted to start by seeing what day next week would be good for me to take her, to make up for the other night." I explained, thinking it was the least volatile of the possible topics. He answered quickly but he wasn't going along with my plan.

"There isn't one." He answered like it was no big deal. I was instantly confused.

"You're not going to be taking her at all." He insisted coldly, no beating around the bush. I went from slightly confused, to petrified in a split second! Again I felt just like I was on and old amusement park ride, only it was less of the exhilaration and much more of the terrifying feeling that I was getting that time.

It reminded me specifically of "The Turkish Twist." It looked like a giant washing machine and it would spin madly until the gravity would shift and the floor would suddenly drop out from underneath you, relying on the centrifugal force to keep you safely plastered to the wall! You knew at that moment that you should be falling, but somehow you stayed suspended in place. Your brain knew it wasn't right and not to trust it though, and *that* is where the fear comes from.

Just like that ride, there was suddenly nothing beneath my feet to support me, but disbelief held me frozen firmly in place. I knew at some point reality would set in and drop me to the ground.

"*What?!* What do you mean?" I asked incredulously while his attitude started to sink in. I didn't want to believe it though. I couldn't accept that he was really going to go there! After every effort we had made to avoid that ugly, *ugly* place! I tried to put a stop to it as fast as possible, before it could become real.

"Look Ben, I let you push me around the other night to keep

the peace in front of the Liliana and the crowd. You know that. But do *not* make the mistake of thinking that you are going to do that to me on a regular basis, because I *promise* you, I will *not* stand for that bullshit!" I shouted in response.

"Well legally you could try to stop me. As you said, it's well within your rights." He answered much too calmly. That was far scarier than if he had yelled. "But if you do, you should know that I have no problem bringing up the fact that I'm only keeping her from you because I don't feel she's safe around your new "boyfriend." I could suggest to the police, or maybe even the FBI, that they should take a closer look into his activities, just to be sure." He suggested. "Would you like me to do that Simone?" He asked in a falsely innocent tone.

As pleasant as his voice was, the threat was still quite clear. I didn't need my empath skills to know it either. I also knew the FBI would just love to have an unrelated opportunity to build a case against Ethan and take him cleanly out of the equation once and for all. Of course Ben had no idea what he was threatening to destroy. How could he? I took a deep breath and let it out slowly, before I tried to speak.

"You don't have to *do* this Ben." I insisted calmly in a last ditch effort to stop it! "It's really *not* necessary, I promise you! Please just trust me on this! I don't want to have to fight with you over her, but I *will* if you leave me no other choice! I will not let her go through that alone because of your small-minded fears! I won't surrender quietly this time either and make it easy for you, I'm telling you that right now! Listen to me when I say this, Ben!" I insisted vehemently! "I've done more than my share of that already and you know it! But I'm done. You don't want to test me on that." I replied with a confidence in my own threat that he surly wasn't used to.

I had always been the "reasonable" one, the one who preferred to make love rather than war, the first to suggest a compromise. But things were different then, in so many ways! He had pushed me back as far as I was willing to go on that topic. The wall was at my back and I wasn't going, *couldn't* go any further. He was going to have to find a way to deal or it was truly going to get ugly, and not just for me for once!

"You can see her anytime you want to Simone." He replied sweetly, which made my blood run cold. "I'm not keeping you from her, just her from you! That just means that you will only see her here, by yourself and with me present for the time being." He stated and my stomach dropped even further at just the thought of that situation becoming my new reality.

"Know that this is your choice Simone, not mine. As long as you're with *him* and involved in all that stuff, I'm not going to let you take her and sit here worrying each time that I'll never see her again! I mean *why* would you even *think* that I would be okay with that?!" He demanded finally letting some of his anger out. I sighed at the fear that it portrayed then tried again, as sanely as possible.

"Listen to me! It doesn't have to be that way Ben. You're getting ahead of the situation here. Just because something is a *remote* possibility does not make it a foregone conclusion! When you find out there's a 2% chance of rain, you don't go and cancel the whole God damned parade, do you?! Nothing has happened yet to make that a real life issue and it doesn't have to!" I shouted heatedly. Then I wisely tried to reign it in again.

"We can all *choose* to cooperate instead and handle this together! That is still a viable option and with our situation being the way that it is, I don't see why you would want to take that option off the table." I challenged right back.

"How would you feel Simone, if it were you?" He asked quietly and for the first time I could hear the insecurity more than the anger. "How would you handle it if I told you that I had decided to be a volunteer National spokesperson for PETA, or that I had signed up to join "World Vets" without telling you? And that if they approved me and I got called, I might move to South America with her for a while with no notice. Nothing definite, but it remains a *slight* chance." He proposed tauntingly. "How would you react to that?" He proposed frustratingly.

"I know you, your face would drop every time I drove away with her after that like the world might end while you weren't looking and it would be all my fault!" He accused.

"I've seen that face and I've dealt with the guilt that comes with it each time I've been the one to *"force you to go through something horrible,"* because it *always* felt like it was my fault, everything! No matter what the issue was. With your 'preexisting' condition, you automatically always got to play the victim and I had no choice left but to play the realist and be the hard guy all the time! So that's what I did!" He admitted defensively.

"You know I used to believe in the possibility of there being more to the world than met the eye. I used to be excited by the notion that everything wasn't always, 'what you see is what you get.' Then you came along and proved it to me. I was scared to believe what you were telling me, but also intrigued by the unknown at the same time. I know how all that goes." He said, as if he understood how I felt about Ethan because he had "been there, done that."

"But you embraced that "other side" so completely, that I had no choice but to go back the other way just to balance it out!" He declared bitterly.

"Well it gets tough after a while to be the reasonable one and take the heat for every responsible thing in the real world time after time, especially when there's so much of it that I really can't control! I mean I'm just as much a victim of our circumstances as you are in the end." He admitted in a rare and candid vulnerable moment.

I realized at that second that we'd had more in common in our relationship than I had ever understood before, than *either* of us had understood! *Lot of good it did us at that point.*

"I don't have, nor will I ever have, the freedom even as a divorcee, to *really* go and do whatever I want to with my life. We can get divorced and agree to live separate lives, but we're tied to each other forever now by our child and I have tried since day one of our separation to be okay with that. I knew when I married you, that I was agreeing to tie myself to all that came with that, and when we had a child together I knew that 'for better or for worse' we would truly be in it forever. We made those choices together and we have to deal responsibly with the aftermath of that not working out as planned. That's hard enough." He insisted logically.

"Yet now you're asking me to tie myself to *him* too, along with all this craziness that he's fed to you, and quietly accept that otherwise you may see fit to steal her away from me completely! I'm sorry but that's bullshit and it's finally all just too much! Even for me! I tried! I tried as hard as I could to be agreeable about everything as it is now, but I just can't do it anymore!" He stated despondently.

"You on the other hand, can do what you want with your life Simone. Go ahead and have every crazy conspiracy theorist in it that you want!" He added cuttingly. "You actually have that freedom at the moment, so good for you." He accused bitterly and I saw that situation from the other side for the first time too.

It really took me back for a minute. Even though I couldn't deny that I had a lot more "alone time" than he did currently, I instantly and *inherently* rejected the label of what I had as *"freedom."* Or I would have anyway, but he didn't wait for a rebuttal.

"I'm not going to stand idly by and let you do that with hers." He declared. "No more inserting your psychosis upon her and calling it random coincidence because it suits your latest agenda." He spit out. He was reaching by then, trying to convince himself that it wasn't real and I knew it, but I didn't know how to stop it.

The coolness of his tone made an actual shiver run down my spine. It was a convenient excuse for him in the current situation as usual, talk about creating a reality to suit one's own needs! It may have almost been a valid argument too, except that he knew me so much better than that. He seemed to come back at that thought without my having to voice it. With our history, it was implied.

"I trusted you Simone. I was counting on that trust and trying just as hard as you to make this work. Don't try to say that I wasn't!" He argued. "I've never acted out of anger or done anything simply just to hurt you. I've never tried to restrict your visits or to keep her from you before, despite my reservations." He insisted heartily.

Hmpf. It had been a convincing and touching declaration, up until the part about his *"reservations,"* but I expected his callousness on that subject.

"I've tried to respect how much you love her and the fact that you let her stay with me for *her* sake and not your own." He allowed, and that much I had to admit, was a shock. It was the first time I had ever heard him acknowledge it out loud. It was surprising, but still too little, too late. I refused to give him full credit for that statement so long after the fact.

"I know how hard that was for you and I never took that for granted." He insisted as if he had always been nothing but fair, like it would be ridiculous for me to state otherwise. I just sat there in shocked silence. "So why would you allow yourself to be in a situation where you might end up doing those things to me? It's like a knife in the back after all of my efforts to accept this situation and it makes all the work I've done feel wasted." He said, turning it around so beautifully that I almost felt bad for *him!* Almost.

"Most of all though, it's just not like you and it makes me think that you're not thinking clearly right now. Until you are, I don't want Liliana out of my sight. That's all there is to it. If you want to go back to the way things were before all of this bullshit, get out of that town and away from him and his little cult, let me know and we can work something out, over time. Until then, I'm not budging. Take me to court." He insisted calmly.

"The negotiations can be as private or as public as you want them to be, I'll leave that part up to you." He taunted. "But that's where I stand." He said immediately resounding in my head as a direct echo of Dani's current threat to Ethan, then hung up. My only thought when I set the phone down was, *this can NOT be happening!!*

Why did he have to try and make me choose!? No one should ever have to choose between the two halves of their own heart! It was unnecessary and it was just crazy!

I exhaled loudly and shook my head in disbelief. He really was counting on the fact that I didn't want the police or the Fed's snooping around Ethan to keep the ball *and* control of Liliana, firmly in his court. I realized at that moment exactly what I'd done. I hadn't shown myself to be a good co-parent by keeping him in the loop as I had intended. No what I had inadvertently done was hand him just enough information to be in complete control over all of us. *Why was I so stupid?! Errrrrggghhhh!!!!*

I put the phone down and rubbed my eyebrows relentlessly, trying to relieve the pressure that had been building behind them since he'd finally started talking.

Ethan found me a few minutes later staring blankly at the wall and asked me what was wrong. It was worse once I said the words out loud.

"He's not going to let me have her this week." I said speaking slowly and unemotionally, like I was in shock. I guess I was.

"In fact, he's not going to let me have her at all!" I added with more feeling, mostly surprise. "As long as I stay here, and with you, he's not going to let me near her outside of his presence." I told him matter-of-factly. I felt his disappointment come across instantly at the fact that we would have to do things the hard way after all, apparently all around.

I tried not to let that train of thought register but it was no use. Even as he was still trying to come to terms with his own latest dramatic turn of events, I could feel his deep concern for me and for what he knew I must be feeling.

I didn't want to look at him and have to see the pity he had for me as well as feel it, and I didn't want to feel his remorse at all! But he felt it for bringing all of that into my life, and so I had no choice but to feel it with him anyway.

Except that I knew he hadn't really done that at all. The situation had existed in my life as long as I had. He had just made it all finally make sense. That wasn't something he should be sorry for in my book. I turned to look at him then to reassure him of that but the combination of his pain and my own became too much to overcome. I held his face and my heart poured out through my eyes. There were tears, but no sound. I gave it a second to pass, then I choked it down and took a deep cleansing breath.

"Let's get out of here, okay?" I requested spontaneously. "Can we go for a ride, please? Car, bike, skateboard, helicopter, I don't care. *Really*, I don't! Just take us somewhere that we can get out of our own heads for a little while. Can you do that for me?" I begged without moving anything except my mouth and my eyes.

He reached out for my hand and I felt his answer 100%. I

sighed in relief and grabbed my slip-on sneakers and my keys and I followed him outside. We took his car to camp and from there we took the path that led behind the cabins and down to the river.

We went down the stone steps, across the sand and up to the dock. There he operated the keypad remote tucked up inside the suspended structure to lower a boat from the protective housing down to the water. He climbed in and unhooked the chains then raised them back up out of the way. After that he turned back and helped me to climb onboard.

He reached under the seat cushion and pulled out two travel sized bottles of red wine. He poured each one into a red solo cup that he got from under the next seat over and handed one to me. I took a long and grateful swallow then held it tightly with both hands as I sat heavily in the swiveling bucket seat next to his. He sipped his own cup then placed it in the cup holder by the throttle. He climbed around for a few minutes, readying things while I sipped. I normally would have tried to help, even though I didn't have a clue, but he purposely chose to leave me be rather than ask, and since he made such quick work of it, I didn't argue. I knew how lucky I was that he had those things available to him and that he was so willing to share them with me.

I thought about Dani then and wondered uselessly just how many of those things she had found out about, and how long they would *remain* in his possession. By the time I finished that thought he had finished preparing to shove off and he sat down in the Captain's seat next to me. He took out a pair of sunglasses and put them on. Then he took another pair from the console and handed them to me. Oh well, just like everything thing else in life there was no guarantee that it would be there tomorrow so I was extra thankful for that fact that we had it right then.

When he turned the key to start the boat, the radio turned on as well. It was tuned to an oldies station and another Bob Segar classic was playing. It was fitting and I smiled as "*Turn the Page*" rang out from the speakers and my whole being began to unclench. He turned it up then pulled smoothly away from the dock and the cover of shade and out into the glaring mid-day sunshine. My hair flew back away from my face with the breeze and I sighed in relief for both the movement of air and the sunglasses.

Eventually my skin began to warm back to a "living" temperature in the warmth of the sun, despite the refreshing breeze. The shock was beginning to wear off, but the reality wasn't much better.

We didn't talk for a long while and it was perfectly fine. He drove the boat expertly through the markers, slowing in the no-wake zones and accelerating in a most satisfying manner in between. I had no comments and I had no complaints. My mind was free to float along the surface of the water as we skimmed by too fast for any foreign emotions to register. It was the perfect escape, even on a beautiful day on a crowded river and despite the difficulties that came with it, I still couldn't believe my good fortune where he was concerned.

I knew that life with him was probably always going to present me with some pretty serious obstacles, just like the ones we were currently facing. But he made everything hard about my life seem worthwhile so I was prepared to take on those obstacles. I figured that I might as well get used to it and go ahead and get started on actually doing it. My fight for Liliana was as good a place to start as any since it just happened to be the most important fight of my life.

I knew that I had Ethan at my back and on my side and that reliability was not something I was willing to give up or take for granted. I knew how devoted to me he was already and I was eager to be able to help him in return for a change. I didn't know how yet but I knew that I would do whatever I could to help in his defense against Dani and to protect everything that he had accomplished over the last ten years. Even as I thought about it, my resolve in that area added to my building strength.

By the time he dropped anchor in the middle of the river, near an outcropping of rocks I felt measurably better, despite our bleak immediate futures. Not great, but better. More resigned, less in denial. He refilled my drink and we went to sit on the bow to enjoy the sun. The days were already getting shorter and I knew from experience that soon the amazing weather would be nothing but a fond memory. So I was grateful for both the mental reprieve and for the warmth of the sunshine on my skin. I thanked him and I proposed a toast to both.

He clinked plastic with me and we drank. Then he held me for a while in silence while I tried to hold myself together. The current situation was not what I'd had in mind for us, *any* of us, and I needed to rethink everything. Ben had played many different roles in my life since first entering it, but every one of them had been important to me in some profound way. I couldn't help thinking that the incarnation of Ben as "*The Evil Ex*" might just be the most powerful of them all though and the one that finally takes back everything he ever gave me. It felt like he wanted to, *including* Liliana! I knew he couldn't really do it, but the fact that he *wanted* to, scared me to death just the same.

I couldn't let him do what he was trying to do. But how was I going to stop him without him making life even more difficult for Ethan, at the worst possible time! The last thing he would need during a public court battle would be the very kind of trouble that Ben was currently promising to deliver! That was equivalent to risking the welfare of every other "camper" past, present and future by default! I couldn't let all of that be ruined by one stupid, ugly divorce any more than he was okay with it all be destroyed by a previously unbeknownst, disgruntled, long lost half-sibling. Either scenario seemed ridiculous after everything he'd been through to get where he was. But how did I stop Ben from ruining me without endangering something so vulnerable and so important? I absolutely hated the idea of giving him the power to manipulate me in that way but what could I do about it? I was sure there had to be a way to make him see reason again, I just had *no* idea what it was!

Those worries dominated my thoughts then but they were not alone. They were accompanied by the ones where we still had to decide what to do if and when she got sick. I did not foresee him being very cooperative anytime soon and I couldn't even bear the thought of not being there for her during her *heightening!* I remembered what that had been like when I went through it and I vowed to myself right then that he would need *a lot* of people to keep me from her during that! Not that he should *want* to! That was still my greatest point! If only he would listen!

Would he ever understand that? I practically deflated as I exhaled with that thought and Ethan smiled over at me. Then he tried to reassure me in his usual confident tone that we would deal with it. I wanted to believe in him but I was also scared of what that confidence may mean at the same time. That didn't mean I wouldn't utilize those extremes to reach an end if it came to that. I was actually more afraid because I knew I *would*.

It was the possibility of it becoming *necessary* that made me feel uneasy. Having that to rely on, at least in theory, was great. In actuality, the thought of ever really needing it was *terrifying*!

Once a choice like that was made, where could we possibly go from there?! What kind of a future could we possibly have after that?

He sensed my course around the universe of anxieties and as was typical, attempted to put a stop to it.

"Sometimes in life..." He started as he unfolded himself and extended a hand to me. "You have to stand up..." He added while lifting me to my feet. "And say to the world, "This is where I draw the line. What's over there is yours. What's over here is mine. These are the few precious things that I will fight you for. Sometimes, that is the only way that the world knows when to stop pushing you." He finished with a knowing grin. Then he drew a line across the deck with his bare toe.

"Then you have to back it up." He added meaningfully, right before he dove over the line and off the side of the boat into the slow moving current. I stood up and looked down at him when he came back up and shook the excess water off his head. He grinned up at me and waited for me to decide if I would follow his lead. My lopsided cannonball made it clear pretty quickly. My spontaneity and bravery made him happy and we laughed as we splashed around.

We swam leisurely for a while, then we climbed back up and laid on the deck to dry in the sun. It was like a mental time out for both of us and for once there was zero guilt. I felt like we both really needed it.

I also knew it wouldn't last. Everything was fleeting, the good and the bad. It all passes to make room for whatever is going to come next.

He had finally managed to convince me not to spend all of my time worrying about it though, when in return he promised to try and do the same. It was a tall order for both of us but no one knew that better than him and I, so there was no one being duped by the difficulty of the situation we were promising to attempt. That dual acceptance of the challenge without fear or reservation, in the end, gave it strength as well. We made the trip back with a lot lighter load.

The clouds began to roll in right as we got off the river, but thankfully the rain waited until we were back at my place to start. We had a quick bite of simple pasta, and then we called it an early night. I was physically and mentally exhausted and for once, so was he. As we ate, a light rain began to fall. We cleaned up to the hypnotic sound of it pelting the windows, then took a short, no nonsense, just-wash-the-river-off-of-us shower together. We threw clean shorts on and in my case a tank top, then we slid into the newly crisp sheets with still wet hair. I turned on the fan then slid up against him. He wrapped his arm and one leg around me and pulled me in.

I listened to the light *tap, tap, tap* on the glass and I tried just to think about the positive things we still had to be thankful for while I waited for sleep to come.

So naturally that is when everything got decidedly worse, like "this *really, seriously* can't be happening" worse!

But of course, right?

Chapter 31

Sleep came quick but it was not peaceful. It was also deep and full of REM state activity, but not even *remotely* restful. What should have been a good nights' sleep for both of us turned into a whole new hell all its' own. It was hard to believe that life still had a few more hits for us but unfortunately it was true. Since by the end of that stormy night, that distant "possibility" of her becoming *heightened* that we were all hypothetically arguing about how to handle, had officially become a certainty to me once and for all when I saw it in my dream.

Dammit! Son of a bitch, God damned fucking, *mother fucker!!* And I'm *not* sorry! Bring on the best curses you can think of, I guarantee I screamed them all like a drunken sailor with an untreated case of Tourette's! I tossed and turned in between fits of swearing and the sounds of distant thunder. It didn't matter though. It didn't help to expel the anger I had in me at that horrible truth. It was only in my dream that I thought my protests were real and my screams didn't stop it from happening. And I knew full-well that they wouldn't.

Even while still in the grips of the dream, I knew what it was, what *kind* of dream it was. I was always very lucid during those dreams, almost like a separate spectator, consciously watching it all unfold from afar. That's basically what it was, me watching a future event from another time. I'm somehow able to tap into certain major events in my life while sleepiong, where the space of passing time between them doesn't matter.

I believe it's because the fabric of life is not always smooth and flat. I feel like sometimes it has ripples and in that ripple, some of those faraway places will come together and touch. They are connections that I can't always explain, but I will see it from both sides of the ripple at those different times in my life and recognize it for what it is from both sides, so it makes a small amount of sense to me but it's hard to explain. I knew exactly where that ripple had taken me, I knew it was already as certain to be real as what I had eaten for breakfast yesterday, and I knew what it meant.

I also knew that after that night, I would be able to see it all again every time I closed my eyes and I was aware of all of that before I even opened them. It was a definite part of my life story that I was seeing and nothing I could do or say would change it. Those particular moments were extremely clear, physically and emotionally.

That unfamiliar and oddly inexplicable pain that she was feeling for the very first time! That gut wrenching childhood fear of the unknown. The frustrating confusion, hers, mine *and Ben's*, along with Ethan's struggle to help us all get through it intact. I had seen it all in shattered bits and pieces. Not the circumstances surrounding it that would spell out the time and place, just the fire of pain burning brightly within the center of the situation. I knew by then that the vagueness of those small details was due to the fact that those were the types of things that *could* still change. But only the props and the background, never the players or their lines.

I had cursed and fought in my mind and begged the powers that be to stop it and to help her, for *Christ's sake!* It didn't do any good. I didn't really expect it to. I knew I was helpless to change it. My heart made me keep trying anyway throughout the entire dream, to change the way it would go, to go back and try and change the way it would end, which I could sometimes do if I worked hard enough. It didn't always change the outcome in real life, but I would wake feeling a lot better. It was fruitless then, but I kept trying to refuse to accept it. Despite all my efforts to be in a grassy field somewhere flying a kite with her, the pain and the gut-wrenching cries kept coming through!

I woke to find myself sobbing all over Ethan and banging mercilessly on his chest as the thunder cracked outside. He hadn't tried to wake me, poor thing. He had just held me as carefully as he could until I stopped swinging and stopped crying and finally looked up at him in sudden recognition. He sighed and released a huge gust of air in relief then as he fell back against the headboard, physically exhausted. I had just stared blankly for a moment as it all sank in.

My immediate reaction was remorse at having taken it out on him. My spirits fell even further, if that was possible, when I realized that I had inadvertently shared my pain with him *physically*! Especially as I started to notice various, red welts all over his body from the assault he had endured. Even in the dim lighting, I could tell he would have a few bruises tomorrow. Of course all I felt from him was a tired calmness. No regret what-so-ever, and zero anger.

I tried to process how amazingly selfless he was as I sat there listening to the rain, much heavier than before. My next emotion was reflexive and it was a giant wave of relief as it dawned on me that it had all been a dream! Even though it was one of "*those*" dreams, it wasn't *really* happening! *Not yet!* I took a few calming breaths, trying to acknowledge that small blessing. *Deep breaths…* It still wasn't real. Not yet…

The next thing I felt though was his deep sadness for me coming across as he saw me processing it all and I felt that he knew exactly what I had been dreaming about. I startled and inhaled sharply and even though a large bolt of lightning crackled at that exact moment, it had nothing to do with the weather. Once it became a shared conscious thought, it instantly made it real again and a few seconds later I started to cry once more. It was a lot quieter but I was fully aware that time so it was harder for him to watch.

He didn't run away from it though. Instead he reached out and pulled me back against him. I laid my head against his chest and stared out at the wind driven rain and the fantastic light show. I grieved into the early dawn hours while he held me silently and tenderly. He never pushed me to talk about it or made any attempts to stop me or to try and cheer me up, for my sake or his own. He simply laid there with his arms wrapped around me until I didn't need him to anymore. It was a small thing and yet somehow it made all the difference in the world.

I appreciated it immensely, but once both the weather and I had been calm for a while, I found I couldn't stay still any longer. I sat up and sighed, kicking the sheet angrily off of my legs. He didn't react. He stayed put and waited to see what I needed. I looked back at him and smiled weakly. I knew how very lucky I was to have had him there with me through that. I had lived the alternative for quite some time by then and the last thing I wanted to seem was ungrateful. That would be impossible. I looked back at him and tried to somehow vocalize it.

"Thank you for staying with me through all of that. I'm really, *really* sorry that I hurt you, but also that you had to see it at all." I admitted, slightly embarrassed.

"I'm completely fine, trust me. Nothing a little ice and ibuprophen won't fix." He insisted with a small chuckle. "I only let a few of them land anyway. I mostly just tried to keep you from hitting anything hard enough to break a bone on." He replied with an honest smile. "Again, not a totally selfless act." He added with a wink.

"And why would you be sorry for being upset? You have every right to be upset. This is a big deal and you're allowed to react accordingly." He answered without hesitation. "I can't think of one place that I would have rather been." He added seriously. As his sincerity washed through me backing up his statement nicely, my anxiety melted away again.

I was still too upset to be good company though. He was amazingly supportive and understanding but I wasn't going to get over the shock that fast and I was hoping to spare him the encore performance. I reached out and held his face affectionately with one hand. Then I kissed him lightly.

"I don't know how I would have gotten through this night without you. I will be forever grateful to you for your unflinching support. I can't tell you what it means to me." I insisted honestly then I sighed. "But I think I need to be alone for a while. Just to sort out my thoughts somewhat. Is that alright?" I asked with a weak smile using our old inside joke.

"You *know* it is." He assured me confidently with his usual easy grin. I smiled a lot bigger then at how much better his comprehension made me feel. I knew he could use some time on his own to investigate Dani's claims further anyway. I kissed him once more and smiled weakly in appreciation. I laid my cheek against his for a moment as I soaked up the beautiful, loving waves of understanding and support that he was sending. Then I got up and went to get in the shower.

I could feel the change when he allowed his own situation to come closer to the surface since he would be on his own for a while, but he was mostly still just sad for me. He watched me go wishing he could do more, but he didn't try to stop me and I appreciated that at that moment just as much as I had appreciated him staying earlier.

My eyes were red and swollen and the cool water felt tremendous running over them. I stood there for a long time just letting everything run freely through my head. All the worries, all the fears, all the little snapshot previews that I had gotten of what was to come.

The crying, *--Flash--* the picture played alongside each memory. The vomiting, *--Flash--* The *fever.* *–Flash--* All the things that I was sure wouldn't change, flashing brightly in my mind's eye within the fuzzy circumstances surrounding them.

It was a different kind of pain, having been through that particular hell and having to watch helplessly as someone I loved went through it too. I cried some more but my tears mixed so completely with the running water that they were virtually invisible and the salt was rinsed away before it could do any more damage to my skin, making them seem less real and somehow less satisfying.

I remembered feeling that pain, her pain, and recognizing it but then realizing that I was feeling it secondhand! *–Flash--* Seeing the pain and the blame in Ben's *tired*, accusing eyes. *--Flash--* It was too much to take! I understood all too well what she was suffering but I was powerless to stop it. That certainty knocked the wind out of me as a parent. My own suffering was one thing, but not being able to stop hers was a true nightmare for me and it was really hard to know that it loomed so definitively in our future.

Where once there had been many paths with countless forks at each end laid out before her, there was only one path left after that night. And much like the main pathway at The Tree-fort Village, that path had been poured in concrete. Granted, it made it easier to focus from there on out on how to help her, finally knowing for sure. However it was hardly a comfort to have her destiny so firmly set in place while she was still so young. *Especially* not when her father and I were still so firmly at odds about how to deal with that particular future.

I could only hope that we would find a way to work out a truce before it was too late, and that she would still get to turn out to be the amazing person she was always meant to be, *heightened* or not. She deserved that and I swore then and there that I would do everything in my power to make sure it happened, somehow!

Eventually, I'd had enough and I got out. I threw a towel lazily around my body but I couldn't be bothered to get another one to twist my hair up in, so I left it to drip dry on its' own. I was drawn to the kitchen by the smell of fresh brewed coffee. I sighed contentedly and headed that way. When I reached the counter I saw a multivitamin and a note next to the pot. Even though I could see almost an hour had gone by, I noticed that the pot was just finishing the brewing process. I smiled weakly as I picked up the note.

I'm so sorry that you have to go through this, but please don't worry so much. She's going to be fine. She's tough. Gets it from her mother.

I know you won't eat anything now but take this at least, enjoy the coffee, and call me when you want to go for a hike.

-E

Hmpf, it was typical Ethan and I loved him for it. Especially the fact that he'd said "*when*" and not "*if.*" I was starting to actually kind of like how well he knew me. It was slowly becoming less of a threatening facet and more of a comforting one.

I added some sugar and coffee mate to my cup then took the multi-vitamin and washed it down with the coffee. After that I went to stand in front of the windows while I sipped and stared as mindlessly as possible out into the peacefulness of the freshly washed landscape.

I tried to take deep breaths and let it all go for a while but the newly upped seriousness of it had a way of sticking to the ribs. The current situation between Ben and I was my worst fear realized. We each loved her too much to ever let go completely and we both knew that. If we didn't manage to share the parenting somehow, we would end up tearing each other and everything around us apart for sure! If it ever came to that it would not end well for anyone, least of all Liliana! That I was sure of! *We* had talked about it! We had both agreed that we could not afford to let that happen. I couldn't help mentally adding, especially *not anymore!*

We had to find a way around it. That was one fight that I could not lose. Not right when I knew she would need me the most. If he managed to keep her away from me during that, I would be all done. Even with Ethan in my life to try and hold the pieces together, I would not survive that. At least not intact. What would remain of me if that happened, even I would be afraid of.

Never fear the well-adjusted human with a village standing by their side. They will always feel the weight to do the right thing, and usually they will. But you should rightfully quiver in the presence of the misunderstood, miserable loner who feels like they have nothing in the entire world left to lose! *They* are the most dangerous people on Earth! That was how I feared I would end up if that ever happened, and I knew those fears were founded in reality.

I could not allow myself to become that completely broken soul just yet though, not while she still needed me. And I knew that even if by some remote chance I managed to win the battle, there would be so much collateral damage to all parties involved that it wouldn't feel like much of a victory. So we just could *not* let that happen.

There was Mare, Mrs. Negativity, right there lurking over my shoulder, promising to hold me and rock me back to sleep if I would just lay down with her and ignore everything. But I knew better than to choose that option by then too. No matter how tempting it may seem to simply hide from it all at the time, I finally understood that that never had a happy ending either. Things almost never "*worked themselves out.*" She knew she couldn't hide that fact from me anymore and that knowledge took even more of her power away. At some point, I may even stop referring to her in the third person, but I wasn't ready for that permanent separation just yet. It still helped to have someone else to blame things on sometimes. *Hmpf. In... out...*

I lasted long enough for my hair to have dried without my noticing, but that was about it. It was too hard to keep every frantic thought from barging in on every tranquil mental reassurance I gave myself so I finally sighed and realized that I'd had enough alone time. I needed to get out, I needed to *move!*

I called Ethan and he was there in under five minutes appropriately dressed. It was clear that he had been ready and waiting while doing whatever it was that he was doing. I just smiled at him in appreciation and he winked. I grabbed my keys and two waters and we left out the back sliders. We hiked for a good half hour before we spoke a single word and it was perfect. After my fifth or so deep sigh, he could tell that I was finally ready to talk about it.

"I know you're devastated by this news and I understand completely. But if you think about it, not that much has changed really, other than your own surety of a possibility that we considered highly likely to begin with." He offered trying in his own cryptic way to point out a less traumatic view.

"I mean, you're not really *that* surprised that Liliana will in fact turn out to be a *height*, are you?" He asked gently but honestly. It was pointless to pussyfoot around that truth by then and we both knew it. He was just trying to help me embrace it.

"*Hmpf.* I guess not." I admitted with yet another sigh. "But the confirmation was harder to take that I ever thought it would be, I can say that much!" I confessed unashamed. "I thought I was prepared for that scenario, but *boy* was I wrong!" I admitted with a sad chuckle. I gave another deep sigh. He looked over at me and I felt his warmth and reassurance reach out to me an instant before his hand did the same.

"I know." He agreed a little too easily. My instinct was to be disappointed in myself for that, but I could feel how commonplace my misguided assumptions were in his experience. It was clear even before the understanding smile, that he didn't hold it against me.

"All I keep thinking is that, if I took it that bad and I thought myself prepared, how on *Earth* is Ben going to react?!" I asked, clearly in fear of the possible answers. He understood completely but again his experience kept him from getting riled by it.

"I don't know yet but I know we *will* find out." He joked with a silly grin "And whatever the answer is, we will deal with it. I also know that she is still going to be okay, and eventually Ben will too. More importantly, so will you." He asserted with his usual confidence firmly in place.

"At least we have some forewarning now." He pointed out optimistically. "That's huge. It should also give us an idea how much time we have to improve upon the situation with Ben. Granted, he's not in a great place at the moment, but it's a start and that's something, believe me! I still think we just need more time and we will get him onboard." He assured me. They were small things but they did help. I tried to be obliging and also to focus on the good parts. He was more than helpful with that.

"And don't forget that we have an extraordinary team of people here ready and willing to help her." He insisted calmly. "You don't have to "search out" anything, if and when or after-the-fact! We are here and we will all do what we do best and *she will be just fine.* I know she will!" He promised and even though I knew he didn't have any prophetic dreams to base it on, I could feel how much he believed it. Whether that was just in an effort to make me feel better or if it was a genuine confidence born out of experience I had no idea, but I wanted to latch onto it either way.

It would have been nice if I could have really believed it. Unfortunately there were simply too many "unknowns" remaining for that assurance to take hold. Like whether he would even still have all of those things with Dani unknowingly trying to take them away, or whether either he or I would ever get anywhere *near* her when she got sick! That was the scariest thought of them all and I couldn't hold it in anymore.

"What if you're *not* all there to help her Ethan? What if Dani manages to find out about Camp and everything that entails? I don't see her mentally separating your personal assets from your business assets. Maybe there won't be any Camp or anything else by the time she needs it!" I proposed near panic.

"What if that doesn't happen and Camp is just fine but I can't make him listen to reason and he keeps her away from you?" I choked out. "What if he manages to keep her away from *me?!*" I shouted, giving voice to that absolute worst fear.

"That is not an acceptable option for me Ethan, you have to understand!" I insisted passionately. "I can let her go to a certain extent for her own good, but I can't lose any more than that, I can't! Not one more inch! It's too much! Especially not when she needs me most because I'll be the only one in her life who knows what she's going through!" I added thinking back painfully on the fever and the crying that I had seen. Just the memory made my heart wrench. "I've been forewarned for a reason! I can't let him stand in the way of that!" I insisted heatedly.

He stopped walking and pulled me to a stop beside him. I looked up and his determination was fierce enough to block out everything else for a beat and a half. He waited for me to stop panicking and take a breath, then he responded just as passionately.

"We are not going to let that happen. *I promise you Simone!*" He stared at me unflinchingly while his seriousness washed over me. I wondered where his intensity on the subject came from and he could see that easily. He tried to explain.

"As long as *I* exist, Camp will exist, in one form or another. If Dani manages to disrupt the operation by taking away a few of our material things, then we'll replace them, and if necessary even rebuild. She can't take away the people who care about this cause as much as I do and that's all we need to continue on." He stated simply.

"As for him keeping her from you." I felt his intense emotions there register and surprisingly they were even stronger! He shook his head back and forth with determination. "That's not going to happen either because I won't let him hurt you anymore than he already has. That's it. I'm drawing the line here. That's all of you and your heart that he gets to have. The rest is mine. "He insisted passionately. "And I'm prepared to fight for it." I couldn't help the joy I felt at that. He was prepared to back it up.

"Do you remember when Ben and I first met?" He asked gently.

I thought back on that day in the parking lot at Breezey. I was confused by the question at first but I nodded.

"Do you remember that *not so proud* moment of mine, when I was momentarily overcome by that overwhelming, shall we say *negativity?*" He asked with a humble smile. I remembered it then, the fire that had burned so hot that it had startled me momentarily, but he had extinguished it quickly and thankfully I hadn't seen anything like it since. I certainly hadn't forgotten it though. I nodded again.

"I know you assumed that it was simply jealousy towards Ben for being with you, and I won't deny that you're basically right!" He said with a self-deprecating laugh. "But not entirely. Do you want to know what I was thinking about that set me off?" He asked me quietly, daringly and finished with a cheeky grin. He was being intentionally playful but I could feel that it was much more serious to him than that. I hesitated for just a beat, afraid of where it might go since he was clearly taken back by it. My curiosity got the better of me as usual though and I nodded again anyway. All but daring him to verbalize what he was insinuating. I took a deep breath and let it out.

"*Tell me.*" I requested bracing myself. The honesty that followed in his answer was raw and unexpected.

"I was looking at the features of his face, the cheekbones, the shape of his brow, the color of his eyes... and I realized just how much Liliana looks like him. Then I acknowledged to myself that it was because she *was* a part of him as much as she was a part of you. I had only ever seen her as yours before that moment and it was incredibly stupid of me." He admitted with a smirk.

"I had left myself open for a rude awakening and I got it! I was immediately, *incredibly* jealous that he had gotten to create that beautiful little human with you! *Hmpf.* Such an amazing thing, and he got to do that, with *you!*" He looked me in the eye again then and I could feel our earlier conversation about kids of his own swirling around in his mind with everything else. "I'd never been that jealous before in my whole life Simone, and certainly *never* about that!" He shook his head in disbelief. "Another curveball and I had never seen that one coming." He joked.

Well *I* was surprised too! Holy cow! It was the most emotion I had ever heard or felt from him on the subject! He had obviously done an amazing job of keeping that very real desire tamped way down after the initial shock. He wasn't done.

"Of course the next thought that I had was an unwanted vision of him actually "*making*" that baby with you and I thought I would rip the pockets off my jeans trying to keep my hands inside them!" He admitted shamelessly. "So in my defense, it was really a double whammy." His jaw clenched and he took a few slow breaths to calm himself but then he laughed again.

"I'm not an overly boastful man Simone, but I can usually say I handle things a lot better than *that!* It was a new and unexpected experience for me and I needed time to wrap my head around it just like anybody else. That's really why I'm so understanding in dealing with other people in turmoil." He joked playfully. "Because I'm so damn used to upheaval myself that I can easily relate." He laughed again more softly.

"I'm prepared to handle it a lot better now. I know Ben's basically a good guy and even a great father. As much as I inherently want to dislike him, I actually respect him immensely for that." He admitted grudgingly. "My point here is not to try and demonize him." He clarified and I could tell that was important. He stared down at me for a beat, his emotion building.

"My point is simply that I wish with all my heart that it had been *me* instead!" He stated intently with an honest shrug of his shoulders. "That you had never met anyone before me and I had never wasted my time with anyone before you." He sighed then. "I know that's not realistic. I know that we are who we are now because of where we've already been. But I can't help wishing that things had been different." He admitted wistfully with a completely unguarded heart.

"You're right, then we wouldn't be having these issues at all." He added with a melancholy smile. He hardened considerably after that though before he continued. I could feel his strength on the subject building as well and I knew better where it came from then.

"It is what it is now and we *will* deal with it. He may have had the privilege of creating her with you, I can't change that. But I am in your life now and I will not stand by and allow him to take her away from you! That I *can* do something about." He assured me with a confident stare that made me quiver all the way down to my kidneys! It was both petrifying and soul warming at the same time.

"I may not be Liliana's father, but I will never let anything bad happen to her. I simply couldn't bare it. I will always protect her and love her like she is a part of your own *actual*, precious beating heart, because I know that's exactly what she is." He assured me easily with a simple smile.

Coming from anyone else it all would've sounded so horribly cheesy and ridiculously contrived, but of course he really meant it and his deep sincerity was like melodious poetry made up of all the perfect sounding words. It washed over me completely and comforted me deeply.

"Look, I know Ben's not going anywhere, but neither am I. And on that note, if you do have any more children, I'd like to officially go on record as saying, that I would treasure the opportunity to be present for that miracle from the start next time around! It would be amazing to watch a *height* grow up loved and properly cared for and never have to *save* them from anyone!" He added vehemently with a wink.

"I look forward to that, but that doesn't mean that I forfeit the right to be there for this one. I will be there for her and for you! Her welfare and your own are like mine and your happiness, you can't have one without the other. They are all inextricably linked now so I will always protect them both." He insisted wholeheartedly. "If nothing else, you have to believe in that!" He insisted quite persuasively.

Well I guess I finally had my answer to at least *one* question! He did want children! *With me!* On purpose! And he wasn't afraid of them being *heights* like us, in fact he welcomed it, saw the ability we had to do a better job of that as their parents than your average, unprepared *norms*. Wow! I allowed myself to accept it as a real possibility then and the elation that filled me was ridiculous! It wasn't even real yet, just an idea floating in the ether, but it was the declared intention that made a humongous difference and also made me so happy that all I could do was smile hugely in return.

"I will do whatever I need to do to protect *everyone* in this little make-shift family of ours, and by everyone, I mean Ben too. But until he comes around, we're not going to be doing things his way, I can assure you of that." He insisted with a quiet confidence.

In that exact moment I felt his role change from "supportive boyfriend" to "professional champion of *heights*" and instantly my mixed feelings about that returned. Of course a huge part of me was extremely grateful to have him and all of that on my side, but I couldn't deny that when it came right down to it, I felt guilty about putting him in between myself and Ben. Even though the whole *height* situation put us at a hugely unfair *dis*advantage to begin with, instead of evening things back out like you would expect, with Ethan on my side somehow it still felt like cheating. Ben had no idea yet what he was up against and because of that there was still a faint impulse left in me to protect him.

That was a fatal flaw of mine though, a direct condition of my empathic abilities which ensured that I always felt bad for the loser in anything, that proverbial underdog. It was a big part of how I ended up where I was to begin with, because I always forgot to feel sorry for *myself* when my own feelings were involved and I would leave my guard down while feeling sorry for everybody else. I almost always paid the price for that. I did hope that having Ethan on my side from there on out would at least keep me from inadvertently hurting myself like that so much. That I would gratefully take without feeling any guilt at all.

"I appreciate your support Ethan, I really do. But how can you promise? I can feel your confidence but how can you be so sure? You can't *know* what will happen." I pressed logically. His confidence only grew.

"No, but *you* can! And you already do!" He said intently with a slight smile. "We know that you saw her being sick, so we know that you *are* in fact going to be there! Don't we?" He asked simply, waiting for me to catch up. I gave a deep sigh at that, my first real exhale in days, as it finally sank in. He was right as usual but I could not be happy about it that time around as the reality hit home.

I was still beyond worried. My vague and fuzzy visions were still not a guarantee to me that I would really be *fully* present, but I decided to try and stay focused on the positive and to keep an open and rational mind as long as humanly possible. It was hard but its' one redeeming quality was that it was better than the alternative. As I felt the clean air blow through me both physically and mentally I looked up and smiled at him.

"I love you, you know." I stated plainly. I still hadn't really said that to him straight out and never quite so succinctly, but I honestly felt it was the best way to sum up everything I felt just then.

"I have no idea what's going to happen next. *Hmpf*! But I love that the one thing I do know is that whatever happens, you will be there with me!" I admitted humbly as I smiled back up at him. He grinned back and I felt his response physically as well.

We didn't need to say it to each other at the same time. I think we both valued the rare and unprovoked declarations much more than the automatic response type. With our nonverbal communication and *confirmations* so incredibly clear, we really didn't have the need for the extra verbal validation as much as normal couples. It was still *stated*, don't get me wrong, we weren't any different there. It was just different in its format and it was surprisingly fun to explore that in a whole new way too.

Of course the settling of one anxiety quickly gave leeway to the next to rise up. I sighed as I thought about it. "Now I just have to tell Ben." I lamented. "If I go and see her there with him, then I will have to tell him. I won't be able to hide it! Just like that, we'll be right back to that brutal silence all over again, getting nowhere!" I predicted despondently with a snap of my fingers to illustrate my point.

"Not necessarily. Let's just slow down and take this one step at a time." He countered calmly. " What was she wearing in the dream? Do you remember" He asked surprisingly. I thought back with a flinch but easily recalled it like I was recalling a a horror movie I'd seen on TV.

"Her "feety" pajamas. I replied sullenly staring blankly in front of me. "Can't remember which ones specifically, aqua blue maybe, but I remember looking at her while she was sleeping. I had noticed her shiver from the fever and I thought that she needed her feety pajamas so she would be more comfortable without needing a blanket. I knew we didn't want her to be too bundled up because that would just raise her fever." I looked back at him them. "The thing is I only remember wanting to put them on her, and seeing that she had ended up in them. I have no idea if I was the one who was actually there to change her or not." I recited in a slightly detached manner, still looking for more clarification from my dream.

"It's alright." He insisted, picking out the bright side for me. "We still know you're there with her, in *some* fashion. *Plus* that also narrows it down to the colder weather. That means we definitely still have some time. You don't have to tell him that we're sure just yet, not until we get to a better place with him on the subject acceptance-wise, or we get closer to that season, whichever comes first." He advised. "But it does give us *some* time." He insisted diplomatically.

"Yeah, but I don't think it's much." I stated, expanding my personal interpretation a little more. "It wasn't clear enough for it to be immanent, like late summer or even early fall, I agree. Even without the feety pajamas I'm pretty sure of that. But it was far too clear for it to be more than a full year away still, so there's no way we have until 'next winter' either. That means that sometime over this winter, between say December-ish and next April, she *is* going to get sick!" My voice caught a little at saying it out loud for the first time but I tried not to dwell on it. *In... out...*

"So more than three months but less than eight. That's not a lot of time to prepare for a life changing event!" I declared. I could feel his added thought about a possible estate trial somewhere in there as well. I sighed again trying not to get overwhelmed. "No, I have to tell him now." I insisted knowing it was the right thing to do.

"Well then hopefully by the time you two talk again, he'll be ready to accept the next step." He offered encouragingly but not with a lot of confidence. "And if not... we'll adjust and we'll go from there." He added, his confidence still unflappable. I had fears and reservations aplenty, but at that moment I was really liking that "we." It gave me a strength that I had not felt in some time. I sighed one last sigh.

"Yeah, here's hoping." I mock-cheered. We both laughed but it was half-hearted at best.

We hiked for another forty minutes in silence after that and it was extremely beneficial. The peace that he emanated naturally and the personal sense of peace that I always got just from being close to nature, both worked to lift me out of my pessimism. I looked up into the sun streaming down through the thinnest branches and felt the weight of impending doom lift just a little more. I reminded myself again that all I could control for the moment was my own reaction and that it didn't *have* to be the end of the world. At least the forewarning did give us time to prepare.

On top of that, I had recently started to believe that it may be possible for someone like me to have a happy and fulfilling life after all. So why couldn't I still hope that she would someday as well? In spite of her *heightened* future. I still just wanted what every generation always wants for the next one, for it to be better for them than it was for us. I looked over at Ethan and thought about all the other good people out there who wanted the same thing for her generation of *heights*. She *really* wasn't going to be alone. We stood a real chance at that point of making the future better for them before they even got there. That thought gave me so much energy and dare I say it, *hope*, that the negativity all but left me!

It really helped me to feel like I could get past the sadness of the non-negotiable part and onto the excitement of better possibilities for everything that remained. I followed Ethan's lead and I stopped fighting it. I acknowledged and accepted that I didn't have to let that information destroy me. I could chose to be a positive, productive part of the future, instead of a victim helplessly bemoaning the unchangeable present. Just like Ethan, all I needed to change my mind was the knowledge that it was really up to me to begin with, that I actually had a choice in the matter. Change my disposition and my reality changed accordingly. I could get on board with that. I heard Mo/Ma bitch and kick up a fuss when she realized that we truly wouldn't be hanging out together and napping all day again after all. I chuckled out loud just a little at her childlike petulance. *(Try not to overthink that, I don't.)*

Ethan looked over at me, clearly surprised by my outburst, but pleasantly so. He cocked his head to one side and furrowed his brow while he grinned curiously, effectively asking me what it was about without actually asking me.

"Sorry. Nothing specific. I'm just starting to feel a lot better. Mary doesn't like it." I joked humbly with a smirk and his quiet laugh rumbled through me. "Thanks. Again." I said leaning my head temporarily on his shoulder. Then I stood up straight and looked back at him. I filled my lungs up slowly but fully, then I let it back out. "Let's go home." I requested calmly. He was onlt too happy to oblige. He pointed to the right at the split in the next trail and we were officially headed back.

Back to my brand new future. Back to *our* brand new future. Back to *her* brand new future! It all awaited us just beyond that horizon.

It was a new beginning. One part of my life had come full circle and the next waited fresh and brand spanking new before me.

I could feel it in the weirdest but the surest kind of way!

For once though I also felt *ready*! I felt stronger, more prepared, like I was exactly where I was supposed to be and I could easily tackle whatever came next because my axis was back on point. It was liberating to finally be so filled with determination instead of fear. I liked that part a lot.

It was even better knowing that it wasn't just my own strength that I had to rely on anymore. I had a partner beside me who volunteered every ounce of his own strength in addition to mine and that was no small offering. On top of that he provided the might of his whole *specialized* team to assist in any way necessary. And he was a kind and caring man who always made life better for me just by being in it. It didn't hurt that on top of that, he *truly* wanted to be right there beside me, more than he wanted to be any other place on Earth! It was the first time that I had ever felt that without a single doubt, without even one *single* misgiving. It was a completely pure desire and it had an effect on me like no other foreign desire *ever* had!

I reached my hand out to hold his that time and I couldn't help but grin at what I was feeling. He looked up and smirked but again took my hand without asking. He was just glad that I was feeling better. I got that. It was a two way street between us, an open line connecting us.

I thought back then and considered that maybe it was related to that "*string of light*" that Carson could see connecting us. Who knows? All I knew for sure was that if one of us was unhappy, the other was as well by default. But when we were both happy together it could be completely *ozone* shattering! *Hmpf*. I'd take that deal all day long.

We came out into the orchard and were surrounded by the sea of intertwined branches of some of the oldest trees and the sweet smell of ripe apples as they sat, fat and juicy waiting to be picked. A few early pieces of fruit had already ripened and fell to the ground in the rows between the trunks. They sat in the grass attracting bees and the armies of ants that would eventually clean them up. In the meantime the aroma permeated the area and acted perfectly as a natural, early fall air freshener. It was exactly the opposite type of scent from the flowery, pollen filled air of spring and I gratefully took a deep breath of it into my lungs. As we walked down the path under the branches, I felt an incredible energy within its' temporary vitality. You could practically hear the collective heart beating from all the life happening all around us!

All the work the trees had done all summer long was currently offered up humbly to any who wished to partake. When the trees had nothing left to give, they would sleep the long winter away. And as long as there was sun and rain in the spring, they would awaken and prepare to do it all again next season without question or complaint. I tried to capture that energy and hold it within me for later.

It was the beginning of my first harvest on the farm and with all that was going on already and all that was yet to come, I was really looking forward to it. Partially because I knew we still had the whole blessed harvest at the very least, before things changed forever so that officially made it my new "*favorite time of the year.*" But it was also partly because the thought of the physical work and the distraction that it offered had me as eager to dive in as always.

Aside from that I still had a lot to learn about myself and I *finally* had the connections and the ability to find some of those answers! Like *real*, actual answers! That was going to happen and that prospect was also invigorating to me, and not *just* me! I knew my parents were as eager as I was to explore more of those avenues. But it was going to take some time to get through all of that. Thankfully I had some coming up.

I was officially off the market professionally for the winter. There was only one main focus to everything I intended to accomplish between then and next spring and that was Liliana. Getting her back and getting her prepared. All the knowledge that I could gain before her *heightening* would make me that much better equipped to deal with it when it happened. It was the only thing I could focus on while I waited. Learn everything I could, prepare. Keep it and all of us together until we came through on the other side. *If* we... No... until. I was officially sticking with that.

And that's exactly what I would do. I wasn't ready to give up. Nowhere near. I knew at that moment that somehow we would get through it, just like every other obstacle that we'd had to overcome already to get where we were. I wasn't sure where we'd all end up yet, I hadn't seen enough to know that much. But I finally felt sure, that all the players were in place, even the ones I hadn't met yet, and that somehow we were all headed in the right direction towards our happy ending at last. I also felt deep in my bones, that *surely* we were *at least* halfway there!

Deep breath…

I looked down for a brief moment at my feet as we crossed the orchard, and I knew that from that moment on every step we took, brought us one step closer.

I looked up then at Ethan and smiled as I purposefully took another, and *another…*

...to be continued in...

Evolution's Goal

BOOK III

A New Conception

25479185R00305

Made in the USA
Middletown, DE
31 October 2015